My Juanita :)

Enjoy! :)

Free Expensive Lies

And please don't
be late at work :D

Taylor

Thank you :)

Enjoy! :)

Taylor Harding-Jenkins

Free Expensive Lies

Prologue

Main cover by **Andrea Gil Coll**

Author's note and disclaimer

This is the last update I'm doing on this book. So, now, all the possible problems you possibly encountered with the previous versions have been sorted out. However, if you downloaded the book on different platforms, you might have to download it at some point, since the book is fairly long, and you may encounter some glitches. But be not afraid, if you have those glitches, you won't be charged another time...

So some of you might have noticed that, in this opus, that I placed a warning in the beginning, "some scenes might not be suitable for all kind of public". And you may wonder why. For those that ask, this has a link with the fact that I used a nickname and I want to remain anonymous. In this opus, as well as the second opus that is due to be released in 2023, so I prefer to start this opus with a **DISCLAIMER** this time. In the previous version, I was more complaining because I got rejected by various agents, but I realised, now that I'm under antidepressants, that there is much worse in life. **MUCH, MUCH WORSE**. So, this is the disclaimer part of this book.

These two first opuses are mostly based on my personal experiences in life, all disguised under a kind of big metaphor. We're gonna pass through many problems, and sometimes, as I faced some of the issues she faces in the story, it has been for me a therapy to write it down. I lost my father in appalling circumstances in winter 2018, and this left me with PTSD (Post-Traumatic Stress Disorder) that ended up collapsing into a severe depression. I have been working on Charlotte since 2013 but, winter 2018 was the month of all my traumatisms. Everything happened to me, everything in the worst. And this book was a therapy, a way to finally manage to get rid of all my pain, and, I would appreciate people not judging me. I already feel dirty enough for what happened. Ashamed, dirty and, I think, there are not enough words in the English language to define how I may ever feel. If you ever face one of the issues I'm talking about in this book, just, don't keep quiet. Don't do like me. But this book is just, one face of my traumatism. It's like, my traumatism, part 1. **Spoiler alert**, I haven't been blackmailed. Oh, yeah... you'll understand what I'm talking about soon enough.

I am not going to talk about my traumatisms, since they are my concerns. As you may understand.

Second disclaimer, it took me eight years to fully complete this manuscript. And also, many rejections from different agents in London, as, well, I guess my book wasn't, erm... I don't know. I've heard some people giving me feedback about what I wrote, they were overall positive, but, when you're a writer, an artist, it's hard to take what people tell you for granted. Of course, I was pissed when I got rejected (I mean, who wouldn't?) then, I realised that there are no bad ways to publish a book, so why not, just, publishing on my own, publishing my very own book, and doing it, my way. Doing everything my way. So, last March, I finally launched this "Free Expensive Lies" new series, for which I have ideas already for seven opuses to come. At least. My goal was to create a new community, a community of readers, wherever you are, creating like, well... Pretty much my Harry Potter, but more in an "adult" version.

The third disclaimer, this book contains some traces of nuts, milk and shells. No, I'm kidding. It's one hundred per cent vegan (I cannot guarantee this for the paperback edition, which I strongly recommend you to buy, I worked my damn arse off on this, and it's much better to read on paper than on eBooks in my opinion, at least, better for your eyes!) but this contains some traces of humour. Regarding nuts and milk, it depends on the chapter, but overall... yeah. Some of you may not like it, as, you know, I'm not the kind of person to keep quiet. I love teasing people, about everything, I am incredibly open to humour, so I'd like you guys to be TOLERANT to this, I mean I wrote a book for open-minded people. If you're an open-minded person, then, I'll be glad to make you laugh. At least... I'll try to. You may not find me funny too, which is understandable, I mean, yeah, in this case... Well, I guess, close the book? Maybe?

Fourth and final disclaimer and I think not the less important one, this book makes some mentions about suicide (and trust me, not in a funny way). I understand that, given the worldwide situation, some of you readers may encounter similar problems to mine, as I thought about it too. I seriously considered ending my days not long ago, and I realised that I have certainly the most wonderful wife on the planet and, this was enough to keep me away from the drug overdose. If you are concerned about this situation, please call for help. **Several helplines are available in different countries, but I can give you the number of the Samaritans if you live in the UK, 116 123, or for those living overseas, in the US, please call the National Suicide Prevention Lifeline on +1-800-273-8255**. These helplines are free to call, and you can talk to someone anytime. They are professional, trained to help you, even in desperate situations, and they will always listen to you, and never put any judgement. Seeing the eyes of my wife kept me alive, so don't forget, people love you. Don't mess up the floor's carpet because you think your life is over, there's always a solution, there's someone to whom you matter. And you're not alone. We don't give up the fight, never. And if you're not convinced, please keep reading, I may have another solution for you.

Finally, to conclude, I truly hope you'll love this book. Believe it or not, but I'm not that much of a reader, I hate reading, or the book needs to be good, (which is why, after all, that agents did not contact me... well I'm free to do what I want anyway, I'm cool with that now) and I wrote this book as I want a book to be written so I could enjoy it. I want it to be as much detailed for you so you can immerse yourself into Charlotte's experience. It may be lengthy, it may be a big book, but, trust me, I did my best. If there are some things you think I shall improve, please let me know. If you liked it, please let me know too. If you loved... Then something may help me, if you could place a review on the store where you purchased this book, then it would help me! This would be lovely from you, and I'd be thankful for that. Sincerely. And, if you're passing through one of the traumatisms evoked in this book or the next opus and this would help you on how to deal with it, then, I'd be really glad. If I can help people, I'm always happy about this.

So, I changed my mind about a lot of things. This citalopram thing I take is responsible for a lot of those changes. If you want to contact me, then I recently opened a website (https://www.taylorhardingjenkins.co.uk/), where there's a section "contact me". Just fill-up the form and send me your mail. I'd be happy to read it. Still, **if you're an agent or journalist and try to contact me, same rule, don't even think about it**. I'm also available on Instagram, and Facebook, just click on the link here to follow me (follow me on Instagram at @taylorhjenkins or on Facebook at Taylor Harding-Jenkins). However, **please note that I will not respond to private messages sent on Instagram or Facebook**, I will only respond to emails sent through my website.

Finally, my decision to remain anonymous follows many shitstorms I had to face, mostly in social networks such as Facebook, in the past, in my life, and of which I want to preserve myself as well as my wife. I will answer some of your questions, but please, do not contact me to asking me my identity. My decision to remain a ghost must, I think, be respected. So please be respectful. Thank you very much.

And now for the big time...

My love,

Oh, dear! I told you not to open this letter until you would turn 18 and you didn't care! Well, on the other hand, that's not a real surprise, you are who you are and will remain the same, I mean I have no hope that you would even change someday, and hopefully, you won't. I wrote the same for your sister, I mean, slightly different because I know that you are, surprisingly, erm, how to say, more grown-up, I'd say that, so... But it's pretty much the same idea, so be nice, okay, and don't reveal what's inside this letter to anyone. Okay? Do you think you can do that for me? For your beloved grandma that passed away, come on. Of course, you will! But still, I know you, at some point, curiosity will take over, that's sure. You can't resist that.

As you know, and as I just discovered, I have been diagnosed earlier today with pancreatic cancer. Yeah, you know what it means, it's over, pretty much. But it's okay, I mean, I was an old bat, I had a wonderful life, maybe your grandfather pissed me off from times to times, but, overall, I do not regret anything. I had a fantastic child that severely screwed up with you; I know what you will say, and it's fair to me, your dad. He married an amazing woman, your mum, and both of them gave me the greatest treasure I have ever had in my life, nothing could ever be above, you and your twin sister, my two granddaughters. And, I don't know for how long I will have to carry that mess, until it ultimately kills me, (I guess that is the price to pay for having smoked my entire life, which I hope you don't do any of that). Still, the doctor said, given the fact that it's an aggressive form of cancer, then my chances of survival are low. But it's okay, I am 65, you may say that I am young, but at least, I had a happy life, and whatever happens, I will always keep an eye on you. You have this girl that you love, and it seems to be serious, I am glad that it seems to work (because you need to have someone by your side), and even if it's not her, then, I am sure you will find one that will be the one. Someone is always waiting for you unless you already met her. But I have good hopes for her. Claire, right? It's just a shame that your mother is not tolerant of that. But, yeah, you know, conservatives Catholics. You know how they are anyway. And you know you can't change them.

I will miss you, darling. I will miss your smile, your little face; I will miss everything of you. I am also glad that you will be following what I taught you, though. Maybe you won't have any children because you say that having children in this world is just insane (and, although I cannot say that to your sister, I do agree with you), maybe someday you will change your mind on this. Me too, when I was your age, I didn't want children for the selfish reason that I love my mornings and I didn't want to invest myself and give time, money and patience to someone that someday will tell me to fuck off. Well, your dad didn't say it in these words, but it kind of meant the same. But, if I didn't have your dad, then I wouldn't have you, and, you know that we have to mess up before being successful, somehow the rule applies to him. No, don't get me wrong, I love your father... sometimes. I am just terrified for you, as nowadays since the smartphone combined with other social networks and engineering prowess has become the primary plague of our century amongst millennials like you, I am honestly feeling sorry to leave you alone in the middle of that mess. Hopefully, you are different, you are, yeah, just a new version of me, the difference you have with me is that I feel, I genuinely think that you will go through your stuff. And you won't be the perfect housewife and mother of two guys that would love from you to have just sex and good food. Charlotte, please, promise me that you will never make the same mistakes than I do, please! Do never be a person designed for a purpose, remain the renegade that you are, and be proud of it! For the housewife role, leave it to your twin, please.

But since we talked about that, if I were your age, I'd travel. I'd love to visit the Banff national park of Canada and discover many peaks and glacial lakes and certainly pitch my tent for a day or two there, or certainly longer. I'd live my life like an adventurer. I'd also love to visit the arid steppes of Mongolia and certainly meet locals that live with the strict minimum, no more than what they need. I'd also love to buy a horse and start learning horse riding. That must be fun, and it's something I've always wanted to do. But I couldn't because I needed to feed your grandfather and fulfil his needs. Anyway, I'd also love to travel to China, discovering Beijing, the Forbidden City, the famous Great Wall, and if I can go to Japan and visiting one of its numerous Temples. And speaking of temples, I'd love to go to this massive temple in Cambodia. I think it's named Angkor Wat. To be truly fair, I'd love to live in Japan, but in rural Japan. Avoiding all those massive metropoles and remaining outside the civilisation. But you know, I guess I made the life I deserved (and don't get me wrong, I am not complaining. Now I think about what I may have missed). I'd also certainly learn how to fly, I am sure, we certainly have a beautiful planet, but so far, the best place in this planet must be the sky, I am sure that no pilot would say otherwise.

I'd love to visit the Pyramid in Egypt. Or also the Valley of the King, along the Nile. I mean I could have done that, but given your orientation, I don't think this is something you can do with your girlfriend. Maybe someday things will change on

Earth and loving someone of the same gender wouldn't be a problem anymore, but. I shouldn't be that optimistic; the human race is so particular. And speaking of forbidden countries, I'd also love to visit Russia, the Saint-Basil cathedral in Moscow, the Lake Baikal, Saint-Petersburg. To be honest, I'm also curious to check on the Lenin mausoleum. Simple curiosity. Of taking this train, until it ends, you know, the trans-Siberian, that must be a fantastic journey, I guess. I'd love to discover Catherine II of Russia; she was one of my favourite women in history. And also, one of the greatest empresses this country had. It's curious! They are talking about kings, what about queens? Last time I checked, Catherine II, Victoria and Elizabeth I were women...

But yeah, if I were you, I'd be travelling, I'd start a long journey. I'd travel to Central and South America too. And smoke some good weed and take drugs. No, I said, don't smoke, darling! Don't smoke tobacco, it's terrible, unhealthy, and brings cancer. And, if you want, I may have an idea for you and your Claire that you love so much (I mean, you seem to love her since every time we are on the phone, you talk about someone different than yourself): the Taj Mahal. Check this out, such a great history. That is something beautiful, and the story is terrific. It brings a bit of magic in this dark and obscure world, corrupted by racism and whatever –phobia. What I mean is, enjoy your life. Discover the true beauty of this planet. Discover what has been before you, and what will be after you, because this is important, as I always told you, the most important in life is awareness. There are things you need to know; you need to see. Just shut down your phone, throw it away, quit all your comfortable life, and just go to the adventure, discover, there are a thousand things to learn, even in your own country. We live on a beautiful planet.

I wish I'd do that one day with you, but it seems that time for me is running out. I do hope you can do that with your girl, with the woman you love, as this is something to wish. Whichever way your life takes at some point, there will be ups and downs. Still, we have the chance to be a wealthy family. You will have the opportunity to inherit soon of a lot of money as I decided to make you my heiress along with your sister. As what your father has done to you was just unforgivable, but I split everything so there are no jealous. Go to some shop, buy a good bag, some right clothes, some good stuff to survive a couple of days, a good tent, then go to the airport, and choose the first flight for abroad. You have the skills to be a survivor; I am confident in this. You are brilliant and very smart, you have the absolute memory, you know a lot of things, you know how to deal with an emergency, and you keep on applying what I kept on telling you since you're a child: look around. The real wealth of a human is not his money; it's his experience. Since we have never seen any cash drawer following a coffin, and since we know that all tombstones in hundred years become eroded, trust me, don't live your life for other people. Live it for yourself and do never look back. But look around, keep on observing stuff. From times to times, it may save your arse.

Unfortunately, within the following months, I don't know how long I will last, but the doctor said that given my age it may evolve quickly or may evolve slowly, he doesn't know at that moment, I will be gone. I know, I will instruct (I mean, I urged) you not to read this letter prior you turn eighteen, but for now, as long as I am alive, I still have the strength to write and also want to leave you with a good memory of me. I am not scared of what will happen, because this is due to happen, and, I knew since I was born that I was supposed to die, the most impressive now is that I have a more accurate idea about my expiry date. It's impressive. I lost my parents, long gone before me, so, I know that death is a reality. For now, you do not know, but after I pass away, you will, and, Charlotte, as I said to your sister, please, please, don't cry. I am not gone; I just took an early train. I am on the other side, and, someday, we will meet again. That may be painful for you because we had a fantastic relationship you and I, and I will leave this world with all the little secrets you confessed to me, but, please, don't be overwhelmed by the fact that I am on the other side. Please, darling, promise me that you will never be overcome. That is not something that I want you to do. But now you are 14, one day you will turn eighteen, and this day, you will look back at this and tell yourself, this was just a problem. Shall it make you stronger, I hope. What I do expect to see is a beautiful eighteen-years woman, in love with some girl maybe different than Claire or even better if it's still Claire, (because she seems to be a good girl, I like her), and I don't want to see you down. Because I know you, when you are not well, you do not speak, you keep everything for yourself, and how many times did I tell you that it was not the right thing to do? So, please. I want to see you thrive.

Well, whichever the outcome, as it seems unlikely that I'd be around at the moment you will read this letter, there are quite a few things I'd like to explain and some advice I'd spare with you before I go, and before you jump into your new life. I trust this would be helpful. You wanted me to teach you how to survive in this humankind because you used to say that without me, you'd be dead and may not be able to cope. I know that life is pretty much nothing more than a tasteless dish to which you desperately need to add some salt and pepper to make it edible, but don't use antidepressants or drugs or alcohol as a seasoning. Never. To cope with life, first, stay ignorant. Because, and trust me, I know what I say, ignorance is bliss, this is an absolute fact. Knowing seems fancy but having too much knowledge is not fancy at all, if you know all the world and all the problems of it, then it will turn you insane, as you won't want to get out of your house. Let's take it this way, knowledge is like feminine lingerie, at first it looks fancy and attractive, but sometimes, when you're not careful, it may hide nasty diseases. And too much knowledge is like having repetitive unprotected sex with that same person, the lingerie girl with STDs. I remember this guy, a former humourist that I loved, a unique and talented guy, named Pierre Desproges, that used to say that intelligence is like parachutes; when you do not have it, then you fall. But, as days pass, I may acknowledge that even when you have intelligence, if you do not manage it well, then you may also end up eating dandelions by the roots.

We used to say that curiosity killed the cat, and believe me, that is so true. It killed and burned the cat to death. Having answers to everything might be disappointing sometimes, or even frustrating. The problem with you is that when you have something in mind, it turns into an obsession for you until you finally get the most rational answer as possible. Quit that bad habit. It is possible also that you may ignore stuff, it happens, you cannot be perfect, darling. Because, when you get to know the world; when you get to know cultures, it seems fancy. But, as things are, they all have ups and downs, pros and cons, and it is precisely because the cat wanted to know the pros and cons of something specific that it ended up having Xanax. Quit that bad habit, Charlotte, please, and get out of your door, and try the adventure. As I refer to my earlier advice, travel, don't stay home reading books like you do all the time. Live your life, stop overfocus on learning silly things that may never help you and may make you feel depressed. I know that when I got pregnant, I did just like you do on a daily basis, and, erm... Well, I told you the story about my depression after I gave birth to your dad, right?

And problems, let's talk about that. You know, the main issue with people today is precisely the fact that they don't have any problems. Well, okay, some issues, such as, well, problems at work, money problems, relationship problems. But this is just rubbish. If you have someday a problem with money, bear in mind that this is only temporary and if you are wise enough, if you can identify the cause of the problem, understand what's at stake it and correct it, then you can survive and move on. Suppose you have a problem with someone, a girlfriend, a friend, a boyfriend, or another human entity, only one thing to do. Confront him/her first, and if you have no results, then get rid of that person (obviously, through legal manners). If you have some problems at work, then quit and find another job, there are a thousand available ways actually to make money if you are not scared and willing to take risks. (And, when I mean "quit", I also mean... make sure you do your notice period in full... That's just a word of advice!) But by this time, whenever people have one of these problems, they pretend this is something they cannot go over. Trust me, a problem with an immediately available solution is not a problem. If someday (and I truly hope any of these will ever happen to you) you lose someone important to you or learn that you have cancer that may kill you, then now, yes, you have a severe problem. Because, eventually, we may have a problem when we are aware that in the near future, we actually won't have any issues anymore. Keep in mind that we recognise bliss at the noise it makes when it ultimately goes away.

If someday you encounter a real problem, bear in mind that, well, it's here and you have to deal with it. Shit happens. It may distort your reality, you may not see the world as you used before, or at least, the planet will no longer turn the same way for you as it turns for the rest of the humanity. You may see the world differently. Maybe a bit more with contempt, or with hope, it depends how hard the asteroid has hit your planet, and how long the nuclear winter will last. What doesn't kill you make you stronger, this is a fact. It will make you different because it will take time for you actually to cope with the traumatism, but after, life will never be the same anymore. It may have been tasteless, even, but make sure it never goes bitter. The problem is to find the correct dose of seasoning to make it work. You may look back and may have regrets. You may try to analyse what didn't work; what you didn't do correctly, how you would have done things better. Darling, promise me that you will never waste your time with that.

Remember this: when the planet was formed billions of years ago, it was just a living hell, then it became a sustainable planet after millions and millions of years after. In this newly liveable planet, there was a small bacterium that was brought or managed to live or be created. This bacterium evolved and then became a plant. And this plant grew, and so on, and so on. Until that day, named a mass extinction. When everything was wiped out, actually to leave the place to some new living things. And this until the end. Life is in the same process. All the time, the same cycle. Some events may change the face of the world; it just depends on how hard these events are. Some may be soft; some may be fine and bearable. But some others may wipe out the entire world and redesign the face of the planet. When this happens, you can do nothing. Everything happens for a reason, honey. Everything.

You may have remorse sometimes. Or feel sorrow for something. You may need to cry sometimes when you face something that is not fair. Because injustice is *part of the history of humankind, there are winners, and there are losers. If you are sad; if you feel the need to cry, do it. Crying is fine, it's relieving. It happens to everyone to weep; it shows that you have emotions, and thus it makes you a great human being. If things are getting maybe someday too much on you, then just let yourself down. Grab some bottle of good old whiskey, and drink it. Drink it until the end, until the moment you are just so fucked up, and you cannot get up, and mostly, put some music out loud, dance, or do something, be ridiculous for once, in private. And you will see, this is the proper therapy that saves you sixty quid from a moody psychologist. Like I said, shit happens, and do not be ashamed of doing it. It's when we are actually down that we have nothing more to lose. But don't think about suicide. First, because it hurts the hell out of you, second, because you need to be courageous enough, and third, and I think that it's undoubtedly the best reason, you do not want to surrender. People that surrender are not heroes. But you may reach a point where being a hero or being an average person may not make any difference to you. Do not surrender, darling. For anything, you never want to bow in front of anybody, that's not what renegades do.*

Because within years following this traumatism, when you will start pulling your head out of the water, you will realise that the world has changed. You will realise that there are certainly beauties in this world, but you may just have become insensitive to it. You may wake up and realise that, well, yeah, people are who they are, they are just all pretending they have problems and you are in the middle of it. You may hear people speaking but don't necessarily listen to what they say, because whatever it is, it's probably nonsense or not relevant, you may not care anymore. You will wake up from that, and see some people fighting for just ridiculous and absurd purposes; this will be the moment when you will gain what we call a real experience in life. And someone that learns things, yeah, it's okay, but it's different than someone that lives things. Someone with knowledge speaks, someone with experience understands. A person with experience doesn't need actually to speak out to say that life is tasteless. If you reach that point, then be sure as hell that you changed, or, I'd better say, you upgraded yourself. A new version of yourself is now alive, and you have to cope with it. The only thing you can do. Your life expectations may be different, and your goals may have changed because somehow, you're aware that death is a reality. Death does not only occur in books and movies, but it is also something that exists, and having the experience of it breaks the denial. Death is a part of life, and one day, it will happen to you too. So, in between, think about it: the day you will find yourself on your deathbed when you will be about to fall for your very last sleep, do you want to have regrets? Do you want to think about unsolved issues? Do you want to tell yourself that you could have done better and failed and did otherwise?

My point about knowledge is, I remember having read Anne Frank and feeling weird after having read the last sentence of her diary because I knew what would happen to her after. I remember having watched the 9/11 on TV and feeling weird the same night because things were just awful. It was just cruel, cruelty was shown on TV, on the very same TV screen where you used to see your cartoons before going to school on mornings, it was showing pictures of planes crashing on some tower on the other side of the planet. I remember having read that in some countries, it's okay to be gay, but in some other, you can be canned to death or hang because it's just "against the divine laws". That TV showed me a lot of things, and this is why I switched it off. I remember, last year, when you came to Montpellier, and you have been insulted in the street because you wore that day your blue dress. And now I see your parents fighting because my son, your dad, messed up and betrayed your mother, and, you know. Deceived also the two of you, and it's just, I hope and want to tell you, honey, save yourself from that madness. We live in a world where we only have babies today like we buy a bottle of water in the local convenience store. Fairy tales that my dad and yours used to read to make us fall asleep are just so far away now in times; I just found out that Cinderella was pretty much a sex slave of the Charming Prince, a selfish prick. Ultimately, when you think about it, fairy tales somehow do serve their primary purpose: making you fall asleep.

I don't exactly remember where I read that, or I think maybe someone told me that, I could not recall, but this is the absolute truth to me, "Living people close the eyes of the dead, and the dead finally open the eyes of the living". Save yourself from the madness. You will read this letter (or at least you are supposed to read this letter) on the 9th of January 2013, and I already feel like things are going messy all around, and I already feel like it's going to get worse. These life invaders, such as social networks, this surveillance from your phones of which you guys are so dependant. All those people being so intolerant and so uneducated when there is someone different, being criticising everything when someone is new, or not even able to say hello when they come into whatever store or meet people. All those things are just making me sick. It's a reality, and we are all monitored. We all became some malleable white sheep, following orders from people also receiving orders and so on. Belonging to our smartphones, to our clothing, our Facebook page, to our laptops, our banks accounts, and god knows what other shit we all have., honey, free yourself from that. You can do that. They are all becoming insane, and you must be different, you actually can be different. And always remember, I may be next door, but if I am no longer part of this world, I still love you. And I will always keep an eye on you.

Your eternal grandma,

Ninon.

Part 1

So, here's your story. First of all, you popped out of nowhere. At your very beginning, you were not even a spermatozoid, or even an egg, you were nothing more than an idea, split in the mind of two people. Two people that did not know each other. They had nothing in common, except certainly common ancestries (far or close, but if close then you've got your very first real problem, and it depends) and the fact that both of them lived on the same planet, called Earth. You were an idea, nothing more.

To create this idea, to elaborate on what you'd become, something happened. Whoever shared the first fifty per cent of you was to meet whoever was sharing the last fifty per cent of the idea that made you. It was maybe... Maybe because that day, the bus was actually late and both of them were stuck under the bus stop under heavy rain, it was maybe because at that party where he/she brought a friend with whom your future mum/dad was actually very curious about, maybe because his/her boss hired a new colleague with whom your future mum/dad wanted to sympathise and later hang out with, maybe because he/she was dating through the internet and swiped your future mum/dad, or maybe because he/she met him/her in a pub or restaurant or wherever... Imagine the chances of you, not actually being created? You don't see it? Okay, let me put it this way: what if the bus today was actually on time? What if, at that party, the friend was sick and thus didn't show up? What if his/her boss hired actually someone else? What if the algorithm of the dating app didn't show him or her? What if he/she decided finally at the last minute to go to another restaurant or pub? Yes, your chances to see the world someday would be severely compromised.

But let's imagine that they successfully passed the first step, and finally, your mum and dad went along together. Okay, the love story starts, great moments are taking places for them... What if dad was not showing enough affection to mum? What if dad was severely jealous of mum and it would piss her off? What if dad doesn't have enough sex with mum? Yeah, you get it... Then what's gonna happen? Mum and dad would be divided, and eventually would break up someday.

It can be for this reason, but there are billions of reason that a couple may not survive. And what if mum and dad break up? Again, your chances to see the world... yeah, you get it, compromised.

But if you're reading these lines, it means that your parents meet, and were happy enough not to break up at least before your mum was pregnant with you. If they break up afterwards, there's nothing I can do... except telling you that your parents are both selfish idiots. But let's look back and see, how many chances until then you were likely to be created? If you followed, I gave you already the reason why you might not be here today, listening to me. Until now, there are billion of scenarios that would have reduced your chances to be here. But let's imagine that your parents are close, they are having a good relationship, and everything works. We pass to the next step, which I know is your favourite: sex.

Your mum and dad are sexually fine. Mum orgasmed all the time, dad really enjoys (on the other hand, if a man dislikes sex, it means that something's wrong), and they finally decide to create you. Then YOU become a material. You are, again, two separate things: an egg, and a spermatozoid. The problem, at that moment, there are millions and millions of you, and this on both sides. But it remains that you are an egg. Now, with his spermatozoids, your dad must fecund this egg with the genetic code included in one of his spermatozoids. And when it happens, then the real race has started: there are millions of you, how many will find the entrance to the womb? How many of them will be oriented towards the real place where the egg is located? How many of them will be trapped? How many will reach the final destination? It can be one. It can be two, or three... But what's more likely, it can be none.

But again, if one of them reach the final egg, congratulation. If two, like my sister and I, congratulation to you guys. If none, then... Maybe your parents will try again, and again, and again, and again... And if it doesn't happen, then you will never happen. You will exist through your next mum's period, but for a very short time. But, let's be optimistic, your mum and dad went through, and one spermatozoid fertilised the cell. Genetic code received; no problem found; you may pass the next step: the cellular division. Congratulations, you are now an embryo.

But yet again, this embryo must form itself. Now, you are assembled, you do no longer depend on two people. Now, one thing is sure, you have a dad, and you have a mum. The ingredients are there, let's tackle the recipe: this egg will divide itself into millions, billions of tiny little cells, all of them containing the genetic code your new dad provided. All these cells are supposed to go in a very precise place, not another. Now let's theorise: what if one cell did not go in the place it was supposed to go? Or even worse, what if the genetic code your father provided was corrupt? Based on these two possibilities, there are now billions of chances that you may not see how beautiful the world is someday. But there're also billions of chances that you will see how beautiful the world is someday, but in all these, yeah... you'll be fucked up. There's only one chance, upon billions, that things are going right. And let's admit that you passed this only chance.

You are now a foetus. Wow, it's amazing, you managed to get in there. Your mother didn't miscarry, didn't suffer from pre-eclampsia, or many risks she can endure during her pregnancy, but not only... She didn't drink alcohol, smoke cigarette or pot, she carefully put that aside for the next nine months she's carrying you. She was serious. She ate well, good and healthy food, that provided to both of you healthy vitamins that helped to develop your future body and strength. She didn't go to work, so it means that she's more relaxed, which means that no adrenalin or shit like this passed through her blood (which means that it passed through yours). She didn't drink her regular flat white on her way to work as well, she ate a full regular breakfast every morning, with all the ingredients that both of you need... No? Oooooooh, damn it. You are now on the final step to become a real human being. Obviously, your mum didn't miscarry and didn't suffer from whatever illness that could have stopped your development and therefore, kill you straight away. And you stayed enough in your mum's womb, you didn't leave early. No, seriously? Well, if it's a no, then I have some bad news for you. Unless you are very, very lucky.

So, yeah, here's your story. Millions of chances that your parents would have never met, millions of chances that your parents wouldn't get along, millions of chances that your mum wouldn't take the pill or be fertile, millions of chances that they'd decide to have you, millions of chances that your parents would actually have sex, millions of chances that the egg you were would be fertilised by a spermatozoid, millions of chances that it would go through and the egg would divide itself, millions of chances that you'd become a normal foetus, and ultimately, millions of chances that you'd ultimately be born one day. And yet, you're still complaining!

1 *Forward*

Free Expensive Lies: Prologue

A strange and dimmed ray of light came into my room from the outside, popping out of nowhere. Still in my bed, thoughtful, and not properly awake, I could almost collect this soft glow of light with my eyes; it was perhaps here for relaxing me and also announce that the night was over. Passing through the curtains, as tiny as it might be, it came very slightly to light up my room, coming perhaps from far, far away, to finally end its course in here, in a dark place. This very morning light, although weak, was attractive, where was it coming from? Indeed, from far, far away, from a rising sun over the old, and perhaps not awake French capital. Now, the moonlight was over.

It was the beginning of a new day. The warmth under my bedsheets was sweet and pleasant, even though the room was still plunged into the darkness of the blooming dawn outside, but I was still quite cold with just that satin nightdress. It's been at least an hour that I am awake and that my brain doesn't want me to sleep anymore. It's funny how a flow of uninterrupted thoughts that you do not wish to have has the sudden power to wake you up. And you can try your best; you can't get rid of it, and after, even if there is still an hour before you have to wake up, you can't sleep anymore especially since it's absolutely nonsense and stupid thoughts. Anyway, still sleeping, my boyfriend was just next to me. It's been days that I am having troubles sleeping, I think it's mostly because of today, and I am doing my best. Still, I am trying not to fall into anxiety. Yeah, today is my birthday, I am finally eighteen, and, well, I guess for the best or the worst, comes what may, as we say. Today I am eventually responsible for my own life, I mean, in terms of the law. Well, I am not scared, it's just that, I don't know. And I hate birthdays. I genuinely do not like birthdays, with all the people that you secretly hate or do not stand are all coming to you with their funny smiley face and sing "happy birthday to you, blah blah blah"... oh lord! I hope mum will spare me the cake with the candles.

Since my eyes were wide open, almost ready to face up the brand-new day ahead, I swiftly cuddled my boyfriend's back. But nothing changed; he was still sleeping like a log. His name is Florent, and we've been together for the last, erm... yeah, since last October. As I am freshly out of a challenging relationship with a girl with whom I used to be furiously in love with, and since things went messy at the end, we started dating each other. Funny fact, he is twenty-five, which means, from the last October until, basically yesterday, between him and me, it was called in legal terms statutory rape, and now... No, not anymore. Anyway, since we started dating (which was weird for me, because formerly lesbian), we basically settled down together. I mean, he spends most of his time here, so, well, I guess we live together now. Somehow.

But I want to let him sleep; it's an important day for him. Just like every morning when I can't sleep, I look around in my room and wait until that alarm rings—getting back to my regular morning boredom. And for that, I guess to kill time (because in that case, you have nothing else to do), I looked around me. And for some reasons, I told myself that the clothes from yesterday spread on the floor were not right. Also, my desk, just in front of the bed, is a fantastic mess. Even though I'm the only one in this room to use it, it is still a real mess. Sometimes I wonder why I have this desk, it's an old piece, and I use it on average certainly once every four months. Books, various letters such as bank statements and other stuff were stack over there anyhow. I have too many things in my room; I should get rid of a lot of stuff someday. It's pretty much the same for my wardrobe.

There was also my lovely wardrobe, with their mirror fixed on every single door, on the left side of the bed, by my boyfriend's side. I use to contemplate the mess that I am on a daily basis and finally tell myself that it could be worse, this massive closet is composed of five doors, and it's so big that it's almost covering the entire wall, leaving just the gap for the door. The first four doors on the right are for storing my stuff, and the last was for Florent. Yes, he only uses one, and it's merely empty, I left him one because he comes here very often. That's a girl problem, and in my case a poor rich girl with everything she wants, all my closets are full, and I can't close the third door. And yet, I am still complaining that I have nothing that suits me. But my twin sister is even worse than me. And the funny thing is, it's not everything in here, last autumn with my sister we packed many of our summer clothes and put them into big boxes to free up some space to get our winter clothes. The big problem is that I have just too many clothes, the big question is that I am following my sister too often into her clothes shop and I don't know how much I have spent into clothes ever since, but, yeah... I am not the kind of person that shows off with clothes, though, but, well, I don't even like it, since I mostly wear the same stuff every day, I have no style, and... On the other hand, my ex-girlfriend pushed me to buy a lot of that stuff, and now, I can dress up the entire Paris, I think.

Free Expensive Lies: Prologue

But when I turned my head, I could see that the five doors of my wardrobe were at that moment all opened, like a reminder that I'd better clean up this mess, the threshold of the acceptable mess may have been already reached. Because, I may be messy, but I like to keep things organised and clean, which is weird to understand for anyone coming in here, but, yeah, arrived the day when it reached the non-return point, and I guess I was just overwhelmed when it happened. Anyway, there was a relatively large space between the bed and the massive furniture in front of the wardrobe, where was left all clothes and shoes from yesterday, certainly crumpled now, on the small red-carpet appearing purple in this dark because of the light. Then, my bedroom, what else to say... Oh, yeah, above the desk and screwed against the wall, there's my TV, a small flat screen that is merely off most of the time since I don't really watch TV. Unless something is fascinating to watch. And yeah, regarding what I call the window, facing the bed and the wardrobe, right now entirely covered because my curtains were drawn, it's actually two expansive French windows that lead to a small balcony outside. Unfortunately, my room is street-side, which is annoying sometimes because of the traffic. And since we live in a private street, my room is facing the main road, which is always noticeably busy; hence, late traffic can be annoying. That's also the problem here, and it's undoubtedly familiar in Paris, our flat is poorly soundproofed. So, between buses passing late at night or pedestrians walking down and yelling in the street late at night... or, funnier sometimes, insults or people having dramas, yeah, I guess that world is living. But some dramas are hilarious sometimes, especially when it involves two car drivers. Entertaining, really.

But I was exhausted. It's been an hour, and the problem is, I know that if I start sleeping now, first it will be nonsense. After all, I will have that alarm ringing any minutes now, but second, I know that I will just be a zombie if I sleep now when I wake up. For now, I am actually okay, even if my night was pretty short. And, moreover, well, you know the rule, you check the time when you want to wake up, 6.30, you say, meh, I'll sleep for five minutes. Five minutes later, 7.35. You are at school, check the time, let's say it is 3pm. You check the time five minutes later, it is 3.01pm. I really need some sleep. My boyfriend turned himself when I was looking at the window a minute ago, and, his pillow was wet since he drools. He seemed to be like, nothing could actually reach him now.

The funny thing with him is that, when he sleeps, a bomb may explode in the building that it wouldn't wake him up. I used to sleep like him, but then, well, I passed through that stressful period. Then I thought, what could he dream about, at this time? Where was he now, into which hollow or more unfathomed depths of his brain was he now? His face features seemed to be so appeased, and somehow, I was okay seeing him like that. A new day has come today, and this day wasn't a day that will look like any other. Another day, another fight.

I love winter. The thing I love with winter is, the night is coming relatively early, and it's so cold that you really enjoy curling up under your sheets. But the sun sets earlier. The only big problem with mornings here, in this flat, is not the fact that it was actually cold... No, the problem comes from the wild. Mum. Unlike me, she's a morning person. And unlike me, she loves to wake up. And also, unlike me now, she was already wakened up and was probably preparing herself. The problem with her is that okay, she never turns on any lights in the flat, so she does not wake us up.

No, the biggest issue with her is that, yeah, she forgets that singing is better if you do it alone whilst having a shower, it's not something you need to share. Okay, she doesn't sing out loud, but as I said, the flat is not soundproofed very well, and she doesn't care. Last day she dared to tell me that her, singing appallingly, was an excellent excuse to take me out of the bed so I can hurry up to go to school. But, yeah, the big problem with her is that she's always in a terrific mood in the morning, and sometimes it creates, erm, frictions. Yeah, because mum and I are in a kind of a fight over the school. She wants me to be the perfect model student, just like my sister is. Instead, I cut school as often as I can, I have had many disciplinaries over poor behaviour and even have been excluded recently for a whole week after I, erm... reminded to some classmate that sleeping with many people may at some point tarnish her image (obviously in a much rude way) and this in front of the Head Teacher, and it wasn't the first time... The only problem with me is that I am the best student they have ever had, in terms of performances at school, I am the best, my absolute memory saves my arse. So, either way, they can't exclude me, even if I hold the record of detention hours not done.

But I guess my "poor behaviour", "insubordination" and "rebellion against authority", as they said, is somehow related to the fact that I kind of love being alone... In general, my mother and I were mostly in conflict over her divorce four years ago and how they (my parents, both) managed the crisis. It's always been electric between us ever since. But, yeah, in general, I am not a really social person. I don't have many friends, and it works for me, because the big problem with me is, one way or another, I will always push things to their own destruction or to people to finally hate me. No, I am mean, evil, and I don't even know how I managed to be for seven years with the same person. Let's say that I loved psychology, I learned a lot from that, and... I kind of used it, sometimes for fun. From feedbacks I have, apparently, it wasn't fun for everyone. Meh... Oh, and, in case you're wondering, no, things didn't end up because one of my stuff, no. She broke up with me. Because of, well, the girl that, because she sleeps with a lot of people may have her image tarnished.

At this moment, apart for my mother, dismantling some random music in the kitchen in a "silent" sotto voce, I was breathing, and trying to relax with listening to the traffic outside. The problem was that my mother was pretty much at that moment, a noise disturbance. At that hour, like every day, the street is already busy as people are on their way to work, and the many car horns and swearing pronounced by various other drivers because (from what I heard) there was an asshole in front of them still daydreaming in front of the traffic lights were genuinely entertaining. For a second, thoughtful, I thought about this guy, indeed stressed out because he slept on the sofa last night because his wife is done with him or some other reasons. Crappy day at work ahead, and he knows that because his/her manager is a moron... A fantastic day in a beautiful capitalist life. Okay, I cannot really speak, since I do the same, going at school to mess around and dating a guy that loves only my arse. But still, based on this, I may understand why he replied to the guy horning him behind (and said after horning by the way "move your damned ass, you asshole") by something like "screw you, you lame asshole", "dickhead", "son of a bitch", or whatever. So much love on Earth, it's crazy. It's like when your neighbours are having sex upstairs, and you're trying to sleep and watching Netflix on your iPad a couple of days after having been dumped by your newly ex... Mate, you feel so alone at this moment. Well, last time it happened to me... Well, I pretty much recall having said the same words. At least, yeah, terms were somewhat similar.

At some point, I looked at my phone, that I used as an alarm, plugged on my nightstand. Time flies, gosh, it was now displaying 7:29, which leaves me less than a couple of seconds before it actually rings. I looked at my boyfriend again one last time, and I still saw the same expression on his face. I honestly wish I were him... Always able to actually sleep. He was quiet and serene as if he didn't care about anything, as if life never broke him one single day. He seemed happy; and... I don't know, happiness is something that I used to experience, it just tastes weird now, I am not really used to this kind. But it's better that he sleeps, as I said it's a big day for him today.

He has exams today, for training that he was following, for now, four months. Because he didn't find a job in what he wanted to do, and therefore was forced to reconvert himself professionally, and did some training to do, erm... he told me, but I don't remember, and anyway, today is the exam day. What he has, and I don't have, the ability to sleep, although stress is high. Well, I guess the fact that we had sex last night helped a lot also, but it doesn't help me be less anxious for some reasons. Which, when I think about it, is a real shame. Anyway, although I advised him on how to do his stuff, I tried to be there, giving him some advice on how not to screw up, providing instruction about how to stand in front of a jury because he's timid. The thing is, he has a kind of presentation that he had to give, today is the deadline. He has to speak in front of a jury that will ultimately if convinced, will approve the training or I don't know what, the only thing I remembered is that he said that he has to convince a jury. He can do it, I am confident, but convincing is not really his stuff, and... I don't even know if he really listened to me. But, whatever happens, it's up to him, not me.

The big problem with sleeping with someone (like, in, really sleeping, in the same bed, literally...) is that, well, I have a big bed for myself, a king-size bed, and I really love curling myself up under the cover. It used to be the same with Claire, most of the time, she was either stealing all the place or all the sheet. And ultimately you end up sleeping with nothing and you are frozen. Which is somehow an insult, since this happens into your own bed, and... The big problem with Florent is, gosh... I hate this once he pushed me so far that I literally ended up on the floor. It was our very first night, and he was directly appropriating my own bed, and... I took my revenge by waking him up with a big bucket of cold water whilst he had his shower. But he never really understood. Although he is still doing this, leaving me space as ample as twenty centimetres for sleeping every night, colonising most of my bed, at some point I gave up. This is what it is.

And suddenly, the alarm rang. I immediately checked my clock. That was now displayed everywhere 7:30. Well, er... FUCK!

Lips are turning blue... A kiss that can renew... I only dream of you... My beautiful!

Ah, yes, I have forgotten that too. My alarm is, hum, yeah... Somewhat particular. Yeah, it's an app that is a radio and wakes me up that the song on air when I want to wake up. Since several studies conducted by myself have shown that if I use a standard ringtone to wake me up, it would dramatically impact my mood the following day. But it's okay, I mean, this is a good radio, passing some good rock music, not too harsh to start the day. Yep, technology is impressive. So, this morning... Actually, I am, thanks to the app, sometimes able to predict when a shitty day is ahead, it depends on the music played and what the song is talking about. Okay, I get your point, these are just predictions, so, yeah, I agree, this is rubbish. But sometimes, I am right.

Then this morning, it was (one of) my favourite band. So, I can predict a good day ahead. *Sing for Absolution*, this was the music currently on air. Anyway, I turned it off before Matthew Bellamy sings louder one of my favourite songs. The lyrics are soooooooooo beautiful, I love it. It's just sad that their last album was terribly disappointing. But what would also be a shame would be me stopping it now, and even if I love it, it's going to wake up Florent, and I don't want him to be wakened up because of me. I want him to sleep because I am like Princess Fiona in the first Shrek, you prefer seeing me only by day. And I also trust that music would calm my anxiety today, so maybe it would actually be a bright idea. Since in the morning, I am more inclined and receptive to arts. I mean, art, songs that are well sung, unlike my dear mother out there still singing different stuff. So, for avoiding any problem, I immediately turned off the music. But I needed to listen to this song again. Wait... is that emotion coming?

I actually pushed the, erm... part of the cover I was apparently entitled to have because he took all the rest for himself. With the most significant difficulties, I dragged my first leg out of bed to put one foot on the floor. I did the same process for my second leg afterwards, quietly, for then putting the second foot on the floor, and to stand up... at the same time, deep in my mind, I heard my motivation yelling at me, "Charlotte, what are you doing?". And for some reasons, gosh, it was freezing in here, I don't know... Did I turn on the heater yesterday? I don't remember. But I think I didn't if it's so cold in here. Anyway, when I put my two feet on the floor and sat upon the bed, Florent moved, and like every time that I wake up and before standing up, I am always feeling weird. I rubbed my eyes, yawned very deeply, started to stretch my arms, and heard my motivation yelling one more time at me, "you're not supposed to do that, get back where you are!". My mother is annoying me because this year is the year I am supposed to pass my baccalaureate, and the school has threatened that if I go AWOL another day, they will cut me from having my degrees this year. I know... what a threat... But, well, it worries some people, so... Well. I guess I have imperatives in life.

So, yeah, when I sit down, and it's every morning the same, even when I am not going to school on weekends, I am always feeling woozy. I don't know what the reason is, but I am still feeling nauseous, but it's rapid, it doesn't last longer than five to ten seconds. And obviously, this, associated with the feeling of having no desire to work, it makes things worse. Thank God, to cope with school, someone invented Netflix. I have seen a doctor, but, well, after having done many blood tests, they didn't find anything. I have poor health since I was born, contrarily to my sister, I guess that's the problem of being twins, one is stronger than the other. Anyway, like every day, that's my daily routine, I leave my bed in my room to sleep again in my college, the problem is I never encounter this wake-up problem at school, unfortunately. But given the fact that I still need to remain part of the civilisation, although I do not really mind doing the opposite, I also need to go there. I am just done with that.

Anyway, at some point, after having rubbed my eyes and finally telling myself that I can find every excuse in the world, none of them may work, I finally stood up. I made sure not to make any noise, I also took care not to bump myself against whatever I may encounter on the floor, as, even if the sun was setting, it was still dark in here. I progressed very slowly while looking at my feet and being really careful, taking extreme care steps after steps, when I reached slowly but successfully, and also quietly, my desk, for finally getting my headset. It was hidden under a small stack of papers, I remembered having left them here a while ago. The problem was, pulling on the wire caused some pieces to move, which made some light noise, but as I maintained the big pile of books, nothing collapsed. Hopefully *Sing for Absolution* is in my playlist in the Music app, so it's okay to keep on listening.

But the problem is, I listen to a lot of music, and it's pretty much hidden somewhere in an exceedingly long scrollable list. It took me quite a moment to actually find it, and when I had it, I plugged my headset. I select it, and I touched on the title displayed on my phone screen. And whenever it was launched... Yeah, I kind of felt the chills of like when I listen to some good music, and, yeah, that was a kind of good pleasure. I actually stood still for a second, and, yeah, actually enjoyed, whilst my feet were hit by a freezing floor, whilst I was really cold out there but didn't really mind. And I thought, it's funny, but everyone tells me that I have the untoward habit of focusing on the sad moments of my life, as they are the only one that has real meaning to me. There were some good moments, though! So, let's get started, but I decided to put the music back at one minute and sixteen seconds, just before, indeed the symphony of my doomed childhood scrolled before my eyes. Ending today.

Free Expensive Lies: Prologue

Sing for Absolution, I wiiiiiiiill be singing, and falling for your graaaaaaaace, Ooooooooooooh!!!

Seriously, today, the real question that I was wondering was... why would I sing for my absolution? Whilst Bellamy was beginning the second verse, I have deeply thought about this question's exact meaning. I believe that I have nothing to ask for whatever forgiveness... Okay, I didn't speak to my ex-girlfriend yet. One of my precepts says that the mistake is human, but the forgiveness is designed for idiots. Or religious people. But since I have neither Gods nor master, and God is totally meaningless to me, forgiving is not in the values I consider meaningful.

I slowly walked out of my room, while Bellamy ended the second verse, still walking on tiptoe, and keeping the phone in my hand. And I was careful not to turn the sound too loud in my ears, and I quickly looked at the carpet, where we left our stuff yesterday. I don't know why... Yeah, I guess it was a right moment when he took my clothes off and pushed me on the bed. I think so. I don't know why; it was at that moment that I kind of had that flashback.

Sing for Absooooooluuuuuuution, I wiiiiiill be singiiiiiiing, and falling from yoooooooooooour graaaaaaaaace, yeaaaaaaaaaaaaaaaaaah!!!

It was when were thrown the darkest guitar notes of the song, like emerging from the nothingness, from the dusk, that I opened the door and I was now moving towards the corridor after having slid my door, still making sure that I wouldn't make any noise. I slid it back afterwards, to make sure that he wouldn't be bothered by any noise coming from the kitchen. I stopped the music, rolled the wire of my earplugs around my phone, and heard no more noise in the flat, it was a relieving silence. Dusk was now sparkling from almost a thousand fires coming from the depths of the cosmos and corrupted by the sun, that it was now bringing the daylight into the corridor I found myself now. Finding myself in the main hall leading to all our four bedrooms our flat has. That's when I heard the tiny sound of my closing door, "clack" that I knew that could go forward.

I swiftly turned myself. Now, it was me against the low light of the hallway. Now, no lights anymore, no more view of the outside unless I go to the kitchen, where... where SHE is. Or at least was. But I really do believe that I didn't turn any radiator on, I think I completely forgot that, and, even if I do it now, the problem is that the flat is actually so big that it takes hours to heat up the place. Seriously, it's freezing out there, I should have taken some pants. There was no carpet in this hallway, only a white-tiled floor, and upon walking on it, I felt like being on burning embers... Yep, because between too much cold or too much warmth, there's no difference, it's painful as shit. No, this corridor, except some old painting of old family members part of our inheritance, there's nothing really spectacular. Oh, yeah, I forgot to mention, the Kominsky family is ancient and prosperous. Besides, on every door of this corridor and even the main hall except the entrance door, there are large stickers stuck because my mother loves Japan and wanted to create a Japanese decoration, except on my own because I don't necessarily want to display what she likes, it's a bit childish in my opinion. She wants to have a personal space designed with what she likes... As long as it is not reaching my area, I'm cool with that.

So, yes, this corridor (in terms of size) is ten metres long, three broad and has got five doors, plus an opening to the entrance looking to something like two doors on each length-side, all face to face, and one at the bottom, facing the entrance. Let's start by the one on the bottom, it's the toilets, that nobody uses since every bedroom has their private bathrooms, including restrooms. If we walk from the toilets' entrance, my room is the first on the left-hand side. My mother's room is behind the door in front of mine, and my sister's room is the one behind mine, so the second door by my side. Yep, the flat in which we are living is immense, I mean... Yep. And expensive as well. And the last remaining room is the guest room. Not used for a while, except when one friend of my boyfriend or some guest is coming. Otherwise, nobody uses it. It's not a room really used, even if I wanted to turn it into a kind of office or workspace for myself, or a library, but I aborted the idea. Or when our half-sister is coming once every five years, but no, we don't use it.

I walked towards the entrance, making sure that I wouldn't be noisy. Yeah, I may be a mean person, but I still have respect for people that sleep. The kitchen is the first door on the left after the partition between here and the corridor from this entrance. There are three doors in here, leading to the kitchen and, on the same side, afterwards, to the living room. On the other side, right in front of the living room door, there's the reception room, tenfold more expansive than its opposite room, and next to this door, a small storeroom, which is undoubtedly the messiest place of this flat before my bedroom. But to be honest, the entrance is not that big. I mean, big... No. Walls are painted in the same colour as the corridor, this goddamn white, and it's as big as a square of five-metre each side. It's just a classic entrance, whose walls are painted in white, with a yellow carpet covering at least 50 per cent of the floor, without any ostentation. And the main door, I forgot. Besides those access to the other places connected to it, there's the big heavy main door.

Free Expensive Lies: Prologue

It's a reinforced door with many lockers because of security, as we are afraid of burglaries. A small item of furniture that looks like a house hanging next to it with all our keys and badges to enter the building and that's it. And a mirror, also.

Nevertheless, there are two doors made of glass in the separation between the entrance and the corridor. Most of the time, those doors are closed, except when mum or Clarisse, my twin sister, does organise some party in the reception room, we usually close and lock those doors. Since we use the reception room mostly for parties, we never use it otherwise, and it's not used more than five times a year. And yeah, thanks to those doors, we have a perfect view of what's in the entrance if they are closed.

For continuing, every door of each room, except the main door, the kitchen door, and the corridor/entrance doors are all sliding doors made of a wooden frame and covered with paper, like thick paper. The paper doors are charming because they give off an orange light during the dawn and the dusk, which is quite poetic during summer days. I like that. It gives us another way to see this flat and also the capital. Regarding the kitchen door, it's made of steel and glass, but, well, it's because it's the kitchen. And then, between the separation and the kitchen door, there's a mirror, with hopefully no stickers pasted on it or anything. It's just big enough to ultimately see yourself, firmly nailed to the wall. And it is fun to see your waking-up face when you just wake up and are going straight in the kitchen to get something to eat. This is also the thing that I use to do all the time, don't ask me why but I love mirrors, and it's sometimes, what I use to do in the morning when I wake up, pretty much looking at the damages.

And just as I arrived in front of it, just like every morning, I just couldn't resist: now, for example, this morning, when I saw myself in the mirror, it was such a disaster. Like every morning my hair is matted and is such a piece of art, it was in an improbable mess, my eyes and my face were so pale that I have to hide it every day by putting foundation, but... no. That makes me think... Okay, so pretty much, I am 7 feet 5-inch-tall, with blonde hair, quite long and wavy hairs. I have blue eyes, I am really skinny and overall, very pale (I use to hide my pallor with a lot of foundation), but I guess it's caused by some health issues, what else, erm... I have actually somehow a soft but deep voice, and I don't usually speak up loudly. But, physically, well, guys use to say that I am pretty, well, I maybe am, I don't know. Well, I am like any other girls, I am not really different. Now I was wearing my black nightdress, and that's pretty much it, yeah, my hairs are messy, but I guess I have to comb it, and... I need to shave my legs. I had my periods last week, but I think this is not really relevant. And I weight about sixty kilos. Maybe less, I know I lost two kilos three months ago because of, well, break-up issues. It's been a while that I didn't scale myself. Last time I went to my doctor was three months ago, after the break-up, and he prescribed me some Xanax to manage to cope with this sad event. Well, believe it or not, but it's tough to be dumped after a seven-year relationship with someone.

Obviously, now I was just wearing that nightdress. And some panties as well, but it's not something that I could see now. Well, I don't really care about clothing, but, yeah, it's winter outside, and the stupid mind I am has entirely forgotten to switch on the heater, and as a result of that, I am frozen, and yeah. The thing is, mum can cope with the cold, she's British, so it works for her, but... I am British too, but I was born and grew up on the Mediterranean coast. And it was not Gibraltar. Yeah, my mum is British, and my father is French; unfortunately, she didn't give me her ability to survive in the cold.

Anyway, after seeing the disaster in the mirror for a couple of seconds, the time to actually come back to reality was time for breakfast. The Narcisse within has left me, it was time to meet with the devil. But my regular breakfast tea will undoubtedly be an excellent tool to help me cope with the rest of the day, or at least it will be a good start. And just like every single day when I wake up, and I think about what's ahead, I always feel like, I can't wait for this day to come to an end. But I have to hurry up; otherwise, I am gonna be late. It was time to make a tea, to at least try to kick-start my day, I need fuel. And tea is my fuel. I don't really like to disturb my habits: every single day when I wake up, the very first thing that I do is my tea, nothing else. Sometimes I listen to some music, like today, but it's not really regular. After this, so, I came to the kitchen. Astonishingly, nobody was there, and the lights were off. I noticed that detail when I was there... but I was sure lights were on, and she was inside. Hum... Curious. But okay, on the other hand, as long as she's far away... I'm not gonna complain.

It's really on that point that mum is annoying: she hates when we leave a room with the lights still on, or even when we quit a room (even for a few minutes), and we keep the lights on. Mum is that kind of person concerned about the planet and says that we must save energy... Which is funny since it comes from an intolerant, homophobic mind. It's also one of the points where I don't like my mother, and I don't really understand that: she's coming from a religious family, she's protestant (not Anglican, though) and... Since she grew up in London before arriving in France and before meeting my father, I guess I will never understand this, her intolerance. However, even though she's not going to the church every Sunday, she still cares about the planet, but wants a world full of straight people, since homosexuality is disgusting for her. Yeah, imagine when she caught me kissing Claire, half-naked, in the sofa of the living room, she kind of liked it. The holy war against my heretic mind was declared. Every time I went to London with her, I found this city as being much more tolerant than Paris, and since she remains with her 18th century's mind. For fun, once, I tried to drag her to Soho... Tottenham Court Road, she knows that. She should have gone there more often, trust me.

Two years ago, last time we went to London, I came back home with an LGBT pin badge. I do not support LGBT ideas by some ideological disagreement that I won't extend myself on, but I came back home just to provoke her. Listen, I have never been slapped so hard in the face for that.

Anyway... Our kitchen. It's not the largest, but by far it is the lengthiest room in the house. If there were a particular word to describe this place, in its dimensions and its rather strange layout, it would definitely be "narrow". Yes, narrow, it's true, but we can, however, come in with quite a few people. But the truth is, it's in a rectangular shape, and still, with all the furniture and stuff inside, it's not really convenient at some point. We would say that if another place of the flat looks like the kitchen in terms of the same dimensions, regarding proportion, size and shape (if, of course, disregarding all that's inside), it would be the corridor linked to all the bedrooms. But instead of finding the door to the toilet in the background, we can find a door leading us to our small balcony, which also connects my bedroom and the living room. But right now, due to the winter condition, we do not enjoy staying outside, not even for a second.

Regarding the decoration, well, it's pretty much a regular kitchen whose walls are painted in pale pink (you know, that famous diarrhoea-style pale pink... although, if your diarrhoea is pink then I think you need to be seriously worried), but with some high-tech equipment. To give an example of this equipment, we have a table which is connected to computers in the house, which means that I can drink my tea and surfing on the Internet without even using a laptop, in the meantime. Quite fancy. Much like the one we use to see in spy movies (but ours isn't huge, though), it's placed against the wall that separates the kitchen to the lounge, in its perfect middle. It's like a giant tablet. And two chairs are against each side of the wall. On the other side (the side separating the kitchen from my room), there are all our household appliances.

Basically, the kitchen is set up that way: first, the big white oven under the ultramodern ceramic hob. Next to it, the white sink above the raw wooden doors hides all the household pots and products. Next to it, a white dishwasher changed six months ago because the former had a nasty leak that flooded the entire floor. Then, in the same colour, we have a tactile washing machine and its tumble dryer that I am the only one to use. For finishing, at the very end, towards the window, the massive American fridge painted in a blue twilight sky. With all the magnets on the doors of trips that we'd love to make someday, such as Dubrovnik, New York, Istanbul, Seattle... On which are stuck different papers (me and my twin's schedule that we are supposed to have at school under some of my many exclusions certificates, some professional convocations that Florent has, some discounts in the closest pizzeria when mum is not here and laziness takes over...). Yeah, but except our schedule at school, pretty much, whenever there is a paper concerning me stuck on that fridge, it's usually for a disciplinary hearing. If I am proud of it? Oh, come on, you're gonna make me blush!

Right after, a small hole, where there are the black bins into which is written in different fonts "New York, London, Paris" (which is funny when it's written on rubbishes) provided for recycling. Recycling remains a weird, boring thing that my mother, my twin, and my boyfriend are pissing me off to do, whilst I still have a problem distinguishing what waste in going in what bin. So, I'm confused. Then over all the appliances, there are many cupboards (precisely four), alongside the wall, full of products such as different kinds of pasta, tea, and other things, it is also where we store plates and other stuff except above the oven and the hob where there's the extractor hood. And on top of the fridge too, there aren't any cupboards (well, it makes sense), as the refrigerator is actually very tall and very full; instead, there's a lot of dust on the top... And yeah, also, there is the credenza, between the oven and the hood. Always dirty... I may have seen it cleaned once or twice since I live here, but it's still greasy. No wonder if someday I get sick or something...

Facing these, there is a dresser. A small dresser in which my mother used to store some dry food. Our old wooden dresser, definitely ugly, certainly carved in some wood coming from a century that is as old as her mind, and she finds it beautiful, whereas I just wanna see it in the bin... No, it's awful, I am sorry. Every time I see it, I want to... throw it away, trash it, or get a more beautiful one in Ikea. The thing is, we are landlords here, (not only for this flat, but we also own the entire building... I mean I own, because... Well, it's a long story), when mum will leave our flat because one day, I will live alone here with my... self I guess, I mean when I will become more independent than I am today, this ugly dresser will move out with her. I really can't wait for that. Unless I move out first and thus, I'll never see it anymore. Besides, right now, she's waiting for us to find a solution. But it's complicated. I mean, Florent and I are still in a new relationship, let's say that I am kind of afraid of commitment. Let's say that he still needs to complete his probationary period before being signed off.

Just like every morning when I am not actually fresh, it takes me a couple of minutes to even recall into which cupboard I stored the kettle. And the coldness doesn't help either. Moreover, I don't like to walk barefoot on the floor, but I didn't have time to pick up a pair of socks before coming in here. And then... Yeah, it's in here. I went towards the ceramic hobs, switched it on, and took the kettle in the cupboard above the sink. Well, okay, the shelves are high enough (because we have a problem here, ceilings are high, less than three metres high), but I'm tall enough to reach at least the kettle. Anyway... So, I took the pot just like every morning, I filled it up with water, and since the hobs were switched, I just had to boil up the water inside, and wait for this sweet little whistling. And right after this tremendous effort, I actually came back to sit down, throwing myself into one of those so uncomfortable small chairs. The only problem with that table is that, as soon as you just put your arm on it, it switches on and surprises you all the time. Yeah, well, they call it technology, it's fancy... Meh.

I actually relaxed, whilst the water was gently boiling, leaning my side against the wall, and closing my eyes for a minute. Usually, when you wake up, you feel you have hours of sleep missing, and I feel drained. Then, suddenly... Yeah, I realised that I needed my cup to drink my tea, so I stood up, and grabbed it from the same cupboard I took the kettle while hearing some activity coming out of my mother's bedroom. Oh no, she found me. A few minutes later, when the kettle began to whistle, and my cup was next to the hob, I took it out, placed the teabag into the cup. And again, the traditional ritual of every morning, I poured the water, and, waited for a second for it to actually cool down. And, whilst daydreaming in front of the tea, taking its standard colour slowly, suddenly, she, in fact, surprised me:

"Hey, darling! You okay?" she startled me.

Yeah, she never calls me darling or something. I mean, darling, yeah, I do not really hear that often from her, even from my boyfriend.

So, yeah, Mum is today forty-four. She lives with us (for too long now, I wonder is her presence is still required today), and like I said, she's coming from

Elizabeth II's realm, so she always speaks with a strong accent that let people know that she's not French. And, she looks like, erm... Coming from abroad. Since we talk about it, she is tall, blonde like me, with short and straight hair (unlike ours with my twin, long and wavy), and unlike us, she has very slight freckles on her face. And I mean very little because you really need to pay attention to see this. She has got green eyes and has the annoying habit of looking at people straight in the eyes when she is talking to them, which can really be disturbing even if I told her many times. She always really cares about her appearance, she is always well-dressed, wearing fancy clothes, except now, because she was still wearing her pink bath dress where Mickey Mouse is drawn on her back. She purchased it when she went to California four years before our birth, which means it's quite old, but she still loves it. And she always wears her gold necklace with a small crucifix, since mum, unfortunately, believes in God and this has created so many issues here because my twin and I are both strong atheist and, yeah. Which is curious, I mean... To be honest, she's a kind of a contradiction sometimes because she works in the clothing industry which is, let's say, open-minded, and... Yeah, it's been eighteen years that I am seeking what's her true meaning of life. And still haven't got any answers.

As such, she is always or most of the time wearing makeup. It destroys her eyes and makes her skin as soon as she removed it looking like she's sixty years old, and this morning she was truly old. No, I mean it. But, like I said, this is due to her job: as she is a fashion designer, she designs clothes, and thus she has to be "at the latest fashion", always smart, with fancy clothes, it has somehow an impact on herself. I wish it would have an effect on her approach to being tolerant. She designs clothes for pre-adults, like me, and works for an important company. And since she has an important position, she makes more than €90,000 a year after taxes. So it makes sense on why she loves her job; I guess the pay is a good point. But she worked hard for it, so I must admit she deserves it. The thing is, we moved in Paris a while ago, and they divorced with my father, and as both handled the situation like two 12-years-old pre-teens battling over bollocks, it was, yeah, like the Soviets and the Americans fighting at home. Pretty much. This is why we are so divided with my mother because she never wanted to apologise that she clearly messed up and since things escalated so far with her... I actually think today, a reconciliation would be really tough to negotiate.

Anyway, when she arrived discreetly (because she knows how to walk without making noise whilst I don't), I was astonished:

"What the hell?"

"I was just asking how you were, you know, if things were okay for you?" she continued.

"Hum... My sister is still sleeping, I think she wakes up at eight or nine as she starts later today," I was actually questioning myself.

"Hum... I wasn't talking about your sister; I was asking you if..."

"Oh me? Oh, sorry I was confused, I forgot that from times to times you actually care about me!"

"Yeah, and I think I should care about you more often, I guess," she seemed upset.

"Hum, honestly, it's fine, I am really used with the fact that you are an appalling mother."

"I'll just pretend that I didn't hear anything."

"Have it your way... Anyway, what's up?" I asked her.

"Well... Not so bad, despite what you might think. What about you? Are you fine, I mean, better, now you insulted me?"

"Hum... They said you'd ask me that question."

"My baby girl. To hear you, problems that homeless people encounter outside is nothing compared to your relative happiness."

"*Claro que no*, they don't have any problems, because they've got crack and other fancy drugs!"

"Yeah. Ready for school?"

"Just like a pig in a butcher shop, mum, as always," I realised that I was maybe too sarcastic.

"Think about your future, darling!" she obviously lacked any arguments.

"What future?" I was laughing.

"I know you don't care, but still..."

Well, now, this was heading to bollocks. So...

"Anyway, may I drink my tea in peace without talking to anyone?" I was this time formally requesting to be alone whilst remaining smiley and friendly.

"Charlotte, I am fed up to pay a school for you, as you obviously don't care. But anyway, all of this is thanks to your... dearest father."

"Yeah, blame him as long as you want, and God bless the other one that married him as well twenty years ago. By the way, thank you, I really appreciate it, thanks for my birthday!"

"Yeah. Happy birthday, darling."

"So spontaneous, gosh. That shows so many stuff, but fine! Anyway, you want some tea?"

"Please, yes."

There's something I don't understand, and I think most of you guys may agree with me: how comes that our parents have to be fucked up... and how comes that our grandparents are just fantastic? I mean, seriously, my grandparents, especially by my father's side grandparents, gosh, I loved them! My grandma was just, yeah, certainly one of my favourite women on Earth, I miss her so much! When I was a kid, I spent most of my time at their place and... It was such a good time! Maybe there were not many things to do, but, gosh, grandparents have this power to make you feel better, whilst parents, meh... I don't really know my other grandparents, since there's the English Channel between them and us, but still. But I recall them, they are nice too, and their house is big and fantastic. They live in Saint-Albans, a place outside London. My grandma, she was just incredible. Unfortunately, she died four years ago and, well, that's life, I guess, death is part of life, as she used to say. And when I see my mother... I am just like, fuck!

Anyway, she took her cup, her small spoon, her milk (this is also something I never understood, drinking tea with milk, terrible – and don't say it's because I never grew up in the UK...) then, started her stuff. At the same time, I went back to sit at my place on the table, and, well, started to rub my face to wake up again as I was still half asleep. Then she, unfortunately, resumed our conversation, after drinking:

"Anyway, what about your boyfriend? Florent. Our only male tenant here since he spends most of his time here. Is he passing his exams today? Hope he's gonna be okay."

"He will, well, comes what may for him, I mean... This is his stuff. If he fails, then he fails, it will be just another failure in his life, what can I say!"

"Don't be pessimistic. Come on!"

"An exam is an exam, if he fails, he can still pass it again next year, or I don't know. That's just a piece of paper, that's it."

"Yeah, well, an important one. Quite helpful for a better future."

"Better future, my arse. I mean, seriously... Come on, mum, open your eyes. It's always the same at the same position in this country. And look at me, I inherited several million years ago thanks to my dead grandmother, I've been making several times the calculation, and I don't even need to work for my entire life. I don't want kids, I don't want anything like this, and I have no plans for the future because I literally don't know what I want to do as a job. So, who cares about a stupid piece of paper? I am clearly advantaged, and I have that chance to be advantaged, so why shouldn't I be happy and enjoy my situation instead of stealing the bread of someone else's mouth?"

"And before you inherited your millions, yeah, do you remember how hard I had to work to pay the unaffordable rent here, making sure you would eat properly?"

"Oh my, don't put the blame on me, mum, you wanted a nice flat, and you wanted to have children, it was literally up to you to put yourself into that situation. Have you ever heard about council houses and abortion?"

"Gosh, I raised a monster!"

"A lucid one, at least. Regarding Florent, put yourself at his place, also. It's been three months that he works his ass off at his traineeship. Every time he comes back home, he's tired, and... No, I am sure, if he fails, he will question himself, and will be scared. Scared of my reaction. Because I am putting him under pressure... Okay, without even wanting. But still, the problem is, he's an architect at the beginning, and now applied for something in computing... He failed to find a job as an architect because he's a failure, and now, he doesn't have enough available space in his brain to succeed on that. So, yeah, because it's all about fear, I guess."

"You're saying that he's actually dumb. Okay. But afraid of you, I don't get your point..."

"Mum, did you forget that everything, literally everything, for a guy, is about sex?"

"And then you will be rude as usual, to overwhelm as you take a perverse pleasure to do when someone fails."

Yeah, right, if you see it this way... Yeah, that's what may actually happen. It's why I thought, I ran out of options to defend myself:

"Oh God, yeah, it's actually true... You raised a monster!" I started laughing.

"I know you since I created you!"

"Come on... He is my boyfriend, Mum, I won't be so rude. You know I have empathy for people that fail. If he fails and I piss him off, and even worse, if I actually do that, blaming him, it would be only for the pleasure to see him crawling on my feet, and you know that's not my style."

"Yeah, absolutely not, it's definitely not your style, see people crawling at your feet, no, not at all."

"Being a monster doesn't mean I need to be Satan."

"Yeah, may God listen to you!"

"Well, if only he'd be listening to me, and you'd be far, far away from me!"

"Yeah. You'd certainly be happy in isolation," Mum concluded, contemplative.

I stood up as I had just finished my tea. I mean, seriously, on mornings, as I am just back from my night and I need time to wake up, this is definitely not the time to talk about silly stuff or my future. She'd be talking about random things that would be better, the problem is, she never talks about random things, this privilege is reserved to Clarisse. Anyway, I took my cup, and I dropped it in the sink, without cleaning... I'll do it later; I don't want to use the dishwasher for one cup. But I was actually late, I looked on the lock screen of my phone, and even every morning it's the same thing: the race against the clock to be ready at the time. It was now 7:35. I had to go into my bathroom for getting dressed up, then getting ready, but first, before everything, combing my hair and all that classic stuff to look like I'm not actually a wild animal. I mean, it's not because it's my birthday that I'll have to act such as an eccentric. I still remain part of the civilisation. Somehow.

So, I walked back on the cold floor of the apartment. The tiles were still all frozen, and it was on tiptoes that I went back to my room. I pushed the door very slightly, as he was still sleeping, and I slowly went towards the bathroom because it's there that I left my clothes yesterday, that I prepared to be faster today. Actually, I always do it like this: to avoid making noise as I know that I wake up late, I put the clothes that I chose the day before in the bathroom. I don't wanna waste time, and since I know she's spying on me, the faster I'm out, the better it is. I mean... Yeah. Freedom is still very appreciated in these trouble times. And also, I don't wanna wake him up. I always like him and bothering him is not something that I want to do, he doesn't deserve to pay the war's price with her. Even if, yeah... He is not mean when I wake him up by accident, unlike me.

On the other hand, I am pretty lucky with my current boyfriend: he is not a trouble seeker, always there to try to avoid conflicts, and what I love about him is that he's never been afraid of what I'm capable of. At least he is more a morning person than I am. I can literally do what I want with him, he doesn't mind. Even being rude, but... well I made a nasty joke a couple of days ago, and he got offended for the first time. What I also like about him is that he is also a guy who always has an answer, and overall, and I'd say the most important, know how to react with me: he's the only one not to be afraid to face me up without shitting in his pants. He's not weak.

Free Expensive Lies: Prologue

On the other hand, he's been briefed by my sister on the day we met, not to get offended by whatever sarcastic joke I may by accident say. And, well, now, whenever I say something, people that use to know me aren't that offended, I mean, they know me, and they know that I always say what I think out loud, without caring that much about consequences. And it's usually a good test: if you get offended, then to me it means that you weren't that interesting. If you're not, then there's probably a potential.

Anyway, I came in, discreetly into the bathroom while he was still asleep, having his head on my pillow. It's cute, I mean, love, seeking my smell, and everything (big yawn) ... Well, yeah, I came in the bathroom quietly by slowly turning the doorknob, to finally push the door (since doors for bathrooms are not sliding doors). I immediately walked on the threshold of my bathroom, while I heard him turning himself on the bed. I kind of suddenly froze: was he waking up? No... His breath says that no. So, I continued.

The bathroom that we have linked to our bedroom(s) is relatively small and rectangular, all in the length of its attached bedroom, pretty much like the kitchen, but much smaller. But it still remains large. Upon entering, there's a white one-place ceramic bathtub with headrests, hidden behind a big white curtain. Next to it on the left is a small wall serving as a separator, and our shower tray is just behind it. Yes, we have both bathtub and shower tray, as strange as it may seem, but yes, it's arranged like this. I told you this place is posh. All the bathrooms of the flat are designed that same way. It's super weird but yeah, even I, I tried to understand this logic, but there's none. But what I like about the bathtub is its bubble system which is... very much appreciated after a long day. In front of both the tub and the shower, I have two grey bathmats, also facing the sinks and the toilets, next to them. As there are two massive sinks made of marble placed in a large piece of furniture into which is stored towels, shower stuff, and all this, yeah, we have a lot of space, to be fair. And a mirror overlooking the sinks, I, yeah... I used to do that, putting lipstick on my lips, and then I kiss the mirror, in this way, when Claire was still allowed to be here, and I had to leave early, she could see I thought about her before leaving... It's not really often that I do it with Florent, but still, it happens sometimes. No, I know, it won't happen today, don't expect that from me.

So yeah, before going to bed yesterday... I mean, at least before eating, I chose my clothes for today. If yesterday I was dressed differently, actually... My fashion code is a bit the same every day, I don't really like to change, and perhaps it reflects my personality. I don't really like change, and I don't really mind about my appearance. So, this is how I dress most of the time: I have always got a shirt, suit trousers, a suit waistcoat, and a trench coat, and finally, my black pumps. Every day the colour changes depending on what I prepared the previous day, but it remains that it's the way I use to be dressed. And I never tie my hair, I brush them, but I never tie them, I like leaving them floating upon the air. Multiple reasons here again, first, because I don't like it, and second, because... yeah, when I tie my hairs, it's becoming hard to comb it. I think it's good enough for a reason.

Regarding shirts, actually, I have got a whole collection, and for today, my shirt was a very light blue one, and I decided to wear a brown velvet vest, which was looking like my suit trousers, and my black leathered pumps. Obviously, I am mostly wearing dark colours. It's really unusual to see me wearing clear colours. That happens sometimes, but it's really not often, I love dark. Oh, no, I also have my heavy coat, a red one, that I love, I have it for the past two years now, it's like a big trench, and... Yeah, I didn't really change it.

It took me five minutes to get dressed from top to bottom, then, I brushed my hairs and teeth. Like every day, same old ritual, I put some foundation on my face because otherwise, I look like a walking cadaver freshly out of the morgue, my pallor makes that I am awful, and then, finally, after all this, I think I am ready. Sometimes I put some mascara just to look like something, but really quickly. I am not spending an hour in the bathroom; this is definitely not my style. Even if it's really exceptional what I am doing now, I hate to put some makeup to go to school, contrarily to everyone. But I guess today is a special day. No, seriously, it's true, I hate it, I am not a real fan of makeup in general. I don't like to do what everybody does, I consider that I am naturally beautiful, I never have to do more, for me, it's like cheating. I wear makeup when I want to wear it. And it's not really frequent.

After a couple of minutes, I left the bathroom, this time ready to go. The man was still sleeping peacefully and certainly deeply, while me, for my part, yeah, I had to go. I went to my small desk to grab the grey handbag that I left there yesterday evening while I chose my clothes for today, to avoid getting delayed. And it was when I caught the straps of the bag that suddenly, he turned himself and, hum...

"Er... Honey?" he whispered.

Okay, what I wanted to avoid, but fair enough, I guess. I am running out of time, though.

So, I turned back, came closer to his side of the bed where I still didn't remove our clothes yet, and then sat by his side of the bed. He fully opened his eyes, looked at me, and smiled while I was about to give him a hug. Because if I leave and do not give him a hug or a kiss, whenever I am back, he will be like "Oh honey you don't love me", blah blah blah, (yeah, guys... some of them don't care, though) so I want to avoid this kind of drama. It saves my nerves. In his eyes, I saw a little emotional glow before I took him in my arms, at this time I could guess that his mind was pretty much wandering in the roads between Baghdad and Kuwait City. Yeah, he was still completely asleep, but alert... That's a good sign, I guess. And yeah... Hug, done, now... I suppose if I don't have a quick chat with him too... I don't really know how they work, that's the thing.

"You okay?" I said after having hugged him.

"Hey, what's up?" he replied.

"I'm good. Hum... You should sleep, your exam is at 10, and... You're supposed to wake up later. So, sleep now, okay?"

"Yeah, I just need one kiss."

"Sure," I said with a little voice.

And then I gave him a little kiss. His lips were tensed, and his beard was still growing even though he shaved a couple of days ago, it stinks when I touch his face with my hand. It feels weird. Sounds, you know... odd, like it isn't supposed to be here. Anyway, I gave him his little kiss. I really don't like his budding beard. Well, there's quite a lot of stuff that I don't like in guys, but since Claire isn't available, I guess this is all I can have in stock at the moment, so I have to find a way to be happy. After having given him the little kiss he finally wanted, I caressed his stinky face nicely, and I said:

"Sleep, now. You must be okay today!"

"All right, baby, see you later, I love you" he whispered.

"Yeah, hum... see you later," I concluded before standing up again and now leaving.

Yeah, I know, saying "I love you" also sounds weird to me. Anyway, in those words, he closed his eyes. I'm sure he's not gonna remember that, as he seems so far away. I could have told him "you and me, it's over now" that he would even give me a smile. I was already carrying my bag; I took my phone to actually check furtively at the time: it was 07:47, which means... Pretty much... Time to move my arse! I am gonna be late. My coat was on the back of my chair in front of my desk, I quickly took it, wore it, then retook my bag as I had to drop it... And, yeah, time to go.

And then I left my bedroom (finally...), after having quickly looked for the last time at my dear boyfriend who promptly slept after having received his kiss—time to actually face up the truth and the hard reality. I walked to the entrance for taking my badges and keys that remained on the entrance yesterday, for going out and... While arriving at the main door that I saw the sun rising progressively on Paris, the sky was bluer than it was around half an hour ago. Astonishingly, mum was still drinking her tea in the kitchen—time to get the hell out. I don't know, the weather seems to be good today, no clouds far away, I actually stopped by the kitchen (I mean, without entering) that I saw that and, yeah... A good day ahead?

Mum was also looking at the window. Still sipping her tea very slowly, I wonder if now it's still hot, but anyway. At the moment I actually stopped leaning against the frame of the kitchen's door, shortly daydreaming, that she asked:

"You're going out?"

"Unfortunately," I kind of wept deep inside.

"Huh? Now?"

"Yes. Why? Do you need anything from me? Like a hug and a goodbye mum, I love you?"

"You? No... You're too kind for doing this!"

"Appreciate that. Anyway, have a good day. See you tonight."

"See you tonight, my darling. I love you."

"Yeah, yeah, yeah."

2 *Another day*

// *Travelling to school.*

// *Wednesday, 9th of January 2013, 07:53.*

After giving all my strength to close it (yeah, this door is massive, I mean... really), I locked up the main entrance, and I dropped my key into my school handbag. I was actually in a rush; it's why I opened the door of the stairs instead of waiting for the lift to come. Too much time wasted just for travelling one floor, and we say that exercise is still good. It would slow me more down than it could speed me up. So, I went downstairs and arrived at the main hall of our residence. I walked through a corridor for going out. Then I had to go to the closest subway station, which is not far from where our building is but still, I need four minutes to walk there, to go back to school like every day. Wait, seriously, you really thought that my life was that exciting?

And yet again, it was damn freezing outside. Well, on the other hand, it's still January, so what should I expect? So, I live in a pretty much recent building (I mean contemporary, it has been built in the 90', but it is still okay for Paris), that is part of the Rue des Peupliers, a private street (*Rue* means street in French... Poplar Street would be a good translation for the full name) that is within Neuilly, a famous city in the suburb of the capital. Famous, because, well, you live in Neuilly generally when you have relatively high incomes. The building comprises five floors, ten flats, more or less, and I live in the second apartment on the first floor—flat number two. We have ample parking with private garages underneath the building, we also have one in front of the building. Still, as the residence is a private residence, we have a security office that checks who comes and leaves the facility. This is why we all have badges with our keys because if we fail to show the badge or a valid ID, we aren't granted access to the street and then to the building. Though the badge is magnetic, we can use it to open the big portal or door to leave the road.

Like I said, okay, my mum has high incomes, but my sister and I are both heiresses. Well, you won't find anybody living in our street who doesn't have at least a million on his bank account. To make it short, my family (my family name's Kominsky) is pretty much an old family, and a wealthy one. Like, yeah, really wealthy, as my great-grandparents used to have a big company in Europe that they sold after World War II, and since even we reinvested in real estate and that kind of stuff. If you include assets and everything, the entire fortune of the family is that, well, pretty much around 465 million euros. It may look a lot, but trust me, there are people more prosperous than us. We even used to be much more wealthy. Anyway, when we moved to Paris in 2005, my father wanted to buy a building, and for a big bill, he actually bought this one. I mean, my grandparents bought it. And when my grandmother died (because she had all the money), dad inherited, and... And until that fun day.

The fun day was in 2006 when, whilst doing stuff with my mum, by the time when everything was still fine between us, we met some lovely girl, pretty much same aged as I was by the time, but we learned that she was younger, and we also learned that she was our step-sister. My mum loved that. So, yeah, as my father cheated on her it led to a divorce, and... the dishonour also led to the fact that Clarisse and I inherited quite suddenly the building where we lived, after months of judicial battle. I mean, we didn't sue our father, no, our mother did that on our behalf, because, she wanted to remain in Paris because we were at school there, and, as my dad was *de facto* landlord, the battle was about that, as my mother never wanted to pay rent to my father because he was ordered to stay away from us. The thing is, dad imposed her to pay rent as reprisals of having won the battle over us, and she had to pay some rents... high rents, I think his goal was to literally crush her financially. Until that moment, they found a deal: Clarisse and I would have the building, with some money, in exchange for him leaving us alone. So, the building is ours with Clarisse. And it's a great source of incomes, of course, as mum also manages the thing as we were too young until then, but now, I really don't know what's gonna happen with that. We need to decide it with my twin.

Anyway, after that short walk, when I arrived at the Security Office, there's always someone that welcomes me. I kind of know all the five guys that are in here, more or less. Basically, mum found an agreement with the landlord association for that security, as, in 2007, there have been a series of burglaries in the street. And most of the landlords voted to invest in private security, and my mother voted for that. So, security is subcontracted by the landlord's association, and, in exchange for a monthly payment, we have them. Which is actually safe, since... Yeah, like everybody, nobody loves to find his flat upside-down after a long day at work.

So, I arrived not far from his office, and like every morning, I have to show my badge, even if I own the place. To be fair, the guys that work here are adorable, I mean, I never really had any problems yet. I don't know their name since I am not their bosses, but, well. Anyway, at the moment I arrived (because when you leave the building, you come by behind the office, as this small office is within a recess of the building and... it kind or works the same way like when you order something at a drive-thru in McDonald's), he immediately turned himself back after I knocked at the window... because he was watching some film on his laptop:

"Hi, boss!"

"Hi, mate! What's up this morning?" I was looking for the little badge that I saw myself putting in my bag a couple of seconds ago.

"I am alright, what about you?"

I was carrying my handbag, and, the problem is, just like every morning, I am in a kind of automatic mode, and always put the badge in the bag without really thinking that in a couple of minutes I will have to take it out again. Yeah, maybe I have a good memory, it doesn't prevent me from being a little dumb sometimes. I mean, it's the morning, my brain still to fully initialise. And then I remembered that I have let it in the pocket of my coat. Geez...

"Well, I'm fine! I'm eighteen today! I can finally come back home drunk legally from today!" I spoke whilst giving the card.

"Hum... I think I saw you drunk already, many times before..."

"Oh yeah? What you say might be true, I don't recall" I smiled before whispering, "I was certainly too drunk to remember."

Yeah, he saw me coming back home screwed up many times, especially recently, I must confess that I do not really bear celibacy. And it's precisely here that I wish, I mean, I'd give everything to have this little pen that they have in Men in Black, "I'm gonna ask you to look at this little red light over here". Oh, well, after all, being drunk, I guess that it's life... Even if I do not drink that often. I am not really a drinker. For Health and Safety reasons, it's better that I do not drink. And by Health and Safety, I mean more safety than health.

"Anyway, happy birthday, anyway!" he looked at me when I placed the card back this time in my handbag.

"Thank you, I appreciate it," I replied.

"Yeah," he sighed.

Meh, no jokes today. Hum, disappointing. There's one thing fascinating with him, it's the natural tone he has for saying atrocities. I have great respect for people with that ability. For example, on Monday, while he was here, I was coming back home, he was in afternoon shift. And I arrived but was carrying two heavy bags since I went shopping before as mum was not here and I had to prepare something to eat. They were really heavy, full of food because she asked me to buy for at least three days, and I couldn't carry those bags and open the doors at the same time, it was impossible. So, he came to help me, and unfortunately, I pushed one of my bags against him, bag that contained three two litres bottle of water that apparently hurt him. He simply said after being hit, "Ouch, it hurt me! Be careful, I checked this morning, and still, I have got two left!" So, with the smile, I didn't understand at first. I dropped my bag, looked at him, and answered so naturally, "You've got two what?" He replied, "My balls! I've got only two left!" Ridiculous, but funny. Oh, come on. That's stupid. The kind of joke that I can't make, it's a shame.

"You're not looking fine today, are you?" I actually asked him as I saw him kind of focused on his screen.

"No, I'm okay, don't worry!"

"All right then. Anyway, thank you, mate, and I'll see you later okay?"

"Yeah! See you later, Miss Kominsky!"

I pushed the door that he opened, and I left. Yeah, sad...

While I was on the parking lot for going away (and this time getting literally frozen because... for some reason it was actually colder than cold), I was looking for my phone in my bag. Yeah, it was cold this morning. I was also seeking my headset, which I – as usual – have fun unravelling whilst walking. But not today, as I used it this morning. I plugged it into my phone while walking this time in the street.

So, yeah, like I said, it was chilly like every January in Paris. The fresh air moving from the vehicles in the street was freezing me even more as I left the portal a few metres away. I think I was not enough covered. Even if I was wearing my red coat, I feel like it wasn't enough. Whilst I walked down the street, I hid my phone into a pocket of my vest because I have to take the metro, and Paris is still unsafe, especially in the metro. So, I'm always scared to show my phone in the metro. I didn't hear music, I pretended to. Why did I do this? Harassment, I guess. Well, I am not wearing a sensitive outfit, but still, some guys can be rude, and when I have my headset on my ears, I just pretend I cannot listen to anyone and thus avoid problems. As, for going to the metro station, I have to walk about a hundred and fifty metres on the Avenue de Madrid (the street that passes under my window... the busy one, remember?) for reaching a roundabout, where I turn on the left to get to a small square in the middle of the avenue after having crossed a road and then, walking down some stairs, and entering an underground alley that leads me to the metro station. Always the same stuff, but in winter, I usually hurry up because I don't want to get frozen. Like I said, there are still many people walking down the street, but sometimes you have lost people seeking their way or, some other times, rude people that because you are pretty, young or whatever, start being annoying with you.

My bag was heavy. Okay, it's a new one – a medium-leathered grey handbag quite deep that I can close – where I use to store all my mess. A little umbrella, a small bottle of water, my workbooks for school and other stuff to write (which were today the heaviest), some tissues, my wallet and passport, condoms (who knows...), and a copy of the keys of my home, all my moveable mess was here. Plus, my phone and my two headsets (I have got two because I'm always scared to break one and music remains one of my very first necessity in life, along with water and sweets), and some chewing-gums. I still don't know why I keep them, since I never have chewing-gums... oh, yeah, I never wanted to get caught for the time I used to drink.

As I was walking and certainly halfway of where I was heading, the weather was changing, with threatening clouds were starting to invade the sky. In the meantime, I rushed because I was late, and mostly because it's cold out there and I don't want to actually have the rain falling on me. But hopefully, I usually walk extremely fast. My sister sometimes complains because I am too fast, and she can't follow. She says it's such a sport to walk with me. Personally, I don't think so, I still walk at what I call an average speed, she's just too slow. There are only three streets from home to the metro station, it's not a marathon at all, it's pretty much four minutes.

Anyway, I quickly crossed the road, even if there was a lot of traffic, I arrived at the station. For those who don't know Paris, my station is located on a major artery of the capital, the Avenue Charles-de-Gaulle, leading to a big business district called La Défense, from the Avenue des Champs-Elysées within Paris, pretty much. For the record, this avenue is famous for being where Napoleon used to come back to Paris with his troops after significant battles, lost or won. But I guess why today this is a major artery of the capital is that it leads to this business district, straight from Central Paris. So, there's always a lot of traffic, and at that hour, congestions. Anyway, I entered the metro station through the small stairs leading to the entrance, walked down the stairs, entered that vast underground hall to pass the porticos and validate my card, for reaching other stairs and manage to sneak into the crowd to actually find a way to get to the platform. Yes, during rush hours, this station is always crowded, it sometimes happens that I leave two or three metros passing before being able to board the next. Well, that's the capital, I guess it must be the same everywhere. My platform was unusually not that crowded, so I could have my bench available to sit down. And after having sat in this same bench, I always read on the panel that the next train is "in four minutes". Paris' metro has a big reputation for being utterly disgusting. Again, it was a regular morning, just like most of the station the network has you can smell that fantastic cocktail of urine and cheap alcohol. This is something that wakes you up, trust me. Or on off-peak hours you can meet with junkies or other pieces of work here, yeah, that's fantastic. But, like everywhere I guess, the real danger here comes from other people travelling with you.

Hopefully, four minutes later, the metro arrived. Even less. So, I stood up for boarding in the overcrowded train, after having minded the closing doors and making sure that I could sneak in that ocean of people. The metro was empty and was travelling towards the Castle of Vincennes. Surprisingly, it was busy, I'm travelling westbound, and it's usually eastbound that it's active in the morning since it stops at La Défense. Meh, that's line 1, far away from the nightmare that is line 13. The problem of the overcrowded metro is, it's sweltering in here, like... I'm melting. It's the same route every morning (when I decide to go to school), I change seven stations later after *Pont de Neuilly*, in the one called *"Champs-Elysées-Clemenceau"*, for after taking the thirteenth line (the worst line ever) to go to Asnières-sur-Seine where my school is located, travelling for eleven stations, and, erm... It's the daily routine, I hate the routine. I know I can take the bus instead, but the metro remains the fastest option.

I travelled to a station, then another, and another and the metro was stopping every time, announcing the upcoming station in its formal name, opened his doors, seeing people getting off the train and then closing its doors, being in between the prey of that moving crowd. Then the harsh and thunderous beep to inform that population that unless they do not want to hurry up..., but like I said, the problem here comes from the people because, even if they see there's no space available for them, then guess what, they still enter no matter what! Which makes that at the end, you travel like in a pressurised bottle, just open the lid, and it's where the fun starts. Yes, the Paris metro system's right thing is that you can have a good phone signal whilst travelling. Which is why, suddenly, whilst travelling, I felt at some point my bag vibrating. When the metro is overcrowded like it is, you can barely move your arms, which is why, instead of taking my phone out of my bag and checking who was calling (as it rang like in an incoming call), I directly pressed the button on my headset. And I guess I'll see who it is...

"Yeah?"

"Oh sorry, erm... wrong number!" I recognised Claire's voice.

Oh, crap... She found me. Not today, please... I don't wanna talk to you. I actually never wanna talk to you...

"Of course, you know a thousand girls named Charlotte, obviously," I didn't believe her.

"There's only one named 'selfish bitch' on my phone, honey!"

"Oh, my... That hurts!" I sarcastically replied.

"How are you doing?"

"Oh, guess?"

"Bad, as usual."

"Then why do you ask the question if you already know the answer? To be honest, I was fine a couple of minutes ago, then I accidentally took that call!"

"Come on, honey, I just want to wish you a happy birthday!"

"There was no need for that, actually. But hold on a second... you obviously didn't make a mistake when calling. You're calling me for something, I know you. You're everything but innocent. So, what do you want?"

"What does tell you that?"

"I have been with you for the past seven years, remember?"

It's funny that everybody suddenly looks at you as long as you expose certain aspects of your life in a crowded train. It literally happened when I started saying that. This is my problem, sometimes I do not hear myself when I speak. Anyway, I love those primitives instincts that attract people to gossips... Crazy.

So, yeah, Claire, (aka. Miss Claire Alexandra Cobert) is my ex-girlfriend. Although we broke up, I am still at school with her, and, I have to see her until that year ends, and... In my wonderful life, I have ninety-nine problems, and this girl is all of them. If I really managed to go over our relationship? No. If I managed to learn to live without her? No. If we are friends today? I wish I wouldn't. (Yeah, I am not the kind of person to like remaining in touch with my past experience... a failure is a failure, that's it) If I still love her? Hum, pretty much, yes. Okay, yes, I am, and it makes me go nuts. I want to have her back. Even if I have to dump Florent for that. But...

"Yes, I've forgotten that Charlotte Kominsky was a thought-reader, I forgot you can read in my mind like in an open book." She continued, "No, I'm calling you just to tell you that I was in front of the College, waiting for you."

"And this is my interest because...?"

"Shut up. Have you had a good night?" for some reasons, she passed to something else.

"More or less. Why?"

"Because today is the first day of the rest of your life. By the way, since we're talking about that, I wanted to ask you something. Tonight, with Kelly and Sophie, we planned to throw a party for you. Do you want to come with us?"

"Nope! Trust me, you actually convinced me right after you said that Kelly would be here!"

"Darling, it will be fun, come on! And I may have a surprise for you after!" she whispered as if she was telling me a secret.

"Yeah, I see what your surprise would be. I will not mess up my life because of you, darling. By the way, stop calling me darling."

"You fucked it up already, you're corrupted!"

"Yeah, maybe, but at least I try to manage it!"

"Come on!"

"No!"

"Come on, Charlotte! You're eighteen today, it's an important day for you, and we need to celebrate that. So, tonight, you come with us, and you keep your mouth shut."

"I'm booked already. As a matter of fact, Claire, unlike you, I have a boyfriend, I'm not single."

The funny thing with her is that, as soon as I just pronounce words such as "Florent", "boyfriend", "I'm booked", or "I'm not single", she feels destabilised. And I can hear it straight since it takes her at least more than three seconds to think about what to reply without being overwhelmed. And, even now, it worked. But to be honest, I have a terrible hunch. Because I know her, and I know that as long as I wouldn't give in, she will make me angry. I know, when we were together, she was already like this.

"You're not booked, it's rubbish..." she resumed after, well...

"Interesting. What makes you say that?"

"You would have told me straight away. You're not booked..." she was extrapolating.

"Okay, maybe I am not booked... However, erm..."

"However, nothing. You'll show up tonight. Come on, Cha, please, for me!"

"Why would I?"

"Come on, Charlotte, it's been a while that we didn't have fun together, and I know that your life with your new boyfriend is as boring. So, please, come. I mean, seriously, I really would like to spend the evening with all of you, my close friends. Plus, we need it, it's been since we broke up that you're alone and not staying with us. So, is that all right? You wanna come with us tonight?"

"You're pathetic." I just snubbed her.

"Come on, it's just a party, Charlotte!" she answered with a lot of hesitations.

"Don't you recall when I said that I didn't want to see you outside of..."

"Come on!" she interrupted me.

Free Expensive Lies: Prologue

"I know how it ends when I'm out with you, so I want to avoid it... And MOSTLY I didn't even need to know that you were going out tonight. Unless you don't understand, but I cannot make it clearer, either you accept my refusal to go out with you tonight, whether you go do what I think. I'm still recovering from our breakup, so I don't need to be pulled down."

"Okay, listen," she interrupted me. "I totally understand... given the situation. But, come on, get over it, darling. I know we're not together; I know you were in love with me and you probably still are, but... Come on, it's just a party! It's just a moment altogether, and that's it, nothing's gonna happen, you have my word."

Interesting. I knew she would use my feelings against me. At least she seems sincere. Get over it, get over it... Because she went through it, maybe, when she's drunk and cries over my voicemail because she's so unhappy now? How many messages I have on my phone from her telling me to ignore the voicemail she left me the previous night because she was just fucked up! Hiding my emotions is harsh with her, she knows me for... Yeah, seven years.

Moreover, Claire's been my very first true love, that's the first reason why I am so reluctant, she's the only one to be really able to make me weak and pull me down. Since we're at school together and I see her quite often... it's hard to, as she said, get over it. We remained close, I mean, she calls me most of the time to talk about her problems as she's always been doing, because there's a strong trust between us, we know everything about each other. Well, to actually summarise, according to her, we are friends. In my view, we have, erm... what the UN calls a "specific status". If I accept, okay... We will have fun, but with her, it will be a bit more than all the fun that I could expect especially if we drink, and I really don't want it, I have a boyfriend, I'm trying to create something with him, and this girl is just a bunch of problem with a vagina. And the very last thing I am is a cheater, cheating is the absolute betrayal for me and, well, I am not a traitor. But after all, okay... If she holds herself, fine, why not. She's right, it's been a while that we didn't have a party and, yeah, I kind of need it too, yeah. After all, she finished by "you have my word", and she is a woman of her words, so... Let's try it.

"Alright, you idiot, okay, I'm in, tonight. But there's a condition. First, if at some point you try to... you know... I get the hell out straight away."

"Depends on you. But okay..."

"Second, you're an idiot and given how YOU ended up our love story, I'm still mad at you and don't worry, I'm totally healed of our relationship. And now, I've never been so happy in my life."

"Glad to know. I gladly don't care... darling!"

"Fuck off. Anyway, I'll be here soon, see you in a bit!" I said while hanging up.

3 *Oh, I am fine, you?*

// On my way to my college, Asnieres-sur-Seine, near Paris...

// Wednesday, 9th of January 2013, 08:33

Interesting fact: the verb "to work" in French is *travailler*. It is the verbal form of the word *travail* (meaning labour... or a job, depending on the context), which also comes from the Latin word *tripalium*, an instrument of torture made of three piles. Say whatever you want about French people, I may just say that they got it right on this point.

Because sometimes, coming here feels to me like... pretty much if I was going to be hung. Several reasons for that, but I guess the first is because the building is quite old and shady (it's actually an old monastery converted into... I know, yeah), and in second, because, yeah, I am, literally wasting my time here. So, to give you an idea about where my school is, it's in Asnieres-sur-Seine, a town that is also part of Paris' suburb, it is actually located in what we call the *Petite Couronne* (small crown). To get there, you need to go to the thirteenth line's terminus, and, pretty much, after having walked two streets, it's into a small park. All hidden from the city by the trees, at least when you pass in that street, you can't see the building. That's the only cool thing, to be fair, of this place, because, yeah, it's in a park, and at least you can stay there during breaks in spring or summer, it's actually fancy. And safe as well, to be honest, Asnières is, well... It could be safe; it just depends on where you go. And at what time, also.

This being said, this school is a pretty imposing building, formerly a monastery, like I said. Some records state that this building was built during Louis XIV's reign, they aren't sure about the precise date. Even if it still contains traces of the History on its walls because it's made of old stones, some are carved to show some coat of arms, well, most of them today have somehow been unfortunately gnawed by modern pollution, which is, I must admit, pretty sad. It has been refurbished on several occasions throughout history, but one of the biggest was in the '70 and, they are also now refurbishing some parts of the building. Basically, due to its religious purpose at the beginning, the building is made of three wings built around a former cloister, which is now a schoolyard. Classrooms are located throughout the three branches, that are north, west and south (we enter the building through a big door in the south wings), and the "east wing" is pretty much where the church is (yeah, we have a church, and a relatively big one, though), toilets and some, erm, warehouse. Through history this building had several functions, for instance, it has been converted into barracks of the Great Army under the Napoleonic Wars. Then for several years after the downfall of Napoleon, it was left abandoned. Since 1953, it has been restored and turned into a public College first, then it has been bought in 1990 by a local entrepreneur.

Thus, this is a private school. Yeah, it's why we have that church since France is, in fact, a laic country and you are not supposed to receive any religious teaching at school. The difference is, well, you pay for private school and therefore can choose wherever you want to go, unlike public where you have to go to your neighbourhood school, but access is free. Oh, and most private schools are nowadays catholic schools, so they can deliver religious courses, which I obviously do not attend (they said "heresy"), but Clarisse does... sometimes, when she comes early and has nothing else to do. Hopefully, those courses are not mandatory, and if you cut them, it's okay, it won't affect anything. The thing is, it is also widely said here that private schools are more prestigious, but they still teach you the same shit in private schools, so... And bullying is always the same, wherever you go... Even if bullying in College is mostly called "revenge porn" or "sex tape", this is why, you'd better stay out of it, which is what I do. The only difference is, I think she pays 450 euros every three months, and... and yeah, she selected that school because mum wanted us to be taught real values in such a sensitive age that is the final years of adolescence. Yeah, actual values, my arse, come on. Name me only one male student here that thinks about Jesus Christ before, while, or after watching dirty porn. I swear to God, if you find this, I immediately sign up to become a nun.

Anyway, in France, the school system works that way: first, after kindergarten, which is not really a school but let's consider it this way, you have the "Primary school". Like everywhere. There, we have to pass five years (succeeding in this way, first the *CP* – for *Cours Préparatoires*, "preparatory courses" – then after this, we have two levels, *CE1*, *CE2* – *CE* stands for *Cours élémentaires*, "elementary classes" and the number represents the year – then after, to follow the same logic, we pass through *CM1*, *CM2*, which means *Cours moyen* "middle classes", the last step before the high school). Usually, you leave primary school when you're ten years old. But since I was born in January, I was eleven when I left, for some reasons. Primary school is quite the best moments at school, you have only one teacher, and you learn basics but useful things. You have your first friends, and you remember all your teachers since they are adorable. Honestly, I really enjoyed going to primary school. But I went to primary school in Montpellier, a city in the south of France, because we lived there. It's also in primary school that Clarisse and I improved our French. As we are not speaking French as a mother tongue. Our parents were actually quite smart on that, they wanted us to speak English as a mother tongue since... well, nowadays, if you don't speak English, you're just screwed. When we were in CP, I recall, we had someone to help us understand what the teacher said.

After having passed the primary school, you finally brace for High School (yeah, brace for), which is called *collège* in French, contrarily to English, and it's covering only four steps, from the sixth to the third class. Which is quite a huge step in our life, I mean... It's the very beginning of your journey through teenage time. You discover funny things, such as... well, bullying, parents' divorce, first girlfriend... masturbation, yeah, funny stuff like that. And don't ask me about the last. My experience? It turns out that it was a challenging moment because if I attended primary school in the south of France, I moved to Paris for the high school, and it's when I was in the sixth class that my parents divorced. Because of this, the stress at home, I screwed up, and I failed my year, and in addition to that, I was bullied.

Consequently, thanks to that great cocktail, I lamentably failed the sixth grade, and the year after I met Claire and became a bully, and... here we are, now. I guess it's there that things have enormously changed. But since my second, sixth grade we actually were friends at first, then more than friends, I figured out that I was lesbian, and she was bisexual. And, yeah, three months after we met, the very first kiss, then... the relationship. That remained a total secret, I mean, even today, nobody at school except Kelly and Clarisse (the only woman on Earth I will actually truly estimate the day I'll find her in a body bag...) know that Claire and I have been together for seven years, we managed to keep the secret intact, they just think we've been friends. The reason why we kept that secret is, precisely, to avoid bullying. I mean, seriously, have you heard all the homophobic slurs that we hear all the time?

After having passed the high school, we have what we call "College" in English-speaking countries, which is called *Lycée* in French. College is divided into three steps: the second grade, the first and the *terminale* (in English "closing courses"). Upon successfully finishing the second class, we are all asked to choose a specification. As the College leads to the famous baccalaureate (which equals the A-level in the UK), we have to decide how we want to go for further studies in universities. There are a lot of different baccalaureates, such as, in that order, *Littéraire* (literary, the easiest one according to everybody), *Economique et Sociales* (social and economic sciences) and *Scientifiques* (sciences, for the tough guys). But not only these, several others but less relevant. And guess what I chose? I am today in the closing class, because I will pass my baccalaureate in July, and even if I still kept a nasty behaviour, I am the best pupil of the whole region (*Ile-de-France*) according to some rankings. A thing that I could obviously be proud of, according to mum, Claire, and Clarisse, but I obviously don't care. Meh. In the meantime, I am the best student and the worst regarding my days of exclusions and hours of detention... Well, we can't be good everywhere.

And if you ask me about any plans for the future, I don't have any. With my results, I can literally go anywhere because they see me as a genius and this not because I am studying hard, but because I am more gifted. I have the absolute memory, which is, precisely... Well, good and bad. But mostly bad. My brain is like a sponge, as soon as I hear or see or smell something, I never forget it. This is why it's such a mystery for everybody, but, well. I had plans for the future, when I was younger, I wanted to work as a doctor, but I just can't stand seeing blood. I really don't know what I want to do, especially since I know, it's a chance, and I am aware that, yeah, I don't need to work. I have enough money not to work. And to be honest, that's what I lack, ambition, and, not having plans for the future... Yeah, frankly depresses me, especially since I know that I am eighteen today.

I was now slowly arriving within the school park. I was walking all the way along, with my hands in my pockets. I passed the main gate a few moments ago, and God knows how I so desired to actually make my way back home. I mean, the thing is, I never rush to go to school. The park around the College has two entries: the first one is the pedestrian entrance only, connected to the Jacques Prévert street in Asnières, and it's still the one designed for leading to the old cloister that we're still using nowadays, even if it has been built somewhere in the 1600 and threatens to collapse at any moment, as it's making an arch. The second is to access the car park, fifty metres away.

On the other hand, they reinforced the arch a couple of years ago when a stone fell on a student and apparently seriously injured her, but, well, seeing that is actually still kind of bucolic. The massive door painted in green, underneath, also rusty, displayed some inscriptions and the coat of arms of the former monastery, and some papers regarding the work currently carried out on the parking are actually somehow the thing that reinforces the stone arch above. And the second entrance, on the same side of the street but maybe two hundred metres after, was still under construction. Yes, because they want to concrete the parking, as it's currently made of gravel, they took that decision over the many complaints they received from people having asthma. And it's true that when cars were driving there, it was releasing so much dust in the air that it was crazy.

After having crossed the big iron gate's threshold, immediately, there is only one way: a hundred metres' footpath on the left, which leads us straight to the school's main entrance. This path is surrounded by trees on both sides and by a little vegetation, always lovely and relaxing to see. It's quite beautiful and fun. And then, you have to go on the right for going to the main entrance of the building, because what's facing up the path is the church, and right now it's closed. Yeah, they only open it on Sunday for the mass, otherwise, the rest of the time, it's shut. So, after walking this hundred-metre path, when I arrived at the end and before to go any further, I quickly looked towards the entrance, and saw some pupils coming inside the school, as every morning, as doors were wide open. Of course, according to different faces and, well, the way they were heading, I could quickly assess the same level of motivation than mine. And, in the middle of this beautiful mess, like, erm, seeing a star in the centre of a far galaxy, Claire. She was slightly withdrawn compared to other people. As, for coming inside the school building, at least to reach the threshold, we need to walk in a small stair; and she was standing just beside this stair. Yes, she was actually waiting for me. Uh-oh.

So, Claire, a broad topic. The last and lost love of my life. I mean, all the time I see her, I always feel the same, she makes me feel totally dumb and, yeah, she's the blue pearl in the middle of the ocean, for me. And also my most tremendous pain, I mean, it's gonna take me years before I go over it as she said, but, yeah, when I see her today, I feel deep sadness and, I really don't know how to conceal it. But things are over now. Claire is really tall (slightly taller than me), has long and straight dark hairs, and has beautiful green eyes. All the time, she looks appeased, I mean, she has always an appeased face. She is very slim, I mean, she's the kind of person to be overfocused on what she eats... I recall, the very last week of our relationship, she complained because she gained a kilo. On the other hand, I must say that the end of our relationship was extremely tough for both of us.

Free Expensive Lies: Prologue

And, today, I don't know why today, but she was absolutely stunning: she was wearing perfect makeup, slight red lipstick, mascara and... Yeah, She was wearing her fluffy grey scarf, her oversized black coat, that was closed, and unlike me, I am sure she thought about wearing a pullover (well, I am sure she did... She is really sensitive to cold), her black-leathered trousers and finally, small, heeled brown boots. She was looking at the parking, leaning against that small stairs, and for some reasons, her sight was somehow lost, she seemed thoughtful. Her hands in her pockets, like trying to keep herself hot whilst it was cold. And her handbag, similar to mine, was at her feet, between her legs. In addition to that, she had her small pink woollen hat. Now I guess you understand why I don't want to see her, right? Because, at my eyes, she will always be stunning, and... Well, another day, another fight, I guess.

Psychologically speaking, Claire is literally my opposite. Unlike me, she had a very tough childhood (she lost her father when she was four) but had I may say very happy adolescence. On the other hand, we know each other since we're eleven. As my girlfriend, unlike me, she's never been allergic to people. She was mostly going towards them, always listening to everybody without getting involved in one's problems, she mainly had an introvert behaviour and, basically, people trust... I mean, trusted her, overall. She is a genuinely kind person, a good liar, and unlike me, she tolerates people as long as they do not cross certain boundaries. This is due to her great calm, deep understanding, and voice, she always appears calm. Claire has this ability to actually lead people and unite them (she can be a great leader). I saw that many times because she knows how to speak to people. She knows how to be remembered and respected, most of the students trusted her, and on many occasions, she's been elected as a representative of our class to teachers and managed many problems. In terms of the right pupil and good student, she's really average. Obviously, this was when we were together, I guess my harsh behaviour was somehow at the origin of this stability, as I also brought her a lot of things. Now, now that she's single (unlike me she didn't find anybody), she dramatically changed. She's being manipulated by this Kelly that literally brainwashed her, and she's completely screwing around. Rumour has it that she apparently sleeps with many people, she betrayed most of them as well, and now, she's becoming isolated, almost nobody wants to talk to her. Regarding her (apparently) countless sexual partners, I have some proofs that it's not only rumoured. And this is sad.

Taylor Harding-Jenkins

We broke up last year, after a long relationship. There were actually a lot of reasons for that. But the main one is that at the very beginning of the last year, we've been caught sleeping together by my mother, who could not accept that I'd be gay. So, it led to many conflicts as mum declared the holy war, which led to this: one week before we broke up, she cheated on me, apparently by accident... with a guy, and with this Kelly. I wanted to forgive since I genuinely loved her, and she also wanted to give one last chance to our couple, but this week were fights over fights. Although I managed to find a deal with her, or at least a compromise, one day she texted me and, later on, after I travelled through Paris to meet her, told me that it was over, without giving any clear explanations. And the fun started afterwards. It led me to a week of isolation, I also lost five kilos, and they had to drive me to the hospital one night as I was dehydrated and vomiting, I broke two phones, and... And then back at school. We had different plans for the future together, we planned to live together, we even planned to leave this country after baccalaureate so we could start our lives. We planned to live together, even getting married whenever that would be legal in the UK. We even planned to grow old together and buy a house in the countryside. Maybe she was my very first love, and we say that the first love never lasts, but my first love was an unforgettable first love. There's no first love like Claire. And when Kelly came between us, I knew she was a threat. This is why I convinced her to kick her out of her life because I was scared. And I was right. Today, she won the game. And I lost, I'm all alone now. She made me Cinderella, and now I am back in my old nightmare. And, sincerely, I'd give everything, I'd give up my money, I'd give up my life, I'd give up my family if only I could have a chance to come back with her. But days after days, I see the opportunity of this happening going closer to zero, so I'm not hoping anymore. My former reality is now, more or less, nothing more than an inaccessible dream.

When I saw her, like I used to do, I feel like I am the weak one, until I realise that perhaps she feels the same. And I saw her, she was looking around. I really don't know why, all the time, she has the very same reaction, and today was the same: why does she, whenever she sees me, takes out of her bag her phone and pretends to have been on it for hours? It doesn't make sense, sometimes.

I actually came closer, unlike her, I never feel the need to do the same. Her phone on her hand, she was probably scrolling down her Facebook wall... I felt like, yeah, disenchanted. Just looking at her, it's like... Like life is coming to remind me "what the fuck, you lost her!". It's sad to see her have changed so dramatically, Claire became the kind of girl who can't do anything without her phone, she was not like this when she was with me. The smartphone, no-one can convince me otherwise, it remains the greatest plague of our century. But, I guess, now, although I know that she's not in a relationship with Kelly (she'd be in a relationship and she would never behave this way), it's curious that she is doing everything to look like her. This is when I say that she's been totally brainwashed, and the thing is, I have no idea why. I really have no idea of what's happening in her life, why she has become such an extravert, why she sleeps with many people, why she behaves this way, all this seems really dodgy to me. But what can I do, she is not my girlfriend anymore, I guess I left the sinking ship too early.

So, I progressed towards her, still with my hands in my coat. Suddenly, although I know that she observed me before taking her phone, she noticed my presence, but I guess she wants to give herself a style, or shall I say that she pretended to see me. And, obviously, usual, she played like, "oh my god, here you are, so good to see you, blah, blah, blah!":

"Hey, hey, hey, look at you, honey!" she discreetly placed her phone back in her left-pocket of her coat.

"Yeah, what, did I have pigeon poop on my coat?" I was ... actually myself whilst coming in front of her.

"No! What's up, baby?"

"I swear to God, call me baby another time, and you'll go to your party tonight with a broken leg, this is my last warning. Speaking of legs, you're stunning today, I mean, look at you..."

"Ah, thank you... I am surprised that it's the only thing you noticed, my legs," she blushed.

"Well, I actually did, yeah. To be honest, I was also curious about what time they do open for business hours."

"Ha, ha, ha, really funny. Have you not seen the results, by the way?"

"Nope. Which results are you talking about?"

"Come on, you really don't know what I'm talking about? You gotta be kidding me!"

"Cut the crap, Claire, I'm not in the mood."

"Come on, it's all on display, your performances!"

"I'm not in the mood, Claire..." I warned her.

"All right then," she concluded.

This is what she hates, and I know that it's when I call her by her full name. Unlike her, I'm no longer calling her "darling" or "honey", because... SHE broke up with me, so SHE must understand that there must be distances between her and me. However, she called me also "Charlotte" once, and I didn't like it either. But, after all, she decided this, so she must assume.

"Okay, so, what're your goddamn numbers?" I was irritated.

"Er... Actually, it's silly. Now it's over, you're not the first as you have been for so long anymore!"

"The first... You mean of this College? Oh, just a second, could you hang on a minute?"

"Erm, yes... of course... what for?"

"Just give me five minutes. So, I can check whether I care or not."

"Hum, you don't care, I forgot."

"Meh, Kelly may have brainwashed you, you still have some neurons working left, glad to see."

"First of all, she didn't brainwash me, and second, it's sad for me because I've always known you as the best! My former girlfriend is the best in the region. Even in France! You're still the best at my eyes!"

Former girlfriend, huh? Already?

Right now, we were walking towards the entrance of the building. Besides her I-try-to-buy-myself compliment, I didn't know what I could reply to this. To be honest, I don't care about being the best here, I know I already am. Yeah, because, since we are one of the best-ranked colleges in the region, they like to display their results every three months or more with who's the best student. She paid attention to this, yeah, somehow, I know that she still cares about me. But I reached with her and, furthermore, the human race, such a level of disenchantment that, well, you know... My name is not on top of the list, what will it change in my life? Nothing.

After having climbed the stairs together, we finally entered that big entrance. It pretty much consists of a small hall, where doors are everywhere, on each wall, but the one facing the main gate is the one leading to the inside of the building, the cloister, where we were actually heading. The second door, the one on the right, leads to offices, the one on the left leads to some room where they store bikes, and all the entrance is, well, pretty much like the rest of the building, made of big and massive stones. Well, like I said, this building is not new. But today, as we were a lot passing through that entrance, it was harder to actually hear her, which was not wrong when I think about it... Anyway, as we walked, I was already fed up having her around, while we were walking, I really didn't know what to reply to that:

"Well, thank you, I appreciate, I guess," I was puzzled.

"Of the world, even!" She insisted.

"Yeah, the world is big, and there must be better than me!"

"And me?"

"You? What, you?"

"I mean... Don't you have a little compliment to give me back? You always have one for me!"

Suddenly, I stopped walking, as we were now about to pass through the door leading to the cloister. I was now flummoxed, actually, literally surprised by what she was asking me: a compliment. Was she begging me for a compliment? I mean, I spend most of my time seeing her now reminding her what she has become through nasty jokes and... she asks me for a compliment? Man, things have gone crazy recently.

Oh, my. I just started to look at her as a parent could be surprised after hearing that his loving child has exploded the phone bill. She had her lovely eyes showing a single interest in something and her beautiful face full of makeup... When was the last time that I had mercy for someone? Don't remember. Poor little pretty girl, I didn't even want to pull her down, as I had... I don't know. I was now thinking about something really mean that I could send her in return. But I didn't know what to target. Her sexuality? Her lifestyle? Her friendship with Kelly? I'm doing it all the time. On the other hand, if I start playing that game, I am sure she would hit back ten times stronger, and I don't think I'm gonna like it... After having looked at her with, I don't know, a mix between pity and mercy, I preferred to actually startle:

"Oh, well... you're the prettiest girl of the College," I threw that with mercy and absolutely no conviction.

"Oh, thank you, Charlotte! It's truly kind, really!" she replied by playing the dumb thankful by the compliment she received.

"Yeah, yeah, don't force me to glorify you," I sent her back, roughly.

"Oh, I do know you won't. Anyway, I'm thrilled you come tonight like really, it's gonna be a great party..."

"Yeah, well..."

"I really want you to come with us, Charlotte."

"Yeah, that would certainly be a good way to give a break to some parts of your body. I recently heard a bunch of guys speaking about you, and from what I heard, I can only deduce that now, the only thing that didn't pass over you is apparently the metro in Paris."

"That's mean, you know. Words can hurt."

"Well, facts as well. But that's not the point..." I ended.

Hum...

"Come on, Charlotte, I have been your girlfriend for a long time, and... Erm... I'll be careful not to say it aloud."

"Who cares now..."

"No, but more seriously. I am not saying this because I want you. I mean, yes, I want you, but not for what you believe. I am despondent that today, because you have your boyfriend, you have your life, now, that... I mean, I really want to keep you in my life, and it's not because we've been together that we have to break up all the ties we used to have."

"Well, I guess you're entitled to your opinion, Claire," I cynically sent.

"Cha, I really want changes, I really want you to stop hurting me all the time, being mean with me, I mean it. I miss you..."

"Yeah, you want changes. I kind of know what those words mean when it comes out of your mouth. I believe you, for the last couple of months, you changed!"

"No, I don't mean these... I really want to have a new relationship with you. By the way, Charlotte, when will I meet your current boyfriend?"

"You? Never alive. You're too dangerous."

We arrived in front of the stairs. And I was like... yeah, irritated, I guess it's the word.

Indeed, I am trying to get rid of her in some ways, it's certainly not to make sure that she and my boyfriend to make buddy-buddy. I mean, it's been a while she talks to me about Florent, but she doesn't know who he is. Florent knows what Claire looks like, and above all, he knows that she's a massive threat to our couple. And also, since Claire's new favourite game is to sleep with everybody and making sure that I know what she's doing, no, her meeting my boyfriend, ways too dangerous. Even teasing her on this doesn't make me laugh. To be honest, if we would have broken up because of something else, maybe I would introduce her to my boyfriend, but since she's a spy from this Kelly, no, no way she's gonna meet him. It's like unleashing a KGB agent in the White House, it's payday for this guy.

"You're stupid..." she said to me, kindly.

"Regarding my boyfriend, the only advice I may give you should be this one, keep dreaming!" I continued.

"Such a shame. Oh, also, as long as you have not introduced me to your boyfriend, Charlotte, I will not introduce you to mine."

"Oh, that's gonna obviously be a huge loss in my life, darling!" I mocked her.

Okay, on the other hand, it's true, I said she doesn't have any boyfriends, but I don't really have any proofs. She tried many times to actually convince me that she was with someone, and I somehow don't really believe it, because, yeah, some stuff say yes, but a bunch saying no. But the thing that convinces me the most is, yeah, this: she always calls me on Sunday afternoon, and we stay at least an hour on the phone, speaking most of the time about random stuff. And when I tell her that I need to do something, she always talks about something else to stay on call. She always avoided her new life unless she wanted to piss me off when she got frustrated, but it turns out that frustration always goes backwards, like a boomerang whenever she starts speaking about that. So, she doesn't have a boyfriend. Because, since I am with Florent, I seldom call her. She called me at least ninety per cent of the time. And, seriously, she would have a boyfriend... wow. No, no way she is with someone. Anyway, after I showed disdain to that lie, she overbid:

"Is there actually something in your life that you care about?"

"Oh, there must be something, wait... yes! My socks. They're pretty useful in winter."

"Cha, I just want to establish good relations with you. I want to move on."

"Good for you. Claire, just to clarify, we have the relationship that we have, okay? We are what we are, we are who we are, and I currently don't want more from you. So now, I really hope you're good with your toy boy or boyfriend, whatever you call it, continue cheating on him and leave me alone."

"Okay, fair enough. Except for one thing, Cha, I am not cheating on him."

"You actually do whatever you want, it's your problem."

"Meh, I guess I can find your boyfriend easily on Facebook..."

"Yeah, sure, good luck..."

And slowly, we arrived in front of our classroom. There were already some other students waiting. But not everyone, though, because for the first two hours, on Wednesday, we have a chemistry course, and he divides our class in two: the best and the... erm... less good. And Claire and I are with the best (no, she's okay in chemistry, she likes it) so we have to wake up early today, and I have to bear her for the first hour. It's at that moment that I thought, I really can't wait for my sister to come, since I'm already fed up with Claire. She's with her boyfriend right now (unless she came back in the night, I didn't hear her), as she spent the evening there. Lucky her, she can enjoy breakfast on bed, I mean. And sleeping an extra two hours.

As usual, once I arrived, I leaned my back against the wall at the end of the queue formed by the other classmates already waiting here (we were something like ten students here, a bit more), I dropped and pressed my bag between my feet, and was overlooking the window and the trees that were without leaves. A bird was standing in a branch, and it was cute. I was hearing it singing. It was perhaps a starling, but... Why was it singing? Last year, on the same tree, I saw a family of these starlings that had set a nest, and there were a couple of birdies, freshly out of their nest. But they removed their nest on springs, I guess because they grew up. It was good to see a bit of nature in a big city. While I was daydreaming about these birds with my hands in my pockets... in my daydreams, I got disturbed.

"Well, about that, Charlotte," she continued speaking.

"Oh, lord... WHAT?" as she could see that now, I was losing patience.

"Oh, hum, sorry, I mean..."

"You know what, Claire, let's make a deal you and I for today: you will shut the fuck up, and I will have a good day, okay?"

"Okay then..."

"Now shut up and leave me alone!"

"Alright, then."

She could understand, I really hope that this was the final warning. Six months ago, I would never believe talking to you that way, but now, it was really too much, she's become such an idiot that I was fed up. When I was with her, I use to talk to someone smart, intelligent, now I feel like I am speaking to a thirteen-years-old wannabe. I was undoubtedly turning red at that moment, but I guess she understood now. Anyway, she was still talking to everybody, doing her stuff, and I kept on watching the tree in front of me. I was feeling tired, like, really. I'd rather be sleeping right now. And after maybe a couple of minutes, after having spoken to everybody, which is really unusual for her but anyway, she came back to me...

"Yeah, you know..." she was now looking for another thing to chat with me.

"What do I know?" I was really bored.

"I really can't wait for tonight! We're gonna have so much fun!"

"If you say so."

She was turning around me. I really don't get the purpose of that, honestly, to behave that way with me. Unfortunately, it's almost every morning like this since we came back to school, the harassment. Last October, after a month trial with her being around, I asked my mother if she could change me of school since I was done with her, and she tried. But as I have an apparent behavioural problem, nobody accepted me. Well, I guess I'm trapped here. I mean, seriously, go over it, it's not by seeing her every day that I will go over it, like that.

Whilst she was trying to find another topic for continuing whatever pointless conversation with me, the teacher finally arrived. After everybody, except me, welcomed him, Claire came next to me as everybody was now queueing to enter the classroom. I was entering that cold room, having somehow my puppy following me.

"God bless that moment; you will finally shut up!" I was relieved.

"I feel like sometimes you really can't see me," she was kind of overwhelmed.

"No, it's just that you know how I am in the morning, I am a little grumpy, and you're just pissing me off with your stupid conversation..."

"Okay, sorry then?"

"Yeah."

"I just... We're gonna have a party tonight, then fine. Now leave me alone, I just want to have my day for myself."

4 *Speaking of which...*

// *Lycée George-Sand, Asnières-sur-Seine, France.*

// *Wednesday, 9th of January 2013, 10:01*

The first two hours in that hell were finally over. Some pointless chemistry explained by a guy who obviously did not like his job for some reasons, explaining some stuff that I don't think will be completely useful in our daily life. But since it's in the program, we have to do it. And of course, whenever the bell is about to ring, like ten minutes before, I always pack up my stuff in my handbag so at least I am ready to be the first out of here. I know, I am fully aware that it's a lack of respect for, as I said, but to be honest, I don't really know what's the most disrespectful: having a guy that makes you waste your time on the sole purpose of justifying his monthly salary, or me. He indeed lacks conviction when delivering his course, so, okay, I understand it's early in the morning, but still. At least Walter White seems to be more convincing... maybe, yeah... the difference between my teacher and Mr

White is that, well, they both get their monthly pay, but bonuses are more interesting for one of them.

The chemistry classroom is the largest inside the college: all the students are sat on stools lined up behind workbenches, and each row of workbenches has a sink at the very end, useful when we have to handle chemicals, and we have to clean up the mess. In this room, we use to follow biology because sometimes, we have to do dissections, and for the same cleaning purpose, and I like dissections. Like, really. It's like watching House M.D. or Grey's Anatomy, but all this in real life, and without all the blood. But at least teachers leave us the choice between performing dissections or doing works if we are not feeling ready for this.

But this room has been recently refurbished, since most of the things here are news, and the blackboard that used to be there is now white. Well, apart from that, it's a traditional classroom. The periodical table is displayed everywhere, some educative posters as well, I mean, yeah. The teacher, however, is the only thing here that skipped refurbishment. Mister Dupery, same old guy, bald, tall... With his white vest, gosh. Looks like a chemistry teacher, it's odd. I'm wondering whether this guy has a life after work since all I see from him is an old bald man watching dirty porn on his computer after seeing the last conference of the Nobel Prize in Stockholm. Anyway, the teacher is not sitting behind a desk, as all the other teachers use to do, but he's standing behind quite a big workbench dedicated only for him, which was quite messy by the way. And lucky him, he has two sinks on both sides of his desk. I learned that one was for chemistry and the other for dissections, in biology... I don't remember who told me that he found semen taches on one of the two sinks. It's not Claire, for once, as she would say to me to whom it belongs. That's why I have this picture of him in my head every time I see him, I can't get rid of it. Anyway, in the classroom background, behind us, there are huge lockers, chemistry labs style, in which are stored everything like microscopes, Bunsen burners, test tubes, and the remaining useful tools in chemistry.

I kept texting my sister this morning, but she did not reply, whilst Claire was busy studying. And at the end, the teacher gave us our homework for the next course, he wrote it on the whiteboard. I looked at it, and... Well, anyway, even if I knew I didn't need to write it down since I could remember it, it's improbable that I'd do it in the week unless I'm very bored. Generally, this teacher is not known to change his habits: it's always the same ritual, fifteen minutes before we leave, after having been misguided in all these molecular explanations, he use to note the exercise for next week on the board, and after he stays behind his computer. You have any questions? Yeah, good luck! When I was the only one working (that happens sometimes) and everyone in the classroom was either napping, whether having fun, I went to his desk for asking him something, and I saw him watching videos on YouTube. As I said, they are failed teachers. And they are complaining because they are not paid enough... Come on. That's why being the best student in this place, I don't care, because it's easy. My memory will always save my arse. I trained it a lot. And as I am the only one to manage to do it here and I'm called a "nerd", it reminds me that the day the word "nerd" has become an insult that we really should have started to be worried.

It was five minutes before the bell rung, whilst everybody wrote on their books the exercise they need to complete for the next day, even while all my stuff was packed, I started to look at my phone, checking the hour and if my damn sister replied. Claire and I's difference is that one: while my phone is locked in my bag, hers is unlocked on her hand. Watching Netflix? No... Sending a text to someone? Almost, but nope. No, obviously, she was doing what everybody does nowadays, after one hour after she completed her exercises, she was checking Facebook. In the case that something terrible happened, like an attack in Paris or an earthquake in Japan. She's also complaining as well because her phone has a short-term battery. Before we had fashion-victims, and today we have brainwashed-addicted. I don't understand why I still have respect for that. I'd be a shrink, and Claire would be payday. But anyway, she is my former girlfriend, and I mean... Yeah. This is really sad; she was not like this before.

Anyway, whilst she was still checking her stupid timeline on Facebook, almost hypnotised by the dummy latest kitten picture she'd see, she launched:

"Oh, by the way, Cha... you want to come with us, after lunch? This is the first day of the sales today!"

"Definitely not, and then, I planned to eat with Clarisse for lunch," I think I made myself clear.

"Cool, then we could have a reason for eating altogether!"

"What, you really think that you'd remain alive after eating with Clarisse? You're so optimistic!"

"Screw your twin sister, then!"

"Oh gosh, Claire... You know what's fascinating, with you? In the order Nature has established in this place, you want at any costs to be the frog that wishes to be as big as an ox. The food chain here would work this way, unless you didn't notice: there's me, the ultimate predator you think you ate but has in fact eaten you and converted your remains into shit, then there is the class protected by the ultimate predator, like Clarisse, and only below all this, there is you. You're still a young antelope, darling. Clarisse is a lion already."

"Which means that I am the least of your priorities, right?"

"Gosh, I was convinced you wouldn't get my metaphor," I whispered. "But, yes, basically, since we are no longer together, I have higher priorities than you..."

"All right. Fuck you, Charlotte!"

"It's done already. Yesterday evening, I am sure I did it yesterday..."

"Come on, it's gonna be fun!" she was insisting after having told me to, erm...

"You're just my ex. Clarisse is my sister. I need her more than I need you now, to be fair."

"Nice, thanks, from my ex, I really appreciate..."

"My pleasure... Oh, shit, I gotta go!"

At the very moment, I said that I had to go, the bell rang. I immediately stood up while I heard Claire telling me something to which I obviously paid no attention.

Because I received a text from my twin, she was downstairs. So, I left the room, I walked down the corridor almost rushing, I had to hurry up me because Clarisse was undoubtedly already in the courtyard, waiting for me, or not, I have no idea, but I had to ask her finally if she wants to come with me for lunch. Of course, what I told Claire was totally unplanned, but it was my excuse to say that I did not want to be with her. And since I was not the only one to want to get out from the various classrooms everybody came out from, I walked through this little crowd, arriving just in front of the stairs two minutes after. I tried to go as fast as possible, going down through the stairs where many people were already, as I wanted to escape her. And moreover, Clarisse has my books for the next course, and as I needed it... I rushed, went down walking quickly in the corridor along with the courtyard when suddenly I came face to face with someone, dressed in a kind of suit with a short skirt, and like me, black pumps. I raised my head... Kelly.

"Hey, Charlotte! What's up this morning?" she said, after finding me out.

"Holy crap, so you did not have any heart attack last night, damn it! Move your arse, I gotta find Clarisse. Move!"

Yeah, Kelly... The perfect example of what I call a Facebook pre-made personality. Kelly is to Claire what Clarisse is to me, the kind of supervising next of kin, except that I am friendly with my sister. What can I say about Kelly? Oh, nothing. She's insignificant, there's really nothing interesting in her. The only requirement to talk to her is that you need to have a minimum of three hundred friends on Facebook and one thousand followers on Instagram. Otherwise, she wouldn't care about you. But it's because she's actually that stupid that it makes her really dangerous: she's totally unstable, over-using social networks and seems to be the queen on it, and seems to everybody (except me) like a trustworthy person, I mean... it's why Claire when she met her, liked her straight away, she's my total opposite. She's also her complete opposite. It's for these reasons that I totally mistrust Kelly, she's all the type of person I'd be delighted to see in a body bag. I'm not sure whether she and Claire had sex since it's quite hard to actually know what she actually enjoys. Physically speaking, nothing even exceptional: she's quite tall, slightly less than me, she's got blue eyes also like me, her hairs are brown and shorter than mine or Claire's, but honestly, she's really banal. Every day, she uses to wear discreet make-up to at least look like a human being. And wear mostly blue clothes. Not every day, but she mostly wears blue stuff, which is quite surprising. Perhaps it matches Facebook's colour, I guess.

And mentally speaking, she's an evil witch: let's imagine she's someone you've just met, and something happened to her. She always does, making sure that she'll always appear as the victim whatever happens. But no, she's not gonna blame you, but she's gonna do everything to make sure that you would have mercy for her. She'd make sure that you would be merciful for her. So at least she could use you and do whatever she wants. She'd appear as your new best friend until you accept her on Facebook: if you have under a hundred friends, you will send her messages, there are no chances she'd reply to you. If you have between one and three hundred, well, your options are reduced, but she will not be your best friend, for sure. You'd have between three and five hundred, you'd become interesting. And more than five hundred, you're her new bestie. Over a thousand, you're DEFINITELY her new bestie.

Besides being absorbed by whatever new social network, I totally do not understand what made her survive natural selection. She's as dumb as a doorknob. However, due to her favourite game on Facebook, I heard that it created her certain notoriety from many people. And Claire told me that she knows quite a lot of people and mostly wealthy people. And I tend to believe that it's true, I mean, how much times did I see her arriving at school, being dropped by someone in a BMW near our school, it's interesting. Because, yes, obviously, someone that behaves that way can only be interested in money, it's obvious, since, while she lives in Malakoff, the, erm... southern suburb in the south of Paris (like not rich people, not a poor suburb but average-income, you know what I mean). From what I know regarding her family, she lives in a small house, with a single mother, struggling to survive in Paris. Her father was a soldier but was killed in Afghanistan a while ago, in an ambush by the Taliban, like Claire's father (Claire's father was part of the French Marine corps, and he died in 2006 in the Horn of Africa as part of a classified operation against terrorism). So, they have a shared history, both killed in duty, but not the same year. It marked their lives, obviously... But life changed them in some ways.

But I assume she went through this in her way: her way to behave and respond to some events in life is sometimes close to mine since that like Claire, Kelly and I haven't had enough love from our parents. I cannot say that I can compare my disaster to theirs, but when it happened, I tried to move on in the right way, whilst she took another path. But as intelligence and kindness are two values that are not always compatible, instead of focusing on things just as I did, instead of trying to understand what is wrong with life, no, she just tried to seek some friends. Instead of growing up, getting better from what occurred, she did the reverse thing. At school, she's a disaster. She is so stupid that a couple of days ago, I remember that I explained why there were leap years every four years. And after having explained it at least three times, she finally understood. I must assume that we have priorities in life, I guess. Ask her about gossips, the latest album of Rihanna or whom Kim Kardashian is currently sleeping with, she will be able to answer and even giving the juiciest details. Ask her how many planets there is in the Solar System, and then... It's like dealing with a supermassive black hole.

Her love life is obviously at her image. I don't want to give any judgement, but I just see, and I almost have mercy for that. I don't know if she's currently with someone or not, but I know that she had problems recently, as she has been with some thug native from Algeria residing in Clichy-sous-Bois (the very dangerous far southern suburb of Paris), but they broke up. Apparently, this guy was doing rap, the kind of rap that says, "fuck the society, fuck the country", you know what I mean. I don't know whether they were in love or not, but I don't think so as love and Kelly are two different things. He wanted her to be converted to Islam for some reasons, but her mum reminded her that, yeah, having a dead father murdered by a Taliban and being converted to Islam, well, well, well, I don't really think that it went through.

Free Expensive Lies: Prologue

After having pushed her to show her that I certainly didn't have time to speak with her, I continued walking through the crowd of people that were coming. And there, maybe two or three minutes after having left Kelly, and whilst I was looking around like a meerkat, I finally could glimpse my so beloved twin sister Clarisse. The one and only. The one to whom I would give everything... well, I mean, as long as it's possible and it's not over a million. Well, my Clarisse... This girl is not like all of them. In my life, she's a centrepiece, she is the one who gives me the motivation to, er... continue. The best advice that anyone can have. No, Clarisse, she is the one for whom I have real respect. The one with whom I say everything, with our twin link that every twin sisterhood has. It nevertheless doesn't change the fact that my favourite thing with her is this: making her angry and spying on her all the time.

Unusually, she looked annoyed and was walking head down. She was wearing the black shirt with long sleeves that she used to wear, and she was wearing a blue jean that I gave her, well... we sometimes wear precisely the same things without even figuring out why. I mean, yeah, we're twins. We're like an Internet cloud, her, and me. But yeah, we grew up at the same time in the same womb, and even if I was born twenty-one minutes before her, we are always connected even when far away. When I am sad, she is sad. When I am pissed, she is pissed. And look, today, I am grumpy, she seems irritable. We have the same feelings at the same time, we have the same tastes for everything (we like the same movies, the same music, the same clothes, the same food, the same activities). It was a real problem for our parents because when we were younger and wanted something, she wanted the same thing, it's why they used to buy everything twice. Except for clothes, they were buying me a specific colour and to her another to recognise us. Now, we are still trying to separate our envies, but it doesn't change, when I want something, I buy it for myself. She gets the same thing for herself certainly days after.

She's my twin, so there's absolutely no difference between her and me, especially since we really look like each other. Even today, I could see that she puts the only foundation on her face, just like me, and untied her hairs, just like me. I didn't even call her to tell that I would do that. But the only difference between us is this: if I am blonde-haired, she is brown-haired but obviously coloured her hairs, but it remains that we have exactly the same haircut and same length. It led to so many fights about who would colour her hairs, but now thanks to hair it's easier to make a difference between is Charlotte Kominsky from whom is Clarisse Kominsky.

However, there are still a couple of differences between her and me, like health. I have got some health problems, but hers are entirely different. We also have different voices. But we can easily impersonate the other (and we did it several times). Contrarily to me, as I am pale for some reasons, she only has asthma. And she got eyes problems, so she's wearing glasses when she's reading something or working. Physically, she's the perfect copy of me.

Socially speaking, she's literally different than me. If unlike me, she's friendly and goes smoothly to everybody, she has more friends out of school than in school. Clarisse is selective, if you're friend with her, it means that you are not a moron and/or you do something special. What matters to her is that you can talk to her, that's what she seeks. She has a relatively strict personality, she loves results as well, but results are better when done within a group. She's honestly a good leader, which is why she's been given the charge of representing our class to the teacher. She's okay at school, not as good as me, but she's punctual, every day at school, never missing a course even when she's sick. But she's never ill. She's a really hard worker. No, she definitely is like me on some points, but when I mean she's different, yes, the only difference between her and me is that she's not allergic to people. She always gives useful advice, she ever hears my problems for giving them a better answer, and as I said, she is more valuable at my eyes for that main reason: she's our class manager. She is always here when someone's in trouble, and... She saved my ass many times from real problems. And the other thing I love in Clarisse is that she's serious, grown and more than everything, the only girl I know who's today eighteen and intelligent at the same time. I am confident that she will definitely succeed in life, as she has all the tools for that, so if I mess up mine, I can still rely on her...

Her point of view is that she doesn't care about what the others think about her a bit like me. She's been with someone for a while now, it's been more than a year now, and curiously she doesn't talk that much about what they do, she's entirely secret, she wants to keep secrecy on what she does with her boyfriend. I am quite the same, though, I am not really talking about my private life in general... I mean, yeah, I think. Finally, her boyfriend's name is Marc and er... He's twenty-five, has his own situation, and... I heard he was a waiter in some restaurant in Paris. I never honestly know where they met each other, I assume through Facebook or something like this. And yeah, contrarily to me that is mostly lesbian, Clarisse has always been straight but was open-minded regarding my sexuality. She's always been very tolerant and understood that we wanted to keep the secret of our relationship with Claire. She even defended me in front of my mother when she found out for Claire and I. Tolerance, yeah, is the reason why today there are so many conflicts with my mum.

She was the very first to be here when I broke up with Claire. Since she witnessed almost the beginning of our love story, when I told her I was with her, she also saw the end. And it's the reason why she hates Claire now because she considers that what she's done to me was profoundly unfair and she takes her as responsible for how I am now. She was the only one to come and spend hours with me to try to comfort me, to be there and try to understand what happened... It even cancelled a weekend with her boyfriend. Even today, I am really thankful to her to have spent all these hours with me. It strengthened our relationship, even if it was already strong. And she introduced me to Florent.

She arrived alone with her heavy bag on her back, and as she was looking around too, I assume she was also looking for me. But if she was wearing foundation today, it means that the night was short and she was exhausted, so I guess she's gonna sleep this afternoon. Because it's Wednesday today and on Wednesday we do not have school in the afternoon. Unless she planned something with her boyfriend. But I don't think so, according to her face, she was grumpy. So, I sneaked amongst all the people wandering, God knows where in the yard, and I finally reached her.

"Hello, honey!" I yelled for her to be able to hear me.

"Oh, here you are," she replied, yes, grumpy.

"What's up, honey?"

Yes, I always ask questions to which I already know the answer. But it was a way for me to break the ice. It was why at the very moment I asked that she looked at me with a kind of a fake smile and didn't know what to tell me. My penchant for annoying people and especially my sister at any time used to be healthy, so I felt the urge to tease her, even if it was not the best thing to do at that moment. But when I use to piss you off, as she says, it generally means that I like you. Yeah, I have a big heart, I know.

"You, what's up?" she replied straight away.

"Meh..."

"Do me a favour today and don't with me this fucking birthday, okay?"

"The idea didn't even come in my mind. Claire annoyed all morning, I really missed you this morning..."

"Don't tell me you're still speaking to that bitch..."

"Come on, you know I really wanted to avoid her, but she's been harassing me since this morning..."

"You're weak, Cha. You're weak to her..."

"I swear, I really wanted to avoid her... But, you know, she's still in love with me, and she's like a damn roach, try to kill that, and you get a thousand behind."

"Yes, obviously..."

"No, no, I swear."

She was walking towards her locker, for picking up her stuff, as every time she arrives. But there was something wrong. Perhaps it's the reason why I am not really okay today, I guess. She was not really in the mood to be teased. Fair enough, but I don't want to act with her like Claire did with me this morning. And, also, I was seeking peace right now, and isolation as well. It's at that moment that I recalled that I had to ask her for lunch. I could almost feel it, she was looking for some good moments, maybe there was something wrong with her boyfriend:

"Wanna grab something to eat with me for lunch?"

"Why not. I mean, yes, if you're not behaving like an ass as you use to be daily like everybody," she said, sniffing the ambiguity.

"I'm not really in the mood today..."

"For pissing me off, you don't need a special mood."

"No, really. Try me."

"Yeah, I'll see. But we eat lunch at home, I'm drained right now."

"Works for me. And I know, you look exhausted, since you wear foundation today. Meh, don't worry, Chef Kominsky will cook for you her greatest and awarded speciality."

"Yes, the frozen pizza that you bought yesterday since you're a lazy ass, is that it?"

"Obviously, what did you expect?"

"No, it's good, as long as we eat quickly and I go to bed as fast as I can eat, that works for me. Marc was sick all night, I don't know what he had... He's been throwing up all night long, and I could finally sleep at five."

"Oh, damn it, I would have bet on a night of pure and amazing sex... I am really sorry. On the other hand, which explains why you are grumpy right now."

"Well, my scheduled night of pure and amazing sex as you said became a night of pure and amazing cleaning of the toilets. I think he had food poisoning, but, well, he's better now. At least this morning he was okay."

Free Expensive Lies: Prologue

"Oh, dear. Meh, don't worry, *you now have your so beloved sestra*," I took a Russian accent. "Now I really hope it was food poisoning and not a damn gastroenteritis."

"I would have been sick if it were the case! But don't be scared, *your sestra* will not poison you," she was imitating my Russian accent again. "And you, how was your evening?"

"Well, it was fine. We had some lunch, but he was stressed yesterday as he has his exam today. I really hope he won't screw up."

She bent down and opened her locker with her key into which was attached to a childish keychain "Hello Kitty". And, when she was there, I got like a kind of a reminder, it's true that right now, Florent is passing his exam. I really hope he's gonna follow my advice, not to be that stressed out. She took her books, then she gave me mine that I immediately put into my bag. And then told me finally while I was doing this, and I had a kind of *deja vu*:

"I really hope you're not gonna piss him off in the possible event that he fails. He's been working hard on his project, it's been more than a year, and he doesn't deserve you being an ass if he fails..."

"Geez, I feel like I hear mum!"

"I am really serious, Charlotte, I know Florent for longer than you, and he's a good friend to me, besides being your boyfriend," she reminded me what I already knew.

"Be not afraid, darling, be not afraid!" I replied.

She stood up, closed her bag, very slightly made a move with her eyes and suddenly looked at me like "if you do it, I'm gonna kill you"... well, when she looks at me like this, with her slightly closed eyes, and a kind of smile drawn on her lips, it means that I'd better do what she wants.

"Alright, then!" she concluded.

And once all her books were in her bag, she stood up and looked straight at me.

"Besides that, you okay?" She started again, seeming protective.

"Yeah, I guess the same as you, I'll be better after I sleep."

"But at least Florent wasn't sick last night, was he?"

"No, he wasn't, it's just that it's been a couple of days that I am struggling to sleep, I really don't know why."

"Are you stressed about something?"

"I guess. I mean I think, I don't know" I concluded. "Anyway, any plans for you tonight?"

"Not really. I mean, besides calling my boyfriend, and erm... Sleeping. And homework, nothing really exceptional."

"You guys still don't wanna live together?"

"Nah, we talked about it yesterday, but now that I am an adult, we are considering finding our own place to live. And still, I don't know what I want to do in my life, so... I don't know. I don't think I'm ready to do that, it's quite a big commitment. At least for me."

"Sort of. It is also for me, but... Someday, it's gonna happen, you'll see."

"Yeah, I still have time anyway. And what about you? Staying with Florent tonight?"

"No, I planned to go out with Claire. But er... You don't tell him, okay?"

"Obviously, you told me you wanna get rid of her, and you're going out with her... Makes sense."

"No, it's not what you believe, she... This morning she called me and asked me if it would be cool to go out tonight together, with Kelly and Sophie. And I said, why not. She's right, on the other hand, it's been a while that I didn't have some good time, I mean, exit my world a bit. I didn't want to tell her she was right, but... No, it's just for... I don't know what she wants to do, but... Don't worry, I know what I do."

"Yeah... You know what you do, with an ex-girlfriend with whom you were in love for five years... I don't know which game you're playing with her, but I feel like it's a dangerous game, in my opinion."

"It's not... And come on, it's just for tonight. What could happen after?"

"Big troubles, for instance."

"It's not going to happen, Clarisse, I promise you."

"She's dangerous for you. But, have it your way, you're eighteen today, I cannot tell you what you have to do, but I still can advise you."

"Don't be afraid, it's gonna be okay!"

"Be happy, honey. You deserve happiness."

"I appreciate it, thank you."

She uses to be tenser when Claire comes in the conversation. But, I guess, today, we are in a kind of synergy where we can understand each other. We sat on the small steps of the corridor in the courtyard, me next to her, and we started looking at the populace around. All of them. They were almost all gathered in many small groups of friends, even if there were also a few students here all alone, sat on the steps just like us, or somewhere else, playing whatever stupid games on their goddamn phones or indeed scrolling down on Facebook for catching whatever gossips. Nonetheless, some of them that I was seeing with books in their hands, certainly for catching up homework that they were supposed to do yesterday at home. But the worst we could see was some of them with their phones in hand in the groups. All head down, just like drones. I think... It's appalling.

On those words, whilst none of us was speaking and both doing the same thing, absorbed in my thoughts, remembering how my ex became so dumb while looking at a girl that stood up like a wannabe in front of me, I saw Sophie appearing all of a sudden, out of nowhere. Ah, Sophie, the latest product designed by The Kelly Laboratories. This is the only prototype provided with an extra tool: a brain. And finally, er... Actually, I haven't really seen her arriving, she was literally popping out of nowhere. It surprised me. She was wearing with a light beige leather jacket entirely closed, above which there was a red woollen scarf wrapped around her neck, probably because she celebrated the New Year Eve with Clarisse and me with nasty flu. No, she was really sick. She also wore black trousers and brown walking boots. She had black gloves on her hands. I love her gloves; she was looking like a spy with it. Funny. However, she's a friend of Clarisse, I like her, but the problem is... she's still a friend with Kelly. So, she's corrupted.

Physically, she's less tall than me, but she's still tall compared to a lot of girls at school. She has brown and long and straight hair, brown eyes, and she's not as skinny as Clarisse, and I are. But she's not fat either. And when we see her, she definitely looks older than she actually is. I mean, she's nineteen and looks like thirty. She's also very flat, I mean... The most exciting part of her body, the one I use to look straight when interested, is terribly missing. Anyway, Sophie is different, as she's really sportive: she's running every day almost six miles, and during her weekends, she's practising fencing and boxing. But even as a child, she practised a lot of "strange" sports, like football, basketball, even handball... And now, yeah, boxing. She's literally a sports addict, sport is like a drug for her, she's been doing that since she's a child, mostly with her father as he is a runner. For example, last year, they've been taking part in the New York marathon together. Let's say that she has a quite hectic life.

And, Sophie, as I said earlier, she's the last in our "kinship". I admit, I never really understood why she is still a friend with Claire and Kelly. She's a girl who has her own ambition, she wants to work in forensics, and she's keen on science. She even said that if she fails forensics, she wants to be a mortician. Why not, I mean, there's no stupid job. Why? Death always looked fancy to her. She's a gothic. But it's what we like with her, at least she has her passion, making her enjoyable. We've been friends for a while, but she doesn't know that Claire and I were actually together. It's just that it's not something that is actually her business. But I respect her, I mean... she's not a good or a bad friend, she's an acquaintance, and that's it. I'm sure, the day I leave College, she will erase my phone number. In terms of results and best pupil, she's sixth, far behind me in first, and Clarisse in second and three other people. But the mystery for me is, why does an ambitious girl, mad about what she wants to become, is friends with the epitome of such a superficial girl such as Kelly. I really don't understand this. Anyway, she saw us and came to us, and, for once, unusually...

"Hi, sunshine!" I launched.

"Hi darling!" she smiled at me.

"You okay today?" Clarisse asked promptly.

"Hi love, fine and you?" she seemed happy.

"Meh," Clarisse answered.

"I guess it's the same for you, huh?" she knew whilst watching at me.

"Well, sounds like a new shitty day" I was still grumpy.

"All right. Well, happy birthday to both of you, by the way. Eighteen, come on!"

At the very same time and in the very same way, we both looked at her... And I think she understood. I mean, yes, we were happy that she thought about it, but yeah, today, it's just celebrating a year we achieved before to die. One year completed in the rest of our lifetime, and one year less early to pass. Fine, fine... I mean I am eighteen, I could be happy to grow up, but still, nope. The difference is, today, I can do whatever I want. And this is funny, but even, it won't change the world, my life will remain as boring as it's already.

"Yeah..."

"Well, Claire said to me that you were going with us for shopping this afternoon?"

"Jesus Christ, what a... I told her that I'd come tonight, I'm not coming this afternoon."

"Yeah, that's what I thought. I found it also weird that you wanted to come to do shopping with us... But she is annoying today, I don't know why."

"Oh, seriously? Why?" asked Clarisse.

"Lack of sex I guess," I coldly replied.

"Good, so you're coming to the party she's doing tonight. Fine, At least we can talk."

"Talk about what?"

"You'll see tonight."

5 A normal day in a normal life

// Park outside the Lycée George-Sand, Asnières-sur-Seine, while coming back home.

// Wednesday, 9th of January 2013, 12:34

Wednesday mornings are always the same: since we work only in the morning, it leaves us the rest of the day available to relax. I usually don't really like to wake up for going there only four hours, but I guess I have no choice since my lovely mum keeps watching me all the time because she wants me to be serious... And all this just for the two same courses: two hours of chemistry to start with half the group every two weeks, and finally, after a fifteen-minute break, we have literature courses. Two awfully long hours, exceptionally long, since we don't study books that I like. No, I don't especially love to read books (I only enjoy reading articles on Wikipedia or more generally on the Internet). We have a teacher that kind of pushes you to love reading if you see what I mean. All the time, Clarisse and I are going there with a certain nonchalance. Yep, the boring life of a dull student in a boring college...

Usually, when I'm bored during the course, I keep my bag on the table. Except when we are supposed to have a test, but hopefully, it was not the case today. Why am I doing this? To thwart boredom. And I use to do it that way: I leave my handbag on the table, my pencil-case in front of everything just to pretend I'm doing something, and I put my phone hidden in the bag, only with enough space to see the screen. And everyone is studying (except some other people that are actually doing just like me), I just learn my own way... With the headphones that I pass through my sleeve for hiding the wire, I take the earplug on my hand, and I put it in one ear while pressing my head against my arm for at least pretending that I am actually following what they say. The teacher sees and knows what I am doing (come on, they are not stupid either), but as long as I am not a trouble for the class, they are okay with that.

This i
American guy v
videos about hi.
the Great Wall o,
for what purpose,
really like followin
listening to *Madam*
she has to borrow m.
to explain how the au
women social status i,
what case what I was
about the social status o
difference between *Mada*
enter one of them. I m
prostitute, but who read t
literature is an essential cc
translated into English... Oh,
based on the novel in 1964. Al

our teacher is giving them now. When you're curious
same conclusion. Now, I'm eighteen, it's why I am
course, I was so bored, which is why in the
all woke up after the soporific two-hour
woke up, because none of them w
school because they deliver ge
what you learned later. T
already, what the hell h
And, ye
favourite and
pleasure
see

_en
_ made a movie

But don't get me wro   _ say that we do not learn uninteresting things at school, it's essential to know Madame Bovary, at least for the general knowledge. Teachers have a really dull and tedious way to teach us the story and this book's moral. I say that for most of the students in the classroom here, right now with me, studying that book is a real waste of time since they are actually a pure waste of brain cells. They are not gonna make academics later, and I can bet whatever money you want on it. Unless I am wrong, you cannot convert a pony into a racing horse. My actual point is, I learn it for my general knowledge, they learn it for good marks. And the reason why I am not studying is that I actually read Madame Bovary when I was nine, I really enjoyed it, and when I remember that the teacher told us that this book would be for the baccalaureate this year. We need to learn that because it will increase the average points if we pass the literature test, I just feel like this is actually insulting the author. These morons won't honour that book, only for the purpose to pass their stupid exams. But this is the way our school system works.

I really used to love reading before, and I read Madame Bovary when I was nine. And I thought it was really amazing at this time. I know the story, and when I was nine, I mean... Since I love learning, I actually understood the same crap that

it's no big deal to reach the
more into other stuff. During the
d, the class became a bit noisy. They
s-speech of the teacher. As I said, they all
s actually interested in the story. I really hate
eral knowledge only to pass grades and then forget
ere's nothing really challenging in being here. I know
m I doing here?

after these two Chinese hours (actually for me), finally, my
so expected sound rang. The bell! It would have been a sincere
if I'd care, but fortunately, time was over. No, I'm not kidding, it really
ed fascinating, even if I didn't follow. I removed my earphones from my sleeve,
wrapped them up around the phone and closed the pencil-case to put it in the bag, then I locked the bag and finally stood up with my twin who was sat at the same table as me and whom, of course, had followed me. When she's tired, she is a bit like me and only thinks only about one thing, sleeping as soon as she can. And we finally left the classroom.

"So er...? How was what you were looking at?" she seemed curious whilst we were walking down the corridor to leave the building.

"Huh?" I didn't actually get it.

"What you watched when we were supposed to work..."

"Ah. Well, it was fine. Speaking about China. Was quite interesting."

"Hopefully, she didn't catch you!"

"Clarisse, don't you still know her? She doesn't care! As long as I keep my mouth shut, that's all that she wants."

"Yeah, well," she yawned.

And it was when I was about to reply to my sister that we were on our way back home, so it was not that long before she sleeps that I felt something moving in my arse. I immediately stopped walking, surprised. And immediately I saw Claire (I'm surprised not to have heard her coming since she's the noisiest today), and the hand that reached me was Kelly's. She removed it after I saw that and was laughing like a stupid baby. It turned me red, obviously annoyed me, and I felt insulted, but as I was too tired to punch her face, I preferred having another approach:

"Do that again, and I swear, I catch you in a corner, and I slit your damn throat, you lame little bitch!"

And I resumed walking, pretending that this never happened after I threatened her. The thing is, when I said that to her, as Kelly is kind of scared me, she was really like... Oh my god, I really messed up! It was so funny to see her like that. Clarisse whiffled afterwards, and she was now really bothered that Claire and Kelly were following us... I must confess that we certainly needn't them at the moment. They were the very last two people that we needed right now.

And moreover, they were acting ridiculously, just to get everyone's attention. She made me angry all morning long, and now... I really want to get rid of her! Whilst still walking towards the exit, now faster than ever, my sister continued talking to me:

"Uh-oh, they found us," she lamented herself.

"I know, all morning I did my best to get rid of them! I sometimes think I am a kind of moron magnet," I was bothered too.

"Alright, Cha, now go tell your two brainless sluts to get the fuck out of here, or I am really gonna punch one of them!"

"Clarisse," Claire said, "Did you just call me a slut?"

"Why, you're gonna tell me that it's not true, maybe?" my twin looked at Claire.

"Clarisse, shut up!" I said as an (almost) diplomat, "How old are you? Six, or eighteen? Come on... She wants to confront you, don't answer her!"

No, seriously, I am really tired of the fact that they hate each other. And they won't have a fight today. Tomorrow, yes, if they want, but not today, it's my birthday. Yeah, okay, it's her birthday too. And Claire, I know her, when she starts saying these words, it means that she's looking for a fight. And upon calming down the situation between Claire and my sister, still, in the hubbub of the corridor as it was crowded since everybody was also leaving, we were now reaching the stairs just like us.

We had to go through these stairs for leaving the building. The steps were made of old stones sometimes not really even as if we were striding the long corridors of an ancient monastery. They left it like this, I think, to keep the charm of the building. There was also no window in it, it was lit by a kind of old bulb on the ceiling, which looked very dusty by the way, and the light was weak and yellow. But the noise was so loud all around that we couldn't even hear ourselves speaking. Everybody was speaking aloud, and, moreover, we didn't have that much to talk with them. We just wanted to go home with my sister. When in the stairs, I had an idea, as I am sure the metro would be crowded right now: call a Taxi. I grabbed my phone and booked it quickly. I'm sure Clarisse would agree with me, and especially since at least, it would prevent them from following us.

Once downstairs, we saw that the weather had changed outside. It was sunny during the break, and it was now cloudy. We left the building through the main entrance, and it was still a little bit cold out there. Whilst the clouds covered the sky this morning to give a certain coldness in the streets, we left the main door, and the plan was to go towards the metro station, close from here, so the driver would pick us up. I took my gloves out of my coat's pocket after having put my phone back in my handbag, because the cold was starting to numb my hands, and we walked towards the pathway leading to the exit. And, whilst still followed by Claire and Kelly, and before leaving, Clarisse started to complain:

"What a pain in the ass..."

I think I get what my sister is complaining about. Because they were following us, and I really don't get what was the purpose of them doing that. They never do that. And whilst they were talking about what they planned to do tonight, for the party, I decided to enter the conversation, actually. Clarisse said it in a quite amusing way...

"What are you talking about?" I said, amused.

"Oh, yeah, please, Clarisse! We want to know!" Claire went further.

"If you'd have a brain, Claire, you will understand," Clarisse reacted.

"No, it's just unusual that you say something like that in such a way." I wanted to act like a grown-up, for once.

"I know..." Clarisse was still exhausted.

"It's odd, she's becoming like her twin, such a bully," Kelly surprisingly said to Claire, losing all interest from my sister.

"Oh, darling, it's just a question of interests, pretty much!" I added.

"Oh, shut up, Charlotte," replied Kelly.

"But, yeah, I may confess that I may have been a bit far with you."

"A bit far, you better be kidding me! Do you remember when you almost pushed her through a window?" Claire said.

"Yeah, well, I just wanted to show her something in a tree... from closer," I concluded.

Clarisse laughed, whilst Claire and Kelly remained silent. At this moment, when I checked my phone, as we left the park, to walk on the street towards the metro station, the driver was a couple of minutes away from the pick-up point. Kelly apparently seriously wanted to challenge someone more significant than her, so she took her bag, while Claire was still making so much noise while walking. And, at some point, I don't know... Suddenly, Kelly unusually reacted to what I said previously.

"Why are such a bitch with me, Cha?"

"I don't know, there must be a reason," I answered so proudly.

"Which reason?"

"Maybe the reason that I genuinely don't like you, perhaps."

"Why?"

"I don't know... Okay, let's be honest with each other: have you ever felt like... Like you hate that person? Like, really hate!"

"Hum... I guess?"

"Like... You know, you really wish all the worst to that person, for absolutely no reason, you know, just by pleasure, by pure pleasure!"

"Well, yes, there are some... But I don't understand!"

"Like... like... Even the fact of hearing his or her voice irritates you at the highest point, and you would slap just for that reason, the reason that this person is actually alive?"

"Yeah, maybe?"

"And like... like you would just want to hurt that person just by pleasure. You know, just for fun! Like... You know, this person deserves to be hurt, and you would willingly hurt that person, yes, just for fun!"

"I really don't get your point!"

"Well, darling," I suddenly looked at her whilst still walking, and I drew a huge smile in my face, "you're exactly that kind of person to me!"

"You're really mean, Charlotte. That's really mean from you to hear that you would hurt me just by pleasure... That's not nice at all, I mean, I have never been that bad with you and you, all the time, you talk to me like shit, and you hate me. I really don't deserve that from you, I think!"

"Don't forget, honey, that the truth will always set you free, but first will piss you off!"

"Alright Charlotte, now you shut up, okay!" Claire started to act with diplomacy. "So, where are we going, now?"

"In some place, where you guys are not going!" Clarisse replied. "And you?"

"Towards the *Champs-Elysées*," Kelly answered quickly but annoyed.

"Come on, Cha, come with us!" Claire asked me for the umpteenth time.

"Yeah, you wish!" I continued.

"I'm tired, I'm tired!" Clarisse insisted, now really upset, "We won't come with you, especially with the two of you, for some bollocks, so leave us alone now!"

We walked through the small street to go to the metro station, as it was the meeting point. And apparently, according to my phone, the driver was nearby. So, now, it was the bye-bye moment, because taking the metro with them and Claire will repeatedly insist for going for shopping, and it will be for the entire afternoon, as I know her. And right now, I just wanted to be home and relax. Anyway, before joining the metro station, we have to cross a road. It might have been easier if we were in a small street, and not in a road such like this: the road was a kind of highway with four lanes, and right now there was quite a significant traffic. Walking across this way was impossible if the traffic didn't stop, and pressing the button is gonna take ages before the light turns red... And the Taxi is really nearby. Obviously, the two great minds that followed us were standing up in front of the white strip of the zebra crossing, ready to cross the road, and this is while seeing how lazy they were that I understood it was my responsibility to press the button. They were counting on me, as usual...

So, I pressed it and took my phone in my hand. There was a small light around the button that has automatically been turned on after I pressed it, and now we were waiting. But it was long. Awfully long. And my phone notified me that my driver was really close to us, I think he's about to call me. And I was looking and searching for any stopped car, while Clarisse was looking very patiently for the light to turn on. She was now taking deep breaths; it usually means that she's upset when she does that. And right after, she put her hand on her stomach. She has stress management problems, which can lead her to big trouble when she's like this. It would be better today if the two of them were not following us. The problem was, they were really expecting that we would take the metro with us. It would explain why they were following us like this, we don't want to stay with them.

Suddenly, Claire's cell phone rang, and astonishingly for once, it was not in her hand. In the meantime, the traffic light turned red, cars were now slowly stopping before the crosswalk, and a couple of seconds later we crossed the road. Obviously, while walking, Claire was looking in her bag, to take the call what she was indeed about to miss. And Clarisse was still breathing quite profoundly. Once on the other sidewalk, we stopped, the metro station entrance was in a few steps ahead of, and it was time to say goodbye. And finally, Claire could grab her phone and told us to wait once on the other side, and the traffic resumed on the road. She obviously missed her call but called back. Whilst doing that, I could see that the driver I ordered was actually one street away, and perhaps it would take a minute for him to turn around and find a way to park and pick us up. It was when I saw that I couldn't hide my desperate face, and Clarisse had at that moment an idea, "I really want to get rid of them," I spoke with my lips to her, without being heard, and she shrugged. But suddenly, she gave me a wink, surprisingly. I think I get what she wants. Since we're twins, we have our secret language, and we don't need to communicate to fool people around.

So, time was passing, and Claire was still on the phone with whoever called her before, chatting, when I looked at my sister, that suddenly started to pretend to writhe in pain, especially at the moment I pretended to look at something in my phone, so at least she could get Kelly's attention. For one reason: Clarisse doesn't want to catch my attention, otherwise, if I call for help, it might sound suspicious. Catching Kelly's attention is better so Kelly can figure out she has a problem, and later understand that I need to take care of my sister; therefore... we can't follow them. We did it already in a similar situation a couple of months before, to get rid of some guy who was harassing her, for the same purpose. Yeah, as I said, we have this power, to understand each other whilst not communicating. While the driver was still on his way to the pick-up point, which was where we were, Clarisse was performing like an actress. Seriously, if I didn't know it was fake, I'd have believed it.

"I... am... not... feeling well," Clarisse's voice was fading away.

"Holy shit! Clarisse!!" Kelly replied.

And it was my turn to enter in the game, now: I pretended that I saw she had a problem, so I went immediately closer to her, while Claire was still speaking on her phone, not figuring out that there was an emergency. A fake one, okay, but there was still an emergency. But she doesn't need to know that it's rubbish. It's when I saw that I lamented myself on the fact that she really changed. Anyway, now Clarisse pretended to collapse, therefore, with Kelly, we have taken her while she was falling, to avoid her to be hurt by her fall. We were maintaining her, and that idiot made herself as heavy as she could; Kelly attempted to remove her bag from her back, while I was carrying my twin with my shoulder to sit her in the very first bench that I could find. She followed me with her bag, and I kept my sister's arm on my shoulder, for carrying her. And it was at that very moment that my handbag started sliding along my arm. And she was making herself heavy, I mean, it was too hard since I have no strength in my arm. Then I sat her, but as she lowered her head... That's here when I wondered if she wasn't fainting for real, because... it seemed pretty realistic. I tried to keep her, but she was still collapsing from the front, her head was going forward, and she closed her eyes. No, seriously, she plays that very well. Kelly was sat close to her, helping me, and I ordered my sister:

"Clarisse, open your eyes!"

"I don't know, Cha... I don't know," she was kind of confused.

"Okay, Clarisse, drink something..."

While I was still preventing my sister to collapse as she didn't make it easy, Kelly quickly opened her bag to grab some bottle of water. That was nice, I could see that she was not actually that idiot and was entirely devoted in case of an emergency. She gave me her bottle, and at the moment I wanted to grab the bottle, my sister began to breathe a little bit harder. And it's at this moment that Claire arrived, still on her fucking phone, having literally nothing to care about what was going on (while Kelly had at least made this effort, although they don't really like each other that much), looked at us. Literally acting like an idiot that doesn't care, she just came... For just asking:

"Hum, Charlotte, does better contains one or two t, I forgot..."

"Come on, you stupid bitch, don't you see that I am quite busy right now," I yelled to her.

"Oh, yeah, sorry..."

I could see that almost it was fake, Clarisse glared at her very briefly. I cannot imagine how many insults passed through her mind at that very moment. We looked after each other very briefly, and she started a heavy loudly sigh while looking at me gravely, for reminding me that this dumb was formerly my girlfriend, and, erm... she was not like this by the time, she dramatically changed, and it's a shame... whatever.

I must acknowledge that for once, Kelly was ways smarter than her friend. And while my sister was drinking a bit of water, she opened her bag to grab some sweets, as I assume that she thought that it was in a hypoglycaemia crisis. Ironically, without even wanting, Kelly gave us a reason to what this faint might be. After taking the sweets, she gave it to her, and looked at me, like, really worried and concerned:

"Don't you think we should call for an emergency?"

"Huh? No, she should be fine. She is just in a nasty hypoglycaemia crisis; she will be fine in a few minutes, I am sure."

"How often does it happen? I never saw her doing this!"

"Yes, but don't be afraid. She's just exhausted, and she needs some rest. I'm going to stay with her this afternoon. Don't worry, go shopping."

"Alright, then. But I mean... How will you come back home; I mean she looks weak...?"

"I called a Taxi already. Anyway, thank you for your help anyway."

"Ah, well, that's okay, I would never let anyone die, so, erm..."

"No, for sure," I said, looking at Claire who was still on her phone just about to come in the metro station, leaving almost on tiptoes, as if she had something to hide...

"All right, Cha... See you tonight. And Clarisse, take care of you!"

"Thank you," she said, still with her voice fading away.

Kelly left us to join Claire, and FINALLY, they both left. She almost ran for joining her, whilst Claire was still chatting on her phone, and we both looked at them leaving, highly relieved. I put my hand in Clarisse's shoulder, and yes, her recovery was miraculously fast, when we looked at each other quite briefly, and again at the entrance of the station, to make sure they were gone. The only word that came out of her mouth, and this with a familiar but quite pissed voice, was "get out, cunt!". I can understand, Claire's reaction was pathetic.

At that very moment, as I was looking for my phone that I put back in my handbag when Clarisse faked her faint, it curiously rang with an unknown number... Hum, it must be the driver:

"Hello! I'm Guillaume, your Taxi driver. I'm just waiting in front of the pick-up point," said the guy after having taken my call with a strong French accent.

I looked around... And there was a light grey car parked at ten metres away of us. I guess it was that car

"Are you in the grey car with tinted glasses parked in front of the station?" I made sure it was actually him.

"That's me, yes."

"Alright mate, we're coming."

"Thank you!"

I hung up, locked my phone, and placed it back in my bag. And finally, I stood up. After making sure that there was no Claire or Kelly around us, Clarisse stood up, and we made our way to this car. Finally, going back home! I was waiting for that moment at the very moment I woke up this morning!

"You're an outstanding actress, by the way!" I remarked to my sister.

"What do you mean?" she was surprised.

"You scared the shit out of me."

"Meh... You see when I told you I have hidden talents?" I was kidding her.

"Yeah. Let's go home, I am done here!"

6 *Obviously...*

// At home, Neuilly-sur-Seine.

// Wednesday, 9th of January 2013, 13:04

Sometimes, I am pleased that someone created a Taxi. I use it quite often. Because a Taxi means no metro, so no headaches gave by some guy that keeps looking at you and daydreaming with insistence (so you use to think that there's something wrong with you but actually nope), or brainless idiots speaking about some nonsense wannabe or other mindless gossips. Instead, it's a fast ride in Mercedes, from Asnières, for going back home, passing across the Seine, towards Clichy-la-Garenne, Levallois-Perret for arriving afterwards in Neuilly. Passing in front of all those buildings, it's here that I say that the problem in Paris, it's because it's a capital that does not breathe. I don't really like living here. But yeah, the only problem with Taxi is that drivers are paid shit for what they do. And sometimes some of them are rude bastards. But I guess that it is capitalism's reverse medal. Make money, no matter what. When we arrived, the taxi dropped us just next to our building. That was fast, and the shortest the better, because I was now quite hungry. Clarisse too. The weather was still cloudy, it was still cold, and I am sure that it's gonna rain this afternoon. But I don't mind, I'll be home within minutes now.

And my speculations were actually right: at the very moment I opened the door and put my foot on the sidewalk to get out of the car, some drops of water fell from the sky, and I understood that it was the moment to hurry up. When we left the cab, Clarisse said "chop-chop!", and started to run towards the entrance. It didn't take long since we showed our badges, but the guy didn't really pay attention and opened the door as he recognised us. When we arrived home, we first dropped our bags in the entrance, I'll come back later to pick it up unless Clarisse does it in the afternoon, and then I went quickly into my bedroom to throw my coat on the bed. Clarisse did the same. And now, time to eat.

We went to the kitchen together, and indeed, I was hungry. The first thing I have done was to open the fridge, and I checked what was inside. And obviously, as I was seeking something that might inspire me, for something to eat quickly, and...

Taylor Harding-Jenkins

Well, I looked again... No, no idea. The fridge wasn't empty, I mean, no, it's never empty, even if we are four to live here. The most boring fact is that I never know which food I want to prepare for myself. But when I say never, I mean it regarding the number of ideas I have for this. And the very problem that everybody has with me is that I do not eat cold. Never, I absolutely hate that. Except for chips and other shit like this. And when I eat, it must be without any sauces. It's not an allergy, it's just that I don't like condiments, I prefer dry food, except in some cases like burgers and other (obviously, it depends which sauce is inside). And if you open mustard in front of my nose whilst eating, I'm gonna ask you to close the container, because the smell repulses me. I'm not allergic or intolerant to any food, I am just a pain in the arse. Anyway, whilst still exploring the fridge, I decided to look in the freezer underneath, after having taken a bottle of water, and gave it to my twin who was looking at me, quite impatiently... I discovered something relatively simple that meets my criteria in terms of times of preparation. That would make us happy, which is really the easiest and fastest solution: a pizza. As Clarisse said.

In pizza, we trust.

Then, I looked at my sister, and it's while showing her what I found, all packed with ice everywhere on it, that was even freezing my fingers which is why I was also looking for a place to drop it, that I ask her proudly:

"Alright darling, in the *plat du jour* today: a pizza. Is that okay?"

"Perfect, hurry up to put it in the oven, I wanna sleep."

"On my way."

So, I took a pair of scissors from the drawer where we put the kitchen stuff and the cutleries, and then I went to the table, to unpack it. While Clarisse was sat and kept looking at me, I switched on the oven, put it on a tray with a sheet of baking paper, and left it for a while, for letting it defrost a bit oven was warming up. After I took two glasses, I served two glasses of cold water because I was a bit thirsty, and I finally sat down with her. Now, I was breathing a bit. Whilst everything was slowly starting, I started making the conversation:

"So, what's on your mind?"

"I'm tired, I just wanna sleep... And you, what's up?"

"I was quite impatient to be back. Now, it's okay."

"What are you gonna tell your guy as an excuse that you can't be here tonight?"

"Well, really easy: I just can't be here tonight... He doesn't need to know where I am."

Free Expensive Lies: Prologue

"When you were with Claire, you always used to justify yourself."

"Yeah, but I'm not with her anymore. I don't think I need to justify myself on what I am doing or not..."

"You don't love him, do you?"

"No, I do, it's just that... It's still quite different. With Claire, we used to have... I don't know, we were really close, we could understand each other, there was a complicity that I didn't find with Florent yet. I'm trying to make something with him, but... I love girls, Clarisse."

"Yeah. It's gonna take time, I think."

"Maybe... Or maybe not."

"I really wish that you guys manage to be happy and build a stable relationship. Besides, he's a friend, he's a good guy..."

"No, he is. I just need time to forget the life I had before."

"That reminds me, Marc asked me yesterday if he could bring back some video game... erm... I don't remember which one, that he lent to Florent a while ago. Well, I'm gonna tell him tonight if he's back."

Ah, videogames... It's funny, we have a console. I have an Xbox 360, but I played maybe once or twice, no more. He is the only one to use it the most. And I recall, last weekend, on Saturday afternoon when I was home watching series on the TV in the living room, I came back to my bedroom, and it smelled burned. I was suspicious. Florent was still with the controller in his hand but was about to drop it on the desk. And the TV was off. I looked at him, and he told me at that very moment with his face that he usually takes when he knows that he screwed up with something that as he played too much, the console overheated and turned itself off. But it was no big deal, and it was better to wait an hour or two until it works again. I laughed... He's a geek, but he's too proud to admit it.

And guess what, at that precise moment of the conversation, my phone rang. I took it and watched on the screen who was calling me: speaking of the devil...

"Meh, guess what, I'll tell him straight away," I first replied to Clarisse while I was answering my boyfriend at the same time, "Hey, my baby."

"No... Not that, I'm gonna take it later... Yeah... Hey, honey!" I assume he was talking to someone else as I heard someone replying after.

"Alright, you can call me later if you're busy right now, you know!"

"No, I'm done with him. How are you, my heart?"

"I'm okay, what about you?"

"Well, yeah, it could be better. Anyway. Happy birthday... I don't know if I wished you already..."

"Ah, yes, the little note that you left me this morning..."

"Ah. Okay, okay, I thought so!"

Yeah, he was stressed. That was the test, but at least I know in which state of mind he is now. Because he never left me absolutely no note this morning, otherwise I'd remember. When he is stressed, he doesn't listen to me and say yes to whatever I say. He also uses to change his voice and adopt kind words and not be vulgar and stop talking shit. His sentences are short and concise. But nope, he left nothing, no messages, nothing. He was just sleeping. Well, at least he thought about my birthday. But if he was stressed and under pressure right now, it means that he failed. I am relatively sure he's gonna come to me and tell me that he failed sooner or later. Anyway, it's kind of him to have thought about my birthday though, I appreciate it!

"How about your test this morning?" I asked.

"Well. Not really fine. If you want to know, honey... It's a shame, I worked so hard for this."

"I know! What about the oral exam?"

"That's what I messed up. I don't know... I saw them all, with their glasses, their old faces, and I have made a mistake to focus on it... it just stressed me out."

"Did you use my advice?"

"I... no, baby, sorry. I was under hard pressure. And I lost my means, it was terrible. It's a shame!"

"Yep. Well, on the other hand, that's okay. You did all you could. It's alright, don't worry."

"Thanks, baby. I just messed up, that's it, and I was scared about what you could have told me."

"No, honey. Don't worry. If you fail, well... Don't forget that you can do something else, and you'll restart. And we can still get the hell out of this country."

"Yeah, we still can."

"Anyway. Unless you learned that you have cancer or a death in your family, there's no problem. You just failed a test, that happens."

"I don't know if I failed yet... However, I am considering leaving France. I'm fed up to look for a job and find nothing and being stuck at your place drives me mad."

Free Expensive Lies: Prologue

"There's no problem, we can leave here anytime. I am definitely okay with that. Just tell me when, and I am ready. If it's to leave that country, I am already okay, as long as we go to mine."

"We'll see. But anyway, now, it's done. We'll have results soon. Now, everything is done."

"And when will you know the results?"

"I don't know. Next week, they said. But... I am really pessimistic about it."

"Well, you shouldn't be. You'll see what happened, and if you failed, well at least you can tell yourself that you tried."

"You won't be angry if I fail?"

"I definitely will!"

"You're serious?"

No, he was really under pressure: fifteen seconds before, I told him that I won't blame him because he has at least tried, and it's like he forgot, fifteen seconds later, after he asked me if he actually really failed, if I will be angry against him (probably just to make sure, but I mean, he knows that I am so unstable, as I can change my mind at any time), I said yes. He believed it, as seen as the way he answered. That's funny when he's under pressure, he is like this, sure about nothing. That might have been a disaster, what happened this morning. I don't really know what being stressed means, as I don't really care about many things, but... It's weird. He is weird. Meh, let's not be an idiot, I might sometimes have something strange called empathy. And since he was like an overstretched elastic about to explode...

"No, of course not, I won't be angry with you if you fail. God damn it, I said it's just an exam. Don't worry, I won't break up with you because of this. There are worse things in life, as I said. But I might be annoyed if you keep on going not listening to what I say, and you make me repeat myself..."

"Oh, sorry. Sorry, Cha, I know. I am a little bit... Lost, actually, since this morning."

"No way! Remember, I told you about an imaginary note you wrote this morning..."

"Uh... Yeah, I thought so, there was something weird on this."

"Weird? Simply weird? You didn't write anything for me this morning!"

"I... Shit... I thought about you all this morning."

"You thought about me all this morning... Are you insinuating that I am the reason why you totally messed up your test?" I was teasing.

"Baby, er... No, I wasn't, I mean... Damn... Baby, please," he was seeking his words.

"Relax! I was joking."

"Oh, yeah... sorry," he was breathing.

Perhaps I am eighteen today, but he's twenty-three. I know, it doesn't look like this. And he knows that I really hate people saying sorry all the time. But, well... I forgot; he was under pressure. Huh, guys... That's what I hate with them: they behave like babies when they are stressed out. It's why I left him taking a deep breath, so at least I could finally swap to something else.

"Well, anyway..." he started after breathing.

"It's okay, it's just my birthday today" I smiled.

"Yes, eighteen!"

"Yep."

"Well, finally, happy birthday, baby. I am sorry, I didn't bring you a gift, but..."

"It's alright, I don't want any gifts. I was just thinking... You're finally allowed to sleep with me tonight, according to the law. What you're doing is no longer considered as child abuse, it's a great day for you!"

"Well, yeah."

Clarisse laughed. And according to the way he replied, something tells me that he was actually embarrassed by what I just said. On the other hand, I am not sure that he was even allowed to live with a minor, legally speaking. Which is funny, I mean... My mother hated Claire, she did all she could to tear us apart but allowed Florent to live with me, it didn't seem to be actually a real problem for her. While smiling because I was happy of what I said, and him... maybe blushing, I kicked the leg of Clarisse softly.

"Yeah, the law is amazing..." I was briefly daydreaming after smiling. "Oh, by the way, I have a good... I mean wonderful news to tell you!"

"Huh? What's going on?" he wondered.

"Well, actually... Guess"

"Guess what? I don't know."

"So... Well, the first clue, it happened a couple of days ago. Don't you remember, an evening when I left the table suddenly, and I wasn't feeling well, I felt like I was woozy, and everything, the rest..."

"Huh? No, I mean, yeah, I remember, but..."

"Second clue... Well, when your girlfriend announces to you that she has wonderful news to tell you, what do you think it is?"

"Er... Hold on. Oh no..."

"And... Third clue... If you take my mother away from our little family, we will soon be four. You, Clarisse, me... And a new one!"

"No, no!"

"No, what?"

"No, that's not possible? I mean... Are you sure of it?"

"Pretty sure, yeah," I confirmed.

"Oh, Lord... Have you done a test, at least?"

"Ah, yes. Yes, I did. And it was positive!"

"Oh no, God damn it... Did you do it twice?"

"Oh, so nice of you. So, I guess you're not happy?"

"Happy to... No, you're kidding me, now, sweetie."

"Unfortunately, for once, I am not kidding you. I am serious."

"No..."

"Anyway, I am delighted you're apparently looking happy. I'll remember it."

"Happy? Charlotte... Damn..."

"Oh wow, you're calling me by my name, now... Nice!"

"No, yes, of course, I'm glad to hear such news. No, I am worried. I mean, you're telling me that you're pregnant, and... Damn, I mean, I am only twenty-three, you are eighteen, I have got any money, we don't have our own home too, even if you have but still... I have no income, I have no degree, no plans for the future, I have no job, I... Damn, and how may it happen? I mean, every time we do it, erm... You take the pill, right? How could it be possible? I don't think we are ready to become parents!"

"Yeah, so what's the problem?"

I was not pregnant. At least, as far as I know, I am not. No... Come on, I know, this is mean, I know. But at least it's fun! Really. He knows I don't want kids. I hate them, and the purpose of my womb is to annoy me on a 24-days basis. No, my maternity centre is permanently closed (toxic leak, from what I heard) while the playing ground is always open, and no. Having a child in this shitty world? No, thanks. I'll hate my child, and he/she will hate me in return, I'll be a crappy mother. But I took such an enthusiastic and so ambiguous tone that he could believe that there was really a part of him in my womb. No, there's no chance. I take the pill seriously since I am with him, given the risks that I did not really encounter when I was with Claire, so he has nothing to worry about but still... I think it's always essential to assess the situation before it really happens. No, I'm kidding.

Oh my god. His nightmare was starting, and I am sure he was already imagining thousands of scenarios on how to get rid of this or at least trying to talk to me about abortion. And since he knows I'm stubborn... It must have been horrible. Curiously, this was my way to force him to accept that I won't be here tonight: if he's relieved that I am not actually pregnant, (because given his stress level, I am sure he was convinced) he will be more accepting the fact that I won't be here tonight. When the pressure is reaching a certain point, he becomes sweet and takes everything. Yeah, guys.

"No, baby, I... I'm not ready!" he continued after thinking about what he could say for avoiding hurting me.

"You're not ready for what? You should better be ready for it because the upcoming months are going to be tough for me. I will need you!"

"And we couldn't talk about this before? Have you stopped your pills?"

"Huh? Because you wanted to talk about it, I only knew this since like... something like... A couple of minutes ago?"

"Five minutes... Cha, what the hell are you talking about?"

"What I say is that Clarisse wants to be at home tonight alone with her boyfriend. I will not be here, I planned something, so she would like you not to come back home. That's what I was talking about. Why? What did you expect?"

And there, Clarisse started to laugh really loudly. Me too... By the way.

And, no, Clarisse didn't ask for that. But that's the only thing I had to make sure that he would not come home. That's lies... But everybody lies. So, I am not really guilty about lying to him.

"Jesus Christ, honey, I will kill you!"

"I know, but only after I abort, please!"

"Damn it... Don't you dare scare me like this again!"

"No, sweetheart, I promise..."

"Holy crap!" he was evacuating the false alert.

"Oh, damn, my girlfriend is pregnant, I'd better run!" I was mocking him in mimicking his scared voice.

"Jesus goddamn Christ... And this funny for you..."

"Absolutely!"

"Oh god... Thank you, you scared the hell out of me now!"

"My pleasure..." I was satisfied.

Meh, he didn't find my joke funny. No, seriously, there he was precisely between scared and upset right now. As if he still doesn't know me, by the time... Well, okay, sometimes, some jokes can be tricky. But at least I know how to react with him if something unexpected happens, like a pregnancy. So, after laughing, I became more serious once again.

"Anyway..." he said, in conclusion.

"Yeah, as you say," I continued whilst looking through the window.

"And you said that you will not be here tonight?"

"Er... Yep. No. I mean, no, I, no, I will not be here..." I was thinking about the approach I should take to deliver him the news.

"Han. Yes? What's wrong?"

"Nothing. Everything is still okay."

"Okay, then. And you told me that you won't be here tonight?" he was actually not confident enough to ask me what I'd do tonight.

Yeah, believe it or not, but since I consider my independence as sacred, especially since I am with him (I had my freedom with Claire, except that with her it was different, until the end we trusted each other) he knows that asking me what I am going to do can be risky.

"Er, no, I will be, er... Kind of busy," I was still thinking.

"Why? What are you doing tonight?"

"I will just hang out with some friends of mine. Er... I think I don't know how long it's gonna take to be honest for the whole night. But don't worry, I'll be back in the morning, or maybe quite late. It's just that I need to go out. But don't worry, tomorrow, I am all yours, and for the entire day."

"Oh, cool. But when you mean 'friends of yours', I really hope that it does not include some girl named Claire, does it?"

"Claire? Oh, yeah. No, she's not invited. No, I mean... She's busy, on the other hand, so, er... Claire's always busy. You know, and why would I see Claire, really? You know that I don't like her anymore!"

"Because you know what will happen if I learn that somehow you managed to be with her?"

7 *An amazing mess*

// Towards Claire's house.

// Wednesday, 9ᵗʰ of January 2013, 18:27

Anyway, he came back home maybe three hours after having called me, and he was, of course, disappointed that I was not staying with him tonight, but managed to plan something else instead. He was not going to grumble, though, because "my girlfriend is going outside tonight", no, we give to each other absolute freedom in our couple life. I let him do what he wants, and in return, I do what I want. In reverse, the only counterpart that I request is that we communicate whenever there's a problem. And we are sharing a lot, for example when I do something that displeases him, he tells me, and same from my side. The truth is, we never remain, neither him nor I, on ambiguities, or unspoken facts. The only rule is that, apart from school, he does not allow me to see Claire. Until today, that never happened.

Actually, after lunch, I had nothing to do. I spent the whole afternoon in my bedroom to sleep, as I was tired, and had to get ready for tonight, not sleepy, and grumpy as I was this morning. Meanwhile, at least before sleeping, Clarisse was convincing her boyfriend to come home tonight, I don't know if that went through. And Florent came back whilst I was sleeping. I mean, I slept from one o'clock until maybe three or four, because I was drained. Well, last night, I just slept for two or three hours, and... This is why I was so grumpy this morning, even if I was doing stuff with Florent before sleeping, I don't know why I am mostly sleeping on afternoons and not during the night. I mean we didn't make love the entire night, but after this, I was like... Having trouble for sleeping. Just like every night. As, by night, usually, before I'm trying to sleep, I use to have spasms in the belly that makes me move like a marionette for an hour before sleeping. I always had it, I'm scared in the dark and horrified at the idea of sleeping and not waking up. It's why this afternoon I slept, I just heard Florent sometimes coming into the room, once for kissing me, then for taking some clothes. Because I think he will go to his best friend's home. But, yeah, at least, for maybe a couple of hours (it's the reason why I'm going there, it might be silly but I do need it, it's quite hard to confess but it's the truth) I will quit this reality because I know there will be drugs and alcohol. I am criticising everybody, but... I know I need that; otherwise, it makes me mad.

But yeah, I really believe that in a couple, communication is the key for everything: never, when there's a conflict, we remain in our position for long. Even if everyone knows my stubbornness, my wickedness and for the fact that I will no matter what push my interests beyond everything, I never do this in my couple, and I never did. Even at the beginning of my relationship with him, I must admit, it was a change, I could seem a bit extreme with him, a little nasty sometimes, but I always listened to him. Maybe it's since I am still trying to understand most of the people, but in every case, I am overall more concerned above all to the happiness and the interests of our couple before worrying about mine. I was the same with Claire. Even if today I don't really know whether he's my choice or not, but since I respect him and I like him, well, I accepted a lot of things I'd never take before, even on myself. It's why, sometimes I feel like I am screwing up with my life, and I feel like... I feel like whenever things are gonna collapse, I am quite scared to fall from high. Since everything starts, thus everything ends, and I don't know what will tear us apart.

Florent left at some point, but he kissed me once again before he left, and I was still sleeping. I didn't really want to talk to him actually. As sleeping is my way to escape, it makes me forget that everything around is evil, and I even forget that I am alive. And when I'm complaining that I am unhappy, "yeah, it's the same for us, we also have our problems". Maybe we had fun during lunch when I was kidding him about a hypothetical pregnancy, but still, I felt like I was not actually okay. With him, but even with Claire, and I assume it's why I am so withdrawn from the other, I feel like there's something in my mind that prevents me from being okay. I always have a problem, but I don't know which. So, all the time, I pretend that I feel okay, I smile at people, or I am an ass to some other, but there's something that I am hiding from people, something profound and dark that I have trouble to show. Maybe it's why I am such an idiot, I am suffering so hard deep inside that now I cannot contain my pain. Sometimes my pain is so unbearable that it's even hard for me to carry on. Some other times it's okay (like today, for instance) but I am always thinking that another episode of depression is coming, and I am somehow making myself ready. Nothing can cure me anyway, even my sister or whatever love people may give me. I saw a GP about that a couple of years ago, upon the advice of Claire regarding that issue, and they proposed me to get lithium. And, hell no, there's no way I'm gonna swallow even a pill of that.

And then I woke up at five o'clock—one hour before I leave. I heard absolutely no noise within the flat, and I could see that the night was already dark. Still, in bed, I realised that even if I slept with my clothes, I didn't sweat that much. But opening my eyes was already a big problem. I sent a message to Claire to inform her that I will come maybe early. And then I woke up: first, I grabbed a bag, opened my wardrobe, took a dress, a pair of new underwear and shoes. I left my shoes in a small plastic bag, so it's not gonna make my clothes dirty, I folded my dress so it wouldn't be messy and wrinkled, then closed my bag. I went to my bathroom for at least refreshing myself before to leave. 5:45 pm were displayed on the screen of my phone, I closed my bag that I left in my bed when I went to the bathroom, I took my make-up... No, I mean I took my make-up then I closed my bag. And then, yeah... Well, it was time to leave. And I really hope there's gonna be something to drink, as my mood was not at its absolute best at that very moment. I didn't actually want to party, I wanted to stay at home, in the dark, and thinking about my fate. But, yeah, I promised that I'd come, so as I promised, I have to go. Otherwise, she's gonna annoy me every day until we finally do this party. I know her.

And yeah, "the most wrenching moment of the day", if I may say so: after having taken my bag like an explorer going to some new adventures, I took my pumps that I was wearing since this morning, left close to the bed before I sleep, my red coat that actually seemed purple in that dark, and I left my bedroom, coming now into the dark flat because the night was here now. I took my keys, and I left. I didn't know when I would go back, and I don't even know whether I will go back tonight or not, it's why I'd instead take some precautions. Ten minutes later, I left my building, after having chatted a bit with the security guy downstairs, as I was so motivated to go. Then finally I went outside, in the dark, and again, freezing night. Streetlights were illuminating me so I could actually see my way, cars were parked along the road, and like this morning, the same way, I went to my metro station, this time not to go to the same place. To go to Claire's house in Ivry, the southern suburb of Paris. I have to take my line and change at the station "*Palais Royal, Musée du Louvre*", and then taking the seventh line towards the terminus, "*Mairie d'Ivry*". It takes me about an hour to go there. Hopefully, her house is just next to the station, and while I was walking, she replied that she was at home with Sophie and Kelly, and they were waiting for me. She eventually sent me a picture of them all three smiling. The only thing I was now scared of was that the metro would be busy.

Well, the metro... I used to take it every morning to go to school. But I'd rather love them to be much more comfortable. I adore the metro just like I love babies, and it's a real pleasure when both are mixed-up together. But we live in a world where kids have power, which is why it turns our journeys into sometimes real nightmares. I don't like kids anyway, but when you hear one of them crying its arse off for some shit that it actually wants, it just reminds me that abortion is just a fabulous tool sometimes not understood enough. When I say that I'd be a dreadful mother. And, obviously, even if the baby is pissing other passengers off, passengers that by the way are paying relatively high prices for using public transports, the mother doesn't give a shit, even if she sees moving out of your seat for taking another. "Meh, come on, it's just a baby", yes, right, then does it give that the right to be a tiny arsehole? I remember, once in the metro, I almost had a fight with one of these amazing and respectful mums, because I advised her to have swapped her baby for a dog, as it also barks and poops everywhere. And the way she yelled at me, oh my god... I couldn't believe a second that its 7-pounds-package-of-shit-in-a-trolley's life was so sacred!

And believe it or not, but I did not encounter that in the metro. My travel went relatively smoothly, and this on both lines that I actually took. And, yes, in case you're wondering, stations were still smelling homeless' urine. You actually have to deal with the other thing, especially in Paris metro or even in general public transports in France, it's perverts. I used to take the tube in London, and I didn't hear that much about that, so I assume this must be typically French. Obviously, don't get me wrong, it must exist everywhere across the planet. As there's a lot of fraud here, people using the metro system and not paying for that, sometimes it is not acutely safe for a girl to travel alone, especially in off-peak hours. Because she might encounter... Well, quite a lot, actually. The full range of issue starts from the "classic" hand in the arse (that happened to me once, and frankly, I felt like shit many days after, it's something really horrible), to the guy staring at you, that you actually find out that he's even masturbating. To get one of these, you need first to travel and be dressed quite fancy (I mean make-up, high heels, and skirt), travel off-peak but especially after 8pm, and be alone in the coach. Yeah, Paris is not only the Eiffel Tower and the Champs-Elysées with its fancy shops, but it's also colossal criminality and a perilous and unsafe city, and this wherever you are!

Anyway, forty-three minutes of travel and one change later, I arrived. *Ivry-sur-Seine*. It's a small suburban town like mine, but it's in the south of Paris contrarily to mine in the west, but it is composed of pavilion houses and small buildings. We might think that because it's close to Paris; because houses are large, it's expensive, but no. I mean, yes, it's costly. But since Ivry is the low-cost suburb of Paris, it's cheap compared to my place. The terminus of the seventh line is downtown, and I have only two streets to walk, again, to arrive in an area that I used to love and that now recalls me specific bad remembrances, hidden behind a little park.

Still, in the darkness of the night, I arrived slowly at the destination. I was getting colder, and even if I had my relatively thick coat, I was freezing. I still don't know the program for tonight, what Claire actually prepared. I hope that for once Kelly made herself useful and brought some drugs. No, seriously, I just took a dress, (okay, not a light one, but still, only one dress) and I really hope we're going to get just fucked up here and not going out. Anyway, *Ivry* is mostly populated with quite a young populace. Most of the youth living in this suburb are generally in the evening in Paris (usually on Fridays), and come back here usually drunk from the capital, I mean, for all the youth like us. Now, I guess, they were all eating and ready to go to bed early as tomorrow is Thursday, and they still have to go to work or to school, unlike us. Maybe there were some cases of asocial people just like us (and mostly asocial just like me) that were doing the same as we did. But I don't think this party will be really long, Claire just wants to celebrate my birthday, as we have to go to school tomorrow. I walked in the streets, my beige leather bag with its straps that I held in the articulation of my left arm, and through the streetlights, I could see some moisture droplets of water flying like a new sun, I felt like it was almost snowy. Parked cars, streets without pedestrians and roads without traffic, the city was idle, it was the practically terrifying calm that Paris didn't have. Same for my place. She is lucky, she lives in a quiet area.

Claire lives at the *twenty-five, Impasse du Temple*. This is a blind alley within a residential subdivision. A dead-end, more or less. She has a reasonably large house that is recognisable with a large blue gate, a small garden, and a terrace in front. I've been here quite a lot of times in the last years, even if she went on my place more than I went to hers. It's in her house that began our fantastic relationship, and also where it ended. Today, if I allow myself to go to her place, I don't want her to come in mine. In this house, she lives alone with her mother. There's a large garden all around the house, and the large terrace in front of the portal is, like an old Roman street, a stone footpath across a small garden. But it's clean, I mean, it's not a mess, Claire uses to spend a lot of time gardening when she's not with her phone. Although from the last couple of months, it's become a bit messier, since her priorities apparently changed. Anyway, I entered her property and went through this path to knock at the door. I heard some deafening music that came from the inside of her house. Obviously, according to the music and the loud laugh that I could listen to, I quickly deduced that they were all in here. And I don't know what kind of shit they were listening to, but it seemed like a mix of pop and electro. All the stuff I don't like. When I said that the party is gonna be very, very long...

Free Expensive Lies: Prologue

While I was freezing, I pressed the bell behind her door because I knocked three timed and nobody heard, as I was still hearing them chatting and chatting again. Fifteen seconds later, Claire came to open me up. Judging by her voice, I assume that she was not with the two others, but she was doing something in the kitchen.

"Hey, love!" she was opening the door, enthusiast.

"Yo," I said, completely detached.

"Come on in!"

At a glance, I saw her, and she was breathtaking. I guess she was already prepared for the evening, she was wearing a black dress, exceptionally smart and obviously all my type, a classic style, with only a strap in her left shoulder. She released her hair, and I assume she did something since they were now wavy. She reminded me when we were together, her lips were covered with a shiny red gloss, and she was beautiful. I knew that I shouldn't come here tonight. She had put her dark tights below her dress, and she had a small black and white flower on top of her shoulder, in the strap. She was brilliant, it changes to see her like this, I mean... I remember that dress, she wore it when we did my last birthday party. It made me feel like... I don't know, yeah, I just noticed that she was actually dressed the same way as one year ago when we were together and ONLY together that day. And when I say that it was affecting her, I was right: her beautiful eyes, beautifully surrounded and displaying a perfect balance of make-up, actually showed her hidden dilated pupils and her mouth covered of gloss looked even really dry, and the way she was that relax therefore means that right now, she was fucking high.

"So how are you?" I asked her, actually destabilised.

"Well, fine, what about you?" she was out of her mind.

"Well, er... Yeah. Could be better!"

Yes, Claire has got a big house, with more surface than my flat. Due to her father, as he was in the army, he could easily buy a home in Paris that could be that big. Listen, she even has an indoor swimming pool, which used to be my joy when I was with her, during spring break, and we stayed in Paris with mum. But as he died, she inherited the place with her mother. And, yes, she's been living here for a while, almost her entire life, and she really loves her house. Because, unlike me, she was born in Paris. Anyway, when you arrive at her home, there is a small open-space kind of lobby. Through this lobby, you can access any part of the house, everything is connected to it. All the walls were painted in white, and there are trinkets placed on them, looking like African mages, all this universe. Supposedly to repulse evil spirits (doesn't seem to work, since Kelly was here somewhere). The floor is in marble tiles. I stepped inside, and she closed the door behind me and locked the door. The fact that she did it also showed evidence that she was high, as she was paranoid. Claire never closes the door, especially when I am here, as she said that she feels safe when I am here.

"Oh, you like it?" She was glad that I figured it out.

"Yeah, it was the one you wore a year ago when we had our night together. And after you tell me to move on... Anyway."

"I don't actually remember, but if you say so. Anyway, Sophie is here, too. But Kelly is changing herself in my bedroom upstairs. As you took a bag, I guess it's for..."

"Yeah, I'm gonna get changed, I was too lazy to do it home, I'll use your bedroom once she's done."

"If you want."

"Yeah."

"Okay, great. Well, welcome! Now if you'll excuse me, but I have to finish cooking the food..."

"Okay then," I concluded.

Then I went to the first step of the stairs on my right, just after the wall separating the kitchen from the stairs. Yes, Claire's house has another floor upstairs, where all the bedrooms are, and the bathroom. At the end of the stairs' guardrail in front of me, there's a woody pole, into which we use to leave our coats anyhow. I left my bag under the coats that were already there, and then I removed mine, as I was feeling pretty hot now. I was standing in front of the stairs, made of wood like the guardrail, inside a considerable place connecting the basement to the first floor. There was, in the wall facing me, a little higher, a lamp. I was standing here because, despite the music in the background that made a terrible noise in the room, I was trying to hear Kelly. Even if it was not wholly accurate, in the reflection of varnished red painting made by Claire in the stairs, I saw many doors closed. Even if, from my position, I can't really see Claire's entry because it's just after a corner on the first floor, I am sure she closed her door to avoid being bothered. And moreover, since no lights upstairs were on, so it was almost impossible to see through.

After I removed my coat and dropped my bag, I turned back and went into the living room. This living room, it's undoubtedly the place where we had our best moments together. So many things happened here. But this living room is unique since it's mixed up with the dining "space", making a vast rectangular open space, just facing the entrance and, more importantly, the kitchen. The table is, therefore in the shortest way from the kitchen. And this table made of opaque and hefty glass was quite long, had at its centre metal stuff made for carrying hot dishes when we eat here, on which was currently a vase with two roses. Four white metal chairs around the table on which the seat was in wicker, but it's so clean! Claire's mother cleans her house a lot, but she wasn't here tonight. There were two blue thick and heavy curtains behind this table (on the opposite to the living room), hiding the vast window gates, hiding the place from the outside and the street. They're always drawn, only sometimes in summer, they open them, but now... And obviously tonight, they were pulled. Walls of this living room are painted in navy blue, and there is no heavy light in the ceiling, there's instead a long diode string glued across the four walls on the roof, giving then quite a powerful light. It's fancy, though. Just like everywhere, the ceiling is white, I guess like in every flat I've been, even in mine. In one of the walls, though, the one facing the entrance next to the enormous windows, a self-portrait of Claire when she was ten that she painted a couple of years ago, and it's impressive how she does to be so good at painting. She's really gifted in this because it almost looks like a giant poster when you look at this portrait.

Now, regarding the living room, at least... The other part of the living room, next to the dining section: I said that once entering the room, immediately on the left, there was a bay window hidden by thick curtains. There's precisely the very same bay window on the opposite side of the room, facing the other, which this time leads to a small terrace and a garden. Same curtains in front, except for the colour, these are red. Inside the room, there are two black-leathered and quite long sofas, one on the left-hand side of the window and the other positioned perpendicularly to the other couch. There is a small, large table in the middle of this vast space, matching with the dining room's one, and the TV remote placed on it. There is also another small table at the end of each sofa that connects them (on which there's a big bedside lamp), and a carpet in the middle. Opposite to the wall where there's one sofa is where a giant 42-inch flat-screen placed above a white not high but wide furniture on which there's also some random magazines, DVD player and Internet box. Immediately behind this, if you go towards the dining room entrance, even if there's some space.

And as I said, this room saw the most significant moments of our couple. We used to kiss here, we used to have sex in here (yeah... This place saw me naked with her for my very first time in my life), and... When I used to be here, and her mother was not here, she used to take her mattress from upstairs, move a sofa and the table, and we used to sleep in here. Or, when it was too hot inside in summer, we used to sleep outside. I know, it was crazy, but now, when I think back, it was undoubtedly our most incredible moment, when we were so close that we thought nothing would one day tear us apart. And... yeah, better not to recall and to leave the past where it is.

But that night, while Claire was cleaning the dishes in her kitchen, Sophie was sitting on the couch, the one facing the window, it was closed, but curtains were open. The TV was turned on, and Claire plugged her laptop to it (a new one... She has the very latest MacBook Air, she bought it a couple of months ago) to see her YouTube page and what was played right now. And Sophie was with a drink in her hand, legs crossed, thoughtful, and alone. I noticed that she didn't really pay attention to me, so I guess she might be high as well. But Sophie is quite distant with me in general, but especially when she's drunk and high she tends to be quite aggressive and looking for troubles, we need to be really careful when we are talking to her when she's high. That was almost sad to see her like this because I felt like she wasn't looking fine, even if she was turned, I mean, yeah. Sometimes I can feel what people think, just at looking at them. She was wearing a short dark red dress, which had no shoulder strap. Actually, her dress was all black, but around her waist, there had a red ribbon. She had not tied her hair and was apparently barefoot. And I could see a strip of shot glasses lying in the table in front of her, all empty. And a bottle of vodka, also, halfway empty. So, slowly, I went to her, whilst bending myself to look like more sympathetic.

"Hi, you," I said, sitting down next to her was her.

"Hello, Cha. How're you doing?"

"Just as you are feeling, and you?"

"Meh. You're always fine, anyway, I don't even know why I still ask that question."

"Certainly... Any problems?"

"Not actually."

"You told me this morning that you wanted to talk?" I whispered as it seemed overall confidential.

"Yeah... Come with me."

I could see she was not really confident tonight: she didn't put any make-up on her face yet, except maybe her mascara of this morning, but since I guess the two others were in a make-up party and since... I don't really know if she was with

Kelly and my ex that were together during the afternoon, I feel like there was some form of despair in her visage. And it was not only this: when she was sat on that couch, I could breathe an inevitable cocktail of alcohol and weed, but she was not even looking high or drunk. Why was she so desperate? That's actually curious, there must be an explanation to that. Many things are escaping me. And it really intrigued me when she told me this morning that she needed to talk to me and couldn't speak actually for some reasons. I have two theories: either Claire told her something that she didn't like about me, or whether she had some bad news that she didn't want my sister to know. And I think it's more likely to be the first because if she had some bad news, I don't think she'd actually be there. If she was like this, it means that it's something massive, and I don't even know whether I'll like it or not.

She stood up and opened the bay window of the living room. I just followed. She opened, and we went together outside. The garden was plunged into total darkness, it was complicated to have any light perception, even if I could see her. I even surprised her to quickly look at all the windows she could see, I assume for checking if they were closed or not so we couldn't be heard. And after her quick safety check, she closed after me while taking almost the most extraordinary precautions, as if she were about to give me the real name of the President Kennedy's murderer, which seemed odd a bit to me. And after we moved towards the centre of the small terrace, she looked at me quite seriously. Curious, and indeed now more than ever, I started:

"Okay, what's going on?"

"You remember. I had something to tell you," she seemed confused.

"Yes, it's precisely why I'm freezing my arse over here, yes."

"Yeah..."

"No, seriously, what's wrong?"

"Be very careful tonight with that Kelly, trust me."

"Why, you actually found out that she was a whore, just like I told you, a couple of time?"

"Believe it or not, but I already knew that. I knew that Kelly was a cunt, and I saw that she brainwashed your ex-girlfriend's brain. I just pretend to befriend with her, but... I am not sure of what I'm gonna tell you, but I think that Claire is in quite big troubles now."

"Oh yeah? How?"

"Listen, I know that Kelly is sleeping with guys for money, and this for months."

Oh, oh, okay... It's true, Claire changed. Not for the best, but she changed. I know that she's been sleeping with many guys, and I'd say that I believe she has sex maybe twice or three times a week, but no more, and... is she assuming that Claire does the same too? I really don't think so. As we used to do before, whenever she has a problem, I am the first person she talks to. And all the time we've been talking together by phone, she tells me about her very new sexual life, but... She doesn't sleep with that much of people. She still has her life and spends a lot of time painting, and she told me that she now starts to manage to sell her work, which is why she is starting to make money. And, for instance, I even bought her a canvas three weeks ago (that I didn't find a place about where to display, by the way), and I gave her almost a thousand euros for her work. But hiding prostitution, I mean, come on... Sexually speaking, unlike Kelly, Claire is quite reserved and do not really like to talk about sex, and especially about sex she had. She considers it very intimate. And, if she ever lied to me, she's have betrayed herself, and I would have guessed there would be something wrong. If Kelly does prostitute herself, that's her problem, and I honestly don't care. But Claire... No, come on. As I said, she talks to me quite often, and I'd guess that. Regarding Kelly's allegation, I simply replied to Sophie:

"Yeah, breaking news. On the other hand, I really don't see where Kelly would earn money unless she shows her pussy."

"And, as I said, I am not sure about what I say, but I believe that Claire does the same, and this with her."

"Alright, listen. I used to talk a lot with her. And let's be honest a second, yes, since she broke up with me, she's not with anyone, she's having sex, yes, but... I mean, hiding the fact that she's sleeping with people for money, I mean, come on! It's quite massive, and Claire... You know me, Sophie, I'd have guessed it. I'm always guessing how people feel, and if Claire would do that, I'd know already."

"Hum... Maybe."

"Did she tell you something that could have let you believe that she'd do that?"

"Not actually, Kelly didn't do that either, but there are things, behaviours... I mean, did you see how she changed since you guys are no longer together?"

"Yes, of course, she changed, but I assume that... she changed because she wanted so... What's the purpose for her to be dressed that way at school other than pissing me off?"

"I know. Your girlfriend is still in love with you... She told me many times, and she has huge regrets to have broken up with you. And don't lie to me, you, Charlotte, are still in love with her."

"She broke up with me," I actually made myself clear, "She lives her life, and I live mine. There's nothing more I can do for her."

"Yeah. Yes, of course..."

"Let me make it clear, okay, I still feel something for her. But I have a boyfriend now, I am living my life now, and she made a choice the day she cheated on me... It broke me; literally, I was horrible, since we've been together for a while, but she made her choices. That's it!"

"All I want to say is, and it's why I am not sure about what I say, and I really hope to be wrong, but Cha... You have the mean to save her life. So, use it! I'm sure she's in danger, and you're the only one to save her soul."

"What do you want me to do?"

"You should monitor her. Make her be followed. I mean, you can hire a PI to do the job. Or there are a lot of technologies available today to spy on her phone or listen to her calls."

"This is... her life privacy. Still, I did not feel any danger from her. Trust me, if I'd ever feel it, it would be the very first thing I'd do. But I am always assessing the situation, and I do not think that she should be followed or spied on. Yet."

"Alright, then."

"Can I ask you a question, Sophie?"

"Of course, yeah!"

"Why are you suddenly so concerned about Claire?"

"I liked you guys, and I am concerned for Claire because unlike Kelly, that is an obvious problem, Claire doesn't deserve to be brainwashed by that idiot. She's nice, and she was more stable with you."

"True that."

"This to say that, well... She is your ex, okay. But she's screwing around before your eyes, and you don't do anything."

"I'll do what I have to do, don't worry."

8 *Where are you?*

// *Approaching the Nightclub "Le Hive", close to the Panthéon, Central Paris.*

// *Wednesday, 9th of January 2013, 23:12.*

I totally ignored that the plan for tonight was to stay at home for a party for a while and then after going to a nightclub. I thought it would be only for here. And I so HATE nightclubs, these places are just meaningless to me. But before I found that out...

Actually, the party was not as fun as I could expect. I don't know, somehow, Sophie's revelations had left me perplexed regarding Claire. Was she sure about what she said? I don't know. I really can't imagine Claire doing such a thing, because, as I said, she's not smart enough to hide things from me. Or I can be surprised, but this is big. It's not like hiding something she bought or stole from someone. And as I know myself, I'm trained enough to recognise when something is wrong or weird, and I don't feel anything strange from her. I really don't think Kelly pushed her into this. I know Kelly made her cheating on me, but to the fact of prostituting herself, no, it's massive. She cannot hide something like this; she'd be psychologically affected and destabilised by this since Claire is sensitive to the sex question.

Moreover, she'd have to hide this from two people: me, obviously, because doing that would be a great shame, and worst, by her mother with whom she's currently living. And trust me, she doesn't want to disappoint her mother since she's the only survivor in her family, so the pressure would really be intense for her, almost unbearable. If now, she loses her mother, she's basically homeless, as nobody would come to help her. And unlike me who lies like I breathe, she's not capable of such a performance. She's not a professional liar just like I am.

So, we stayed home for a while this evening. Kelly went downstairs, in her turn, when I came back from outside with Sophie. I assume it would be a dress party tonight, as basically everyone was wearing the same thing, even me. She had a classic dark red dress, and for once I may recognise that she was actually pretty. She has already put make-up in her face and was wearing thick black tights just like Claire did. And whilst trying to avoid her, I didn't even say hi, I jumped to Claire's bedroom with the bag I took from home. It was time to get dressed.

And, oh yes, her bedroom... A unique place. A true reflection of Claire's personality. Well, I'm not judging, if she cleans like every day her house because she is literally obsessed with cleaning, it's not always the case for her bedroom. On the other hand, she has a bedroom, but she's more using it as her painting studio, she frequently sleeps downstairs, on a sofa. It's odd, I know, but it's how she works. Actually, without necessarily paying attention, I preferred to let the light off, although it was not advised, I know this place, it used to be a kind of a gigantic and monumental mess. It's awful. I removed my clothes, and I took the dress that I wanted to wear tonight out of my bag. It's a short, strapless one, in white and black. And I don't know... Every time I come here, I remember all the fantastic moments we had together, the fact that we used to call each other "kitty" or "kitten", and it was that evening that, I must confess... Life is not the same without her. But, yes, as I said, she moved on. I have to do the same. It made me... Actually, I had a small tear when I recalled that, and now I see her being corrupted by that cunt that I'd love to find her dead someday. Life is tough. And whilst it makes me more upset every day, I have to tell myself that she's now part of my past.

The very first thing I actually did when I came back downstairs, and I could see Claire glaring at me when I was in front of her with that new dress, was pouring for myself two shots of vodka and drinking them straight away. And I went quickly outside, pretending that I had a phone call, just to wait for at least five minutes. So, I could calm down and start getting drunk, so being more... in the accepting mood of my fate. They were all there, sitting in the two sofas, dining the petit fours that Claire had prepared after shopping this afternoon I think (or at least bought it in a store and made just to say that she has done at least something interesting, but I didn't want to eat, I didn't want to sober up), then all we have distilled our turn at least six beers. Ironically, they were all messed up, but... yeah, that's a fact, as I am twenty-five per cent French, and seventy-five per cent British, I have a kind of natural ability to bear alcohol better than them. Also, a kind of better training, the very first time I actually drank (of course in secret) was when I was thirteen. And my family name (at least the first part) is Kominsky, which means that my father's dad was Russian, so I have like a third superpower. It's maybe the reason why vodka tastes actually like water to me.

Six beers, three shots of tequila and believe it or not, but I was not fucked up. After speaking, gossiping, talking actually shit, laughing all evening, they decided to go to "Le Hive", a nightclub in Paris's old student neighbourhood. No, I hate nightclubs. I really do hate those places. But that was okay for me to go there, actually. What convinced me? Well, actually... Nothing. I was not in spy mood, I was mostly in a happy mood, and I didn't even care, just like all of them, I actually felt like it was maybe good to go there because we only have one life. And, tonight, I almost even forgot who I was. And what I wanted. They actually proposed, I just followed. And also, for another reason, actually. And although I remained quite conscious, you know that you just tend just to follow the pack whenever you are drunk, you do not take actual decisions for yourself. But even drunk, I have quite an immense self-control, and usually, I never appear leathered, which is the chance I actually have. Kelly wanted to go to an exact place. Because she had, at nine o'clock, received a text from I don't know who, which was saying, "Hey, why don't you guys come at the Hive". I assume she posted again a picture of all of us on Facebook, (which was highly prohibited from me since I do not want to appear under any forms in Zuckerberg's mass-destruction toy). When Kelly received that text, Claire immediately added, "Oh, cool, I have the VIP access, so we can get more drinks for free"... Oh yeah, cool, I didn't know she had a super pass to go into those places... Three to say yes, I didn't really want to ruin their party. And, I was thinking, at that moment, I could get a final drink and then going back home...

At the moment we decided to leave, it was maybe 10.30pm, we all stood up and grabbed our coat and shoes, and I took my credit card, passport, and phone in my pocket. In case something happens, I can still call my boyfriend. Claire was quite drunk, euphoric (she's like this but at some point, she stops drinking whilst I continue to the end of being sick), Kelly was so high that it was hard to see if she was drunk, and Sophie... even if she's the most sportive of all of us, she was really fucked. Kelly went upstairs with Sophie to refresh her make-up, and whilst they were doing that, I was downstairs with Claire. I still needed to ask, as... curiously, what Sophie told me earlier about her... it was even turning around my head.

"Could I ask you a question... Like... A personal question?" I started to ask.

"Yeah, of course! Tell me?" she was definitely out of her mind, even if she ate quite a lot.

"If you were... By any chance... I mean... I know, I am your ex, there's nothing you owe me, like any explanation... Everything is obvious to me... But if you were screwing around... You would tell me?"

"Of course, I'd tell you, but I don't really see what you're talking about," I was too drunk to analyse what she meant by that.

"I just... Never mind. Let's go?"

"Yeah!"

And after having waited for the two others to get ready, it was now time to go. Although we've been waiting for them maybe something like ten minutes, after they went downstairs, Claire turned off all lights, turned on the alarm and locked her house whilst we were outside. I don't know, I was on another planet. You know, the kind of world where I love everybody, even my mum, where I just like my boyfriend but he didn't seem like very important in my life... Being drunk changes totally your perception of the world, it's why I so like it. And Claire, oh my god, she was so beautiful tonight, I mean... No, honestly, she was really awesome. I really cannot understand what happened, how comes we are no longer together. And then, whilst walking in the street on the way to the metro, I saw Kelly. Anyway, I have a boyfriend. I have a boyfriend; I have a boyfriend. I was almost wondering if we could take a Taxi, but I know that on the backseat I will have to deal with my ex and that, well.... No, I think, the metro is a good idea, actually. Even if there're also perverts and babies inside.

To be honest, the travel was really fast, I was feeling like.... I was actually following them. I didn't know where they wanted to go. Time was flying. And even me, I was surprised to see that the metro was so fast. I really hope that... Damn it, I'm gonna be really hangover tomorrow if I go to school. And the hangover is gonna be harsh. If I'm not sick tonight, I really hope not.

Anyway, we were now near the nightclub. And like every time we want to come in those places, it's not as easy as we wish. But it's everywhere the same. There are bouncers at the entrance dealing with the relatively long queue of people alongside the nightclub, asking for an ID. It's why I took my passport. That's when Claire took out the two VIP passes that they had with Kelly of her bag, and we all took the IDs of our coats, and we joined the quite long queue. This nightclub is located actually in a relatively fancy place, really close to the Pantheon in Paris. Not that far from the *Quartier Latin*, place where the most important universities of France are. Kelly and Sophie were behind us, and even though there was quite a lot of people in front of us, I was leaning against the wall and observing all that's around me. And, again, I was seeing her, and I don't know... I felt like no pain, I felt like there was no past between us, there was also no future, there was just this moment. Sophie's "you're still in love with her" was bouncing back and forth in my head whilst I was confused by the noise coming from the inside of the building and the street all around. Indeed, I was bewildered, that must be true, but I don't know, this moment, even if I was cold and my feet hurt because of these damn heels, I mean, this moment was kind of unique, and I felt like my soul, and my body were two separate things totally disconnected. There was only her, she was the reason to go on and move forward.

Still in the darkness, in the sad and dark but quite wet streets of the capital, we were all in a certainly disconnected world. The night all around, only streetlights were giving a semblance of light. Still, some cars were passing by, bouncers were now allowing more people to come inside, and whilst still leaning, I could feel the loud music from inside passing through every wall and making them almost vibrating. Altogether, I with Claire monitored by our two watchdogs in front, we were waiting for our turn to come in, even if there were maybe fewer than three groups of people. Every guy was escorted by at least one girl, as places like this are quite selective, and they were not allowed to come in otherwise. And still, in that place, I was telling myself, what the heck am I doing in here? It doesn't make any sense, if Claire would have said to me that she'd do that tonight, it's sure that I'd have said no. But I'm sure it was scheduled by Kelly, and since Claire has become her puppet... and tonight, curiously, I was Claire's puppet, then here we are. Droplets of water were floating in the air and brought a stronger feeling of cold. We could hear, when it wasn't the chatter noise of the two others behind, the music inside and the conversation between all the people around us, it was quite loud, and even the slamming in the ground of our heels. But I don't know, I was not actually feeling now in the mood of partying anymore. Even now, I usually feel better when drunk, and I felt like... I don't know, a kind of a hunch, that I put myself in troubles. Meh, come on, it's just a hunch, caused by the fact that I'm drunk, there's nothing rational since that right now, I am not really logical, I'm out of my mind.

Alongside the wall, more and more people were now queueing after us as long as time was scrolling, just before our eyes, we saw in the most total blur the end of the queue that was about to enter and didn't cease to grow. I didn't think it would be so busy on weekdays, it's curious. The façade of this place was actually odd, accessing the nightclub was actually through a little door trapped at some point inside a pretty huge building that looked like a kind of a hangar or a warehouse, and it was surrounded from side to side by a grocery store which was closed and a bank, closed as well. But we could see of a kind of super stretched neon just on the top of the entrance, at a few centimetres above our heads (I don't know how we call the sort of neon-light stretched along a wall), which were written the name of the place. "The Hive", in a handwritten style, was shining in a weird dark yellow colour.

We were now in the top of the queue, and behind the bouncer safeguarding the entrance and checking IDs or passes, there were sands and a red carpet that indicated that it was the entrance. And the bouncer, a big black man burly and frankly tall, wearing an expensive suit and sunglasses even if there was no sun, remained somewhat stoic and did not actually calculate. And to be fair, he wouldn't be the kind of guy with whom I'd seek troubles. Geez, he was impressive. I was almost as tall as he was, thanks to my heels. Anyway, we waited after our turn, or at least for some people to leave the nightclub, for finally entering. Sophie and Claire were chatting about some people they know, and I remained withdrawn, behind them, I was feeling a little tipsy because I was drunk, and I could feel that this cold was sobering me up, which was not necessarily a perfect thing.

Anyway, we were assured of passing whatever it takes. Why? They had their VIP cards. I don't really know how it works; I mean, I know how nightclubs work, but since it's maybe only my second time in my life that I go in places like this... If I could follow them because I didn't have that card. Well, I guess I can, given that I am with her and I am quite a hot girl, especially the way I am dressed, I don't think that would be a problem. Girls like me are always admitted. Claire didn't even need to talk to her, but since I was honestly so detached from what was going on, as I was in a state of deep relaxation and nothing around me was actually real, I genuinely didn't care. If it doesn't work, well... It's gonna be the time to come back home and sober up a bit. And, whilst I was just listening to the gibber-gabber of the three other girls but not really paying attention, I was surprised by the bouncer's deep voice, "ID, please". I gave Claire my passport that she shared with hers to the guy, and everything was okay. After having checked their VIP passes, he let all of us coming in. Finally, we were no longer waiting outside.

"Well, okay, you see, we managed to come in," Sophie said to Claire.

"Why? What were you afraid of? Four girls dressed as we are, trust me, it's like holy bread for them, they're gonna attract people thanks to us, so I'm not actually scared" Claire quickly explained.

"Meh, maybe. I'm thirsty, I need to drink, guys... Let's hurry up, I need a shot, Kelly's life may be in danger!" I was seriously sobering up, and I really needed a shot now.

"Alright then... The bar is just upstairs, on the right-hand side, but the first round is on you, huh?" Kelly started to play with me.

"Of course, you idiot, I want you just as drunk as I am... It's gonna be fun!"

"You bet it is!" Kelly told me, friendly.

She laughed. But as the music was thunderous, I don't think she got the "stupid whore" that I added at the very end. We then all entered, after that the bouncer allowed us to pass. We arrived in front of a large dark room, and the loud music that we heard outside literally increased at the moment we passed the threshold of the door, but as it passed through the walls, it made a strange noise, like I heard my own heartbeats, since only the bass and drums could be heard. There were two doors. The first in front of us at the end of a very black corridor led to the nightclub and the dancefloor. And the second in our right where we had to go through a black staircase parallel to that corridor, was giving access where we had to go, the VIP club. But before reaching that part, there was an office with a woman to whom we had to give the passes for coming in, as she had a laptop with an ID scanner. Because for accessing the club, a thorough identification of your identity card was required. Was it a pledge of safety? Who knows? But it's the same everywhere. Then, for the VIP club, the admission was with Claire's pass, but we could all go through because she was a member, and we were her guests. But the room was plunged into total darkness, I mean, I saw absolutely nothing. Just some other bouncers guarding both entrances, and the brightness of her laptop, and erm... Yeah.

One thing triggered my curiosity, though, as I found it quite odd but... Why Claire had such a pass? Before she didn't like nightclubs as well as I do, we went there once together just to see, but she told me she didn't like it. And now... Was Sophie right, was there actually a life that I was unaware of? Meh, I guess it's part of her change. And, God damn it, if she's in trouble, it's her damn problem, I really don't care. After Claire discussed over that woman and telling her that we were her guests, we could pass. She proposed us to take our coats, and I said yes. We actually all said yes, and Claire told me that since it's a VIP club, drinks are for free as we are women. Fine, that works for me, free alcohol. This was pretty cool. We gave our coats, and in return, she gave us papers with a number that we had to give her back if we want to take our jacket back. So, we walked towards the left line, to finally access the stairs, and eventually, my thirst could be fulfilled soon...

I went up through the eighteen steps that were quite a reminder of my eighteen-year-old just passing today, and I perceived a noticeably light mist, which annoyed me as I couldn't see where I was walking. A walk, two steps, and I felt my legs a bit heavier. And I don't like stairs, especially now. I love it less when I'm drunk, and with 3-inch heels, yeah, it was almost survival, but I could see that I was still doing better than Sophie who was ways more fucked than I was. Anyway, this staircase was straight, not in a spiral, and the more I was progressing through it, we could see that there were already a few more people on the lounge. Hopefully, there was a handrail, but blue neon lights turned on pointing towards where we were due to go. But the stair was still very dark, I mean, these neon-lights were providing a significantly dimmed light. So, I went up, steps after steps, and it was really exhausting, but I remained like I was not feeling any pain or other things, I stayed inflexible and professional.

At the end of the stairs, another black-suited guy kept an eye on what was going on in that floor. After having walked the stairs and... continuing suffering with those shoes (a reason I rarely wear that), I arrived in front of him as we were queueing to walk upstairs, and I felt like... Well. He watched us coming in, smiled at me, and with a deep voice said, "Welcome to the VIP Club, ladies".

It's usually much more challenging to walk through a stair when I wear heels. I mean, I don't wear heels, it's infrequent, especially these high ones, I don't like it. And as I was drunk, so I guess my inexperience in there made it worse. Upstairs was quite colourful. There were four quiet walls, some neon lights suspending from the floor, giving a futuristic impression, and some diodes across the border changing their colours randomly, displaying like a wave. This electro music was resounding everywhere, so loud that I could almost feel its vibration coming within me, and the room was quite dark, it was a very, very dim light. Claire and her band came following up afterwards, and we were all four standing in front, like in a kind of survival story, four against the world. It was hard to perceive all the details since we perceive everything either very dark, whether clear, but not at its real perception when we're drunk. This VIP salon was a kind of balcony with a pretty view of the populace below, dancing happily as if nothing could happen in their life. But it seemed like, I don't know, an entirely different place, at a glance I didn't see that much of people dancing here. Perfect, I don't like dancing. First, the mezzanine appeared as much more prominent as I could think, I mean, for a balcony, but it was perhaps broader (I believe this feeling was because there were many people here, it was quite busy, but not a lot unlike downstairs, it seemed quite selective), it actually seemed more like a lounge or something like this, a lot of tables, a lot of sofas, and obviously, on these tables, a lot of drinks. And it was quite busy. Also, when I said it was quite selective, I mean that most of the girls here were dressed almost like us, it was just for the guys that it was quite different.

Ah, fashion... Clothes are the perfect thing to have a better understanding of anyone just at a glance. Understanding clothes that someone is wearing is like understanding the person. About that place again, the floor was black, but oddly, not slippery and the bar was just behind a counter only on the left, after leaving the stairs. In front of all these, quite a vast space, I assumed used as a dancefloor, which was the first part of this place. And behind, the first tables, with all these people. Behind the bar, three bartenders, two women and one guy, all wearing suits, very smart. And on the other side, some people speaking with them, I assume ordering drunks or talking about other shit. And, yeah, so, behind this dancefloor, this long and deep lounge, extending across all sides of this place, with many leather sofas, and many people sat, with the average of at least three girls for one guy, and er... Yep. There were still some tables with more guys than girls, or even table with only guys or girls, but it was less common.

Obviously, as I desired, the first move we made in that place was towards the bar. I wanted to get drunk. As I was not feeling really comfortable with this place, I needed to drink. But I don't think I am gonna stay long. And at some point, Sophie began to shout out loud to Claire:

"Hey, Claire, is there Joris around?"

"Uh... Yeah, I think? Normally it is the bar. But he didn't text me, so I am not really sure if he's here or not," Kelly replied immediately even if Sophie asked the question to Claire.

"He didn't send me any text either. I really don't know. Anyway, don't worry, you will see him at some point I'm sure," Claire finally replied to the question.

"Who's this guy?" I was intrigued.

"Um..." Sophie said, hesitating.

Yeah, right, they brought me here, I guess to meet their acquaintances or people they slept with, but I still don't know anybody. Even from now, they mentioned quite a lot of names, that apparently Claire knows, and curiously she never, ever talked to me about any of them. Well, as I said, she has her life, now, and it's good for them, but it's just very curious. But at the very moment, I asked that question, I felt like the dumb that didn't know anyone, and I also felt like it was the question not to ask. As when I asked who was this Joris in question, I felt that Claire touched my shoulder, in the strap, by two small pulsations. So, immediately, I was kind of surprised as she stood behind me, I turned back and looked at her, and she put her finger in front of her mouth for actually telling me, "Hush!" but why? Why for Christ's sake? Is that guy a kind of criminal? But according to the way she looked at me, it kind of showed me a little feeling of threat suddenly hanging over my head. Meh...

"Actually, Joris is a friend. We know each other for, well... a couple of months, maybe! And he's often coming when we're here. Well, maybe, wait... You can meet him if you would like?" Claire was seeking a quick explanation to the bothering question I asked.

"I'd be curious, yeah," I replied, determined.

And whilst Kelly was looking otherwise, Claire, whilst explaining to me who this Joris was, her sight was pointing straight at the bar. Hum that means something.

Generally, I always have a hunch when I meet someone... Well, I mean, before meeting the guy in question, I know that it will be him or her that I am supposed to meet, and not someone else. And amongst all the people that were here that I could see in the darkness of the bar, except waiters, I felt like this guy was here for a reason. If he was here, he'd be in front of the bar, since Sophie asked for him, and Kelly replied to her question, that means that he's someone quite important within their group, so he should be in a place where they'd find him easily. That should also explain such secrecy. I recall, Kelly was invited here by two other guys, I don't remember their names, but Joris was not mentioned. So, let's find him, from right to left... From left to right, I mean one man sat in the bar drinking a pint of beer, who obviously wanted to be discreet and alone. After him, a girl in a white dress and heels similar to mine, a tall brunette with straight hair and she was pretty, who was laughing... I saw actually her gloss that was so shining on her beautiful lips... But she was busy: there was a guy with her, I think a student at *La Sorbonne*, according to his quite expensive suit and his glasses, who was leaning on the bar. Since this man was undoubtedly focused on being inside the charming girl that he made laugh, he couldn't be this Joris. The suit and the girl mean that he'd have no interest to Kelly, so he's not someone she wants to meet. She was quite hot, though, it's a shame she was speaking to that guy. I'd arrive earlier, I'm sure I could get the prize.

That's a quick analysis, but usually, I am quite right. There was another girl, more classically dressed, with shirt and trousers, not like the first I saw in front of the bar after them. Well, she seemed a bit older than the couple before, I think at least twenty-five or twenty-seven, she was brown and long-haired, more protracted and curlier than mine, but she was there just to dance, having some fun after a difficult day, because I think that for her, dance is like practising a sport for me, a way for relaxing. Honestly, she was hot. According to her body language, I don't think sleeping with a girl should be a problem for her. Hum, no, that can't be Joris, and moreover, that is only for me, just in case I don't want to come back alone if you see what I mean. A kind of a note for myself. Afterwards, a guy was just about to speak to the lovely blonde waitress, but he seemed like a loser, I mean, it was apparent that she didn't want to sleep with him, but still, he was insisting. He really should go to a strip club. This fact simply excludes him to be Joris, as Kelly does not like losers. However, if he is there, it means that he has money. But no, the non-speaking body language of that waitress meant a clear nope. It can't be him...

The guy that actually held my attention was the first I was talking about, and I don't know why, but I felt that Claire would lead me to him in the bar. It is a hunch, and I am sure of what I say. Why? Because while drinking, he was looking everywhere. He looked at everything all around him, as if he were looking for someone, so maybe he was looking for them. As they texted him, so he was obviously expecting to see them. Curiously, he watched everyone as if everyone were a target, and it seemed like he was making sure that everything was right. That's interesting, as, at a glance, he did not seem really trustworthy, at least he wouldn't be someone that I'd trust. He looked like a cop leading a strange activity undercover: he was not especially big or strong and was young, I think something like twenty-five, the same age as the girl next to him, and seemed like detached from everything, his pint in hand meant that was either single, or he is in an unusual relationship or, otherwise, following an unmoral rule. He was a cop, it was apparent. Or a PI, but it's more likely to me that he is a cop. He was wearing a sweater, underneath which there were a white shirt and some jeans. And running shoes. Then he, yeah... Brown and short hair, that's mainly why I say that he works in the security or in the police, he was shaved, and... Then Claire stopped me while I was looking for this famous Joris, for showing me the answer, with her finger, - not really friendly - and took me in her arms. And guess who she showed me...

"Alright, here he is; follow me!"

"Okay," I said, still looking for this guy even if he didn't even see me.

"Hey, Sophie, Kelly, look who's here!" she yelled.

"Oh!" Kelly turned around as I don't know where she was heading.

Oh, nightclubs... I dislike these places: too much noise and loud music obliging us to yell for communicating because we hear nothing from anyone when we're not speaking naturally. So, I followed Claire, who seemed glad to see him, although... I don't know, I found this guy weird. He appeared quite dodgy. So, hello Joris, my name is Charlotte, I am Claire's former girlfriend. Nice to meet you! Two things came actually to my mind, "Claire, what the hell are you doing with your fucking life", and "I so want to go home and sleep". But it was meaningless right now to say any of those.

"Hey honey, you all right?" Claire was just coming beside him, taking him in his arms briefly.

Wait... Honey? Actually, I don't want to know.

"Hi, Claire! How are you doing? Oh, I see you've brought me a surprise!"

"Hey, Joris! We are here! Don't tell me that you didn't see us!" Kelly, a narcissist, as usual, was screaming as if she wanted to become interesting whilst she was everything but the concern right now.

"No. I mean, yes... Well, you know, I'm not at my first beer." He replied. "Well, anyway, you're ready?"

"If we are ready? Of course, we're ready, yes!" Claire enthusiastically said.

"Hi, Sophie!" Joris has seen her.

"Joris..." she almost whispered; it was quite awkward.

Hum, interesting. So, Sophie asked Claire is Joris was here... because she doesn't like him. There must be a juicy story behind that, I need to find that out very soon. He looked at Claire, who came in front of him like an immature puppy, whilst Kelly leaned in the bar... in a quite bitchy way, trying to get his attention. Hum, curious. But I was quite overwhelmed... I had a moment of weakness for a few seconds because I realised the perverse game of Claire, even if I don't know if doing this is a deliberate attempt from her to embarrass me or if she actually ignored me. Still, I kept seeing all this with extreme though hidden contempt. And Kelly... he so ignored her whilst he was touching Claire's body... That... Yeah. I looked at Sophie, the one that followed all of us, and she remained next to me, withdrawn from the pre-orgy scene that was scrolling before my eyes. They were chatting, and whilst Claire was leaning in front of him, and when this son of a... put his damn hands over my... ex, I was really irritated. And Claire kept touching her hairs, just like that, witnessing that triggered a feeling of fury, but... I'd be in a normal state, and I'd put my hand in her face... When actually, suddenly, I had a moment of awakening and enlightening:

"And... Hi, you!" he said, looking at me after leaving my ex.

"Hi!" I remained brief in my answer, trying to hide the fact that I was distraught.

"What's your name?"

"Erm, I'm Charlotte," I shyly said.

"Ah... What a nice name, I love it! Well, welcome. I hope you'll have some good time with us!"

"Seems like it already starts," I smiled.

"And the thing she didn't tell you," Claire said, "is that she turned eighteen today."

Yeah, I think it was that: she really wanted to bother me. The thing she doesn't know, it's just... It's not a good idea to have me pissed when I'm drunk, I can do something that she may not like sooner or later.

"Oh, seriously?" he was given the thread to make a conversation with me.

"Yes, seriously!" Kelly looked at me, saw that I was annoyed, but insisted deliberately.

"Wow! Happy birthday to you, then! And congratulations!" Joris then smiled at me.

"Oh, thank you, I appreciate," I remained calm and straightforward.

And at this moment, Joris and Claire looked at each other and exchanged a smile as if they wanted to add something. And he made a move with his hand, which actually meant like "I wanna tell you something private, come here". So inevitably, as Claire was taller than him as he was sat, she leaned herself and gave her ear to him. Obviously, so I couldn't try to catch through his lips what he'd say, he hid his lips with his hand. But I could hear him whispering, even if it were not precise, I couldn't understand. In the meantime, Kelly was still looking around, which was a sign that she knew what Joris and Claire were talking about, she wasn't curious. She used to be more curious... and I hate secrets and unspoken words. But I don't mind, they must be talking about shit, I mean... this is none of my business, and honestly, I really don't care. However, Claire was carefully listening to what he said. Not much approving, as seen as her face, but actually somewhat embarrassed. Puzzled, as if it were something with which she was not really keen on. So, I guess he asked her a question regarding something embarrassing. And after she unbent herself, she actually said, feeling like she was now more severe:

"Well, not yet. It's a matter of time."

"Okay, I trust you then," he said then, as assured.

Kelly nevertheless saw my reaction when she was looking around, and she knows that I was pretty embarrassed by this situation. And, somehow, I guess, even her face changed, I felt like she was less immature, and she wanted to reassure me on something:

"You don't have to be worried. Joris is a cop. So, if someone is annoying you, you just call him, and he'll be there. If you see what I mean?" she looked at me.

"Yeah, if an arsehole just comes for pissing me off... I see, thanks for the tip," I replied like impressed by her even if I don't trust cops in this country.

"Yeah, Charlotte..." he continued, "you shouldn't be worried. If you're in trouble, you call me, and I'm on it. You're safe here."

"Awesome. I'll think about it."

"Yeah!" He said, smiling at me, thinking that I fell for his charms.

"About that, have you seen someone that you or we know, here tonight?" Claire asked with a seductive voice to Joris.

"Yeah. There are Christian and Dylan in the lounge, over there. Well, it surprises me that you didn't see them yet, I mean..."

"Claire, they sent me a text earlier, remember?" Kelly helped Claire to remember...

"It's even the reason why Kelly wanted to come so badly!" Sophie added.

"Oh, yeah, I see them!" Claire actually looked around. "Okay, well, you know what will happen now?"

"Yeah, I know you're going to join them. Well, I guess you're gonna go dance downstairs?"

"Yeah, maybe, I don't know! Come on, well, catch you later!" she seemed impatient.

"See you, darling!" Joris said to Claire when she was actually leaving. "Before you go, Charlotte, I was glad to meet you, and hope to see you again. I mean, unless you're in trouble and I have to take you to court..." he suggested me.

"Well, it's more likely to be the place where you might see me next," I actually joked whilst looking discreetly at Kelly, "but I was good to meet you too. A real shared pleasure," I remained polite.

"Come on, see you later, girls!" he finished.

"See you later" Kelly finished.

Nightclubs are like this universe: moving from someone to someone else. A group of women, a group of men, this is only in such a place that we can see that the whole mankind is reduced here to its basic instincts: a group of girls are sitting somewhere, when comes a group of boys, which will settle with these girls, and then it's here that is applied the ruthless Natural Selection law. Except that, for once, that was us who were chasing a group of two guys, and erm... That was pathetic. Especially since Claire was playing that meaningless game in front of me, I really... Anyway.

We walked through the small dancefloor with the three others for going towards the big lounge, which seemed to be more comfortable than the seats on the bar because this place was almost looking like a fancy restaurant, with little tables and armchairs in leather. What I liked in this place was that it looked like futuristic. I quickly counted how many tables there were. Twenty. Every table was surrounded by four armchairs, and on the middle of each table, there was a lamp, as those tables were circular and relatively small. But although the number of lights present, it was still very dark, I guess to prevent the use of drugs or other stuff like this. I don't know for how long they've been open, but I was quite surprised to see how busy it actually was for a Wednesday. And at some point, we saw a group of two guys sitting in a table. I guess they were the Dylan and Christian we were looking for.

And then we finally arrived where we had to crash, our short walk appeared to me like several miles travelled: these two guys. They seemed, however, to have a kind of family connection, according to their resemblance. Probably two brothers, both young, I think one of twenty-three and the other of twenty-one, but yeah, they were at least two years older than I was now. One of them was looking more mature than the other one. So, yeah, I think they were brothers. Both wearing a suit, sitting in a kind of big black leather chair, which was quite brilliant, and since they were sitting next to each other, they could see us coming. Yeah, that's funny, guys don't need many things to look smart, just a suit is enough. The first one was wearing a dark night suit, had a light moustache in his face, looked tall enough, had blond and short hair, and had two cute brown eyes. A bit like Australian, Australian guys are all blond.

On the other hand, a guy with long blond hair is really, really, really weird in my very own opinion. I saw once a guy with long blond hairs, and I thought at first that this man was a girl. Long brown hair, okay, fair enough, but blond, no... It's kind of weird. Anyway, the costume he wore seemed like having been made bespoke. Thus I assume quite expensive. And the other was wearing a blue striped suit. The other, so the younger one was probably a little more attractive. And he was a brown-haired boy, shaved, and yeah... A bit more my type of guys.

When we arrived at their table, first, Claire and Kelly became hysterical, and they both stood up as if they knew each other for a while. Before me, Sophie was so I could see it better: it was the hugging party, and I could see the blond guy putting his hand over my ex's ass. They slept together. It's obvious. Wow, just five months were enough to swipe me entirely from her life, fantastic... Kelly received hands from both guys (what a surprise) and Sophie, none. Yeah... Well, I don't care, anyway. Then I looked at the guy in the navy-blue suit, I gave him a little wink so obvious but discreet so that Claire could notice and I sent him a discreet "hello" with my hand, then he answered this by a smile I then replied by the same way. She saw that and treated it with disdain. And, pretending to be shy... Actually, let's backfire.

"Hi!" I said, sheepish, to the guy to whom I gave a wink.

"Hello, you!" he replied, sure of him.

At their table, I actually found out that there were two or three cocktails cups, many glasses whose three-quarters of them were empty. There was about maybe something like almost ten. Yeah, it was like, I don't know, fully drunk. Meh, I guess they started ways before we arrived. Yeah, well. Okay, I have met their friends, I think it was the evening's purpose, I assume it was now time to go home? There was actually nothing more interesting, and I was kind of feeling a bit drained and done with all that. This place is not a place for me. They were all friends, I mean, I could see that they knew each other, and they remained altogether, I clearly had nothing to do with them. Because I don't know them, and I don't really care about them. And, after that evening and Claire's way to behave with me, I was actually kind of sad, and I'd instead want to stay home than staying here. It was not entertaining anymore. And, yes, whilst daydreaming, because I was actually upset because of what I saw earlier, at some point, since nobody was like interacting with me, I withdrew myself, standing up, and crossed my arms, and nobody really cared. They were chatting, I couldn't hear what they said because of that loud music, and I was seriously considering going back home now. I was right this morning; I shouldn't have come. But suddenly, something woke me up, when my former girlfriend began to shout to all of us:

"All right, girls..."

"Yeah? What?" Sophie replied very playfully.

"What do you think about dancing a bit? We will not stay there like that, seated... I need to move right now!"

"Meh..." I said, confused...

"You can stay here, if you want, you, Charlotte!" Claire kind of reassured me, as I felt tired and obviously not in the mood to dance.

"Meh, I don't know... I'll stay here for a bit, and maybe I'll come back home later. I'm tired."

"It's up to you. Okay then, the rest of you, are you coming or what?" Claire felt suddenly, enthusiast.

"I don't really know either, I don't feel like dancing. I'm gonna stay here too. But go on if you want, I might come later," the younger brown-haired brother said.

"Well, I see, you wanna stay with her..." Claire has concluded.

"Alright then, let's go!" Kelly shouted.

"See you later, Chris, and... If you go home, see you tomorrow, Cha!" Claire concluded.

I just said yes. I don't really want to see her after that. Finally, the blond-haired guy went downstairs with them, and... Yes, maybe I'll get a final drink at the bar, and I'll call a taxi to go home. And yeah, I looked at them going downstairs, all of them, dancing... I don't recall Claire liking dancing. Meh, everybody changes, as they say. Well... I sat on a sofa, just next to where the guy was actually sitting, but I asked if I could sit since I'm polite. And he said "yes, of course!" with a smile. I actually sat to rest a bit, I didn't want to stay with him, maybe I'll go at the bar, but at least five minutes, just... to relieve my feet a bit.

Yeah, well, we had quite a fun party, but, yeah, besides being pissed, and not understanding what I was doing there but coming because they wanted to come in here, I was drained. Even if I slept this afternoon. But, yes, at some point, this guy, the one with whom I was seated, started talking to me. But he didn't really know where he wanted to start, I mean, I could feel it, I felt like he wanted to talk to me, but... we don't know each other at all. Because, after I sat, maybe a couple of seconds happened between the moment they left, and he started talking. And honestly, I was not really in the mood to speak with him.

"They are nice, aren't they?"

"Yeah, they are. I know them for a while, and... Yes, they are nice."

"How long have you guys been friend?"

"Oh, quite a while. I know Claire for several years now, but Kelly and Sophie... Yeah, I don't know, maybe two years."

"Oh, okay. I heard that Claire was with some girl before maybe five months!"

"Yeah. I was that girl," I just said, quite sad.

"Oh, sorry. I mean, I didn't think... I'm really sorry."

Yeah, starting with Claire's story was not really an excellent choice to start a conversation with me, especially at that point. But, well, he couldn't know, it's not written on my face that I was with her. I mean, I don't look like a lesbian, since in France there's this cliché of lesbian looking like truck-drivers. And moreover, this love story was now the reason why I wanted to leave. But, yeah, he seemed quite embarrassed by what he said, and... yeah, it's always embarrassing, especially since I know that he slept with her. He didn't tell me, but... Imagine yourself at his place. That wouldn't be comfortable. But, well... I don't care anymore.

"Don't be... You couldn't know..."

"Yeah, but situations like this are always harder, aren't they?"

"Yes, but... I moved on. It's been five months; I went through it. Moreover, I don't really want to talk about that."

"I can understand. Anyway, wanna drink something?"

"No, not actually, I think I'm gonna go back home, I'm quite tired," I said, because I wasn't sure what I actually wanted, I was keen on going back home now.

"Really? Come on, just one drink!" he was quite insisting actually.

"Okay, then... Just one drink..."

He called one of the two waiters roaming amongst the tables around us to collect empty glasses by just raising his arm. The guy didn't actually see him at the first moment he rose his arm, but whilst he insisted, he came. I was actually quite impressed to see the waiter because honestly, carrying such a heavy tray full of empty glasses and not dropping a single one, yeah, it's okay. I wouldn't have such a balance. Anyway, the guy came immediately.

"Good evening, guys, what can I do for you?"

"Well, could you get me... erm... Yeah, a shot of tequila would be fine..." I started in first.

"Wow, just a shot of tequila?" he was actually surprised.

"Yeah, why? Is there any problem with my order?" I justified myself.

"No, I mean, why not!"

"Yeah, so my travel home will be faster..."

"Yeah, make sense!"

"And for you, sir?" the waiter was asking him.

"Meh... I don't know... Just a beer, I think I'm gonna go with that."

"No problem, sir, on my way."

"Could you actually also add a shot of tequila with that? I mean, as I'm gonna go dancing after... You know!"

"All right, sir, on my way!" the waiter actually left.

Yes, I think a shot of tequila could be great for finishing my birthday. He was surprised by my order, but that's honestly all I want, that will be more than enough for me. No, seriously, when I asked for my stuff, the way he replied, I felt like... I don't know. Meh, after all, he just wanted to talk to me, so let's give him a chance. I am not that mean.

"Could I ask you a question?" he started after the waiter left.

"Depends which question you want to ask..." I replied, straight away.

"What's your name?"

"Charlotte, and you?"

"Christian. But you can call me Chris."

"Fine. Nice to meet you."

"Nice to meet you too. And how can I call you?"

"Well, you can call me Charlotte, since it's my name."

"You don't have a nickname or something?" I was laughing.

"The girls use to call me just 'Cha', but it's not really often. I mean..."

"And where are you from? Because, no offence, but your little accent says that you're not French."

Hum... He noticed my accent. I used to take my accent back when I am tired. I mean, unlike French people that do not roll the "r" like English do, I assume it's the thing that betrayed me. Regarding him, there was no doubt, he was French. Just like Claire, and all of them, with his appalling accent. Meh, curiously, he seemed friendly to me, and I was okay to leave him a chance. Well, I'm not offended, as long as he doesn't announce me that he's a damn racist that votes for the far-right... But British people aren't really targeted by racists here. And I'm not entirely British, I was born in France, I just don't have the country's citizenship, that's it. But according to the bespoke costume, I don't really think it's the kind. So, yes, he was interested in me. Okay then. Let's play the game.

"Well, yes, I'm British. But ironically, I was born in the south of France. I just spoke English before French, it's the reason why I have my slight accent I guess" I explained.

"Alright, interesting. And you live in Paris now?"

"Yeah, we live in the suburb, yes. And you, what about you?"

"Not in the suburb, I have a flat really close from here..."

"Lucky you, I wish I'd live close, so I wouldn't have to take the metro and everything!"

I could see from far away the waiter coming with, well, the two shots and the beer. It was for us. Well, yes. And the two limes on the side. He came to us and brought everything. Christian actually specifically requested to leave the tray on the table, and as soon as the guy left, Christian took our two shots, placed mine in front of me, and, I assume it was now the moment to start drinking. We took the shot glasses, looked at each other, and I said "Cheers!". And I had my very last shot of the day. I mean, from the moment, I decided that it would be the last. Maybe I'll get another one later. So, as usual, we drank it, took the lime to reduce bitterness, and... whilst I felt like the alcohol was going down my throat, I don't know... He felt like, more sympathetic, suddenly.

"What are you doing, like... like as a job, as occupation, what do you do in your life?"

"Well, I'm actually into a business, more like various businesses. And you?" he curiously took the same position as me, as apparently, it means that he wanted to enter in contact with my mind.

"I'm just a lost millionaire seeking what she wants to do with her life. That's it..."

"Yes, of course," he laughed.

Well, he didn't seem to believe me. But, that's the truth, I mean... he's not the first person to whom I served that as an answer upon asking "what do you want to do in the future?" or "what do you currently do?". Even, a couple of days ago I met a guy once... God, this guy was so awesome: first, he was very banal, physically, he was really bland. He was a friend of one of Claire's friend, and we invited them both to grab some lunch. He asked me that very same question, and I replied the very same answer. Man, he started to tell me that he was earning ten thousand euros a month as he was an engineer. My mother's best friend is an engineer as well and doesn't get the same money. Claire told me not to believe him since this guy lives with his brother in a flatshare in Central Paris. After that, I thought about how much I earn a month (to be honest, I don't know, even today, since it's increasing and decreasing all the time), but I thought that this guy who seemingly wanted to impress me, well... When you have the main course, a starter is not really impressive. Especially since it's not credible. But whether he believed in me or not, I didn't care.

"Yeah, this is the way the world works."

"I think so."

"And you, what do you mean by being into business?"

"I'm investing in companies, doing trading... It actually became quite a big occupation..."

"Yeah, I imagine."

"Yeah... Anyway, it's the first time I see you here, with Claire and Kelly."

He was switching the topic almost straight away. Now, the reason why I am here tonight. Interesting. At that very moment, I started to feel weird. I mean, no, not the envy to throw up, although it might be really likely given all what I drank this evening, but nope. I know I am very resistant to alcohol, which is quite funny, but I felt not really comfortable. Like... Excited. But since I must show that I have colossal self-control, especially in front of a guy that was obviously seeking to sleep with me but using reverse psychology. Again, it was not scary, I know that feeling, it's just that I cannot really explain it right now, why it happened now. And whilst I started to feel increasingly hot, I mean, it was bizarre since I was feeling rather cold a minute ago... I continued:

"Yes, I got trapped by Claire and Kelly. Trust me, never again!" I kept an Olympian calm.

"Trapped? How comes you've been trapped?"

"Well, really simple, it's my birthday today, and Claire used to throw a party for my birthday. So, yeah, it's why I drank maybe a bit too much, and I am here stuck with you, unable to move now."

"Oh, really? It's your birthday today?"

"That is."

"Well, happy birthday then. How old are you now?"

"I'm turning eighteen."

"Great, that might be an important day for you then!"

"I don't see what it will change in my life except that now, I don't need to ask someone to buy me alcohol. Yeah, I can do a couple of things, it's true."

"True, you're now freer than ever."

"Yeah, I am!"

Two things from now: he mentioned earlier that he was living nearby, and now he says that I am free since I'm eighteen. And I'm also not stupid, I know he drugged me. Or maybe he didn't, but someone put something else in my shot of tequila, but I couldn't feel it when I drank it. That would be the only explanation to my increased heart pulse right now, my feeling of weakness and the fact that I am boiling now, almost melting. And also, to the fact that I'm not tired anymore and that I want to rest. No, he obviously wanted to sleep with me, I mean, the way he was looking at me, he was obviously trying to manipulate me. Let's play the game, Claire slept with this guy. I'd be actually curious if she learned that I also slept with him. Before everything, I am a manipulator, which means that everything, in life, to me, is a game. Let's play the game, then. Let's pretend that I was ignorant then:

"And you, Chris, tell me about you." I was now playing the game.

"Nothing is exciting..."

"Yeah, obviously..."

"What do you mean by 'obviously', Cha?"

"I mean... You're an investor, and your quite expensive bespoke suit doesn't tell me that you're doing only this. I mean, I know investors that are earning quite good money, but... I don't know... There must be something different."

"Well, unless you work for taxes, I mean."

"No!" that made me laugh... "But I assume you have hobbies, stuff you do in your free time..." I tried to find a more comfortable way to explain myself.

"Well, if you consider watching series on Netflix as a hobby, then..."

"Well, it's okay, I sometimes do the same. But that's not a hobby, that's killing time."

"And you, what's your thing?"

"Well... I like listening to music. And playing, as well..."

"Playing... playing like videogames?"

"Yeah, sort of."

He was actually surprised. That's not a hobby, I don't really have hobbies besides being a pain in the arse, learning and reading a lot. Yes, that made me actually realise that my life is really tasteless.

"Okay then, that's quite surprising, looking at you, I'd imagine that you'd have a thousand of hobbies..."

Well, look at me: I am here, I understood you wanna sleep with me, I understood that you drugged me so you may think it should be like an easy way out because you are not fully confident on yourself and you don't know how to take the right approach with me, and all you're speaking to me is about my hobbies. Now, let's go to this, how to turn me on... There's actually not a thousand ways, since I am overly complicated, I consider you're an ass, and I have by extension not an adequate consideration of guys. Yeah, actually, I'd flirt with me, I wouldn't know the right approach since I am so complicated. I am allergic to people... But the way he was behaving, I mean, indicated that he knew who he had in front of him, it's why he indeed used drugs, just to make sure he'd succeed. I still didn't show any signs of weakness since... I trained myself over keeping strong self-control.

But even, I almost lost total control of myself. I was fragile, and I could see him luring at me. And, honestly, I felt like disconnected to the real world. There was nothing around. Was it a good sign of trust, I mean... should I trust him? Well, life is life, and if mine had to finish today, then I'd rather be happy to be done now. He seemed just like he wanted something from me, it was okay, I mean, I could be okay with that. But I felt like there's no past, no future, there's no point of being here anymore. I don't know, suddenly, I was feeling depressed. And, being depressed is something that I'm gonna have serious troubles to hide.

"I like psychology, as well" I continued, focusing on actually... going where he wanted to go.

"Oh yeah? Are you studying that? Or I mean... Will you study that?"

"It's not studying that, for me, psychology is just on observing."

"Is it?"

"Yeah. Okay, let me give you an example. You seem like someone to whom everything is quite successful. You're young, but I don't think that you're doing only legal stuff."

"Hum... I don't know how to take that, honestly."

"It's okay if you are laundering money... I don't really care. I love people that fuck people, they are the only one that has my respect."

"Interesting," he just looked at me.

"After, I could see that you had sex with my ex."

"Nope..." he denied the obvious.

"Of course, so when you frankly touched her ass when you were hugging her, it was just like that," I argued to prove that I was right.

"I never touched her ass..."

"It's okay if you did that with her, I'm okay with that. She's not my girlfriend anymore..."

Hum, yeah, Claire was quite a sensitive topic, and this for both of us. I don't know why, I mean, usually guys are rather proud of whom they slept with. Hum, maybe I guess because given my position... Well. It's odd, beyond that, I had almost no limits. I think that now, I felt like super drunk like all the drinking night was now coming... I felt like surprisingly invincible. Nothing could reach me right now. So, I continued...

"You also find me quite attractive."

"Hey, darling, look at you! You look amazing tonight."

"I appreciate that... Thank you."

"Claire talked to me about you once," he restarted with her.

"Oh, really, what did she say?"

"Well, she said that you were crazy. You were really special..."

"Well, that is not a secret!"

"You look like... I don't know, you don't really care about a lot of things."

"Not really. I'm living like each day of my life like I'm gonna die tomorrow. I guess it's the reason why I'm so special," I justified myself.

"It's unusual to see a lot of girls like you. I mean, to so openly not care!"

"It's true, I'm not like everybody," I appreciated what he said.

"So, does living like today is your last day on Earth includes doing what you want daily?"

"Yeah, obviously... Oh, wait... Do you mean, like... Me, sleeping with you tonight?"

At this point, he started to blush but remained quite... damn, don't know what to say, I mean, he was not actually embarrassed by what I even spoke. Hum, I was wrong, he was actually confident, it's just that maybe I was predictable, and he used this against me. Geez, damn, upon saying that, I was like, god damn it, so confused. Come on, that's what he wanted. This was not a secret.

On the other hand, even me, I was acting weird, I was sweltering, touching my hairs whilst looking at him, so it was apparent that he had all my attention. I was too drunk. But at the very moment when I said that I was actually speaking to myself, "comes what may".

"Well, if that is an invitation, then I would accept it, yeah!"

"Oh, dear..."

I actually didn't realise that, and at that very moment, I was still not realising what I was completely doing: I am incredibly drunk, and everything's out of my control. But, somehow, something told me that everything was fine. I was feeling okay with him, he didn't seem like a freak or a weirdo. Even if my judgement was altered by the considerable quantity of alcohol I swallowed, I don't know. Honestly, I don't remember... Yeah, I was weak.

"You're quite straightforward, aren't you?"

"Yeah. Let's say that I don't like wasting my time..."

At that very moment, my head was about to explode. I mean, my heart was beating so fast that I wasn't even feeling good. I wanted to leave that place; I was drained. And, still, the sound of that music was quite getting on my nerves. He had what he wanted, I also had what I wanted, I think that, yeah, it was time to go. And, I was severely drunk, I was not about to throw up, I mean, I was still conscious, and I was okay, I'm gonna sober up, but it's just that I was so drained and my mind was so confused that I actually did not really know what to do next. I just wanted things at the moment, and that's it. And, even, it's true, I was over. I don't know actually what caught me, whether it was tiredness, or something else, but I needed to leave. I needed to get some fresh air. I was really feeling weird. And, really, actually, I didn't feel like going back home, to be fair. If I go back home, as I am so drunk and I don't know what I am clearly doing or even wanting, I may fall asleep in the metro and miss my stop, and... Meh. Maybe I'll sleep with him, perhaps I won't, but either way, I needed to leave this place, I needed to walk.

"Music is shit over here, isn't it?" I told him.

"Yeah, it's not what I actually like, to be fair."

"And I'm quite fed up being here, honestly!"

"Okay, then."

"Let's bounce? I mean, unless you know another place around... I'd actually be okay to get something to eat or grab some coffee..."

"I kind of know someplace. So, let's bounce?"

"Sure!"

9 *Et lux in tenebris lucet...*

// Between the nightclub "Le Hive" and this guy's flat, streets of Paris.

// Probably Thursday, 10th of January 2013, about 01:00... I don't care, I'm drunk!

We just stood up and left. Yeah, now, I don't know, standing up made things worse: okay, I was still on balance. Yet I don't know how I managed to, but I still was. I mean, I was really drunk, certainly about to fall, it's why I took the formal resolution to stop. I actually wasn't fully aware of what I was doing, when I stood up, I was just like a puppet to whom you could say whatever you want, I'd do it on command. But obviously, let's get out of here, for him, meant, "let's go home so I can fuck you". And since I was certainly struggling to gain my self-control but the amount of alcohol that I had was so huge that I couldn't actually cope with that, I was flummoxed and... He was the one that drove me. And, yes, at the moment I was going down the stairs, I could feel him following me, like... yeah, monitoring me. And my chest was in such pain... I could feel my heart beating, I could even hear it since I felt so heavy and so light at the same time. I was shivering as well, but I didn't feel it. I was just responding to the envy of the moment, although he wouldn't have been my first choice, right now, he was undoubtedly exploiting me to his advantage. When downstairs, he asked me to come to his house for the last drink, after I got my coat back again. Awaiting for my answer, he had his ears wide open, and his eyes plunged right into mine, and I don't know, I completely lost all notions of what could be straight from what could be wrong, and I was just at the mercy of my primal instincts. Okay then, I mean, I am so drunk that I cannot go anywhere else. And he drugged me, also, so, whatever I say, I mean... He wants to have sex, but if I want that to go away, my heart about to explode or anything, I need to do it. It's odd, but I was no longer myself.

"Um... that's what you want, and I am too weak to go elsewhere, so, go on!" I was just replying whilst we were on our way out.

"Ah! Great, cool! Well, let's go!" He replied immediately.

I was neither feeling good nor bad, I was just like frozen in time. I couldn't be either sympathetic, whether a bitch. I felt like higher as I have never been before, because of my heels, I guess. He was lurking at me like I was an achievement, and curiously I was still responsive, I was really responsive, it's just that there was absolutely no connection between my answers and my real me. I was put in automatic mode. I was like discovering the world for another time as if I came from another planet. Everything seemed to be unknown to me, and I was torn apart by this deep desire that I needed to do it with him.

"Alright then, follow me, sweetheart!" he said while we were about to move.

Curiously, being out was like a relief. Although I was melting inside, at least the coldness of the winter made me feel better. I was feeling better, honestly, and I was feeling like I was sweating. I don't know, I never ever felt that way, and it was weird, but I wasn't worried at all, because I only couldn't. It was icy, certainly colder than when we entered that nightclub, and I needed to put my coat, to check if everything was still there, and I wanted to close it because I was feeling a bit cold. I checked... My wallet, okay, my phone... okay. I took the reflex to always check if nobody stole me nothing, especially when I am drunk, to avoid nasty surprises. No, everything's here. I closed my coat and put my hand in my two pockets. And then, as he was now driving me, I walked next to him. I didn't know where we'd be going:

"So? Are you living far from here?" I was curious.

"Huh? Oh no. No, I am close. Just two streets away from here!"

"Okay, then. Let's be quick because I'm not actually feeling okay."

"Are you? Do you wanna stop somewhere before we come back?"

"No, no... The faster, the better, actually."

"Sure!"

I swiftly turned back whilst we were on our way out. I mean, I don't know, I just looked at the bouncer, and recalled that barely an hour ago, maybe longer, I don't know, since I also lost all notion of time, I was trying to enter there with Claire and Kelly. Now, I was out with him, going, God knows where. We walked along two narrow streets to go to I actually don't know where, and these streets were still looking so alive, although they were in the absolute darkness. Everything was so bright, although very dark. Without saying anything, we walked together, really close to each other, and I honestly don't know whether he was carrying me or not, since I felt like he was taking my arm. And as we left the nightclub, we could still see quite a lot of people waiting to come in, I mean, yeah, although the bouncer handpicked all that and denying some people the entrance, I was like, yeah, it's like natural selection. It was very odd. I was really struggling to stand still, and even, I felt like I was bouncing back and forth, I was like a weird puppet. It was like if my life was going away and I could not control it, but on the other hand, that as the feeling I was seeking.

We kept on walking away from the nightclub, located in the *Avenue Trudaine*. Actually, the name of the street was the very last thing I paid attention to. But Christian, still guiding me, mentioned that he lived on the *Rue des Martyrs*. I kind of know, it's not that far away. But always, that seemed to be quite a long walk. But I was fine, I mean, at that moment, everything seemed fine, actually. I wasn't thinking about anything else, my head was utterly empty of all the problem it used to contain, I was just living in something perfect, so perfect that it might frighten me.

I don't know what was motivating me. Nothing really mattered. At least, at this time, I was like flying leaves flying because of the wind. I was perhaps uninhibited at that moment, but that's what I actually wanted. With a guy that wanted sex, I don't even know what I wanted from him, but I was accepting that, curiously.

On the other hand, sex never really attracted me. It was just something I had to do. I don't know, I never talked about that, but yeah, maybe with Claire I was okay, but I never saw sex as something meaningful for my survival. If he wants that, then, fine, but I never felt any pleasure doing that. Sex is for me like cleaning dishes, it's like a chore, I have to do it, but I really do not want to. What attracts me is the appearance and the conversation, sex has never been quite interesting to me. I mean, especially for the last couple of months, sex has really become meaningless.

Maybe I'll enjoy with him, or perhaps I won't, but... I don't know how this evening is gonna end.

At some point, we arrived at the final destination: his place. The name of the street was strange (martyr street), but, since he stopped in front of a door, I guess he lived there. Meh... So, we walked towards the entrance of the building he is currently living.

"Interesting street name. I hope not premonitory," I digressed whilst he was looking for his keys in the right pocket of his jacket.

"Well, who knows. Depends on you, actually!" he replied after he found the keys.

The coldness tingled my legs and made my feet and my hands almost numb. Here we are, at the threshold of his door. It was like entering a hunted building because his home was actually within a broad Haussmann-style building in a district of the capital not very posh, but into which we must have the means to live. It was quite gloomy, actually. I think it would have been the perfect place for ghost hunting. But, finding out the actual location where he was living told me even quite a few about him: first, as he was living within the city of Paris, so I assume the price of the rent must be very high, I don't really believe that he owns the place. Second, this place was perhaps within Paris, I don't think he must be paying a lot, as the entrance of the building, I felt like, yeah, entering in a spooky place. But despite the scary atmosphere here, the entry of this building was made of a massive carved wooden green door with its paint left in poor condition, I think due to the time it's been painted, with a bell on the left side, at a human size. The top of the door was covered by cobwebs. I wanted to press the bell button while chuckling, but he grabbed my arm, which actually made me understand that it was not a particularly good idea.

"Oh no, don't do that Charlotte... you might regret!"

"Huh? Are you serious?" I said still out of my mind.

"Oh yes, believe me, you're gonna wake up the ghost!"

"I ain't scared of ghosts!"

However, before entering, I quickly checked the keypad of the building. I saw that he lived in flat number 4, as it was the only flat with someone who had a "C." before the family name. I didn't actually fully see his family name since it's not even relevant. But this keypad seemed very antiquated. Also, at the top of the entrance, a gargoyle was there, as it's often used on the Haussmann-style buildings in Paris, which looked like a giant lizard with a human head. The sculpture was not monumental, though, it came out of the wall above the entrance gate and was quite nightmarish, as the reflection of the moonlight above it was somehow distressing. For a moment I was entirely absorbed by that sculpture, remaining motionless as this was undoubtedly the most impressive beauty that I've ever seen, whilst he actually opened the door. And I don't know why, but I thought about this:

"Geez... If Zak Bagans comes by, I'm sure he's gonna have enough for a lockdown!" I said, pointing the finger to the sculpture.

"Who's this guy?" he replied.

"Who? Bagans?"

"Yeah?"

"Oh... Hum... Well, it doesn't matter, actually. Chop chop, I'm cold!" I made himself hurrying up.

I really don't know, something somehow convinced me that there was maybe a kind of an evil spirit in this gargoyle. He put a type of magnetic card in front of a big black button down the keypad, and it magically made the door being opened. As I watched the gargoyle, he was now entering and, my obsession increased for that thing, he may have stared at me for like the ten seconds I was imagining that Satan was living within this gargoyle. I felt like a big baby. And it's when I saw him at the very beginning of a corridor that I told myself, "yeah, maybe it's time to come in!" He was still carrying the door for me. And, as I expected, the corridor was very dark, it actually seemed like entering an old manor, which every door leading somewhere were closed. After I came in, he closed and locked the door.

The interior was weird. Not any light except the moonlight. And a constant noise of water drops that were freaking me out. Plus, the noise of my heels, I had to be incredibly careful whilst walking. Or trying to be silent, which is gonna be quite hard.

"So, you're living with ghosts!" I remarked, quite loud.

"Yeah, and be careful, don't speak out loud, you're gonna wake them up otherwise!" he whispered.

I remained close to him since I didn't see where I was heading, and I felt in this dark that he started to put his arm over my shoulder. And I was kind of focused on this noise of water drops whilst still trying to be quiet while walking, it frightened me. We both passed through the hall completely dark, so dark that I could barely see the tip of my feet, only the reflection of my legs and other things that were lit by small windows. Through which I could see quite a giant cobweb, by the way. The last thing I was actually expecting given that this place was undoubtedly haunted would be to hear bats flying. For someone that was into business, I must admit that he was even living in a shithole... but I guess that he's here because he enjoys this place. At least he carried me, that was really nice of him.

While being guided in the dark, we actually passed that small corridor. We were now in a small indoor lobby, where mailing boxes were along the left-side wall, leading us the final stairs to reach the upper levels of that place. But this place was still creepy, especially since we had a full moon tonight, it was perhaps giving an idea of the hour it was now, maybe it was the middle of the night. And, yeah, my heels were echoing in here, and this noise of water droplets, coming from big pipes that I could see above the mailboxes was absolutely deafening. But the stairs were actually in another room, and upon entering there, I felt like walking on something different, softer than usual. I was right: there was a long carpet on the floor, that with this darkness appeared black, like incorporated on the floor. That was actually odd, but at least it killed my heels noise, leaving me only scared by the drops, which made even much more noise for some reasons. Even if there was that little light down there, the decoration from inside was different because of the Middle-Ages-style, assembled, dusty, and naked stone walls. God, has ever this place been refurbished? Okay then, it was better actually not to touch those walls.

"So, this is your place," I asked him after coming in where we were.

"Yes, I know. The light in the entrance is dead for two days now. That's why we were in the dark," he was giving me justification regarding the light.

It was actually quite hard to describe how I felt. Now, my senses were utterly spinning, and I was really exhausted walking these stairs. I was kind of exhausted, but on the other hand, relieved to be finally here because I know that I can rest soon:

"Oh, uh... Okay. And on which floor are you living?"

"Um... fourth floor."

"Oh, okay."

"I know it's quite long."

"Meh, it's okay, I'm gonna survive!"

"Yeah. We have to."

I was actually following him in the stairs. In my mind, it was like... totally empty, there was just this moment. The more we walked, the more I no longer heard that noise, even if it was still very dark. And I felt like I was in total peace, an inner peace that I've been seeking for so long was now there. I don't know, everything seemed strange, but okay, it seemed irrational but totally rational, I was like in a surrealistic place where... It was like a dream. For once, I was feeling good. Whatever I do, I'm not gonna hurt anyone, whatever happens, it's gonna be okay, I was so enjoying that moment that I almost felt the need to extend it. I sometimes wish my life would actually be like a living dream, where there's nothing, just calm, where I can do what I really want to do. This peace of mind was actually quite strong, it was amazing, it was like... I certainly experienced that before, but yes, this parallel reality is so much bearable than the rest of this life. Yes, Claire was right, tonight was my night, tonight was the moment where I could do what I want, and I just want to do what I want. Fuck the rest, fuck that spooky place, I just wanted now to enjoy the moment. And the more we were walking the stairs, the more I looked at him with a certain kind of desire, maybe I was not craving for this guy, but... I don't know, I was like, something told me that I was about to have something exceptional with him tonight.

Whilst multiple scenarios came into my mind regarding him, the pain I experienced whilst walking through these stairs was killing me. And after the second floor, I noticed the blue LEDs that lit in front of each step. Pretty neat, and actually useful. And after quite a long and energetic walk, we arrived at his floor, a corridor with four doors. At this point, I was kind of very lost, I was breathless and exhausted. This corridor was also dark, and everything seemed incredibly old in that building, I just saw that ceilings were white, the passage was something like thirty-two feet long, and amongst these four doors, there were two on each side facing one another. This place was definitely old, and very classic, I mean, it looked like a derelict place, almost like a squat or something. It was so weird that the more I saw that I felt like I was in a dream. But it couldn't be a squat, I mean, it was hot, the warmth was okay. I just followed him, because he wanted to lead me somewhere, without asking any question. This place was actually odd, it didn't seem real. I mean, I felt like I was in a kind of a nightmare, there was something that didn't make sense. Let's recap: when we were in the nightclub, we first had small talk, then... Then, god... Something's wrong. At that very moment, I was genuinely confused. What the hell happened... Oh, no, yes, I had a drink with him. Then we left. And... No, I just remember the big building, a kind of vast building... How comes I'm not wet, I mean, isn't it raining outside?

So, we walked, entering that building... I mean corridor, and at some point, he stopped in front of some door. So, I guess this was where he lived, the first door on the left side, after leaving the stairs. I was thinking, now, I mean... Something happened to me, I'm sure, I mean, I couldn't have followed him for... There was some reason. While I was focused on, well, my mind, I was actually baffled, as I was just following like a sheep, he just said, at some point, having his key in his hand and waiting in front of that door, his face lit by the moonlight...

"Hey, Cha, are you okay?" he was looking at me.

"Hum... Yeah, I guess... Yeah!"

"You do not seem fine..."

"I'm just drunk right now. Can we come in?"

"Yeah, of course..."

He saw that I was confused, but curiously, he didn't seem to worry that much. That seemed quite odd to me, but maybe it's normal. It's quite curious, it's the first time I am feeling like that. I couldn't recall some events, or perhaps I do, but I just need to focus, that's really weird. I really don't know. Also, something seemed curious to me, I was not panicking. I was quite relaxed as if my confusion were like a game, and I had to find the answer. I just looked at him whilst he was looking for the right key to open the door.

"You know what?" I actually asked, really confused.

"Yes, tell me?" he stopped and looked at me.

"Do you know... erm..."

"Yes?" he saw me hesitating.

"I don't remember, why did I follow you here?"

"Oh, darling, don't you remember?"

At that very moment, I looked at the window, just behind, to see the moon. It was so bright, I mean, it was like... I've never seen the moon that way. The window through which I saw this was like dusty and full of cobwebs, but I could see the moon very brightly. And the more I saw it, the more a kind of new feeling was taking me: confidence. Seeing that moon tonight, I mean, it was like the most beautiful thing that I ever saw in my life. I watched it for like ten seconds, almost seeing all the craters the moon had, and when I turned back... The guy I saw, he looked like Florent. I don't know... I mean, he looked like someone to whom I could give my entire devotion.

"I'm actually very drunk, now," I just replied.

"That's okay, we're gonna come inside, and everything is gonna be alright?"

"Yeah, sure. It's gonna be okay!"

"You know you can trust me, right?"

"Yes, of course! It's okay, open the door, please," I replied, weak.

That is weird, I mean, I heard Florent's voice, at the very end. He told me to trust him, that's odd, Florent doesn't need to ask me to trust me. He was like playing down my anxiety or at least killing it straight in the egg. While he was still looking for his key, I saw like a shade at the very end of that corridor. It was weird, like as tall as a human. It didn't have the shape of a human, but it seemed quite tall. And it was peculiar to see it, it seemed like it was coming towards us. But didn't appear as threatening. I don't know, as my eyes made themselves to the darkness here, now, I saw things certainly better than before. I turned my head, and I saw him, again, and I was wondering... I don't remember Florent came tonight. I think I told him this morning that... No, I told him... Damn, no, I said to him that Clarisse wanted the flat. Geez, yes, maybe he was with me. That would explain why I heard his voice. I mean, it wasn't his voice, because his voice is more in-depth than... That's impossible, did I drink my glass with him? And Claire? Oh my god, this was really confusing.

"Charlotte?"

"Yes?" I answered to... Florent, I guess.

"You don't remember, we drank that glass together. I had my beer and a shot of tequila. You just had a shot of tequila. You don't remember?"

"No, yeah, I do, I really do, but I just don't remember... having had it with you?"

"I told you this morning I wanted to meet Claire!"

"Did I say, yes? Hum... That is confusing, really confusing," I was trying to recall, but it was tough.

So, tonight, I had a drink with Claire and Kelly. Then I remember, Kelly received a message. So, we went here. I mean, at the nightclub. We've been waiting outside... And, yeah, we went upstairs, and... Gosh, I remember, Claire, when we entered, she introduced me to... No, no, we had a drink. Wait, did we really have this drink? What did I have tonight? I know, I had a couple of beers... I remember I had a shot when I saw Kelly at Claire's house coming downstairs because I couldn't bear it... Why is that all blurred to me now? Geez... Okay, so, we went to two guys. Amongst those two guys, there was... There was Florent, I mean, I guess, he's the one that I followed... Where did I follow him? I remember, he told me we were in someplace... That's really weird.

"Hey, baby?" I was now a bit worried.

"Yes, lover?" Florent replied, looking at me straight in the eyes.

"Where are we?"

"We're home, now!"

"This doesn't look like it's home, honey."

"Well, that's where we live for the last couple of months. Where do you want to be? I called you a Taxi to come back home because you texted me, you were really drunk!"

"Did I?"

"Yeah! Anyway, we're home, now, we're gonna get a tea, and we're gonna sleep, okay?"

"Okay, then!"

"You're safe, now," he finally found the right key.

He unlocked and opened the door of the flat. No, it must be Florent, I mean, this was his voice, this was... This was him. I think it was him. But where were we, we cannot be in our flat, this is impossible. I remember, this is not our flat, I'd remember if I would have been here before. So, what was this place?

The entrance of his flat was a large room where walls were painted in a quite flashy yellow, but the style differed completely with the decoration of this building's hallways, and from what I could imagine from him, as I thought at the beginning it would be a squat. At least from what I saw. It was quite large, yeah, with this awakening yellow wallpaper on the walls, a small chandelier hanging from the ceiling in the middle of the roof with African motifs all over it. Still, walls were unusually high, it much seemed like a hall, but of course, less impressive. Finally, the ceilings were at least three metres high. Two doors, one in front and the other on the right-hand side, and a wide opening on what seemed to be a living room on the left-hand side, Next to the left-hand side door, a coat rack. I don't remember having ever been in this place before, it was totally new to me. After having entered, I was feeling so weird that I actually gave him my coat. He closed the door, took my jacket, and before putting it on the rack, he looked at me and said:

"Are you okay, darling?"

"This is not home, why were you lying to me?"

"Cha... This is actually a surprise!"

"Is it?"

"This is actually... Damn, I didn't want to talk about this before, but this is our new place! You know, recently, I've been speaking to you about this place, a place that I wanted it to be ours."

"I didn't think it was that serious that you actually bought a place."

"I did, you know, I'd do anything for you."

"That's amazing!" I remained still sceptical.

He put my coat and his on the rack, and it's with quite hesitating footsteps that I went to his living room. I think I was in a dream, as this was quite hard for me to understand. Regarding the living room, yeah, same colours as the entrance except that the yellow of the walls was much paler. I didn't know Florent's taste for the yellow, I thought he didn't like this colour. But it was a little messy, though: he had a rather large room, with huge windows that gave a view over the roof of the buildings nearby. It was both a living and a dining room, just like in my house. It could be impressive. It was a relatively big table, looking like Claire's table at her home, but there was actually a mess in here. Quite unusual for him. There were two black-leathered sofas in front towards the windows, which seemed even quite cold but were wide, one facing the other, with in the middle a small glass table, with a black metal frame. And before the windows an item of small furniture where the TV was. It seemed ordinary. But the sky, this place seemed actually more welcoming than the rest of the building I had to pass through for coming here, I couldn't actually see the sky as there was the flat's reflection through the windows.

Also, because of that, and because of my vision that was now slightly altered because of my state, I could barely perceive through the window that he had an expansive terrace. A giant sunshade, folded up, as it was quite windy, a wooden table and four chairs. It reminded me of someplace; I don't remember which one. When I saw that, I thought it might be cool to have sunbaths there. I couldn't see everything, as the light inside was reflecting on the windows and I didn't want to go out to visit, it was actually quite weird. What am I doing in here? This is odd, really weird. And I was feeling increasingly bizarre, and weaker and weaker. My heart was beating weird, like faster, I was hot as hell, and I was now really struggling to keep my balance right. My state of confusion did not improve, since I was still trying to understand what happened, why I was here, what pushed me to come here. I don't remember having taken a Taxi. Right now, I don't even remember where I am coming from. All I remembered now was Claire.

"Take a seat, darling, as I can see that you're not feeling all right..." he advised me.

"Okay," I answered.

As I was standing near the table (and obviously he was somewhere else but not with me in the living room or the entrance), I actually hesitated to move.

Free Expensive Lies: Prologue

Because my shoes were now more comfortable than ever, and I feel like I'm gonna fall if I make a move. But on the other hand, I could no longer stay up as my legs were heavy and my feet hurt a lot, I tried very slowly to move towards the sofa. Once I managed to be close enough, I collapsed like a card castle after maybe something like ten seconds. My strength was gone, I was almost crawling, when I watched myself, I looked at my legs, and I thought about what I was doing now. In my mind, it was the big misunderstanding, what the hell has just happened, why am I feeling so bad? Nothing had answers, and it started to worry me a bit. Immediately after I threw myself on the sofa, after maybe five seconds, as I have been quite noisy, he asked through where he was:

"You okay?"

"Yeah, all good, I just... I'm just seating," I struggled to reply.

I managed to turn myself, as I regained some strength after having thrown myself, and I managed to sit appropriately, watching the very empty wall in front of the opposite sofa in front of me. Okay, fine. I heard him pouring some drink in a glass, I really hope this is not alcohol, because I am not sure I can manage another glass. And whilst I actually put my head backwards to relax myself a bit and crossed my legs, he came back, now I guess from the kitchen. And when I heard him coming back, I rose my head, to see first what was in the coffee table in front of me. If I miss information about the place while I still can, so I can try to gather my memories later, if I don't, I'll be fucked up. There were many magazines, mostly talking about finances, markets, and stock exchanges... I remember something about finance, and markets... Hum, yeah, but I cannot say actually what it is... I don't know. There was also a *Charlie Hebdo* number left in his table, with a cover drawn by Charb saying, "North Korea hunger" about Depardieu, a French actor. He moved to Russia because he was paying too much tax here recently. It was a mess. This table was not tidy. When he was coming, after having quickly glanced at the table, I saw a weird detail, since he didn't wear his coat anymore, he was wearing a blue waistcoat. He looked at me, gave me a little wink, and I saw him carrying a small tray with another two shots. This was served into whiskey glasses. And when I saw the shots... I had a kind of revelation... Something told me that there was an answer in those two shots.

"So, voila... One of my beautiful guilty pleasures."

"What is your guilty pleasure made of?" I asked with a small voice as I was now really exhausted, about to fall asleep.

"It's something really nice, you will see. It will give you a bit of strength, as I can see, you are literally exhausted."

I saw that glass, and I was feeling like, I can't. But he says this will give me strength, so maybe I actually should. I had no power, I really don't know what has hit me, this confusion... I was still wondering what happened to me. When I saw the glass, I remember... I had a kind of a flashback; I saw Claire and Kelly leaving in a dark, crowded place. I saw them going with someone.

"Okay, then!" I replied whilst raising myself to get that final drink.

I drank, not really sure of what was inside. To be honest, I was not really in the state of asking myself questions, given that I was so drunk and so confused. And, God, I don't know what he gave me, but it was actually powerful. Although I could listen to another voice when I heard him speaking, my mind thought so hard that I heard Florent that it was really confusing. All I had now in my mind was this spooky place, and my vision was blurred. My heart was beating amazingly fast again, I feel like I'm gonna collapse any minute now. And he sat in front of me, quite sure of him, He seemed perfectly normal. I was trying to, but it was almost impossible.

"Honey, how do you feel, now?" he kept on asking me as if he was trying to keep me alive somehow and alert.

"I don't know... What's with my heart?" I was feeling a pain in my chest.

"I have no idea!"

"I don't usually feel that way when I am drunk, it's curious!"

"That's okay, it's alright, as I said, you're safe!"

"You never talked to me about this place!"

"As I said, it was a surprise!"

"You never said that... Even, I thought... How did you manage to find that place, that's very curious!"

"Honey, when we love someone, we are ready for all the sacrifices!"

"You're weird tonight... What's going on..."

"As I said, we are home! I mean, do you like this place?"

"Not actually!"

"It's okay, it's just a dream..."

"What the hell happened, I mean, where are we coming from?"

I must admit that... Okay, again, he gave me alcohol, which made me drunker than I actually was, but it somehow made me stronger. Maybe not more alert, as it worsened things, but at least I regained some of my strength. Was it an illusion? I really don't know. I was actually lost in a flow of weird memories. The only questions that kept on coming to my mind were... even, trying to remember the very last thing... I remember seeing myself in those stairs, walking, going upstairs. I was really about to collapse since those memories were quite unclear.

"We've been here for hours, honey!" he simply replied, confusing me more and more.

"I feel like we've been elsewhere..."

"No, we stayed there. I mean... We've been drinking home, you wanted to stay here tonight, don't you remember?"

"Nope."

"It's okay darling, you're gonna get better."

"I don't know, I'm... I'm feeling really weird now."

My chest pain was increasing. My heart was beating faster than ever, and at multiples occasions, from now, I was feeling huge vertigos, even if I was sat, I felt like some strength was pulling me down. I was trying to resist, but it was actually stronger than me.

"I'm not okay, I'm gonna collapse..." I started to panic.

"You're here, with me... it's gonna be okay."

"No... It's... You're lying to... me."

And, suddenly, I felt like I was pushed. I collapsed.

10 *Crimes and punishments*

// *Christian's flat, Paris.*

// *Thursday, 10th of January 2013, 08:20.*

It was new dawn above Paris. The weather seemed promising, as I could perceive a small white light through my eyelids, like the one of a new day, coming through my eyelid, although I was still asleep. Yet again, something here, one of my severest headaches that I could never feel... It was... Yeah. Like a big one.

Oh no... Actually, the sun woke me up. Or at least activated my mind somehow. But I'm not sure it's the sun that woke me up. I was, no, not fair at all, I really wanted to blow up my face against a wall as my headache was so intense and so horrible, or I wanted in first to run towards the restrooms because I was about to throw up everything I had in my stomach. But the problem is... Everything was moving now around me. I was trying not to move as it might be very perilous. Well,

well... I don't know. I tried to avoid thinking that I had a headache, even if it was actually more challenging than ever. I can survive to a hangover. Generally, this is strange, but when I have a headache, it's generally when I have my most fantastic ideas, and obviously an increased tolerance to the humankind in general. Why? How? I don't know. Geez, the one of yesterday must have been amazingly strong, I mean, it's the first time for a while that I wake up like that, actually.

I could smell everything around me, even if my eyes were closed. And I was slowly trying to recollect what I had from yesterday, gather all the remaining memories. The alcohol smell was terrible like a nauseous smell, highly likely to come out of me all around me. And I don't know, I didn't, well... it was very weird that I was still nauseous. Then yeah, there was this; also, I was feeling really tight in the clothes that I was now wearing. But as my hangover just got started, I barely realised what the hell was wrong with me. My head was resting in a pillow, and I was in the sheets of a bed, I was almost curled up in a weird bed, by the way. It didn't have the texture of my real bed, one on which I sleep most of... No, seriously, I was not at home yesterday? Uh-oh, I don't remember what happened! Or maybe I slept in the couch in the living room... but I never do this thing, because this is really cold, and even, I'd have been woken up by someone or something, but as I was drunk, none of these could have made sense... Impossible, I might have slept on the entrance floor but not on the sofa as I sometimes do. I still kept my eyes closed, as I felt like that the truth will not amaze me.

There was a nasty smell of alcohol, nevertheless, and the smell around did not indicate me that I was home. It could only pop out of myself; I just hope that I didn't throw up that much. No, otherwise, the smell around might be more pungent than it is now, and I recall some surprises that happened after I threw up because I was too drunk, that I was keen on wanting to avoid. I could feel something odd under my pillow, something rigid, so I passed my hand underneath. And I felt like a little thing, like a square that was familiar to me—a reasonably stiff thing, smooth. But rounded at the corners. Hmmm... my phone. It's odd; usually, I never sleep with my phone under my pillow, since the wave disturbs me from sleeping. Then the noises around me became more explicit, I heard... some water flowing, in a shower tray, not far from me. But really not far, maybe in a room next to the one I was. It was perhaps the shower... Hum, looks like home but doesn't taste like home.

I kind of enjoyed the warmth of the bed, and I turned myself around. I tried to touch in front of me, to know if someone was there, but no. Of course, no... He has a shower, I am stupid. But at that stage, I was barely waking up and recovering from yesterday. So, still, in the bed, my eyes closed, and now pretending that I was still asleep, I tried to reassemble the events that occurred yesterday: I remember, we went at some point with Claire to a nightclub. I remember having drunk quite a lot, as I have a massive hangover right now, and yes, so at some point we went to that nightclub, I think after Kelly received a text.

After, I remember we entered, we went upstairs to some private club, and... Yes, we met a guy, don't remember his name, apparently a friend of Claire... I recall that after, erm, I think we went to... No, yeah, Kelly was seeking the person that sent her that text, don't remember their names... No, yeah, we went to them. What the hell happened after? I have no idea.

On the other hand, I remember, as I drank quite a lot, I don't exactly remember what I had yesterday, but I remember that I had a lot, so this would explain the blackout. Now, what would explain the fact that I am now here! Yes, as I mentioned, I was feeling tight, it means that I slept with my dress.

My dress was pulled up. When I sleep after I am drunk, weird, but I have the reaction to putting myself in the recovery position in the bed, on the side, so at least I do not choke if I have to throw up. And I am not moving. But I was like... I started to sleep, and even now I was still feeling slightly tipsy, I mean, my body did not evacuate all the alcohol in the blood yet, but I was more conscious, and I think for the next hours, I shouldn't drink or eat, it might be perilous otherwise. I felt that my dress was coming down a bit below my chest, even if I still had my bra. But I felt like I was not wearing my... Oh, god, no, don't tell me that I... Yeah, there were two guys, with Claire, Kelly, and Sophie. Yeah, now I remember, I stayed with one of them. And I drank. As I don't recall what happened after I drank with him, it could be possible that I came home and had sex with him. It would explain everything.

Suddenly, I felt that my phone was vibrating under my pillow. So, I started to mumble a "God damn it, no!" and then I took my phone. Time to wake up, the reality is now back. And I didn't want to open my eyes. I touched the two corners to make the difference between the top and the down, and then I answered. Yeah, I know, my phone, I'm so used to it... Anyway, I replied:

"I really hope it's an emergency; otherwise, you'd better fuck off and die!" I was annoyed.

"*Lycée George Sand*, hello, Charlotte," someone said more clearly than me the voice on the phone.

"Jesus damn Christ, what do you want?" I whispered.

"*Lycée George Sand*. Am I calling Charlotte? Charlotte Kominsky?"

"Yeah, what's going on, are you guys lost without me?"

"Yes, hello, Charlotte. How are you?"

"Still living in the age of denial, just like you guys… hey, hang on… Really, hold on, what day are we today?"

"We are precisely Thursday, 10th of January 2013, it's 8:20 am, and you're supposed to be here for the past twenty minutes. I obviously mean 'supposed to' be here."

"What? Are you serious?"

There, suddenly, to make sure that what she said was right, I felt the need to check. I gently removed the phone from my ear, which made the screen to turn on. And I look at the time on the small side on the top of it. It was 8:20, yeah. So, she could only tell the truth about the… Shit! Yes, it's true, it's Thursday and, er… My boyfriend's maybe at home! Oh, gosh, I am dead…

"Oh, fuck, yes, you are actually serious!" I laughed after verification, nervously.

"Unlike you, yes, we are. What's your excuse today?"

"Hum… I'm not feeling good, actually. Some moron mixed cat food on my chocolate birthday cake yesterday, and I spent my night throwing up. That was so messy, mate, oh my god!"

"Well, it actually wouldn't surprise me if it were true, since most of the people here hate you and spend their time complaining about you…"

"I know, a victim of my own success!"

"Yeah, yeah. Alright then, if you can try to catch up what you missed today, I mean, you know, I have to tell you the things you obviously will not do."

"Yeah, I know, if only you didn't sleep at school, you'd have a better job and wouldn't have to tell me this."

"That's right, yeah, exactly. See you tomorrow," she was annoyed.

"I don't know, I'll see it!" I concluded by hanging up the phone.

Finally, I actually opened my eyes, and put myself flat back in the bed for a few minutes, while even figuring out what shit I actually was now: Florent didn't call me or text me, which means that he is still not home. Well, I have to get back home, even if I don't actually know where I am. Regarding that, since I don't recall having had sex, it actually never happened. Hiding that I was unfaithful, it doesn't seem to be actually a big deal. Even if I have evidence that it happened, I felt like I feel after sex, especially down there, no, it never happened. For being successful in lying, I have to convince myself that it never happened, it's gonna certainly require an hour or two, the time I find another story to cover up where I slept that night. And still, in that bed, I rubbed my face a couple of times, indeed to make sure my eyes are used to that new bright sun. I moved my legs and arms, making sure that I was not that rusty as I used to feel after a night of excess, and looked around, in the hope of finding my panties, but impossible. So, to hide what the public didn't have to see, I lowered my dress, as I wanted to get up. The guy with whom I slept with was still in his bathroom. God, I don't remember his name. I am sure he told me... Or maybe he did not. I don't actually recall him telling me his name.

At a glance, his bedroom seemed relatively small. I mean, there was the bed, just in front quite a vast and very tall wardrobe... Yeah, it was relatively small. His bed was quite wide but had a metallic frame, and his mattress was hard, I mean... Mine is ways softer, and I know I slept on something hard, my back was really fucked. The frame of this bed was white, and as the room was quite cold, not like freezing, but it was slightly below the warmth I could accept, the frame was freezing cold.

On the other hand, next to this bed, on both sides, two nightstands, both the same, fake-wooden with one small drawer, not that big actually, and a relatively high bedside lamp. That was actually really dusty, I don't know how often this guy must be cleaning this place. But it did not seem pretty clean.

The floor was wooden as well, made of quite long slats that were slightly curled, cold as well, but even if it seemed waxed, there were still splinters and tiny holes all around, so I need to be careful where I put my feet. Next to the bed, on the right, actually, by the side I was sleeping, and on the same side, I found my heels lying on the floor, nothing in fact, except a blue-painted wall whose paint was breaking up at some points which showed the moisture below... On the middle of it, the window, above the heater, covered by white quite thick curtains... Well. And the heater, I mean the pipes that were heading to this heater were all dusty... I'm sure if I stay longer in here, I'm gonna get sick. The dust was so thick that it turned almost black. He seemed to have a very old heater... Well, that's a shame.

His wide wardrobe was in front of the bed. Well, nothing except five doors, it was pretty high as the ceiling was high and this wardrobe seemed massive since it almost covered the entire wall, leaving the remaining space for the switch and the white wooden door, but nothing except mirrors covering every single door and empty luggage on top of it... Well. Yeah. That mirror was quite broad, and I'm not sure he's using the entire space of the wardrobe given the fact that he does not seem to be actually someone that loves fashion (guys are not that much attracted by fashion in general, except some cases... and gay people, of course). I am not sure he has a girlfriend or something. Plus, he doesn't seem gay, so there must be other things in this wardrobe other than clothing things. And the mirror in front... Well, I assume it was something really fancy for last night, for him. As the bedsheets were actually somewhat smelling weird, I guess that most of the things happened here.

Finally, to complete everything, nothing on the right-hand-side. I mean, except his bedside lamp. Walls seemed derelict because moisture was attacking the paint, and I couldn't see any pictures of whatever, and personalisation of the room in general. It seemed empty. Looks like mine, no posters on the wall, no flags, nothing, hopefully, no cobwebs. It says a lot about him, as the bedroom is the most personal space in a flat or a house, no. As if he was attached to nothing. Or maybe the things he might be connected to are not important enough for him to be displayed and remembered in his bedroom. That would explain his behaviour, I wouldn't say this guy is a womaniser, given the fact that I don't feel like he's confident in himself enough, but he seems detached to a lot of things. I knew womanisers, quite a few of them, and they are entirely different than this guy. If I slept with him, it means that one of us exploited the other's weakness on the purpose of having something.

The existential question, though: womanisers, by definition, are actually having multiples affairs with women. How do we call the reverse, a woman that has multiple affairs with men? Oh, yeah, I know... a whore. Why does it have to be an insult in the other way round? And what if I sleep with a thousand women, given my gender, would I be a womaniser? That's a curious question... I'll check that out. I should try that experience; I'm sure Claire would love it and Florent as well. And my mother too... No, that's a bad idea, actually. Pleasant, but wrong. Well, on the other hand, I'm sure, if I do that, my mum will believe that I'm possessed, and she'll call an exorcist. To remove the evil within, unfortunately, I'm afraid she'll have to kill me.

Anyway, upon putting my two feet on the ground, I had suddenly a kind of violent but very swift vertigo, which carried me away, but it didn't last more than ten seconds. It was violent, though, I felt like my eyes closed on their own and I felt like weak... But it was okay. Boom! It was at that very moment that I heard him being done with his shower, while I had a black veil beside the eyes, and my headache was actually much more powerful. Yeah, I was still a bit drunk, maybe going to the toilets (because I wanted to pee) will help me sober up, but I felt like my stomach was threatening. And, also, upon standing up, I was feeling like, yeah, all the blood that my body contained was now feeling up and down, and on my feet, I felt a wooden floor, recently waxed. Still, the thing I actually did, just the time I gather enough strength to stand up, I put my head in my hands, my hands before my eyes, and was thinking.

At that moment, I heard him actually leaving the bathroom, walking towards... somewhere, and he was whistling. Hum, yes, if he was whistling, it means that we had sex. The way he was walking, very straight, it means that he knew where he was going. I have no idea what he was whistling, but he seemed quite happy, he doesn't seem threatening. Which means, yeah, I don't think I'm gonna have troubles with him for leaving his place. Also, I still have my phone, it means that yeah, I was just too drunk, and I slept with the first guy I met. That never happened to me, it's the very first time. Meh, it's still essential to make experiences in life. I just hope that I'm not gonna get disappointed by the material I actually slept with.

Curiously, I was neither feeling happy nor sad, not even guilty or... Yeah, I have a boyfriend, but... Meh, it's a secret. I mean, well, every couple has secrets and how many women at that very hour have actually made the same mistake that I did and hid it for years? I'm not alone, I just have to be careful of what I say, now that I am aware that I slept with him. Lying to Florent is gonna be easy, as I had sex when I was in a blackout, so this possible thing was purely imaginary. Or maybe I was definitely not sober enough to actually realise that I in reality cheated on my boyfriend, and... Like Claire, when she cheated on me, the only difference is that I even caught her doing that. Meh, as I say, comes what may.

Actually, I was hearing his whistles coming towards me... And he went into the bedroom. Whilst I was still waiting to get ready, I heard him coming to the bedroom. Oh... What I actually wanted was to avoid this guy. I felt even disturbed when he asked me, on a very amazed and relaxed tone:

"Hi, Charlotte. How are you doing this beautiful morning?"

Yeah, I get it. It really happened. I mean, even Florent doesn't feel that way after sex. Okay... I just turned around, feeling still like a zombie, to actually look at him. Here really came the huge disappointment: he was looking like a... Not fat, but he seemed to enjoy life, according to the shape of his belly. Hairs everywhere, on his legs, on his torso. Not even muscles, not... He was quite tall, though, but was good-looking. Meh, okay. Oh boy, I must have been really fucked up last night then. He was just wearing a white towel wrapped around his waist, not to show his stuff. So, yeah, disappointed, I just looked at him:

"Okay, then we slept together, right?"

"Yes. That was awesome! I couldn't imagine lesbians being so hot in bed, it's crazy!" he replied with a delighted smile.

There are some things, you know, in life, that you'd actually prefer not to hear. Like, what he said at the very end I asked that question. Okay, let's focus, he seems to be an idiot, obviously, but a happy one. What really matters to me right now is to recollect what happened yesterday, how comes I slept with that guy and not with a random girl? I mean, a girl would have been my first choice, not a guy, that's totally just not me, and impossible that I became straight only during the night. Well, I know that alcohol is powerful enough to make me straight and tolerant, but, I mean, this guy, come on... Something must have happened. That's sure. Let's take another approach and see what's going on: to get what I want, let's pretend I'm devastated, and I am feeling really guilty because I just found out that I cheated on my boyfriend. I want him to be more serious, and thus guilt is a reliable way to get what I want, if he feels guilty, he might be helpful.

"Oh, no, damn it... please tell me it's not true," I said for once more softly, changing my voice on purpose, almost in whispering, while rubbing my face with my hands to show him I was feeling bad now.

"What do you mean?"

"If you want, erm... I... I just have a boyfriend, actually!"

"What?"

"Yes. I am in a relationship. And I love my boyfriend. How could I do that to him!"

"Holy crap! I'm really sorry!" his tone seemed... I don't know, like fake or something.

Then I stood up from the bed, still with my headache, and I wanted to... Well, I could see that he was everything but sorry. The small rictus drawn on his lips when he said that he was sorry actually betrayed him. But, if there was a rictus, it meant something. Something happened, but as he seemed foolish but not that much of an idiot, I'm not actually sure I'll ever know. My approach was wrong, that is sure, I didn't find the right way to actually get what I really want from him, because he obviously had no mercy for the fact I had a boyfriend, he simply didn't care, what actually mattered to him was the fact that he had sex with me, and that's all. Okay then, and since I need to get out of here, it's better not to trigger a fight or something. So, I took my phone, and the conversation continued between us.

"No, it's not your mistake. It's mine, I was drunk, and I didn't tell you anything about him..." I absolved him.

"Meh, it's okay anyway, he doesn't need to know," he just said with total disinterest.

"Yeah, maybe. Anyway, I gotta go. Don't you know what you've done with, damn... my panties?"

"Huh? No. I am sorry. Look under the bed, maybe it's there. Wait, I'll be right back, I'll just go to the bathroom for a minute."

When he walked back to the bathroom, I searched everywhere in the bed, under the sheet, the pillows. In case it still is in here. It was much better to find it because... even if I just have my dress and coat, I cannot travel that way. Also, do not leave compromising pieces that may jeopardise something else later; like my couple. It was better to take it with me. You may find me paranoid, but I prefer being careful, I don't know this guy or his intentions. So, I watched under the bed, I crouched myself, and... Except for the only used condom of that night, I saw nothing. I don't know if it could reassure me (I mean yeah, of course, because I don't want to catch any disease or becoming pregnant because of my mistake), he still thought about protecting himself. Surprising, for a guy like him. Guys usually don't like condoms, all of this for genuinely stupid reasons. Putting my head upside down was not that a good idea, so I quickly rose my head. Yeah, I was still tipsy, even if I was ways more conscious of the situation and I was on my way to sober up, I still need to go home and get some sleep.

Anyway, while looking under the bed and seeking the missing thing, I heard him return. In my head, I was like "wow, he was fast". And whilst I was still searching, and... wait, what's that black thing other there? Looks like fabrics and lace. Oh, gosh, good, here it is. It was within my reach, fortunately, not that far away, so I guess I am saved. But as it was all folded... and if I was drunk yesterday... When I actually touched it, it felt like all cold and wet, and very slightly slimy. Oh, gosh, disgusting. But, well, at least I'm saved, this is not gonna stay here, it remains with me. Nothing more compromising left in here, I'm good to go. But actually, he came to me, this time dressed up with... well, a black suit, no tie, white shirt, all perfectly ironed... He was looking like someone doing business or finance. How comes it took him such a short time to get ready? Anyway, this time, he was feeling slightly compassionate:

"Well, I am... quite confused, you told me you didn't have any boyfriend. I thought you were with a girl."

"Well, with whoever I might be with, a man or a girl, you know, it's still cheating, what we've been doing." I actually was condescending.

"No, but seriously... Well, it doesn't have to be known, you know!"

"Nope, and it won't, trust me! Oh, by the way, I found it!"

"Cool, I'm happy."

"So, the good thing is, it will prevent silly things being done like masturbating or something, you know?" I was feeling like... the real me was back.

"Why would I do that?" he actually blushed.

"Because you're a guy, and you guys are all the same!"

"Geez, I didn't believe you would actually be... Well... so nice to me!"

"I know, there's even a fan club, you should check it out. Anyway, I gotta go!"

Now, I'd actually quite want to hurry up. Seriously, I had to hurry up, because I don't know if my boyfriend was at home right now or not or on his way back home, and if he is, well, that will be funny. He certainly doesn't expect to see me dressed that way, and if he sees me like this, it is gonna raise numerous questions, questions to which I didn't find the lies to cover up. Regarding him and keeping the secret, I think I can trust him (it seems not right for me to say that I can "trust" someone), I know he will not be an ass with... I'm not even sure he may know anything about me or my life. Except for my name, maybe, but I don't think he's smart enough to find out where I live and who is my boyfriend. And what's the interest in being a jerk with me, for him, by the way? None. I just went to grab my shoes, because, yeah, it was time to go. This thing that was still in my hand... No, I can't wear it, I'm gonna get sick otherwise. Time was running out now. I really wish I'd stay further, but, you know, obligations...

"All... right. But wait a minute. How are you going back home?"

"Oh, I'll take the metro. Why?"

"Well, if you want, I have an appointment nearby. I don't know where you live, but I can drive you to the metro if you like, as the station is pretty far away from here, and you have to walk towards *Montmartre*, and it's gonna be a pretty long walk for you! I mean, unless you wanna walk, but I think it might be more convenient."

While looking at him right in the eyes, I thought that, well... Somehow, he was right. I still had my heels, and... as I looked from his windows, Montmartre doesn't seem that far, but I don't think my shoes would manage to get me there. It may slow me down, and... It is why I thought about Florent: he's likely at his best friend's place or at his mother's home, and it's barely nine. Usually, unless he has something scheduled, he wakes up at ten, so I may expect to see him home at around twelve today, for lunch, I don't think he should be here before. Wherever he was, I am sure he played on his console all night, which means that he may be tired. I know, he can play until late, and I'm sure he did that. He played once with Clarisse's boyfriend until four of the morning. I also checked my phone, and it said the nearest metro station was Abbesses... at a pretty significant distance, actually. There are just two lines, I change at some point, and I'm home quickly. If I take the metro, I may have a chance to arrive before 10. If I walk, even if I leave now, I will be late. Hum, okay. After having fully considered both scenarios, I looked at him, like inspired, I told him, straight but hesitating:

"Hum... Okay, then."

"Okay then... like a yes, you want to come with me? I drive you to your station, and that's it!"

"Fair enough. It's okay if we leave now. I don't wanna wait because I am in a kind of a rush."

"Yeah, of course. I have to rush as well, I'm also late, I'm not sure I'll be there on time actually."

"Okay then, let's go."

"Let's go!"

Meh, that's nice of him. No, I mean it.

Anyway, as he was ready, perfumed and everything, we were prepared to go. I had everything; it was time to go. I took my phone as it was still on the bed, and we went into the hall, which was directly connected to the bedroom, because both my coat and his was still standing there, on a rack near the main door. It's curious, I had a kind of impression of déjà vu, of that place. I mean, I certainly saw it when I was drunk, but... Yeah. Now it seemed quite dark even if there was some light, but it was still the morning. The French capital's misty morning light was heavy and has let appearing a strong light into intense darkness, provided by his living room's drawn curtains. It dimmed it. My red coat was still there, and he gave it to me. He had a kind of long black coat, business-style. I really don't recall anything from yesterday. I was just following him, and whilst wearing my jacket, he was looking for his keys to open the door. I placed my phone on the left pocket, and I checked the right, my wallet was still there with my keys. I put the wet thing on that pocket. And yet I quickly watched the living room and the table... Chairs were moved, there was a couple of empty shot glasses on the coffee table between the sofas, and, well, that must have been a crazy night. I was not actually in balance, I felt like I was walking on a wire as a tightrope walker. I think it must be the reason why I am so mean today and in an unbelievably lousy mood, I'm gonna take some pills once at home for my headache.

He finally unlocked the door with his keys, when I was next to him, contemplating the remains of the last night in the living room actually. Don't ask me if I was proud of myself. Obviously, I was not, and... I have to think now, but there's no chance he might discover what I was doing last night unless he is now at home and waiting for me. It's improbable. He will ask me what I did last night, and that's it. After unlocking the door, the guy with whom I slept with actually looked at me:

"Here we are!"

"Uh... Yes. Hurry up, please, I do not intend to stay here all night," I remained cold and distant towards him.

"Well, well, ladies first," he actually pretended to be a gentleman.

When he opened the door, the feeling of déjà vu of this damn corridor was like... wow, I saw it yesterday. I just can't remember how I was. When I passed through it moments later, I noticed that the floor was covered with a white carpet. I curiously recalled having walked somehow on something smooth. I observed that place as if I knew it like my entire life, saw the walls painted halfway down in green, and halfway up in white, to have the same colour as the ceiling. It looked dirty, and the paintings were done a long moment ago, just like his bedroom. But I don't know, in my memory that carpet was associated to something, and the thing that actually came to my mind was, I don't know, I felt like I was confused at that point. Maybe it is true, perhaps it was fake memories, but one thing is sure, it's that I cannot trust those "flashbacks" as they happened during my blackout. So, they might be corrupt. But surprisingly, he told me to take the other way in this corridor, as I was walking towards the stairs on my right upon leaving because something told me that it was actually the way out, but we walked towards the lift. I didn't really understand why something told me to go through the stairs, but it doesn't really matter, I just said okay and followed him without asking any questions.

He pushed the button to call the elevator, which arrived maybe two minutes after, as it was actually quite busy. Fine. The lift was noisy like really, we could almost hear the machinery from upstairs, and it was apparently as old as the building was also. This place seemed to be old. Again, "ladies first" where I could almost feel this guy's nasty sight when I walked in, he came in a very few seconds later and pushed the button of the floor he wanted to go, -1. And once the doors of the lift were closed, he just looked at me, and... actually, whilst I was searching on something in my phone, I was even checking quite a few things, he remained silent.

As I said, this lift was old, and I felt it going down quite slowly, which made things actually worse because of my headache and my hangover, I could hear noises much higher, and for something that seemed banal, it was really deafening. The lift was nothing more than a square-shaped coloured metallic cage painted in pale yellow with a floor made of black not seriously strong, with a safety guardrail at human-size all around. This thing was actually tumbledown and was threatening to collapse any minutes now. Next to this guy and on the left side, a grey metallic control panel included all the buttons from 4 to -1 and two buttons down, the first one to hold the doors opened and the second one for an emergency call.

While the lift was going downstairs, I was checking my phone. Yes, my position and I was close to a street, *Rue des Martyrs*, something told me that I went there. It didn't seem unknown to me, at least I was not that surprised to be here. Hum, yes. I also checked the settings, checked my Wi-Fi, and saw that my phone has not been connected to any other networks except the network at home. I went to check my bank accounts, and still, I was over thirty-two million. Nothing actually happened. Astonishingly, I didn't spend a penny last night. Oh, yes, because obviously, (and I must admit that it's thanks to my mother; otherwise I wouldn't have thought about it), my money sleeps in a bank account in the United Kingdom, especially in the city of London. You may ask me why... it's for tax avoidance purposes. It's not illegal, it's just that France is seeking so much money that it taxes poor millionaires just like me. That's immoral? Come on, I invested in that country! I mean, someone invested for me, and I negotiated... but I'm providing home for people, so I'm not an arse, okay?

I also checked my Internet browser, just in case something surprising may have happened. And, no, except YouTube, Google Translate (yeah... I sometimes lose my French, there are words that I seek as I speak English more often than I speak French, which actually drives Florent nuts since he's the only one at home not being able to speak the same language than us at home), and the website of a coffee shop where I get rewards when I get a flat white there. It's a new business that recently opened, and they launched that system through a website, that's quite amazing. And their coffee is nice, to be honest. Or my favourite hot chocolate with oat milk. By the way, it reminds me that I have free coffees. Maybe I'll get there later.

Taylor Harding-Jenkins

At the end of our little trip from the fourth level to the garage, we heard a small "ding" after having felt like a pretty hard stop. Well, I was already good, I mean, my stomach was indeed already good, I felt like everything going up, but for a short time after bouncing back again, it was like a real pleasure, geez. The automatic doors opened themselves shortly afterwards, and it's at this time that I was thinking about, erm... hum, yeah, before to leave, curiosity took over:

"Erm... could I ask you a question?" I was hesitating.

"Huh, yes?"

"At least... Well, I was drunk, okay, but... how was it?"

"Ah, huh... Well, fantastic, I mean... Yeah. It's odd you ask such a question!"

"I'm inquisitive..."

"You know that you drool when you sleep?"

"Someone told me. I also speak, apparently."

"You speak when you sleep?"

"Yeah, but I didn't sleep well in your mattress. You should consider changing it. Anyway, I don't wanna... You don't need to know more about you..."

"But wait, seriously... Don't you remember anything?" he seemed sceptical.

"I don't even recall having met you last night in the nightclub I was," I was honest with him. "I don't even recall your name..."

"Well, in case you want to know, my name is..."

"No offence," I immediately interrupted him, "but that's not relevant information to me. I actually prefer to forget who you are."

"Okay then... It makes sense."

Before to leave the lift, I turned myself back as he walked away, because there was a mirror just behind me, to actually assess the mess. A kind of self-assessment, yeah. But I must consider the fact that I didn't eat yet, I didn't even pee or even had a shower, it's why I looked at myself with delusion: I still had my makeup from yesterday applied in my face, even if it was mostly fading away, my red gloss was gone, and my foundation... I actually looked like a revenant. My hairs were messy and voluminous (they usually are, but not like that), geez, now everybody will look at me in the metro. Because people here are so silly that whenever you're not looking like the rest of the populace, they look at you like you're coming from another planet or you are an animal that escaped the zoo. It's something I hate with French people, to be honest.

It was actually damn freezing in here, as walls were only made of concrete and this place within that building was leading to the outside. I put my hand on my pockets, putting back my phone in my pocket. So, yes, the garage. White walls, the corridor is actually about five metres long, and a door was at the end. It's actually the only corridor of the building that seemed modern, maybe this garage has been refurbished recently. On the ceiling, noisy pipes, all exposed and all heading to the garage, wrapped in a kind of strange foam that has taken the dust and was falling on the floor. Hopefully, I'm not allergic. And, yes, at the very end of that sixteen-feet-long corridor, a massive black door. Small windows on it actually displayed what was next.

He and I went out. He was leading, and I followed. Because, yes, although I knew we were going to his car, I didn't know where it was. There was a kind of deep silence in that corridor, though, no ventilation noise as we used to hear in a parking lot, no noise of water passing in the pipes above me, nothing. Just the noise of us walking, and it was quite loud. After a couple of steps, he opened the door for me, and some fresh air came straight to my face. We finally managed to arrive in that very dark, poorly lit, and all concrete garage. But when he actually pushed the door, as I assume that the light switches were by motion sensors, I could perceive a dimmed light that made the place certainly brighter. However, this parking was like linear and small, just one corridor leading to a ramp leading to the main door. Maybe five garages on each side, all the door closed. Well, all the garages are always the same, all made of concrete walls, pipes appearing under the ceiling and making such a labyrinth above our heads; our garage is the same, more or less. There was still that very strange foam all over the ceiling that made the floor dusty. On the floor, the traces of different vehicles that passed here.

Regarding walls, they still contained the remains of the time when the residence was under construction: the traces of the printed strings that workers placed against it to make markings, scraps of writing in pencil against paper walls and... Well, it was a garage, more or less. I actually remained near the door leading to the lift, whilst he was picking up his car.

Meanwhile, I took my phone to see the text messages I received when I put my phone back in my pocket, as I heard it vibrating. I heard it vibrating often, and I was even surprised to get signal in here since concrete kills the waves. I realised that I honestly didn't check my messages in case I did something I may regret. When I took it, I immediately saw "one missed call" and just below, "four new messages". The missed call was from Clarisse. In general, if she calls me in the morning, it means that... But yeah, shit! Oh no, I completely forgot!

Then I look at the messages. Obviously, the first message was from her, of course, "Charlotte, I WILL KILL YOU: we had a presentation to give back to the English teacher, and we had to do it together. You didn't leave me any notes. Now I look like an idiot because I made a mistake to trust you. I swear to God, I'll kill the hell of you!" Okay, she will be upset for a few hours, and then it will be all right. Yeah. I know, sometimes she can be such a perfectionist at school that she's screwing up with everything. I returned to the unread messages, and I looked. The second was from my mother, the third from Florent and fourth Claire. Let's start with mum, who told me, "You turned eighteen yesterday, and yet you're not at home, and the first day you're supposed (I mean supposed) to be responsible and going to school you are not reachable. No comments!" Geez, like there's nothing else in her stupid life more essential than spying on me. As if I really cared about school. Meh, anyway. I just wanted to remind her that it's gonna take five minutes to get a plane ticket for a country far, far away. I should consider it, though. What the heck am I still doing in here? I must be masochist somehow, I think.

Meanwhile, I heard him opening the door of his garage whilst I sighed. I somehow needed inspiration, I needed to find something to tackle the "be responsible". Geez... So, after having thought a couple of seconds whilst watching him opening that door, I started to type, "Oh dear, I'm so sorry, I missed school today. Then what, you're gonna call the police to force me to get in there? Come on, go on, do it!" hell. Anyway, back in the unread messages, I looked at Florent's one, now: "Hi honey. How are you? I guess you're at your friend's home, sleeping. Well, just to tell you that I will come back later because I am waiting for my results, I'm passing by the school before to come. I missed you last night. I love you, sweetheart. See you tonight, I love you :)." Alright, so I got the confirmation that he was on his way to come back home actually late. Fine, that's perfect, that's even better, that'll leave me plenty of time to sleep then. And get my miracle recipe for the hangover.

And for finishing, Claire. Miss Claire fucking Cobert. What on Earth does she want, now? That's her favourite game, she knows that it's harder for me to read her texts that she writes in French phonetics since I am a foreigner, she sent me... well... I guess that looks something like... erm... give me a minute, actually... okay, so "Hi Cha, I hope you're doing great, congrats for last night, I knew you could do it! Don't forget to come to pick up the stuff that you left home. I love you!" Well, well, well, she knows. It's not actually... Well, I'm surprised, I mean, how could she know? Well, on the other hand, I had a blackout last night, so everything becomes possible.

While I was reading, I actually missed the fact that he started his car, and when I put the phone in my pocket after having done my best to decrypt Claire's message, I saw his car in front of me ready to go. Well, well, well... His car actually reflects his personality. For men, cars are like what's the most important in their lives. I saw in front of me a BMW series seven coloured in a metallic grey, leathered interior, and I'm not an expert on cars or mechanics at all, but I can always recognise this car. Now, actually, was this guy rich or not, that's quite hard to say. Especially since his car seemed new, I mean, it was not a second-hand car, I could see that, as it appeared to be a new generation. It was like jumping back in the past, as our father used to be the same (his car was his life), and he had a car similar to his, even if this was years ago.

I turned around, got in the car, and we were ready to go. Even if my journey on board would be relatively short, I still fastened my seatbelt, while feeling the seat cold for my legs, I immediately afterwards took my cell to call my twin sister. Yes, because his car engine was quiet, and I wanted to avoid having to speak to him. So, I called her once, but she didn't answer. I insisted, calling a second time:

"Hello, darling!" I immediately said after she took the call.

"What? What the hell is happening to you? I'm at school, for fuck's sake!" she whispered, actually embarrassed.

"So that's even better, I'm gonna make your morning much more fun: let's admit that I had probably done something stupid last night. A kind of foolish thing... What would you do in my place?"

"I don't have time to deal with your piddle-ass problems! I am busy. Catch you later," still with the same tone, she said before hanging up.

Hum. She's busy right now, she won't listen to me, even if I insist. Okay, then, it's better not to insist if she is with that mood. He was now on the ramp, leaving the garage, and used a remote controller to open the door. And at the moment that door opened, when we were about to go out of the garage, and I could see how cloudy the weather outside was, see how it was and how Paris was busy as every day. But obviously, as the sun was up now, the very first light that came to my eyes was so powerful and so strong that it kind of dazzled me. I was like... Fuck, I forgot my sunglasses. Especially since I saw this morning that my eyes were red because of that hangover, it was like... yeah. Actually, pretty intense.

He left that ramp once the door was fully opened a couple of seconds later, making the vehicle move pretty harshly. I actually said thanks for the ride, and he was like, you know, being modest, "it's okay, don't worry". But... obviously, the road was congested, however very slightly. Meh. The leather chairs were cold, against my almost naked legs. However, it seemed to be quite chilly this morning actually, as I could see through a screen on his car dashboard that it was actually two outside, no wonder why seats are so cold. But there was the air conditioner, but as it was starting the airflow was still pretty cold, and... well, it's just maybe a metre away, it's not that far anyway. So... Wait, my boyfriend's school is nearby. I was thinking... He used to tell me that he used to leave the metro at this station to go there for his exams... Holy shit, I'd instead make sure that he is not there. I immediately took my phone whilst he was starting to drive on the road, on the way to the station. I immediately called. Once. It rang, no answers. Then a second time, still nothing. Then a third. Alright, it was when it started ringing that I actually thought... is it a good idea to wake him up? I mean... Well, if he's waiting for his results, maybe he is already there, or he is on the way. It rang once... Twice... And then...

"Hello, sweetheart?" Florent replied, although according to his voice, he seemed asleep.

"Hey, darling. Hum... What's up?" I was not actually sure of myself, whether I wanted to talk or not.

"I'm okay... why do you call me at that hour, I'm still sleeping?"

"Hum... Well, just checking up on you! I mean... I'm... You know..."

"Checking up on me? Oh, wow, it's certainly the very first time you do such a thing!"

"Well, I mean, you know... I am waking you up?"

"No, I'm outside, but I mean... I sent you a text this morning. You're not at school?"

Okay... Okay, I said it, I shouldn't have called. Now, it's becoming suspicious. He's right, I never check what he's doing, since I don't mind. Now, I do... Hopefully he's not like me and will never harass me until he finds out why I have been acting weird. But he may wonder. But he will leave me the benefit of the doubt. Okay, so... The perfect lie... Let's take yesterday evening, I have been with Claire, Kelly, and Sophie. He knows Sophie. Not personally, but he knows she's a friend of mine. So, let's say... Oh, I know, Sophie proposed me to go to a party yesterday, with friends of hers, and I said yes. I told him I wasn't home, so it could cover-up that I was not home. It's close to the truth, actually. We've been drinking with Sophie. It's a new approach of the fact, easy to cover up, for him it will be okay because he's aware that since I am with him, I almost cut contacts with most of my friends, and Sophie has been an old friend. It may make sense. Let's do it this way. It's something credible.

"No, actually, I'm slightly hungover. I'm going home now!" I felt now surer of myself since I had something to hide the truth.

"Slightly hangover, the party must have been juicy!" he was intrigued.

"Yeah, well. You know, I was with Sophie, and we drank a lot actually, it was a pretty great party!"

"Okay... Well, good, I spent my evening playing videogames with an old friend."

"Oh, really?"

"Yeah."

"Anyway, when are you going to be home? I mean... what hour?"

"I have no idea. I don't know, I'm going to the school, now, so... I don't know, maybe later. Hum, maybe for noon I'll be there!"

"Um... okay. I'm pretty tired, we stayed awake until extremely late, so if I'm sleeping when you come back, just... You know, wake me up."

"Okay. Honey, I love you, but I gotta take the metro now."

"No problem, honey, I'll see you later. I love you!"

He hung up after having given me a kiss by phone. Okay, so he's gonna be home by noon, which leaves me plenty of time to change myself, drink my tea, and sleep. That's even better, I mean, at least I can relax, do what I have to do... And enjoy a shower. No, I need it, I stink alcohol, and it's terrible. And I really need that. That, and a nap as well.

We were close to the metro station. I mean, I could see it. The problem, he needed to find someplace to park around. Because the avenue on which we were was quite busy at that hour, and I don't think stopping, even if it is for a couple of seconds, would be a great idea. This metro station, well, I mean, it was in a place. It was undoubtedly the place that had the most the real spirit of Paris: paved streets which, when you're driving on the pavement, makes your car vibrating, in between, in this place, many temporary shops, a carrousel, it had its charm. And the station seemed like an old one, with written on top of it the old and famous "*Métropolitain*", I actually love these places in Paris. For me, it really looks like Paris. Montmartre and this place, yeah, this is Paris. Again, that's my opinion. But although we arrived, the road was still quite busy, and as the traffic flow wasn't stopping, he actually couldn't stop. But he saw a bus stop. Maybe, if he had enough time, he could stop by.

And whilst he was manoeuvring to actually exit the traffic for parking behind that bus, and whilst still keeping an eye on the road, he started to say, focused:

"So? Relieved?"

"Relieved for what?" I didn't get what he meant.

"For your boyfriend?"

"Oh, well, yeah. Yeah, relieved."

"Yeah."

"Thanks for the ride, anyway, I really appreciate..."

"That's okay. I mean... That's just a couple of minutes for me..."

"Thank you very much..." I was starting to breathe.

"Okay then, have a good day."

"Well, you too!"

He stopped the car. And I didn't see, the door was locked when I tried to open. He figured out and opened the door for me, and he was looking at me, like... I don't know. I opened the door and left the car. Now... time to go home.

To be fair, I actually didn't want to go back home. Because believe it or not, but I do not like to lie. And... I have to hide something to Florent. So, well, okay, yesterday was my birthday, I actually drank, I had fun, and I don't know how my party ended, but all I know is that I woke up with this guy. What actually makes me angry is that... I may be a manipulative bitch that lies all the time, but I love to remain loyal. And what I did to Florent, that's unfair. Claire cheated on me as well, and when I found out, well, I got really hurt. It was horrible to me. But I loved Claire. I like Florent, and I wouldn't say that it's okay for me to have sex with someone else since I don't love him as much as I loved Claire, but still, he doesn't deserve that from me. And, starting our life whilst hiding something... The thing is, he loves me, he trusts me, and I acted this way. No, I felt a bit guilty, but if I want to preserve my couple with him, I have to keep on behaving as if nothing really happened. The thing is, I really don't know where things between us are going to go, I really don't know how far we will go, because I am kind of forcing myself. I am not entirely filled with happiness. Claire had the power to destroy my depression, she could put it on mute, by elementary things. And Florent doesn't have this power. And I do not hope I may find someone that may make me happy. I couldn't be like "let's forget and shrug off", no, I cheated. Now... Well, I can deal with that. I just don't like to.

As I left the car, I turned around to walk towards the metro entrance. My shoes were really painful, and I was quite impatient to get rid of them. But suddenly, as my phone was back in my pocket, I felt it vibrating. Someone was calling me. So, I took it to check who it might be. Well, an unknown caller. Hmmm... Who could it be? The last time it ever happened, it was Claire that made me a joke. So, I answered quite promptly to make sure that it wouldn't be lasting long.

"Geez, I really hope this is important, otherwise..."

"Happy birthday!" a masked voice suddenly started to say.

"Thank you, but who are you? As you apparently want to play the game..."

"Don't worry about that!"

"I really want to know who's the son of a bitch that wishes me my birthday with a day late, just to kick his lame arse?"

"Meh, you wouldn't."

"Try me, mate. I can still kick your arse!"

"I know, but, Charlotte, don't make anything that you may regret!"

Yeah, that's obviously a joke, an arsehole who's changing his voice on the purpose of scaring me. That happened already, and I found out who it was the very last time. But obviously, someone that knows me, otherwise he wouldn't say my name. It would be probably Claire or Clarisse, Claire because she's always having fun to bothers me when I am already bothered or embarrassed, and she knows that with what I did last night, it would be entertaining to piss me off right now; and Clarisse because she's angry against me and she wants to make me a nasty joke, just like she did once. That's a prank, that's it if he really thinks I may be scared. But I'd rather bet more on Claire than Clarisse since Clarisse is at school and I think she may be busy doing something else. Or it could be Kelly. Anyway, let's see how far it goes. He wants to play? Fine, I like playing too.

"Yeah, Clarisse, you're pathetic!"

"I'm not your twin sister. Do you think I actually look like a girl?"

"Okay then, so Claire, hang up this goddamn phone, you're definitely stupid. You did that prank before!"

"I am not your former girlfriend, either. But, yeah, nice try, try again!"

"Um, okay, so who are you? To know that Clarisse is my twin and to know that Claire was my girlfriend?"

"I am someone!"

"Well, it does actually make sense. You'd tell me you were a tree; I wouldn't have believed you a second!"

"I'm nobody. But, in the meantime, I am all the entire people around you. I know you, but you don't know me! You may or may not know me... You will, soon!"

"Okay mate, so when you want to tell me who you actually are, leave me a message, okay?"

"You think I maybe am not serious? You think I am here to mess up with you? Okay, I think I may surprise you. You will have some of my news soon directly at your home. And for answering your question, who the hell am I? I am the last person you will see alive!" he told me coldly.

"Oh, is that threats? Who are you, for threatening me, you shady arsehole? You think you are..."

...scaring me with your goddamn threats, you idiot? The guy with whom I spoke hung up the phone. Geez... what the hell was that?

11 *This means war*

// At home, Neuilly-sur-Seine.

// Thursday, 10th of January 2013, 14:00.

Nobody was at home when I arrived. And, actually, when I arrived, everything was quiet. Even the metro, there was almost nobody, the peak hour was now over. When I came back home, I immediately went to my bedroom, removed my shoes in first, my coat and my dress after, I peed (I couldn't contain myself anymore) immediately had a shower. I put a nightdress... oh yeah, no high heels anymore, no short dress, just the feeling of the water flowing along my skin, and... Frankly, that was absolutely relieving. It's funny, that feeling you have when you remove heels after having worn it for quite a long time... you feel suddenly tiny. I actually finished sobering up when I was in the metro, but my hangover was still here. But now, at least, I was feeling fresh, I was not smelling like alcohol anymore. Back to my bedroom, I just wanted one thing at this moment, going to my bed, and sleeping. No more parties, no more heels, no more... Even if I was starving. For that, I assume that I'm going to have to wait. After all, I know that if I eat right now and sleep after, I may wake up later to actually throw up because my stomach is not ready for food. Yeah, it already happened, and the very last thing I want is mopping the floor of my bedroom and changing the bedsheets. No, really.

Free Expensive Lies: Prologue

But before sleeping, I actually... made quite a wise thing, to make sure that life will restart as if nothing happened: I made sure that the shoes and clothes I wore yesterday were stored in their correct place as if they never moved. I removed my panties and took all the dirty linen we had (because there was actually a bit) and made a machine, and I put my coat correctly where it was. So, nothing is gonna appear as suspicious if someone comes back home. I'm here, a machine is on its way... Yeah, I was only tired after coming back from a night of excess with Sophie. That's the rule; when you're paranoid, you always assume that everybody around you is paranoid too.

I have just drawn the curtains and slid myself in the bed. At least, this was much more comfortable. Again, I put myself on the recovery position, as we never know, and I just closed my eyes. It was almost ten of the morning when I started to sleep, making this time my whole night. It was challenging, but after turning many times on myself, I finally closed the eyes, because my stomach was actually in pain, and I felt it like bouncing back and forth because it was still full of alcohol. I even started to go into sleep quite quickly. I mean, I was so exhausted that I needed it, what I had last night was almost like a sleepless night. I removed all thoughts from my mind, I just started to imagine myself walking in the street, in a warm day, on the summer, in a remote village, where there were terrific trees all around and a river flowing next to the road I was walking along. It was so amazing, it almost put me into my inner peace.

And then, the blackout. My phone was plugged in my bedside table, and I was just sleeping, quietly. I was just enjoying those moments where I was almost reprogramming my mind, erasing the fact that I was with Claire and Kelly, I've never been to that nightclub. And I never slept with that guy. It was time to convince my mind that none of that actually happened. It happened, but in reality, I live, it never happened. I don't know for how long I've even been sleeping, but all I know is that at some point, at two, my phone rang out loud and it woke me up. "What a man, what a man, what a man..." It was Clarisse. Yeah, that's her ringtone. I was like... Geez, what does she want? I replied.

"Hey, honey?" Clarisse answered in first.

"What?" I was pretty cold.

"Okay, what did you want to tell me this morning, when you called me?"

"Actually, give me a minute..."

Well... My door was closed, I didn't hear any noise in here... But I know that the flat is poorly soundproofed, so before engaging myself in a   sensitive conversation that I didn't want anybody to hear, I preferred ensuring that I was really alone. So, I started to scream as loud as I could, this:

"IS SOMEONE IN HERE?"

And I waited. Trust me, I yelled loud enough to be heard everywhere. I waited something like ten seconds... No. No answers. Okay, so, where were we?

"What the heck was this?" Clarisse was surprised.

"Safety measures. Okay, so, last night, I slept with some guy!" I actually spoke relatively low voice... Just to make sure.

"Wait... ARE YOU SERIOUS?" her tone actually changed...

"I know, call me whatever you want to call me, or whatever you want... But it was an accident. I was drunk, and I had a blackout when it happened. I don't even remember how and where it happened."

"Charlotte... This is a joke, isn't it? You're kidding, right?"

"As I said, it was an accident!"

"Oh, my fucking dear Lord and all His saints..."

"I know I messed up. I really know, I mean, I just realised that I'm just jeopardising everything, I... Fuck!"

"Okay... And now, what are you going to do?"

"Hum... Well, of course, I'm not gonna tell him, if it's what you want to know."

"You'd better not!"

"No, I mean... First, it was an accident. Second, as I said, I had a blackout when it happened. So, it shouldn't be that hard to hide..."

"I told you yesterday that going out with these two brainless things wouldn't be a good idea. Now, see how it went? Seriously, Charlotte... You cheated on him!"

"Clarisse, not that loud..." I told her to lower her voice as she was speaking loudly.

"I'm coming back home... I'm gonna kick your arse, seriously. You don't remember when Claire cheated on you with that guy? You didn't get the lesson the day it actually happened to you? When you were crying so hard that it took me days to make sure you wouldn't kill yourself or one of them!"

Well, I must admit that on that point, she was not wrong. She was actually right. I have been in that situation before, and I know what Florent may experience if he finds out what is going on. Because I know he is actually in love with me. Clarisse is right, I should have said no for that evening. I must acknowledge that it went too far. Okay... And, given her position, as Florent was one of her most valuable friends, yes, that was actually a pretty embarrassing position for her. Okay, well then...

"Okay, I get your point. And you're right..." I replied.

"Of course, I'm right! Okay... What's your plan now?"

"Well, I kind of assessed the situation and estimated that there are actually a very few chances that this information might leak, or he might be aware of. Hiding this, it's not gonna be a big deal. And, for now, except Claire, Kelly and Sophie, nobody knows. Oh, and now, you, of course. Florent is not friend with any of the populace in the College, so it should be okay to hide this."

"Jesus Christ... You 'assessed' the situation..."

"Of course, why do you think I am not actually crying right now?"

"Charlotte, seriously... This is all just strategies for you? Don't you feel a bit of guilt?"

Hum... Well, meh. I think the priority for me now is to cover that up the mess. On purpose to avoid this, guilt. Otherwise, it doesn't make any sense.

"Clarisse... This is not the moment!"

"Geez, you're a monster..."

"Okay, but right now there's an emergency. So, either you're by my side, whether... I tell you all to fuck off, and at least the solution will be swift."

"You wouldn't do that, Cha. We are much too valuable for you. But anyway, yes, of course, I'm here for you... So, what's your plan?"

"There's no plan. What did you do last night?"

"Well, I was with Marc, what do you think I was doing last night?"

"Here, at home?"

"Yeah, I don't see what it would change, actually, to your story..."

"Okay, so what we're gonna say is this... You were home with Marc. I was out with Sophie, and I stayed with her last night for some reasons. And... That's it. Nothing more happened."

"Yeah. Do you at least remember that you told him yesterday that I wanted to stay home all alone with my boyfriend!"

"I do, but in case I fail to be convincing, and in case he becomes suspicious, would you cover my arse?"

"Cha, you're my sister, I'll do everything for you!" Clarisse remained reassuring, despite the terrible news I was giving her.

"Good. Okay. So, I was with Sophie last night. And nothing happened."

"Yeah... Nothing happened."

I heard that the lift started working. Hum, well, something told me deep down that it would be here, since Florent told me he actually would be home for noon, and he was not. As I was still all alone in here, it might be him. Okay, then, it was time to wrap up, Clarisse. I have to make myself ready just in case.

"Besides that, is everything okay for you?" Clarisse continued whilst I was busy hearing that lift.

"Could be better, actually. You?"

"I'm good. I mean, how's your mood going today, since you're all alone at home?"

"I'm coping. But don't worry about me, I'll be okay!"

Let's be honest. I was not feeling well. No, right, I mean, it could be true that what I did last night affected me, but I feel like it was not only that. There's something else. I mean, no, I woke up, and I really feel like something is not right. And obviously, she felt what I think. So, yeah, the lift stopped at my floor. And I heard someone moving towards the flat's door. Yeah, I was actually right, it could be only one person, Florent. I mean, he was the only one that I was expecting now. Still sat in the bed, I now stood up.

"Well, Clarisse, I have to go, see you later!" I said, now in a rush.

I heard the key in the locker, and then the door opened seconds later.

"Why? What's going on?" she continued almost distraught.

"I love you, catch you later!" I hung up the phone.

So, he was here. It's the first time that I see him since yesterday morning. But he was late, this was surprising. He opened the door, and I went to the entrance, at least to show him I was also here. And yes, it was Florent. He had some shopping bags in his hand, I guess he went to get some food... Oh, shit, the list... I forgot.

Surprisingly, when he saw me, it was like he actually expected me not to be here. I think I made him the surprise of my presence, even if he knew I'd be here. He was all wet, I mean, I could hear that it was now raining outside. I assume that he carried all the stuff from the metro station to here. He had his oversized grey coat and, well, it was only after putting the bags on the floor, and it was after he saw me that he actually smiled at me and in return, I whispered a very tiny "hey". He even opened his coat... And touched his back, which means that the bags were heavy. There were actually three sacks, all full, I mean, he could have called me. He dropped them on the floor, and after we kind of saluted each other, whilst leaning against the door frame between the corridor and the entrance... I actually made him notify that...

"You could have called me for helping you with your bags. I mean, I wanted to go shopping now, but..."

"That's fine, I was on the way, and it's like heavy rain outside. I just thought about it and did it, so we don't have to go later. What's up, honey?"

"Fine, I mean, better than this morning."

"Yeah... Hangover, right? Did you make sure that you didn't throw up anywhere in the bedroom, so I am avoiding surprises?"

"No, I'm feeling better. Moreover, I slept like a log this afternoon."

"You're not gonna sleep tonight then!"

"No, I think I will, I'm still pretty tired, and honestly, I don't wanna do anything today."

At that very moment... Actually, well, I thought when I was in the metro this morning that after I woke up, I'd go to get some food for tonight, so at least this would lead me to Claire's house, as I had to get the bag I left yesterday. But I don't know if Claire's at home, I think she must be since it was late yesterday... On the other hand, unlike me, she's an early bird, and even if she sleeps one or two hours by night, she wakes up and feels like perfect and okay, ready to tackle the day ahead. I'm more of a night owl. Well, in many cases, I... I don't know yet, maybe I'll go later today, perhaps tomorrow, but I need an excuse to go there Either way. Because otherwise, he's gonna ask questions. Well, the justification can be "oh, you forgot something, and I need to go to get it, I'll be right back". That can be it. So, I helped him carrying bags towards the kitchen:

"Fine. Then we can stay at home and watch TV!"

"Yeah, I don't know. I more feel like I want to stay in bed, actually!"

"Fair enough!"

"I don't know, I'm not in my very best mood right now!"

He could see it, I guess. When he opened the fridge, he just looked at me, and I showed him a face which meant that's certainly not the day to piss me off. He didn't want to annoy me, sure, but... He knows me the day after a hangover, we've been drunk together several times, and the following day I am generally depressed, and I prefer staying home and doing nothing.

"Yeah, I can see this. You had a little nap? And you're not tipsy anymore?" he started putting the stuff in the fridge.

"No, I'm okay now. But I think I'm gonna stay away from alcohol for the rest of the week."

"I know that feeling. After a hard night, it takes me ages to recover."

Yeah, mostly that very last one...

"Yeah" I was checking what was inside a bag.

"Did you eat something since this morning?"

"No, I will. It's just that I feel it's not the right moment if you see what I mean."

"I know."

I don't know, it was heavy rain outside, and in the silent of the flat I could hear the water drops coming from the sky hitting extremely hard the floor of the small balcony, it almost made the noise of a waterfall. And, he was still unpacking the bags, looking for putting the items at their right place in the fridge. And I was thinking about what I may eat later because my stomach was calling for some food now. And Florent, yes, doing what I wanted to do. As mum consider that she's working for all of us (or at least for Clarisse and Florent, she believes me as relatively independent since I am the least obedient here), we established this system here; we need to participate in housekeeping activities. As we are not working full time like she does. So, in return of providing to this house an income, she wants us to do the cleaning, and she usually leaves a shopping list for the things we have to get. Yeah, we don't have any cleaning lady, and mum doesn't want one, she considers that having a cleaning lady will turn us – Clarisse and me – into lazy arses. Depending on how much we had, she decides on whether she refunds us or not. Florent is the only one to get refunded all the time since he's the only one to have less than a thousand on his bank account here. It depends on whether I am friendly with her or not, I am generally the one who pays all the time without being refunded. This to say, last year, she refunded me only twice on maybe ten times I went for shopping.

To be honest, as I said, since we have money, we are not actually really used to it. I could hire a cleaning lady, or even a driver, or a wealth assistant, but nope, I don't want to spend money on this, I consider that cleaning, driving and dealing with my money are things that I can do on my own. I actually prefer living my simple life, and I don't see the actual reason why I should change just because I have money now. I'm not that much of a spendthrift, I'm more selfish. For now, as I calculated, and as I am convinced, I will not have an exceptionally long life, I can spend my entire life without working. I don't want to have children, so there's no need for me to actually make sure that I'm gonna have a job and perpetuate my inheritance so my children will have money. Last time I checked; I could still clean my arse on my own. It's something that people don't understand sometimes, but for me, it's like, it's the way everything works. I don't want to change. Anyway, after removing the eggs from their packaging (yes, mum wants all the fridge packaging to be removed, since people in the supermarket do not wash their hands and mostly don't care about others' health, and she's scared of germs... Well, I gotta admit, she's not wrong on that), Florent looked at me, with one egg still in his hand:

"Are you sure you don't want a quick breakfast?"

"No, sweetheart. I appreciate that, but my stomach is not ready yet!"

"Fair enough."

That's really kind of him. No, he's really kind, sometimes. Really thoughtful, that's what I love, sometimes.

"Anyway, how was your evening?"

"Well, it was okay. I mean, you know, drinking, speaking... Girls stuff, gossips, and all that kind of stuff, you know," I restarted with conviction like it was normal.

"Oh. Did you sleep at your friend's place?"

"Yeah, I did. It's why I didn't actually sleep well, her mattress was as hard as a stone, it literally broke my back," I touched my back to make it more credible.

Sometimes, tiny details make the difference. Moreover, I spoke like everything was okay. I gave some details to make this more convincing and more credible. If you want to be a successful liar, make sure that you use small pieces in everything, as long as they are relevant. Not too many, but only the most pertinent. Otherwise, if you use little irrelevant details or worst, if you use too many extraneous details, it's gonna make your story the reverse effect, and it's gonna raise the suspicion around you. I know, it's terrible, but I must admit that this is the truth: everybody lies.

"Oh, I see..."

"And you, what about your evening?" I shifted his attention to himself as I made sure that all I could say regarding my party would be boring.

"Meh, I was at mum... Well, regarding eating, videogames, and YouTube, you know, nothing exciting!"

"And by YouTube, you actually mean... porn videos?"

"No, come on!"

"Alright then!"

For instance, when I asked him about porn, yes, he was actually lying. Many reasons tell me that: first, he is a guy. I know it's cliché, but I was not with him yesterday, so I assume it's a reason for him for doing stuff I wouldn't imagine him actually doing. Meh, he does whatever he wants, it's not my problem, I really don't care.

"So, finally, you went shopping?"

"Yes, of course. Your mother didn't plan to come back tonight, as she will go out with some of her colleagues and called me around twelve. And she told me by the way that she's upset with you because you're not at school, t's why she didn't want to talk to you. And Clarisse will stay in the evening with her boyfriend. So, I thought that as we could have the flat for us, we could have our evening."

"Okay, but don't expect anything from me tonight. But that means that we'll be only together tonight?"

"I know, but don't worry!"

"Fine then, if you want to cook, it works for me..."

"I know I won't expect anything from you, you look drained."

As he was now done with putting all the food in the fridge, he took all the bags to wrap them up for finally making a ball. And he threw them away. In between, I don't know, I was feeling like... Weird, actually. There was something on my mind, I felt like not okay at all. But yet again, as I use to do, hiding it, what's on my mind is anybody's concern in this house. After having thrown the bags, he looked at me, standing by the rubbish:

"Something's wrong with you, honey!"

"No, it's just... Don't worry, I am fine. I'm surviving in this world."

I gave him a little smile, and he came closer to me. As if he was concerned, he hugged me and kissed my forehead, whilst I put my head against his chest. I don't know, there was something weird in my mind, actually pulling me down right now. Maybe it was the fact of simply see him, I was feeling just down. I almost wanted to tell him, "don't touch me, stay away from me," but it won't make any sense if I do that. I will never get rid of my depression, that's a burden that I carry every day, and I do not complain about, because nobody cares whether I am okay or alive.

"And what are we going to eat tonight?" I simply asked whilst still in his arms.

"Oh, um... It is a kind of surprise!"

"Great..." I sighed.

Free Expensive Lies: Prologue

For a short moment, I could hear his heart beating, usually. I could hear him breathing, and I could also enjoy the silence of this apartment. I so appreciate that, the actual silence. Hearing the rain falling... It made me almost daydream, my real dream is to live in a remote place where it would be silent all the time. Where I could have only the necessary to survive, just a chair in my wooden-made house, a cover, and a chimney, where I could hear the fire. Just a good book in my hand, and the noise of the fire burning and heating me up. The book would be, something like an encyclopaedia, where I could learn things. Fiction? That's a colossal waste of time, come on! No Internet, no cell or smartphone, no TV, no laptop, nothing that contains electronic circuits that may connect me to the civilisation, just my chair, my book, the cover, and the chimney heating me up. And mostly, so far, the most important, I think... No human being living within the next two hundred miles around. I could easily survive, I mean, coming back to the basics, hunting and fishing, if I have to adapt myself, I could learn... Unfortunately for me, this dream is never gonna happen. And whilst I imagined the most perfect life for myself, I heard his chest vibrating slightly, and him then saying:

"It's okay now..."

"By the way, I wanted to ask you, erm..." I was now leaving his arms, seeking my words.

"By the way..." he actually started at the very same time of me.

We both looked at each other, face to face. Okay, what I wanted to ask was if he actually didn't forget my soap, if he went to the pharmacy, because... Since I am slightly anxious in my life and overthinking about problems I have, I sometimes have issues... well... To pee, and it irritates me. But he seemed to have something more important to tell me, so...

"Yes?" he asked.

"No, no... You first!" I told him.

"Come on, honey..."

"No, you first! Please!"

"No, my princess, you started, you finish. And then it will be my turn!"

"Well, did you go... To the pharmacy?"

"What for?"

Okay then. Well, I can understand, it must put him in an embarrassing situation, but there's no shame today. I mean, that's just a soap, it's not like he would go to get my pills or anything, it's just that it's quite essential for me. I don't wanna get infections or anything. Well, as I wanted to avoid saying the word, I used another way to actually ask him:

"It itches. And, you know the place I'm actually talking about!"

"Oh, your stuff?"

"Yeah, But... It's okay if you forgot, I mean, I can go to the pharmacy to get one. It's my mistake, I should have told you about that!"

"It's okay... I can go, give me just five minutes!"

"No, I will go. Because there are other things that you forgot, and I need to go to the supermarket to actually get it."

"Alright then... Fine."

"Now, you, what did you want to tell me?"

"Alright, then... Give me a couple of seconds!"

He gave me a light kiss and then went somewhere. According to the footsteps, it was to the living room.

I sat on a chair next to the kitchen table. And I was feeling like, yeah, okay. A bit better than earlier. I was now feeling kind of weak. Like, the black veil in front of my eyes... It's been since I am a teen that I actually think that. It's curious when I speak to Clarisse about that, she never experienced any of my symptoms. We've been consulting doctors and doctors about that, and they thought it was an iron deficiency, so they gave me medicines, and, well, it didn't actually make things better. Many blood tests showed that it was, yes, a part of low iron deficiency, it's why they gave me pills to balance the iron, but it didn't erase my main symptoms. Yeah, for instance, it's been years that I feel tired or have low motivation. So, my doctors explained this by my untreated depression. I pee a lot, even today (it's why I have this specific soap) because I am drinking a damn lot of water. For example, when I go to school, at least on an average day, I top up my small bottle at least five to seven times a day, and I still find it very odd since I'm not that much of an eater, and it happened that I spent days without eating and being hungry at all. Sometimes, when I stand up too fast, I feel weird, like dizzy for a couple of seconds, which is funny. It happened for the last time a couple of days ago. My psychiatrist thought that this would be linked to my depression and that I am a psychopath, but there was not enough medical proof.

Whilst he was away, I was actually relaxing by focusing on the droplets' sound and the little traffic noise, cars were passing by... I had my eyes closed, so I could again place myself in the house of my dreams. I really can't wait to go to bed, but it's not for now. Everything I wanted to do right now was to make my head totally empty, like a total vacuum. And this noise helped, it was crazy, I was almost feeling like, I was in the middle of the street, it was raining all around, I was all wet, but it didn't actually matter, and I was walking. I was just walking, in the footpath, and I heard someone running to me. Visualising it was so relieving, it calmed me down, and... And I opened my eyes. Florent. Standing in front of me.

"Baby?" he whispered.

I immediately opened my eyes, and the day seemed brighter than before. Yeah, I am drained.

"Huh? "I was startled.

"Yeah! You'd better go to bed!"

"Yeah, maybe later, I'll go there early tonight because I have to go to the pharmacy!"

"Can it wait until tomorrow?"

"No. Meh, it's okay, I want to move a bit. Going outside, I mean, I didn't go outside for like most of the day, I wanna be alone for a couple of minutes."

"Fair enough... Hum, honey..."

"Yeah?" I was looking at the window.

He started suddenly to kneel down in front of me, one leg towards me like he was a knight. I was like "Okay. Okay, okay... It must mean only one thing, and I am unsure if it is what he actually wants. First, I am eighteen, and thus not fully ready to get married. Second, he wants to have babies with me, and I made myself clear at several times that I do not want to have babies one day. Third, I am everything but stable. No, right, I mean, I love isolation because I am allergic to people, I am a pain in the arse, and I am aware of this. Forth, well, I have no friends and then have no idea who my wedding witness might be. Fifth... In the likely event of a divorce, I will have to split my thirty-two million with him, making only 16 million left. If he wants to marry me, I have to see a lawyer and discuss how I will keep my money safe as I do not wish to split nothing with anyone. Because I am the richest and, yet again, I may not care that I have money, I remain profoundly capitalist and not at all someone who shares. Imagine, even paying food for a homeless hurt me, so imagine me sharing all that... Impossible, it's gonna kill me! All this to say, we are ways too much different him and I, we do not have the same aspirations for living our lives... But he's been talking about making our relationship official for a while. Well, well, well... And sixth, my conversion into bisexual has not been fully completed yet.

And then, hidden in his right hand, a small black box, which he opened softly like it was a kind of magic. Inside, a really (I mean it, it was really awesome) beautiful ring, shining despite the relative darkness here... I saw many rings in my life, but never such a beautiful one. To be fair, no, I was really stunned when I saw it, I even whispered "Oh my fucking God..." straight when he showed me this... I am sure he must have paid this one quite a lot. It was totally set with tiny diamonds, all around the ring, and on the top of it, there was a small, dark blue... Actually, this, was totally unexpected, I must admit. I didn't think that he would do it one day, as I said, he was talking about that, but I didn't know he'd actually propose me! Anyway, as I said, saying yes or no would be a real big deal, at least for me given my situation, which is why, after having seen the surprise, I actually let him start speaking:

"Honey, I... now, it's a long moment that we're together. And I know it's a bit too early. But I don't care. Now, every day I wake up with you, in the same bed as you, every day that I live with you, there's only one thing I'd say... You know, it's... You're part of my life, and I want to show it to the world!" he was uncomfortable

Okay... Okay, okay, okay. He wants an answer now. And erm... So, it's why he's not so focused on being curious about what I have done yesterday evening. Usually, he's more interested, but now, no. He was planning that I could see it for a while, it's certainly been days that he's thinking about this. Two options were here for me: saying yes, and then accepting... this, I don't curiously see myself being divorced at 20, that would be actually weird if I meet someone after him and saying that I am twenty and divorced. Saying no, and... That would be the safest for me, but saying no will raise suspicions that he may have about me regarding whether I love him enough now... I know that if I say something like "I'm not ready now" would break him.

"Okay!" I actually pondered.

"So... I just want to formalise our union, our... and the fact that we are together, I just want to be with you every time, then, yeah, I just want to make sure that our love will last and..."

"Okay, okay, okay, all right..."

"What?" he actually saw my face.

"Things are not... That simple, actually," I remained pragmatic.

It is perchance the moment to dump him, what do you think? Hang on... No, that would satisfy Claire.

Free Expensive Lies: Prologue

Again, I was assessing what would be the outcome if I come to say no. If it comes to a no, things will lead eventually to our break up, that's sure. I mean... I don't want to hurt him, he doesn't deserve that, but he would be greatly disappointed, and I would totally understand why I'd undoubtedly be the same. That's not the only solution, I mean, he can ask me to become his fiancée, but we do not engage anything like a marriage within the next three or four years. Because I need to make sure he's the right person. Being his fiancée do not engage me into anything if we break up until then, and it would make things more official for both of us. More importantly, I think that's something that wouldn't actually be too much for me... I know someone who would heavily and tremendously be upset: Miss Claire Cobert. Oh my god, the day she will learn that news, she's gonna be mad. I can say yes, but it's under my terms, or it's nothing. He would accept it, and we would find a deal.

"Are they?" he became now timid.

"Okay... Now shut up and propose me formally what you want," I actually surprised him.

"Charlotte Taylor Allison Margaret Kominsky, would you accept to... Do you want to become my fiancée?"

"Meh... Fuck, let's do it, yeah!"

Oops, this is serious, I never thought he could remember all my names. Okay, now I said yes. Here I am, fiancée to him. Great. Here we are now, yeah.

Slowly, I approached him. He was still in front of me, kneeled, he was standing up, and I also stood up, because, yeah, it was the moment for the hug and all this. Ironically, and it's true, I didn't feel that much transcended, I was like, okay, he proposed to me. I will become his wife (only if he successfully passes the probationary period that I will establish in my terms), but it was not like... I am not even sure this is going to work. But let's see if it can make him happy, okay then. He took my face with my two hands like it was precious, and I kissed him. Well, let's say the fairy tales start, I mean, I cheated on him yesterday, I was so fucked up that I do not recall shit, but now we're gonna get married, it's on the way. Somehow, I was feeling like very sceptical, and for me, it's never gonna happen. I just said yes to please him. Because if I don't please him, he's gonna talk to Clarisse, Clarisse is gonna make me angry, I will feel like I am under pressure, because she likes him, and... Because Florent is incredibly determined, when he wants something, he's a bit like me on this, it doesn't matter the way he's gonna use to get it, but he will get it.

"But... If you want me to become your fiancée and someday your wife, there are conditions that you need to accept, otherwise... I won't do it."

"Whatever you want, love!"

"First of all, I'm okay to become your fiancée, but I don't want to engage any marriage procedures within the next five years. It's been only three months we are together; I understand you love me, but I'm barely eighteen, and I want to make sure you are the one I really want to get married with."

"The idea was actually..." he actually wasn't so sure regarding what I wanted.

"Yeah, I know what the idea was... The thing is, it's been only three months we have been together. And, whether you want it or not, you are still a big change in my life. Since you're a guy."

"Oh, I see... I didn't see things that way!"

"For the rest... Well, I want to keep my name, and in case it ever happens, you keep your name, and I keep mine!"

"Fair enough!"

"All right then, we have a deal!" I took him on my arms.

At that very moment, I was thinking, "what the hell is wrong with me?". Clarisse is also engaged with her boyfriend, it's been a while, but they adopted the same agreement as us for the same reasons. But I remember her the day she announced us (yeah, it was last summer, so I was still with Claire) that she said yes, she was thrilled, almost crying. I mean, I remember, the emotion was taut. Not for me, when she told me that, I was of course, incredibly happy for her, but now, at that moment, I do not feel like Clarisse when it happened. I feel like, yeah, it happened. Clarisse will undoubtedly be happy when I will tell her, but I do not feel like I want to party to celebrate this. Two things might explain this: first, I am still having my tremendous headache, and...

I think I'll take paracetamol or something because it's gonna kill me. Seriously. Second thing, well, that I know what I did last night. Things like this do not really affect me, I mean, as I still don't feel anything regarding this, I am like... Yeah. I think that must be because I am actually drained. I don't know for how long I had been sleeping last night, but if there's anything, it must be because of that. Florent looked disappointed. I actually didn't know what to say... But, yes, that's what I want. Maybe I am eighteen, but I am not naïve, I know that most marriages today end up in divorces, and I do not wish to file papers for divorce. Take me for an idiot if you want, but I prefer remaining pragmatic.

Free Expensive Lies: Prologue

I simply gave him my hand, and he took my ring finger. Now, the proof of love was here when he actually slid the ring very delicately... I don't know, I just looked at him doing that, and I said to myself, the ring is stunning. The colours, the diamonds... Okay, I'm not sure it would be real diamonds, but it was terrific. Even if there was almost no sun, it was shining, even if it was raining, it seemed like there was somewhere a sun shining. After he did that, now I had my very first ring around my fingers of my both hands (I do not wear jewellery), I just stood up, just as he did. And I gave him a kiss.

And after the kiss, the hug. At least, it was okay, I said yes, everything was okay. Now we were engaged, fair enough, everybody's gonna be happy. Between the "I love you" and deep breath sonata that was sounding before me, this moment was astonishingly fine to have. I love him, but... but whilst thinking, a new call disturbed that extraordinary moment we had with Florent. I left his arms, and checked the screen, as I took my phone with me and left it on the kitchen, and... Oh, as if it was the right moment. Florent saw that, and... Well, I took the phone, he sighed because he didn't like the name written on the phone. And I took the call:

"Yeah, what?" I was showing that it was not the right moment.

"Hey, darling, what's up?" Claire replied, as usual, in a fantastic way.

"Well, I must admit that the day started pretty well until I saw your name on my screen!"

"Ha, ha, really funny. So, where've you been? And speaking of the day starting, as a matter of fact, it's actually 4pm now."

"Yeah, well, a day can start at 4pm, no? And regarding where I have been, I've been hunting dragons, more or less."

"No, I'm talking about last night! We lost you at some point!"

Hopefully, I do not put my call noise very loud, because he was next to me, he was actually seated on the other chair next to me, on the other side of the table... Well, she couldn't know, on the other hand, but sometimes it actually looks like she does it on purpose. I almost wanted to say: "My dear Claire, could you do me a favour and shut the hell up?". Now, I have to find a pirouette to make sure that my secrets are not that exposed. Florent still thinks I have been out with Sophie, and only her. If he finds out I have been with Claire, he's gonna piss me off. And will tell my mother who's gonna do the same too.

"Okay, then be quick because I have my boyfriend next to me!" I pretended she actually wanted to tell me something important.

"Oh, okay, sorry, I mean, I didn't know he was here. Sorry, so yes... Erm, it's embarrassing, of course. Awkward."

"That is."

"I am dumb, sometimes, Cha..."

"In denial would be the more appropriate term, actually..."

"Bitch. Anyway, can you come to my place?"

"When?" I made a pretty short answer.

"At seven today."

"Why?"

"Oh, it's just that I need to see you. It's important. I mean, yeah."

"What could be that important?"

"You'll see if you come at seven. And take your swimsuit because we've opened the indoor swimming pool with Kelly ..."

"No, there's no need for that. I mean, I know there's pretty heavy rain, outside, but... You know..."

"We will swim a little! It could be good after what happened yesterday, right?"

"If you allow me to drown you, of course, yes."

"Yeah. As if you could."

"I'll see what I can do. See you later then!"

"No problem, baby, see you at seven!"

12 *It's a match!*

// *Towards Claire's home, Ivry-sur-Seine.*

// *Thursday, 10th of January 2013, 18:29.*

There are things I sometimes do not understand. Like... Maybe it comes from me, even if I went to consult some doctors regarding this... And even if it's pretty awkward to actually realise, but I do not enjoy sex. I mean... When I hear others talking about this, even my sister (and trust me, I know quite a lot about her dirty secrets), I do not feel anything about sex. For example, unlike many people I know, I never watched any porns (and I really don't understand why nobody believes me when I say that), I never did... the thing alone, and I never felt the need to try. And even with Claire, I never really enjoyed sex. She did, just like Florent does now, but, for me, it was just... Let them make me naked and having fun with me, whilst I was actually thinking about the things I have to do once they have done.

Free Expensive Lies: Prologue

Claire knows about this, we talked many times about that, and I insisted on telling her that it was not her, I was just made upside-down. Florent doesn't, and I prefer hiding this from him, because... because he's a man, and he may not understand what it actually means, he may think it's because of him, while it isn't. Nobody has ever had an explanation, and... What actually attracts me on a person is the beauty and the conversation—nothing else. Sex is the very last thing that may attract me.

Anyway, after Claire called, we went with Florent back in my bedroom, having some moments together. Now, I had to go and get my soap, but it was four, I actually could go later. We just watched some videos on YouTube, and I could feel that my eyes were pretty heavy. At some point... I told Florent that if I fall asleep, he can wake me up at six. But I was exhausted, I mean, I really lacked sleeping, and I needed to recover.

And when I woke up, at six, as Florent remembered what he had to do, I saw that he went actually back to the living room and was playing some games on the console. But he was totally in the dark. I just heard the TV's gunshots' noise, so I guessed he was maybe in the middle a war. But I heard him speaking... I mean, insulting and rude, so I assume that he was in a multiplayer session. Which is funny... I love insults in French because whenever French people are insulting you in French, it still sounds so romantic... it's the same for Italian people, in their tongue. It took me at least ten minutes to emerge. And it was all dark in the flat, whilst it was still heavy rain. I was supposed to meet her at seven, I had fifty minutes left. I might be like ten minutes late. Anyway, I woke up without making any noise, I checked on the wardrobe to get some heavy clothes and a pair of boots. And, yeah, whilst still being quite cold here because the heater was still not on, I actually walked towards the bathroom to get dressed. It took me a couple of minutes. There was actually nothing really unusual, I just took a top, one pullover, above which I took my blue sweater and a pair of jeans. And after peeing, getting dressed, peeing a second time, and wearing my boots, I finally went out of that bathroom. I took my coat, and I closed it, and my purple umbrella left in my office. It's when I was on my way out of the bedroom that I actually saw Florent, walking out of the living room:

"Hey honey, are you going out?"

"Yeah, I need to stop by the pharmacy... And erm, Clarisse sent me a text, she has to give me my works for tomorrow. You know, for school."

"Oh, okay. Will you be back soon?"

"I think so... It shouldn't be that long, I think. I mean, depends on Clarisse, you know her..."

"Yeah, she's a chatterbox!"

"Yeah, she is. Anyway, I'll text you when I am on my way back home! See you later, I love you!" I gave him a kiss when I was now about to leave.

I took my keys and my wallet, my badge, and I left. I actually saw him going to the kitchen. But... Damn, I told him many times to stop playing in the dark, like he does, he's gonna destroy his eyes. Meh, maybe someday, he will understand.

So, yeah, I left, I went downstairs, showed my badge, and I left. There was no wind, so it was okay, I could deploy my umbrella, it's not gonna break. I had my phone in my pocket, I didn't take my handbag, because it's quite late and it's not recommended as I am going to Claire's and using public transports, and my wallet in the other. But I was still freezing, I mean, it was icy out there, even if I were wearing clothes like I'd go to the north pole. Through the rain that was clapping over my umbrella, I walked outside, and the streets were quite busy. That was quite a good idea to wear my boots, it was protecting me to my knee, and yeah. One hand carrying the umbrella, the other in my pocket, I was progressing through the rainy streets.

Then, as usual, after crossing the big roundabout, I went to the metro, for the same journey as yesterday, towards Chateau de Vincennes, and changing in the Louvre, for taking after the seventh line towards Ivry, as I use to do when I go there. And at the very moment I arrived at the platform, my phone rang. My mother... Gosh, what does she want?

"Yes?" I actually got quite disturbed.

"Wow, always so welcoming!"

"What do you want, I've always been bad at greetings."

"Yeah! And even in being social..."

"Meh, I cannot be perfect on every point, right?"

"Yeah... How are you, honey?" she nicely asked.

"My psychiatrist told me to never discuss that with strangers..." I actually made fun of her.

"Strangers... Wow, that's nice. Well, on the other hand, the last time you called me 'mum' was maybe three years ago."

"And I also told you that same minute to get used to it. And you, what's up?"

"As if you cared about..."

"I obviously don't, yeah, that's true, but it's just because... I was looking for something since I don't really want to talk to you! I was trying to be nice..."

"Try harder, you may get results!"

"Yeah, I'll think about this!"

"Well, I shouldn't have called you!" she started complaining.

"Yeah, indeed, it's true, you shouldn't have..."

"As I know, you were out yesterday, and since I assume that... somehow, you were with your dear friend Claire Cobert..."

"Of course, I did, what did you expect!"

"Anyway, I called you today to tell you... Actually, to congratulate you, I am pleased that you got engaged. Florent is a good guy, and I trust you guys will be happy."

"Meh. We'll see. Maybe it will work, maybe it won't, I have no idea."

"At least he's a wonderful guy that will put you on the right track."

It's odd, she can be such a twat sometimes. I don't see where being with him will make me a better person than... any goddamn heterosexual. It's actually why... After having shut up for a couple of seconds because I was thinking... She must know that it's when I don't say nothing for a short time that something insulting is on the way. It's why I actually replied, being very calm that time, that...

"Yeah, being with guys will put me on the right track! And according to the fact that you're nearly forty and still on a dating app because you're still alone in your bed, I assume it really worked out well for you then!"

And it worked, she actually didn't know what to reply. It's why she was now thinking. And then said:

"It's why I want it to work for you," she was actually more brilliant than I thought.

"I am a tremendous pain in the arse that do not want to be here just to cook food for some moron, and you think it might work out well for me? Impossible. At least, Claire knew what I wanted. Florent, it's still his trial period."

"Trial period. Yeah. I really wish he'd never know what you're telling me."

"Well... Actually, me neither. That's really mean."

"Well, darling, you are who you are, and I assume that... Since you became worse after you broke up with, erm... Her, I think it may take time!"

"I don't know."

"That's gonna take time, it's sure. And I will be immensely proud of you."

"No, this is rubbish."

"What is rubbish?"

"You're not proud of me, you don't care about me. You don't care about me, since I am who I am, as you say, you don't really care."

"Charlotte, you are my daughter, and you can trust me, I'd do anything for you! Whoever you are, whatever happens to you, I'll always be there for you."

"Yeah. Okay, I gotta go," I really didn't want to break her heart. "See you later."

"Honey?"

Yeah, it was becoming too emotional, so I hung up the phone straight away. It was time to get out. Honestly, it's curious, it's not that I hate her, I just want to break the ties we have together. I want a break between us. Why? Because both of us cannot cope with the other's lifestyle. I want her to be my friend because maybe she loves me as a daughter, but I cannot love her as my mother. I want her to stop being so patronising and admitting her faults and apologising for this. We actually both want the very same thing, except that... None of us wants to give in. It's why this situation will never end.

Anyway, after my usual forty-five minutes journey through the metro, I arrived, and even though it was still heavy rain, I was feeling different. Except for my bag, that she could have brought back tomorrow, what was so important that I needed to come? It's okay, I mean, going there, I'd rather be home instead of walking under that heavy rain. I really hope that this is not crap, but Either way, I do not plan to extend myself here anyway. If she made me travel through Paris a rainy night to see me for some bollocks, I swear to god, she's not gonna like it. Anyway, I opened my umbrella when I was outside, but I was careful as it was windy. And my headache was still here, even if I took a paracetamol. And while walking through the rain, I had this weird hunch, the same I had yesterday: something told me that going to her house would be a mistake. A couple of minutes later, I arrived on the step of her door, and I was completely wet, cold as well, and I wanted to be really brief with her. But something tells me that I'm not gonna like what she's gonna tell me.

I knocked at her door, three times, quite loudly, and I folded my umbrella. Because what I could hear was corrupted by the showers' noise falling and the loud music coming from the inside and loud laughs also. Suddenly, a very first thunderstorm banged through the sky. Come on, hurry up! After I knocked another three times, I heard the laughs stopping, and her turning her key in the lock, for finally opening. Obviously... Well, as I said, I shouldn't have come: she was wearing just her pink and red bikini. What crazy mind would open an indoor swimming pool right now... In January? Jesus Christ. Even though seeing her like this, and obviously opening the door since she wasn't wearing anything else, but this made her quite cold for a few minutes, I told myself, stop being weak in front of her. It's nothing. Anyway, once she opened the door and slightly got cold for a minute, she just smiled at me, but I felt like it was not real, it was really nervous:

"Hi, Charlotte!"

"Hi, you idiot!" I treated her with the contempt she deserved.

"How are you doing today? I mean, you wanna come in?"

"Meh... I must admit that seeing you freezing your damn arse is quite pleasant, do you mind if I stay here for a few?"

"Come on in, I'm gonna catch the flu!" she actually grabbed me by the coat.

The flu is a nasty word for her. Last January, she caught it, and she was so sick that I even carried her to the shower to wash. Yet, she still doesn't get the jab. And after, I am the idiot. After she dragged me inside her home, she immediately closed the door, but she acted really weird, I mean like someone was actually watching her. It's really unusual seeing her that way, something was stressing her out. I threw my umbrella under the coats, at their regular place, but I didn't want to remove mine, I don't have time for her tonight. However, I still opened my coat because now I was hot, she turned on the heater and honestly, there was a real difference in temperature between outside and inside. And she looked at me:

"Hum... Do you want to get upstairs, I mean, if you want to come with us to the swimming pool?"

"No, Claire, that would have been with pleasure, but I don't really have time."

"Oh, really? It's not gonna take long..."

"No, Claire, I am sick, because of yesterday, I don't think swimming would be a great idea."

"Oh. Okay, then!"

"Yeah. Hum, did you see my bag? Because I came for picking up that."

"Yeah, I actually put it upstairs, in my bedroom. Oh, I didn't see, that's a nice ring that you have, over here!" she actually took my hand.

"Oh. Oh, yeah, I forgot to tell you. Florent and I got engaged."

"Erm... What? You guys... got... Engaged?" she actually turned white, and suddenly let my hand go.

Yeah, geez... how can I forget to tell you such a thing?

Yeah, I was sure this wouldn't be some news she'd actually welcome. Mostly since she actually wanted to marry me. It is still not possible for now, but one good thing I even think about the new President Francois Hollande is that he wished gay marriage to be voted in parliament whenever he was running for president. He got elected last May, and the next day (as he promised the bill to be voted soon), Claire proposed the idea that we could actually get married, and she would propose me the day the bill to be adopted. Yet the bill has not been voted, there are still protests everywhere because of homophobic morons just like my mum with their corrupt family values... But I am sure the bill will pass. Unfortunately for her, things are going to be different that day.

After having obviously felt really disappointed... She just started, with a very tiny voice:

"Well, congrats..."

"Okay... My bag is in your room upstairs, right? I'm gonna get it," it was really awkward.

Let's cut the crap. I was like, she may or may not enjoy that, I had to get my bag and get out, that was the primary mission for which I came today. Anyway, her room is upstairs, the swimming pool is where the garage used to be but has been refurbished and transformed into a pool. But first, I went to her room upstairs to collect what I had to collect, while she went back to join her dear Kelly that I didn't see. Once upstairs, I walked towards her door, pushed, and I turned on the light. And the thing I love in her bedroom is this when it's rainy, we can hear the rain coming banging in the roof, and all that was held as a long and peaceful repeated music just like it was now. I really wish I have this in my home, but I'm trapped in that flat. It can be weird, but I love this noise, I feel like it's reassuring. It's peaceful. When I was a child, I had the same on my bedroom as it was also under a roof, it made me sleepy. Yeah, childhood memories, whatever your life is, there will always be something that will hold you to your past.

Her bedroom is not big, but Claire loves painting. Her room is more or less converted into a kind of painting workshop. In front of the door, she has her bed on the right side, close to her little window. Well, upon entering the room, you actually arrive on the right side. The rest of the room is dedicated to her work. That has always been her passion, and she spends hours painting. Honestly, she has a real talent for this, and if she keeps on doing what she does, I am sure she will become a great painter someday. Astonishingly, she doesn't have that much furniture in her bedroom except her bed and her wardrobe. She doesn't even have a bedside lamp, she used to leave all her stuff on the floor. Her wardrobe is on the left side, right upon entering, next to the switch and the door; it contains three doors, but they are all closed. In front of the window, her painting easel on which was put a quite big canvas. I don't really know what she was painting, since it's pretty hard to guess what her painting would become when she starts it.

Alongside the opposite wall to her bed's wall, all her painting stuff dropped on the floor. Some of her paintings that she actually finished, but... Nothing personal. Claire gives a lot of her time to her work, unfortunately, less now since she's under Kelly's influence, but she used to be very prolific. Her bedroom is a kind of vestige of the personality she used to be. She didn't really care about social stuff, she didn't really care about many things when we were together. What mattered to her was her paintings, because somehow, Claire doesn't care about quite a lot of things, but unlike me, she doesn't show it. It's why we have so much in common until she completely switched to become who she is now. Her father was a soldier who has been killed on duty, and her mother works a lot, certainly much more than mine, which is why she is not often here, at home, as she works in hospitals, she's a nurse. Yeah, she grew up in this house, and she said that she'd never leave here.

It's actually pretty sad to enter her space since there's no personality in here. I mean, she still keeps one of her father's tee-shirts when she sleeps, but yeah, she has a temperament, mostly reflected in her paintings. You need to be quite clever to find out what she really believes and how she really feels, even if now she wants to appear like an idiot, she's everything but an idiot. On the wall on top of her bed, there's the decoration earned by her father (he was major) granted by the army and the government for the accomplished mission he did, and ultimately there's the *Légion d'Honneur* that he had posthumously because he died for the country. All these are suspended by adhesive tape on the wall. Yeah, we've been sleeping together several times, and all the time she used to have her father's shirt with her. Otherwise, she cannot sleep. Today, she doesn't really remember her dad, except some pictures she has (and she looks like him), but she is really proud of him and, yeah. She always said that growing up without a dad is something odd, someone is missing. But, as she said, he died for the country. Or... he died for their countries.

I didn't stay that long in her bedroom. I don't like that place. One of the last times I came here was to find out that she cheated on me. Like me, she was drunk because we had a fight (because of Kelly) and slept with the first guy she met. Unfortunately, she did it at her home, doesn't remember anything, and I came the following morning whilst they were still here. She said that it was a mistake many times, and something told me to believe her, it would have been a mistake, but the error was still made, and as Kelly was behind everything, it ended seven years of relationship. It's why, when I say that I hate that Kelly, it's true. But that bitch is surviving thanks to Clarisse because I was ready to pay someone, to set a reward for her head. But if Kelly disappeared, it would have led me to big troubles, and I would have lost Claire for sure.

I took my bag and went downstairs next to the stairs. And I was hearing them both chatting. Once downstairs, I saw that they were both sat on the edge of the pool. Some dimmed lights illuminated the veranda to bring a sort of yellow sunlight, somehow contrasting from the dark night outside, accompanied by the clicking noise of the rain that was undoubtedly louder than upstairs. Both of them were already drinking something – as if yesterday wasn't enough – and when they saw me, they were almost about to propose something. The heater was on in the veranda – it's also why it was so hot – and it almost blurred the veranda windows because of the fogging. Curiously, Sophie was not here. It was just Kelly and Claire, Kelly wearing a one-piece black swimsuit. As always, she looked pathetic. I don't think Kelly is gonna swim, given that unlike Claire, her face is covered with makeup. When I came, I actually put my bag on the floor, next to Claire and far away from Kelly, and I sat on it.

"Here I am!" I said while seating.

"Here you are!" Claire noticed my arrival.

"Alright, then, what's up? What time did you come back home yesterday?" I continued.

"Well... What time did we come back home?" Claire asked Kelly.

"I don't remember..." Kelly replied.

"Fine. Has any of you seen my sister today at school?" I asked.

"No! We were too tired to go there!" Kelly softly retorted.

"Oh, were you?" I acted as if it was surprising even if it was not, "For my part, I came back home a bit late this morning. That was quite annoying..."

"Yeah! Yeah, we learned that!" Claire actually continued.

"Apparently, Christian and you..." Kelly giggled.

"Oh, so Christian was his name? Meh... Anyway, if I hear any of you talking about what happened that night to whoever, I swear that... Yeah, I will make you dig your own graves for so I can throw your dead bodies after, is that clear?"

"Still, that was surprising... And fun" Claire argued.

"Especially you," I looked at Kelly.

"Don't worry, you don't have to fear us," my ex concluded. "Anyway, did you have a good day, Charlotte?"

"Well, I came back home, did my stuff, slept, saw my boyfriend, slept again. Even now, I'm still pretty tired."

"After the night you had, it does make sense, yeah. You've never been that drunk!"

"I know, it's gonna take me days to recover from that. But still, I came back home alive, that's the most important I guess..."

"Actually, she's a cunt with us, she hates all of us, treats us like shit and like being isolated, but damn... She knows how to party! I mean, from what I heard last night..." Kelly actually looked at the water.

And what did that piece of work hear exactly last night? Be specific, I mean when we talk shit about people, we better know what we mean. She mentioned that she heard something from someone. So that is actually quite interesting because when she says something like this, it means that someone told her something about me. More likely, some private information. If Claire knows my dirty secret, I may have a chance to keep it secret. But if she knows something... Okay, she is not really a danger, I mean, she doesn't know anything about my boyfriend... I mean fiancé now, but still, she has a significant influence within the school and since guys love gossips such as "she slept with him or her when she was drunk" ... Let's find out, let's make her talk.

"You heard stuff, you said? Tell me more about this!" I quizzed her.

"Wait, did you really blackout?" Claire wanted to make sure something.

"That's not the point..." I wanted to start.

"No, that is the point..." but she interrupted.

"Yeah, but I'm not talking to you, I'm talking to that wicked bitch next to you: what did you hear, and from whom did you hear shit?" I regained control of that conversation.

"Someday, you'll regret insulting me, trust me..." Kelly seemed quite inspired saying that.

"I don't think I'll regret anything, it's always a pleasure!" I smiled at her.

"Yeah... We'll see that sooner or later..."

"So, anyway, talk: what did you hear and from whom?"

"Because you really think I will tell you? Charlotte, if you want something, either you are a little nicer with me, whether you can go away!"

"Be really careful, Kelly... If you retain information, whatever it is, you may hurt yourself!"

"Is that threats?" Kelly looked at me, for once, not amazed at all.

We actually glared at each other, and it was like... Perchance, all the hate and the contempt of the world was in both our sights. And the fact that she was speaking calmly indicated something: she was actually really nervous, but on the other hand, she knew something that I needed to know. I could see that my lips were tights, and my jaws were closed, but she just looked at me like... And Claire actually intervened:

"Okay, ladies, let's relax! Kelly, stop it, you don't see she's provoking you? And you, Charlotte, stop acting like a cunt with her."

"I'll take it easy when she stops being a cunt..." Kelly stopped looking at me and lowered her head. "I really don't understand why she hates me that much..."

"Right, yeah, keep on acting like a naïve idiot. When you grow up, you'll understand," I muttered.

"THAT'S ENOUGH!" This time, Claire yelled at us.

When Claire yelled, we actually remained quiet for a couple of seconds, and all looked at each other. Kelly is definitely hiding something, as, when I am mean to her, she turns that into a game. She always sneaks out of that situation by acting like an idiot so I can have more fun of her, facing me up is not something she does. It means, there's something wrong. But today, no, she's provoking me. Saying that I would regret insulting her is not something she usually says; instead, she is playing fools when I insult her. There must be something, I mean... It's been several months I know her, she never, ever, acted that way.

Moreover, something was really wrong today, as I said, Claire was annoyed when I arrived, I mean... she was embarrassed by something. I could feel it, and she was trying to hide it, but it was apparent. Her body language is the thing that betrays her the most. And now, she yelled. Claire usually yells when she is under pressure; otherwise, she never does that. That is really curious. If I want to find out what is wrong, I shouldn't put it straight. Kelly was actually happy, and Claire was not. I am sure it must be linked to the vital thing Claire wanted to talk to me about when I was on the phone with her earlier. I preferred looking for another approach:

"Hey, what's up with you?" I actually touched Claire's shoulder to tell her to relax.

"Nothing, I'm not really in my mood today. So, relax, and erm... Stop seeking problems because there are none," she was pondering.

"Okay, then. Fine."

Astonishingly, she looked at me but made sure Kelly wouldn't. And her eyes were red, she was holding her tears. She did so in a way like, I did something wrong. Two theories: either it's the fact that I announced to her that I got engaged with Florent since she really wanted us to get married, affecting her. Okay, that was amusing, informing her of that, so at least she could get pissed, but I didn't want to reach that point. Annoy her to make sure she would react, yes. That could be it. Problem: I didn't announce that by phone, I told her when she saw the ring, and she didn't look at my ring a single second since I am back from upstairs. If it would be it, she would be staring at my ring and would have told me to come with her in an isolated place, where we couldn't be heard, so she would speak to me. And another problem: she was already sad when I arrived. Which leads me to the second theory.

It could be something else. The question, what could it be? Let's consider what I have from now: she is pissed and now about to cry, and Kelly's reaction. Kelly was actually pretty happy now, she didn't seem that much annoyed or disturbed by the fact that her best friend was not right today, and she provoked me. It's something that Claire cannot talk about. So, I am looking for something that makes Kelly proud, but that really annoys Claire, at the point to almost make her cry. It can be a million things. I need to know, now, which is why, Claire was affected, I needed to know what her problem was, no matter what it would cost:

"Claire, talk to me!"

"She's okay, don't worry..." Kelly was actually amazed.

"Kelly, that's my last warning, you should shut the fuck up," I coldly reacted. "What's wrong, Claire?"

"I'm alright."

"You're not."

"I just had a bad day, that's it."

"What bad day? What happened?"

"Nothing!"

"Claire, it's been seven years that I know you! And I know when you're lying or are hiding something from me. So, if there's a problem, I want to know it now."

This was actually the very last warning for her, and also the last opportunity that she would have to speak. If it's something personal, her usual reaction after I said this would be "let's go somewhere, I need to talk", because it would be private, and Claire still holds some secrets from Kelly. She has no secrets from me. After a few moments, after she actually turned her face to me, always hiding from Kelly, and she started sniffing. She gave me a wink, which seemed more a loving signal than anything else, I didn't really understand why. Yet, she was not crying. And, in her turn, coldly replied:

"Nothing that concerns you, Cha!"

"I want to know."

"Charlotte, please bear in mind that since the last 18th of August, you are no longer my girlfriend. And you're annoying me to attack Kelly all the time!"

"Yes, but it doesn't matter to me, it's just that..."

"Okay, you want to know the final word on how we know that you slept with Christian? Because you're gonna piss us off until then!" she interrupted me and made me refocus on the first issue I had with Kelly.

"Is that the reason why you called me this afternoon to tell me you apparently had to see me because there was something important?"

"Yeah, it is. Open your bag!"

"What bag... My bag? This bag?" I showed the bag I came to pick up upon which I was still sat.

"Yeah, this one, yeah!"

At that very moment, at the moment she pronounced her last sentence, she made her lips moving. She knows that I know how to read on her lips. She first said my full name, "Charlotte", and then, with her blushed face and her eyes that were red, the fact that her hand was holding her forehead, and then added, "I am so sorry". I actually understood that she was ashamed of something.

I immediately took over the bag that was under me. And when I took it, actually, I heard something folding in it, like... It wasn't my clothes. There was supposed to be only my clothes in that bag. I took it and opened it, as it was closed by a zipper. Maybe she slid it into it, but there was a small white envelope that wasn't here yesterday hidden under my shoes. I looked at Claire, and she seemed really down at that moment, I heard her starting sobbing, but she still contained her tears. She knew what was inside the envelope, that's sure. Whatever it is, I don't think I'm gonna like what the envelope contains. As I said, it was white, small, but seemed slightly thick (but not rigid), there was like... I don't know, some kind of notes inside, tiny papers, all piled one above another, and where the address was supposed to be written, there was instead a big "CHARLOTTE" handwritten. My name was written in uppercase letters, with unknown writing to me, perhaps the one of a guy, using a black pen. Now, the question, what the hell was this. I took it out of my bag, merely looking at Claire, still holding her head and appeared apparently overwhelmed by the situation, and asked:

"What the hell is it?" I asked, intrigued.

"Open! It's from Christian, your very first gift," Kelly really enjoyed that situation.

I wasn't waiting for any gifts from him. So, I tore the top of the envelope as it was sealed, and without looking at its content, I simply put my hand in, while still looking at Kelly, to check what was inside. And, actually, at the very moment that I touched... It felt like a weird pile of paper, that looked like notes, I mean banknotes. And then I saw what it was: ten fifty euros banknotes. From Christian, the guy with whom I slept. Thus, five hundred euros. Which means... That either this is a joke, but a nasty one, like the kind I'd be able to do to really offend someone, or either... And then I recalled Sophie, what she told me yesterday evening, about Kelly that slept for money. And the reaction of Claire, why she is so ashamed and overwhelmed right now. Oh, gosh... Don't tell me this wasn't a joke...

"Oh my... To be honest, I really hope... I sincerely hope that this is a joke!" I was now upset.

"Joking? You earned that money, Charlotte!" Kelly smiled, certainly savouring her victory.

"You'd better give me a damn explanation about this."

"Cha, yesterday... It was your initiation! Come on, you still don't know that Claire and I are doing that for months? It's okay, I understand it might shock you, it was the same for me, but... Come on, that's so fun!"

"You guys are doing... prostitution?"

"That's not 'prostitution'... That's just services, easy money! And so much fun!"

How comes she could hide this for me... Okay, yes, I was now feeling filthy, but my feelings are not something that I show. So, I preferred hurting deep down, so... He thought I was a prostitute, there must be a big misunderstanding. It's... Yeah. But I don't know what actually shocked me the most: this, me getting insulted by that, Kelly in total denial for that, or Claire... I really hope she's kidding for Claire. I really hope so.

"Claire, please, don't tell me you're doing that. Tell me she's joking..."

She didn't even reply. Instead, she has done yes with her head, her hands covering her face. From that moment, a wave of massive anger suddenly rose within, my muscles got tensed, and I felt like I wanted to break something. First of all, I have been humiliated, ridiculed by the wickedest thing that can knock out my integrity. It's me, I have been really offended, I actually slept this guy, and he thought I was a damn whore. I just looked at Kelly, and there are a thousand scenarios that came to my mind involving me and her death. My jaws were so closed, my muscles so tense, I certainly became red, and I started to see red and hear my heart beating.

There was actually nothing right now, but a tremendous fury. I was just feeling nothing that the need to break something or hitting her. But now, if I get overwhelmed by my rage, and if I actually do hit her, because she is in the most potent situation, she might reveal everything and starting to contain that secret, it's gonna be huge. She's gonna use it against me. So, I just looked at her... What I need to do is make her disappear. I need her to get kidnapped or something. I can do it, Florent knows some people who know people and pay someone to get rid of her. I must play this in a tricky way, but I must act fast. But Kelly must disappear. I was like, I will find a way to get finally rid of you, cunt! And Claire... She let her do that, she was her puppet yesterday, everything was calculated... Oh my...

"Well, congrats, Claire. Your father must be proud of you!" I spoke whilst being really mad.

"That's not funny, Charlotte," she was speaking with her hand in front of her face.

I was still feeling my fury taking me, and my heart was beating so fast that it couldn't contain anything when I looked at that envelope. So, the party of yesterday was actually organised. I mean, that could be the only explanation, since I remember that we went to that nightclub, the place I met that guy, and we went there because Kelly received a text and... Geez, I can't realise that bitch won the battle. She's not gonna win the war, though. Claire was in there; she's been used as a puppet. Maybe Claire wanted to have a real party with us, have some good times, perhaps this was just a trap, but... I need to get an explanation from her. But Kelly, she was contacted by this idiot, and she did it anyway, she pushed me into his arms or managed to make sure that something would happen... Geez, that's... Okay, I was really pissed now, because first I have been a whore. But what made me more upset was that I have been trapped by Kelly, the lowest form of human this mankind ever created. Because it's sure, if I slept with this guy, it means that something happened. It means that there must have been a deal, and Kelly wanted to get something from me. She fooled me around. And now, she's gonna pay the hefty price. Because unlike her, I can hit hard, and I won't let such a game pass before me without fighting.

"Okay then..." I just said, still with the money in my hands.

"Charlotte, please, don't take it wrong! It's just... I know that you don't need that money, because you're already millionaire, but come on," Kelly was trying to develop a new idea.

"Hum, yeah, tell me more?" I actually wanted to see how far she'd go.

"It's just for fun! I mean, it's just getting free money, free parties, free alcohol, it's why we are doing this with Claire! You cannot imagine how much money we earned thanks to that! And we know the people we do that with, you can't imagine how much people we know now! It's not brainless students that we have, we know many influent people! I mean, that's really useful for us!"

"Kelly... If I got what you said right... Are you asking me to join you?"

"Yeah! Come on, it's just for fun!" she was actually serious.

"Fuck you. Fuck the both of you, actually," I stood up and left.

13 *Deal or no deal?*

// On my way back home, in the metro.

// Thursday, 10th of January 2013, 20:50.

It was late, and I think it was definitely enough for today. What I actually learned; it was peculiar. I felt like everything changed, I mean, okay, I can survive after I got insulted. This is collateral damage. But now, I understood that I was at war with Kelly. I wasn't even aware that I was at war with her. I mean, I didn't like her, I never liked her, but I never attacked her in such a way. She actually successfully fooled me. I can be at war with her, it's okay for me. I have nothing to lose, but she has a lot to lose. The thing is, for making sure she would take a great leap, she secured Claire. She has her, as a great asset, and she knows that she'd use that against me. I have to make sure that Claire is safe before attacking her. And when I start my attacks... I will dismantle her. I will crush her. I will collapse her; I will simply but forcefully wipe her out. I'll make sure she would never survive to that. When mum used to say that revenge is a fabulous dish best served cold, I must admit that she wasn't wrong.

After the revelation, I just left. I didn't even say goodbye to anyone. I actually went away as fast as I could, as if I were hunted by zombies or something like this. On the other hand, Claire was feeling so bad when she understood the seriousness of this. I'll try to call her later, check her out. I was really feeling weird, I didn't know what to think. Everything was just totally unexpected, finding out such a thing, it was really the very last thing I'd expect, to be fair. What may I say, what may I think? Claire is obviously not really proud of this, she never wanted that. I don't know, I was a bit confused when I left. But now, Kelly has an incredible power on me, because she knows what I have done, and can exploit this against me. And if it comes to emerge that I whored out one night, well, at school, it will be funny; I'm sure I'll become the target of harassment from everybody, as I am not really loved at school. I can survive this; I'm simply scared of myself.

On the way back, I took my phone in the metro, plugged my headphones, and listened to some music for relaxing, but I actually didn't listen. I may be Claire; I'd be crying right now. The problem, I cannot cry. I really wanted to get Christian's phone number to call him and insult him, but things are already messed up, it was not the moment to make things worse. And ironically, I was mad, yeah, but not that upset. And I was thinking, actually, should it be a good idea to call Claire right now? I'm not sure this would be a great idea since Kelly should still be there. At least, when I left, she was still here. Moreover, I don't know, Claire lied to me, and even if it's true, everybody lies, Claire lying to me is actually something that I would not imagine one day. Especially about that, it's not hiding something insignificant, it's big. When I changed the metro, when I took my line for going back home, whilst walking through the corridors, I finally decided what would be my next move: not contacting Claire or Kelly and leaving things as they are. Nothing happened. If they want to seek me, they know where to find me. Because if I make the first move, it's like... You see, I am looking for something. It's better to let Kelly enjoy her victory for now.

This journey was actually pretty long. Besides the shock of the discovery, well... and obviously the insult I got, well... I was just listening to some music to relax. Because if I come back home nervous, I know that Florent will be suspicious. And he thinks that I am with Clarisse, if I tell him that we had an argument, he will try to find out what happened, and I really want to avoid this. Because he's gonna question my sister, and my sister will act weird, so he will understand that this is just rubbish. When I am upset, I usually listen to classical music. Actually, I used to listen to classical music a lot, I love this, and I have a vast preference for Mozart. I don't know, it's weird, maybe I am funny, but sometimes I feel like his music speaks. Like, when I am very pissed, I used to listen to the 38th symphony, called "Prague" – maybe not his most famous but one of my favourites – and I am feeling literally different. It switches my mood. It makes me feel like, meh, nothing really matters. Also works with the 20th piano concerto or the 24th. It's like, I don't know, it's like him talking straight to you and telling you, "that's life, you know"—no wonder why we call this guy a genius. No, Mozart is my favourite. I also like Beethoven and Bach, but their music seems too complicated for me. And, I am not really a fan of metal, unlike Beethoven.

However, don't get me wrong, I also enjoy all kind of music. I love classical music… it's not a type of music that I am looking for, but more the melody. For instance, I am not a fan of metal, but I like some metal bands. The only kind I really dislike is rap (again, except some of them like Tupac) but I mostly hate rap. Especially French rap, that's a crime against music.

On the other hand, I am mostly neophobic (it means that I hate what is new or seems unfamiliar to me) and it generally takes me time to get used to something new. My neophobia applies in many things in my life, like food also, and it's something odd. Or technologies. Sometimes, that's a problem when people come to me and ask me "oh, did you hear the latest thing of her?" or "did you see the latest film…?". Unusually, I go to the cinema, for example. Because, generally, I don't really know what to watch. And not knowing is the thing that scares me the most in my life. Last time I went to the cinema, it was for Avengers last April.

Anyway, when I arrived, I went to the pharmacy (because I had to), and still under that heavy rain that didn't seem to actually end, all wet, since I realised that I left my umbrella at Claire's place, I then walked back home. Man, it's gonna take ages to dry everything.

When I came in, everything was quiet in the flat. I opened the door, and I heard a kind of background music, like classical music. Again… But it was not something I knew; it was mostly something quite jazzy. It was not that loud, though. I was surprised because Florent doesn't like that kind of music. Yeah, everything is actually fucked up today, I really need to sleep. Florent is weird, Claire is funny, the next plausible thing that may happen to me tonight is that a dragon comes to attack me, or I may break one of my legs. I dropped my keys in the entrance, all wet, so wet that I think I'm gonna need to mop the floor to avoid it to be slippery, in the little basket, and the first thing I did was to remove my boots and leave them in the entrance. Then I went to my bedroom, then to my bathroom, to remove my coat and my jeans, obviously whilst taking off my wallet and my phone, and I hung both of them on the towel radiator. Again, I peed after, my bladder almost couldn't contain itself. Hopefully, my sweater was not wet, and I found some old pants that Florent left here. I had nothing else, so I wore it. I dried my hairs in the bathtub... And all the water that was there made like an odd big noise when it fell on the tub, I was like, man, how comes my hair could contain so much water?

And then I went back to the living room door, as Florent was still in there. He was still playing his game that he bought recently... And curiously was fighting with a dragon this time. When I actually leaned against the door frame, he paused his game and looked at me:

"Oh, hey, honey!"

I smiled. Now, I was more relaxed; but famished as I could smell that he actually cooked something. And I was very thirsty, I mean, it's been since I left for Claire's house that I didn't drink. Since he loves my console, at least I know where he is when I am not here. I slowly entered the living room.

"What's up?" I said, exhausted.

"I'm alright." He dropped the controller on the table.

"How are your eyes going?"

"Well... Fine, yeah. I need to get glasses."

"Ha, told ya!" I smiled.

"Your mum texted me. And I completely forgot this. Do you remember she wants to introduce her new collection to her guests? I'm not sure she said it was on the 16th of January. She told me that she wanted you to wear a wedding dress."

"Damn it, I completely forgot. Holy crap. Yeah, but it's been a while that it is scheduled, she planned it already six months ago. And why me and not Clarisse, for her wedding dress?"

"She said it won't fit for her. Since between the both of you, you're the slimmest. I really don't understand why she called me, and she didn't call you for that..."

"It won't fit... Bollocks. She's exactly the same as I am. No, I think she called you because when I was in the metro, she called me, and it didn't end up well."

"Shocking!"

"Yeah. But yeah, why not, I mean, if she needs me, of course."

Yes, and I remember that she told me that she wants to do a kind of reception because she's been working really hard on her new collection. And would like Clarisse and me to use as models. I was okay initially, but, yeah, I completely forgot she wanted to do it within the next days. And honestly, my mind was elsewhere, at that moment I was thinking about something completely different, it was just, yeah, the thing with the least priority. But I suppose she's going to hire some of her staff to help her prepare everything, she wanted to use our reception room because it's the only place that is wide enough for having at least fifty people. I don't think she needs me on anything... I mean, she would have told me otherwise. She's always very organised, whenever she is organising something, it takes her days to make sure everything will be perfect. Still, in my thoughts, I continued:

"I mean... I guess..."

"Something wrong, honey? I mean, you look quite different now. I feel like there's a problem."

"No. I am just drained. Any chance we could talk about something else?" I got annoyed by his comment.

"Okay, okay!"

After having leaned for a while in the door frame and whilst he was still sat in the table (even if we have sofas... I think it's for a question of immersion in his game), I walked in.

Unusually, I come into the living room, it's been maybe three or four days that I didn't go in there. But unlike the reception room that we close when we don't need it, the living room is always open. It is the second-largest room in the flat (and I mean it, it's like big), obviously after the reception room. But according to the plans that we had when we first visited the flat, it was supposed to simply be a dining room. Because the kitchen is just the next wall. It kept that purpose for a while, but when dad left, we slightly changed the setup and the goal with mum, as we were just living together, the three of us, thus it was meaningless to have this. And since that, it stayed that way. The shape of this room is like rectangular. And like my room, it has a balcony. And, yeah, now, this room is like, where the life in this flat all come together, it's usually where I had my biggest fights with my mum, where I spend hours in front of the TV when I have nothing else to do, it's generally the lazy place. It's not that I like or don't like this room, it's just that, well... Many things happened, and unfortunately, I have the tendency to remember better something that pissed me off than something useful.

The wide window is facing the door, all along the opposite wall. Upon entering, immediately on the left, there is our corner sofa. But the corner sofa is actually pretty broad. All woolly grey has the same length on both perpendicular sides and is even turned in a specific way to make a small alley between the door and the dining area, towards the window. It actually clearly delimits the living area from the dining area, and we turned it that way, making it more comfortable when we carry something hot from the kitchen to the big table near the window. There are at least no obstacles in between. We could have made it the other way around, but this table is so massive that when we moved it a while ago, even if we were four (mum, Clarisse, Claire and I), we needed the help of our neighbour to carry it.

So, let's start with the living area: within the perimeter drawn by the big sofa, there's a small coffee table (I mean small... A square of at least one metre fifty) where we drop many magazines or books, many pieces of stuff, or papers, that mum complaints all the time because we usually leave this table messy. This is a glass table, like a classic glass table... This table on which Florent sits all the time he is playing. Now, it was not that messy. On the wall facing the alley leading to the dining area, our flat screen, quite a big one, fragile, attached on the wall, under which there is a small piece of black furniture, where the console and other things like the Wi-Fi box was. All a set of games that Florent invested recently in underneath the console... Yeah. Oh, yeah, and a big carpet covering the floor of the area. A big cardinal red carpet. Everything has been made by designers here, and, well, it's okay, honestly, but I am not quite a fan. I mean, she would have asked me my opinion about the furniture and everything, I would undeniably have chosen something else.

Now, the dining area, just facing the big French window leading to the balcony. And this table... Obviously a glass table, but it's so long... Oh my god, I don't even know how they managed to bring it here. It's like five metres long and two wides. It's the main thing in that area. We only eat here when we receive guests or are all four to eat here. Eight black chairs assorted to the table (since its frame is black), all them covered with a white pillow. On it, right now, nothing else but a flowerpot with obviously fake flowers on it dropped over a small grid that protects the table when we put a hot dish from the oven. Apart from that, on the edge of the TV wall and the French window, there is a large white halogen lamp, "design" as they say. We turn this on only in the evening or on the night principally for its delightful soft light, generally when mum sometimes watches her programs on TV. Or when she has a Skype call with her friends in the UK. And she brings her laptop in here. Ironically, even if we can see the facing buildings and the neighbourhood through the window, mum decided to leave this window without curtains. But since in this country windows have shutters; (unlike the UK and the US) in summer we draw the shutters to keep this place cool.

Florent turned on that halogen lamp as he was playing. The night was weak, and I honestly don't know... he's gonna screw his eyes someday. His game was still on, and... As I was in the alley, with this floor really cold made of big white tiles, well... I actually looked at him, exhausted:

"Cha... I know there's something wrong" I felt like, for once, he wanted to speak.

"Yeah, well... I don't think you want to talk about her," I was quite sad.

"Oh, I see. Let me guess; I am sure this is about Claire."

"Yeah."

"Okay, what's her problem?"

"She has no problems, it's just... When I was in the metro, she called me and, you know, she was somehow depressed. I mean, I feel like she's been doing something bad recently and, you know..."

"Why does she have to be that close to you! She cheated on you, she deceived you, she... And yet, you are still close to each other."

"Florent, Claire, it's different. We had a very long story together, we've been together for a while, and, yes, she cheated on me, yes, it didn't end very well, but still, I made her the promise that I'll always be here for her."

"She's your ex, for God's sake!"

"I understand your point of view, honey," I actually reassured him, "I totally do. I know that she's my ex, and you see her as a true target. I do understand that. But what if you too were with someone that... You know, you were so close with each other and... You know."

"She's a threat to me..."

"You hate her because you heard my mother talking about her with her homophobic point of view, yes..."

"No!"

"Then tell me, why would you hate her?"

"I don't hate her; I don't even know who she is! The only thing you showed me was her Facebook, and that's it."

"All right, baby..."

"She remains a threat to me. To us."

Several times I have been trying to make him accept that Claire is not the devil my mother used to depict him. Again, I hate my mother because she's homophobic, if you are not anti-gay like her, she will persuade you that these people are mad. Therefore, before I told him about her, she made sure that she would say to him all the worst about Claire. And I hate that, even if she changed, Claire used to be someone adorable, she is still someone nice. That's a shame. And I understand she is a threat for him since she's my ex-girlfriend, but we broke up. And even if it was hard for me to accept, I finally agreed and moved on.

"Claire is not that bad. I'm sure you guys would love each other if you'd finally meet and talk."

I saw him going to the kitchen. I don't really know why I was talking about her tonight... Well, actually, yes, she's the reason why I got pissed tonight. And if I am pissed, he will harass me until he knows what's going on. But, right now, I don't know why, but I was in a kind of peace and love mood, I mean, Claire, all that stuff, all that mess, what if everything would come together?

On the other hand, well... Okay, I said it, but sometimes I wonder if I really moved on, I sometimes also wonder if I didn't come back in a relationship too fast after having broken up of such a relationship. I must admit that I needed something, I needed someone by that time, because I was feeling alone, and I got scared. Now, curiously, when I was with Claire, I already hated everybody, but she made it bearable. Since I am with him, I must confess that first I hate everybody, and second, I really want and need to be alone all day. Maybe mum is right, it's gonna take time. Once in the kitchen, I was not that angry. I saw him removing something from the oven... But, yeah, I was hungry in the metro, but thinking back about all that story, all that happened, it actually killed my hunger.

"I really don't think I'd love your ex, no," he continued.

"Well, anyway..."

"But seriously, what was her problem?"

"Well... She called me, it's about Kelly."

"Kelly... The girl you hate because you told me she's behind your breakup with her?"

"Yeah... She actually found out that Kelly was doing stupid stuff and... Well, it doesn't matter. Kelly lives her life; Claire lives her life, and I live mine."

"Yeah. It's still a shame that you're still thinking about your ex."

"Sorry, love. I didn't think about that this way," I apologised.

"It's okay!"

I think speaking about Claire wouldn't be a great idea. I'm certainly too idealistic, I mean, in my perfect world, well... Claire would still be my girlfriend, and

Kelly would not be existent. Unfortunately, I'll have to deal with the fact that I am with him, living under a shitty household, and as I am engaged with him, I am still loyal, and I don't want him to be collateral damage of my relationship with Claire. As I said, I like him, and yet I am still living with him, sometimes just because of loyalty. Being engaged with him, yes, but it's gonna take time to accept and find out what I should do. I don't know, right now, in my mind, it was like, I needed to be alone, but... He is my boyfriend. It happened already, with Claire, that I was with her and I needed to be alone. The difference is, with her, I had a symbiosis that I still don't have with Florent. It took time to have it. Why I am still with him, it's because also somehow, I think I can create it. If I fail, then I will tell him that it's over. Mum is right, and even Clarisse is right, and I must admit, he is a beautiful guy. When I said yes to be his girlfriend first, and after I said yes to be his fiancée, I just don't think that I was doing the right thing at the right moment. Now, it's too late!

Yet I have no plans for the future. I had plans, but everything collapsed last August. I still don't know what I want to do in my life, I don't know what I want to study at school, I yet don't even know if I want to remain at school. And I am eighteen, I mean, I am not the only one, but nothing pleases me. I feel like there's nothing I want to do because there's too much choice. Also, in my ideal of life, I expelled the idea of having children one day, and this is a strong point of disagreement with Florent, he wants to get married and have children. I saw my mother's life, I see my sister's life, and I just feel like, I have enough money to survive. I have incomes, I am not worried at all about the future. I can spend my life without working. Yet, since I inherited, I barely spent the quarter of a million, I have so much money that I feel like I'm never gonna get rid of everything.

The problem is, nothing really attracts me anymore, because I see the fact of living as a permanent threat. After all, my parents messed up with me when I was a child because I have been in love with someone now totally brainwashed and I failed to keep her on the right tracks... And today I found out that she's doing prostitution. My life is sometimes meaningless. The only thing I want right now is, just stay home all day, in a dark room, hearing the rain all the time, and being alone in my bed. And sleeping, again and again. Even if I have to buy sleeping pills, but just sleeping.

"You know..." I was feeling inspired in the exhaustion, "I'm actually going to go to bed. I am drained."

"You should eat, honey!"

"I'm not that hungry..."

"You're not okay tonight, are you?" he looked at me, now more concerned than ever.

"No, not really. It's just that I am feeling depressed, it's gonna be better tomorrow."

"Do you want to talk about this?"

Several things were pissing me off right now: first, the fact that I was paid for sleeping with a guy that I don't even know. It was quite a hard blow. Even if I didn't really speak about that, I felt weird about this. Second, Claire's discovery that she hid from me this. And I couldn't see anything, I couldn't even guess what she's been doing. And third, Kelly's proposal, even if it was rejected, I felt like I fell last night in a trap. I remember my grandma, she used to say that "a human is a wolf for humans", and even if I placed myself in the predator category, having a prey revolting against the predator is still a blow for me. It's like, there's something weird, something that doesn't work. I was still upset, like terribly upset, but I passed the moment when I wanted to break something. Now, I was in the moment when I want to withdraw and think. And... being sad since I cannot cry. It was undoubtedly the moment when I was the most dangerous.

"Why not. What do you do when... let's imagine someone you already don't really like pissed you off... Like, almost betrayed you. What do you do for a retaliation?"

"What do you mean? Something happened with someone you don't like?"

"No, but... Let's imagine this person might, what would you do?"

"I really don't get your question. Someone that I don't like, well, first, I would stop being around this person, so there's no way he might make me angry someday. And, well, if he might, then... I don't know. But I don't get you, someone pissed you off, and you don't like this person, and you want to retaliate?"

"No, it's... Well, actually, you know what? Never mind."

"No, there's something wrong! Tell me!"

"Okay... This Kelly had spread craps about me at school. Or at least intends to. And I really want to stop her."

"I remember you telling me that knowledge is power, don't you recall?"

"What do you mean?"

"Well," he looked at me. "whatever crap she wants to spread about you, just make sure you know something better about her."

I seriously thought about blackmailing her if that's what he means. But I created a fake account on Facebook, and all possible social networks she might be on to gather information. All I could get was an extraordinary life, amazing pictures of fake life and all that bollocks. Contents made for her to make sure she'd be famous; I didn't find anything quite useful. I seriously considered hiring a private investigator, but I rejected that idea because it would have caused more harm than anything else by the time I thought about it. After all, the primary target was destroying all possible relationship she'd have with Claire. And as Claire is not dumb (I mean, not entirely), if something would have happened to Kelly, she would have suspected me, which would have worsened the situation. Now, I can still hire a PI, but the problem is what she has against me, it's big. And yet, I didn't assess the situation thoroughly. Because I am sure, she hides something bigger against me. She wouldn't be so confident otherwise.

"Well... it might be helpful, but I don't think she might take a bow if I blackmail her, to be fair" I considered his idea but rejected it.

"Well, then I guess it's gonna cost you some money!"

Killing her or making her disappear would be the riskiest idea, but that would undoubtedly be the best idea, but as I said, the most perilous. The only problem is, she said that now, she knows quite a lot of people. But what kind of people does she know? I remember a guy that we met when we arrived at the nightclub, just before I had my blackout, which was quite imposing. And, if I am not wrong, he seemed like a cop. Kelly is narcissistic, and if she's really doing prostitution, she's seeing rich and influent people. Again, I don't forget that day when she showed up at school brought by a guy in a luxury car. We all wondered how she managed to do that, but she lied to us about who this guy was, or any of her explanations were coherent. Since we all know that she's single (at least that's what she says on her Facebook or other shit like this), I feel like I only see the tip of the iceberg, something bigger must be under.

I must confess that I made a mistake to underestimate her. She was a more severe threat than I thought. And now... To retaliate the best way to that little cunt, I must fully understand who she is. But I must do it discreetly. Otherwise...

"I considered it, but... That may be dangerous. And I don't want her to lead me to jail."

"Ha, ha! You said 'her', no I assume you may speak about this Kelly, huh?"

"No, someone else. Kelly is no longer a threat. And you know I am not really popular at school because of... many things, actually."

No, he doesn't have to know that it's Kelly. Because he knows that Kelly is related to Claire and I don't want him to be aware that this is Claire-related. It will raise suspicions otherwise.

"Hum, I don't believe you."

"Honey, whether you believe me or not, I don't give a crap," I used reverse psychology to make sure that the doubt would be created on the identity of the person I am targeting.

"Uh, okay... Then who is that person? I mean, you can tell me!"

"I will tell you who that person is when I will be sure that she actually wants to fuck me."

14 *You're probably wondering...*

// My home, Neuilly-sur-Seine.

// Sunday, 13th of January 2013, 10:12

There have been a couple of days, obviously, before that Sunday. To finally celebrate my eighteenth birthday, at least the week that marked my eighteen birthdays. And I must confess, I was quite happy to finish that week.

Finally, Thursday night, I was eager to go to bed. But even if I drank for most of the day, I was still quite hungry, but not that much, so we ate what he prepared. But my mind was actually focused on how I could respond to the earlier aggression, I ate but without really enjoying. He made some pasta with salmon, which was nice, really lovely, but I was so exhausted that I went straight to bed after I quit the table. He was not so tired, he played on the console afterwards, but I was already sleeping like a log when he came to bed, I didn't even hear him coming here. Falling asleep didn't actually take long, as I was swaying myself into sleep with the noise of the raindrops exploding themselves on the balcony and the window. Although my bedroom was lit by a candle (I took some from the kitchen) when enjoying my bed's warmth, it was much more pleasant and comfortable to sleep. And strictly no idea came to my mind that night, except, maybe, well... accepting what was going on, because it was a new reality, and all I can do for now is just taking it and say thanks.

The next day (Friday, then), well... Yeah, the first stage of failure for Claire! First, I did the same thing that I use to do every time, I woke up bored because I have to wake up. On Friday, it's different, I mean on the week, we use to start courses at eight, but this day, as a teacher was absent, we could start later, at 10. I got up, obviously not awake, and it was raining again. After waking up, I had my classic cup of tea with milk for breakfast, then I got dressed, and of course, my brain was still studying a solution for getting the advantage of the background situation. And when I was on my way to the metro, heading to school, again... I surprisingly received a call. Miss Claire Cobert. Okay.

"Hi, Charlotte," she started when I took the call, not really confident of herself, with a relatively severe tone.

"Claire. What's up?" I replied the same way, very cold.

"Hum... I am quite embarrassed about what happened yesterday, to be honest."

"Okay. Then what can I do?"

"I, hum... We're gonna be at school today, and hum... I really, erm..." she was seeking her words.

"Claire, why did you lie to me? Why did you conceal such a thing?"

"I... Trust me, I really wanted to avoid this, I mean... Damn... Charlotte, believe me when I say this, but... I really didn't mean to do that!"

"By doing that, you mean inviting me to a party with that brainless stuff, then pretending that you guys are called by two stupid morons and finally pushing me to the bed of one of them? That was a nice trick. A genuinely nice ambush."

"You're mad at me..."

"The thing is... I'm not even mad at you!"

"I am really sorry about what happened."

"I am not mad at you; I just don't even want to hear from you."

"Cha, please, you can't do that, I mean, I've been here for..."

"Yeah, yeah, yeah. Now Claire, do me a favour, and kiss my arse, okay? Fuck you!" I hung up the phone.

Obviously, she wasn't at school today. I don't know where she was, and I don't even care. Kelly wasn't there either. This, for the entire day. My new strategy was to actually isolate her. Make sure she could have no help from me. And make sure she would remain in a long friendship with her Kelly. Using reverse psychology with her could work, I mean, losing me would matter to her.

I must admit that my bad mood remained for the rest of the day, as I was still recovering from the hangover of my birthday. It's always the same, the first day after the party I am feeling weird but not that tired, it's generally the day after that is the worst because the tiredness usually takes over. And I am not in my best mood when I am tired. But at least Clarisse was with me, so we stayed the day together. Sophie was here with us also, and we went all together in the closest fast food during lunch break, close to the college. And... Yeah, I kept on thinking about what she told me. Telling her what happened would be a mistake since I didn't even tell Clarisse (I was quite ashamed of what happened, to be fair, and I didn't really want this incident to be known by someone) to avoid much more problems. However, Sophie knew that I slept with someone else. She told me that she actually didn't stay that long during that evening, she took a bus to go back home because she was exhausted.

However, I was kind of curious, I asked her to tell me more about Kelly. Without being paranoid, Sophie doesn't like Kelly that much, which means she can give me useful information. She knew that Kelly was an escort, and she apparently did it for a while. Clarisse was shocked by what Sophie said, but when I asked, like, what does she know about her, she just said, "nothing". Although Kelly's life is widely exposed to social networks, this seems to be kept in high secrecy. And she wasn't lying. This is what I think: Claire knows more about this. She tried to call me at least ten times since I hung up, but I didn't reply. She sent me many texts, most of them telling me that "I am so sorry, I regret" and "Please call me back". I honestly don't know if I may trust my ex or not. It was hard for me to do that to her, but keeping her under pressure could be rewarding, she could give me juicy information because she would be desperate to regain our "friendship" back. And either way, Sophie advised me not to trust her.

After that short lunch, we went back to school for the last four hours of the afternoon, as we had two hours of art courses and two other math to ultimately end this week. Well, as usual, it was boring, and again I was really impatient to leave. After that, just like every Friday, we took the metro in peak hour, to make our way back home. And the evening, surprisingly, for once, everybody was home. Mum didn't have any date tonight, Florent was here, Clarisse too, because she apparently had an argument with her boyfriend, and yeah. Mum told us that she's gonna start on Tuesday to prepare the reception room for the ceremony she does next Wednesday, for her collection, and she's finishing the wedding dress. Nothing really exceptional during that evening, we were all in the living room, watching TV, we actually all ate in front of the TV, eating chips and some French charcuterie, and we all went to bed. Again, I was undoubtedly the first to go there, because if this day wasn't that annoying, I was exceptionally drained, and I really wanted to go to bed. I think, yeah, maybe at 9pm I was already sleeping.

Free Expensive Lies: Prologue

Saturday morning... My sister almost killed me. That was so funny! Just because she has got, in her bedroom, a big canvas. Like, really big, it was part of the stuff we inherited, some old family stuff that she actually wants to keep for some reason. Yeah, because except money, we also inherited lands in a department in the south of Paris (but a bit far away actually, sixty-nine miles from here) and many paintings that belonged to the Kominsky family. To make it short, we used to have many possessions, and we had a castle on these lands, castle that has been bombed by the Nazis during World War II because it was hosting resistance groups. Nonetheless, we still own the grounds, and we rent it to the department as a public park. Anyway, in this castle were many paintings, which includes the one Clarisse has in her bedroom. We have many paintings from that castle that we store in the garage (and I don't want any of them in my bedroom), but Clarisse had to fall in love for the biggest one. Because when she has free time, she likes to restore those or make sure that it will not fall into decay.

And this one, she spent a lot of time in it, watched videos on the Internet, and even, it's been almost two months that she's on it, she even changed the frame and... No, she did a lot of work. This painting is one of our ancestors. But the problem is that she ordered a frame in a workshop at *Porte des Lilas*, far from home, and as they obviously don't deliver, we had to pick it up. As my boyfriend has his driving licence, we had to wake up and leave home early because he rented a van for some specific hours. We had no other solutions, the frame was massive, and we couldn't rent a car. So, driven by my fiancé, we did it on our own because mum was still working on the most crucial piece of her exposition, the wedding dress. As it must be done before Tuesday afternoon. Anyway, going there took us almost our entire morning, but it was fun.

It's only once at home that things became much more complicated: to go through the ground to the first floor, it was really tough and rigid that we couldn't use the stairs as the thing was cumbersome. The only solution was the elevator because we couldn't carry it for such a long distance. It was a fun moment, even at three, since the thing she ordered was bulky, difficult to handle. Problems began when we arrived in front of the elevator because I was sure that the frame could come in as it could barely pass through the door. When we saw the door opening, we weren't that sure. But it was the only way, so we pushed. And, to motivate while she was afraid to destroy it, I said, when she pushed:

"Go, for God's sake, Clarisse, push, come on!"

"It won't come in, we're gonna break it!"

"No, it will!"

"It is rubbing the ceiling, don't you hear, we're gonna break it!"

We didn't damage it. Hopefully, I made sure we didn't damage it. Once it was inside, I pressed the "1" button, and my twin started to examine how the structure was inside and how we could take it out. And once the lift was on, just to laugh, I made her panicking:

"Damn... This frame was heavy, how could it be possible?" she was out of breath.

"Totally. Oops, yeah... Actually, well... you were totally right!" I looked at the frame as if I had the best idea in my life.

"What?" she started to panic after my remark.

"The frame... Oh yeah!"

"What, the frame?"

"Well, yeah... It couldn't come in, you were right!" I was laughing.

It took her an hour before speaking to me again. She was really fed up. Geez, sometimes I don't feel it, but I can be such a bully. But at least she handled the thing well, attached it to the canvas, and put it back on the wall. I even helped her. The rest of the day, well... Nothing really exceptional. Staying home, looking for some shit on the Internet, I watched Black Mirror, Gossip Girl and Breaking Bad. Yeah, in that order. Yeah, I know, Gossip Girl, but I like it. Florent did some stuff on my iPad because I used the laptop, and... Well. Still no news about Claire, or Kelly. And I wasn't seeking any. Before we went to eat as mum prepared a cottage pie at the end of the day, my eyes were truly fucked up. I asked Florent, "what's your secret?", for staying hours in front of the TV. However, at the end of the day, I had to update my laptop. Because, yes, again, when you actually want to turn off your computer, and you find out that you have to install these updates... Damn, I hate Windows 8.

And Sunday. Sunday is never a day like any other. It's definitely the least productive and the laziest day. It used to be for us the beginning of the week. But as we are in France, this day is considered the end of the week, and... Yeah, try to make a French person work on a Sunday. Everything is closed, on Sundays, the entire country is dead. Above all, Florent and I use to stay in bed on the Sunday morning until late sometimes, as it's a kind of ritual. As it's the quietest day of the week, we can spend some moments together, discussing, for example, or other things when I am in a better mood. But it wasn't actually the case today; it was only me and myself in the bed. He was gone.

Free Expensive Lies: Prologue

And this morning, I was curiously feeling better, and fully recovered. The warmth under the sheets was pleasing, curtains were drawn, I just perceived many tiny lights coming into my room through the seams of the thick curtain. It was dark everywhere, but not so dark, and I could figure it out through the room's deep dim light that it was not sunny outside, today again. The sky seemed threatening. I was still enjoying the warmth because unless something happens, this won't last. I opened my eyes, but I didn't move my head. It was the moment, now. Again, for another day on this planet, my brain needs to start and face the new day. I felt now a little better, my hangover was definitely gone, and for once I was better than the last days. There was no noise around me, neither inside my room. I still don't know if anyone if awake since I really didn't hear a noise in the flat. Maybe they are, but they are elsewhere, or they closed the living room to make no noise.

But usually, I mean, at least when I am not woken up by this damn phone, it takes me a couple of time to properly wake up. Otherwise, I am in a nasty mood if someone or something disturbs me. After I opened my eyes, I stretched myself and yawned, stretching myself again; and yawning, now louder. Here I was. I actually put my arm next to me, at the place the gentleman is usually sleeping, and... I turned my head. My hand was reaching nothing. He wasn't here with me in the bed. Hum... Weird. I checked my desk chair, and... His clothes weren't here. Meh, fine.

Fair enough. He is obviously up already, and maybe in the living room, which happens sometimes, and, well, I was not worried that much. Or probably in the bakery for buying some *pains au chocolat* or something like that, especially this lazy day. I kind of like that, it's just a shame that he has to go far away to actually go to a real bakery and... Well, this is actually typically French. He uses to buy some for Clarisse and mum, and he used to buy something else for me, that he usually brings straight in the bed. But still, to make sure, I took my phone that was plugged in the bedside table, to call him. And when I took my phone, no missed calls, or unread texts. Fine. I like it that way.

I called him, and actually on his voicemail as he missed the call. "Hi, you've reached Florent. I'm not here right now, so come on, don't be ashamed, and leave a message, bye!" I actually tried again, just in case... And this time, after the fourth ring, he took the call:

"Hi, baby!" I started when he answered.

"Hi, love! How are you doing?"

"Good, where are you?"

"At the bakery, I'll be back in a bit."

Taylor Harding-Jenkins

"Oh, great. Okay then, I'll see you in a few!"

"See you later..."

Well, that's what I thought.

As he was speaking as if he were busy, I assume that he was indeed paying. Okay then. So, I put back my phone on the bedside table, and, yeah, I relaxed. Sometimes, well, it's crazy, I really miss having my bed for myself. I mean, waking up alone, going on YouTube watching some videos for maybe like an hour or two, I sometimes miss that. But, anyway, it was time to wake up. I mean, perhaps I'll return to the bed soon, but at least it was time for my tea.

I got up and stretched myself again. But the thing I hate... I mean, when I use to do that, I use to have a black veil for a couple of minutes before my eyes because I stood up too fast. But I was in a good mood today. After that, I took my phone, went to the door of my room, and then to the kitchen. There was still nobody, I guess they're still sleeping. And yet, I actually saw that the weather was weird: the sky was dark, but the sun's rays could go through the clouds, it was bizarre. Radiators of the whole flat were all burning, making some water droplets suspending on the window due to the temperature difference. Because this morning, it was hot in the flat, and this everywhere I was. But the silence all around was pleasant, I mean I could hear TVs turned on in the bedrooms, as no-one was in the living room, they were all wakened up but staying at bed for a bit. It was like moonlight, the sky, today, I mean, the light seemed coming from the moon, when I approach the window. I went to get my kettle for my classic morning ritual, a cup of tea, on a cupboard, afterwards.

And after I took it, as usual, when I wanted to pour water into the kettle, first problem: I pressed a little too hard on the tap for getting water, and the stream of water was so strong that it splashed onto my nightdress. I was just like, "fuck it", but it was actually too late when I reduced the flow. Because in winter, through the tap we do not receive only cold water... we receive almost freezing water. This tap has a real problem, actually, or maybe it's the heater. Because when the water is hot, it is as hot as the lava from a volcano, and when it's cold, just like today, it's so freezing that you can almost leave a finger in it. There's no in-between. Obviously, this annoyed me, so I closed my eyes and breathed a little stronger and a little loudly because this is not the first time it happens, and every time I am surprised. I told mum several times that we need to do something about that. Anyway, my kettle was filled, I put it on the burner, switch on the gas, closed the lid, and wait until it would be ready.

Free Expensive Lies: Prologue

My mother subscribed a while ago to a French newspaper that we receive once a week, it's called *Le Monde*. "The World", for non-French speakers. It's a daily newspaper, but for some reasons, we don't receive it daily. Curiously, it was dropped on the kitchen table already, so I took it whilst the water was gently boiling. Let's have a look at the news today. So, the French anti-gay marriage lobby will protest again across Paris today, the Justice Ministry Christiane Taubira who is going through movements with a law that anyone wants and, well. Well, it's crazy, since this started, it's like everybody has become so homophobic. It's in the trends to be a racist homophobic and intolerant. I began to read the articles, and, meh... Seriously, why do we care about two guys getting married, why is that so sacred, marriage? Heterosexuals are already screwing this up, why wouldn't we be allowed to do the same? I mean, I honestly don't really mind, since I didn't invest myself in politics (I am still not registered to vote and I do not want to, because to whoever you vote for you actually serve the interest of a sole and same group), and... Well, mum should be happy. Honestly, sometimes when I read this, I just want to kill myself. Because you finally figure out that the world is just focused on piddle-arse problems and doesn't make any sense. All this for money or God.

The water was still boiling, and the newspaper even in my hand that I actually saw my dear sister. She entered in the kitchen, wearing her pyjamas, black pyjamas with a pink bow tie on the neck, her hairs messy and barely wakened up, and sat in front of me, her back against the wall, watching me. She maybe has found out that I was already using the kettle because she usually drinks a tea just like me. The only difference is that instead of the semi-skimmed milk that I pour in it, she uses oat milk. Disgusting. She was still sleepy, though. Meh, I actually thought that it's gonna take a couple of minutes, I guess, for her to be able to communicate. But it's only when I dropped that newspaper that I smiled at her, and... she was actually wakened up.

"Hi Cha," she smiled me back.

"Hello. How are you?"

"Waking up, and you?"

"Yeah, could be better," I took my phone to look at the time.

"Where's your future husband?" she looked at me.

"Not here, actually. He bought some *pains au chocolat*, so I assume he will be back shortly."

"Cute..."

"Yeah, cute. Where's mum, by the way?"

"No idea. I heard her leaving this morning, so I guess she went shopping or something..."

"On Sunday? Everything's closed here..."

"I know, but... I don't know. She actually didn't leave a while ago. Why are you looking for her?"

"No, I just want to know for how long she's gonna be away, so I can enjoy this amazing morning without her."

"Of course. Of course," she actually seemed annoyed by my answer.

Clarisse hates that situation. Okay, since I am twelve, I changed, and I rebelled against the authority. The problem is, let's say mum is the USSR and I am the US. We are both messing up because we both want our ideas to succeed; unfortunately, there's gonna be only one winner. She hates being in the middle of this, as she said that someday, things will be really fucked up. Since tensions between my mother and me increased as the result of my relationship collapse with Claire, it seems like no diplomacy could save us from an inevitable nuclear war. She was not personally responsible for that, but she's one of the causes that led Kelly to be more successful with Claire as I couldn't be with her because she behaved like a cunt.

"I really wish someday you will stop that. It's annoying everybody here, seriously," she said like a diplomat.

"Yeah, I know. You guys are in the middle of this."

"You say this as if you don't actually care..."

Okay... I think this the moment. She seems ready for this.

"It's true, I actually don't. Oh, yeah, I didn't tell you the breaking news, I forgot to mention that... The discovery I had last Thursday."

"Yeah, what happened? After you..." and she lowered her voice, "cheated on him."

"Yeah, well. I actually found out that miss Kelly Royer is actually sleeping with guys for money."

"WHAT?" she was shocked.

"Yeah, when I said Kelly was a whore... I actually didn't think I was that accurate!"

"How did you find this out?"

"Erm... Well, you remember what I told you... When I, erm... on Wednesday night..."

"Yeah?"

"Well, I went to Claire's on Thursday night because I left something there. And Kelly was there, with her, and erm... She actually confessed that, well..."

"Okay, stop lying to me!" she actually figured out that I was saying craps. Or at least was about to.

Hum... She's clever. I am sure she understood that I was about to lie because I was seeking my words, and I said that she actually confessed something. Kelly would never acknowledge this. And she knows Kelly enough to be sure that she'd never admitted such a thing. Hum... What if I actually tell the truth? She's my sister, she's the second most clever mind that I know, so maybe she might help me find a solution to my problem?

"Okay," I whispered, "so, yeah, when I came that night, last Thursday, I found out that Claire left in my bag an envelope of five hundred euros. I was wondering what it was. Kelly explained to me that actually, I slept with a guy that thought I was an escort just like her, and..."

"What the fuck, Charlotte!" she seemed pissed, and pretended to yell when whispering.

"What?"

"This is serious, I mean, I'm not joking. Why didn't you talk about this to me earlier?"

"I really don't want such a thing to be actually known, as you may understand."

"I am your twin sister, it's not like I am a stranger... Damn, it's why I got so pissed Thursday night, I was feeling humiliated, but I didn't understand how and why," she actually recalled.

"Oh my, don't tell me you had a fight because of me with your boyfriend!" she interrupted me. "Because if I was the cause of your fight, I am really sorry."

"No, no, it was not you, don't worry about it, he was just moody. But that's not the point. Are you telling me that Kelly actually fucked you?"

"She won a battle, yes. But I'm gonna fuck her," I refused to admit she won.

"Who did you talk about what happened?"

"Nobody knows, except Kelly and Claire, because they were both here when it happened. And you, now... But, otherwise, nobody knows!"

The kettle started whistling. When I felt my twin sister looking at me, I got up, certainly upset by what I just revealed. I thought that she was actually pissed, but not that much. I just arrived, switched off the gas and removed the kettle from the burner. Then I took two cups on the top shelf above me, and I began to fill them with boiling water, like every morning. Clarisse took the tea bags, as I think mum made herself a tea this morning and as she knew I'd have one, she actually left the cup where she usually leaves the bags on the table. I took two saucers for the cups because leaving them on the table would damage the screen, and then, I returned to sit with one cup in each hand. She took two spoons, and yeah. I assume we were now all ready to start this fantastic breakfast at the time of my problems with Kelly and finding a solution to a quite disturbing problem. And, I really don't know why, but at the very moment I sat, the very first thing I saw was the saucer of the cup. And I was literally... hypnotised by this.

I had a real fascination for this: it was a drawing, like an old one, sketched in blue paint, displaying two farmers that had stopped working for praying, looking like *The Angelus* of Millet, a religious work so fascinated by Salvador Dali. When mum bought these cups, it was to an artisan, it cost quite a lot, and I really admire this, as it seemed to have been hours of work. Because this was handmade, it was not printed or designed by a machine. When we went in Alsace a couple of years ago, she bought it to an artisan working porcelain, and I recall what he used to do was absolutely fabulous. And, I don't know, I love this cup, it seems to me like... I don't take religions seriously since God doesn't exist for me, but I am still overly impressed by all work related to religion, especially Christianism. God might be bollocks to me, but I enjoy going to churches because, there are nonesuch places on this planet where you can actually find calm, peace, and finally great appeasement. And being surrounded by notable works that bring you back straight to your human condition. Yeah, I know, I have a weird approach of all that's religious. I might go to some church a bit later today.

And whilst I was like, for some reason, literally hypnotised by that saucer for a while – perhaps it was God's call of today – Clarisse kept calling me. So, I raised my head, to finally see, standing next to her...

"Charlotte, are you okay?" Mum was almost shouting at me because I was not responding.

I actually didn't see she was there. Standing in here, with a bag full of things, no idea what it contained, and a couple of envelopes that we received yesterday but none of us went to check the mailbox.

"Oh, you're back!" I said, disheartened.

"Yeah, I'm back, and really happy to see you! Do you realise that these are your very first words you actually tell me since that weekend started?"

"Yeah, I haven't been that talkative."

"You actually don't wanna talk to me, that's the only reason... You almost spent the entire weekend trying to avoid me."

"Okay, let me get this straight: did you come today here to piss me off, or was there another reason?" I was feeling attacked.

"I just want to see my other daughter, is that too much to ask?"

"No, you just saw me, here, you're happy now?"

"I just want to check on my other daughter, since there's only Clarisse that comes to me recently."

"I am kind of busy, right now, it's maybe the reason why I don't want to see you!"

"You're always 'kind of busy', Charlotte. But it's okay, I'm used to it anyway."

"All right, then," I poured some milk in my tea.

"By the way... That's for you. I don't know what this is," she dropped an envelope next to my cup.

Okay, someone wants something from me. Whoever it is, what was it? I was inquisitive. I mean, when I receive letters, it's only for claiming me something, like taxes, bills, or things like that. So, I took the letter and examined it. A white, A5 format envelope, with my name and my address written in white with the Times New Roman police, at the address space. No logo, no address of whoever has sent that letter whatsoever, nothing. Hum, curious. There was also something quite strange, there's generally a postmark on the letter that we receive, at least the postmark notifies when has the letter been sent, and usually the location, but it was missing. No stamps as well. Even administrative letters have both stamps and this postmark. It means that someone other than the postman dropped that letter inside the mailbox. The problem, letterboxes are within the building, and you need to pass through the security gate to access them. Could be someone from inside the building? I am curiously not in touch with anyone, and they don't know my name, so it seems impossible. Only the postman has access, and I haven't been called for any suspicious activity within the building. There was also a string of numbers under my name that actually looked like a phone number. That's weird. Anyway, I took a knife for opening the letter, whilst mum was discussing with my twin sister about something that I didn't hear and actually care.

And here I opened it. I took what was inside. Four goddamn pictures entirely developed and, in crystal-clear quality. I just looked at them, like, very quickly, before pulling them back in the envelope, because the content of these pictures was... actually the moment I blacked out. I didn't even look at them, because it seemed clearly me, having sex with the guy with whom I slept that night. Although all these pictures were very dark, we could clearly see my face and his face.

When I saw what was on the printed pictures, I felt colossal vertigo triggered by stress and embarrassment. I certainly blemished by what I just saw, because I actually found out the trap it was. Kelly went further than where I could even believe; she really trapped me, and I didn't see it coming. Because I remember that, I mean, I didn't actually go everywhere in his flat, this was a mistake, but some pictures have been taken of me when I was weak. They used the fact that I was drunk against me, to trap me. Now, this is obvious, I am in deep troubles because whoever sent me that letter, or dropped that letter in my mailbox, wants to blackmail me. I just made sure that my mother, still close to me, wouldn't see those pictures. So, they got me. I felt like... Really weird, actually. Because if I received those pictures, other images of me exist somewhere, or worse. And whoever sent me these pictures wanted something from me. It just took a couple of seconds, not exceptionally long, to recall that prank call I had when I left this guy's flat. So, it wasn't a joke.

Still that letter in my hand, my tea that was undoubtedly cold in front of me, I actually... I was now shaking everywhere. Now, I was scared. I honestly didn't see my sister, who was still in front of me, when I started to scream:

"Clarisse!"

"Cha, what's wrong with you, I'm here! What? What's going on?"

"I... You... I... I need you to follow me, right now," I was seeking my words.

"Hey, honey, what's wrong with you, why are you so white now? Have you seen a ghost or what?"

"Yeah, and an evil one. In the garage. Mum, can you give me the key?" I looked at her, overly concerned now.

"Your ghost is in the garage? What do you wanna do in the garage?" she was confused.

"Don't ask any questions, and give me the key to the garage, I need it, mum, please."

"Yeah, all right, then," she sighed.

My heart was almost bombing my chest, and I felt like in the biggest rush of my life. I heard her walking to the entrance, seeking for the keys in her handbag. Meanwhile, I immediately closed the envelope under the eyes of Clarisse, looking at me and trying to understand what situation was actually ongoing. I whispered very quietly, "I'll tell you in the garage". After a couple of seconds, I heard mum finally finding the keys and coming back to the kitchen, when I stood up and prepared myself to leave. And when she arrived, she was still curious:

"What's her problem now?" she looked at Clarisse.

"Nothing, mum. Thank you," I interrupted a possible conversation very swiftly, after having taken the keys out of her hand.

"Well, well. But what will you do in the garage?" Clarisse asked.

"Nothing, I mean, I need your help on something."

"Okay. Just, don't mess everything up, please," as mum was still worried.

"It's okay, don't worry. Thank you," I cut short the conversation.

Still, with the letter in my hand, my legs were shaking. And Clarisse stood up, always seeking to understand what was ongoing. But I saw her quite reluctant to come. Surprisingly, she seemed really concerned about me. I mean, I could see she was now under some pressure, but she remained actually quite confused. Whilst I was about to go, she was still standing in front of her chair. My behaviour was weird, now, I mean, everybody was actually suspicious, even my mother. But it's when I saw my sister being still reluctant to come that I actually asked another time, this time more imperative:

"Clarisse, are you coming with me? What are you waiting for?"

15 *This is gonna hurt*

// In my building, towards the garage, Neuilly-sur-Seine.

// Sunday, 13th of January 2013, 10:12.

I took my phone, and mum saw us rushing out like the fire was on my arse.

I actually made as fast as I could, actually, to leave the flat. I didn't even get my coat; I was just with my nightdress and ready to go. I don't know, on my mind, I kept on thinking, what if the guy that called me when I was about to take the metro last Thursday morning was actually the guy that sent me the pictures? I was doing my best, again, to try to recover what happened that night, but it was impossible, I really forgot all that happened. God damn it. And what could be this phone number? I had an unbelievably lousy hunch coming. Whatever happened, whoever was the guy calling me and masking his voice, I could only say one thing, things were actually getting harsher than I could believe.

After a moment of feeling weird, Clarisse followed me. We just went to take the elevator. Hopefully, Florent was still not here, and I really hoped he would be as late as possible today because I need to calm down. If he sees me like this, it's gonna raise questions and I am so stressed today that I do not want to say anything to him. As my sister quickly understood, she finally got that the ghost she was talking about was actually in that envelope. It's why, when I closed the door, she looked at me and said, "What could contain this letter?" but I did not reply, I just pressed the button to call the elevator as fast as I could. As she saw I was not responding and was really acting weird, she actually kept on asking, with more insistence this time:

"So, what's your problem right now?"

"Just wait two minutes, and please don't speak out loud."

When the lift arrived, I walked in first, then I pushed on the button for going into the garage, while Clarisse was just following me, confused about what was ongoing. My lips were closed, my legs were so shaken that I almost couldn't hide the fact that I was horrified, my nervousness and fears increased really quickly, everything was reaching a certain threshold that it was tough to hide. I was increasingly nervous, and this couldn't stop. Clarisse, now next to me, started feeling the same, a feeling of total insecurity. I thought back again of the call that I received when this distorted-voice-asshole wished me a happy birthday. Who could it be? I don't know. I have absolutely no idea what was happening, everything seemed to be out of control. And while holding my phone a bit harder, I fell again and again into a feeling that I don't exactly know, which was fear. I didn't experience that for a long time. This is something that I always underestimate.

A few seconds later, the lift reached the garage and stopped quite abruptly. We arrived in the garage. I quickly came in, Clarisse followed me like a little doggie. But I focused on the ongoing events that I progressed headlong into the small hallway between the elevator to the garage. And it was only from that very moment that I actually decided explaining to her what was going on. By giving her that letter, and thus she could have a look at the content. Meanwhile, I was hurrying up to go to the garage entrance, so we could be alone and not heard by anybody. As I didn't want to speak in the lift by fear of being heard.

There was a small room when we used to arrive that connects the lift to the garage. I actually pass through this as fast as possible, before I pushed up the red door in throwing myself against it because it was heavy and difficult to open for me otherwise. Yeah, here I was.

"That's... Well, just have a look at this."

"I... Oh damn! What the hell is that?" she actually opened the envelope and saw the picture whilst walking.

"These are pictures of me. You see, now I remember what I have done the night I blacked out..."

"Who the hell has sent you these pictures? Do you think it could be Kelly or the guy with whom you slept?"

"I have no idea, Clarisse. There's a phone number under the address, I think that if I call, I may know who is behind this. But this phone number doesn't seem to be Kelly's or... a phone number I even know."

"So that's it? Someone is blackmailing you; do you realise? I mean, that's what I start to understand. Because if it's the case, you're in real troubles, you know this. Why the hell do you place yourself in such situations, Charlotte..."

"I don't know. I seriously don't know who's fucking up with me."

"Things are now out of control, Cha..." Clarisse started to make things more straightforward for herself. "This morning you told me that Kelly fucked you up, and now you find this out. This is insane!"

After a short walk, we arrived in front of our garage door. The good thing is, the garage is not that far away from the lift door, which is the best thing when we have to bring the bags upstairs when we go shopping. The key still in my hand, I quickly opened the door and pushed on the top to open it once unlocked, and obviously, I took the key with me. Otherwise, I won't be able to take it back. Then, once the door was fully opened, I invited Clarisse to come in. And yet, the shock was still here, and I must say this for both of us:

"Whoever it is, Clarisse, I will not let them win. But I must understand what's going on."

"Cha, why don't you let that go and go straight to the police?"

"Because... There are actually too much at stake. Claire knows that I want to cover this up, Kelly as well, they know I have a boyfriend, and... And mostly, I do not know what this guy has with me. He sent it straight to me because he showed me those pictures, so it may only be the tip of the iceberg. I will go to the cops if shreds of evidence show that this is a prank, but the problem is, if I go to the cops, things won't be private anymore. And I want this to remain private, or at least the minimum of people aware of what happened."

"True. If Florent, or worst... mum, find out what happened, yeah..."

Yes, Clarisse, this is what I want to avoid. This is the thing I am the most scared of: finishing on some pornographic website or stuff like this. Since I am clearly naked on these pictures and, well, it's obvious. I think this would definitely be the worst that would happen to me, it would ruin my life. Okay, my life is already ruined, and I may not care about a lot of things... But I don't want someone to completely nuke what I am trying to create. Because I am trying to build my life with Florent, even if it's hard, even if it may not work, but I am trying to clear my mind of Claire. I need to know what the sender of that letter wants from me, so at least I can try to tackle or negotiate. That seems to be the only way out.

"I must be strategic."

"You really don't remember anything from that night?" Clarisse was seeking for a solution.

"No, I don't, I was drunk, and... I don't know, I wanted to be drunk because I couldn't bear staying with Kelly... I should have said no to her."

"Well, I am sure, even if you said nope, she would have trapped you for another occasion. If Kelly wanted to do that, she'd have done that anyway. We both know her, and we also know that whenever she has an idea in her mind..."

"True..."

"What's the matter with Kelly?"

"The matter is, I hate her because Claire explained to me that when she slept with those guys, you know, before we split up, well, she was having a party with Kelly and it was through her that she met that guy and... Kelly destroyed my relationship with Claire. I just want her dead; I don't want her to win that."

"And what tells you she is behind this? I mean, this could be just someone else playing with you, not necessarily her!"

"No, that must be her. I am sure she must be behind this."

Her theory of a third person could be okay, unless, things look like being done by her, it clearly smells like Kelly. Now that I remember, Claire insisted so much for going to the nightclub that evening, so I assume it was done for a reason. Using my feelings to get something from me used to be something she did successfully at many times, and if I were Kelly, given the fact that I know Claire is my weakness, I'd definitely use her for targeting me. Then the party, she knew that I needed a couple of drinks to tolerate her during that party so she could start playing that thing with the guys, especially with the guy with whom I slept. And manipulating everybody, it was easy as we were all drunk. We came there, and... But there something weird, I mean, why would I sleep with this guy? I actually mean, why would I sleep with a guy in general?

God damn it, yeah, that's actually something quite important, it doesn't make any sense at all. The very last thing I remember from that party was us, walking to a group of guys, two guys, sitting on a table and drinking cocktails. I remember having seen a girl that actually raised my attention that night because she was pretty. And when I saw this guy, I didn't feel anything; he was just a regular guy in a nightclub. Why did I stay with him if I was drunk and didn't go to that girl that attracted me? Because I am not bisexual, I am still lesbian, so why would I sleep with someone I am not attracted to? There was something, that evening, something that actually pulled me to... Oh... I see. Yeah, there's also this, I recall feeling weird at some point, so they drugged me, it's the only thing that truly makes sense.

Let's say it happened that way, Clarisse must be right. Her third-person theory could be explained since I really doubt Kelly to be intelligent enough to make such plans. Someone helped her. Because, yes, I don't actually believe that she would be... I mean, this plan is really tricky.

"But hold on..." I actually realised that she could be right.

"What?" she stopped thinking.

"You may be right. Because some things don't actually make any sense at all."

"Such as?"

"Such as, why did I sleep with a guy that night? I am naturally attracted to girls, and I remember that night, there was one that actually raised my attention."

"Well, I thought about it. Actually, I was astonished when you told me you cheated on your boyfriend with a guy."

"And I got a call at the moment I took the metro on Thursday morning to come back home. Some guy with a distorted voice that wished me my birthday, and... It was actually bizarre."

"Yeah, a damn prank call."

"That's what I thought, but it seemed very serious."

"Oh?"

"Yeah, I thought it was either you or Claire, but... Well, I didn't take it seriously because, well, that's not the first prank call that I receive, but that's actually... That could be the guy that sent this letter today, that actually called me."

"Maybe. Do you remember the name of the guy with whom you slept?"

"Nope. I mean, I remember because I heard the name Christian from Claire or Kelly, but to be honest... I know where he lives, but I wouldn't be able to actually go back to the entrance of the building where he actually is."

"Okay," she showed me the phone number under my address. "I think it should be better if you try to call that number, underneath your address, over here. Maybe you'll know more."

"Yeah, give me a minute, then."

That's the only way to know what this person wants. I need to learn more about this because the string of number under my address was obviously a phone number. It started by +33, which is the indicative number for France. God damn it. I unlocked my phone number and put the keys of the garage on the car's hood. I dialled the phone number, and, yes, my phone didn't recognise the number.

Meanwhile, Clarisse had an app on her phone – she used to be harassed by unknown phone numbers last year, allowing her to trace and recognise which phone number belongs to whom. And she typed the phone number that was below... it was actually a temporary SIM card. The kind of SIM card you can top up. Obviously, the person did not want to be identified, and since we cannot triangulate the call... So yes, after I dialled and she showed me this, I called. And when the person took the call...

"Dear Charlotte Kominsky?" the person promptly replied with his obviously distorted voice, same as before, "I couldn't wait for your call!"

"Yes, Kelly Royer. Don't be that timorous with me. You know, I'm much cleverer than you," I took the defensive approach.

"Oh yeah?"

"Oh yeah!"

"Uh-oh, I so wish you were right. But nope, again, I am not that Kelly. I am not the friend you actually hate."

"Oh yeah? Prove it."

I really had no idea to whom I was answering right now. But if this person wants to take me for an idiot, so, let's go, let's play the game. If he wants to impress me, I will need much more to be impressed, so he's gotta find serious stuff, and mostly, he'd better know me better than Kelly does. Even if I am sure, Kelly spoke a lot with Claire about me, the thing is, she may know much more than I think, so it might be tricky. I really need to pay attention to what he says, I mean, how he uses words in his sentences, the way this person speaks. Because Kelly always uses the same words most of the time, she will betray herself at some point. She's very predictable, so I really hope she's going to do that. However, the first time I spoke to him, he seemed quite informed on me. Maybe through stuff that he found on social networks even if I don't have Facebook, people still can find me there. And knowing about my relationship with Claire, as I remember he did the first time I was on a call with him, well, that's not really a secret. Not many people know about this, but it remains that since we broke up, this is no longer a secret. No, if he really wants to impress me, he'd better find something that is not a secret.

But given the existence of Facebook today, it's no longer difficult to get information on someone. I asked him to prove that he is not Kelly, and it took him a couple of seconds to think about what he may say. Let's see where it goes:

"You want me to prove what?" the guy was starting to be confused.

"That you are not Kelly. Prove it. Tell me something about me, and then maybe I will consider you more seriously."

"Um, okay. Although it's been four years since you definitely left Facebook, you met your current boyfriend a couple of months ago a few days after you broke up with Claire in arranging yourself by deleting your account and all the rest. You actually are in a relationship with your current boyfriend since the 4th of September 2012. And Florent, his name, is a friend of Clarisse, your twin sister. Quite an incredible love story for a former lesbian... And, Claire, yeah, that's one of the biggest dramas of your life. You still love your ex, and you hate this Kelly because you accuse her of being personally responsible of, erm... yeah, bringing the guy that fucked your ex-girlfriend the day you found this out. Anything else I can do for you?"

Okay. This asshole's really, really well informed. What actually shocked me was when he said the special day when I started going out with him. Even Claire doesn't know precisely when I began my relationship with Florent, she knew it a month later. So, it may give me a clue about who could be the guy with whom I am now talking: someone really close to me. Because I remember, this thing is really classified, I mean, I never spoke about that day to anybody. And I don't think I did when I blacked out, which means... Except for my mother, my sister, and obviously my boyfriend, who could have sent that letter, and, precisely, knowing the day when I started seeing Florent? Someone close enough to me. This clearly excludes Kelly from making that joke to me. Okay... What does he want, money?

"Well, nice try, mate," I replied, terrified and wanting to confuse him, "but you're all wrong..."

"Oh, even you don't even believe a word of what you are just saying. Yeah, the Tuesday 4th of September 2012, a sad rainy day, when you actually kissed him for the first time in your bedroom."

"Who the hell are you?"

"No matter how I know. And call me *Rising Sun*."

"*Rising Sun*, man, that's a ridiculous name. Looks like a shitty spy movie. But okay, fair enough, that's gonna be a nice nickname when I will find you and kick your arse."

"Well, don't be so optimistic, you need to find me first..."

He was using sentences... it was like a mess. He didn't seem like someone I know. And I was also paying attention to the background noise. Hopefully, through my phone, I can hear things very well, I mean the background noises and anything, and as I heard nothing, I assume that he was indeed in a room. I didn't hear him typing things on a keyboard or anything, but I could hear him at some points, for example at the moment he gave me the information about Florent, I could hear him taking some papers. And actually, seeking some information on these papers, to make sure I wouldn't be sceptical. It means that maybe I have been followed by a PI, but one thing was sure, this guy, whoever he was, was well-informed about me. And if he had papers, it means that either he took notes or stuff like this, whether he hired someone to do the job. So, well, the danger was real.

"What do you want from me?" I was scared.

"You know what? Let's play a game together! You will love it. It's been three days that you allowed yourself to some big party for your birthday that ended actually pretty well... or pretty bad, I don't know And the next day, you went at your ex's place to get a bag that you left the day before. Remember, there was also Kelly, and your ex wanted you to go swimming with her. No? Don't you remember?"

"You son of a bitch!"

"Remember that proposal, when she asked you to join the party... just for fun!"

"Oh, I don't remember. But please, refresh my memory."

"All right, then. Three days ago, the guy with whom you had an affair, Christian, offered you some money for your wonderful night. And that must have been a pretty fantastic night according to the pictures I can see now. Still don't remember anything? Well, even if you don't, this is precisely where we are going to start this game."

"Oh, don't play with me!"

"I'm not, you are playing with me! From now on, I actually give you forty-eight hours to call Kelly and tell her that you finally accept her offer. You will tell her that you are interested in her offer that she was about to propose after having seriously considered it. As she said, it's just gonna be for fun!"

"I will not."

"Oh, trust me, you actually will!"

"What if I do not do anything?"

"It's really up to you. No, I mean, it's true, we live in a free country. If you don't want, well, then, it's fine. It's just that the amazing movie of your affair will be published on the Internet, you know, one of these amazing websites. That also includes Facebook. Regarding those pictures that your sister is currently holding, the string of pictures I have of you will also be sent by email to your mother, Amelia Kominsky. Also, to your father, Adam Kominsky. And, if it's not enough, I'll do it to your surviving grandparents Caitlyn and George Campbell in the UK, to your boyfriend Florent Bruggen, and finally... Yeah, to like most of the guy in your College. I'll select ten of them randomly. I'll also do it, and this, just for fun!"

"My grandparents do not have any email... Or at least they don't know how to open it... Nice try, mate," I actually played my cards.

"It's okay, thanks for letting me know, I appreciate that. Do they still live in St Albans, north of London? Hum... 45, Willow Street?"

He even knows the address of my grandparents. Now, the world was collapsing all over me. This guy knows a lot, and his threats, well, they are serious. He knows all the names, he knows everything. Also, how could he know that my sister was holding the pictures, right now? For a couple of minutes, I looked around me because maybe he is spying on me, through cameras, through devices like this that I may not see. But... Nothing like this, at least I didn't find anything. Oh my god... So, I took an entirely different approach. Indeed, a calmer and... Because what this guy clearly wanted was me admitting my defeat. I will not, but I will try to use his feelings against him, maybe it will reverse things.

"This is too much... I really can't do that."

"It's really up to you. I mean, yeah. All the cards are in your hands, you do whatever you want with that."

"And who tells me you're not bluffing?"

"Well, let's say I had the balls to send you the pictures already. Hiding behind my screen and uploading pictures to download it on a funny website or on my phone to send it to your relatives. It doesn't seem to be a big deal for me."

"What do you want from me?" I pretended to start sobbing.

"Oh, dear, are you crying?"

"Seriously, what do you want from me?" I continued pretending sobbing, as it was undoubtedly my only way to get rid of him. "I have money, I can pay you if that's what you want? If you want to attack me because I am rich... I can give you whatever you want!"

"Well, I want you. I know you have a lot of money; I know you can try to defend yourself by trying to identify me, but unfortunately, it's gonna take you months! It's gonna take me a couple of hours to destroy your life. So, I don't really care about your millions, I don't really want it. What I want is you. I want your life. I want to destroy you."

"What do you want from me?"

"Oh, and please, stop pretending you're crying. Everybody knows you can't cry!"

He hung up the phone. It cannot be Kelly, then. It must be someone but on her behalf. If I regret having insulted her many times? Of course, no. I need a couple of minutes to try to find an exit strategy. Because, well, this guy wants me for some reasons, and it's now a war. Obviously, we do not have the same weapons, and for now, I don't actually see how I may try to counter all this. I must admit that he has bigger weapons than mine. The problem in a war is that if you do not know who your enemy is, you might lose. Knowledge is power, as I say, and in my case, I might lose a lot. And this situation, I cannot just shrug off and pretend it never happened, there are too much at stake. Well, actually... there's always a solution, there must be a solution to this problem. At the moment I left the phone, Clarisse, who followed everything literally as during the call I left my phone on speaker, whispered to me:

"So, conclusion?"

"Conclusion? Just swear that you won't tell anyone what is going on, even to mum?"

"Why do you want me to tell such a thing?"

"Swear it, Clarisse, I need to hear that from you."

"Yeah, okay, I swear that I won't tell anyone what happened, even to mum."

"Thank you, Clarisse..."

"So, what's next?"

16 *Listen, darling...*

// Back to home, Neuilly-sur-Seine.

// Sunday, 13th of January 2013, 11:12.

We say that the most important man (or woman) in someone's life is not the first, but the one who will not let the next exist.

We left the garage a few moments later. Here I was. The war just got started, and the first bombings took already place. However, before leaving, we took the lighter that we use to keep in the garage, burning the envelope and the incriminating pictures. So at least, this never happened. I took the decision to do it; I preferred to see this consumed by the flames instead of being somewhere where whether my boyfriend, whether my mother could find it. It's actually too dangerous to keep this somewhere. When we took back the lift with my twin, when we came back upstairs, my boyfriend was here, arrived apparently a couple of minutes ago with his little *pains au chocolat*. Fresh from the bakery and just seeing him was enough to help me feel much worse as I already was. Curiously, it took him so long to come back from a bakery, though, but, well, I assume that he went elsewhere. And when I saw him, I felt like I needed to leave. Sometimes, we lose battles, and this fight, I was actually surprised that my enemy could be more informed than I was, I thought it would be easier to manage. But yet again, I pretended that nothing really happened, as nothing was actually serious. While arriving in the kitchen, I made as if nothing happened, but Clarisse was somehow overwhelmed; unlike me, she cannot really contain lies. She does not have that ability.

I was actually doubtful and didn't really know what to think about this. I honestly didn't want to justify myself regarding that mysterious letter, and why I acted that way after I opened it, I just wanted to leave that as it was a total mystery. Usually, I give them lies so they can leave me alone, but spending my time saying bollocks to the entire world, at some point it becomes too much, you can't handle it anymore. It seems that rule has changed now. Curiously, everything seemed upside down from now. It was like, battle to survive. Many things were at stake now, and I have to win. For once, losing is not an option.

Florent was happy to see me. He was sitting on a table in the kitchen with my mother, and they were both eating their pastries. As usual, he made his small coffee, and they were talking about some random stuff. He saw us coming, looked at Clarisse, mum also looked at Clarisse, and they somehow understood that something was going on. In my mind, I was feeling like, I need to be alone today. I really need to think about what I should do, evaluate the real situation, and seek an answer. Because accepting means that... Well. Again, who the hell was this guy. When we entered the kitchen, mum looked at us:

"You're back already? Why did you need to go to the garage?"

"I just wanted to check something. Maybe I'll go for a ride today, I mean... I need to go out today."

"Oh yes?" she looked at the window, checking the weather.

"Yeah, I think I need to go for a run, maybe, instead... It's been a while that I didn't run."

"You may or may not have seen this, but it's cloudy, it's cold and windy, and you want to go for a run? Maybe it's going to snow in a bit, but you still wanna go for a run? You know, the flu is still out there, you should stay home. Because you're gonna get sick."

"Well, I'm gonna have a perfect excuse to cut school tomorrow, then," I said, smiling.

"Obviously, why didn't I think about that!"

"I'm lazy anyway."

"Well, darling, even sick you will go there, I really don't care. If you want to deliberately get sick for cutting school, just deal with your flu, but I will put you at school. Anyway, what's wrong with Clarisse?"

"Huh? Nothing, we just had a fight."

"About?"

"About the fact that Charlotte is a stupid, selfish bitch, and she should start acting like a cunt!" Clarisse intervened, pissed, and looked at me, almost proud of what she said.

"Language, Clarisse!" Mum looked at her. "I know your sister doesn't have any limits, but I am still struggling to save one of you from the dark side."

Are you actually serious? Because this situation would never have happened today if I were still with Claire. And I am not with Claire because mum declared us a stupid war, that led Claire and me to have several arguments. Because of her. Those arguments divided us, and Kelly sneaked in between to make sure we would really be split up, you know, ensuring the job is well done, with no mistakes. If Claire met Kelly and made her a bestie, it's because of my mother. Kelly just made a profit of a terrible situation, and if I am here now today, it's because of her. She has her part of responsibility today.

And seriously? She fucked up with me, I know that. When I went in her bedroom, I read one day, when I was twelve, that she didn't even want to have us or have twins, when she was pregnant. I know she never wanted me; I know I have always been a problem. She's struggling for Clarisse because she wants her to be made the way she wants? Fuck that, fuck her, and fuck all that she is. Now, it made me feel... well, mad. Like, literally mad. This was really not funny.

"Oh, I see," I continued, "you want to make sure that Clarisse is perfect because you admit that you totally fucked up with me, huh?"

"That is not what I said," mum started acting like a diplomat.

"Of course, that's never what you said. You just said that you want to save one of your daughters because the other is just hopeless today," I actually wanted to trigger a fight, so I could have the perfect excuse to leave that flat.

"I didn't say you were hopeless, Char..."

"Say whatever you want, you always preferred my sister to me. I know you never loved me; I am just a pain in the arse for you!" I started to get upset.

"Hey, Cha, calm down, what's wrong with you?"

"What's wrong with me? My mother is a whore, my dad is a coward, and my sister is a bitch. This is what is wrong with me!" I was now involving Clarisse, deliberately. "You guys are a nightmare, and I really don't understand why I am still staying with all the fuck of you!"

"Did you just say I am a whore, Charlotte?"

"You are a damn whore! Every time there's a problem in this flat, it's never your fault. Dad left, not your fault, your daughter is not feeling right, it's not your fault. Nothing is your fault today, you're just here and contemplating the situation, everything collapses, but you're just here, Charlotte, go to school! Fuck your damn school! I don't care."

"Charlotte, just to make sure... To make sure that I heard that right... Did you call me, your mother, a whore?"

"Fuck you, mum," I just launched at her, with indeed all the hate in the world.

Mum has learned to remain calm, whatever I say. And today, it was not the day to seek troubles with me. Ironically, she remained calm. And whilst I was standing up, now really upset, so upset that my legs were shaking, my arms as well, and my jaws were really tight... Things exploded in a brief time. I don't care who she is, she is today the source of all the problems. And having said that, literally, to my sister... Usually, I am suffering in silence, but I couldn't contain my pain anymore.

She actually stood up and went in front of me. It's really unusual, I mean... Usually, when it happens... At the same moment, Florent stood up and went next to Clarisse, who was undoubtedly now backwards because she didn't want to get involved in that situation. But now, I made her upset. I could see that. And I could also know that she wanted to slap me, like really, but she couldn't because she knows that she will lose all the credibility if she does that. And if she does that, she knows that it will lead to a fight. We already had a fight a couple of months ago, and Clarisse went to separate me because I was... I actually couldn't stop. Ironically, I was waiting for her to touch at least a single strand of my hair. I really needed that... But instead, she was very frustrating. Standing in front of me, she breathed and then started to speak:

"Charlotte... You who knows everything... I really wish someday, when you'll have kids with Florent, that your son or daughter comes to you and calls you a whore. I really wish that to you," she was speaking in an unbelievably soft way, which means that she was now furious and couldn't contain her anger anymore.

"Surprising. Unlike you, I'll make sure I'll have an abortion before!"

"You are a stupid cunt, Charlotte!"

"The example comes from above!"

"Get out!"

"I am, don't worry."

"Get out of here. I don't wanna see you anymore."

17 *And God created lesbians*

// At home, in my bedroom, Neuilly-sur-Seine.

// Sunday, 13th of January 2013, 15:14.

Meh, she can say whatever she wants... this is my flat anyway. So, I can do what I want. But I must confess that when she told me that, the only thing I really wanted was to get my stuff and get the hell out of here. I actually had no destinations. And regarding that fight, well... It's gonna take her a couple of hours, she's gonna cry, and she'll be better after that, like always. When we have a fight, she frequently acts that way. She'll be mad at me for a while, and then will be back. Because unlike me, she wants to restart a relationship with me. So, even on Wednesday, she will need me. That's sure.

Free Expensive Lies: Prologue

I went into the bathroom after that, and I had a shower. Ironically, Florent avoided me because he knows that I am more likely to seek problems with others when I am having a fight with someone. It delivered me some moment of real peace. They left me alone. I went to get some stuff on my wardrobe, like my pink vest, another grey light pullover, a scarf because it's freezing outside, my pink hat, a pair of trousers, and some sneakers. After all, I need to walk. And some white socks. I went to take a shower, peeing, getting dressed, and... No makeup, nothing else. I went to get my red coat, my phone still plugged in my nightstand, my wallet, my earphones, and then, fully ready to leave, I left.

Florent was in the bedroom when I left. He actually didn't talk to me. I gave him a kiss before to go because otherwise, it will raise questions, like "why you didn't kiss me, blah, blah, blah" ... And even, he didn't really want me to leave. But whatever it was, I needed that.

I actually went to take the metro, and, well, I didn't really know where to go. When I was on the platform, I could see that the next train was in like 5 minutes. I waited. And, well, it was there that I realised that I forgot my gloves. So, well, I'll stop by a shop to get some... I know there's one in the Champs-Elysées, so I will go there. After, I'll see where I can go. And the metro arrived when I turned Spotify on. After I searched, for like a couple of minutes for what I wanted to listen to, I gave up as the choice is relatively infinite. After all, why not enjoy the people's authentic sound for once (you know, like in a zoo and spending time on your phone, it doesn't make any sense, you cannot see a giraffe every day!), instead of destroying my eardrum. And, yeah, I travelled. Four stations later, it was my stop.

I realised that I loved those moments, being alone like this. I mean, at least today, I was free. I didn't have anyone on my arse to tell me "oh, let's go here, let's go here..." For the very first time in a while I actually stopped in the first McDonalds, I found to get some food. This is not something that I usually do, because it's very unusual for me to go there, but I felt like I wanna go here. And for the first time in maybe a couple of years, yeah, I ate that. And believe it or not, but this meal had a kind of taste of freedom for me. I stayed in there, for maybe an hour or two, and I read some shit on my phone, I went on YouTube to watch some videos about ghost hunters and paranormal... Well, it may sound spooky, but yet I still don't dare to watch it in the dark. I used to watch the American TV show *Ghost Adventures*, but, well... I don't believe in ghosts, and I really hope that sometimes, this is fake. I mean, I don't believe in ghosts... I do believe in ghosts, but not in a religious way. I do think there must be malevolent ghosts, though.

Afterwards... well, I went to get my gloves, actually, because it was freezing out there. Then, still, with my large coke from McDonald's in my hand, I was slowly walking down the Champs-Elysées, heading to the *Jardin des Tuileries* after the Concorde, when, well, problems of the morning went back. I was texting with my sister in the meantime, she was feeling better but got pissed when I called her a bitch. I apologised because she didn't deserve that from me, as I acted impulsively, and... yeah. Whilst walking down the avenue, I was still thinking: he got me. At least, they got me. After having thought about this, yeah, actually... I do not have any other choices but saying yes.

Because for that reason: it's true, I do not know anything about whoever is blackmailing me. I do believe that it must be a guy. The problem is that it could be everyone. As he got a lot of information about me, he knows where to target... And he has those things. Those pictures and apparently films. And it's true, he has all the names so it suggests that he might have their address... At least he has the address of my grandparents in the UK. Which means I don't really think this guy is bluffing. The problem is, what does he want from me? I have money, why isn't he interested in this? If he knows most of my life, this guy knows I am rich. I mean, over thirty million... It doesn't mean this guy is interested in money; he doesn't do it because I am rich or something like this. This guy wants to destroy me, it's pure revenge. On the other hand, it would make sense because Kelly seeks vengeance on me. After all, I spend all my time belittling her. So, revenge is his motive.

He also said he leaves me forty-eight hours to say yes to Kelly, which means, he wants to humiliate me. He wants me to become, well... Yeah, a prostitute. Let's say that if I actually do what I want, and I do not say anything to Kelly, then these pictures might be published. He will target everyone. First, my boyfriend will never forgive me. And, well, as I pretended that nothing has happened, that will make things worse because, yes, I lied to him, I deceived him, that will be the worst. So, I will lose him. I'm gonna hurt him and hurt him very badly. I don't want to do that; he doesn't deserve that. My mother... Well... Here, the disgrace will actually be significant. Because receiving this... I honestly don't know what her reaction would be, but since she likes valid familial values, what I did went against, and she wouldn't forgive me. Well, I'd become like the pariah of the family.

I sometimes dream about being alone, but the problem is, I need someone. I'm scared of being alone, and, yeah, I need someone to live with me. I want to have someone I could rely on, the problem is, as this guy wants to change the order in my life, and wants to destroy everything... I am sure that once he publishes all those stuff about me, he's gonna want something else from me. Because these are threats, I am taking them seriously, and since this guy is more interested in destroying me than ruining me, he will want something more from me. If I say no, first, these pictures will be published, given to my relatives, but there will be something else. Because I believe he knows that I can bounce back from this. It could be challenging, but I can still bounce back by leaving the country and changing my identity. The problem is, if I do that, financially speaking, that will involve quite a lot of things: if I change my identity, I am not multi-millionaire anymore. And if I want to fight this guy, I will need money. Vanishing, yeah, why not, but restarting from zero, it's gonna be more problematic.

And if he finds me, because it will take time, he's gonna find me. Honestly, I don't really want to play with him. It's quite risky. Because maybe this is all bluff, maybe there's nothing behind, but there were still these pictures of me that I received, so... Maybe I am worrying for nothing. Maybe not. Well, doing that will be more secrets to hide to my boyfriend. But, if I say yes, that will be, first, doing this. Second, if my mother finds this out, I'm just dead... And who tells me that this guy will not try to play with me at the end? He may still lure me, and I would have to say yes. That's the problem.

It's when I was walking down, in the *Jardin des Tuileries*, that I actually thought about Claire. The park was unusually not that busy for a Sunday, and the sky was still threatening, darkening minutes after minutes, and I was even thinking about her. Why did she do that? I mean... the Claire I knew wouldn't accept this, so I assume she's been trapped as well. As I have to say yes... It was actually better to ask for advice, on how this might be going. And it was in this unbroken calm that, well... I sat on a bench and checked on my phone. Last time I called Claire; it was for telling her to fuck off. It's true, I didn't really want to speak to her anymore, especially since the very last time I saw her was, well... that Thursday evening, she usually calls me every Sunday on the afternoon. Usually, she likes to talk about her week, what she's been doing, who she met, and how she thinks about people and other shit like this. She used to call me at around one, and it was two now. She still didn't call. Maybe she had the same envy as me, just to call because we need each other. I don't know what may be on her mind right now.

I am not someone that likes texting. Hiding behind a screen is not something I love to do. And... After having thought, after having seriously considered what to actually do, well... I called her. And ironically, it rang only once... She was waiting for a call.

"Hi..." I said after she took the call.

"Hi..." she replied in an actually weird voice, like the first time I called her after we broke up.

"What's up?"

"I'm bored."

"Same here..." I used actually the same tone as she did.

I noticed, however, that she wasn't home. I heard her being outside, like in the street or something. She usually stays home on Sunday, because it's her painting day, but today... Well, I don't recognise her since last Thursday, so everything could be possible right now.

"Wanna catch up?" she asked, surprised.

"Yeah, why not, where are you?" I accepted.

"Somewhere. Where are you?"

"Somewhere too..."

"Well, it's gonna be constructive then."

"Yeah..." I led this conversation into a stalemate since I wanted her to reveal where she would be first.

"Well, I'm actually close to you. I went to *La Défense* today, as... Well, I guess shopping was making me think about something else. And you, where are you?"

"In the Jardin des Tuileries. Come, and... If you want, we'll go for a drink somewhere."

"Yeah... Okay, I'm coming then. See you in a bit."

I hung up the phone and waited. If she's there, it shouldn't take long for her to come here, she just has one line to take.

I like to come here, in this garden. It's like, yeah, one of the only parks in Paris that I like. Overlooking the famous *Place de la Concorde*, leading to the end of the Champs-Elysées and the French Parliament. This place is mostly renowned for its obelisk, lights at night, and, more historically speaking, when French revolutionaries here beheaded King Louis XVI more than two hundred years ago. Every time I come here, I remember that argument I used to have with a teacher when I was in high school because they used to depict Louis XVI as a moron. In my opinion, he was one of the greatest kings this country has ever had. But the problem is... as they say, I am British, I come from Britain (which is wrong, I was born in the south of France...) so giving my opinion isn't generally a good idea.

Free Expensive Lies: Prologue

Basically, I am both British and French citizen. I hold both citizenships. As my father was French, I could have French citizenship. My parents actually met in France, as my father just finished his finance studies in a school near Montpellier, and my mother was doing a linguistic exchange program to learn French. They actually met because my French grandparents used to be host family, and by the time she was there, as they had a really close age difference (my father is like... 3 years older than my mother), they somehow fell in love. Instead of going back in the UK, my mother decided instead to remain in France, with absolutely no money in her pocket because she didn't finish her studies, but... love has its reason that reason ignores. She almost gave up everything, to stay and build a family with Adam, my dad.

Within their first years together, at least before mum got us, it was quite challenging for her to find a job in France since her French was terrible, she was struggling. But to learn, she found a cashier position in supermarkets, bakeries, just to find a way to get home. And, she used to say, and I tend to believe her... by the time she was settling down in here, she was struggling with the country's administration. In between, my father finally got hired in a bank and was banking advisor. After three years of relationship, mum got pregnant, and instead of having one baby, she had two, my sister and me. That was a surprise. She wrote in a diary that it was hard for her to learn that she was pregnant of twins because she had no savings, she had nothing, and, although the school is free in France, healthcare as well (there are no private doctors here), she was scared because she couldn't afford to have two kids at once. Even my father, although he had an excellent job in a bank, he didn't earn that much money.

When we were born... Actually, there was some problem: even if I was the first to see the world, twenty minutes before my sister, I almost died. Because I was the weakest, Clarisse took almost most of my strength when sharing mum's womb. Clarisse is the strongest, and when my mother delivered me, there were several problems. Surgeons could save me afterwards, hopefully, but I was not actually scheduled to survive until then. While my sister didn't have many health problems, my first years were almost a battle for my survival. For instance, I got dehydrated when I was two, had chickenpox and almost killed me, and at four, I entered into a four days coma after an unstoppable fever. Since then, well, even if doctors managed to stabilise my health, and I got stronger, I remained very pale and, for example, my sister can do better things than me. I don't practise sports because, for instance, running, I get breathless before her, same for sports like basketball or anything.

If on the plan on survival, Clarisse would definitely be stronger than me. If there was a natural selection, I would die for sure; however, things are slightly different regarding our intellect. Unlike my sister, I almost learned everything on my own, such as reading, writing, and counting things. Unlike her, a kind of a troublemaker when she was young, I remained always very calm in my first years, and my mother told me that I was watching everything. She used to say to me that I was literally fascinated by animal documentaries. When I was a baby, I wasn't crying that much by night, and I was such a sleeper that sometimes, my parents thought I was dead so woke me up by night to make sure I didn't pass away. I remember the first thing I loved in my life was the books my mother used to read. I used to love dictionaries because the pictures were teaching me what was what, and on my own, even if Clarisse spoke before me and I spoke actually quite late, and I started reading things quite early, I was maybe three. Clarisse could only read when she was five. I already understood the principle of division at her age and could calculate it only with my mind. Today, even if it's quite incredible, I can calculate with my mind complex stuff. The thing is, I am unable to explain how I could get by the results. I never used a calculator in my life.

But unlike her, I remained always isolated, I was not seeking the company of other people. I was just reading, all the time, and staying all alone. In addition to that, our parents decided that we should speak English as a mother tongue, (my father spoke English... at least he learned with my mother) and my grandparents thought it would be a great idea. Because as the world speaks English, so learning English would be making our lives easier. It was a significant advantage for us and a big problem because when we arrived in primary school, we could not talk to anybody since we couldn't speak their languages. We had a translator during our first years at school, the time teachers could teach us French. It was quite challenging for Clarisse, who had normal development, she learned French quite quickly, but my teacher used to try to teach me how to read. The problem, I knew that already. I was reading things a couple of months before I turn four. However, as I learned French by phonetics and learned the English alphabet first, it was hard for me to write correctly.

When I was seven, I mean, when we were seven, my sister and I finally spoke French fluently and could manage to understand and be understood. Whilst we evolved when we were at school together, I was more and more isolated. Our parents took the decision to colour Clarisse's hairs to difference us because the problem was... When I was wearing some clothes, or she was wearing some clothes, somehow one of us wanted to be dressed like the other, which led to dramas. And it was tough to distinguish who was Clarisse from me. And we started our lives here, in the south of France. I was still reading a thousand books, I read so many books, it became like a passion. Unfortunately, as I was labelled as the nerd, I didn't have many friends, unlike Clarisse, that was more socialised than me. But I liked my isolation. It raised my teachers' concerns that saw my potential, they called my parents to check if everything was okay, and, well, apparently, I was born that way. Even to the teachers, I wasn't that communicative. They thought I was autistic because even in class, I was almost not speaking. They tested me, and, even today, they are not really sure. When they diagnosed me as a psychopath when I was twelve, it showed that I was not using any emotions or affection after having done a functional MRI. This zone in my brain was bypassed when I was making a decision. It's also a theory that I might be autistic. It is also said that I have no notions of danger.

Yeah, it's true, I never felt any emotions. For instance, I do not cry—for example, love. I know what it means, I am just unable to experience it. When I have sex, (and this has always been the same with whomever I am having sex with, a man or a woman), I do not feel anything else but something going down. If I moan during sex, it means that it's likely to be false. I never had any orgasms in my life, I don't know how it feels like. But I feel an attraction for girls. It's tough to explain – I am probably asexual – but taking decisions such as this... It's weird to explain because it's not the fact that sleeping with people that scares me the most. It's something I can undergo. What actually scares me is the aftermath of this.

But sex wasn't a question when I was in primary school, and we moved to Paris when I was eleven, we finally found out what was high school. My father got promoted within his bank, he was now in charge of investments, earning much more money than previously. The problem, my father, in between – nobody knew about this – was having an affair with one of her colleagues. None of us knew about this. And we found this out a long time later. When we moved to Paris, the first year at school, Clarisse was with her friends, but... although I got some primary school problems because I was the nerd, problems became much worse when in high school. This time, I was targeted by bullying because I could not adapt to the new challenges. It took me one year, and as they saw that they could actually do everything with me and I wasn't affected at all, it was quite discouraging for them.

However, I wasn't showing that I was pissed by that, but I still got the humiliation, I was deeply humiliated, for example, the day they covered my locker at school with unfolded condoms... And everybody laughed. The problem was, I couldn't defend myself.

And in between, it was not even a year that we settled down in Paris that someone knocked at the door on a beautiful day of September 2006. We were living here for two months already, and we opened to this person: a ten-year-old girl seeking Adam Kominsky (Adam is our father's name). By the time, we were both with my twin eleven, this girl was ten. After having actually questioned her why she was looking for our father, it's when she replied with an innocent, "He's my dad too" that everything literally changed within our household. Mum was over there and did not believe a second this had happened. And from that day, the war, a terrible war that changed the face of the family.

And it's here that divisions started between my mother and me. Because usually... For example, I know both my grandparents, from both sides. They met, both after World War II, and still today, they are together. My French grandparents are dead today, but my English grandparents are still alive, yet they are a loving family. But yet, even my French grandparents remained together until the end. Even if death did them part, but until the very end, they were together. I don't know if one of them cheated on the other, but I honestly don't think so, because although there were many disputes, many arguments... when they were both apart, one was looking for the other. I am not that close to my English grandparents, but they are the same, two old people that spend their time fighting and arguing and complaining... but when there is one without the other, it's like the end of the world. I love seeing that it's actually so cute, they are adorable. They went through thousands of things in life, but still, they are together, united, and always as strong as the very first day.

Unfortunately, both my parents were born in the '70s. And, I am sorry, this generation is undoubtedly the shittiest the humankind has ever seen. I mean, don't get me wrong, but parents coming from the 70' are the shittiest ever. Like my parents, they got married, and had kids, and are both appalling parents. Why? Too much time at work, becoming the slaves of their managers or bosses means that they didn't care or didn't have enough time to focus on their children's education. And obviously... If it weren't one of them having an affair, it would be jealousy problems, it would be misunderstanding problems, it would also be disagreement... They go through that sometimes before they get married. But this problem is nothing... it becomes worst after the wedding. And it's precisely here that we come to my generation, paying the price of their idiocy by serving as postal services. You see your father, "oh, you know, your mum..." so you hate your mum. And you go to your mum, "oh, really, your dad said that? But you know, your dad...". When they exploded within our family, these kinds of problems tore my sister and me apart because my sister took my father's side, and I took my mother's side. And as none of us found an agreement for us because they were all fucking stupid, so they had to go to a court, and the judge ordered that Clarisse would live with her father and I'd live with my mum. The thing was Clarisse forgave them. As I am a psychopath and I am totally unable to forgive anyone, here is the situation today.

Today, I am making my mother pay the price of her mistakes. Insulting her, it's nothing. After we split with my sister, I literally changed, I became out of control, and things were worst during the year Clarisse was not here. Because I needed her, she was necessary to me, I couldn't grow up without her. Because Clarisse and I are incredibly close to each other. And splitting two twin sisters at the very beginning of their adolescence is not really a good idea. She will pay the price for as long as both of us will live under the same roof. So, we both use tools such as humiliation, intimidation, and today, the war is still ongoing, except that I am the new enemy, and for her, it's undoubtedly the worst. Because she can just do anything against me, Clarisse and I are landlords of our building as she wanted. Today, she somehow uses Clarisse against me, but it doesn't work that much. Maybe she won many battles, like the fact that Claire and I are not together anymore because she said that homosexuality is an awful sin, the battle is still almost daily because none of us will give in. And I will not give in until she fully apologises and recognises her disastrous results as a mother. Because I know that I am right. And she is wrong. But she doesn't want to apologise because, yeah, she's a mother.

Thinking about this... It's probably my most significant pain today. Because, as I said, I am not someone that tells what is wrong. I bear the pain, I carry the heavy burden, but... I am never talking. And, somehow, well... I was looking at a bird, covering a nest, incubating the little new babies. Little birdies. It was at that very moment that, when I was looking at that bird and actually being in my thoughts, that, well... I heard someone disturbing me.

"Excuse me! Terribly sorry..." I heard a 25-year-old man voice.

"Hello?" A young lady.

I was in my dreams, and I turned my head. Well, a young couple. I mean, they were a couple as they were holding each other's hand. They seemed nice, actually. But not from here. French, but not from here. He had a nice girlfriend, though.

"Hey, guys, what's up?"

"Doing okay, what's up?" the guy started.

"Yeah, fine. Can I do anything for you?" I kindly asked.

"Oh, yeah. We are actually looking for the *Musée d'Orsay*. And I think I lost my way."

He had his smartphone in hand. Hum... Old school, huh? I looked at that. And... I know it's close, but the exact way to go there? Well, honestly, I have no idea. Erm, my phone is in my pocket. And I am sluggish to the job that someone else can do.

"Hum... That is really close from here," I started to reply. "I am not sure, but you need to walk towards that way, open Maps, type *'Musée d'Orsay'* and... It should give you the right way, I guess."

"Oh..." he looked at his phone, "Oh, you don't know either. Sorry about that."

"My pleasure."

They left. Well, I don't think I have been actually rude... was I?

Yeah, if there's a thing I keep from childhood, I do not speak that much. I am always observing things, hearing things, and I keep them always in secret. Sometimes, I feel like my brain must be a museum of unnecessary items. When I was young, teachers were still surprised that I didn't involve myself within groups, I was always apart, in my books, or watching everything. It's actually through watching that I learn most of the things. I only learn by understanding the logic of something; otherwise, I do not understand anything. Sometimes, it's weird, but it's why I hate going to school: they teach us stuff that we have to learn. I never learn by heart; I always try to understand things so I can remember. And my logic is sometimes tough to understand for teachers, this is why they are actually giving up.

And logic always prevailed in many of my choices, because for me, if things are not working, it means they are not working for a reason. The problem is that it applies to everything. And Claire actually understood how I worked amazingly fast: we eventually met during my second year of high school. The reason why, I failed my first year as I couldn't focus correctly on things since my mind was polluted by my parents' problems and also by bullying, and I started my second year with people younger than me. Claire was amongst the new pupils beginning that year. And it's actually odd, although she had many friends because she knew many people already, she came to me naturally. Meanwhile, I changed, I started to take care of myself, and I began to open myself to the others, which were like the first time as I never cared about my appearance and anything before. She came to me, became friend with me, and, I don't know, there was, yeah, something else.

This other thing, well, it was actually attraction. Maybe after a couple of months of friendship, it turned out that our strange closeness was hiding something. It was actually weird how our love story started. The thing started with a bet. The bet was on a memory test; it was a game she downloaded on her phone, and she pretended she could beat me. She ended up at level 10 whilst I had to stop at level 50. The issue of the bet was, if she wins, she would actually give a kiss to some guy she actually liked. If she lost, she would kiss me. On the 14th of December 2007, a few days before the Christmas holidays, she was so ashamed to actually kiss me in her living room, so we waited until being in her bedroom, and it was something that none of us had regrets to do. Well, okay, on the very moment when it happened, it was somewhat different.

Because on the moment, it was like, "shit, sorry, what the hell happened? I am really sorry", and, even, because I was spending the weekend with her by that time, I actually cut short and went back home relatively early. Claire replaced my twin sister by the time because she only came back home in Paris in 2008. And this thing, well, we actually didn't speak to anyone. When she kissed me, as for Claire, as a bet is a bet, she, well, kissed me for real. It was not like a small kiss, no, not at all. We both loved it but were too young to admit it. And it shocked us. And as we were in the same class, we had to go back to school the days later.

And until the next Friday, we didn't speak to each other. I resumed being all alone when she said with other friends and this guy for whom she had a crush, and... And what was supposed to happen actually happened, on Friday, one week after, she came to me, like, "can we talk in private?". I said okay, and we went within the school building to speak without taking the risk of being heard. And at that moment, she actually confessed that she had a real crush on me, and this guy was not finally that interesting. Even if we knew that being lesbian was actually a fact, we couldn't think it would happen to us. It's why we were so shocked. But this Friday would be the last one until we go on holidays for two weeks, and she also said that since that very first kiss, she couldn't stop thinking about doing it again. And honestly when she kissed me... It was not the same anymore. Because me too, by the very moment I couldn't stop thinking about what happened. So... We kissed again. And, that 21st of December 2007, a couple of days before Christmas, as if it were for sure my most beautiful gift ever received from someone, started my new relationship with Claire. This, obviously, in total secrecy.

Yeah, she's an essential part of my life. Or at least she has been. Still sat on that very same bench, I was still looking that nest in the middle of the park. It's like, yeah, the nest, what I have missed in my life. Creating mine. And, at some point, I felt my phone ringing in my pocket. I took it and saw "Claire – Incoming call." Hum, she must be nearby. I immediately answered:

"*Ja?*" I replied with a German accent.

"Where are... Oh, don't move, I'm coming."

And she hung up. At the very same moment, I heard someone running towards me. Like, running quite slowly.

I turned back, looking a bit everywhere, and then I saw her. I don't know why she always used to run when she is coming to me. Meanwhile, I put my phone back in my pocket. She was still very tall, all dressed in black, with a closed leather coat which perfectly reflected the streetlights near to us, but it seemed quite heavy. She was awful with it. Ironically, no makeup today, which means she was actually not right. Usually, even very slight, she wears makeup, but today, nope. It means she was seriously affected by the situation. She was wearing warm clothes though, she had her usual grey pullover with printed on it "be nice or go away", a pair of black jeans and, ultimately, a pair of burgundy boots. No heels today. She ran towards me meant that she was happy to talk to me again, even if she likes to keep her distance (this must be common in French woman... I mean, even if I never had any other girlfriend from any other countries, but this is something I noticed on many women here, if you do not open yourself to them, they will never open themselves to you), she seemed quite happy. She didn't smile, though. But I really don't know why this coat, it was awful.

"Here you are!" I said at the moment she sat on the bench next to me.

"Hey! How are you doing? I hope better since the last time!" she didn't know where to start this conversation.

True, she was placing some kind of barrier between us, meaning in her language that "if you attack me, I leave". Claire, come on... You're no enemy to me, which is why I started to bend myself towards her, placing my head over her shoulder, which meant that, in my body language, whatever happened, you will always remain my Claire. She didn't wear any perfume today, and as she was carrying bags from a *pret-a-porter* low-cost shop from Sweden. Not the Irish one, it still doesn't exist in France, for the moment. According to her smell, she woke up quite late, got dressed, had her Kellogg's as usual, and left. I was just very pissed last day, I was just, mad, that's the reason why I reacted like this. And whilst still hugging, I started:

"I am sorry for what I told you last day on the phone. I didn't mean to be that rude to you..."

"It's okay, I..." she was sincere for once although she remained quite melancholic, "it's my fault, I mean, I should have told you this long ago... I promised to never hide anything from you, and I am sorry for what happened."

"Yeah, everything has changed..." I thought so, somehow agreeing with her. "By the way, I considered Kelly's offer."

I actually wanted to see that reaction, though. However, I needed to confirm whether she was or not my blackmailer. Because although she can be my ex-girlfriend, it doesn't exclude her from the list of suspicious people. Let's start: why would she do that? Claire has never been interested in money, and even if she knows how much money I have on my bank accounts, it has never been something that has interested her. Destroying me, why? It may make sense because even if we are no longer together, I know she still desires me. She dreams just like I do to come back with me, so she would have all interests of breaking up my couple with Florent. It would make sure that she would be the first to talk with her about what happened, seeking reassurance, and then I would fall for her arms. The thing is, this is credible, but using this way to get what she wants, it seems quite extreme. Then, regarding the information... She knows most of the people my blackmailer mentioned by phone, except that I am not sure she knows my grandparents, and their address and I know for sure that she doesn't know when precisely I started my relationship with Florent. She still could be *Rising Sun*, but, well, there are still a lot of "but" in this. Things show that she may be, but other things show that she couldn't be. Let's exploit this.

"You're kidding, right?" she said thoughtfully, using reverse psychology. I could genuinely see her embarrassment.

"Well, why not, after all?"

"Well..."

"I was upset on the moment, but after having considered it..."

"Hum..." she started before yawning.

She actually didn't know what to say. And, she was yawning, which seemed that she didn't sleep very well. Her hairs poorly combed showed that she was quite anxious right now, and the same as her breath. She was really nervous.

I feel like... That's just my feeling right now, she actually wants me to do that. For the sole reason, she thinks that if I do that, I will be more nervous, just as she is right now, to create tensions between my boyfriend and me. Which will lead to a breakup. Because Claire knows just as I do know, truth always appears. And my relationship's collapse is like her dream. But on the other hand, it seems like she doesn't want me to undergo this, it could be explained by why she was almost crying when she saw me the last day and said with her lips that she was sorry. The fact that my relationship explodes, it is definitely the thing she seeks, because unlike me, since we broke up, she couldn't manage to find a new boyfriend. And the Claire I knew is not a fickle woman.

"Sleepless night?" I was trying to change topics.

"More or less, I just can't sleep now," she started. "What do you want to do exactly regarding this?"

"I have more considered your offer, and I said to myself... It's true, it would be quite fun."

"I don't really believe you!" she knows me.

"Well, yeah. I need new experiences in my life. And I thought that... Well, it's not the best thing to do, but it can be fun."

"Charlotte, please, don't take me for an idiot. When we had sex together, which was not that long ago, you told me that sex doesn't do anything to you, because you're asexual or something. And now you are talking to me about doing this?"

"Well, I may... I am not asexual... I just want to discover."

"Huh..." she sighed, nervously. "You know what, it's up to you!"

Interesting. She doesn't believe me and acts like a sceptical. It's true, she knows this, regarding me not feeling anything during sex, she is fully aware of this, but still, she didn't advise me not to do that. Instead, she acts like this is a sensitive topic for her and like, "do whatever you want, I don't care". It's interesting because she actually cares, but she doesn't want to say why she cares about this. Because it's why she cares that is actually the sensitive thing. I don't think she acts like this on purpose, I think she acts like this because she's been instructed to do so and totally disagrees with the instructions. I know this, I know her, and I saw her acting like this before. But deep down she wants me to say no, whatever the price of it, but there's something. I would bet whatever I can, but I am sure she must be blackmailed too. It would explain why she's been acting so secret for the time, why she changed like this because what I feel from her, it's fear. I feel her fear, she's petrified but doesn't want to admit anything, because it may be dangerous. And when she took her phone out of her pocket and told me after seeking someone's phone number, it confirmed what I actually thought:

"If you want to go further, then, you need to call this number. Joris. He's the guy behind the scene."

Joris... Wait, I know that name! It seems familiar to me...

"Hum... Okay then. What do I tell him?"

"It's up to you, either you call Kelly and speak with her, or either you call this Joris and tell him that you're a friend of us, and you were the one with Christian. The guy with whom you slept and that gave you the five hundred euros."

"Well, I'll see. Thanks for the thing."

"Yeah," she didn't seem amazed at all.

She became increasingly nervous. I mean, the more I was talking about this, and the more she was tensed. Even if I was still close to her, still hugging her, she was nervous. And I remained that way to actually hear her breath better and feeling her pulse. Because, discreetly, I was taking her left arm and trying to touch above her hand, where I could feel her pulse.

On the other hand, it's the first time she speaks about that with me. I don't really know what would be in her mind, how dumbstruck she could be, but... I had to do that, so, this is done. Now, let's speak about something else. Because she won't be at her ease. It's why I resumed.

"You look very tired," I started.

"Huh? I just can't sleep now! It's been maybe a week that I am having big troubles to sleep."

"You should check a doctor, it's been a while you are telling me this that you can't sleep."

"Yeah, I could. I mean, I could see a doctor tell him that I am feeling appalling every morning because I regret having broken up with my ex-girlfriend and now, for having fun, I am having sex for money. And now, you're getting married. Soon."

Oh... Well... And after I didn't go forward. Seriously, what should I say about this?

"Well. What can I tell you?" I actually started and stopped hugging her.

"I know! There's nothing to say," she was on the edge of crying, again.

"Claire, we had this discussion a hundred times before."

"I know, I slept with them, I did something wrong, it's all my fault. And I broke up with you."

"I never said it was your fault. What I say is, I tried to rebuild things, I tried to forgive you. But for some reasons, you said that it was over, and I never really understood that."

"I hope you will" she was sniffing. "I am sure, someday, you will. I have so many regrets, Charlotte. I... I am so sorry."

"Tell me!" I understood that she wanted to tell me something big.

"I... I can't," she was crying.

"Why, you can't?"

"He's everywhere. I gotta go, Cha. See you later, I'll call you later. And don't follow me."

"Who's everywhere, Claire?"

She immediately stood up. She didn't run away, but... Damn. Oh my god. She actually managed to not show me her face.

"Claire, come on, what's going on!"

"I can't talk. I'll call you later."

So now, well, I think I can dismiss Claire as being my blackmailer. Her behaviour, the way she acted, definitely said otherwise. But the way she reacted... It's the first time she openly talks about me, missing her as a girlfriend. I am indeed the cause of her not sleeping at night, it seems weird to me. This was unprecedented, honestly. It even shocked me. And the fact that she leaves suddenly, like this. Man... That is really weird and totally unexpected. And what she said, yeah, "he's everywhere". For now, my theory would be that Joris, to be my blackmailer, even if I need to confirm it. And if she is under their influence, it almost confirms what I think: Kelly is definitely behind the fall of our relationship.

Every time I see Claire crying, it's... nope. I really hate this. I didn't see her crying that much, but my heart bleeds every time I see her crying. I mean, there are a few things that affect me in life, there are a very few things that make me like pissed that way. But Claire crying is one of them. And, despite confirming what I already thought about Kelly and her in this thing, this was... Claire was weeping because of someone, so I must act. It's weird, sometimes I am feeling like a guy saying that, but, whenever she is crying, I cannot accept anything. I swore when I was with her that whatever happens, I'll be there. She's been here for me at many moments of my life, and I can't give her up like this. It's why my decision was taken: Kelly, no matter what, this means war. She attacked my girlfriend, she used her against her wishes, she used her for her stupid things, she dishonoured her, and this. It may cost me a lot, or it may cost me nothing, but I won't leave Claire alone. So, I had a plan. They want me to do that? At least Kelly and my blackmailer? Fine. I will do it. Not for me. But for Claire. It's for her that I am battling now, even if it has to cost me a lot, I don't mind. Whatever the cost, whatever the price, Claire is Claire. I will infiltrate this because so far, I know that they are obeying to Joris. I must know more about this Joris. Gathering proofs, and then... I'll find a way, but I'll dismantle that. I'll put Claire safer. My priority is to remain discreet because I don't want anybody to know what I am doing. I think, doing that, it's possible. And if I have to leave Florent if it explodes... Well, it will. But I must remain discreet, no matter what. Because I still don't want nobody to find the truth. As I am attacking myself to a prostitution network, it may be perilous if I fail being discreet whilst doing my infiltration.

But instead of confronting this guy straight, I actually wanted to call Kelly. It's unusual, I never call her, but she is expecting my call. I don't know what to say to this Joris, and Kelly seems to be a better opportunity to come to infiltrate this. I cannot tolerate Claire being harassed by them, and I will do my best to make sure she does not suffer anymore. Because she's a victim, she's also a victim just like I am, and I cannot let her down. Sophie was right, I must act, and even if I have to undergo this, I don't care. What I want is to make sure this guy is no longer causing harm to her. So, after I saw my ex-girlfriend leaving, and honestly, seeing her going away was heartbreaking, I immediately grabbed my phone. It is now time to counterattack.

It rang twice.

"Hey, Kelly?"

"Hey Cha, what's up?" she seemed, so friendly and hypocrite...

"Could be better!"

"Oh, what's wrong? I hope there's nothing big!"

"Me neither. Hum, regarding your offer..."

Well, well, well... I actually didn't know where to start. I was somehow in a vengeful mode because I kept on thinking about Claire. And, I felt like, yeah. For the honour. Whatever happens, from now... The day I kissed Claire; the day we promised assistance to each other, I swore in an oath to defend her whatever happens. And even if we are no longer together, this is still my duty. Today, the danger has a name, more than ever and now clearly identified, and its name is Kelly. Claire may or may not admit it – but I think she did today – but we need each other, and especially today. Today certainly more than ever. So, whatever happens, whatever the consequences, even if it has to destroy my life, I cannot let that whore overthrow my Claire Cobert. Kelly wants the war... At the moment I saw Claire crying another time, I said, the battle is now declared. It's like the Royal Air Force against the Luftwaffe. Yeah, I could speak about the Armée de l'Air, but unfortunately, things happened to them.

"Oh. Are you serious? You finally want to join us?"

"Yes," I said coldheartedly.

"All right then... Well, okay, but do you feel ready for that?"

"Well, it's not like I didn't do it already. Remember last Thursday?"

"Yes, but first I need to know you won't give up after having started, or that you won't say anything to the Police or something like that. I really need to know that I can trust you. There's quite a lot at stake right now, and I really want to keep this alive, otherwise..."

"Oh, darling. If I wanted to call the Police regarding your business, trust me, you'd be rotting in jail already!"

"Of course, it makes sense... Yeah, for sure. Forget that. But I need to know that you won't give it up once started."

"Why would I?"

"You need to be cold-blooded to do such a thing. Do you think you can do it?"

We used to say that there's nothing more dangerous than a woman in love. For Claire, I am ready to do anything. But I need to draw a plan, I cannot do this on my own, I mean, I need to think about it. Well, I had no other options but to accept it, I am aware it's gonna be a hefty price to pay, but it's for a good cause. I think, once I get to know more, I can act consequently, and thus respond as things go until I find something interesting to finally draw an exit strategy and saving my ex's arse. I continued:

"I am tougher than you, darling..."

"Okay, I ask this because, well. As you are currently in a relationship. I just don't want this to interfere with that."

"There are no chances. My boyfriend still doesn't know about anything."

"Okay, then. You think you can hide this?"

"Darling, I can hide your mother and even put a chocolate cake in her arse, if I want."

"Yeah, true," she laughed.

"Are you reconsidering my quality of being an incredible liar?"

"No. Of course not. You're the evillest person I know, so, no, I think you're cold-blooded enough for that job."

"Thank you. Now, how does it work?"

"Hum, yes, I will speak with Joris, but I think it may work out. What are you doing tomorrow? Because I have something for you in the evening."

"Already? The evening? No, it's not possible. I have many appointments after school and... No, sorry, but I can't."

"Ah. Too bad."

"Yeah, I am sorry."

"Um... The truth is, I need girls available at any time."

She needs girls... Then who the hell is Joris? She may be organising stuff, arranging parties, and Joris takes the money. Hum... I really need to speak with her, find out who is doing what. The problem is... I don't think I may be in a position to refuse, given the fact that God knows what's the next move of my blackmailer.

"I can understand that you may already need me, but the problem is that I have a medical appointment, and I can't miss, this is really important. Come on, Kelly, you know I am sick."

"Well, darling, you'll have to miss, I am so sorry!"

"You ain't serious?"

"I am!"

On the other hand, nothing told me that I have to accept this, she just leaves me no choice. Even if I used the fact that I am sick (I am not ill, I mean not really, and I don't have any medical appointment, I just don't want tomorrow) against her, she said she can't. Because she imperatively needs me. My blackmailer wasn't really precise on whether I have to accept the first job or not, I just want to prepare myself for this. Prepare what I have to tell everyone what excuse I want to give them, and everything. On that point, Kelly is a bit like me, whatever the tool used, we need an outcome. She's a bit like me when it comes to serving her own interests. Maybe trying to make her feel a bit guilty would work. It's why I started:

"Okay, is it just because it's me or you are always so bossy like this?"

"I... no, what do you mean?"

"I just told you that I couldn't do anything tomorrow evening. I have an appointment that I can't miss, and it's important. I will be available after at any time, but I have my life, and I want you to consider this more seriously. Don't forget that I can withdraw myself at any time, because I do not do that for money, unlike you."

"Charlotte, all right..."

Ah, sometimes, speaking about money... So, it means that I think she might get some sort of bonus on that. If I find this out, I can put her damn arse in jail for a while.

"So, let me make myself clearer, either you let me choose when I can and do what I want when I want, whether you can fuck yourself. Don't forget that you need me, and I don't necessarily need you."

Okay, I must confess that what I just said was somehow dangerous: as I am the blackmailed, so I expose myself to a more dangerous situation if I do it. But, on the other hand, I said yes to do her stuff. She wants me in, so whatever I say, it's gonna be always a yes since she needs me and she knows that as I am shifting, and I can put her under pressure as I wish. On the other hand, she can also put me under pressure. It's why refusing the first thing would be proof that I still keep the control. Now, I have to accept the second job.

"Okay, sorry. On Wednesday afternoon, I will have something. Claire is gonna go for tomorrow then. It's in the south of Paris, *Rue du Lever du Matin*. From three to four of the afternoon. Is that okay?"

"Fine, as long as it's not after five because I have something scheduled after."

"Oh, don't worry. I'll give you the details tomorrow."

"Okay, then."

"Of course, don't cancel at the last minute, because it's gonna be... Really bad."

"Don't worry about it."

"Okay, so, Charlotte, you said yes. I can manage your conditions when you can't, I won't give you any jobs... But if you screw up with me, once, trust me, there will be consequences. I really hope you bear this in mind."

18 *Self-sufficiency and sustainability*

// In my bathroom, at home, Neuilly-sur-Seine.

Free Expensive Lies: Prologue

Having no emotions may be helpful in life, sometimes. It avoids being worried or concerned. Unfortunately, it does not avoid fear.

I was preparing myself. And fear was at its climax. I kept on convincing myself that it would be a wrong time, it's just an hour. It can happen, I mean, we are all doing bad things in life, maybe not as awful as this one, but I am not the only one to do that. It can happen, to screw up. I'm not the only one, some others are doing this to fund their studies or even living, I'm doing that to save my ex's arse. Whichever the outcome, now, it's too late. If I go back or if I say something else, I am in serious troubles. Despite knowing that the hour was coming close, I remained somewhat calm, it's like accepting my fate because... That's gonna be an experiment. Even if I have no idea what I am talking about, even if... As I said, it was not doing the thing I was actually most afraid of. I just still don't know what this is.

Anyway, back to Sunday evening, which was crazy, after I came back home. I actually understood that I officially embarked into something quite dangerous, but I was, in fact, trying not to think about it. I didn't remain long outside, as the night fell quite quickly, I came back home fast. And when I arrived, well, everyone was smiling, happy, except my mother that didn't even say hello and pretended I was not here. But I didn't want to be such a troublemaker, I didn't want to make problems. Unusually, when I came back, I tried to clean a little my room because it was a mess, for now, a couple of days; I asked my boyfriend to give me a hand because it was my mess and his. But I was freeing my mind of what I saw, I mean, Claire crying. He distracted me, talking about his friends, their problems, and their joys, and I actually realised that, well, in my life, I don't have any friends. Claire is not a friend, I mean it looks like, but she's not a friend yet, well, maybe my sister for now. But yeah, except my boyfriend, my sister, and Claire, well, there's no-one else in my life. On the other hand, I recall my beloved grandma that used to say, "Charlotte, do never forget that the lion moves alone, while the sheep moves in a herd."

Meanwhile, My mind was somewhat changed. For the very first time, I was considering dumping him. Seeing Claire overwhelmed was just too much, and seeing him not being aware of a single thing, being that innocent... There was something that was actually odd. The real problem is, I really like him, I really do like him, he's a fun guy, and I really need him as a good friend. But I don't love him enough, and, there's no need to conceal it. Being a friend would definitely be the best relationship we could have together. The problem is, I cannot just say this that way. I cannot go like, "Florent, it's over" because I am his fiancée, now. I know I should never have said yes, but something odd would have appeared if I haven't. And... Whatever I do, especially now, I have been hiding the fact that I cheated on him, if I just break up with him, things would go, like... And, yet I am still lesbian. We really can't get along; I mean as boyfriend/girlfriend. We can be best friends, but... I'll find a way. But if I break up with him now, this will raise immediate suspicions. First, my mother will automatically suspect Claire to be behind this, which may lead to discovering the secret nobody wants to find, and Clarisse... Because Clarisse knows, and she will explain to him the reason why. And moreover, honestly... if this relationship has to end, I'd rather him to end it, so it will ensure that his future relationship will not be ambiguous. And by "ambiguous", I mean, he's not gonna seek by any means to sleep with me. This story... Well, it can be an opportunity.

The rest of the evening, after putting my hands in the dust accumulated in my room since the previous cleaning, I went to clean my hands and ate something in the fridge, and I changed myself for going to bed. We stayed a couple of hours to watch something on TV with Florent, I mean, after the first film they passed, there was *CSI: New York*, so I watched it for thinking about something else, thinking about something other than Claire and all this mess. But as I was too tired and I fell asleep in front of the TV, Florent woke me up at some point and we went to bed.

The sun rose for a new day over Paris, and, of course, I slept only two hours during the whole night after Florent woke me up to go to bed. And whilst turning many and many times in my bed, I turned on the TV, zapped between programs for the whole night, then turned it off, and took my phones to watch some videos on YouTube. The only moment I actually slept was after going to pee for the fourth time in the evening and topping up my bottle of water, again and again, I forced myself to sleep between five and seven in the morning. I have to wash it, by the way. And Monday morning, even if I was tired, I got up with my red eyes, because I had to go to school. Because I actually need to think, and it's been since yesterday, with all that happened that I was not feeling genuinely safe, I didn't want to remain at home. I didn't really believe that either Claire or Kelly would actually be there, but I wanted to go there to think about a plan.

And so, we went there, we had the first two hours English and then maths. Meanwhile, I was slowly setting up my plan, I didn't waste my time for everything. To be efficient and sure that this has a chance to work, it's essential to gather all I know so far: first, I know that my downfall was organised, and this from the 9th of January. Everything was fully scheduled. Second, I have been filmed that night, and I do not recall anything. Third, I actually think that Claire is actually blackmailed too, which is why she was part of that plot against me the night of my birthday. Fourth, they do not appear to be really interested in my money, what interests them is actually to seek to destroy me, it is why I have to counter to avoid this. Fifth, he said he has videos against me that may jeopardise everything and plans to tell everything to make sure my life would be destroyed. Basically, and that's what I think, he wants to push me into suicide. Oh, and sixth, this Kelly organising apparently everything, and the name I heard from Claire the day before, Joris. I recall who that Joris is.

And what I recall so far is that this Joris is a cop. I don't know to whomever he is the closest in the Claire-Kelly network, but she said he's the guy behind the scene. It means, he is the guy earning money, and Kelly might just be the one that assigns tasks to her force. But I also know that Kelly is sleeping with guys, it means that she's still also a prostitute in the network, but she's the leading one. Joris, being a cop and even a pimp... That is quite a dirty secret. Unfortunately, if I want to expose this, I need to gather proofs against Joris.

As now I had two days left before the very first time, the thing was, doing it. I do believe now that Joris is my blackmailer, for the sole reason that as a cop, it is relatively easy to investigate on someone's life. So, he may know a lot of things about me. But I must confirm it because as he's a cop, it's like a goldfish attacking a shark in admitting that I am the goldfish from now. First, I need to identify and prove that Joris is the pimp, so I must do the first job. Because if he's the pimp, the guys will give me my money unless this has already been paid, and I must provide a part to Joris. His percentage. And I must take proofs of this. But I must first see how things are going on, and are organised because it's also possible that he may ask me to give Kelly the money, so Kelly dispatches it after. First, my very first time on Wednesday, I must observe how things are going.

Regarding the risk, I think... Well, I will drink after. Because on Wednesday, there's also mum's ceremony for her work, and I must wear her wedding dress. Where she's gonna present her new clothesline and everything. Because I think, somehow, this will affect me, I mean, this is gonna be, well... And I must remain pro and pretending nothing happened. So, it would reduce the damage, at least for that day. And to cover up the thing, well... Maybe I should sleep with Florent, so at least it will kill any suspicions.

So, first things first, two priorities: I must confirm that Claire has been blackmailed. So, I must steal her phone and try to hack it. I know her passwords, and I think it's unlikely she changed them, so I must steal her phone. The problem is that her phone is something that she keeps all the time with her. Maybe, if I find a way to be alone with her... I may get a chance to have her phone. Gaining her trust.

Regarding Florent, the second issue, the plan is simple: if we have to break up, then, fine. The thing is, if we break up, I think I will tell the raw truth, so he will break up with me. Because there are still chances that things do not go as I want them to go with my blackmailer, and I do not want him to find out the truth by anyone else. If I confess the truth, I will remain the victim, and then it's likely that he forgives me because I have been admitting the truth. And I may need him in my fight. But for now, my two priorities are to identify whether Claire has been blackmailed or not and find out how I may find a way to prove that Joris is behind this. Florent, if I have to tell him what's going on, I will, but if I manage the thing well, I can hide it for years and make sure nothing happened. And as I said, I want Florent to break up with me, I do not want to dump him. Yet. But if at some point I have to, then I will.

During the lunchtime break with my sister, we went to the restaurant with Clarisse, and I explained to her the actual situation and my plan. I think it may work... Clarisse insisted about one thing: what I am attacking, it's big. It's not attacking simple burglars or thieves. But the problem now is, whatever happens, I can't actually go back, because she suggested that it's also possible that something terrible happens, and this even if I pay someone for my protection. Everything must remain discreet, I have to be as I am every day, to avoid others to be aware that something is ongoing. Maybe I underestimated the actual danger of the thing I am attacking, perhaps I play it down, but somehow, I do not feel that this might be dangerous. It's like acting undercover, if I follow the plan, it shouldn't be a big deal. And all this is for saving Claire's arse, it's not only for dismantling Kelly. Even if there's quite a big deal at stake, but I don't really care about this. I don't care about me, I care about Claire, and that's all that matters.

On the other hand, life is just a game, a game where there are winners and losers. I am not scared of playing with them. And if things do go wrong, if I finally mess up with everything, well, they can destroy me, I don't really mind. I can manage this. If they want to annihilate my life, then, they can go, I mean, I am already broken, there's nothing left. I just want to make sure Claire is safe. And even if I have to pay someone to abduct her, I don't care.

She said that, nonetheless, it remains that it's David and Goliath, even if we know that David defeats Goliath. Besides, the thing to do was not something that everybody wants to do, it was a dirty job. And this, if played well, would be very, very tight. And if successful, I'll be a hero. But chances for success were still slim, but at least I have a plan. No, literally, she told me, "you're at war, so good luck". And I felt like Churchill saying that I have nothing to offer but blood, toil, tears and sweat. I must admit that this is probably the most perilous enterprise I have ever done, but on the other hand, if I am successful, I get Claire back, I wipe out that Kelly and, well... The pride of saying that I dismantled a prostitution network. But before saying any of those things, there were, well... Things that were supposed to happen.

Later that day, in the evening, we returned home pretty tired after a whole day there. Mum wasn't here, she texted all of us to let us know that she had plenty of things to finish. And Florent was there with a friend, unusually for doing job hunting. Apparently, he told me that he had a job interview for the next day. That was actually really good, he said to me that even if it were in a supermarket, it was still a job, and he could finally get money. It's a shame that... Yeah, even if he's been in a business school, he cannot find anything in what he wants to do. He keeps saying that he misses going to work, and I actually can understand. Anyway, once at home, Clarisse has done her homework in her bedroom, and I went to my bedroom, doing my favourite thing when I come back home, taking my iPad. For instance, I read something about World War II, precisely regarding the Battle of the Coral Sea in the Western front. Yeah, I know, I have some weird readings for relaxing. But, well, I love history, that's my passion, I love to know what happened and World War II is a massive part of our history, which is the reason why I am so interested in this. Interestingly, we still didn't find the Lexington, the US aircraft carrier that sank that battle.

You may ask me why this battle? Because I found a video on YouTube when I was in math class talking about Port Moresby, the capital of Papua New Guinea, and they spoke about the Japanese invasion of the country during the war. And what fascinates me with this, is that this war was obviously one of the deadliest conflicts in human history, but it's also the only conflict where... it was the first significant global war. Because everybody, literally everybody, was at war. And sometimes, if you're savvy enough, you may learn from this.

Anyway, after maybe two hours of reading many things about the war, I waited until his friend left and then went to the living room, for playing videogames on his console with him; I sometimes do that... That happens sometimes. And as mum asked us to make some food because she will be back home very late because of work, I went in the cuisine, cooking the dinner, whilst Clarisse and

Florent stayed in the living room, this time watching TV. I made burgers as I had no ideas on what to do, and everybody here loves that. I like cooking. No, seriously, I always liked it, and it's something that I love to do to relax. So, yeah, I cooked, we ate, I went to pee many times again, as usual. And I cooked my patties separately because I love them very salty. I don't know why I eat so much salty food. And, well, we ate, and Clarisse went to bed.

Florent watched something on TV in the living room whilst I was actually feeling tired. I continued watching stuff on YouTube until I eventually fell asleep.

Tuesday, a new day, also the last before the beginning of the actual war. I must admit that the stress was slightly rising, but I was trying to forget it or hide it. During the morning, nothing was different. Waking up at seven, I took my classic waking-up tea, but now I know one thing: Claire and Kelly would likely be at school today, to avoid missing too many courses even if they don't really care. On the morning, moments before to go, I accidentally broke my bottle of water. And if I don't drink, if I don't have my bottle of water, it's gonna be a disaster, as I need a lot of water. It fell on the floor, and as it was full, it literally broke the plastic of the bottle and spread the water all over the floor. It took me ages to clean the mess, wipe the floor correctly and dry the water... Next time, I'll consider buying a metallic bottle. On the other hand, well, this bottle was quite old, and as I don't clean it that much... now I may start to drink clean water.

But this morning, I was exhausted. Clarisse used to keep some vitamins all the time in her handbag, for me. And even if I took a pill, I was still drained. My back was killing me, and I was slightly nauseous. Hum, maybe this morning won't last exceedingly long at school. I don't know, sometimes, I am feeling like this, and even if I went to the doctor and he saw that my blood pressure was relatively low but still acceptable, I don't know. Sometimes I feel like my diagnostic hasn't been done correctly. I think that nobody knows what's my problem. And, yeah, actually, when I was at the school's threshold, I started complaining to my sister that I was not feeling good. And she could see that, I mean, I was feeling like my tea wanted to go back where it was from, I was about to throw up any minutes now. And, yeah, straight away, I took the metro, back to home. And once back home, as I used to do in that case when I feel like I am about to throw up and I feel like it doesn't come out, I force myself to throw up. I know, it's not right, but it was nothing other than my tea. I really don't know what I have, but all I can say is that it's a daily pain in the arse. A month ago, I calculated based on what I wrote on a paper daily for an entire month, I drink an average of three litres of water a day, and I go to pee at least seven times. And when I speak to my doctor, "it may be stress". Yeah.

As I was now feeling better after having thrown up, I knew that it was safe now to go to bed. And like yesterday, I took my iPad and watched something on YouTube, until I actually fell asleep before the end. I slept until late, like one or two pm, when I heard mum coming back from work, obviously surprised that I was here whilst I was supposed to be elsewhere. But I explained to her why, and even, she saw that I was not at my best today, which is why she didn't actually insist on why I wasn't there. When I woke up, for example, when I stood up from the bed, the fact to just standing up made me feel really dizzy. Well, instead, for the afternoon, as we were together... believe it or not, but it was not the war. She made me try some of her fabulous dresses, and I asked for her wedding dress, but told me that it was still at her warehouse, she still needs to make some adjustments before it is actually fully ready.

Florent was not here for the entire day, as he said that he had his trial shift straight away, he came back maybe half an hour before Clarisse, at around five. Unfortunately, for him, it was not that successful. Well, I mean, they told him that they will call him back, which means that, well, I don't really think it might work. And for the rest of the day, well, I made and ate some cookies, and mum, well, she worked in the living room whilst Florent and Clarisse were there, actually playing chess. Oh, yeah, because still, Clarisse is excellent at chess and Florent wants to take revenge for the... well, actually, the five times she beat him. I know the rules, but I wouldn't pretend I am a good player... I wouldn't even pretend I am a player at all, but my sister is absolutely unbeatable at this. He thinks he may have a chance. Yet again, even if they have been playing for up to four hours (none of them would give up, Florent by cowardice and Clarisse by honour), for the very first time, my boyfriend won! And he was so happy about this. Like, honestly, it's been months that he is seeking to defeat my sister. He did it.

After a while, while Florent was still enjoying his victory over my sister, we ate some croque that I did with my mother, and we went back to bed. Again, sleeping. Oh, no, before that, I took a shower. But I went to sleep after that.

The alarm rang at the usual time today, at 6.30 am. And here I was, Wednesday, the day where everything is due to start. One week since this mayhem started. Anyway, I woke up, and then I went to the bathroom to get some pants because it was unusually cold in that flat. I got up, and I joined my twin, who was drinking for once a coffee in the kitchen. I arrived for my morning tea, we discussed a bit about the weather, things like that, although she knows what I was doing today. Mum was already gone; she had many things to do. Clarisse knew what was supposed to happen today, but she remained quiet. Unlike me, maybe she was aware of what I would do. Then, as every morning, I had to go to school. As usual, I mean my regular look for school, a pink shirt, black waistcoat and black pants, black sneakers for once too, while my twin sister decided to wear, today, well... a pink shirt with a black waistcoat, black pants, but white sneakers... I looked at her, smiling, and I told her kindly, "Stop being dressed like me, please." At least, if we want to fool people today, it's gonna be... No, yeah, I forgot we have different hairs.

Metro, the commute of every morning when we have to go to school. I was okay today, at least I could sleep yesterday. However, I am still pretty impatient to go back to bed tonight, but the evening will be actually pretty long, as I think we're going to have many guests and it may end up being a long evening. This morning we're going to school, Florent still has his job stuff to do today, he has an appointment at 11.30am and mum will surely be back at two, it leaves me plenty of time to get out of here without being seen. But in the metro, she asked me undercover how I felt about this, and, yeah, I was quite nervous. As I said, one week ago, I didn't think this would actually happen, and, yeah, I was anxious. I was between, yeah, it's just a job, and also between the fact that, yeah, for the very first time in my life, I'm gonna have sex on command with strangers that I do not really know. This is quite scary. And it's why I was scared, because sex is still something quite intimate for me and, yeah. Right now, I was just telling myself that this would be only one hour within the next twenty-four, but I still have to do that. As it's the first time... I can go there, but tipsy. I mean, at least it will make this more bearable. I don't honestly know what to do, to be fair.

I honestly have no idea on how to approach this.

On the other hand, I don't really know what to expect. No, I mean, Kelly texted me the details, like the address where I have to go, and it's apparently some guy alone in a flat. He apparently paid for one hour, and she said that he should be alone. She also mentioned that she and Claire know him, he is not a bad guy. He just wants, yeah, to have sex. Maybe this guy will be kind, I have no idea. She said, well, he lives in the south of Paris. I didn't ask that much of question, to be fair. I was expecting to see her this morning, to actually find out what I should expect, what I should do, and everything. I mean, I know what I have to do, I am not that stupid, but I don't know... I mean, I don't know what to expect. I am relatively ignorant regarding being an escort since this is how she calls the activity.

Thirty minutes later, we arrived at school with my twin, and we were actually late, even if the main gate of the school was still open and the door leading to the yard. While Clarisse was impatient to go to the classroom because unlike me, she cares about all these bollocks, I took my time to arrive. I had to go to the lockers to get some books. But the yard was still empty, and I saw a couple of school supervisors coming out of the building when we entered. Ironically, whilst Clarisse was seeking to hurry to go as fast as she could when I went to my locker... I realised that I have been escorted:

"Miss Charlotte Kominsky. How are you?"

As usual, I get bothered in the morning. In response to that, erm, aggression, I acted as if I didn't hear anything if I may say so. They were three, three young women, charming... No, really, they were looking lovely. All three were pretty much dressed the same way, like the classy outfit with a very discreet makeup. But it was the first time I saw the two others, so I think it's highly likely that the two others are in a traineeship or something: two brown-haired and one blonde. I just kept on taking my notebooks.

"You know, Charlotte, I don't really mind, to be honest," the supervisor began to speak to me while I was not answering, "I mean, I don't care, I already have a job... But you, you can have a bright future ahead."

"Oh, my, just by saying that, darling, you are freshly destroying my Charlie's Angels fantasy!" I closed my locker and looked at them.

She knows me. So, she's not really offended. But the two others, well... That was funny.

"No, to be fair," I continued, after having looked at their silly faces and almost laughed, "it's true, unlike you, as I have almost forty million and I can even buy the building if I want, yeah, I need a job to ensure my future. That's a huge concern, yeah!"

"Your many unexplained delays, your countless hours of detentions, your unjustified absences... Do you know that when you came here for the first time as a student, we brought you a small book with a list of rules that you have to follow when you are here?"

"The book... Oh, you mean, that book?" I pretended to remember something.

"Yeah, that book!"

"Yep, I remember. I use it to wedge my desk at home." I cynically replied.

"Don't be an idiot, Cha, seriously. You know that with your excellent results, you can easily get degrees, you can go really far..."

"Oh wait, are you telling me that in this country there are still some jobs?"

"You can get important degrees, you can get a really nice job, yes, Charlotte..."

All right. I decided to come closer to her. Okay, let me make this clearer... So, I started:

"Hum. Okay... I remember the day when you came to me and told me, you've been working your arse off when at school for becoming a medical researcher. What happened?"

"I told you, I failed my exams..."

"You failed. And now, what does it tells about you, honey? You are working here, having a job in a school, being a state-arse paid that barely earns nothing more than the minimum wage and, obviously, since you are a woman, you could be paid more, but earn less than your boyfriend. This being obviously the result of many sons of bitches that you called teachers that offered you a spotless future. A spotless future that is now full of greasy spots."

"Well, following that logic, Charlotte, what the hell are you doing here?"

"Oh, well, to please my mother first, and to meet failures such as you are, to make sure that this is not the life I want!"

"Well... get the hell out right now. And quick!" she said after turning herself back and left.

I know, I can be really mean sometimes. I mean, it's not everybody that can remain calm and patient with me just like my mother and... hum, yeah, Claire as well. And Clarisse. She was really pissed. On the other hand, it's the truth, if she cannot face the truth, it's not my problem.

Anyway, after she left the locker area quite pissed by what I said, I packed my stuff in my bag, and as it's Wednesday, we have chemistry course in first, and as I am here because he reunited both groups this morning. After all, there's a test, I was expecting to meet Claire today. I went upstairs, to the classroom, and when I entered, I came in without saying hello even though the course just started. And my bottle of water was already empty, I wanted to pee, but I could contain myself at the moment. I went to sit next to my ex-girlfriend, who was obviously there. Then, well... Yeah. Here she is. I took my stuff, then the teacher has continued its course after being disrupted by me, as he was accustomed to my delays and the fact that I never apologise for it. Unusually, Claire was, well... First, all alone, we usually are together on Wednesday morning, today, she was actually... I could see she was feeling better, but not really happy to see me. When I sat next to her, whilst whispering as the teacher was speaking, she actually started:

"I should have bet... I was sure you'd come!"

"And why didn't you?" I replied, whispering too.

"Where's your bottle of water?"

"Well, I broke it this morning. I'm gonna buy a new one later today."

"Oh..." she said, apparently disappointed.

"Why?"

Seriously, what was the thing with my bottle of water? I know I carry it all the time, everywhere I go, but, come on. I bought it for a euro a couple of months ago in a supermarket. Meh. Anyway, today, it seemed like her mood was low. Maybe she knows what I am about to do, it's the reason why. Unlike the other days when I see her, nothing, today. Just a black hoodie that she had a while ago, some blue jeans and black converses. Her hairs were untied, no makeup, nothing. That is actually pretty curious.

"Well, since you drink too much, I just don't want you to get dehydrated, that's all..." she actually resumed after I looked at her.

"Oh, don't worry about me!" I started to seek my words.

"What's up today?"

"Meh, just one more day of life on that planet. And you, what's up?"

"Meh. Same as you, I guess."

"You don't seem to be actually okay!"

"What do you mean?"

"Your look, last week you were in a more provocative mood. Now, you look like me a week ago here for doing your hours and then being impatient to come back home because of your presence..."

"Oh. There could be a reason for that, I think. It's true, I know you are the master of analysis. So, I think I can give you an explanation for that."

"I'd love to, honey..."

"Maybe it's because I know what you're going to do this afternoon," she stared at me.

"Oh, you mean my meeting with Angela Merkel, huh? Well, she said she wanted to postpone, she was feeling sick this morning."

Taylor Harding-Jenkins

"Yeah, and by Angela Merkel, you mean the Russian guy I had to meet last week, same day, same hour, for the same purpose? I know, accents are somewhat similar."

"Oh, you know about that, then..."

"I know everything, Charlotte."

Obviously, she knows everything. So, as she spoke straight about this, it confirmed that this is pissing her off. Unfortunately, I, well... I can't tell her everything. I saw that this was a big problem for her today. She went through the same, but the thing is, I do not have to lie to her, unlike her who did that to me. It's a torture for me, to be honest, because I really wish I'd tell her that I am doing this to save her arse. After all, I want her back, even if it involves dumping my boyfriend. Unfortunately, this would compromise her, because if something wrong happens, they will attack her, and I don't want that. If she knows what I want to do, she'll know too much, which will definitely jeopardise my plan with all the consequences that go with that.

I didn't want to show myself as being clearly affected by this. First, because I was quite worried about this, I wasn't concerned that much, and it would be lying, and second, because... Well, I actually needed her for advice:

"Speaking of which... Now that I know you're a professional and an insider..."

"Shut up!" she understood that by my words, she should still be ashamed of what she's doing.

"How should I take the thing... As you know this guy?"

"Well... I don't know, he's a guy, he's nice. He just wants sex, that's all."

"Should I be worried?"

"No. Because... Well, at some point, you'll get used to sleeping with people you don't want to. You'll be used to have no dignity. To be just a tool. The first time is different, but since you have absolutely nothing about this, I mean... Sex for you is just waiting for the other to finish, so, you might go over it easier."

"I don't know..." I spoke almost inaudibly, just like her. "I'm still quite nervous. I don't really know how to behave."

"You'll see. It's just an hour, and after, you're free."

"Yeah..."

The course continued, the second half of the hour was a test, as scheduled. Well, it's like, well... We had a break, and, oh, yeah, Kelly was absent today. Surprising. So, yeah, during the break, we actually remained together, because

Free Expensive Lies: Prologue

Clarisse was on the phone. We bought some pastries and a coffee and went to sit somewhere in the yard and speaking. I wasn't trying to interrogate her, to be fair. At that moment, she was more seeking comfort because she confessed that she was ashamed. She was feeling bad, and she explained that she went to her GP yesterday afternoon to talk about that. Because she was crying, exhausted because it's been a week that she doesn't sleep and (the very last time she did it was on Monday) explained to me that she regrets. Officially, and even to me, she said that she accepted to join Kelly in this, but I think, the truth is elsewhere, she's lying to protect herself because she knows how I will react. And she also explained to me the reason why she concealed it for months before I found it out last Thursday. Even now, she's scared that I may speak to anyone about this.

That is not my intention. But that morning, during that twenty-minutes break, we were really close. It reminded me like when we were together, talking about what we may do later or when she was feeling bad and needed me. And, automatically, all the conversations we had, all the words exchanged were all leading to... our couple, us. Unfortunately, she said that she respects Florent and does not want to interfere with our relationship, especially since I look happy and I'm going to get married someday. That reminds me of *My Best Friend's Wedding*, I just don't really want her to be Julia Roberts in this. Yeah, she does not want to interfere. But if the possibility of interfering in my couple to get me back presents itself, I am sure she would definitely be willing to breach that promise she freshly made. Especially since I know – she doesn't – that this occasion will reappear soon.

The last two hours, as usual, literature. The only two hours of the week, and we sat together again. Well, for once, I actually helped her in her things. This morning, she was studious. To be honest, I felt like I had my girlfriend back, there were not all the things she used to have as soon as Kelly is nearby. I must admit that it was quite pleasant to have her back, I felt that she also wants me back somehow. We both need each other right now. But as there's Florent in the middle of this, I guess this would just remain a fantasy in her mind. Well, things can change, I think.

And then, twelve, my daily commute back for home. When I arrived, as predicted, nobody was here. During the break at ten, Clarisse was with her boyfriend, and they actually decided to lunch together. Fine, when I arrived home, I removed my shoes, and threw myself on my bed, it was time to relax. I mean, relax, focusing on that nonsense and meaningless life, I did it while I remained with my eyes opened, and I capture every single moment of the silence here. Sometimes, I am fed up that things do not go as they are supposed to go, I am fed up sometimes also that some idiots could be victorious... This is the time, now.

Hopefully, in events like this, I always have the solution in things that I wouldn't actually love to experience. A couple of years ago, I did some works in my bathroom, behind the bathtub, I could hide behind a tile a kind of mini drawer, where there's an old pencil case, into which I leave some pills of diazepam. No, I got prescribed it a while ago, and as this had such an effect on me – like I was feeling high for many hours – it was initially to deal with my depression. Unlike Kelly, I am not a fan of low-cost drugs or sophisticated chemical stuff, I am more into medical stuff. And this diazepam, as I don't have it quite often, I feel like in another universe whenever I take a pill. I mean, I am not like stone or something, I am just not fully aware of what I do, or it kills any possible emotion or remembrance I could get. It's like the consciousness-withdrawer for at least six hours. I took one, and as usual, I need at least a couple of minutes for it to actually takes effect. I used it quite often, for example, last time I had one was for the first time I slept with Florent. It was useful and worked. Yes, because the first time of doing this, given my past, was still something I somehow apprehended. Yet today he doesn't really know. He doesn't even know about the existence of this pencil case.

Yeah, who forced me to actually follow the treatment protocol?

It was now twelve o'clock. My phone rang, and I received a text from an unknown number. That said, "Hey, Charlotte. This is your reminder for the meeting of this afternoon, at 4pm. There's one door, just knock, and they will open. Before you leave once it's done, wait for me outside, because he must give you something for me. Send me back a text if you are still on it – Joris." Hum, okay. The very first time this Joris was contacting me. But, as suspicious, as I still had the phone number of the blackmailer (that I had to call that last Sunday morning), and I compared both numbers... Nope, that was not a match—both quite different numbers. Anyway, I assume this will be monitored by Joris, so whilst the medicine started to be effective, I just replied, "Copy that, I'll be there". Whilst sat on the bed, a couple of minutes later after I rub my face and sighed, I decided that it would undoubtedly be better to take care of myself and have a bath. I don't know, I was feeling slightly different, but remember that before to go, I needed to be completely relaxed. So, I was like, let's have a bath. It may help.

I was everything but hungry. After having stood up of my bed, and obviously experienced dizziness for a bit, I went to my bathroom, turned on hot water, removed my clothes, and took a bath bomb with me. I put my morning's clothes folded adequately on the table under the sinks, and whilst the water was pouring, I went to pee. I still had my bomb in my hand, I was waiting for the bath to be full to place it. And, whilst still sat on the toilets, with my bomb in my hand, I was actually daydreaming, the noise of the flowing water made me almost drowsy. I was still tired; I am fed up sometimes to be that tired. And it took several minutes, I could feel the water actually somehow warming up the bathroom, still quite cold. I remained sitting on the toilet for a while, like, something was sticking me onto it. I don't know how mum will manage to place that wedding dress in my bathroom, I mean, she said the dress was quite heavy, I mean, I really hope it's not gonna be that heavy. At some point, the bath was ready. I actually stood up to stop the water and threw my bomb into the water.

And then I went into the tub. The bath was quite hot, but it's okay, I love it when it's like scorching, almost burning. But my mind couldn't focus on anything else, and for some reasons, I thought about the meeting place. I never use to go there because it's facing the buildings belonging to all the capital's riches. But to be fair, I was more apprehending the moment than I was scared of it to actually happen. I even closed my eyes and started to think. Enjoying that silence, a moment of deep calm, I tried to stop the flor of thought in my mind, but... Yeah, I guess it is true. I have no notions of danger. As, well, I think I'd be Clarisse, and I'd be peeing on myself, but... I wonder if Claire was scared on the first time? Oh, I'm sure she was. I guess, because... if he blackmailed her, she had no hope, she freshly broke up with me and was pretty much screwed, and had no hope, no plans where she may escape. But, on the day she proposed me to become her girlfriend, I made it clear, I made the promise that whatever would happen, I will always be there, whatever the outcome of our relationship. This is my duty to honour my commitment, otherwise, what does it make me, a coward? Will she remember her ex-girlfriend as being someone that talked and never acted? There's no way I would ever be that person.

Moreover, the more I see her, the more I feel like, the day I will find out what really happened. When I think about how she was on the day I accepted her offer (I mean, Kelly's), she was not like usual. When she goes shopping, she always comes back with the smile, and now, she was crying and left, I mean, ran away. Claire, running away, it just doesn't sound like her. Something happened to her, and, I am sure Kelly made her life into a nightmare. She's blowing up more and more every day, and, even though she pretends her new life is satisfying and memorable (curiously, she didn't pretend that today... and stopped pretending that since I accepted), there's something weird. And since I know what's at stake, I just cannot close my eyes and pretend everything's okay, there's potentially someone's life in danger.

Anyway, a couple of minutes later, I actually opened my eyes. And I checked at the time, on a clock over my sink where I put my clothes, and it was time to leave the bath. I know that Clarisse and her boyfriend will be the first to come in here at 3:30 pm, but happily, I'll be already gone. It was now nearly two o'clock, and I'd better hurry up, because, at 3 pm I must be gone. I think it will certainly be safer to take a cab to go there, as I don't really see myself taking the metro in the outfit I will wear. After a relatively long bath, I left, actually more relaxed. I thought about this, and, well, something switched me. I have a mission, and it was time to actually achieve it for my girl.

When I left my bath, I saw myself in the mirror facing the tub, and I had a kind of moment of absence. My face. White as it has never been. I really tend to believe that I have something serious, I mean, this is not normal. I spend my time peeing and drinking. A doctor said that perhaps I was overeating salty things, but, well, I crave for salty food. My last meal was yesterday evening, I didn't eat any lunch today because I was not that hungry, which is weird. Anyway, so I stood up, and I went to pee. And all over my body, I could see the water leaving my skin quite red, because of the intense heat. And now, I was certainly better. I mean, in my mind, all the processes that were processing into my mind actually stopped, suddenly, to leave an empty space of relaxation. It's true, this bath was really relaxing, but I assume that the two pills that I took before helped also. I was feeling light, like, really. As light as the sunlight would be. I was undoubtedly high at that very moment, but I was not actually aware of what was going on, and this was something I didn't actually want to be mindful of. I wasn't even feeling being myself, I felt like, yeah. Not weird, I was feeling dumb, but to be serious, I didn't care at all.

After I peed, I actually dried myself with my towel left on the sink (there was water all around the toilet), and I went into my bedroom, and my wardrobe, to take my clothes, for the next two hours. I'm gonna change myself several times today, I just hope I won't have to wear heels for my mother's dress. I took my bra, a black one, and it gave a contrast of black lace and white skin, I am sure she would have loved it. Because I was obsessed with Claire at that moment, she was the only one in my mind. Then the rest below, my panties. It could be weird, but I seriously thought, is it necessary to put it for that occasion? I mean, we already know how it will finish, the purpose of why I am going there, maybe she wants to do it while I am still dressed? As I said, sex for me is just to know how to please the other.

But meanwhile, if I choose not to wear one, I'll appear like the enterprising one. On the other hand, I don't really care how I will appear, I am not here to appear today. I first started to put it. I don't think she would love it; I don't think she would be okay with that, and... She loved it when I was enterprising. Allow her to freely explore the territory without having to pass through any borders, that's what she always wants. Maybe it's gonna be the first time I will actually enjoy this, so let's make this fun as it should also be for myself. If she wants, I may discover myself. I may show her that I am not afraid, and I am strong and independent. That's what she wants, that's what I want.

It was the time, now, I took my chosen dress for the moment. A deep red dress that I wore probably once or twice since I have it. This dress had a nice colour contrast. Its harmony was perfect. The two shades that I love. Two colours: the blood in a forgotten vineyard in the forest of the night, it seemed like the red of the melted blood flowing along with a black wooden cross. It used to be one of my favourites, it also used to be the dress I wore for my first time with her, and now I was wearing it today again, I don't know for what reason. This dress was made of a gradient of two colours, black and red, and made of some fake leather fabric. Black and red, my two favourite colours. Red, to evoke a thousand things that have happened, the injustice, that I have the luck to have money and I am literally powerless, to seek the love of someone that I cannot reach. Black, like an answer to all those issues I have faced until then, meaning a future without stars, a night with no lights. Even if my mind was undoubtedly flying now into some kind of deep and uncontrolled vortex surrounded by chaos, I have spent a couple of minutes actually looking at myself and telling, whoever you are, you have the chance to be an heiress. You have the opportunity to have someone that loves you, and all that you do is just fucking up every chance you had in your life? This black sounded like the end of the world, like the answer to what I am. I can't actually describe what I'm gonna do, but all I can say is that... I am balanced. I am between them, and I don't know which one to choose between Florent and Claire.

After I actually looked at my face like it was fading away, I started to put makeup. Today, let's make it dark like the actual mood: the gloss to bring back to my lips a shiny dark red, like the angel of chaos coming to me, will overthrow all my fears and make me invincible. I actually put everything, like foundation, I made my eyes very dark, as dark as possible, and I even found out, that, yeah. Is this meaningful? I mean, I was meant to do this, I was born evil, I was born mean. I hate everybody. I consider that the most dangerous people in my life are the people living with me, because everything is dangerous, and everything is a threat.

Does this actually reflect who I am? The decisions I took, the evil things I've made... Nothing really matters because I keep thinking that everything happens for a reason. And the reason today is that I have to save Claire's arse. I will give my body to save her arse. I really hope that she will see and realise this. That I will succeed, but somehow, I am sure she's aware of this. And Florent... Whatever happens, for what it worth, I have a plan. I really wish that this plan will be successful, that I will collapse Kelly. I really hope he's going to forgive me for what I've done because hurting him is everything but my intention.

I decided to wear some expensive shoes that I bought not a while ago, obviously a pair of black heels, and, yet, when I saw myself fully dressed, I just said to myself: what is going to happen, it's big. I know that these people are not joking, and I am doing this for the honour. For Claire's honour. And for my glory. This situation may be dangerous, since I know that Joris is apparently a rotten cop, and I don't think if he finds out that I am messing up with him, he's gonna have any remorse to kill me or destroy me. Today I may make a sacrifice, but it's for an innocent. This is why I have a plan. And this plan must prevail. Kelly is a whore that doesn't care about anyone's reputation, she just wants to play with people and destroy lives doesn't seem to be a big deal for her. And now, I know that this Joris participates in this. I must be cautious with whom I have to deal with. Because even if I didn't fully assess the situation, even if I don't really know who I am dealing with, this may result in much worse than my debauchery being exposed on Facebook. They may kill me. Or worse, they may kill her.

19 *Game over*

// 15th arrondissement of Paris, south of Paris.

// Wednesday, 16th of January 2013, 16:00.

I actually called a cab for going there, that was faster. Because, yeah, taking the metro, first because of the heels, second, because of, yeah, the outfit. Okay, I was not that provocative, but my makeup and everything reminded me that it was better to avoid public transports. Yeah, we're in Paris.

Free Expensive Lies: Prologue

Actually, once I was ready to go, I called my taxi, took all my stuff in a particular handbag, took my coat, and left my pockets all empty. I deliberately didn't take any of my passports, for safety reasons if they decided to steal it from me. I took my regular stuff, such as my phone, my wallet (obviously, I left my important credit cards at home), a bottle of water that I'd better not to use otherwise it's gonna ruin my makeup. And... some device I bought actually not long ago, a small chip at the end of which was a micro. This chip can record up to three hours, and I slid it in the handbag's hidden pocket. But, hopefully, we can still hear very clearly what is said. I keep it, and tonight I'll put everything on my laptop or my iPad, so at least I'll have the proof of what happened today. I could use my phone, but... I don't think it's a good idea. I know that phones can be compromised, and I cannot exclude the possibility that I may be listened to or under surveillance. That may be paranoid, reacting that way, but I prefer taking no risks and going my way. My laptop or iPad can also be compromised, but I can log them off from the Internet whenever possible. And to make sure it does not reconnect again; I can place them in the safe on my wardrobe. I am the only one to have the code, and putting it in a safe (as it's a metallic cage) will act as a Faraday cage and will kill any possible signal that may come. So, no possibility to hack the laptop.

Where I had to go was actually in the south of the capital. It's located in the fifteenth arrondissement (like south-west), in a residential street. This "fifteen arrondissement" is known primarily by me for being the end of a park where we went walking with my mother when we just arrived in Paris when things were fine during this period, the *André-Citroën* Park. Also, there's a fun water park where I used to go almost every summer with Clarisse, near the station *Balard*, and I love going there. This park is massive, I mean, there's everything in there, obviously swimming pools, waterslides, even a beach (yeah, within Paris... They tried to do the same on the Seine banks, but it was not that successful). And in the compound, there's also many restaurants, shops and even a cinema. Like, last summer, with Claire and Clarisse, we used to spend days in there. Like, entire days. And that was so fun. But, unfortunately, it was not near this place I was now supposed to go. I miss that time, though. We can still go there with Clarisse, but, well... It's not the same.

To be fair, I don't really like this part of Paris, except this waterpark. Because it's mostly residential and all the buildings we can see there, even though it's not offices, they are all soulless. It feels like it's sad. It's not a beautiful district, in my opinion. It doesn't even look like Paris. But, well, it's been since 2006 that I live here, so it became actually ordinary in my eyes. I see the Eiffel Tower every day (Believe it or not, but I've never been in there, I'm scared of heights... And I recall Clarisse being sick after going to its second floor) and it feels like, you know, so familiar. But, well, people here are friendly, my ex-girlfriend was born here, Florent as well (okay, Versailles is not Paris, it's about 13 miles from here, but still) and, well, I've never had many problems with locals here. And this city is alive, I mean, there's always something to do. They don't have this horrible accent that you can find in the south of France, and you can go out by night... well, I mean, if you are with someone, otherwise it's not safe at all. But I told that already.

My target was a small street behind a relatively new building, *Rue du Lever du Matin*. It was at the eighteen, and I requested the guy to drop me in front of the door. And, well, when the driver stopped the car to drop me in front of the door, I actually said to myself "here we are now". I felt like, yeah, this is real now. It's not virtual anymore. I still had a ten euro note, I actually gave it to the driver as a tip and left the car. I even arrived a couple of minutes early, and... I remained a bit far away from the building, and mostly the entrance door. And, yeah, I don't know, arriving in front of that door somehow impressed me. It's why, still carrying my handbag, I decided to actually call my sister.

"Yeah?" she replied, apparently eating something.

"Hi, sister," I said.

"Hum, Cha, you all right? What's going on?"

"I don't know... Just wanted to hear your voice."

"Hum, last time I heard you saying that it was to Claire," she actually laughed. "I really hope you're not trying to flirt with me now because I am still your sister, last time I checked."

"No, honey. I just need my sister now. I don't know, I need a hug."

"Well, okay, but... Hey, what are you doing? How dare you!" she was speaking to someone.

"Stop eating that! You're gonna get fat!" I heard her boyfriend, in the background.

"Geez, taking out my tiramisu off my hands... What are you seeking, death, or what?" Clarisse was replying.

"He's damn right when you have this in your hands..." I teased her.

"Oh, you shut up!" she was talking to me. "Give me my tiramisu back, honey!"

"Yeah, yeah," his boyfriend replied.

"Jesus Christ..." and she complained.

So, I assume that she stopped by her favourite bakery when she left school. Because, yeah, tiramisus are so far her favoured pastries and, yeah... She could eat that all day. I like it too, but at some point, it's just too much.

"So, what's up, baby?" she came back to me.

"Well... I'm out, for the things you know. Whenever I am back, do you mind, erm... Like, I'll ring your phone when I am back, do you mind jumping to the main door and make sure nobody sees me when I come back?"

"Hum, hum, yeah. Of course, no problem, it makes sense. I'll make sure I keep an eye on my phone."

"Thank you, honey."

"It's okay. Anyway, love, I have to go. Hum, good luck for your, erm... thing."

"Yeah, thank you. I'll see you later, I love you."

"I love you too, bye," she hung up.

It was time to go. I was now walking on the street where I had my kind of meeting. The weather was sunny today, even if it was a bit cold, and as my legs were uncovered, I was actually freezing, since winter is still here, and the cold temperature won't stop until maybe the end of February. I was due to go to the number 18, my destination.

Number eighteen led to a black wide painted door, looking like a garage, even if the door was split in two. There was actually a building over it, I mean, maybe a three-floor building, looking relatively modern just like the various buildings in the surroundings, with flowerpots at almost every balcony. Balconies were actually making nearly three parallel rows. When I arrived in front of the garage door, I was obviously seeking the entrance, when, maybe after ten seconds I was examining the door to try to find out how I may come in, I received a text from Joris. Hum... I checked on the screen, and curiously, I assume that he may be relatively close to me, if he texted me when I was about to reach the threshold of the door. He said: "Charlotte, this is the big gate just in front of the number 18, where you need to go. You'll see a keypad on your left, press the button three to come in, and once inside, you will be in a courtyard. Search then for the third flat." There was a description of the inside of the building after. Well... So far, it seemed more evident to me. He was actually right, I turned my head and saw the keypad; in between, I even heard someone who played music out loud in his flat (it was not coming from the building I was in front of but the one facing it, and the music was

Killing In The Name). I actually placed my phone back in my handbag and went to press that button on the keypad. And, well. After hearing a small buzz, I turned my head, and the door was unlocked, but not opened.

Still, before entering, I checked briefly along the street, on both sides, if this Joris was somewhere. Honestly, I wouldn't recognise him since the last time I saw him I was totally drunk, but... Amongst the many buildings all around, all moderns, many windows were open, but I couldn't see anybody standing before any window or balcony. However, all along the opposite footpath of the street, there were several cars parked. Most of them were urban cars, where you could actually see that there would be nobody inside, however, on my right and at maybe less than thirty metres away, there was a big black SUV with tinted glasses. I cannot actually say whether there is someone inside or not, but this car... I don't know. It seems like a window was open, but I am not pretty sure. Anyway, I'll find this out eventually.

Here I was, now. The door was hefty, as I almost had to throw myself on it to push for the opening. Hopefully, Joris was accurate in his description. He said, "you must pass the door next to the garage entrance, it will lead you into the courtyard." Okay, done. Then, "once you are in the yard, you must walk to the small stairs next to the three other garages within this yard, it's gonna be right in front of you, and you will be at your meeting point, it looks like a veranda. Just walk on those stairs." Okay. To be fair, the yard was fairly wide, I mean, okay, the three garages were right in front of me, facing the main door and the big garage door, and... yeah, those stairs leading to that veranda were right next to them. So I walked on this small paved-floor. Hopefully, it was broad but not too much, as I could clearly see where I was heading. But, yeah, now that I see this, it's quite impressive. The building is kind of made in a square-shape with that yard in the middle, has two floors, and, to be honest, at a glance, I'd rather say that this looks like a retirement house than a young student flat or whatever it may be modern. I mean, the small veranda leading to the entrance, the flowerpots on almost every balcony, with sometimes faded flowers. Well, on the other hand... I don't know who I'm supposed to meet yet.

It was silent, however, within this yard. No external noises... Interesting.

This yard was almost reminding me of some lovely places in the country's southern countryside, like old-fashioned buildings, it looked like the place we used to live in Montpellier. It seemed relatively calm, though, I mean, except the garage, we didn't hear anything from the street. Also, there was a small recess under the stairs where were left a couple of bikes, three of them, like mountain bikes. When I found that was also parked in the middle of this courtyard a blue van, I quietly walked in. Well, this van seemed old, and I'd say antique. It seemed being parked here for a while, maybe more than a year or maybe less, as I could distinguish a leak of oil underneath it. Hum... Given the flowerpots on the balconies and, the bikes, the van, and everything, there were no tire tracks on the floor, it means that the garages are empty, and this building is inhabited by, well... The average age of the people living here, in my opinion, should be fifty or above.

However, the air here seemed more breathable than the rest of the capital, even if we weren't in a greenhouse. This must be explained by the number of plants all around. I kept walking, and the calm of the building was relatively impressive. Well... I also have no idea where I was supposed to go, given the fact that the stairs were leading to a passageway that also served to the adjacent building, the one above me when I entered. But as he said in his text that it was the third flat, I just have to find where it is. I walked up the small stairs leading to this passageway, and the calm relaxed me, I kind of heard the sound of the capital differently, without the permanent noise of sirens of the police and emergency services. And at the end of the stairs, I carefully looked around me, progressing slowly. It was important to actually find out where was my actual destination, when three metres away, I found a door, like a glass door.

This door was made of heavy and thick opaque glass, it seemed thick, and a wooden frame was all around. The knob was made of steel. I could see through the door that this was leading to a relatively dark corridor, or at least poorly lit, it's why I checked the inscription on this door. It was written in some old-fashion letters a list of flats here. "Flat 1 to 4". Hum. So that should be this way. Before entering, I checked all around as not sure of myself, and I felt like, "should I continue?". I touched the knob, and this door doesn't seem to be locked. I looked all around me one more time, I breathed, and even if the diazepam helped me relax, there was still a bit of apprehension inside me. What will I find? What kind of person they want me to have sex with? It's why I breathed one more time, closing my eyes, telling myself that "it's gonna be fine, nothing bad should happen", as long as I follow the desire of, well... My new customer.

So, I pressed on the knob, and actually... The door was locked. So, I knocked three times on the door because I didn't see any button for any bell or something around me. And I waited. I took the straps of my handbag in my hands, so I could hide my legs. Meanwhile, I heard someone walking on that corridor, and I could see a human-shaped shade coming closer to the door. Still there, I made a step back, in case she wants to open the door. Until... I could distinguish through the opaque glass at the very last second an old lady actually unlocking the door from the inside.

An old lady. It was the first face that I saw: perhaps a seventy or seventy-five old lady, beefy enough, for not saying... yeah, "fat" would have actually been the most appropriate word, she was fat, I don't understand how she was still standing on her two legs. To be honest, I know ladies that looking better than her at the same age, she was quite repellent. Even if she was wearing clean clothes, a grey sweater, black trousers, I actually really hoped she's a janitor here and not the one for whom I came for. Yes, she looked as old and exhausted as the van in the courtyard. Awful. But I was embarrassed, I mean, maybe I disturbed her from her nap as she seemed to be actually waking up, at a glance I'd say that she's not really happy to see me. And her face, her dry mark of slime in her lips, her hideous glasses on her nose with her skin covered of blackheads, her double chin, hum, yeah, I was surely waking her up from the little afternoon nap. When she opened, I was actually, erm... Not impressed, but I was looking for my words.

"Hi, hum... Sorry to disturb you, miss... Someone is waiting for me here."

"Yeah... And you are?" she asked me with a rather strange Russian accent.

"I... My name is Charlotte. I... erm, I think it's in flat three," I was like, damn, what the hell should I tell her!

For like a second, at the moment I said this sentence, I was thinking, please, not that! I mean, not her. This, well... No, I don't think I am ready for this. I don't think I came for her, because Kelly mentioned (Claire too) that it was a nice guy. But for those who believed that homosexuality was a disease, I had just in front of me the absolute cure. Even the treatment for a heterosexual. Because I was like, yeah, I just imagined myself doing to her like... Oh, no. I can't say much more. Anyway, she processed what I told her about my name, for at least a couple of seconds, then she said again in her weird accent:

"Ah, yes... Joris must be sending you. All right, so come in. My nephew will welcome you!"

"Thank you very much," I replied, quite nervous.

Her nephew will welcome me, so her nephew must be the guy. Well... All right, then. When she said this, I was relieved, because just the image of going down to her made me actually nauseous. I began to be nervous, but I was telling myself that it was something that I'd better hide. For the reason that if I don't show myself confident enough, this will be a nightmare. And they'll be using this against me for sure. Anyway, when I said thank you, she actually opened her door wider for allowing me to come in. I stepped in, making sure I wouldn't touch her, and the very first thing I could smell from the inside of that corridor was a kind of strong incense smell. I walked a bit further because of the small carpet that was at the entrance. The gallery was narrow, and I saw a few metres away on my right, a shoe rack. When she closed the door, and when I turned myself back to her, I actually asked:

"Um, uh... should I take my shoes off? Or..."

"Not necessarily. My nephew will tell you what he wants," he replied.

"All right, fair enough."

"Follow me."

She passed before me. And still behind, following, I could hear that everything was quiet here, except my footsteps that echoed, as the corridor was quite long. I was almost feeling like in an empty church. Absolutely no music, nothing but my shoes and some background noise, like maybe a couple of TVs that were on, speaking inaudibly in a specific language. But, yeah, the sound and everything, it didn't seem like the French TV or at least the channels I know. And still, this significantly more pungent incense smell, I mean, didn't indicate that the average of age living here would be below 45. And of course, this corridor was not lit by any lights or even single window to the outside, it was somewhat scary. This place was actually quite eerie, and even this lady, the first human I met here, seemed very cold. I don't even think there must be a French person living in here. Anyway, there were at least five doors on both sides of the corridor, all of them not facing one another. There were decorations on the walls with pictures of dusty frames, paintings of landscapes, but all of them were actually small. At the end of the corridor, a door was slightly opened, where I could perceive a burgundy light, which seemed almost purple. And I think that this room should actually be my final destination. Especially since she seemed to lead me there. I was not dazzled from the difference in light between sunny weather outside and a dark and spooky corridor. However, my eyes still didn't actually make the difference, and I could see everything even very black. However, at the end of the corridor, there was a pretty big painting of the St. Basil Basilica of Moscow by night. According to her accent, the smell of incense, the several pictures of landscapes and this cathedral, I think I should expect meeting some Russian guy, as my customer. Let's just hope that he's not fifty or beyond.

At the end of a long seconds' march in that walkway, she arrived at the level of the slightly opened door. I suddenly stopped and looked at me:

"Here we are, hum... Charlotte, huh? So, where do you come from, Charlotte?"

"I am from here," I tried to contain my nerves after I heard her saying my name twice on purpose, still speaking in a low-pitched voice to seem sympathetic and confident.

"Your accent says otherwise," she actually noticed.

"No, well... not completely. It's a long story." I didn't want to extend myself on who I was.

"Fine. Come in. Sit where you want, just relax, and suit yourself. My nephew is on his way, he shouldn't be too long."

"All right, then... Thank you."

After having softly pushed on the door to open it, she smiled at me. I smiled back, and then she actually left, for going back to some other room; I didn't follow where she was going. Now, my mission starts. I just had one thing to do: coming in and getting ready. Hopefully, I had diazepam, because even if I am feeling nervous right now, it would have been worse if I didn't have it. I made a few steps into the room where now everything was to happen when she was going away, and I saw... A vast space that turned out to be a single room, a bit bigger than my bedroom. Indeed a guest bedroom, even if I didn't know well where I was inside this building. But I know that I will go out once everything will be done. I just walked in.

This room, warm but not too much, was actually like that: four walls, no other access to anywhere else, no windows, just a bulb of light on the top, and was quite chic, actually, to be fair. The decoration was posh, on the classic seventeenth-century style, and the burgundy light was coming from the bulb in the ceiling, reflecting against the gilding furniture of the room. It actually felt like burgundy from the outside, but it was, in fact, a golden light. The fact that there were no windows in there would be good, at least no observers or witnesses of what's gonna happen. High and white ceilings all surrounded by carved frescos, a gold and red carpet covering the entire floor drawing various symmetric patterns, to be fair, I'd actually feel like in a luxury suite room in a five-star hotel in the centre of Paris. The bed was on the right side of the door like just behind when you open it, it was readily covered with golden satin sheets. Two nightstands on each side made of black wood, small, with two drawers in each. Well... Facing the bed, both being separated with a pretty wide space, there was a sofa, all black and made of leather, in the room's style, like old centuries. Maybe in mid-space of all this, a tall Japanese windscreen, actually a pretty tall one, not covering any light but I guess to separate the place in two, with birds' patterns drawn on it. Apart from the bed, the sofa, this windscreen, and a small cube hidden behind it and a coat rack behind the door, I must say that this room seemed pretty empty. Nothing on the walls, no paintings at all, I was actually feeling like in a bedroom in Versailles castle. Odd.

But it was quite hot here, and unlike the corridor in front, it didn't smell this disturbing incense everywhere here. I removed my coat and went afterwards to sit on the sofa, as the entrance here was quite a long walk. So, I'm here for a nephew. I don't know, somehow the atmosphere here was not that reassuring, I was wary of these people. Every time I hear about Russian people on the news, it's generally mafia or KGB related. I was now wondering, where was it better to wait for him? These were quite uncomfortable, I mean, waiting for the guy, it was like, I don't know, I was feeling under surveillance here. And again, hopefully, I took that, because otherwise, I'd start panicking severely. What's next, only they know. And when I thought that Claire knew this place and was here last week for the exact same condition, whilst I was quietly sleeping in my flat at the very same hour, well.

I was breathing, again, and again, and again, trying to contain all today more than ever all feelings of apprehension and maybe fear or even embarrassment. I just stared at the door, waiting for it to be opened. And, yeah, all this for, yeah. Five hundred euros, I don't know how much Joris wants to take on this unless he wants to take everything. Well, on the other hand, no, I'm gonna take twenty, I just need twenty, maybe I'll ask to stop by a shop on the way. Or thirty, I need to leave a tip for my taxi driver. Seriously, five hundred... Well, I'm aware that for some people it's a lot, but for me, in my position, it's just petty cash. Or I can give it to Claire because she seeks money. Because, no, I don't wanna cash in that money. I shall leave it in my safe. On the other hand, if I give it as a gift to Claire, well... She might get pretty offended. I always offered her money for developing her projects, she always refused just because she is independent and wants to do everything on her own. I think... Yeah, she still didn't get the principle of patronage.

For maybe ten minutes, I've been waiting. I was trying to avoid biting my lips, which I do when stress is pretty high – for not removing my makeup. And I was waiting. Waiting today... Well, I felt like waiting for the doctor to finally announce to me that I have pancreatic cancer, and I just have a month before the end. And I kept on thinking, what should I do when this guy comes? I don't know how to do, I don't know if I have to go towards him directly, I don't know, it's the first time. This was actually really awkward.

Because basically, when we think about this, it's almost like a date, except that, yeah, he knows what he wants to do with me and I will have to obey anyway, it's more or less that principle. Some people say that this is the oldest job globally, and if this is the truth, there is no need to wonder why humankind is so fucked up today. And yet, after maybe twelve seconds, whilst I was actually still thinking about maybe a thousand things... I heard two guys walking. If I heard them speaking, as I heard them opening the door at the end of the corridor, the door through which I actually came here, it means that walls are not well soundproofed. And, yes, two guys, speaking to each other. They both had deep voices, but they seemed relatively young, I mean they were indeed both in their thirties and as they spoke quite loudly, suddenly... I was quite scared. I knew for one guy, not two. However, the first one seemed quite drunk, which was a problem because it's gonna take hours to be with a drunk guy, I mean... To get what he wants. Yet again, they didn't speak French, they were speaking a language that I don't know. Hum... Maybe it's not for me, perhaps it's not, maybe it's actually something else. Because at some point, I heard them stopping walking, for chatting, again and again. Hum, no, it may not be for me.

I really don't know what they were talking about, but it seemed fun, according to the fact that one of them was laughing as it was undoubtedly the joke of the year, which was the thing that confirmed me that he was fucked up. And, yeah, for a couple of seconds, they stopped, spoke, and... Maybe he was looking for the keys to something. I started to look at my shoes, staying in the same position, and this time more stressed, I really hope it's only one of them, or even better, none of them. When, after maybe a couple of seconds, maybe twenty seconds later, twenty or thirty, I don't know, but I heard them walking again. And this time, towards me. Oh my god, no. I started to breathe, close my eyes and breath, repeatedly, for now, getting ready... As they both came in, damn...

And at some point, I saw the knob of the door being opened, as I closed the door for more intimacy. And through the darkness of the corridor, I could see two guys coming in. Regarding their age, I think both of them were around their thirty, no more, according to their faces and their approach. Okay. Well, it could be worse, two guys aged the same as the derelict wreck that opened me the door, which would have been a nightmare. Two guys, well, at least that detail was kind of hidden, even if I don't really know what's gonna happen if both are here for me or...

I really don't know, I just forced myself to smile as soon as I saw them. I smiled, because there was nothing else to do, I mean, yes, the apprehension was now at its peak, since I do not know what's next and not knowing this terrifies me. At this point, I thoroughly assessed the danger of the new mission I was into, to save Claire: if I'm gonna meet guys like this, that was actually seeming quite dangerous and hostile towards me, then it's gonna be, well... I really need to find a way to protect myself. Because they know this Joris, and Joris, if he has connections within mafia circles, well... As the very first thing I was actually feeling, at least when the first looked at me was, well, I better shut up and do what they want me to do. And mostly, not speaking. This is why, remaining cold-blooded might not be enough, actually.

They came in. And amongst these two guys, at least the very first one to enter the room, he was a tall guy, but when I mean tall... I mean very tall. Even ways taller than me right now, even if I am wearing heels, and he seemed quite impulsive, as he was rather massive. Blond hairs, the same colour as mine even if mine is natural, but, of course, much shorter. He seemed to be the perfect archetype of evil misogynistic guy who just wants sex and good booze and nothing else, usually getting this from prostitutes or... God knows what. He was wearing certain clothes, like famous brands, which means that he was probably an heir, just like me. This guy smells money, he doesn't need to say it to prove that he has money, his clothing speaks for him. Now, he was wearing a black biker jacket, short enough, a white shirt, and blue jeans almost faded. At his feet, a pair of expensive sneakers. All these were surely coming from luxury shops or brands. And even, behaving that way is the perfect type of an heir, as he was still carrying a bottle of vodka, had red eyes certainly because of the alcohol consumption or certainly the lack of sleep because of a rough night, and above all, he looked... I mean, he gave the impression of being such an arsehole pursued by his own devils. All the type of heir I certainly do not want to become. Oh, and also, as he seemed immature... That evokes many family problems and indeed linked to the mafia, certainly a power struggle.

I could see anything other but misery when I saw this guy. He was undoubtedly a descendant of a prominent family, given the fact that his immaturity could only mean that he was an heir and not someone that struggled to get his own money like an entrepreneur. He also had probably other brothers (what I call a brother is not in the way the word means, by "brother" here, I mean "business partner") fighting within the same family for the power. And he was probably failing as he seemed to be the legitimate one. As he was impulsive, I think that alcohol must turn him violent because I feel that this liquid must be his only strength to affirm his authority, which is why he is immature, he is not respected. However, I could see that he seemed to have a specific power or influence over the second guy present today. What tells me he is from mafia circles are his many tattoos that I could see under or through his clothes, his behaviour, and the fact that the second seems to follow him like a puppet. Blond, green eyes, tall guy, curly hairs, and fancy clothes, and his behaviour, all those sounded suspicious to me. Yes, when I see this guy, I think I should consider submitting myself, or otherwise, nobody will ever see me again. Whatever it may cost me.

I read many things about mafias around the world, and I know that for what concerns Russian or even Slavic mafias circles, tattoos are basically signs of achievements, where they have been, and whom they worked for, more or less like a CV. But this guy, no, seemed rude and disrespectful, but I do not actually believe that he's ever been to prison. He looks tough, but not tough enough, unlike his acolyte. Contrarywise, his mate, seemed to be more like someone... I don't know how to explain, he seemed ways harsher than he. Maybe his mate has been to prison, maybe his mate made more than he actually did, but there was something. Perhaps the other is plotting something against the "brother". For once, I actually felt like, well... I knew these mafias existed; I just wasn't that aware that this was even real. And that also confirms that I didn't come here today to play cards.

As for the second, who was much more discreet than the first and certainly wiser, he was wearing a classic suit, a black one, white shirt, and... Okay. He had tattoos on his fingers. Something which is honestly... Disgusting. And horrible. To be fair, I said they were Russians, but nothing clearly tells me they are from there. I suggest they are from there. This second guy was a brown-haired guy and had a more perfect haircut than his colleague, he seemed more dangerous and, yeah, perhaps more academic, somehow. But the way he behaved, as I said, I still didn't understand what they meant as they were speaking in another language. I don't understand Russian, he was probably one of the servants of the first, I guess, or one of his enemies who pretend to be his friend, as it's typical for any family that has influence and power and control those kinds of stuff. A nice suit, a neatly ironed shirt, he seemed however and was watching everything like if everything was dangerous, and wasn't drunk, or high. But when I mean, observing everything, I mean... Obviously, whilst he ensured that the tall one didn't see anything.

Free Expensive Lies: Prologue

When they entered, my breath rate actually slightly increased, as the panic started. And I recalled because the more I saw them and the more I was feeling threatened, I remembered that Claire was here a week ago, certainly with the same guys, or... I don't know, and she's still alive. What I have to do is just, well... Listening, and not speaking. Because this guy seemed like someone who controls, I mean the tall guy, he appeared as the alpha and certainly wouldn't accept a female would resist him.

On the other hand, he is paying for having me, so I am supposed to do what he wants at least for an hour and shut the hell up. I just smiled at them, I didn't know what they knew about me, I didn't know what they wanted from me, I didn't know what to do, I just looked and smile. And yes, I was not at my comfort; I wasn't wet, I wasn't ready. This situation was really stressful.

They both came in. Obviously the first kept on drinking whilst speaking to the other, and the second, more discreet, was following. However, I noticed that the second closed the door after coming in, so, well... Well at least for what will happen next, it's not going to be a spectacle. After he closed the door, I uncrossed my legs and immediately stood up. Because I trained myself many times on this, on stressful situations, whatever the danger is, I must always show myself as confident. Hence, it disarms the adversary on whatever attempt he may want to have to push me down. Now, it was time to apply what I learned. Well... And once stood up, the guy with the costume came just in front of me after they kept on speaking in this foreign language with the tall guy, as he pointed me with his finger with a pronounced contempt. He looked at me, smiled, I smiled back to show that I was sure of myself, and at the same time, his pal went back, closer to the door, to lean and watch what would be going on. I said nothing. Not a word, as I didn't know what the protocol would be in such situation, and I thought that as I wasn't a man, I was not allowed to speak in front of two misogynistic sadistic that they could be. And breaking this rule would certainly be a terrible idea.

Quietly, like a predator, he came closer to me. There was a gap between me and the sofa, I saw that he didn't seem to want to stop. Instead, whilst still ambling, he started looking at me. I was so stressed that my bladder was about to explode, but I managed to keep terrible self-control. Right now, if I mess up with something, my life may be at stake. Except for Joris and Claire, nobody knows where I am, and if something happens to me, it can be life-threatening. He started to ogle me, like, beginning from my shoes to my hairs, and whilst still slowly walking, he started turning around me. I was... Well. Not reassured at all. And pressure must not overcome me. He was still chatting with his friend, in this language and as he was closer to me, it was like, when he spoke, almost deafening, but I remained poker face. And whilst still spinning around me, at some point, when he achieved his first round before starting the second, he started speaking to me, in French:

"Hi, you..."

"Hello," I convinced myself that nothing wrong would happen so I could use a slow voice and show that I was not terrified.

"You look so pretty!" he continued, still like the predator he was.

"Hum, thank you..."

And whilst behind me, I started to feel the zipper of my dress slowly going down, after he pushed my hairs. His hands were, well, I could feel his other hand touching my right shoulder, and it seemed to me like an attack, and the comfort was definitely gone. I was almost petrified, I mean, many electric shocks throughout my body, and I felt like, I don't know, at the exact place where he placed his hand, I felt like it was dirty and my skin would never be cleaned again. When I felt my zipper being at the half of my back, as I didn't see him, I felt terrible because he removed his hand, and I just kept on feeling, how is this going to end for me! I must remain deadpan. It was like torture, which started so suddenly and that I had to undergo until the end. And at some point, the zipper reached the bottom, and my dress fell on my feet. And at this point, whilst the tall guy remained leaned against the door and was watching what was happening and when I kept on smiling to him, but this time nervously, I was hearing the suit guy, behind me, breathing increasingly fast. And this breath just made things worse, this was like a terrible threat to me, like some pervert that was on his way to attack me. I was still feeling his hand on my shoulder, even if he removed it for a couple of seconds now, my shoulder was like where all the world pain that I could have ever experienced was directly located. I felt so dirty and so ashamed that this hand has ever reached this place of my body. And, I was like, this is a nightmare, and it was now just a beginning. As I was now only with my underwear and my shoes, still terrified to make a single move, he came actually in front of me, for ogling me again one more time:

"Well, you are really hot, actually."

I just smiled to conceal a mix of embarrassment, shame, and fear. Apparently, yeah... The best thing I had to do was closing my mouth because speaking would lead to even worse and unleash my fear. I felt like the victim of a crime, and the only thing I had to do now was to let it go and let them do. Suddenly, whilst standing in front of me, he started to remove his jacket, for throwing it in the sofa just behind us. While still smiling (maybe like an idiot now), he went just behind me and started to touch my back. He was merely pointing his finger. Was he on the way to remove my bra, was he on the way to... I don't know? When he actually touched me, I just wanted to do one thing, it was to turn back and push his goddamn finger and tell that I am getting out. But instead, as the danger was omnipresent, I just closed my eyes and raised my head, pretending to moan. Because, yeah, I was terrified. He started to take the strips of my bra, taking them for letting them slap my skin. At some point, when I began to breath stronger because, in my mind, I was scared, I was terrified, I was assaulted, and I couldn't say anything but thanks, he started to push my hairs on the other side, on the shoulder he actually touched me a couple of seconds ago.

At that moment, I lowered my head. I kept my eyes closed because seeing the tall guy still leaning at that door was increasing the pressure, the pressure to which I was not supposed to give in, I was feeling that he was pushing my head, and removed every string of hair that he could find on the other side of my neck. And this was absolutely terrible, I could feel his hand, his repulsive and disgusting hands, as he came closer to my body, I could start to feel his whole body against mine... And I just wanted to move, to move away, to leave, as I could smell him, smell his guy's smell, and... On my bottom, through his pants, I could feel that he was hard. This is gonna be just for sex. When, in my mind, whilst the terror was everywhere, as I could feel him all behind me, when I lifted down my head, at some point, I got surprised by the fact that he actually gave me a kiss on my neck. It was terrible, I mean, now, the aggression was real, I was really aggressed, I was feeling under attack, and I couldn't get away. I just had to remain there, terrified, feeling him attacking all that's intimate to me, my very own me, I was feeling his lips against my skin, his penis through his pants on my bottom, and this was just the most disgusting thing that ever happened to me. I continued moaning, softly, and this was a moan of fear, of "get the hell out of me", but this was slightly different to me. And then... When he stopped kissing me, when the mark of his lips and his genitals, of all what was disgusting in him, was now spread on my own body, he just stepped back and said:

"Perfect. Now, come with me."

20 *To whom it may concern*

// Rue du Lever du Matin, 15th arrondissement of Paris, south of Paris.

// Wednesday, 16th of January 2013, 16:15 maybe.

Again, I called the cab on my way back home. And honestly... Yeah, I was just speechless. I didn't know what to think, but to leave my head against the window and see the driver driving me back home. In my mind, well... I never thought I'd actually experience something like this someday. And yet it happened. I guess I'm gonna need more important things now, to cope with, well, the rest of a couple of days ahead.

Obviously, this was a disaster, at least for me. Basically, I was here for the guy with the suit, and nobody else, I was here for one person. And given the language, they spoke (I am not quite sure they spoke French) and the tall guy's behaviour, communication was something impossible. Basically, he drove me towards the bed, where I actually lied, well, facing the tall guy, on all four in the bed, above the sheets. He didn't say a word, just kept on speaking with his mate, whilst I was just doing what he wanted me to do. He spared my legs so he could have a place to sit behind. He didn't undress in front of me; obviously, I was the only one to keep my underwear, even if he removed my panties. And then, well, just the simple fact that he posed his hand over my body, I felt deep repulsion, I felt like the aggression was even higher like this was probably the very worst assault he could do to me. Whilst still on all four on the bed, I just closed my eyes, listened to the noises around, and the very first noise I could hear, I remember because that went so slowly, I heard him removing the belt of his trousers, get the fly down and slightly removing his pants. The brother, still in front of me, was almost gloating. And after, whilst I kept on my mind that I was almost all covered with a kind of decayed mud all over my body, everywhere he put his hands over me. I couldn't get rid of it, the very worst actually started, because the shame was intense, he touched me where he was not allowed to, where I did not authorise, and I felt like my skin was almost instantly rotting, I was still saying on my mind, "carry on, it's not gonna take long".

Because what happened next was horrendous. He started to touch on the most intimate parts of me, and... And he did it. It was exactly like I got stabbed. Because even though he actually managed to wear a condom (and it was undoubtedly the best thing to do since I was not wet at all), it was so rough that, well, I actually moaned in pain and it was like being moved from everywhere. The pain was so intense that I was feeling tears coming out of my eyes for the first time of my life. And obviously, his hands were all around my pelvis, and he bounced me, again, and again, and again, and again. It was like, I was actually feeling like on another planet. A planet where danger, desolation and chaos are nothing else but a daily routine. I kept my eyes closed, did what he ordered me to do, while the brother was still in front, speaking out loud, and felt, again and again, his own hands moving my pelvis. The pain was horrible, I felt like an intense heat down below, and it was so itchy. But he didn't actually care, he was still doing what he had to do.

I can't actually describe what was on my mind at that time. It was, I don't know... For once, it was like nothing. I mean, nothing and everything at the same time. Usually, when I didn't want something in sex, I just say, "don't", and he/she stops. But now, I was not allowed. I was only not allowed to do anything. At the moment he started, well... Putting his thing in my vagina, I was just like, "you can't", but he just did. It was already too late. Just the fact to feel him, well, penetrating me, was, I don't know, I don't really have words to explain. Well, it was horrible. For the first time of my life, I got forced in that, and I just couldn't imagine this would be something absolutely terrible. Until then, sex was, yeah, something fun, but now, someone was just destroying anything that could be fun, only for his own purpose. He changed the rules, he just... My mind was for once empty, just praying for it to stop as soon as possible, and this very quietly. I wanted to say, again, maybe ten times stronger, get out, get the hell out, leave me alone, but, no, I couldn't. I just had one thing to do, give in to the pressure, because when it's gonna be over... I mean, I hope, it's gonna be the end. I couldn't actually believe that this would be so hard. I just assumed that, well, sex is just sex, and that's all it is, even if I feel nothing, it was the very first time I actually felt something. And it was for sure the worst way to actually discover the thing.

And I couldn't get away because of the fear of the tall guy still standing in front of me. Obviously, both, during the act, kept on talking. He went actually so fast with me that I could even hear my legs slapping against his skin, whilst the pain was just horrible. Nothing actually came to my mind except this word, I was a coward. Doing what I am doing, to Florent, he's never going to forgive me. What I am doing right now, it's just abject. It's just betraying him. Even if I was forced to accept, I mean, what I am doing is not even forgivable. And he doesn't deserve that from me. It's actually horrible, even me, I am... It's gonna take me months to recover from that. This humiliation, this... all this mess, I mean, how can I see Florent straight in the eyes after? I don't know, for once, I actually realised that maybe sometimes, even if I had no other choices but accepting that. Well, whoever blackmailed me, for now, I couldn't imagine that he would take such an advantage. I must remain cold-blooded after that, it's just an hour, it's just... It's gonna be over soon. I must remain cold-blooded as I am now, things still must be in control, because otherwise, everything will be gone and it's gonna be over. And I am fighting for making sure things are not that over.

I had actually no idea for how long it lasted... He was just gripping me forcefully and doing his stuff, whilst the pain was absolutely horrible. But to be fair, I actually had no longer any notion of the time or anything anymore. I was just impatient for him to end that as fast as possible, but it seemed like an impossible dream. I start to understand why Claire hid this from me now. What has it been for her, the very first time? It was certainly much worse. If I am right, if she has been blackmailed, just like me... It must be the reason why she is now acting this way. She's been traumatised, I mean, this could still be a traumatism. But I must remain the strong one, as I've always been, and this, again, whatever it might psychologically cost me. But, yes, that's... To be honest, I don't know what to think, it's like, I don't know. Time stopped, and... I just have to wait until this is over.

Until that moment, I don't know for how long after, even if it was quite long but, I don't know how long it was... When he speeded up, for like a couple of seconds. The heat down there became increasingly intense, and... it was just awful. It burned. When, yeah, he speeded up, hurt me ten times more, when suddenly... He was done. At the very end, he moaned pretty harshly, his mate laughed and started to clap his hands almost on slow motion, and... And I thought that it would be over, but actually, at some point, I felt him literally crashing on me. Okay, I am done with him.

When he actually crashed on me, I let myself collapsing too because his muscles made him actually ways heavier than my back could support. And, yeah, I heard him breathing. And now, I was kind of hoping that this hour would be over, so I could get out of there. He collapsed for some moments, and, whilst still inside me, when his friend stopped clapping, he actually found the strength to raise himself. And at the same moment, when I was still in a brace position, with my hands protecting my head and almost covering it, the friend said, in a crystal-clear French and perfectly audibly, always with his Slavic accent:

"Congratulations, my brother... You fucked her very well!"

"Oh yeah, really?" the other one replied, behind me, recovering. "Well, do you mind now getting the hell out whilst I get myself dressed?"

"Okay. I'll be in the courtyard!"

Free Expensive Lies: Prologue

I assume that they looked at each other because I heard any movements for some seconds, then I heard him leaving, the door slammed. It actually startled me to be fair. At the very same moment, he withdrew himself, and I guess I was definitely now in a state of shock... Because it seemed to be definitely over. To be honest, that door slamming gave me some moments of peace of mind, because... It appears to be over. And when he withdrew, I let myself collapsing for some moment, because, what happened, it was unbelievable. Many things came to my mind now, I was feeling dirty, disgusting, and I felt that I have actually been used against my will, which was terrible. I was defenceless, I couldn't defend myself. At the same time, I was angry but just too empty, too strengthless to actually express my anger. I was also feeling completely useless. I have no idea of what was going on in my mind, and, well... I was simply scared to look at him. Wow, this was what I accepted. I don't know what the worst could be: the pictures released, or me still doing that. Whatever it was, I have no idea who is my blackmailer, but this guy really wants me to collapse.

Unfortunately, I still have things to do, and it was not the moment to actually lament on myself, it was time to continue my mission and get out of here. Once he was out, he left the bed, and I needed some moments to actually recover from what happened, it's why I remained on the bed, still not moving, and I fell on my right, to lie entirely on the bed. I actually needed some moments to think about what just happened and try to go over it... I felt it almost like trauma, I was feeling totally repellent, and I felt like all the parts of my body that he touched, yeah, it was so dirty, it was like the mark of the shame of which I couldn't go over it. In the meantime, I saw him going away, I don't know for what, and I heard his mate leaving the building. I actually... I was feeling like, I must remain strong, for the rest of the day, even if it's gonna be lighter, there are still things that I need to hide. I cannot talk to anyone about what has happened because there will have consequences. Literally, I am trapped in a terrible situation, a situation through which I cannot get away. If someone hears about what has happened today, it will be a total dishonour, and except suicide, I do not see any other option to cope with that. Still, I was feeling disgusting all over my skin, down there, I cannot describe how awful it was, mostly since I was not fully ready for that, and... All these thoughts came to my mind. Again, I will have to hide it, pretend that nothing happened.

Again, now, I don't know how long I remained there. My body was all covered by this feeling, I couldn't escape that, and I was just feeling cold. I could feel my clothes on me, my shoes as well, and some kind of small wind that travelled through my skin, almost like cuddling me. I heard him putting back his belt, doing his stuff, obviously behind the Japanese screen so I couldn't see... Until that moment. Now fully dressed up, with his vest, all I could see was his horrible fat fingers all covered with ugly tattoos. He actually went to take my dress, which was still left down there, on the floor. And obviously, just the fact of seeing him was enough to feel like, yeah. A mix of repulsion, anger, fear that he may touch me again and disgust. He actually came to me and dropped my dress, now so messy, right in front of my nose. And with his strong accent, still standing up in front of the bed, and taking his wallet out of his pocket, he asked me, coldly:

"That was your first time, right?"

"Yeah," I whispered.

"Where're you from?"

"From here."

"Hum... This is for you," he said whilst he actually gave me a couple of banknotes. "And try to stay alive again."

"Why're you saying this?"

"You'll understand soon enough. Now, get dressed, and get out," he was on his way out.

Still in there, well... Still lying on that place, on that bed, at the same position, I actually saw him leaving. And, yeah, now, it's over. I don't know how long this took place, but... I don't even care, I just need to get out. Immediately, I gathered all my remaining strength and... And, well, I actually put my dress back. Obviously, the zipper was behind, so it made this harder for getting ready and longer. My panties were on the floor, I wore that back, and yeah. It's over, now. It's done. And, down there, it was horrendous pain, I will go to the doctor tomorrow, I think if it does not get away. I was in such a state of mind that I actually didn't feel relieved that it was over, I don't know. This was just huge. But I must continue. After I wore my dress back, I just felt one feeling, get out as soon as I can. So, I stood up, took the money that he gave me, took my handbag, because Joris was supposed to get his part of the job, left that bed, and took my coat. After wearing it and closed it, making sure that nothing would be visible, I actually opened the door and left.

The door of the corridor was open, and given that I didn't hear any noise in the courtyard, I presume that they're already gone. And it's better because the very last thing I wanted right now was to fall on one of them. I was almost rushing, I need to leave that place as soon as possible, I almost felt like I was chased or hunted down, and... and the darkness of that corridor was just making things worse. I put the money in the handbag and took my phone. I saw a text of Joris, received ten minutes ago, saying "Charlotte, I'll be waiting for you outside, just in front of the door. I'm in a black van, just come in when you're out, cheers". Yeah, cheers. When I left the money in my bag, I was just feeling like, this was... I didn't deserve that, I endured this for just a couple of notes. It was just something disgusting. I actually walked fast, as fast as I could, to get out of here.

While the courtyard was empty, I walked towards the main door, the door through which I entered, when I pushed it with the force of my body, I was feeling like, I don't know, a kind of freedom regained—a sort of different feeling of safety. And, yes, when I left, I actually saw his van parked in front... Yeah, it was precisely the black van that I saw when I was out there. At the moment he saw me, he honked, to make me notice that he was there. So, immediately, I walked towards the front door, and I jumped in the car.

And I was rediscovering him. Yeah, I remember his face, the last time I saw him, I was with the three at the nightclub. Before things went messy. But today, he was actually watching the road, with sunglasses, so I couldn't see his eyes. His car was pretty cold, and the leather seats were obviously so cold that it gave me a burning feeling on my legs. I just sat, opened my bag, took the entire package of notes, and gave it to him. I wanted to be brief, I didn't plan to extend myself in here:

"Here you are... I assume that this is the thing you were waiting for," I still used a soft voice... yeah, again, because of what happened.

"Yes, honey! Exactly the right amount. But there are some things for you in here, to compensate you for your effort."

"Take everything, I don't give a crap."

"No, no. That's not the deal."

"I insist, leave me alone with that money."

"Fair enough."

"Okay... Anyway, how was it?"

"How was what?"

"Well, your experience of today?"

How was my little experience? For the first time of my life, I had sex without my consent, this just killed me, and I think it may have traumatised me, I was scared, I feel awful, I feel like I am a damn mess, a whore and a traitor... Oh, yeah, but I forgot, I cannot say that. No, because if I say this, even though I went until the end... even if he abused me. In front of his mate, even if the guy was speaking whilst he was just fucking me in that language I don't know, I must remain happy of that because this was just a job. And if I say otherwise, if I confess that I am not feeling good, this will stop everything, he will tell me that I am not ready to continue. And my blackmailer will publish the pictures and ruin my life. And now he certainly has shreds of evidence that I am also doing prostitution, this will be...

I couldn't even believe that I could be in such a humiliating situation. And I don't know what's worse: having undergone what I underwent, or having to shut up, say it was fine, whilst I am feeling absolutely terrible and right now, I just want to kill myself? Because I cannot speak about what happened. Maybe to Clarisse, but I must take heavy precautions. Destroyed, and pretending to be happy, I faked a smile and said:

"Yeah, it was okay..."

"Good. Did you like it?"

"Yeah."

"Awesome, so we can start for something new tomorrow then."

"Already?" I was like... No... Please, no...

"Yeah. Some friend of mine is throwing a party, it's actually near the Champs-Elysées. A perfect place, a big flat. You're gonna love it."

At the same time, I was taking my phone. Ordering a Taxi. Because, yes, I need to go back home. And I certainly don't want him to even believe that he could drive me back home.

"What are you doing?" he asked me when he saw my phone in my hands.

"Now? Ordering my taxi for home."

"Come on, I can drop you. I mean, you live far away from here?"

"I really don't want to. That's nice of you, but I don't want you to drive me home. I want to get some food, and, you know. If you don't mind, don't get it wrong, but I kind of want to be alone now."

"Okay. Anyway, you're okay for tomorrow?"

"Hum... Any chance we can postpone? I, erm..."

"No, I really need you. The guy today was actually really happy with you, and I really want you on my party tomorrow!"

"Oh, so it's your party?"

"No, I mean... Yes, well."

"Okay, then. I'll be there tomorrow," I concluded.

21 *For the blue of your eyes*

// Back home.

// Wednesday, 16th of January 2013, 17:28.

I was not feeling better or worse, to be fair. Just the fact to be out for a while, to watch Paris, calmed me down. The rest of the day started, now it would be more enjoyable, I actually didn't know how to take it. To be fair, right now, I just wanted to stay in my bed and take a maximum of sleeping pills, to sleep, again and again. I just couldn't hide anymore. It was just too much, what just happened.

The thing is, to be fair, I was not feeling guilty for what I did. I was just feeling dirty for what I did. Well, yeah, I am a traitor to Florent, because I cheated on him, but being a traitor is something natural for me, betraying and deceiving people is not something that prevents me from sleeping. I was just feeling genuinely dirty. But one thing was sure, I was not ready for tonight. I mean, now I was back to the civilisation, I felt like a new day has started, with new rules; basically, the world was still turning, but I was just feeling disconnected from this. There was no beauty anymore, just nothing, just the remembrance of what happened. Again, and again, and again, and again. I was just telling myself at that moment, I'm only done with this. I mean, behaving like this, always making sure that things are going right for everybody, saying this not to hurt him or her. This has been all the entire story since my parents broke up and divorced, and... It's been years that I am coping with a breakdown, but now, it's even worse. I mean, I was really unable to deal with anything directly, and... I just wanted to tell my driver to drop me somewhere to come back home by walk. I just don't care about anything. But I can't, first because of my outfit, and second, because I really want to take a shower. I need one. But right now, for once, my brain was restarting more slowly. Restarting to cope with everything. To give an example, it's like... Imagine we just nuked a city. How I was feeling right now, it was after we finally managed to extinguish all the fires. It's all chaos and death everywhere.

Anyway, everything was already well-calculated: as Clarisse was aware of everything, she knew that her role was, basically, that she had to wait for me behind the door after receiving my signal because it's obvious, if my boyfriend sees me in this outfit although hidden by my coat, that's gonna raise thousands of questions for which I do actually not want to answer. And as this day is essential for my mother, today is the last day to screw up something. Everything must be all right because that's for her job. I actually rang her phone seconds before the Taxi driver drops me in front of the building, and she hung up. It means she acknowledged my call. Immediately, she sent me a text saying, "red light". It means I could enter the building but not my flat. That's what I did, but for once, I took the stairs and waited in there for the signal. I carefully removed my shoes before coming in, to make sure I'd be more discreet. She was supposed to keep an eye on Florent and make sure he'd be busy with someone else.

The light, in the stairs, is on for at least a minute. If you are not close to a switch before it turns off, then you find yourself in the obscurity. Curiously, I was feeling like... You know, when you are fourteen and making the wall for coming back home when you were actually supposed to be home but instead you went to out with a couple of friends. Well, today, it was certainly less exciting than any other days, because the mood was definitely killed, and the thing is, I shouldn't take another pill because I might actually have an overdose. The light went off, and... I actually enjoyed the quietness of the stairs. I just heard myself breathing, until that moment, maybe a minute later... Clarisse, "Greenlight, chop-chop!". I hurried up, opened the door of the stairs, and then, rushed to my door. Clarisse should be waiting for me now.

Daylight reappeared a short time in the corridor, and before coming in, I could hear all the noise of all the guests invited to that private ceremony talking, like nothing happened or everything was normal. I knew mum had asked at least sixty people tonight. But for now, basically, as she had models that she hired that were changing in the fourth bedroom that she redesigned for the occasion, they were still in the dress-up and make-up stage, the fashion show didn't start yet. For the moment, everybody was still drinking and speaking. And there were already a lot of people, maybe they were all here. I just hope this will finish before eight, so I can go to bed early, I didn't feel like having a party now. Before pushing on the handle, I put my ear against the door, just for checking if Clarisse was alone at the entrance. Amongst the noise of everybody chatting, laughing, plotting or I don't know what... However, I heard Clarisse being close to the door, meaning that she was in front of the door. So, I pushed slightly, to notify her that I was nearby, very slowly, when I heard the noise of her footsteps coming closer to the door, and she opened. And when we looked at each other, as I was certainly not at my best mood, she understood that something was not actually right. Ah, come on...

"Well, you're here, come here right away!" she whispered to me once the door was just half-opened.

Free Expensive Lies: Prologue

Immediately, she took my left arm very tight, pulled me inside, and let the door closing itself. She drove me inside very quickly, making sure that nobody would actually see me, even if actually a very few guests noticed that I was there, as the door of the reception room was still wide open, all the other doors were closed, and I think, locked. I just turned my head quickly to glance what was inside, and, well. The parade was about to start, and as I am wearing the wedding dress, I was the last to go over there. But actually, at that moment, she held my arm so firmly that it was quite hard for me, when she dragged me to my room, certainly in the space of ten seconds, no more.

Today, I must admit that she was dressed slightly differently than the rest of the guests. Well, I mean it's not for her a usual manner, even for a ceremony where everybody was almost wearing ties and suit, or black dresses and heels, no. She had a black skirt, half extended, arriving on the top of her knee and departing below her belly. White shirt and a black jacket; she was dressed like a businesswoman. That's my sister, well, I guess this is something we have in common, never wanting to do like everybody else. I do not have the required balance for that. Yes, on many points, she's more skilled than I am. She was pretty, and if her boyfriend is here tonight (I do think he is), I mean, he must have been happy to have such a cute girl for a girlfriend. I used to have that feeling before, and everything changed. It's not frequent that I find my twin pretty, but today, as rules have changed and now, I was in the worst mood ever, I mean... The beauty of the world remains right now at my eyes deeply corrupt.

So, whilst she was still holding my arms, when we arrived in my bedroom, she immediately locked the door with the key that is all the time on the door's lock, and I rediscovered my bedroom as I left it three or four hours ago. It felt like I went here for maybe a month or more, or even years, I was like, I don't recognise this place, even if nothing moved. I just walked in, dropped my shoes on the carpet of the floor, and walked, sadly, towards my bed. The background noise of everybody laughing actually shocked me at that moment, I was feeling like the world was still turning, and I was certainly not a part of it right now. I was just sat on my bed, still recovering from what happened. Always somehow feeling his hands touching me or still feeling that this just never stopped, I just wanted actually a moment to heal, to deal with this. Now I was secure, now I was at home so nothing may ever happen to me, nothing wrong at least, I just saw my sister, once she locked the door, looking at me, and remaining in action:

"Go to your bathroom. NOW!" she actually ordered me because we were together hearing that everyone finally noticed that I finally arrived.

"Um, I..." I was hesitating.

"Cha, please, this dress is fucking heavy, and it's gonna take ages, so please, don't screw up!"

Sometimes, she can be such a little cunt: she sees that something is wrong, and no, she just wants me to wear that bloody dress. Fuck the fact that we are running out of time! But I didn't really want to argue. So immediately, like totally compliant and acting like I was about to be hung, I got up nonchalantly, and she remained like at a metre away, following me towards there. After I removed my coat that I left lying anyhow on the bed, I stood up to go to the bathroom, and... remembered that I had a bath before going in there. I was really destroyed at that moment, I mean, there was nothing that could cheer me up. I was definitely not ready for the rest of the day, but the truth is, when Clarisse knows and sees that I am pissed, she uses to kick my ass for telling me to carry on, and to go through events. I honestly don't know if this was an excellent idea at this very moment. I don't even know if she actually found out that there was a problem with me.

And here we were, in the bathroom. I actually found the wedding dress hung in the shower stall, in a big and really thick black pocket, but the first thing I did upon entering the bathroom was to actually head to the toilets to pee. I just couldn't stand anymore. When Clarisse entered the bathroom, she locked the door, again, and went to lean against the sink. The way she looked at me, as I was head down and almost watching how I peed, she could understand that there was a problem. I think she was about to change her approach because I don't want to act like a bitch as I use to be with her when she is mean, and there's something wrong. Now, I need to be alone, but I can't. She didn't look at me like I was carrying the plague or another dirty disease. Still, the fact that she was standing up, near the sink, crossing her arms and didn't come closer, she probably felt that I didn't want anyone to come close to me now. I raised my head, to look at her, and understood that she has felt what I felt during that moment. She seemed pissed, but merciful for me, and mostly, was standing far away from me. Until that moment, we looked at each other's eyes: there was a little between her and me a huge shame, but in between, I could feel like she was feeling like me, dirty and repellent as she was crossing her arms. When she crosses her arms, it usually means that she is upset, and she's feeling weird. It happened once, already, after I made her a bad joke and had the exact same immediate effect on me, I was feeling like, don't touch me. So, it means that she somehow also lived the same thing with me. As seen as the way she wears make-up, even if she is pretty and prepared herself carefully, she didn't wear that much make-up. Because when this thing happened to me, she was perhaps preparing herself by that time. And, whilst still on the toilets, after having peed and obviously lifted my dress to avoid peeing on it, she kept on looking at me, feeling actually weird.

"Give me a minute, please," I said, lowering my head one more time, with an exhausted voice.

"Charlotte..." she was upset because she understood that I was in shock and certainly couldn't talk.

"What?"

"Talk to me!"

"Talking about what?" I preferred avoiding the topic.

"Or at least answer that question. Because this is... Why the hell did my mood switch when I was preparing myself, why does nobody touch me right now, and why I am feeling ashamed and upset even if nothing actually happened. Let me get this straight. What the hell happened in there?"

"Clarisse, I... I really don't want to talk about that now."

She actually glared me, as if she were about to tell me "you'd better talk", but she didn't. I lifted up my dress and gave it to her, and she put it on the left sink, next to her. And, answering her question, I really did not want to talk about that right now. But she felt what happened, I mean, we are twins, so what I have, she has it too, and I guess this is why I was somehow looking at her like I'd see myself in a mirror, regarding her mood. That's scary.

At the moment I removed my dress, I had some flashbacks in my head. All that happened bounced back into my mind, especially when the feelings all across my body of where he just put his hand over me reappeared like a hot flash. I just couldn't get rid of it. I was undoubtedly crying from the inside, I mean, maybe my brain was crying or at least wanted to express what it was feeling, but I couldn't. I was feeling some kind of mercy from my sister because she could differentiate the fact of my anger, my fear, from the fact that I was obviously not feeling right. I will definitely take a shower, maybe it might help me cope with the fact that I am feeling so dirty, or... I don't know. When she saw me down, almost inarticulate and hanging over the toilets, heavily depressed, she just said to me:

"Charlotte, whatever happens, I am here for you."

"I appreciate it. Thanks," I replied, exhausted.

"But there's something I don't understand. You told me you didn't get anything with sex... And now, I am feeling embarrassed and weird. What happened? And I know it cannot come from me, as I didn't have sex today."

"I don't know. Things certainly didn't go as they were supposed to go!"

"Look at you, honey!"

"Huh?"

"You're just totally out of your mind, I've never seen you like this! Ever!"

"I'm not okay now... Just give me an hour, it's gonna be better."

Clarisse was definitely right. I mean, okay, this happened, and this was terrible. But this was a part of the plan, even though I had to pay the price. It's hard, but I must move on. I must keep on going, and... This is over, so I can restart an everyday life. This is done, over, and I can pass through that.

Clarisse gave me a hand, she actually took my makeup-remover, and put some on some cotton pad. She told me I was awful and looking like a zombie. Maybe removing this could be the first step of accepting what happened. I actually stood up after I took the cotton pad, and went towards the cabinet where the sinks were, to look at myself in the mirror, At the same time, I could see that when I came closer to her, my sister actually stepped back. And frankly, seeing myself in the mirror was, I don't know, I had some kind of shame when I saw myself in the mirror. I immediately switch on the sink's water, I soaked several pads, and without trying to see myself, I just removed all that mess. I need at least an average of six pads to get rid of all make-up, and today I needed eight before I washed my face with hot water. Clarisse was still next to me, and, at the same time, took a black towel under her, so I could dry my face again. Yeah. And when I looked at myself one more time in the mirror... Well, I had the feeling of, you know, a dethroned princess looking at herself in the mirror. It may perhaps take some time before my mind swaps to something else. Usually, when I got out of my diazepam trip, I used to feel better, but now, it's kind of strange. So I tried to find another approach, deep down, with, you know, my usual speech:

Okay, Charlotte, you're over it. You passed through that. Now, it's over, you're done, you removed that dress, that make-up, and you will make it disappear. Just, look at yourself, breath, you're a warrior and a renegade. A warrior always fights until the last minute. Like you told yourself when you were in the bath, you must not give in, you must not fall, because if you do, Claire is fucked. Claire's sake is on your shoulders now, and if you collapse, you will fail, and this is not what you want to do. You're a fighter. He made you feel dirty, right, he humiliated you, but you know what humiliation looks like, you know what feeling dirty means, and you always survived. You may not take your revenge, but it's okay, you're doing for a noble cause. Now, you lived it, then accept it, because whatever the outcome, there are no other options than accepting that you did that. He did that to you, he's a fucker, but now... Think about Claire. Think about the one you love, and... come on, wake up, life keeps going, and you must not give in. SO MOVE YOUR ARSE!

Hum... curiously, I feel better now.

"Darn it..." I actually shouted when I opened my eyes and saw the dethroned princess that I was in front of the mirror.

"What?" Clarisse remained impassive next to me; still, her arms crossed.

"Why on Earth do I have to be so doomed?"

"What do you mean?"

"All those bollocks and craps that happen to me all the time. Why me? I mean, seriously, is it written 'fuck me, please' on my forehead or it's like my fate or something?"

"No, Charlotte. Can I tell you something?"

I actually turned my head when she said that to look at her. And I don't know, I mean, the way she said it, it felt like... Yeah, she wanted to say something important. Because even if she knew that, even if she knew what I would do, she never disapproved me. And I don't know why she actually smiled now and uncrossed her arms for actually taking my hand, I mean, taking my arm... And I don't know, this was powerfully cheering me up.

"Yeah..."

"To be honest," I actually gave her my hand, "you're not a whore of any kind or whatever you may think of you. You're simply different and, well. I'd be your ex-girlfriend, right now, if I knew the least of what you were doing for me..."

"Yeah, prostitution, yeah."

"Believe it or not, love, but... If only someone could protect me the way that you are fighting to protect Claire's arse... I'd be devoted to that person until my last breath. Whatever this person is doing or has done."

"Yeah. Well, I really hope she's gonna ever realise that I am doing that for her, even if it costs me a damn lot today."

"I am aware that it does. But, hey... You're her saviour, her guardian angel!"

"I ain't a fucking guardian angel or anything, this is rubbish, Clarisse. Seriously, I am fed up with everything. I am at the end, now, there are too many years that I just wait for one thing, the moment I'll die. Why am I fucking alive, and why I didn't die in the womb of our mother? Or why didn't she get aborted?"

"Just as a reminder, we were two sharing the same egg, so if she got aborted, I'd be dead too. My point is, today, you're enduring pain for your ex. Whatever your situation is with her, I mean, someone doing the same for me, yeah..."

"I am not a heroine, Clarisse! I am nothing of the sort."

"The only thing I disapprove, Cha," she continued, "is the fact that you are doing this, whilst being with someone."

"Well, in wars, there were always many collateral damages!"

"I am and will always be by your side, Cha. This is something I will always be," she actually spoke this time very slowly, so she thought her words may have more impact. "But... I am just asking you one little thing. Please, please, if you want to go on, if you want to protect Claire's arse or if you want to have her back... Please, don't break Florent's heart! He's an amazing guy."

"Clarisse, it's too late, now," I said with disenchantment.

"It's never too late, Cha."

"It is. Imagine the day he will find this out? Or imagine if I dump him and my blackmailer finds this out and sends the pictures anyway? I will break him if I do that! I have to go through this whatever the cost, so I can save both of them... And my soul, at the same time," I concluded.

I am not paranoid. But I know that he certainly won't make my life easy. Given the apparent motivation this guy has to the envy of destroying me, he will not make my life easy, that is definitely sure. Anyway, I had no idea how long I had to get ready, but it was time for a shower. And, honestly, I really do not want to go there, this is just torture right now. I removed my bra and everything, and, well, I was actually sluggish at that moment. I was about to ask her to go there at my place, but the problem is, if something changes in between at the very last minute, it will appear as unusual, and I will have no excuse to say that I sent my sister at my place. And I paraded already for my mother twice, I did, it is why I know maybe certainly half of the people present here today, and they know I would be here. I like doing that, helping her on her stuff, this is something I love, and if I do not do that today, it's gonna raise questions and mum will certainly not appreciate that I change her plans at the very last minute.

But one thing may have been sure right now, was that I was undoubtedly delaying everyone. Today, there's a lot at stake for her, for instance, she is about to negotiate a big and juicy contract with some big luxury company here, and everything must remain perfect, because if she fails it... I mean, okay, I'm at war with my mother, but she's been working really hard on this and collapsing this just because I'm not okay or I'm seeking revenge is nothing but the bitchiest thing I could do. And I'm not that person, I really want her to succeed. Especially when the CEO of this big company is present today. Anyway, on my way to the shower, I continued extrapolating:

"But yeah, seriously, I am fed up. I am done with this..."

"You still don't know who your blackmailer could be?"

"I have some ideas, but I actually don't know... I mean, this must be, I think, bigger than, just my close friends. I think I'm attacking myself to something huge."

"Do you?"

"Yeah. I mean, this is big. But I think I should exploit Kelly's relationships. When I called her the other day about today, she spoke like she was the leader. And her role within this network is not well defined. I should speak to Claire, as she knows much more than I do..."

"How long do you think this is gonna take until you can finally have strong evidence against them?"

"No idea. It can take days, months... I have no idea, Clarisse. But given that I met Joris, the apparently head of that network, it might lead me to something. I think this guy is the head but uses Kelly as an organiser. Like, you know, he's the CEO, and she's the COO. Because this guy is a cop and cannot really involve himself in the management of all this, this is why he must be delegating."

"A cop is the head of the network?" Clarisse seemed surprised. "You mean... like a rotten cop or something?"

"Yeah, it's why I need to be careful. Because, as a cop..."

"Yeah, I see what you mean."

"Collapsing a rotten cop will be hard. Especially since I know that now, he has links within some kind of mafia, the Russian mafia."

"How do you know that?"

"Oh well... I think that if you found me so bad earlier, then I assume that you'd guess with whom I was today..."

"Oh, hum... Oh, dear," she actually realised.

"This is why I need to be incredibly careful in my approach. If he is a cop, whoever I am, making me disappear can be something really easy for him. Especially, given my situation."

"Cha, if something happens to you, I'll always do my best to find you no matter how."

"Yeah. The thing is, as I worth thirty-nine million euros, it should be easier to find me because I am not like the futureless philosophy-studying student that sucks dicks to pay her bills."

"Are you saying that your life matters more than any others? If this guy wants to make you disappear or to kill you, your money ain't save your arse."

"Oh dear, Clarisse," I said whilst entering the shower tray. "You still don't know that in this 'humankind', it's all about money? Come on, open your eyes! We are no longer humans today; we are just credit cards with legs, born to consume. What saves my arse is just that I can strike harder than the common of the mortal over here."

Unusually, I used the shower tray. Even, to have a shower, I use the bathtub, but I guess today was different. And, in the meantime, the shower helped me to feel better: I mean, the hot water, sliding along my skin, was acting like it was almost swiping away all the feelings I still kept on having of him continuously touching me even though he was not anymore. I was feeling gradually better, and eventually, I was feeling ways better. It was all gone. And gone for good. I don't really like having showers, to be fair, I am more someone who takes baths (come on, it's all our guilty pleasure), but I never enjoyed so much for the first time of my life a shower. I still had my dried soap; meanwhile, my sister left, she actually went back in my bedroom (as she left the bathroom door open) to get some stuff in my bedroom, I don't know what. I didn't actually hear her properly, I mean, the flowing water's sound was far louder than her shoes walking around. Honestly, this moment was almost to die for, I actually took my time to enjoy the warmth, because it was still pretty cold out there, and... I just forgot to tie my hairs. Well, fuck it. I still have my hairdryer, and... And yeah.

Maybe more than ten minutes later, I opened the shower doors for getting out, as I was actually done when I heard Clarisse still on my room. I was out, now, just looking for my towel that I actually found on the seat of the toilet. My sister thought about everything, she even put a towel for my hairs. She has dropped the dress still in the package hanging over the bathtub, and I looked at it, it seemed really heavy. On the other hand, it's a wedding dress. But when I touched the packaging, it didn't seem that heavy on the top, but it seemed very thick on the bottom, at the skirt's level. I really hope it's not going to exhaust me, but as it seemed to be a considerable dress, then... It would hide the fact that I am not wearing heels. I was okay to parade in a wedding dress, even if it's my first time, but I really hope that she would understand that there would be no way I'd be wearing heels for that. You know, I am more of a con than a model.

Because, yes, when I carried the package, (and hopefully my sister is here), it was like... Like really heavy, like it's gonna crush on me. Hopefully, *meine schwester* is more robust than me, so she's gonna be accommodating. After I wrapped myself in the towel and wrapped my hairs in another towel, I just looked at myself, back to the mirror above the sinks. My face was paling increasingly, my blue eyes stood out like never before as if it were blue diamond lost in the middle of the desert. I am petrified, sometimes, by the fact that I am that pale. My slightly damp skin and the little mist that was leaving my body because the water was burning and it gathered all the heat, the light of the room and everything made me feel maybe sicker than I already was. Meh... Obviously, she came back into the bathroom many seconds later.

Thank god she thought about me... And brought me my black pumps. Great. And upon entering, she threw it on the floor. And when I saw her, I said:

"Clarisse," I told her sadly.

"Yes?" still standing near the entrance of the bathroom.

"I really don't know how I'm gonna deal with Florent tonight."

"What do you mean?" she didn't get what I meant.

"I just... I don't know, it's gonna be hard. I just don't want anyone to touch me... And I really don't know what to say to him."

"I understand. I do. The thing is... If you tell him just 'don't touch me', it's gonna be like, quite suspicious. And... I am afraid to tell you that you're gonna have to deal with it. Because, well... You're his girlfriend, and... When was the last time you guys actually did... erm... you know?"

"Maybe a week ago."

"Wow... Until then, nothing?"

"Nope."

"Oh, dear. Well... Say that you had a big day, and you are just tired. For instance, I told him that you were at Sophie's this afternoon because you had to help her with some stuff. Did he text you?"

"Surprisingly, not... But that's fine. I mean... I'll think about it that I was at Sophie's!"

Right now, unbelievably, I don't know, I actually... Well, I realised that this was just over. Believe it or not, but I just hate lying, especially to him. I already served him maybe a thousand lies whilst, with Claire, I never lied to her. Ever. I looked at myself in the mirror one more time, whilst I was thinking, the sink and my dress on my left, still packed. I was waiting for Clarisse back to help me to wear my new dress. All those lies, all the time, it truly makes me sick. And I really don't even feel that I want him to touch me, to... do anything, or even be close to me. But this time again, I cannot get away, I guess.

Again, Clarisse was looking for something, back in my room. My new underwear, I guess. When I actually thought that, well, I hide a knife below the sink, just in the cabinet where I store my make-up remover and other shit. And I don't know that my psychological state was suddenly worsening increasingly. The more I actually looked at myself in the mirror, I just felt like I do not deserve anything. And, in addition to that, I suddenly had a kind of flashback when I heard this guy still speaking, going around me, ogling me again, and... Geez, I just can't get rid of it, I felt like I can't escape. Now was definitely the moment, given the fact that she was away, I still had time! And I must confess, given all the things that I gathered in my mind since I was born, all the knowledge I have, I just can't go through. Mum used to say that ignorance is bliss, being stupid allows you to cope with the unintelligent and dementia into which this world is driving daily. Now, this is just too much for me. My brain began to make by itself the total sum of everything at the time, and my desires of the moment, divided by the shame, was pulling me increasingly down. At some point, it's just unbearable, and I actually reached that state for now too long. I'm done with being alive.

I just grabbed the knife firmly from below the sink. As my twin was still elsewhere, nothing can actually stop me now. It's a dark and quite a thick dagger, finely sharpened, and it's been a while that I even think about this, that I keep this knife in case things goes totally out of control. It's like the poison capsule for a spy, but this dagger is the manipulator's tool. Sometimes I just have to look at it to convince myself that life ain't worth to be lived at all, now, after what happened, I didn't need to convince myself any further, my life doesn't worth to be lived. I had the knife in my hand, whilst my mind kept putting me back actually a few hours ago when it actually happened, just to convince me that what's left of my dignity was now ruined forever, and there was no need to continue. Now, my lies, whatever the outcome of that conflict may actually be, I will never be forgiven for what I am currently doing, so it doesn't really matter to keep on fighting. Florent will never be my friend, and Claire will never come back, I just have no hope. And when I looked at the shining blade, the metal colour gave me certainly much more convictions and more decisive resolutions. Even though I am scared of the pain, the manufacturing's furrows appeared as golden highlights, my cowardice was gone, and I don't need to hide anymore, I just can proceed.

Whilst holding it, I convinced myself to step forward, while having, in perfect silence, the echoes of my fears and my apprehension for tackling myself to the final solution. Checking on my other arm where my little veins were, still appearing as blue confused in a white ocean, crushed under the weight of my muscles that allowed me to move my wrist but compressed under several layers of my skin. It was now the moment to finally quit that nightmare, to leave that body that was still a pain every day. To stop that rotten and corrupt mind. I kept looking at my mind, then at my blade, and I was just like, it's gonna hurt for a few seconds. Should I do it? Is a failure of this process necessarily an option? Whichever the solution could actually be, staying here and continuing to lie, say yes next time to Florent even if I will still think about when I was almost raped before. Is it living an actually wonderful life? If I tell the truth, I am fucked on literally every point, and lies are actually like a poison that kills you, even more, every single minute. If I quit now, well, whatever it will be, it's not gonna be escaping a problem like a coward, it's not gonna be an abandon, it's not gonna be fleeing, it's just gonna be a surrender. I prefer to surrender. Because I just kept imagining Florent, in his beautiful suit, waiting for me over there, wearing a dress that he actually dreams me to wear someday for being married to him, and I just can't, I can't, I cannot deal with that, because that's not what I want. The girl I want is not available anymore, because she's now collapsing in the rotten foundations of a hell designed specifically for her.

I can't deal with anything anymore. I can't deal with myself. I can't deal with Florent because I don't love him as a lover. I do not trust anybody on that planet. I just trust myself, and everybody is still a potential threat to me, mostly since the threat level has been increasingly raised at "imminent attack". All the problems were all connected, everything had a link, and unfortunately, I cannot go back. I went too far, I just... Yeah, when I saw myself, again, in that mirror, all I could feel from me was just repulsion and absolute hate. My life is a nightmare, I am unhappy, I am in love with a whore, my boyfriend wants to become my husband, and I don't want, but I have to deal with this. I have money, but no plans for the future that comes with it, everything is a waste of time. Now, even the beauties of the world were like extinct or absent. Many people wouldn't actually care if they were in my place because they think that I am a part of that population lucky. But luck, there's no luck, there's just maths and ways to reach an achievement. Oh, yeah, and there's now this: I am having sex for money just because I am blackmailed. The kind of situation that was absolutely never supposed to ever happen, it actually happened. There are just no ways out. What the hell should I do?

Masks are now falling. It was time to say goodbye. Suddenly, now more convinced, I actually hold the dagger fiercely in my hands, both my hands, the blade pointing towards me, and to make sure that this would succeed, I immediately pushed the sword as hard as I could towards my heart. It was not even a second, it was undoubtedly half a second when I felt a sting. For after increasing in the space some moments, experiencing like the most immense pain I have ever felt in my concise life, like the pain of a foreign object entering my body, it was huge. Still, it didn't appear like straight away, it just blew me up maybe a couple of seconds later. I was just pushed back towards my bathtub behind me, just a few steps back, but I didn't fall, and suddenly, I was feeling like, very cold, increasingly cold, even if the pain was totally unbearable, but it's not gonna take long. I just lowered my head, checking the damages, when I saw a massive leak of blood flowing along my chest, my belly, and along my leg. The floor started to be covered. And, although I actually managed to stand up now for maybe the space of a few seconds, certainly ten, or twenty, or less, I don't know, I collapsed, and I was actually feeling that blood was running out now. I just fell on my back, on the carpet, the small rug I had before my bathtub. Now, it's over.

My body was now in shock because the blood pressure decreased dramatically and couldn't supply every organ. They were all collapsing one after the other. I have no idea if my heart was still beating, or not, but it was about to end. I changed the balance, forever now. I just couldn't hear any noise around me, I could barely have my eyes open, I was still struggling to keep them open, by the way, maybe in case Clarisse could come, so I could say bye. When I collapsed, I actually curled myself up, when I saw her coming, rushing towards me and screaming "HELP, I NEED HELP IN HERE!". But I was in a state of profound misperception, my eyes were now definitely closed and couldn't be opened anymore, but somehow, I started to feel better, maybe I was feeling lighter. I lost my strength but was feeling safer. I couldn't speak anymore, I couldn't be able to move anymore, I couldn't do anything anymore. My body was just nonresponsive.

Clarisse just kept on panicking, and was definitely afraid of what was happening, her sister will die before her eyes. But there was nothing she could actually do now. I had no idea of what she was actually doing, as my eyes were closed, and I started to see the light at the end of the tunnel—a dark tunnel into some snowy mountain. Nothing could stop me from running there. I just heard her voice, "Charlotte, open your eyes". I tried, I really tried, but I couldn't. I had no longer any feeling or perception of my body, and I was suddenly feeling all right, the shock was now over, but I was still so cold. It was time to leave, time to go, and I was so willing to do so. Everything disappeared as fast as it appeared, I suddenly saw no tunnel or even no light, I just heard my sister keep on calling me, oppressively, with a "Charlotte, wake up! Are you daydreaming or what?". When suddenly, on my very left ear, when still in my thoughts, I actually heard her yelling at my right ear:

"CHARLOOOOOOOOOOOOOOTTE! WAKE UP!"

Oh my god... Suddenly, I opened my eyes. Damn it, she broke my ears. And when I actually "woke up", I was still in front of that mirror, naked, and thinking about what's next. I had this feeling of expulsion, like the one you experience when you are wakened up like too brutally from a deep nap... And, when I actually turned my head, she had in her hands one of my numerous black laced bras with a panty. But the time to come back to my mind...

"Huh? What?" I said with a small voice that brought me back into my mind as if I was daydreaming again.

"Are you all right?"

"Yeah. Yeah? I am fine. Uh... What do you want?"

"What happened?"

"Well, I don't know, I was kind of having a fantastic dream. Anyway."

"Yeah, anyway... Is that okay for you or you want some other?" she showed me my underwear.

"Well, okay, but I really hope that either you or mum are going to come to help me get rid of that dress."

"I'll be there, yes, don't worry..."

Right now, I was like... How can I say, I just breathed, like, very deep, like, it was the time to go. I was still in my mind, like, yeah. My sister gave me my underwear, and at the very moment I wore it, I mean, when I was almost ready, she went actually back, towards the bathtub, and on her own started to unhook the huge packaging of the dress, to lie it down on the floor. From there, she began to unzip the edges. It made a kind of noise, and I felt like, okay, time to discover it. To be honest, I was quite excited because I love mum's creations. She's really gifted for that, and I really wish that this will be the most important thing and the dress that will ensure she's gonna get her contract to be signed. She designed many of my dresses, many of whom I still wear today for great occasions, and she's really talented. Whatever the problems between us, I mean, I must recognise that this is something big and I really want her to be successful. And, whilst Clarisse was unzipping that massive packaging, I was actually discovering... well...

It was a massive dress, and incredibly long too, which is good since I really don't have to wear heels then. To be honest, as a wedding dress, it seemed more like a kind of princess dress, the kind of dress that princesses would wear in Disney cartoons. And even though Clarisse was bending and actually struggled to open the package as it was relatively wide and very thick, basically she couldn't walk on it as the dress was covering the entire alley. To be honest, this was really breathtaking, but it seemed very fragile, as it was massive, it seemed to me like... I should really be careful with that. At the end, when we took the dress out of its packaging; when Clarisse managed to open everything, I looked at her:

"God damn it!"

"What? Yeah, I know, it may be heavy for you, but at some point, you won't feel it anymore!"

"No, I'm just... This dress is fabulous!"

"Oh. Yeah, it is. When she showed it to me, I was like... I don't think Charlotte will want to remove it."

"To be fair I already want to remove it, but I must confess that, yeah, this is incredible."

"Okay. Anyway, I need your help, now!" she said, now bossier.

I was literally impressed, and, yeah, if I marry someone, I would certainly like having the same dress with the same style. But it was a good surprise. First, it was quite long and had different colours, which was quite unusual. It was composed of a bodice and a long, voluminous, and stately skirt below, both obviously linked by an almost invisible and very hidden thread. I think she tried to do it according to my personality, as I love all that is official and aristocratic. And it was curious: the colour code that she used to compose with her fabric was mostly dark red, almost burgundy, and black. Unfortunately, it would be very tight, and I'd better not move too fast with it, as there was a sort of skin-tight closing just behind which was laced and now attached with a tiny knot, so I needed to untie it, for slipping myself inside.

So, first, as it was a bodice, I'd better remove my bra; otherwise, it's gonna be awful. And second, we carried it with Clarisse, we just turned it upside down, for loosened the knot and the lace just behind. Also, mum hid a very discreet zipper at the pelvis level, that we opened, so I could slide myself in the dress without breaking anything. On her own, she actually carried the very thick bodice and left a space so I could put my two feet inside, and I helped her afterwards to hold it until the skinny and light strap made of lacework reached the top of my shoulder. Curiously, she made it amazingly comfortable for me, I mean, even if it was a bodice... for now, it wasn't tightening my chest. Okay, it's not clamped yet. And this operation took us several seconds.

And when I had this on me, I actually rediscovered myself: from the top, the strap (only one, on my left shoulder) was already made in a fragile red lace with black patterns stitched all over it, giving a lightly thick shape. Multiples flowers are drawn on this lacework, all connected by the same roots, and all going from the top of my shoulder to the top of the skirt, passing through my bodice, while still completely covering a side of my body, leaving my other side free. I assume that the skirt was allegorising the root of these flowers. The design of this was actually quite unusual, as the strap covered my chest, letting it slightly appear, but it was stunning, it was hiding my chest.

Mum thought about everything: the bodice was therefore below, designed in a much more resistant frame though really heavy, covered from the inside with a lovely piece of fabric, incredibly soft, and on the outside with satin, all this covered with this massive lacework. I don't know, she really adapted that with my body's shape; I don't think it's going to be that thick. And it felt so comfortable, not hot, oh my god, it was terrific, a real pleasure to wear. On the burgundy lace, between those lines surrounding my body, we could distinguish several different floral patterns attached with some shiny golden wires even on my back. She has designed many roses that emerged out of nowhere, many gladioli and mimosas, but those flowers were a kind of allegory about me, at least it seemed to be. All those flowers were still strongly connected, even if some were leftovers and weren't connected to anything, I could almost see a beautiful allegory in that. And finally, at the border between the bodice and the full-length skirt, above my bottom on my back was made a big bow tie, hiding the link between the bodice and the skirt, made with a full burgundy thick fabric, which at least could hide everything. The dress also had, both in front and behind, everywhere on the body, many sparkling diamonds, shining, certainly evoking the constellations in a burning dark sky, and they were literally around throughout this dress, embroidered within the lace.

And finally, the skirt. As I said, it was exceptionally long, like leaning against the floor, certainly designed for my size as I was tall enough. However, from underneath, I could feel several layers, one that was full of something, the second top of other things, but I was unable to actually find what it would be. Through certainly a third layer, all this to display that the dress was actually entirely recovered with various flowers made of the same lace that was making my strap. These weren't embroidered, they were all stuck together to form a kind of flowers bouquet, also made of different burgundy tones. Throughout the dress were presented almost the very same colours, but all in significantly different shades. There were burgundy flowers, then after there were dark ones, after a burgundy one, a light burgundy, it was so much more harmonious and so much lovely and dark... I was voiceless, I mean I have never worn such a beautiful dress in my life. Yeah, it was making a kind of enormous mountain of flowers. That was a fantastic creation, I mean, I cannot say anything else. And, well, on the other hand, as this is the piece onto which she worked the most, I mean, there must be something else that must also be amazing for that dress: its price.

Obviously, I didn't see that at first, but for finishing there were also this, these long gloves. The kind of gloves that start beyond your forearm. These two were made in some sort of burgundy velvet, making my finger thinner and longer as they already were. I had to remove my engagement ring, the only ring I am wearing. Obviously, Clarisse had to finish with an essential thing for wearing it: tightening my bodice. And obviously, as usual, I'd like to say when I wear a bodice, to make it tight she has to pull on the wires, she loves doing that firmly, and by surprise. And it was when I removed my ring that, well, suddenly, I felt like an immense pressure all around my chest, tightening myself very forcefully. After I slightly complained, she just said, with the astonished but delighted air:

"Oops... Sorry, darling!"

"Jesus Christ, Clarisse, you're gonna break it!" I yelled... actually very softly.

"Oh, darling, trust me, you can survive. And if you are still complaining, stop reading your iPad and practise sports like me!"

"Oh, well, I can actually do both and throwing my iPad into your face. Apparently, some people call it relaxation! And depends on the force, we can still consider it as a sport."

"Of course, and after I can take your damn arse and balancing you through your balcony. Some people also call it relaxation, and it can also become a sport. But they also say it's illegal, I never understood why!" she laughed.

"I can kick your damn arse, Clarisse."

"Yeah, and then complaining because you broke a nail."

Meh...

She gave me my black pumps. The problem is, I couldn't bend, I couldn't actually do anything, so she put it on my feet. And, meanwhile, I was combing my hairs. I was happy to be like that. But it was true, okay, the dress was fabulous, but I don't think that I will move a lot, because it was too tight, and I couldn't really move that much. Obviously, to avoid any damage, I cannot really bend myself or even sit. Well, for bowing, I just checked, I just couldn't wear my shoes. Anyway, the ceremony will take place any minutes now, so I actually hurried up. Clarisse finished with my hairs, she tied them to make sure that no hair would hide my strap and put all them on the other side, in front.

During this, I put my make-up. It was slightly different from earlier because I didn't wear any gloss but instead a dark red lipstick that matched with the dress. And when everything was ready, when I was ready, I wore my gloves finally. And now, time to go.

And right before I actually left, at the very moment I was ready to go, Clarisse looked at myself and, whilst contemplating, said:

"You're amazing, Cha..."

"Oh... Am I?" I shyly replied.

"You are. And... I know one person over there that will be really happy to see you like this. Even though it's not your wedding!"

"Yeah. Even if my heart is beating for someone else," I actually thought, sad.

22 *On the brink of collapse...*

// Still at home but now in my bedroom, after the ceremony, Neuilly-sur-Seine.

// Wednesday, 16th of January 2013, 22:10.

She was actually right, there was one guy, at that party, who was just with stars in the eyes when he saw me parading on the small scene made for the occasion. But in my mind, I really wished she were there. Obviously, by she, I mean... Claire. She was indeed the only one missing today. Perhaps I was fantastic tonight, but of all the stars that were shining through the tiny diamonds on my bodice, there was just one star that was not glowing anymore. And this was sad.

Obviously, there was a lot of people tonight. And when I mean people, I mean, mostly her colleagues. I think we were about sixty or something. I knew some of the models parading tonight, I mean my mother worked with them already, and it was great, I mean, in the end, I saw mum leaving with the big boss of the company to the living room whilst the party continued. And when she came back, I went to her, and she told me that she actually signed her contract, everything was now official. And I was like, great. I even congratulated her because she worked really hard for that. Basically, at this party, she hired thirty different models, for trying sixty-five different outfits. I was just for the very end of the spectacle. Photographs obviously shot me many times, and... I saw Florent, and he was jealous. But hopefully, this didn't lead to any problems.

After I paraded, and when I was still on the scene, my mother came to me to conclude the ceremony and speak to the audience. We both left the small scene a couple of minutes later, after her speech, and Florent immediately came to me. As a dominant male, he started touching me, but I repelled her hand. Curiously, that hand reminded me of this guy's hand, but he was surprised by my reaction. I just said that, basically, I was hot, and I needed some air. I actually went to a group of people, with my sister... Until we came back to my bedroom, with Clarisse, so I could wear a lighter dress. I remained with the wedding dress for like, yeah, two hours, and at some point, it was just too much for me. As I said, the conditions were not there, I was just like, please everybody to get out, because I was done with the party. I just wanted to be in my bed, and that's all. Unfortunately, my desires were slightly different from what actually happened. And... It was awfully long. It's why I hate parties at home, it never ends.

But things went actually different, I mean, whilst Florent was having fun, I just came closer to him, when I saw the time scrolling and scrolling again, at some point the music became like a lullaby, and I came to him. Because I was really exhausted, and it was 10 pm. I ate a lot, I discussed with almost everybody here, when at some point, seeing that the night fell and I had school tomorrow, and... I also had other things tomorrow, I was just feeling like, I need to sleep. So, I went to him whilst he was still discussing with guests, and just said:

"Hum, love... I'm tired, I'm going to bed, I'm drained."

"Oh, already?" he looked at me.

"Yeah, I'm tired. Well, if you don't come with me, I'll see you tomorrow, I guess!"

"No, no, I'm coming. Hum... Give me a few minutes, I'm coming."

"Okay, but I am going to the bedroom, so don't look after me, okay?"

"Sure!"

And, drained, exhausted, I went to the bedroom. Even if I kept my dress, I went to my bathroom to remove my makeup, and after I went to my bed. Of course, I removed my shoes when I thought that nothing was ready for tomorrow. But, when I let myself fall on the bed, I actually enjoyed the guest noise still as background noise. My face was washed, and I just covered my face with my hands and told myself, "what a day!". Huh, a tough day. And I hope a day to never have ever again.

Florent came a few seconds later. I kept the light on, for him, so he could be sure not to actually fall. And when he came to me, with his nice suit, he just did the same after he closed the door: dropped his jacket and throw himself at his place in my bed. Yeah, that was a hard day. He saw I was still awake, not yet asleep, and after maybe a few seconds of silence, he just looked at me and said:

"It was an amazing evening!" he was still amazed, I assume imagining me in my wedding dress, his ultimate fantasy.

"Yeah, it was," I just replied, exhausted, and pissed as I recalled my day was horrible and long.

"I love you!"

"I love you," I finished, laconic.

We actually turned ourselves, facing up each other, looking at each other's eyes. And he seemed like pretty sad. And, okay, perhaps it was a shitty day for me, but at least the evening was a bit fun, it counterbalanced the day somehow. But, right now, for me, the pressure was decreasing. I mean, reducing, for now, tomorrow is, unfortunately, another day, and it will have its new messy package. Even if I don't really know what will happen tomorrow, still... But for now, the pressure decreased, and honestly, I was feeling weird. I was feeling lighter, and, on the other hand, I know what to do, to cope with all that. At least, now I know. I still kept on thinking about what may happen again tomorrow, because... But for now, it was time to enjoy the fact to be alone, with him. So, let's enjoy this.

I don't actually know how his day went. And all I heard was his breath. Like a topic of what to say to me, he was seeking something just to engage a conversation. And, spontaneously, I thought about this:

"By the way, baby... I found something weird last day behind the desk... It was a calendar, wrapped in your stuff close to the desk the other day, hidden behind, in your papers, where you highlighted weird dates. All this with the two letters CP on each day you highlighted. And, well... You know, I'm curious. What does that mean?" I asked in a somewhat amused and playful tone.

"Ah... I don't know. I let you guess what it could mean, you'll find by yourself," he replied in the same tone, having put his hands correctly like I did and looked at me tenderly.

"CP, CP, CP... I don't know, the Conservative Party?"

"I'm not in politics, honey!"

"Yeah, right... Chicken Pox?" I was still seeking what it could mean.

"Nope!"

"Yeah, and it makes no sense too, honey... Commercial Paper? You probably found a new job."

"Ah, ah! Perhaps!"

"No, that's not it... Central Perk?"

"We're not in Friends, come on!"

"Yeah, right, but I don't know... CP... No idea!"

"Isn't that obvious?"

"Child Protection?"

"No, no..."

"Wait... I remember about the dates, it was regular, every twenty-three days... Oh no, you gotta be kidding me..."

"Charlotte's Periods, that's right. You've found it!"

"Oh, dear!"

Meh, I'm not that annoying when I have my periods. I mean, sometimes, yes, but... Or maybe I am not aware, but I am a real pain in the arse. But he should be used, I am a pain in the arse daily. I mean... Am I? Oh, come on, I hate having no answers.

"That's unusual, I mean, am I so annoying when I have my monthly gift?"

"Well, it used to be, but since you're all the time a pain in the arse!" he was kidding.

"Oh... So nice of you!"

"No, I mean... Don't get me wrong."

"I got it, honey, don't worry," I whispered, and gave him a wink, showing that I understood his joke.

"Anyway."

"By the way, darling. I have a question to ask you," something actually came to my mind... A new idea.

"Yes?"

"You can joke as long as you want about me being a pain in the arse, even though I don't think I am the most annoying girlfriend, but... How do you actually love me?"

You probably know that feeling, like, erm... how to describe. Yeah, well, you know my life overall, and you have someone else on your mind, like the forbidden fruit, and someone else in your bed, a person with whom you actually promised to engage and... Yeah, somehow, yeah, now that I see, he does love me more than I do love him. Or, I don't know the reason why he loves me, there is certainly one, but, deep down, I was confused. My two hands under my head over that pillow, I was like, well, now that we're together, convince me. Like, convince me that you love me and that I may fall for you. I need comfort right now, and let's find out whether he's able to give that to me. Maybe I love him somehow, and I am just waiting for something to trigger feelings, as they do not come naturally... And, astonished, he looked at me and seemed confused:

"What do you mean?"

"What would you do for me?"

By the "what do you mean", I actually got the very beginning of my answer. I asked several times the same question to Claire, she'd never say "what do you mean". But the problem was, would Claire be able to do the same if it were to save my arse? That, I think, will remain a life-long mystery.

"And what will I earn after confessing my sins?"

"Oh, because you're looking for a reward to say how much you love me? And you say this is a sin?"

"I'm kidding. I love you, Cha. I'd do anything for you."

"Oh yeah?"

"Yeah!"

I just moved my head in the same position so I can place my hands under my pillow. Yeah, sometimes, this is what I feel. Men and women do not have the same conception of feelings. And I could see that today again. When I was with Claire, we were both equal. It didn't take long before we could understand each other, and generally, it was just at looking at each other that we got what we meant. She used to tell me as often as she used to show me how much she loved me. And, yeah, I talk quite often about her, I compare both of them because Claire used to do better than him on many points. On many occasions, when I was attacked, Claire used to be the first to take my defence, whatever it might cost for her... Even once she wanted to fight with a guy because he pissed her off by being too close to me. Claire wasn't jealous, she has never been or at least never showed that to me but was fiercely defending her territory. Instead, Florent (for using the same comparative) has a realm but just shows off with that. I reproach to Claire that even if feelings are still there today and maybe more concealed, she only pretends nothing ever happened after breaking up with me. On that point, yes, she's definitely French. Okay, yeah, I know, I'm playing the same game.

On the other hand, given my past, Florent used to be warier of my female friends than my male friends. He knows that it's implausible to happen that I could be attracted to some guy. And, he is right, I don't see guys as a potential target. On the other hand, when you're a guy or a black woman (it's not racism, I like black women, black people are good friends, I am just not attracted to them), you're relatively safe with me. Florent is more into... I don't know. First, he is older than me, we are five years different, and sometimes I don't feel like, also, given my past, it was a good idea to be with him. I don't say that it would be a bad idea, but I just say that I am indeed too young for him, or at least I didn't... I mean, when I met him, it wasn't love at first sight. On many occasions, when I am beautiful, he pays more attention to me than when I am in nightdress and staying at bed because I am tired. I am tired quite often, that's the problem, but it was the same with Claire. Well... Life is life, anyway, and today this is my situation.

Anyway, after furtively watched the ring, I put my hand under the pillow, and I just looked at him. And he resumed speaking:

"What happened to you this afternoon? Where were you before coming back for the ceremony?"

"What do you mean? Oh, hum..."

I was thinking... Damn, yeah, she said I was at Sophie's, right?

"Well," I continued, "I was at Sophie's. It's been a while that I promised her that I'd come and help her for some stuff."

"Hum. That's certainly the first time, I thought you didn't care about your classmates!"

"Baby, I..."

"I didn't even see you coming back... And to be fair, I sometimes felt that your sister was almost spying on me, throughout the afternoon, when I came back and helped to prepare."

"Well, I was late when I came back, so, it's why I actually rushed towards the bathroom, as I knew that Clarisse was waiting for me to get dressed. After, if

Clarisse was spying on you, then I have no idea why. But I'll ask her tomorrow if you want!" I concluded.

Well, he's not stupid. But playing his game that I was late and, in a rush, would give him a good explanation. And it was the truth, I was really in a hurry, we didn't have that much of time, so, I really hope he is satisfied with this because I don't have any better answer to actually give him. Yeah, I'm tired of this, to try to provide any explanation, the explanation that everybody wants to hear.

But deep down I was thinking, "you're definitely wasting your time with me". I mean, I am too young for him, or he's too old for me, and, yeah, I must admit that the mere reason I actually accept to start a relationship with him was that I wanted to take revenge over Claire as she was still single. I wanted her to know about this, and also, yeah, let's not conceal it, I'm scared to be alone. I mean, I need someone, I need someone to stand by my side just like Claire successfully did for seven years and, finding yourself alone at the end of a long relationship is definitely scary. At first, I thought he would be right, but now that I see things, three months on, well... I don't know who's wasting his time the most with the other, but... Yeah. He continued:

"There's no need for that... Don't worry!"

"Okay then," I replied promptly.

Here we are. Of course, Clarisse was spying on him, but... Now I know that she wasn't discreet at all. Well, she did it for me, on the other hand, she could also have shrugged off and tell me to go to hell, but... Well, that's my girl. For a few seconds, at the same time, we heard that the party over there was over, and I was really exhausted. I was about to sleep. As I sometimes do when I want to fall asleep, I just listened to his breath, hearing someone breathing reassures me, as I am sometimes scared in the dark. And I must confess that right now, I wasn't really at my ease over there. And, in the silence of the room, we could hear my mother saying goodbye to her guests, as they were leaving. I yawned... when suddenly:

"Huh?" Florent heard something.

"Yes? Anything wrong?"

"Did you speak to me?"

"I just yawned!"

"Oh, I thought you said something. Sorry..."

"It's okay."

"You're tired? You wanna sleep?"

"Well, I feel like my eyelids are pretty heavy right now, to be fair."

"You don't want to change yourself?"

"Yeah, I will... Just, give me a minute, before."

Oh, yeah, I have to change myself. Even if it happened many times that I slept still dressed up. But this was when I was alone, and conditions were pretty different. But I don't know, I feel him distant, now. I mean, yes, he didn't get right the moment when I told him to back off when I was with the dress, and he wanted to come closer to me, maybe because I didn't say it "in a nice way", but it's been several hours now, I think he can manage to go beyond this. It's not the first time that I am talking to him that way. But he actually has this problem, I wouldn't say that he is immature, it's just that when you have a problem with him, it can take hours before you reach a compromise. As soon as I don't say something like, erm... the "s-word", it takes hours before things to go better. He knows that I am not a person that present any excuses because basically, I consider that he needs me more than I need him. I don't really need the three things he is in love with me: sex, love and... sex, again. I can live without sex, and regarding love, the problem is that... well, it's a deeper problem.

"Is there any problem that you may have tonight?" I continued.

"What problem?"

"I don't know, since I told you not to touch me, you're acting weird."

"I am still trying to understand what's going on, that's all."

"I told you this dress was weighty; I couldn't really move, and I was sweltering..."

"Okay, fine, then no, there are no problems at all!"

He gave me a little kiss on my forehead, maybe to actually state something like, fine, calm down, it's okay. Maybe, telling me to take it easy. He finally put his second hand over my back, and still, he was cuddling my hairs. Perhaps this was what he was actually seeking, an explanation. Anyway...

"Anyway," I actually kept on asking, "How do you love me?"

"Erm... What if I showed you?"

"Why not, if you prefer acts than words."

"I actually do, you know, I'm not someone that talks."

"True."

I don't know what went through my mind, right now, I mean, I was like, let's let him do whatever he wants. He immediately pushed me back and started to kiss me, like, you know, kind of ferociously. We were both in front of each other, still kissing like it was clearly our last, and I let him do whatever he wanted to do with me. I was holding him, my right arm on his back and my left remained along my body when he had me, like, his two hands holding my head, like, "do not leave". I don't know my feeling when he kissed me, to be fair, there were a thousand things into my mind, and I was so tired. And maybe after a few kisses, he just left me, when suddenly, he just ordered me to come above him, a thing that I did. And, whilst now lying over him, he just kept on kissing me again, and again, and again. And, this continued until, at this very point when I felt his two hands reaching my butts. Okay... Things are going there, now. Fine.

To be fair, I was neither bad nor good, I was just like, I kept going. I was not forced at all, I was okay for him to continue, even if I was drained and I don't feel like I'm gonna make it. Still kissing me, I repeatedly felt him seeking the down of my dress very slowly. Usually, yeah, I know what it means. On the other hand, it's been a week that we didn't have sex and, well, if I refuse, he's gonna be like, come on, so I just let him do whatever he wanted. Unfortunately, the down of my dress was out of his reach, so for helping him, I just pushed myself again towards him. Yeah, since I am slightly taller than him... Yeah, I actually took myself to the game, he wanted to go there, so, fine. When I felt his hands now on my leg, I was still on him, I actually put myself slightly above him, still to kiss him, when I opened his jacket and started to caress his torso. When, after some moments later, I actually felt him touching the very end of my dress... and he slowly lowered it.

Just the fact that he pushed my dress made me thrill, it was... I don't know, somewhat intense. Meanwhile, I actually slowly opened the button of his neat white shirt. One, two, and then from the third to the fourth, always went downwards to watch his impressive body with his slightly drawn abs. I didn't open my eyes, keeping my imagination running. At the same time, when I was moving to go down, as I couldn't reach the fourth button, I felt him starting to remove my dress, at least putting it a bit higher, higher than my pelvis. I was slowly breathing just like him, sure of myself and finally, I kissed him, on his torso, where his shirt was still open, and I kind of felt like it was certainly not the moment to stop, as he closed his eyes firmly and rose his head. To be fair, he actually turned me on, I was like, yeah, why not. And it's usually when I am tired that I am apparently more performant in there. Somehow I was like, I need it, like, if I had to end up that day in a better way, this would certainly the way I'd choose, occulting certainly all that actually happened because I cannot explain this to anyone. I was just launched; nothing could stop me. So, I kept on going, down and down, kissing him again and again. And I went down, until the point, where... Well, he knows that I am not the kind of person that actually does that. After I completely unbuttoned his shirt, I went back to him, and after I certainly killed one of his most feral hopes (no, there's no way I'm gonna do that), still all four on him, I just said:

"You wished!" I actually whispered and smiled at him.

"I didn't!" he smiled back.

"No, you didn't, I just heard you thinking out so loud..."

"That is not true!"

"Yeah, yeah... Come on..."

I was in the mood, now, of doing that. To be fair, it's okay, I am tired, but I can manage it, and he is there. My dress was now entirely folded under my chest, and still, his hand was over there. It made me feel weird. Not, badly odd, no, it was a good strange, like all the time I'm turned on. I just placed myself next to him, lying on the bed but all against his body, when I dropped my hand on his torso. And whilst I just put my head on his torso, I heard his heart beating faster and faster. I just didn't do that much so far, except cuddling his torso, whilst he was fondling my hairs, we were just breathing at this point. But it's still a kind of a dangerous game to play. As I saw that he was now more tensed, a perilous game was on because of what was going on. And I was feeling like, should I continue, should I keep on going? My next target was his trousers, as his next target on me was my panties. But if I pull his zipper down, he will want me immediately something. And I am not fully ready for that.

His torso was wide exposed, now. And my dress was quite annoying to be all packed above my pelvis, but I was sluggish to take it off. I was in the mood of, yeah, I needed hugs, kisses, and affection, I was not really into sex right now. And I was like, yeah. I was probably just next to him for a minute, lying down, and listening to him. And to the outside world, as well. At the same time, I could hear my sister going with her boyfriend towards her bedroom, and mum was still leaving. But Clarisse closed the corridor door, which meant that we absolutely heard anything of all the guests coming in there. We just heard her and her boyfriend laughing. Outside, we could hear that it was pretty windy, I mean, I could listen to the flow of the wind whistling against my window. But it was astonishingly not that cold. I heard that it forecasted to snow tomorrow or Friday. Well, I'll figure it out soon.

And, still there, with my hand where his heart was beating, more calmly this time, after the small moment of slight excitation, still in the same position, I was actually enjoying the calm of him cuddling my hairs. To be honest, my hairs are my weakness, whenever someone cuddles my hair, it makes me, well... At least more obedient. And he knows that it calms me down almost instantly. I just said, when I heard my sister and her boyfriend entering their room:

"Well, I guess we know what they're going to do in the next minutes!"

"Yeah!" he chuckled, "a bit like us in a minute..."

"Maybe. Or maybe not!"

"But maybe yes."

"Yeah, maybe. Baby, I'm feeling weird."

"What do you mean?"

"I don't know, I'm just feeling like..." I actually hold him harder. "I need protection. I don't know why I'm feeling like that, unsafe..."

"You're feeling unsafe with me?"

"No, that is not what I meant... I'm just feeling like, not safe. I'm scared, I mean, I feel like everybody is a threat and I just can't defend myself."

"And you're saying this because...?"

Well, because of a thousand things, actually. I don't know, I'm always feeling like this when something like this happens when I stop, I'm feeling like insecure. I mean, when it happens in normal conditions, I'm always feeling anxious. Okay, the period is quite an anxiety-inducing, but still... I really don't know why I am feeling that way. Somehow, something tells me that I should continue, but on the other hand, I do not feel like I really should continue, I'm actually really shared on what I really want now. I just sometimes overthink, and that is not even good.

"I don't know, I just realised today that, you know, many things could happen to me, and... I really hope that you'd be there is something bad would happen to me. That you'd never judge me?"

"Why would I judge you?"

"Just... I don't know, I... I'd like you to solemnly swear an oath tonight, actually," I thought about that.

"What do you mean?"

"For instance, Claire and I, when we were together, we promised to each other that whatever happens, even if we are no longer together or we are far away, that we will always give assistance to the other. I swore that oath for her, and even today, if something happens, even if I am with you, I'll always help her, because this is something I swore for her, which is really important to me. It's a matter of honour."

"Yeah, baby, yeah, Claire, again..." he was pissed.

Well, whether he wants it or not, and as I explained to him several times already, Claire has been and is a part of my life. If he wants me, he also accepts my past and my problems. Otherwise, there's no point to discuss. For me, honour is something important (I mean, this is weird to talk about honour when we manipulate people, are morally wrong and deceive everyone without even giving a damn). Whatever happens, I will always place that oath before everything. Yes, I know that I am a disgrace already. But... Well, somehow, I'd like him to swear the same promise, even if I am sure, if someday we break up, he won't give a damn anymore. Because I am just some attractive girl with a cute accent.

"You know what I told you about Claire and my past, you have to deal with it if you really want me..."

"I am not complaining about that, it's just that those recent days, you actually talk a lot about her, and... I really find it annoying!"

"I am not talking that much about her!"

"Anyway, please, say it."

"Say what, something that I already told you a thousand times, because I love you and... That's it, of course, I'll always be there for you!"

"Okay, then. Thank you, I appreciate," I just said, with disappointment.

Yeah, sometimes... I really tend to forget that men and women do not work the same way. I mean, as long as I didn't have sex with him, I cannot be wholly fulfilled with love and... being satisfied. I just need to empty his balls first to make sure that I could get what I want. But, okay, fine. Let's get what he wants, I don't mind. I'm just like, I have to do not care. They are all the same anyway. After a short moment of silence, I actually thought. Let's talk about something lighter, let's think about something else. Because if I continue, seeking to even get what I want from him, I will be disappointed. And, well... Until that moment, I actually thought about the classic question...

"Anyway... How was your day?" I continued.

"Oh, hum... Well, I woke up when you were out this morning, I received a call for a job interview tomorrow."

"Oh, really?"

"Yeah, well. It's actually to get a position of supervisor in fast food, near Notre-Dame."

"Oh, nice!"

"Yeah, she saw my CV and given the fact that I did some studies, she said that I'd be perfect for the job. Which is surprising, I did architect studies, and not management studies..."

"Yeah, but you still did studies, so it proves that you are serious."

"Serious, you said? I didn't even get my degree!"

"Yeah, but... Meh, you know what I mean."

"Well, anyway I said why not. On the other hand, it can be good to start my life. It's quite interesting, she said that I'd earn almost ten euros an hour."

"Oh, nice. Since I never worked, I don't know what it actually means, because, for me, ten euros is like the crust of bread, but... I assume that it's pretty nice for you! Well, either way, good luck for tomorrow!"

"Thank you!"

And suddenly, I don't know, I was feeling like, weird. But, like, really weird. I felt like severely dizzy, I mean, I kind of had the black veil before my eyes, I felt that my eyes closed by themselves. Well, I was still next to him, but for a couple of seconds, he was actually speaking, but I was unresponsive. I mean, I heard him talking, and... everything seemed like blurred, and really confused. In myself, I was like, "god damn it, not that again...", when I actually pushed myself from him, to go to my place and remain flat back.

"Yeah, and... Hey, Cha, are you okay?" he actually stopped speaking, seeing myself unresponsive.

"I, hum... Yeah, give me a minute..." I actually whispered.

Whilst being flat back, I was actually having a hot flash. I placed my left hand over my forehead, to check my temperature, and I was freezing. And I put my second hand over my belly, as I was feeling nauseous. Meanwhile, I don't know, I was feeling like, my chest was like... softer than usual. This is the very first time it ever happens to me. I mean, I never experienced such a thing. I used to be nauseous, feeling weak and dizzy, but I've never felt this in my life. My body was literally boiling at that moment, I mean, I was feeling like almost inside a pan heated up at more than a hundred degrees, and as I didn't eat that much tonight, usually, when I have a hot flash, it makes me throw up. So, I may expect that this is why I was touching my belly, I mean, sometimes, just the fact of touching my belly helps me to deal with that. But I was not feeling good at all, and I felt that Florent, next to me, was moving towards me. I closed my eyes to actually save energy, and I was thinking: is that my periods back again? It's impossible, my last periods ended on the sixth, and as I am still regular, I'm supposed to have them at the end of the month.

And, I mean, my periods... That never does that. Usually, I feel like a massive pain in the belly that kills me for a day, and after I'm feeling better, I'm not like this, I sometimes have hot flashes but not as hard as this one, and mostly, I never feel that nauseous. I'm never sick at all when I have my periods, actually, maybe when I was younger but not anymore. Florent was still next to me, and to be honest, I wouldn't do anything anymore but sleeping for today. Today has definitely been a shitty day, and this until the end, and as I know that tomorrow is not going to be better, then... I really don't know why I still didn't hang myself yet or done something like that. And, really, this hot flash was incapacitating, I mean, I was feeling like fragile. Hopefully, I am in my bed when it happens, but I felt like I was sweating many seconds later. I felt like a cold sweat, like tiny drops of water forming all along my body. This is really weird. What the hell is wrong with me?

"Are you okay?" I could feel panic in his voice.

"Nope," I replied, concisely and without any emotion.

"What can I do for you? Can I help you with something?"

"Actually, yeah, erm... Could you bring me a glass of water? I feel like I'm melting, and I'm thirsty."

"Okay, then, give me a minute!"

Whilst I was still away, my eyes closed and undoubtedly enjoying that very fucking hot flash, I felt like he stood up. When I thought, "lucky him, he doesn't know those problems". Yeah. Hopefully, he was still swift. And I am not sure, but I think my bottle is still in the bathroom. Anyway, after he stood up, I actually slid my hand from my forehead to my eyes, because the light seemed a bit aggressive.

Meanwhile, I was feeling a bit better, I think I just passed the peak of the flash. I heard him opening the door of the bathroom, rushing in there... And, I was like, yeah. Also, I need to pee, again, so I'd better manage to get better because I don't really want him to escort me like a 90-years-old lady heading to the toilets. I also drank quite a lot during the party, I mean, my glass was full all the time. Even though it was mostly coke (mum wanted explicitly that there would be no alcohol, so there was none), it was the only sugar-full stuff. I needed sugar that evening, so... I remember, at some point, when I paraded, I was feeling weak, but this was hypoglycaemia. I recall, after I drank a glass of coke, I was feeling a bit better. I don't drink a lot of soda, I mostly drink water all the time, but, yeah, today... It's been since the party started that I was feeling weird, but it was manageable.

Free Expensive Lies: Prologue

But hang on... My breasts, soft... Holy crap. That hot flash, that nausea, my chest, and... But I take the pill... Holy shit, because of that, it's been a week that I completely forgot that. My mind is so elsewhere that I completely forgot that. Oh my god, I really hope it's not what I think it is. Hopefully, I have a pregnancy test, I bought it a couple of months ago as I started my relationship with him, and I am not that confident with the pill. And, since the last time we had sex was for before my birthday, as I slept with that guy and I have no idea if this guy protected himself, but I think he actually didn't... Okay. Okay... And as Florent and I no longer have protected sex (except for the first time, but now, I trust him, so I told him that I was okay with that) and I didn't take my pill the following day. Okay, I may not be pregnant. Yeah, so, yeah, I need to check, but... It's been a week the last time I had sex (I mean... before today, but you cannot get pregnant in a couple of hours, I mean... It takes time), and, holy crap, I really hope that this is not that because otherwise, I am in deep shit. My mother doesn't want to hear about abortion, (because obviously, when you are a fucking homophobic retard, you are against abortion, one doesn't come without the other), I could use my sister's help, but... She is cool with that, but... Okay, let's not think about the worst, it could be another thousand things. It could be millions of things, actually, let's not think about the very worst.

It didn't take long for Florent to actually find my bottle, let me actually know even if I didn't even care that he had my bottle, I just wanted water, fill it up, close that damn bottle, and coming back to me. Simultaneously, I felt a bit better, it actually did improve, but instead, I was seriously thinking. Thinking that me being pregnant was the very last thing I ever imagined in my life and especially in that plan, the very last thing I want right now and the last thing I actually think about. And if I am, who did that? Who's responsible for that nightmare?

On the other hand, I don't know what's an abortion, but, surely, there's only one way this beloved baby will be if I am actually pregnant, gonna be out of my damn womb. I just hate children, it's not for having one myself, especially since I know that I will not be a good mother. I am not stable enough to be a mother. Because, unlike my own mother, I already know that I am going to be a mess, so if I really want to love my child, I'll make sure that he's not gonna see the world with me as a biological mother. But as I said, it can be something else. And I really wish this is something else.

Anyway, when he came back, he actually gave me the bottle. At least, as I was lying down, he put the bottle on my nightstand so I could get it once sat down in the bed. At the moment he actually left the bottle, he just looked at me and asked:

"Honey, do you want a hand to sit down, or it's okay?"

"Hum... Yeah, I'd appreciate if you can give me a hand, actually!"

At that moment, he actually took my dress and lowered it. Yeah, sorry, no sex tonight. I helped him, moving my pelvis, so he can fully complete this. He immediately took my hand, placed his other hand behind my back, and raised me. At that moment, I just slid so I could put my back lying down over the top of the bed and sit. But, making that effort, it's weird, I kind of felt like all my blood going down over my head and my body. It made me feel dizzy, but for a short time. Meanwhile, Florent suddenly crouched next to the bed after taking the water bottle and gave it to me. When I had that weird feeling, I closed my eyes and breathed. After a second, I felt better, but the envy to pee was still there. I drank two, three sips, and I closed the bottle. I looked at him, like, what's going on, and whilst staying how he was, he just said:

"You're very pale, now..."

"I'm always pale..."

"You should go to the doctor tomorrow, I think!"

"Yeah. Maybe. I'll see it. But what do you mean, I'm pale?"

"You're as white as a piece of paper, now. Well, you're usually white, but not as white as this."

"Well, on the other hand, I'm feeling kind of weird now. It's unusual, it never happened to me."

"I can call a doctor if you really need to. I mean, if you're feeling sick, I prefer calling a doctor to make sure you're okay."

"Hum. Call Doctor Gregory House, at Princeton Plainsboro. He might get the right diagnosis. And if not, call Dr Cuddy," I ridiculed him.

He looked at me, like... Dumb. I mean, come on, doctors are following me since I'm thirteen, and even if I am convinced there's something wrong with me, nobody has been giving any better diagnosis than depression or flu. Well, I'm sure House could actually find out what's wrong with me, maybe. As he is so brilliant.

"Yeah, why not Doctor Foreman as well?" he laughed, apparently not understanding that I was not serious.

"What I mean, honey is, it's gonna be okay. If you find me with my eyes closed tomorrow and not responding to anything, it meant that there was a problem. Until then, there are no problems. Okay?"

"You mean if I find you dead?"

"Hum... Okay, maybe it can be worrying explained that way, to find me ready for the coffin next to you for breakfast, but I can assure you, for me, in this state, there are going to be absolutely fine for me, it's just going to be a fresh start! And fresher than fresh..."

"I just can't imagine finding you dead next to me, that's the problem... And me? Have you ever thought about me?"

"Of course, that's why post-traumatic stress disorders are here for, darling."

At this point, he actually stopped talking, looked at me, and smiled. But he smiled for something like, "I really don't know what to say", whilst I smiled for "You see, things are going to be okay". Okay, yeah, I can be harsh, sometimes. But, well, it may happen, what if I have a heart failure when I sleep? He's going to find me dead, wetting the bed and maybe adding some extra solidified gravy with that, but this is what is likely to happen. Okay, my doctors recently checked my heart, and they said it was okay, so a heart failure or a heart attack is quite unlikely to happen, but it still might. You can die anytime. Seriously, I didn't find any better think to actually reply to that. I really had nothing more in mind. He asked a question; I gave him an answer.

"Okay... Anything else I can do to help you to deal with your morbid thoughts?"

"Yes, getting the hell out because I'm going to wee-wee, again," I actually ordered him.

"Sure!" he approved.

He actually stood up and went back to his side of the bed. In between, I was feeling ready to stand up, it would be relatively safe. So, I put my two feet on the floor, prepared to rush to the bathroom. Well, I certainly have five metres to walk, that wouldn't be that hard. And when I put my two feet on the floor, at the very same time, and I'd rather say, as usual, when Florent goes back to bed, he almost throws himself on the bed. How many times did I ask him to be more careful, but yet, he doesn't actually care. He loves that as the mattress is exceptionally soft, then it makes waves and sometimes when he throws himself so hard on the bed, and I am sat like this, it makes me fall. And he loves that. I turned myself, looked at him and said, "be careful, for fuck's sake!". But, well, whatever I say... I'm sure someday I'll come back home, and he's gonna be crying because he exploded a slat or two.

The reason why I do not want to see a doctor is that I need to confirm something before. If it's not what I want to confirm, then yes, we can call a doctor. I just walked to the toilets, and for once, I actually closed and lock the door. Usually, when we are together, I just close the door, but it's just that I don't want him to see me with a pregnancy test in the hand. Even if he pretends that he doesn't want a baby right now, he still wants a baby, he wants to have a little girl, and if I announce that I am pregnant, oh my god. Or, even worse, if he sees me with that test in my hands, he's gonna insist to stay until the result is displayed. Or even worst, as I slept with two different guys, what if the baby is not his? And it's the baby of the guys to whom I don't even know the name? Oh, well...

I arrived in the bathroom, and I opened the two doors of the drawer under the sink. That's here that I left the pregnancy test. I took it and dropped the box next to it. After that, I lifted my dress, like it was a minute ago when Florent was still excited and was expecting something that I could not deliver from me. I removed my panties, sat on the toilets, and finally grabbed the box, and opened it. Okay... So... Remove the plastic cap to expose the absorbent window. Okay, done. Point the absorbent window directly into the urine stream, and take a sample for at least seven to ten seconds... Or collect the urine into a clean container and dip half of the absorbent window for at least ten seconds then remove it... Okay. As I really want, peeing for ten seconds is something I can do, I don't have any clean containers here. So, I started. I placed it, and... Okay, that made things harder, to be fair, peeing is something like a right moment for me, and when I am disturbed doing something else at this time, it's annoying me... Okay, done. And then? Okay, three, re-cap the device and place it horizontally on a flat and clean surface. Wait for at least five minutes for the test to finish processing.

I actually left the thing next to the sink. At the same time, I obviously washed my hands, because even though I was meticulous... Okay, now, I have to buy another one. Geez, all the problems we can actually avoid when we are lesbian. After I thoroughly washed my hands, I went back to seat on the toilets. Obviously, I lowered my dress. Still the box in hands – the test was on the other side; I didn't want to see anything until it's like fully completed – I actually checked what the result meant, with the colours and everything. Okay, if I got knocked up, then some colour should appear next to the red line. If nothing happens, then I need to go to a doctor tomorrow because this was weird.

Unfortunately, I didn't have my phone with me at the moment. It was still plugged on my nightstand. And, well... I cannot really check how long it has been, so... Well, in between, I just sat on the toilets. I yawned. I didn't even want to look at the test, to avoid any possible pressure that may come out of it. Okay, what to do with the box, now that it's open... Unfortunately, it was sealed, and I had to break it when I opened it, now... And if I throw this on the rubbish, and Florent accidentally opens it, that will lead to a drama.

What to do, what to do... Hum, replacing but on the other side in the cupboard, like, on the side the package is still sealed? That could work. I mean if I leave an empty box and by accident Florent takes it... Well, I mean, come on, why would Florent take the package of the pregnancy test? I mean, for what reason? Well, he could, because behind this package, which is straight in front of the cupboard when you open it, there is his stuff such as razors and shaving gel, he never leaves it elsewhere. And he uses it daily, so if he sees the package open or missing, this is gonna raises questions. But I need to check, I need to make sure that this is not something... I mean, I could have checked tomorrow, or... Why the hell did I do it now? And what will I tell him... Or unless he doesn't care and won't notice a change. As he always does. But, I mean, a pregnancy test, as he is still too interested into me having a baby, I am sure that it's going to be something he will notice.

And, anyway, what if this is the case? Hopefully, the test will say if I am pregnant or not, not with whom I am actually pregnant. Well, how could I forget my pill for seven days in a row? I usually think about that, I am really conscious of this and always cautious, how could I simply forget that thing? Seven days, and as I had unprotected sex... I should have thought about this. I usually take it before dinner, always at the very same hour, but... Damn, my gynaecologist was damn right, I should have thought about setting the alarm on my phone. If I am pregnant and restart the pill now, it's not gonna change anything. But seriously, I know it's important, I know that, and... Especially since I am with a guy, I took all my precautions when I went to the doctor for all those checks when I was with him, and... And I was doing that every day. Taking that pill, and... Okay, I did it before having sex for the last time with him, so it may work, no? Well... Oh, actually, if it worked, it's even worse then. It means that it's not his baby and... Oh my god, no. What does it make me then, a slut or something?

And even... Oh my god, what if I am actually pregnant. Okay, I have two choices: either I tell him, or whether I just simply shut up. I can still hide a pregnancy, I mean, it's not tomorrow that I'm gonna get that fat belly and... How to deal with that until I get an abortion? Because I will abort, that is something that is not negotiable. Abortion is the only way I will go if I have a pea in the pod. And one more thing, one more... As if it was the moment, now.

Anyway, it can be this, or it can be something else. It's curious, I've been waiting for a particular time, now, after having thought, when I realised that... I don't know what Florent was doing, and as I didn't want to leave this pregnancy test unprotected. And it's curious, whilst the test was still processing, I just looked around me, to seek something available to make the time scrolling. Because five minutes, when you have absolutely nothing to do, it's long. It may not seem long, but it is. I mean, seriously, it's really long. Usually, when I am bored and waiting, I take my phone and go on YouTube, checking on videos, but as I don't have my phone, time takes longer to scroll. Yeah, it's usually when you have nothing else to do that you start seeking something available around you... And erm... Meh, nothing.

I anxiously looked at the test, when I reminded, that may be my periods coming in advance. So, I checked the toilet, as I didn't flush yet. And, nope, no traces of blood. On the other hand, that would have been quite surprising to find something like that. As I said, I have them regularly, and having them in advance would have been really surprising. Or maybe there's nothing, and... But I am not feeling like having my periods right now. Okay, anyway... It has possibly been something like four minutes, now, and, even if I don't have a clock in my bathroom, I mean, it's been long enough for me to look like it was actually four minutes. It was, well, the decisive moment.

Around me, I heard the silence. I don't know what my sister was doing, or even my mother... I assume she took her dating app back and was texting someone. I didn't hear anybody speaking, as the guests were all gone. I just hope that the reception room is not that messy, because... Well, she said that she's gonna handle this tomorrow. Okay... My arms were slightly shaking, because, yeah, I was apprehensive about what I may see in the upcoming minutes. I took the packaging first, as the instruction paper was still in there. I remembered that if there is something in front of the line, like a blue shaped form appearing, it means that I am pregnant. I didn't see what there was on this thing, as I was still sat and too lazy or stressed to move my arse. Okay. So, I dropped the package quietly next to me, when, well... I took the pregnancy test. And... Oh my fucking god.

At that moment, it was like all my strength lost me. I could clearly see a blue line appearing before the red line. I just... When I saw that, the only thing that I did was to actually say out very loud "FUCK!", obviously in English (but as everybody knows what it means so...), in a very panicked way. Oh, my, god. Okay... Okay. I was just speechless... until my boyfriend actually heard me. Oh my god, the unbelievable has just become a truth now. I mean, me, pregnant? Well, now I actually was, it has become a truth. Oh, my fucking god. At the moment I said that f-word panicked, Florent just said, after a minute, "Is everything okay over there?", to me, in French. He doesn't speak English, so... Okay. I just replied, through the door:

"Could you call Clarisse?"

"Why, is there a problem over there? I can't help you with that?"

"Not actually, I need Clarisse. Could you call her?"

"Erm... I'll try to."

I actually heard him leaving his phone down, standing up from the bed, and quickly, leaving the bedroom. At the same time, I was like... Now, standing up, and going towards the sink. Now, the situation is really fucked up. I still hid my pregnancy test, so if I have to open the door and Florent unintendedly comes, he will not see it. It will be hidden. Okay, now, question... When did that happen? And, mostly, how to deal with that? I need my sister, as an advisor, for that. For fucked up situations such as this one, Clarisse is perfect. In the meantime, I was like... Fuck, why me? Why the hell does it have to fall on me? And now, abortions, how does it work, in here? I mean, I don't want to have the baby, and... Florent must not know that. Because, first, we are not ready, second, I am definitely too young to be a mother, third, he is in the age of having a baby and will want me to keep that shit in my womb, okay. I just can't tell him what's going on. I can just pretend that I have my periods in advance and that's fine, at least, he's not gonna piss me off with sex for another week. If he asks what's going on.

I assume Clarisse would be pretty busy right now, I mean, she must be busy with her boyfriend. So, well... But I really need her, right now, because I have a real situation, and I can't really deal with that. I actually heard him knocking at his door, but it took a couple of minutes before someone opened. In the meantime, I had this test in my hands, and I couldn't even look at it, I actually turned around towards the bathtub, looking at myself in the mirror required, well... To still have dignity. Maybe a few seconds, I heard my sister, gasping (so she was pretty busy) and opening the door. There is definitely no intimacy in this flat, it's a shame. Florent explained that I had a situation and asked her to follow. Obviously, she was not like happy with that, so she replied pretty harshly, "okay, what's her problem now!".

I also assume that she was ready when she opened the door as she left her bedroom almost straight away when Florent called her. I know, it's terrible, but now it's actually a matter of emergency. I heard both of them coming afterwards, entering my bedroom, and as I heard someone suddenly throwing himself again on my bed, I assume my boyfriend. I still heard some footsteps towards my bathroom, so it was Clarisse. She knocked at the door and seemed pissed. Okay, I guess I just ruined some excellent moments with her boyfriend, but still, no need to get mad at me. I rushed to the door as it was closed, and the fact that she heard me unlocking the door actually triggered that question. She turned to Florent and said, "she locks herself, now?". As I opened the door at the same time and told her to come in, I saw Florent not replying. But if she's a bit clever, she may understand that it also means that I have some big new problem if I locked myself.

When she entered, I closed the door immediately after me. At the same time, she entered and walked towards the toilets, but noticed the pregnancy test package being open. But she didn't pay attention. Instead, she looked at me, and, in French, although making sure that she would not actually be heard, started to say:

"Okay, what's going on?"

"I actually have a kind of womb problem..." I said, in English, and whilst whispering.

She looked at me, like... "okay, and the real problem is?" because she remained quite sceptical. Basically, now, well, I have ninety-nine problems, and pregnancy is a new one. And the fact that I interrupted her during sex didn't really help her actually be kind and understanding. Sometimes, I feel like it's a gift to disturb people at their best moments. Frankly, she would have been someone else, I wouldn't mind, but now, I felt a bit guilty. Will I show it? Of course not! Anyway, after she looks at me, we'll I had the confirmation that she actually ignored the package. Otherwise, she'd have understood almost instantly. So, after I declared the womb problem, she replied:

"Darling, if it's your periods, it's normal, it happens to a lot of women on this planet, don't panic for that, okay?"

"Oh, really? Anyway, whisper and speak in English as fast as possible, I don't want to be understood..."

"Are you done with all your secrets? Because I'd rather go back to..." she whispered and complied to what I asked.

"Clarisse, there are important things, and right now, this is an important thing. So, if you don't mind, you're gonna finish your boyfriend's blowjob later, because right now, I am in deep troubles and I need you."

"Fuck you, Charlotte."

"Okay, come on, now, look."

"What?"

I came closer to her and grabbed the pregnancy test that I just carried out a few seconds earlier. And I just gave it to her.

I don't know why, but at that precise moment, I just thought about the day I bought that stuff. When I bought it, I was in the spirit of, I really hope I'll never have to use it. I just bought it as a safety, only in case someday I would be feeling weird, and, well, the very last thing I imagined that day was that if I use it, it would be positive. Life is funny sometimes. I bought it because after our first time, when we had sex, Florent told me that he was not okay with condoms because it's too tight for him, so I feel forced to comply with his desires. And now... Here we are.

Clarisse glanced the test, and the window mentioning that it was positive. She knows what it meant since she used one a couple of months ago. And it went negative. At the moment she saw it, she actually understood. She dropped it, and slowly, looked me, for after, seeking her words:

"Oh, erm... Okay. I assume that, erm, congratulations are not the thing you may expect at that moment... I mean, well..."

Hum, no, congratulations are not the right thing to say at this very moment, honestly. I just didn't actually reply, I just, well, lowered my head, and shrugged. Even if that baby's future has already been decided for my part, the only problem is that given the fact that I didn't get pregnant on my own, I still... Well, I don't know if I need to get the father's consent, given the fact that there are two potential candidates for this position: my boyfriend, or the guy of my birthday. It is not really clear about whom this baby belongs to, but as for Florent there's only one possible truth: I am a faithful girlfriend, and that never, never I could have cheated on him, he will want this baby for sure. And obviously, I will not reveal the dark truth. Because if I do... Well, that will actually be funnier than it's already fun.

On the other hand, whoever the father may be, this is still my womb so my decision. Florent pretends he is not ready to be a father, but given the fact that I am landlord, millionaire and still student, he may be okay to keep that baby. What he wants is a situation for himself, but the thing is, I already have that situation. My problem is; first, I do not want to be a mother, second, given the fact that this world is a shitty world and god knows what may happen further, with all those new technologies threatening to collapse someday on our faces, I do not want to bring a child to this world. Third, I inherited that money, so my money is my money. It belongs to me and no-one else, and certainly not to a possible heir that I may give birth to, and that will tell me someday to fuck off because I am an awful mum. Also, I don't feel like having a baby for the sole reason that Florent and I may be in a relationship, but we are not a healthy relationship. I am not seeing myself in the future with him, especially with what's ongoing right now for me. I am a liar, I cheated on him if I manage to hide it, okay, but if things explode... Well, having a baby in all that, and raise that baby on my own? No fucking way.

So, whatever happens, that's a no. Problem is, I know that I need someone to be there for my abortion. I cannot rely on mum, Florent as well... Clarisse, yes, but the problem is if it comes to be known, mum is going to kill Florent and us may never forget the fact that I hid my pregnancy and I got aborted, and will not understand why, and... I could also ask Claire, but if she comes to know that I'm pregnant, my blackmailer may know this and use it against me. And this information, it may be... He will put her under pressure to get to know what's going on with me, and she will give in. And also, she's going to turn eighteen next April, she is still minor. Then she can't sign the papers for me.

Clarisse remains my best option. When she saw the test and understood that this was, well, another funny event of this funny period for me, she was still seeking her words:

"Okay, well. Well, well, well... Erm... What do you want me to do?"

"I really don't know what to do now. I mean, this is kind of huge!" I was down.

"Well, Cha, you're pregnant. I mean... I assume that you don't want to keep the baby!"

"No way!"

"And erm... is he the, hum... father?" she pointed out the bedroom, I assume to say, Florent.

"I'm not quite sure..."

"Holy crap... How come you're knocked up? I mean, you still take your pill, don't you?"

"Well, it turns out that... Believe it or not, but I am so stressed and as I have thousands of things to think about right now that if I am pregnant, now, it means that I forgot it!"

"Okay... Erm, shit. Why do you need me?"

"If I get an abortion, I'll need someone. And as we have a fantastic mother, you and me, that consider life as sacred no matter what its form is, I'm gonna need you to be there the day I'll do it."

"Of course, Cha. Of course. I mean, you know I'll be there. And what about, erm... him?" she showed the bedroom again.

"If he asks you, tell him that I had my periods in advance and I was worried. And erm... Well, what should I do, what would you do if you were me?"

It's really unfair, to Florent, if I deliberately retain that information. But given the fact that the identity of the father is unknown, holding that information is better. Better for me, because I know the truth, a truth that he doesn't. And if this truth comes someday, he will leave me alone dealing with that shit. I was lost, really lost. Hopefully, after having thought about it, Clarisse gave me the solution.

"Hide it," she replied, sure of herself. "Because if you tell it... Things are gonna be really messy and be out of control!

23 *Drifting universes*

// *Avenue Kléber, near Joris' penthouse party.*

// *Thursday, 17th of January, 22:41.*

Well, he started to wonder stuff about why I went to the bathroom, suddenly... And, I told him, I had my periods in advance, which was unusual. He understood that, thus, there would be no way to have sex tonight. Although it was not my periods... I just went to sleep, with a really heavy mind. Yeah, now... Well... Rules have changed. And, I was just speechless, I was just, yeah. No "why me?" anymore, it was just, yeah, it's on me, it's my shit, and I have to deal with it. Now, I have twelve weeks to do this; otherwise, it's gonna be too late.

It was now half-past seven. There were at least three hours that I was awake, idly, in my bed, disturbed by the recent events of yesterday. My arms crossed, turning many times on the bed, trying to actually find a solution to reach the goal of abortion. The problem was not actually the abortion. It was to find a way until there. And after at least two long hours of reflection, thinking about yesterday's events in their globality, from the two Russian guys until the discovery of my pregnancy, it actually became urgent to find an exit plan, since, in the past few hours, things went almost out of control. They remained under control, but what I mean is that it was emotionally challenging. Through the morning, on many occasions, I looked at Florent, sleeping next to me, and he seemed calm, still holding a pillow against him, he slept peacefully. Until that point, it was half-past seven, and time to go to school. The alarm was today the sound of "Bella Ciao," like, yeah, the Italian revolutionary song. Yeah, well.

Quickly, I woke up. Even if the envy to stay home was quite tempting, waiting to wake up with my fiancé was not actually a good idea. And, to be fair, I didn't really wake up in an excellent mood today, as nothing was prepared from yesterday, I just didn't have time, and, erm, well, the spirit was just not there, I was not fully ready for any contact with a human entity today. I stood up out of my bed, left my room to go to the kitchen where my twin sister was already there, in her pyjamas, and was obviously like me, in a bad mood. We just said hi to each other. None of us was available for a conversation at that moment, given that she was checking her Facebook. I took my kettle, poured my water, turned on the heater, dropped the kettle on it, took my cup, put my teabag inside, dropped it on the table, and sat in front of her... when suddenly... she unexpectedly woke up.

"Hello, Charlotte."

"Yeah?" I was surprised by the fact that she woke up.

"Feeling better?"

"What do you think?"

"Well, I actually don't know why I'm asking you that question. You are never okay since Claire dumped you. So, well... I shouldn't have asked."

I just looked at her, in a way that meant, "continue saying that Claire dumped me, and I swear to God that you're not gonna like that morning". Until I remembered that, well...

"Clarisse, please don't start with provocation, that's not a really good idea today," I warned her.

"I know. When I meant 'feeling better', I meant, in a healthy way?"

"Oh, hum... Well, I am moving on. Yeah, I mean, I am not nauseous, I am okay now."

"Hum, okay. And did he ask you questions about, well, you know, this?"

"I told him it was some issues that were none of his business. Pretending it was my periods."

"Okay, so, what's next?"

"Well, what's next... You know what is next. Cleaning my, erm..." I didn't want to be more precise, by the fear that my mother would hear me as she was awake.

"Did you check what you could actually do, I mean, because it is quite sensitive!"

"Yeah, I checked, and, well..." then I used a tiny voice, "First, I get an appointment to make sure I want to get rid of that little crap, second, I choose what way I want to get rid of it, and third, you get the point."

"Hum... And you need me?"

"I need one person major to be there with me in case things go wrong. I mean, that's what I heard. I am not fairly sure about this, but I prefer taking precautions."

"Yeah. Well."

"Now, shut up because the devil is nearby!"

"The devil... Who are you talking about?"

"The old racist, intolerant anti-abortion bitch that serves here as a mother!"

No, I heard her walking around. And as I don't know if she was getting closer or not, so I prefer switching topics.

"By insulting her, I wonder who is the most intolerant here, to be fair," Clarisse defended her mum.

"Well, last time I checked, I was not homophobic!"

"Yeah, but last time I checked; you were the cause of certainly ninety-five per cent of the conflicts within this house..."

"Dear, this is just a detail in history. At least I am not imposing you to go to pray for some bollocks every Sunday."

"She doesn't even go to the mass!"

Whilst I told her to shut up because I felt like she came closer, she drank her coffee while I drank my tea. But she didn't seem to come closer, even if she appeared to be in a rush this morning. After that, with my sister, after certainly a few seconds of silence whilst I was trying to hear what she was doing, we talked about other topics, funnier things, as she saw that whatever happens today, I wouldn't be in a good mood. She wanted to entertain me, even though today, absolutely nothing would entertain me at all. The only sentence that actually came to my mind was this one, extremely popular in France, I think it was from Lamartine, an old writer, that wrote that "miss one person and everything seems empty". Right now, everything was so real. Only one woman was missing. If she would be there, even if it was dark outside, then the sun would shine, the spring would be there, and birds would sing. If she were there, the tea that I was drinking wouldn't be that bland, and I would feel hydrated upon drinking it. If she were here, as well, the Eiffel Tower would feel like a prowess, the Arc de Triomphe would appear as majestic, the Champs-Elysées would be full of people, the Notre-Dame Cathedral would feel so deep; instead, it looks like dead all around. If she were here, food would be tasty, and I certainly wouldn't take recreational antidepressants sometimes to season like salt and pepper the tasteless dish that is my life. It's why, even though I was speaking to my sister, now, I felt like, yeah. It's all empty and worthless. Nothing makes any sense. I miss her, especially today.

Anyway, still in that mood, after fifteen minutes, drinking my tea, I went to get dressed, but first pick up my stuff in my wardrobe, wearing what I use to wear when days were still amazing to live, a white shirt, black trousers, a brown waistcoat. And some white sneakers today. As usual, I went to my bathroom, getting dressed, but I did not feel like I wanted to wear any makeup today. When I was ready, I took my bag in my bedroom, whilst Florent was still asleep, and, as every morning, Clarisse was waiting for me. We left the flat together, went outside, heading to the metro, as usual, and it was almost eight, and we had to be at school at nine. As usual, the metro was overcrowded... I don't really know why, but today, I felt like habits would certainly kill me. I was exceptionally depressed, and I immensely needed love or being alone, at home, in the dark, with Claire. Still, instead, I was outside with my sister, in an extremely hot because overcrowded metro. And I realised that you could have all the money in the world if you want, it's true that when someone is missing, everything is meaningless. And, curiously, when I was out of the metro, I checked my phone, and I had a missed call. Yeah, Claire. Speaking of the devil... So, I called her back.

"Hey, love!" she said, quite happily when she took the call.

"Hi," I coldly replied, disenchanted.

"Oh... Let me guess you're not okay today. I can hear your voice!"

"Maybe... What do you want?" I didn't really want to be friendly.

"Hum... I won't be at school today, erm... I don't really want anything, I mean, I called you to check if you were okay, but, erm... If you want to come today, I'll stay home until tonight, if you feel like you need to talk or anything, I am here. I mean, you know I won't leave you that down."

"Thank you very much, Claire. I appreciate."

"Hum. Yeah, you know."

"Yeah. Is there anything important you need to talk about now? Don't take it wrong, but I really don't want to talk to anybody now."

"You're going to school?"

"Yeah. Do you need anything from there?"

"Hum, no... Just to let you know that, as I know you're coming tonight. I'll be there too."

"Great!"

"I, hum... It's near the Trocadero, it's, erm... You will see, it's going to be fun."

"Hum, Claire, would you hold on a second?" I wanted to say something to her in private.

"Yeah, sure."

But the problem was, as I was escorted by my sister, I couldn't speak that loud. In the street, well... Behind me was a house, and in front as well. The college was at the end of that street. So, I told my sister if she could go before, I'll be joining her. She agreed and walked before me. I just waited until she was at least several metres away so I could restart. Now, Claire, let's cut the crap. And whatever the price, I don't care if I am currently listened to, but I want to know.

"Are you still there, Claire? And all alone?"   ,

"Of course. And, yeah, I am still in bed, now, so, yeah, I'm alone."

"Now cut the crap with me, okay? In what sleeping with people for petty cash is actually fun for me, and especially for you?"

"It is not... I mean..."

"You lied to me, you stupid moron! Since we broke up together, you are having sex with several guys, just for cash. Why? What the fuck is wrong with you? Did you lose your mind, or how does it work! It's been months that you are in trouble, it's been months that you are doing that, and now, you act just like that bitch of Kelly and pretending that it's fun?"

"Charlotte, I... I just couldn't tell you anything. I can't tell you anything."

"Claire, come on. We've been through seven years together, and I know you. I certainly know you better than anyone. And I am not judging you, please do understand that. It's been since we broke up that you act weird with me, even if I do understand that we broke up for completely absurd motives. You cheated on me, and after said that I don't deserve you. So cut the crap, now, Claire!"

"Cha, I... Yes, I said that because that's the truth. You're fantastic, and I cheated on you, even today, I can't forgive myself. And I love you. I really do. But I cannot come back with you, because I am the cheater, and I am ashamed of what I have done. And it's just impossible."

"I fucking forgave you for having slept with some wanker, Claire, I didn't care, what I wanted was you, and, yeah, me too, I love you, I want you back, and I don't give a shit about that! I want my girlfriend back, whatever it may cost me. Even if I have to dump Florent, I will do it, but I want you back!"

"You're with Florent, I don't want to be the bitch that destroyed your couple. Anyway, see you tonight!" she hung up.

"Hang on, Claire, I'm not done with..." I actually... well.

Well. Actually, no comments.

Then I arrived at school. I wasn't late at all, I even had time to pick up my stuff in the locker. But the rain was now quite heavy, and surprisingly, it wasn't that cold. For the first four hours of this morning, mathematics. I mean, two hours, plus our break, plus the last two hours. Four hours, because for the baccalaureate, at least in my section, maths is an important thing, and... And God knows how much I don't even care. Baccalaureate, today, it's like... even when you sleep at school, they give you your baccalaureate, it's just nonsense. Still, we are in January, I know that in March they will ask us where we want to go, what choice we want to have for the university in case we pass the baccalaureate (in case, they say, because... yeah, they still play the game, like, you know, you can fail...) and I don't even know what I want to do. Clarisse knows, she wants to go to an engineering school in Toulouse, because there's Airbus there (if you don't know, they make planes), or is considering studying law. Which are two different things, actually, making planes and defending criminals, it's like quite different. But, fair enough. Or she wants to study chemistry.

Well, given my results, basically, I can go anywhere I want. I even thought about studying the military, as there is a famous military school in Brittany. No, studying war, yeah, I know, it doesn't sound like me, but... Because I have to do something in my life, and my mother wants me to do something. The army always seduced me, I have been learning a lot about military, especially during Napoleonic wars, and I am fascinated by this. Problem is, I am bad at strategy. But I am extremely good at maths. I mean, I kind of have a gift in maths, it's why I choose to go in scientific for the baccalaureate, it's the easy way for me. Clarisse opted for science because it's also the most prestigious. Oh, or maybe I could go to medical school. Problem is, I hate seeing blood. And I hate people. And I hate waking up early in the morning, so this is not for me. No, I need to find something that actually fits me, that makes me happy, that makes me forget my life, and... Or I can do some sports. I wanted to start Krav Maga and martial arts this summer, just to have something to do. Because, usually, every summer, we are busy with Claire, we used to visit or spend times together, but as I am heading to my very first summer without her, I'd better start thinking about something I can do on my own. Doing sports is better than eating some shit in front of the TV series on Netflix.

Through the morning, well, yeah. Tonight's party was not enchanting me that much, especially when I saw Kelly with us all morning, but hopefully, she stayed away from me. At least for the two first hours, we had a test, where I think it's gonna be quite hard for me since it's equations and... I am particularly good at equations; the problem is that I am totally unable to explain how I managed to find the result due to my math particularity. It went actually pretty fast, and I remained withdrawn from everybody. I was staying away from many people, even at the point to hide myself during the break within the college corridors because I really didn't want anybody to talk to me. The two last hours, then, lunch break. And when I left the college, this time without my sister who finally decided to stay at school as she was not that hungry, I received another call when I was out. Florent. In the beginning, I was like, I wanted to pretend that I didn't hear my phone or something like that. But if I do that, he will call back again, or leave me a text and at some point, I will have to talk to him. Because this morning, and even today, especially since I know the programme for the evening, I really did not want to speak to him at all... So, as there were no other ways, I took the call.

"Hi," I replied, still not that friendly but not unfriendly too.

"Hey, lover?" He replied, obviously he was in a better mood than I was.

"You okay?"

"I am, but you, since yesterday, you're feeling bad!"

"Yeah, well, I've had better days, it's true."

"What's going on, honey?"

"Nothing, I am just done with quite a few things, that's all."

"Like me?"

"Yes, for instance, yeah," I was laconic.

Oh, erm... Well, I shouldn't have said that. I don't know why, but when I am depressed, I am in a sort of automatic mode that makes me say many things that I do not necessarily say. At the same time, when I took his call, I sat on a bench on the alley leading towards the exit and was watching some squirrel climbing over a tree eating a nut. Squirrels are unique, I love these little rodents. And erm... When I actually figured out that I shouldn't have said that.

"Oh, well, that's really nice of you!" hopefully he laughed.

"I was kidding," I actually remained laconic.

"So, what do we do tonight?"

"I really have no idea for the moment..."

"Are you okay? You feel like really depressed. I mean, can I do something for you now?"

"Leaving me alone would be a good start, actually, darling. I mean, I am tired, I have my periods in advance, so it's quite painful, so... Please, just, you know..."

"Oh, I see. I'll call you back later then. See you, I love you!"

Seriously, that squirrel was funny. I mean, I don't know why, but I kept at looking at it. It was climbing through a tree, where there was an abandoned nest. I don't know, it was weird: the nuts in his mouth (let's assume that he is a baby boy), he was just climbing, and then saw the nest. He saw me down below, and I looked at him. For like, several seconds we looked at each other when in my mind I was like "Will you go? Won't you go?" ... But at some point, even if he didn't see I was that much of a threat, he left. Well, he stood up to actually finish his nut and then left. Oh, my. These animals are just funny.

To be fair, I was still not that hungry. I was always thirsty, and I just stood up to go to some small market next to my college, and I went to get a bottle. When I left the shop, I was feeling like, I don't want to go back. This squirrel actually entertained me, to be fair. And, curiously, it was the only thing that I was missing right now. I was tired but didn't want to be back home. It's why I actually sat on a bench near the shop where I went and took my phone. There, the very first thing I opened was Claire's texts. I started scrolling up to see our texts. And I read. My bottle was left next to me, and, well... I read, the texts I sent her the day we broke up. I left her twenty-five different texts to tell her, I love you, just don't do that. And... Above, our lasts messages, when we said to each other, I love you with the several <3, all the time. It's funny, we didn't text each other a lot when we were separated.

I used to text her when I was bored, and immediately, she used to reply, "what's up kitty? <3" ... And, we always had something to say to each other. Something to talk about. Kitty, she ever nicknamed me like that. I mean, in private. Otherwise, it was just "Cha", or "love". And... Yeah, it plunged me into these good moments when we were together until... Clarisse came to ruin everything. "Charlotte, get your arse over here, you're fucking late!", she just texted. Yeah, yeah, coming.

Two hours of biology and two of English were on the program for this afternoon. After, well. Going back home. I asked Kelly about this afternoon about the party tonight, and she told me that she would call me at six because she still doesn't know what's the plan. Okay. In between, Florent texted me, telling me that he will eat with his mother tonight because he has some stuff to do at his home. And I was just like, yeah, fine. My two hours of English, and, yeah, back home. I am sure that this routine will kill me at some point. But, it was actually not that long, we left school at around 5, I went to the store where I went for lunch to get another bottle of water and some cookies because I was actually kind of hungry (I didn't have lunch), and, well... We took the metro, we arrived back home, and... I went to my bed, closed the curtains, heard the noise of the wind, read some stuff on my iPad, until 6:20 pm. Yes, because... Kelly actually called. Well, she told me she'd give a call at that hour. So, I took the call.

"Yeah?" I coldly answered.

"Yeah, Cha. Still coming tonight?" she seemed like out of breath. Like she ran after something.

"Um... Yeah, I am still all right, what about you?"

"Ah, excuse me, sorry. How are you, Charlotte?" she slowed down.

"Yeah, like you care about how I am. Anyway, yes, I am coming tonight."

"Perfect!" she had her answer, all that mattered.

"Where is it?"

"Okay, so basically, he told me that it would be near the Metro Station Kléber, some building near the station. He didn't give me much more information about where it is precisely but told me that they will come both together as he must see Claire for some reasons. Oh, and it starts at something like ten or eleven, so you have time to get ready, actually. Let's say, come for eleven."

"Claire has to see something with Joris?"

"Yeah, apparently he told me that he wanted to invite her to the restaurant. I mean, I don't know why. Meh, maybe they are doing something together, I don't know. He will probably date her. Anyway, oh, maybe you want to eat something with me at my place?"

I don't like hearing that.

"What, you really think I will come in your shitty working-class suburb?"

"That's what I thought. Anyway, why don't we meet each other at the Champs-Elysées Avenue, at 10 pm?"

"Well, we could. If you want, wait for me near the station for like 10.30, I will be there. I just hope Claire and Joris won't be late... As she's always late when she's with him, I don't really know why."

"We'll see. See you later."

I immediately hung up before she had the time to reply to something.

So, Claire has a meeting with Joris, that's interesting. On the other hand, the way Kelly said that, well... I am used to this kind of provocation. Like Claire is going to date Joris... The day she announced me that I have been trapped and when she told me about the envelope, I remember having seen her almost crying and making with her lips I am sorry. And then she dates that guy, no, it just doesn't make sense at all. Maybe she's with him, but it certainly not for dating. Or I am foolish, but I don't think I was born yesterday. She changed, yeah, but she unquestionably doesn't have Stockholm Syndrome.

Moreover, Claire never dated anyone since we broke up, so unless that rule changed – she keeps on saying she doesn't feel ready... but, yeah, there's this detail I forgot, she's French – I don't believe she broke that rule. Well, I mean, I still have a doubt. Well, if that's the truth... Joris better start thinking about what he wants to be written on his tombstone.

This evening, again, I was almost alone in the flat. Almost, because Florent was seeing his mother, and Clarisse texted me, as she wanted to spend the evening at her boyfriend's flat so won't be there. Mum was the only one to be there, and like every evening it's just the both of us in this flat, she remains in the living room, and I remain in my bedroom, we prefer avoiding each other. I watched some TV series on my iPad, to kill time. Yeah, it's quite fancy in here when it's only the two of us. As the night fell already, I actually remained into the darkness for like, yeah, indeed the entire evening, and I was not hungry. Like, literally, the only thing I ate today was cookies and nothing else, I was just too much processing my problems today, it just killed my appetite. It happens, days like this, when I am everything but hungry, and that I don't eat through entire days. My record is still four days without eating. It ended that I actually fainted away when I was peeing, as my sister was in my room and heard a loud "bang". Yeah, it was during their divorce. My parents drove me to the GP afterwards, and even if they explained that it was more or less their faults, it just ended up with "Charlotte has stress disorders". Yeah. Because I stressed myself on my own, maybe?

Free Expensive Lies: Prologue

At around nine, mum went to eat, and then to sleep. Strictly no words were exchanged through that evening between us. And it was nine, and I was due to meet her at ten. Taking the metro to go there would take me around twenty minutes, so I went to my bathroom to get ready now. And it was like the very last day, but this time I am certainly up for all night, I couldn't take anything with me but my bag. And even in my bag, I need to be extra careful as I am due to go in one of Joris's places or parties, so I should be cautious with what I carry. Into the darkness, I stood up and opened my wardrobe, and I saw a dress I wore not a long time ago, in December, at the beginning of the month, a party where we've been with Florent and his friends. It's a relatively short black dress, thick enough, with a broad strap over my left shoulder with on the top a small little flower. The dress is also crossed with a white stripe on my body from top to bottom starting on this flower. That could be fine. I also took some underwear and the same shoes that I wore the very last time, erm... yeah, actually, yesterday. Yeah, if I have to throw away some clothes in a future, I prefer throwing some stuff that I don't really care about, as these clothes will remain in my mind associated with the ongoing events.

I actually realised that I didn't have that much of time. I went into the bathroom for changing myself, I made it quick. And when I left, I was ready to go, I just took the very same bag of the last time, and checked if everything was inside: my wallet without any of my IDs, my credit card where I just have a thousand on it, my bottle of water, and yeah. Curiously, it was still the bottle of water of yesterday, I just didn't drink. On the other hand, what I know so far is that tonight will be a party, so it's going to be different from yesterday. Basically, I can choose with whomever I want to do that. I put my makeup into my handbag, so like my shoes (I still wore my pumps from two days ago, I tried to remain discreet), and then I can go. My coat, my phone, my pass for the metro, and I left. I don't know if mum heard me leaving, because she was still in her bedroom watching TV, and I actually left furtively to avoid questions such as "where are you going?". And to make sure that my escape would be faster, I took the stairs, as the lift was busy. And, after I passed the entrance, I forgot how Paris' streets could be so cold on a January evening. But it was not that cold, okay, it was cold but bearable. I heard that tomorrow, it's apparently going to snow.

I don't usually go to that part of Paris, the 16th Arrondissement. Basically, if you ask a Parisian what 16th Arrondissement means, he will tell you that it's the only place within Paris where you have to clean your shoes before entering. Yeah, it's like Kensington in London. I mean, Chelsea and Kensington, these places where you can smell money more than you smell the rubbish bags in the street. Okay, I cannot really say anything, because I am living in Neuilly. In this country, you say Neuilly, it will automatically be linked to millionaires or these people. I am not sure about what I say, but I heard that Neuilly was the wealthiest place in France. Basically, to us, the 16th is more or less low incomes compared to us. The 7th Arrondissement is like the 16th, but it's more an aristocratic place, I mean, it's rich as well, but more of a noble place. Basically, if the 16th is the place where you need to clean your shoes before entering, for the 7th, you need to do that as well and be able to hold a spoon with only two fingers. Even in my school, Clarisse and I are the only two coming from Neuilly, and when we say that we are from there... It usually places distances between people. I never understood why even if I am an heiress; I am still a human amongst the rest of them. My boyfriend and my ex-girlfriend were both poorer than me and, well, I loved them anyway.

The 16th is mostly known for being the high-society place, and I am not sure, but I think it's one of Paris's biggest arrondissements. It's mostly known for being where the Trocadero is (it's a kind of small palace facing the Eiffel Tower, it's lovely), many museums are and also the most renowned schools, and... Behind that, there's the Bois de Boulogne. Okay, basically, it's where two hippodromes are (Auteuil and Longchamp), but in the common culture, the Bois de Boulogne is mostly associated with Brazilian transgender prostitutes. For some reasons, I've never been there. You may wonder why, but I'm not that curious. Hopefully, the avenue where I was supposed to meet Claire, Kelly and Joris was basically the avenue that goes from the Place de l'Etoile (the Arc de Triomphe) from this Trocadero. So, it's mostly an urban place.

Only two lines. The first, and the sixth, for reaching the metro station Kléber. For those who don't know, Kléber was a former general during Napoleon's Egypt campaign before he became emperor. The avenue is actually silent: even if it's a high street, it's mostly residential, there are not a lot of shops, but what I like in this street is that from each part of the road, there are a bunch of trees on the footpath almost hiding the buildings from the street. Although this street is quite busy, right now, it was not. It's not that far away from the Champs-Elysées and the Place de l'Etoile. The travel took me almost fifteen minutes, and when I arrived, I was the first to be there. I actually waited next to the stairs, and I texted her, "where are you?", but had no answers. And, yeah, leaning against the metro entrance, I actually looked around: the street was actually not busy at all. There was not a lot of traffic, but many cars were parked on the side of the road. Although there was still some activity within the building as I could see through the windows all lit, the street was still noticeably quiet. Not far away, beyond those cars parked and those trees without any leaves on it, I could see the bright Arc de Triomphe, lit in a kind of yellow light, shining in this cold. I actually stared at it for quite a few moments.

My mind was actually astonishingly empty at that moment. I mean, I had no thoughts that came to disturb me. Perhaps I was just waiting in the cold over here, I was just, yeah, it's quite hard to describe: I have no idea of what's going on, and I somehow reached a point that I don't care anymore. To be fair, I didn't have that much of apprehension for today, unlike yesterday, because I feel like it's gonna be okay, I am not going to go through the same things as yesterday, I mean, regarding my "customer". I actually didn't feel that threatened or scared. I was quite confident. Since everything started, since I turned eighteen, I just don't realise how things actually went out of my control in just a couple of days. I really should have left everything behind, leave everything, and quit my life. Quit Claire and everything, except that, yeah, I just realised that I have been trapped from the beginning. While looking at the Arc de Triomphe with insistence, I felt like my phone rang in my pocket. Kelly was here, she actually sent me a text. Well, then.

After a few seconds, I saw her finally exiting those tunnels from under the ground. The first thing I noticed was her coat, a long black one, a bit the same as I use to wear, but with a belt around her waist, contrarily to mine that has a fake belt on my back. It seemed like expensive stuff, her coat, I mean, I would find the same in expensive clothes boutiques, it didn't seem like she bought it in some cheap place. Astonishingly her coat was rather long, almost reaching her knees, longer than mine, I couldn't really see what she was wearing underneath, as her chest seemed free. I have never seen Kelly dressed that way, to be honest, and, well, she was quite pretty tonight. Still, not really my style, as my type of girl, but I must recognise that she was lovely. She straightened her hairs, but her make-up remained exceptionally provocative, though. That was what I didn't really like, even if mine was quite the same. It does make sense somehow, we are here to be identified tonight, we are not supposed to be here just for fun. High heels, just like me, I mean... I really don't know how she managed to travel that way in the metro, especially from where she is coming from. Funny thing, when she left the metro, she was followed by two guys, that actually stared at her arse when she was climbing the stairs. Well, as they did not speak, and as I saw them obviously not being that indifferent to that, I assume she felt them, as she played the game. Acting like a whore. Yeah, well... I just prefer not giving my opinion about that.

Now only Claire and Joris were missing. Basically, obviously, when she arrived, she was still on her phone, checking I don't know what shit on Facebook, even when climbing the stairs, I had to call her so she could notice me. She asked me how I was but was so hypnotised by her phone that it almost cut short any possible conversation I could have with her. And even, I didn't want to talk to her. Afterwards, she just came next to me, waiting for them while still looking around me. And she remained on her phone. But it was fine, I don't really want to talk to her. While she was absorbed by her phone, I was still waiting. I mean, I observed her at some point, thinking about if someday I ever become a person like this, I really hope someone brings me to Switzerland to end my days. It's funny, I mean, I looked at her screen, and all after what she scrolled was just a bunch of shitty memes and... Yeah, it must be me. I mean, it's been a couple of months that life has become a burden and I don't really know how to deal with it, but, seriously, I mean, what's interesting of losing such times to look at some shitty stuff and like it?

And half an hour later – Kelly was right, they would be late – I saw Claire and Joris arriving. They didn't take the metro, I actually recognised Joris's car parked in the street nearby, Avenue des Portugais, and they both walked towards us. I don't know what they could say to each other, but Claire laughed as she never laughed. And to be really honest, I was so not in the mood. But as I have to pretend to be so, I could still be part of the group, seeing them both actually rose some kind of sudden envy of murder. Even today, I really have a problem with whoever is close to Claire. And, as they were kind of close together, as she actually held his hand, I felt like, yeah, insulted. That will be something for which he is going to pay, eventually.

So, after passing through a zebra crossing, they arrived together. We could only hear Claire laughing and the loud sound of her heels. At the same time, I wore mine. I found infamous that they looked like when she was with me, and we were walking down the street. My ex-girlfriend was wearing a short, black dress, on which were some small diamonds or sequins made the dress shining in the night. And I was like, "you're such a bitch" because she bought it when we were together, for one of our numerous times when we went to the restaurant after leaving the cinema. She saw that I remarked it, but I said nothing.

Meanwhile, I was just like this is just a game, it's all orchestrated by Kelly and Joris, to make sure we split apart, they are just taking us for two idiots, it just doesn't work with me. A beautiful and shiny red was colouring her lips, and her eyes were gorgeous. She uncurled her hair (she's slightly curly, but her hairs were straight), so I knew that she took the whole day for getting ready, or she did it for her boyfriend because they spent some moments together. That made me so boiling... But I guess this is the price I have to endure for some reasons. And, given the fact that I find her tenfold more attractive when she releases her hairs, so, what was the final objective? Pissing me off, or what? It kind of worked well either way. I just saw her, I just looked at her at some point when she actually came to us, and... Only by seeing me being in a mix between embarrassed and deeply upset made her stop suddenly laughing. If it was a game for them, it was not funny for me.

Whilst Joris was wearing a beautiful black suit with a little bow tie like he'd go to a wedding, they were coming. He was smart, and if it were the first time that I saw him, I could guess that maybe he's rich or something. His clothes actually suit very well with the avenue we were into. Well, I assume being a pimp must be a lucrative way to get money, over my ex-girlfriend's arse. This is why I couldn't be upset with Claire, because the way they actually behaved, they didn't need to speak to manipulate her, it actually worked. It doesn't work for me because I do not believe that Claire is dating him a single second. Claire is not attracted by money, and certainly not attracted by such a loser like Joris. If you make some women sleep and gain money on that, in my opinion, you are a coward. And especially when I try to speak about that with her, she starts crying and deliberately avoids the subject, so it means that she cannot be dating that piece of shit. When she actually saw both of them, Kelly started to scream like an idiot, and rush towards them. For the first time in that evening, she put her head up, locked her phone, put it in her pocket, and ran. But what actually shocked me was that Claire, when she saw me, suddenly stopped laughing and swapped. And quit Joris's arms. When Kelly started to run towards them, I actually saw my Claire looking at them, both of them, Joris and Kelly, with a slight disgust before continuing being a hypocrite with them. Should I see in this the end of an enormous friendship?

Obviously, Kelly gave a hug to Joris, and then a hug to Claire. Claire, curiously, didn't hold her immediately. I mean, Kelly was holding her fiercely, like she hasn't seen her for several years, but Claire, no, she kind of hesitated when she saw me. I don't really know why, but I feel like when she saw me, she had somehow the same reaction as I had when I saw her. From both sides, from my point of view and hers, it's the first time we see each other but only as prostitutes. What we couldn't believe something we never saw became a kind of weird, distorted reality, and it was a shock. After their hug, she actually walked towards me, somehow dubious and definitely ashamed. Unlike her, I had no shame at all. Walking towards me, but not smiling at me, she actually said more with a severe sight when she was a metre away from me:

"Hi, hum... You're pretty tonight!"

This moment was actually so awkward. It was, yeah, like I found out she had made some mistake and, I just discovered that. I have never seen her in such an outfit since we've been together, and usually wearing this would end up in bed. Because yeah. Now, it was for some different purpose, and just discovering this was, yeah. For her, it was sad. For me, it was curious. For her, again, I could feel some huge jealousy coming out of her, she wanted to release it, to scream it, but deep inside was so scared so she just couldn't do anything. Deep inside me, I just wanted her to scream her jealousy, and let her talk to me, whatever it may cost me. Because, right now, I was fragile, I was upset, I was jealous as I have never been, and... I must confess that I never imagined her doing that. Tonight, I will witness it, which will be just, yeah, horrible. Still confused by all this, I just, yeah, replied:

"You too, I mean... Yeah, you are!"

"I miss you, honey. I really miss you," she said, looking straight in my eyes, with a small and confused voice.

Hum, well... Well, well, well... What was ongoing was like, yeah. Heavy. Massive. Erm, yeah, more awkward than ever. Especially when she said that whilst looking straight at my eyes and, erm... I was disoriented. Like, really, I was disoriented. Of course, I miss her too, especially when I know what she is going to do, now, I was feeling a kind of intense, very intense desire. Mixed up with huge melancholia. I may not cry, I may not be able to do so, it doesn't mean that I cannot be sad. I suffered a lot when we broke up, even if I am hiding it. But now, I was feeling like, all the pain in the world, all the pain someone has ever felt. She is the only person on that planet to actually be able to destroy me, there is no one else who can do that. I genuinely hope she is sincere. I was just, yeah, speechless. It's why maybe fifteen seconds took place between the moment she said that, and I actually retorted:

"Claire, let's get out of here, together."

"I really do want that. I just can't, for the same reasons as you do."

"Let's go to Roissy, let's take a plane, let's just get the fuck out of that shithole, and... We can do it, I mean, I have enough money so we can restart our lives, I just want to leave, I don't care, there's nothing meaningful in that bloody planet without you, Claire!" I was really inspired.

Free Expensive Lies: Prologue

She looked at me, like... Yeah, it's true, I never said such a thing. When I was with her, I was living like nothing could ever happen. She just, when I said that, she was like, she wanted to hug me, but she couldn't. I could feel, she was holding her tears, the pressure between us was so intense. She simply said:

"I just love you, Charlotte. I can't stop thinking about you. But before anything, there are things you can do. You are the only one that can do that."

"Do what?" I cautiously answered.

"Tonight, look at all the guests, you should see a tall woman with hairs like mine and a green dress. A dark green dress."

"There might be a couple of them..."

"She should also wear on her dress a four-leaf clover brooch," she continued, "Talk to her in English, and only in English, don't say a word in French, and make sure you use your British accent so nobody can understand you. She should reply with an Irish accent... Just, stay with her, and make sure you leave with her."

"Why?" I continued.

"Listen... Trust me, she's our only way, honey!"

"What do you mean, our only way?"

"Cha..." she started to whisper. "Be my hero. Save me, because I know you're the only one that will have the guts to do so. And just behave with her like you're a professional and don't talk about her. Just do whatever she wants. She will call you back later."

"Ladies, let's go?" Joris actually called us.

Hum. At that moment, we looked at Joris, together, and followed him.

Be my hero, save me, what does it mean? I am already trying to save her arse! Unless... Yeah, she's been... Oh, my god, I think I get her point. Well, if it is, that's really bad from her. Or maybe... Maybe both Kelly and Claire that evening co-operated together, but not for the same purpose. Both of them wanted me to do that, but not for the same reason. Claire wants me to save her and thinks that given the fact that Kelly tried to trap me that evening... Oh, my, that would explain a thousand of things, now. And confirm that Claire has been trapped by Kelly.

Next to the Kléber station entrance, there was a zebra crossing to actually reach the other bank of the road. We crossed it but stayed away from Kelly and Joris that were still talking in front. I really don't know, but, suddenly, I felt like a heavy pressure, like, whatever I will do tonight, it will actually matter. Because, the way Claire looked at me, the way she was talking, the way she was behaving, it just didn't lie, Claire needs help, and I am sure it's the reason why she approved Kelly when we've been doing my birthday party, she wanted me to enter the game, so I could help her to exit. It confirms that she's blackmailed. I mean, she is sincere, now. Claire cannot just act, she can hide things, but she's a horrible actress when it's for lying to me. Kelly and Joris were walking, maybe five metres away from us, and we remained together. Whilst walking, I actually furtively took her hand. Very discreetly, I made sure that both Kelly and Joris couldn't see us. According to Joris, it was quite a long walk, but on remaining on the Kleber avenue. Fine, then. So, whilst we've been walking, still hiding behind the noise of our heels, we resumed talking, far away from them, discreetly.

"Claire, I cannot tell you everything right now," I pondered. "But be assured that if there's someone by your side, no matter what happens, it's me! I am... I was your girlfriend, and whatever happens, I will never give you up."

"I know, I know! Me too, I mean, there are things that... I regret. But I just... Just, you know, behave like normally with that person. She's nice. Don't talk about me, just, you know, do what you have to do," she continued, switching topics to avoid the thing she desperately wants to ask.

"Okay, sure. I will, thank you."

"She's nice, you'll see."

"Sure. Hum, Claire, could I talk to you about something that you won't say to anybody?" I actually wanted to explain to her why I was in such a bad mood today... until...

"Oh, hum, Charlotte!" Joris suddenly came, "I need to talk to you about something. Hum, in private. Sorry, Claire, do you mind if I take your friend for a minute?"

"Sure, no problem!" she suddenly smiled and switched her mood.

Claire moved and actually took Joris's place when he bounced back with me. Hum, yeah, ironically, I think it's the best to do. Because, yeah, I don't really think it's an excellent idea to talk about my pregnancy, it will destroy her, and given how we've been speaking lately, I think she's broken enough already. Curiously, Joris has been smiling at me, I don't really know the reason why... He indeed wanted to talk about yesterday. Well, if he smiles at me, it means that I passed my admission test very well. For tonight, at least, I have a plan. And there's nothing that he can really do to kill that plan, to be fair. So, we bounced back, and whilst we resumed walking (as we were now standing in front of some office, we were walking towards the Trocadero, opposite to the Place de l'Etoile), I actually started the conversation.

"Is it gonna be a long walk again?" I was exhausted to wear those heels again.

"No, we're nearly there," he acted like a fake personality. "Also, I wanted to congratulate you for yesterday, the two guys were thrilled. You did a great job, thank you."

"Meh..." I remained still very laconic.

"But, today, I mean, I saw you with Claire, you don't seem really fine. Is there anything I can do for you?"

"I am okay, what do you mean by I am not fine?"

"No, I mean, I just saw you and Claire," he started to talk in a low voice whilst Claire and Kelly laughed in front.

"Yeah, and?"

"Okay, hum. I have quite a few things to ask you, actually. Well, not to ask you, but... I want something."

"And what do you want?"

"I would like your ex-girlfriend... You know, as my girlfriend."

Of course, and I want the United Kingdom's crown, the nuclear weapon as well, and if possible, I'll also take a private army. Yeah, my ex-girlfriend, yeah. You so wish, my dear. But, okay, let's not be actually stupid. Of course, we had a kind of intense moment with Claire, but at least, he knows that having Claire, because he was obviously flirting with her, but if he asks me this, it means that she refused whatever he did with her tonight. So, he was having a hard time with her because he knows that she's still loyal to me. Hum... Finally, we have a point to discuss. Yet, we have a point to negotiate. He wants Claire, and obviously, he expects that I may not be in a position to refuse. It would have been twenty-four hours earlier, that would be okay. Now? Well... Basically, he needs me. He needs me for something. That is so sad... If he wants Claire? Oh... That is actually something that I could play at my advantage.

"And why do you want Claire?"

"She's... You know. She's damn hot. She's huge, I mean, I really want her!"

"And what do you want me to do?" I was actually thinking about a strategy.

"I don't know, I... Just find a way."

"And what if I don't?" I was still trying to coax him in an imperturbable calm.

"Well, if you still want to do that... Or if you still want to actually see Claire alive, you will do it. Because, Charlotte, I still have some, erm... powers. And you know, I don't really care about the law."

"Oh, and I thought you were a cop. Well, nice."

"Just do what I want you to do."

He is bluffing. He uses threats because he doesn't clearly know me and clearly if Claire disappears, it's not in his best interest. But, okay, let's pretend that I am intimidated and that I believe him.

I was thinking. Clearly, this guy is misjudging me. Because, for obvious reasons, he didn't sleep with Claire. Why would he come to me and ask me to help him deal with Claire if he already had sex with her, it just doesn't make sense. First, as he wants something from me, he needs to deserve it, and Claire, he's never gonna have her. That's just impossible. But I can use Claire for that. Because, and he is right, I am not in a position to actually negotiate with him. However, I am in an excellent position to fuck him like he's never been fucked, just because he wants something from me, it's actually quite a mistake. He may not be aware of that, but I am an evil bitch, which means a manipulative psychopath, and my mission is to protect Claire. And contrarily to him, I use my brain.

Second, as he thinks that I may be overwhelmed by several things such as what happened yesterday and like the fact that I saw Claire with him, I know that it's part of the strategy to destroy me. Even if I don't really know the motives, somehow, they are becoming more apparent, I was targeted because this guy might have been a stalker that uses quite elaborate strategies to get what he wants. Third, given that he knows our shared history, and since it's no longer a secret that Claire and I are still in a very ambiguous relationship, I think I have my exit strategy. Let's actually play the game: let's push Claire into his arms. So, let's start their weird romance, their stuff, their thing... And then, let them sleep together. Then, I will gather enough proof with Claire to report him for statutory rape and pimping. That's gonna be hard for my girlfriend because I really don't want her to undergo that... But that could work. That could actually work. Especially since Claire is still seventeen and thus, she's always minor. Wow, for a cop... Man, curiously, I was feeling lighter, all of a sudden! However, I remained like, pretending I was sad or something. But in between, before establishing that strategy, there are a couple of things I must set in place, to make sure things work as I want them to work. Especially, meet that woman.

"Okay, well... As I don't have any other choices... However, I still need some time. Just give me a couple of days to accept it, and I will do what you want to do."

"Wise decision, Charlotte, a wise decision."

"Just... Don't be an arse with her, okay? She's awesome, she doesn't deserve to be with an arsehole!" I concluded with some fake embarrassment.

"Don't worry about that!" he concluded. "Oh, by the way, ladies, here we are!"

We were now in front of a Haussmann-style building, like many buildings that are on that Avenue. It was not that far away from the station through which we arrived, to be fair, but it was far enough to be annoying. This building, like a four-floor building, was, well... It didn't actually seem like inhabited: next to the keypad, I could see that there was on the first floor a law firm, and the second floor was a medical office, apparently some neurologist, cardiologist and a gynaecologist. However small, the building was compacted into two other buildings, the first on the left was built with more contemporary architecture, and the second on the right was another Haussmann-style building. Still, we could see that the façade walls were actually brighter than this building. Obviously entirely made of stone, we could see only three rows of windows, (one on the left, one above the door and the last on the right, each were asymmetrical) and through the two first floors' windows, we couldn't see any lights. But for the third and fourth, well, we could see lights, and also hear some music and people speaking. I assume this is the party where we are heading.

I remained withdrawn. Claire saw that, and whilst Joris went to actually call the flat through the keypad, Claire looked at me, and I smiled at her. She noticed my smile. And she knows that when I am smiling, it means that I have something. As I told her earlier, I cannot tell her anything, but... Now, I am feeling more confident. And I was thinking, like, I will take her out of that mess, I will pull her out of this. And now that I can see that she understood my goals and she helps me on that, well... I still need to find out if this bollocks or not. I will see tomorrow how I can establish the exit strategy, I need to speak to her Irish lady first, before making any decisions. Joris pressed the button actually several times, until... Until someone responded. "Hey, it's Joris!" he said. And suddenly, the voice of a lady appeared, because he was speaking with a woman, replied, "finally, you're here. Come on in, you know where we are, right?". And I heard a buzz. The door finally opened. And now, Claire became nervous. Again, one evening that she's going to have to keep in mind. One more time that she'll have to do that, and that's just, well... Too much for me too. But now, it's just a question of patience.

After he pushed the door, I mean, after this buzz, he pushed the door, and, in that order, Kelly came, followed by Claire and then by me. We arrived in a kind of dark corridor. Even, at this point, I was feeling like, I know this place, it recalls me something. Like, some old Haussmann-style building, with obscure corridor when you enter, I don't know, I had a kind of a flashback. What I actually really paid attention very well was that green door, this green reminded me something in particular, but I have no idea what. Anyway, we actually entered, walked in, and the journey wasn't that long because, immediately on the left, maybe like four or five metres away after the main door, there was a lift. Joris called it, I mean he pressed on the button to call it whilst, still, with Claire, although there was a ray of moonlight provided by a small window above the door, we couldn't see anything into that darkness. I could see Claire standing next to me, whilst the noise of the lift coming down was quite loud. In that noise, she whispered to me:

"Remember... The Irish clover."

"The Irish clover," I repeated.

The lift arrived. Ironically, it was undoubtedly as old as the building was, as it was relatively narrow and putting four people inside was quite tricky. Basically, we were not stuck to the other, but we were really close to one another. I was the farthest away from Joris. He pressed the button, the door closed, and the lift started to go up. Quite roughly, by the way, it wasn't like a soft lift like I have in my building. Anyway, the travel was truly short, like a few seconds, before we actually arrived on the floor where we were supposed to go.

And when we arrived, yet again, we had that loud noise of music – that we couldn't hear downstairs when we entered the building – resonating on the walls, it almost made them vibrate. The music was like, I don't know, some electro music. And as it was loud, I really hope that I will not have to dance. I left the lift and walked. Basically, still, it was like another corridor, pretty much the same, but shorter. Still obscure. And there was nothing else but green walls and a brown door, as the passage was probably something like two metres long.

"Here we are," Kelly started.

"Yeah," Claire continued, laconic.

"Well, girls, are you ready for having fun?" Kelly continued.

"Yes!" I concluded, enthusiast.

Free Expensive Lies: Prologue

"Okay, so, basically, the rule is, we all split ourselves, and as soon as we see someone that looks rich and obviously alone, you guys know what you have to do!"

"Yeah, as usual," Claire ended, still very terse like she was depressed.

Joris passed in front of us and opened the door. Well, I don't know whose penthouse it is, but if he enters without knocking, it means that he's familiar with the place. And when I entered, after Claire and Kelly, I found myself in a kind of ample and wide-open space. And, yeah, when I mean, wide, I mean, really wide, but somehow it was only one of its kind. Nothing to say about this place but it was busy, indeed more than fifty people, and there were just the walls, really tall, and sofas all along the four walls. Basically, yeah, on the left side was a small mezzanine, with a small stair to go over there, and this mezzanine was heading to the rooftop. This mezzanine was entirely surrounding the place, and I could see, well, quite a few disturbing things. I am not sure I will go there. Or I don't know.

That was a kind of weird duplex. Hopefully, I did not arrive on the mezzanine floor, I reached under. Basically, yeah, it was wide, it was like extensive, and the floor was covered with a full red carpet. At least it seemed to be red. Along the wall, on my red, there was a kind of a bar, with two bartenders, and three people sat on stools facing the small bar, obviously, behind the bartenders, a sort of giant vitrine exposing all kinds of alcohols. Next to this, many sofas, where many people sat, chatting, I remarked that it was a bit more than talking for some of them. Basically, he said this was a penthouse, it looks more like a nightclub than a penthouse, except that there are no bouncers—Hum, weird. Oh, and after the sofas, there was the stair of the mezzanine floor.

There was nothing but an entrance to the toilets on the opposite wall, that seemed busy now. Like, the bathrooms seemed to be like a separate room, within this open space. Nothing more than these toilets. But, in the middle of this, a considerable number of people dancing. Like, yeah. Many girls, many guys, but quite a few people were dancing over there. I have no idea how many people could be there tonight, but if I have to give the average age present here, we were definitely 18-25 years old. And I assume, twenty-five must be like a maximum. And, yeah, I was feeling like in a nightclub, on the guys, most of them were dressed quite the same way, like a shirt, trousers, and shoes, whilst girls were with dresses and heels. I really have no idea why this party was thrown tonight, I mean, for like a couple of seconds, we remained near the entrance door, and actually discovered where we were. And wow... Seeking that person, the one Claire told me about, it was like looking for a needle in a haystack.

Taylor Harding-Jenkins

And the music was damn loud. Yeah, it was like a nightclub. Even if all lights were off, we could see a huge chandelier hanging from the ceiling, in the middle of that square-shape mezzanine. As the mezzanine was square-shaped, we could see that chandelier hanging from the top roof. However, there were some light spots under the mezzanine, but it was strong enough for bartenders to see what they were doing, not light up the place. But the chandelier was off, I mean, no lights were coming from it. I couldn't see any window as there were so many people in front of me, but the only light was the artificial lights made by special lighting made for parties. Now, it was a kind of dark blue, purple, but absolutely no lights were on. This place seemed like a massive contrast of its own: when there's not this lightning, this striking lightning, this place looks more like a hall of Versailles Palace, now it was a mix between a brothel and a nightclub.

And finding girls with green dresses, yeah. There are quite a few; I just need to observe. Overall, yeah. When we entered, we were all like... Yeah. We need to split each other. Basically, from now on, I don't know any of Claire or Kelly, I feel like... Yeah. I don't know who's taking the cash here, but so far, from what I've seen of the people here, it seemed quite selective. It seemed to be only rich people or at least rich young people. Well, at least it was not the two kinds of 35-years-old wrecks that I had yesterday, I was feeling like, whoever I meet tonight, it won't be that bad. Especially since I know that I have to meet someone. I just wonder if that person expects to see me. And I really hope she's not on the mezzanine. I don't really want to go there.

"Just look very carefully and keep your eyes wide open. She is actually waiting for you," Claire whispered in my ear.

Yeah, I think I got her as she seems to have spoken to that person, so I may expect she's waiting for me. And she's also here for me. The problem was, there were many girls alone, many guys as well, but overall, most of the people here were either in couple, whether... well, just two people about to have sex. I really hope that I won't have to do it here, in the middle of everybody. Even though basically, nobody was having sex, I mean as far as I could see, on this floor, it was mostly preliminaries. But, yeah, as the party seemed advanced, already, I really have no idea on how I may approach that green-dressed lady that is waiting for me.

"I'll find out. Good luck, Claire, I'll see you later!" I looked at her, this time full of hope, something I lost a while ago.

"Take care, honey!" she actually left.

Free Expensive Lies: Prologue

In the meantime, I actually looked around. Basically, at a glance, there were only five women on fifteen that wore a green dress. Two of them wore a dark green dress, which actually matched the description that Claire gave me. Hum, did she say a dark green? I don't recall. Anyway, let's say that I'd be here and supposed to be waiting for someone to be accosted. Hum... I'd certainly not be dancing in the middle, as I must remain visible, but not too much visible. So, I walked. In the toilets? No, there's no way she must be waiting there, or maybe she is still here. But one thing is sure, I would never be in the mezzanine, it's too isolated, and I do not want to be isolated. So, let's recap...

If I'd be waiting for someone, I'd be alone. Some twenty-seven women are currently alone or seeking someone, whether on the dance floor or elsewhere. Amongst these, twelve are now looking for someone explicitly, which makes fifteen left. Three of them are wearing a green dress, but none of them is wearing a brooch... Even if there is one with whom I am not really sure, given the fact that she's turned, and I cannot see her face. The first is dancing, and as I said, maybe she's seeking for someone, but as she is dancing, I wouldn't be dancing so... And she doesn't wear any brooch on her chest. So, it leaves only two of them. The first one, the wone turning her back, is at the bar, currently ordering something. The second one is sat on the bench. Hum... Let's try the one at the bar. Because I cannot see any brooch on the second, and Claire insisted on the brooch, apparently, it's the thing that will make me recognise her.

So, let's find an approach. Flirting with a woman is different than with a guy, especially given my current role here tonight. Claire said that I must leave with her, I mean, at least made me understand that I must go with that girl, which means that she must find an approach with me whatever happens. I walked, and then, slowly, I approached the bar. Hum... let's order something, and maybe, I should propose her something to drink, I think that can work as a right approach.

There were currently only her and some other guy at the bar. I approached and specifically choose my words because I must talk first to the bartender to raise her attention. And let's make it theatrical, even if I've never been in a pub using a British accent:

"Hey! Double scotch, mate, please!" I said to the bartender, some guy with a suit.

Mate... Yeah, cliché. I feel like a guy saying this.

But somehow, that worked, I immediately raised her attention. Oh, my... Obviously, I started with her face, a brown girl with brown eyes. Green eyes are more likely to be my type. Very slim, not skinny like Claire but very slim. So, brown eyes, turned-up and slender nose, light and beautiful red lips, and her hairs were untied, very slightly wavy. She had some very discreet freckles on her face, but it was almost charming. Even if she had a straightforward makeup, she didn't wear any foundation. Her body, skinny legs, and she was quite tall. I think she must be twenty-five years old, as she looks quite mature, but I may be wrong. Like, she was wearing heels but was definitely as tall as I was, maybe more elevated than me, but the difference was pretty hard to make. A skinny chest, she didn't actually have breasts, I mean, it was very slim in there. Oh, and, speaking of this... She had a brooch. A four leaves clover made of shiny diamonds. Yeah, I was right, this would undoubtedly be different than yesterday, at least it was more interesting. So, she should be a person waiting for me. Nobody wears brooch here except her... Okay, I didn't go upstairs.

At the very moment I ordered my drink, she already had a drink and was watching her glass with insistence. Obviously, I didn't look at her straight, but I looked at her glass and noticed it was empty. As she was focused on her drink, she was definitely thoughtful, and at least it gave me the pretext to talk to her. Hum... Now, she knows that I am here. And if she is waiting for me, for sure, she would respond. She would be the next to respond. And, after having spent indeed a couple of time thinking about what she would actually say... Whilst the bartender started serving my drink, I had, yeah, a kind of an astonishing surprise.

"Oh, wow, I thought you'd be Irish, but your accent says otherwise!" she replied with an actually deep male voice.

Suddenly, yeah. The surprise was actually total. I, erm... Really didn't expect that. I just looked at her, like, she looked at me straight in the eyes, and we just, erm... I really don't know what to say. When I looked at her, in the beginning, she really looked like... Oh, my, that's actually well done. I mean... Or maybe that's a guy undercover, but... I kind of felt some transgender waves coming from her. I reacted, like... I just tried my best to hide my surprise, but it was actually astounding. If I appear as surprised, she'll be upset (god knows how transgender people are sensitive), so... Okay. Okay, okay, okay.

"Hum... Oh, wow!" I said, smiling at her.

"Oh, yeah, that's my voice, darling? I know, that's pretty unusual."

"No, I was actually about to say, that's, erm... Well, congratulations, I mean, it's very well done. I would never believe that... Wow. I mean, yeah."

"Cool. Now please don't ask any questions about what happened, because that's not gonna work between us, darling," she seemed quite defensive.

"Yeah, I heard about it. Google has many answers on how transgender people transitions. I am not stupid like the commoner with his nasty curiosity, be not afraid," I replied, actually sure of myself. "Anyway, Charlotte, nice to meet you, hum...?"

"Allison. I'm from Dublin. Nice to meet you, Charlotte. Where are you from?"

"The south of this country. Some city, I forgot the name... Starts with an M..."

"No, you can't be from here!"

"You might be surprised, actually. My mum is from Devon, but she grew up in London, and even if I was born here, my sister and I spoke English before speaking French, and... Well, that's a pretty long story!"

"Okay, interesting."

I actually think I made a good point on automatically switching the topic, introducing myself straight. I have never met any transgender people in my life, but I am sure that there must be fed up with stupid people asking thousands of questions about how they did it. I mean, if I were in her position, replying to invasive questions from strangers would piss me off at some point. Responding "there's Google for that" when I said that, I really made a point as I could see on her face that, yeah, at least I was not one of these people. But I don't know, there is something weird, from her. Not odd, like... She defended herself because I assume, she's been approached by many strangers and turned them away, and...

Given that French people are still too restricted regarding LGBT issues on their globality (this is why, unlike me, mum loves that country), at least according to the protests outside against the gay marriage and as transgender people are too different from being accepted, well. Showing that I am friendly and that I do not care that she's transgender, I think I made a good point. Okay, I usually know how to approach people, but transgender people are still different. Don't get me wrong, I never said, different in bad... If I do not find something to say to her, she's going to turn away, so I must keep the conversation for a while. For that, let's go straight to the point, actually. I feel like she likes people going directly and not turning around something to ask something.

Coming back to this, to give an example regarding French acceptance of trans people, the latest crap I heard from one of those commoners is the chromosome excuse. Like, you know, guys are XY and women XX. So since you were born XX, then you are a woman no matter what... You know, like they can see your chromosomes through your skin or something. I have also been told recently that being trans is pretty much a new fashion coming from the US. They certainly never heard about Iran. Hum... They tend to have forgotten that trans are the kind of "legacy" of former transvestites and, well... What about Philippe d'Orléans, or the Chevalier d'Eon. Meh... Whatever it is, you cannot take seriously a country whose people protesting in the street because gays can get married, I mean... I always said that France is a beautiful country, a massive history that must not be forgotten, a tremendous culture, outstanding gastronomy, gorgeous countryside; nowadays France's only problem is French people.

"So, how do you find Paris, young traveller from the rainy lands of Ireland?" I continued.

"Cool. That's actually nice. Okay, people are a bit, erm... Weird, here, but, well, that remains a beautiful city!" she continued.

"I know, I always said that the problem in France is French people. Otherwise, that's a great country! There are so many things to do here!"

"Yeah! The only problem is, I don't really know anybody here. I mean, I am here for a couple of months already, and still, I feel like, you know, I'm all alone here... And, sometimes, you know, with all those protests against the gay marriage."

"Yeah, that's why I say that French people are the problem in this country. But, meh, anyway. I know what you mean, I feel the same. And what are you doing? Studying, or working, or something like that?"

"Well, I am studying computing and, you know, programming. All that kind of stuff!"

"Oh, I see!"

"And you, what about you?"

She starts asking me stuff. Basically, I'm acting with detachment with her, which means, she started defending herself over her transition, I strategically replied, "yeah, I can find my way to get my answers". Then, I asked what you are doing here, meaning that I don't care what she is, I really care about who she is. She felt less abandoned. Less, I mean, she felt like unlike other people with their unwholesome curiosity, for once, whilst speaking with me, she felt like she was an average person and not, a transgender person. I understand why things actually went very well with Claire when she met her, given the fact that four years ago, one of her cousins transitioned the same way, from a man to a woman, and she really helped her doing her transition. Claire is very tolerant of transgender people. I don't care, they are just human beings like any other human being, they just have a different history. But seeing the fact that she actually replied back to my question, "And you, what about you, what do you do in your life", means that she has interest for me. Which will make the thing certainly easier.

"Oh well, many things, actually..." I continued, taking myself to the game. "Technically, I'm just a student, I mean, I will pass my baccalaureate. But I really don't know what to do for my future."

"I don't know. I imagined you as a lawyer or something like that!"

"Yeah, only if I can defend criminals and get paid by the mafia!" I laughed.

"Oh, yeah. You actually look like that kind of lawyer, that's what I wanted to add, actually."

"Oh, thank you, dear," I still played the game, "But I am not really into reading law stuff and shit like that. No, I really don't know what I want to do for a living."

"Meh, you still have time to think about that..."

"Yeah..."

"And... Your ring in your finger shows that you're in a relationship, am I right?" she actually noticed my finger

"Um... I... No. Not really, actually," I replied, sure of myself.

"Aren't you? Such a beautiful girl like you?"

I actually started drinking my double scotch, whilst thinking, could I see myself with a trans? To be honest, I don't really know how they are working. I am attracted by all what's female, there is just the voice that can be a bit disturbing, but I can live with that. I don't really mind, that's just a detail. Unfortunately, I have someone in mind already, and this person is my one and only. But given the fact that I was here to earn money for my boss, well. Sleeping with her wouldn't actually be a problem for me. I mean... I didn't ask, and that's the very least question I'd ask if she had surgery. No, yeah, that could actually be a problem, is she had a, erm... Yeah. Unless we have no sexuality for a while because I have a real problem with, well, the thing. No, I think I could be with a trans woman. The most important thing is what's in the heart; the packaging always lies. I don't know, but, well... But, yeah, as she was now obviously flirting with me (I mean, it was not, like, obviously, but it actually seemed like it was), maybe I could use this at my advantage: I am not in a relationship, but I was. Because she knows that I was. Or perhaps she doesn't. Meh, let's try. Meanwhile, I actually wanted to pee. Like, quite severely.

"Oh, well, that is a... Well, a gift from a friend; it's not what you think, I just use it as a bait. But, no, if you want to know, I was with a girl for like seven years, and, well, it ended like last summer." I lied whilst thinking about Claire. "But it's fine, now, I mean... I managed to move on. Erm, do you mind if I use the loo for a bit? I mean, don't leave, I'll be back!"

"No problem, Charlotte, I'll stay here, I don't move!"

"Thank you, darling. I'll be back soon."

"Okay!"

To be fair, I looked at her another time, before to leave, as I walked back and smiled at her, and, well, I would never believe that she was trans. It's, erm, wow. But I don't know, there must be something with her, because, yeah, I felt like she was here, I know she was waiting for me, but, I don't know, I was feeling like she mostly needs something like a girlfriend instead of having sex. I mean, she doesn't seem to be that much interested in this. I really don't know how to approach her, at least, to make her understand why I am here tonight. Because Claire has been specific, I mean, she told me to go with her. But, yeah, either way, I feel like she's hiding something. Like me, she is also here for a purpose, not the same as I was (because she was all alone), but she was here for a purpose. But not for Claire's purpose, another one, a deeper purpose. I assume I'll find out soon.

Anyway, I walked towards the toilets, opposite to the bar, where she was actually waiting, drinking. I didn't have that much of a walk to do, to be fair, the toilets were in front of me, and as it seemed to be relatively small, I assume these toilets are unisex, they were at least ten metres away from the bar. And while walking, I observed the situation very furtively around me, looking for Claire, Kelly and Joris. First, I could see that my former girlfriend was drinking a champagne cup with a young guy, but curiously they were drinking in the same cup. Well, at least it wasn't long as well for her to get what she was supposed to have. Meanwhile, Kelly was discussing with two other guys, they were definitely something like twenty-five, but unable to actually know what was going on, or where it would lead since, I assume, she just found them. I was the only one with a girl... Oh, and, unable to actually find Joris. I looked at him everywhere around, but I couldn't see him. But I made it quick, just not to be seen doing nothing. Yeah, I just looked at them, and felt like, well, I don't know in what state of mind Claire must be now, but... Well. I will talk to her maybe tomorrow or later in the weekend.

And then I arrived (hopefully, toilets were open), I pushed the door of the restroom slightly, and I came in, while still keeping an eye on Allison, when I actually heard when I entered, as the light was off, that it was no longer carpets on the floor. I turned on the light, and before closing the door, I looked at her, and she ordered actually two other drinks. So, I locked myself, turned on the light, when I found a real surprise: sat on the toilet, obviously not peeing, or doing anything, he seemed to be waiting for me, there was Joris. Immediately, when I saw him, I got actually scared.

"Here you are, beauty!"

Seeing him was almost like seeing a ghost. I mean, he just surprised me, and, yeah, it actually made my heart beating slightly faster. I was already under pressure, I was like, yeah, I actually needed for a short time to lean myself against the sink fixed really close to the light switch, and after a brief moment of recovery, I simply said:

"Fuck, Joris... You scared the shit out of me!" I actually whispered.

"How's the business going tonight? I saw you with Macready," he actually raised his head and looking at me like I have done some mistake or something.

"Macready?" I was now okay.

"Yeah, the guy dressed up like a girl, at the bar. Easy choice, tonight, huh? I didn't know you enjoyed trannies!"

"You should be careful with what you say, Joris," I warned him. "Especially if you want to sleep with Claire, try to be a bit more tolerant because the use of that word with her won't pass."

"Meh... This guy or girl or whatever it is, it's just a wallet at my eyes. But, fine, he knows me already, I will just text him to collect the payment. Anyway, I feel like you are stressed, just like Claire... Is everything okay for you?"

"I'm fine," I remained concise in my answers.

"Hum, I don't really believe you..."

"Okay then," I really didn't know what to reply.

"Unfortunately, tonight, the big boss is nearby. And I want all of you at work, bringing a lot of money. I want to make good money tonight, and I really don't want you to mess up with anything, especially since you are new. So, I don't know what you are plotting with Claire, but if you fuck with me, Charlotte, you are going to be in big troubles. Is that clear?"

"I am not plotting anything," I just defended myself.

"Sure. I saw you with Claire when we arrived earlier, and suddenly, when she saw you, she switched. I gave her good products to make sure she would be high enough, but... It's why I split you both because I know that you're a danger. Let me make it clear, Charlotte: the boss told me, if you fuck with me, I'll fuck with you. And remember that I have all your pictures and I know where you and your family live."

"Oh, so it was you, the *Rising Sun* moron that blackmailed me. Oh, wow, what a discovery. On the other hand, I was expecting that, since, well, you're a cop and having that information doesn't seem to be a problem for you."

"I am not that moron, as you call him, but I have a copy of everything. So, Charlotte, I am explaining things to you calmly, for now. Believe it or not, but I have a boss above me... I am just like you are! So, don't fuck with me, because believe me, I am opposed to all forms of violence against women."

"Such a funny threat. But, okay. Of course, instead, you make them sleep for money for your account..."

"Not my personal account. But anyway, it's bigger than you think, and it's also none of your business. Anyway, give me your arm!"

"Why?"

"Give me your arm, I said," he actually started this time to be more aggressive.

It was weird: he was feeling under some pressure, now. Claire was acting strange, which makes that, without wanting, I actually triggered something interesting: I don't know who took the pictures of my wedding party, but I assume he did, but now, I know that he is also working for someone. On the other hand, he's a cop, and... Running a business with only three girls is like being an amateur. I'd be at his place; I'd have more girls. Especially tonight, as he said that the big boss was here. But he was not lying, his body language told that he was not lying, from the way he sat, how he was actually holding his hand like he has a big problem... Now I understand the conversation we had earlier in the street: he was actually, yeah, splitting me from Claire so I couldn't talk with her. He understood there was some pressure between us, and... Okay, so I now understand the situation a bit more. I tend to think that we are part of something. Joris, Kelly, Claire and I are just a cluster within a vast organisation. I mean, that's how it looks like. But if that is the real case... Then it's possible that I may not know the guy blackmailing me.

At the moment he actually asked me my arm, he took out of the inside pocket of his coat a syringe, full of a yellow liquid. If he was asking me my arm, it means that it was drugs. I forgot to take some diazepam before to leave, so... Yeah, it can only be drugs. And, yeah, whatever could be in this syringe could not kill me, since, well, finding a dead body in the bathroom, especially mine, would certainly not be a good thing for him. Since he is a cop, that wouldn't do his business very well.

"What's in your syringe?"

"Come on, I drugged you once already, and you know it's not lethal!"

It was the first time that I saw him as an anxious guy. His nails were bitten, and, for the very first time, I could see some white hairs in his short dark hairs. He was suffering from tremendous anxiety, and even if he was managing it, it was still extremely hard for him, this is why he is giving Kelly some extra power. He actually took a short blue tourniquet with the syringe, and whilst was standing in front of him, thinking about this, I was discovering this guy under another angle: he was a moron, obviously, but a moron under colossal pressure. This explains a lot, now: he cannot blackmail me, because Kelly is his assistant. This is why Kelly broke our couple and saw in Claire a potential victim, she actually trapped Claire for that purpose. Because he needs girls, but cannot recruit them quickly, using Kelly, that comes to you and pretend she is a friend and traps you. Yeah. He could be my blackmailer, this is obvious because he needs me. I am a girl, so he needs me. I just looked at him, still thinking about that strategy, and thinking that it will definitely work. Then I actually removed my coat, dropped my bag, and gave him my arm. He tightened the tourniquet and started looking elsewhere. Still, before he put the needle into one of my veins now more obviously displayed, I needed to make sure that what he was giving me could be enough to make me high enough, without any risk of overdose or even worse:

"Still, what's the liquid, in your syringe?"

"It's, erm... Don't worry, it's not gonna kill you, I gave some to Claire as well, it's not dangerous."

"How can I know that I can trust you?" I started to take my arm back whilst he was distracted.

"Come on, don't be a pussy," he actually took my arm back, "This dose will not kill you. Otherwise, Claire would be dead at least five times. You will not die, don't worry, you'll be just high enough like on your birthday."

"You still didn't answer my question!"

"For the love of God, Charlotte."

"Okay. Okay then, do what you have to do."

Whilst again looking elsewhere, I started to feel like a very slight sting into my arm, and I just didn't move at that moment. Yeah, well, I don't know why I was like, yeah, in a trusting mood, I really don't trust him, but, well. He already drugged me on my birthday, so being drugged is something I actually became familiar with. It just can't be poison. And, well, even if it is, well, then... The easy way out will be taken faster, I am not that much attached to being alive, to be fair. Then, after a few seconds, he removed the needle out of my arm, removed the tourniquet, and whilst I stepped back, he actually placed everything back in the very same pocket where it was coming from. Well, it's going to take time to reach my brain, as it is directly. Maybe less than the last time they drugged me, but... Well, I don't know, I'll see what will happen anyway.

"Here you go. Now, have fun and enjoy," he concluded.

Still thinking, and whilst he placed everything back in his pocket, I leaned against the sink. And I was like, yeah. Yet in that flow of understanding the situation. I just didn't want to reply, because, whatever I say, well, it doesn't make any sense. Afterwards, he stood up from the toilet, finally releasing them, and left the bathroom. I locked the door after he left.

I don't really know, now, suddenly, I was kind of, well, overwhelmed. I just sat on the toilets so I could finally pee, and, I figured, yeah, Claire never left me, it is why she is like this today, they forced her to break up with me. And this, yeah, it was hard to accept, because they were just confirming what I actually thought. Claire became the victim of a human trafficking scheme, even if she was free, she was not free to do what she wants to do, and it's why it's been days she doesn't come to school. He said, earlier, that he was threatening to abduct her. He can't kidnap her, because he needs her too much, and it's why my exit strategy can work: if we target Joris, Kelly will fall, and it will trigger an investigation on whom is behind this, which will highly damage Kelly's reputation or even better, send her to prison. Because, yeah, tonight I saw the real face of Joris, and to be the head of a human trafficking network, you need to be a leader and a good liar. Joris is everything but this, however, he is a perfect tool. He can quickly bring some useful information and blackmail people because he works for the police, so accessing information such as the one he gave me the first time he called me. Tonight, I saw someone under pressure, but under hard pressure. It was just out of his control, and I couldn't miss that. So, okay, he understood that Claire and I being together is a danger, this is why they are doing their best to destroy any possible relationship we may develop. Kelly knows me better and knows much more the real reasons why and how strong our couple was. Damn, this is just insane, I mean, I only didn't realise that the iceberg would be so massive.

Free Expensive Lies: Prologue

After peeing, I actually stood up, obviously flushed (and I think I was the first to do that), wore my coat and took my handbag back, and I left the toilets. And Allison was still alone, standing at the bar, and when I went to the bathrooms, she actually saw me and smiled. I smiled back, thinking "so you know Joris...". Well, I also felt that she knew him because I assume that she had sex with Claire already, so she had to pay her. I walked towards her, still giving her many smiles, and remaining as friendly as possible. Ironically, I had a hot flash at that same moment, but I had an idea about what it has been caused. Coming closer to her, I started to say:

"Sorry about that, Allison... I was a bit long!"

"Stomach problems?" she smiled.

"Yeah, something like that... But I am sure you don't really want to have the details of the situation."

"I must admit that it's not something I am curious about, yeah, indeed! But at least you're okay now, so it's fine for me!"

"Be not afraid, dear, I'm not sick!" I sniggered.

"Well, I hope so! I don't really want you to dirty your shoes or something."

"Hum, yeah, these?" I showed my shoes. "That's okay, I need to change these shits anyway!"

"Well, expensive shit, apparently," she suddenly looked at me, this time more serious.

"Well, expensive, what do you mean?"

"You look like rich. Or, I mean, you look like the rest of them."

"What do you mean, you look like the rest of them?"

"You are wearing expensive shoes and carry a pretty handbag, I can see that your coat is made of a kind of special fabric, you didn't buy it in a pret-a-porter brand. The way you walk, you look like, you have manners, so I think you are coming from an aristocratic family."

"Oh, my..." I pretended being impressed.

Hum... At the same time, I drank again. Okay, he found out that I bought my shoes in a luxury shop and my coat in a shop near the City. Finding out that I wear expensive stuff, for a woman, at least for someone that is becoming a woman, is not that difficult. Everybody can find this. It's, yeah. Pretty easy. If she wants to impress me with cold reading, I think that's not gonna work. I know how to cold read someone as well, (oh, yeah, for people who don't know, basically, cold read someone is basically what I am doing most of the time, analysing people from their hairstyle to their clothing, their gender, their age... If you want to become a great manipulator, you need to know this – mentalists and psychics are using this, for instance), so it's not going to impress me. Unless it's done well, and... Guessing that I am lesbian might be tricky, but it may be possible. Anyway... Let's pretend that I am impressed, let's keep the game going, and let's see what cards she has on her hands. Then, I will see what I can do.

"Yeah, well," she continued, almost thinking that she reached a threshold she was not supposed to reach.

"Wow, you can guess me!"

"It's no big deal, to be honest. I also see that you are high right now!"

"Hum... You can see my eyes, huh?" I was suddenly confused.

"How do you know that I can guess through your eyes that you are high?"

"My dilated pupils, right?"

Yeah, when people are high, they have their pupils dilating, that is something familiar. That and their behaviour are the two tangible ways you can recognise them. And, at that point, I really don't know why, but I felt the need to actually lean myself against the bar because I was feeling really weird. Okay, I felt that double scotch almost intoxicating me quickly, until I reminded that my only meal for the entire day was two cookies. So, obviously, as I didn't eat and my body doesn't have enough vitamins, I am getting drunk and high almost instantly. I felt like a kind of hot flash, I was now baffled, which came so suddenly that I was like, I can't. I need to go out, take some air, and whatever happens, I just need to leave.

Meanwhile, she remained calm, was still standing next to me, but didn't dare to touch me. It was only the two of us at the bar, but I needed to actually get out of that place. So, I just, erm... I just continued, now we were only together.

"Yeah, that's right, yeah. Also, according to your current dress code, I'd guess that... You're here tonight as an escort girl, am I right?"

"Oh, my, how do you know that?" I was feeling a bit better, but it was still not the paradise.

"You're provocative. Pretty, but provocative. But it's fine, I mean, I need someone for tonight, I am scared coming back home alone..."

"Oh, really?"

I was boiling. I mean, at that point... The other day, when I got drugged, it took longer to actually work, I remember, because I was drunk, and I ate quite a lot at Claire's. Now, hot flashes upon hot flashes, it just didn't stop. I just really need to get some air. So, yeah, she guessed that I was an escort, and she's scared to come back home alone, fine. I was melting, like, really melting, it was just terrible. I don't really know whether it was for sex or not, but, either way, she wants me to come back home with her... Anyway, she knows Joris, so she's used to that process. Still harshly struggling with my hot flashes, I actually saw this opportunity to leave as a so sought freedom.

"Okay dear, whatever your price is, you wanna come back home with me?" he said.

"Yeah, I actually need to get out of here..." I was sweating, feeling trapped and desperately needed to leave.

"You think you can cope with the lift and everything before we go out?"

"Yeah. Let's get out of here!"

24 *Gosh, it stinks!*

// I don't know where I actually crashed.

// Friday, 18th of January 2013, 10:10.

It's been nine days that I turned eighteen and, basically, in nine days, my life was already upside-down. Already a mess. What did I achieve since I am major? Oh, quite a few things: being a prostitute, and also be pregnant. Oh, and, yeah, there are so many lies that I am hiding that, well, if someday the truth explodes, that will be funny. Also, I blacked out twice, I got drunk, erm... Okay, once, we cannot really count yesterday as being one, because I was not really drunk, I just didn't eat, but one thing was sure, it was, now, I was still not that hungry. Once I'm back home, I'm gonna eat. Otherwise, I'm going to fall, and that's not going to be a fun idea.

And this morning, it was actually hard to describe how I felt. I can only say that things actually worked out well, as I don't remember anything. I just tried to recollect my last memories, when I was still in that penthouse, with her, and, yeah, from the moment Joris drugged me, I am lost. I mean, I recall having talked a bit afterwards with Allison, and, after, it's the blackout. I don't know why, but when I remembered her name, I feel like, yeah, a kind of feeling of protection, as if that person was protecting me from something. Why did I have the word "cop" coming and being associated with her name or anything? Well, on the other hand, I went to her on purpose because Claire asked me so. It's funny, I don't remember anything afterwards, it's just black. Even if I tried, I mean, I really tried to pass the film of the events in my mind, from what happened, I just remember, yeah, speaking to her, leaning on the bar because I was not feeling well, and that's all. Losing your memory, yeah, because you never know what you have done and you may have done something harmful, it's a shame. But curiously, I don't really feel like I did something terrible or appalling, I feel like, Allison carried me in a safe place. I feel her, she was protecting me, she was caring, so I assume that she made sure that everything went fine before things went really messed up.

Obviously, I wasn't home. I felt wrapped in cold satin sheets, as my bedsheets are in cotton (okay, synthetic stuff, we got it at Ikea), and my bed is always warm. Well, I was expecting something like this, not coming home for the entire night, and hopefully, Florent is not home. I was slowly coming back to my mind, but actually very slowly because I was not feeling well, but I could not feel where. So, yeah, as expected, I assume that I am at her place, but it's kind of weird, I mean, satin sheets, if she sleeps on that... Well, I guess there's nothing, like... I don't feel like I am really at her place or something, I may be elsewhere, in a neutral location. My belly was hurting because I was hungry. And, I was so cold, I mean, it was freezing out there. Does she leave the bedroom without any heater turned on for me? Because it's curious, I mean, I was freezing, it was crazy. Which is why, I was curled up, now, in the bed.

Curiously, I did not feel like something happened. I just didn't have my shoes and my coat, but I was basically sleeping with my dress and my underwear. Like, basically, as if I came back home after a night of heavy drinking. And, even, I don't feel like I had sex last night, I was just perfectly normal. I could only feel myself, especially since I was curled up to actually gather the remaining heat that was available. But, curiously, I felt fatigued, like tired in, I didn't sleep that much last night. It's possible, maybe I was sick or something, but I feel like I didn't actually sleep that much. It happens a lot when I am drunk that I don't really sleep the following night because either I become sick and I throw up or have night terrors. Speaking of night terrors, today, I need to call the abortion clinic, to get an appointment. I'll do it certainly later today.

But I felt that, yeah, I was increasingly cold. I touched next to me, and, it seems like, I slept all alone in the bed: the other side was cold, and it was almost like, the pillow was at its correct place as if basically nobody slept in here. Well, that actually raises curiosity on who is Allison: basically, this person was seeking me, so I assume that she must be a cop in undercover. Now, for what reason, I presume infiltrating that network. And appearing as a customer. The problem is, how to confront? No, I mean, the question is, should I confront her? The best is to wait until how things are going on and pretending I know nothing. If she needs me, she will call me. Right now, I mean, when I was waking up, I heard some music in a room next to mine and someone typing on a keyboard. On the other hand, she might really be working as a programmer, or whatever she said to me, being like a student. The music I heard was, yeah, basically, some cool and classic music.

After a few moments of, well, enjoying a mix between the warm and the cold, I heard a combination of sounds between someone typing on a keyboard and some classical music. After smelling my own odour after I wake up and seeing through my eyelids that I was in a room where the light was somehow dimmed, and it didn't seem nice weather outside, I actually lifted the cover of the bed with my arm and opened my eyes. As I was curled up, and basically executing my very first move for the day, I felt like an urgent need to stretch my entire body. I put myself flat back, put my arms to the sky, and, forcefully, I stretched myself. I even yawned at the same time, when after some moment, after a kind of black veil left my eyes because I stretched myself up maybe with too much strength, I was feeling slightly weak. Like, I need to eat something. I don't know, but if I can, before coming back home, I may stop by some fast food and ask for breakfast, because… Maybe the journey to go back home might be too long, wherever I am. But this weakness was not incapacitating, I can still walk and stop by to have some fast food or a shop where I can get something to eat.

When I opened my eyes, and when that black veil went away, I actually discovered the room where I was now. Yeah, on the other hand, which confirms that we crashed in a hotel or something because I was in a place that seemed totally empty of personality. It was a small place, with, in front of me, the door, maybe at less than two metres away from the bed on the left-hand side. Right now, it was closed, she surely closed it to let me sleep. I don't know why, but I rather have the feeling that I am in a hotel suite instead of a flat. On my right, on the edge of the bed was maybe a two-metre space, and a relatively tall window just before the wall, above a radiator that didn't seem to be switched on. Covering the window, two quite thick and embroidered curtains, in a dark-grey colour, letting passing through feeble light of an apparently cloudy sky, even if it seemed whiter than grey at that moment. Curiously, nothing else. No wardrobe, no portrait, no personalisation of the room means that we are in a hotel, we are not at her place. Except for her laptop, she may rent the room for a couple of days, preparing this.

It did not smell good or bad, but one thing was sure, it didn't smell sweat or anything that could give me a clue that "we had sex". I just smelled my own odour when I wake up, and especially when I saw the bed: only my side was messy, not hers. It means she never slept in here that night. Now, two questions about this Allison, whoever she is: she certainly guessed the purpose on why I came to her. I remember, she figured out that I was, yeah, here for that. Joris knows her. The fact that we didn't have sex, the fact that Claire sent me to her, actually start to make sense.

But on the other hand, I didn't have enough proofs that she was indeed a cop. She still could be either someone involved in that network, near or far, either a cop (I feel her more in this role, the fact that she practices cold-reading and stuff) or whether, ultimately, my blackmailer. But if she would be my blackmailer, that would explain many things from the beginning, because she seems to be another manipulator just like me, maybe less trained, but that would certainly not explain why we didn't have sex last night. If I were my blackmailer, of course, well, having sex with the person I am blackmailing would be the ultimate thing.

Curiously, I didn't hear that much traffic outside, and even not a lot of people. I listened to some car passing by, but they were driving slowly. What actually intrigued me was the white light coming from the outside. I really have no idea where we could have crashed, but if I were fucked up yesterday when we left, I am sure we wouldn't have gone far away from Kléber Avenue. Well, that doesn't mean anything, on the other hand, we could have taken a cab and gone on the other side of Paris, or even outside Paris. But, meh. I started to touch my face and... Oh, god, I drooled last night again? If I drool, I don't get it, it means that I slept very well, then how comes that I am that tired, actually? That is weird.

I yawned a second time, after a couple of seconds watching all around me, and I turned my head towards the nightstand on the other side, when I remarked one thing (a weird one, actually): my phone was there, plugged. I was in charge of a charger that was obviously not mine because I didn't take it before leaving yesterday. She indeed lent me her charger. I stretched my arms another time, I rubbed my eyes by instinct, and here it is, time to get up. But as I was desperately hungry, I first sat up, and it was tough because, given the fact that I am feeling a bit weak, I felt dizzy. Like if I was feeling all the blood stored in my head suddenly going down or a lack of blood pressure, but it didn't take long. I feel that almost every morning. In the meantime, I heard her still typing on her keyboard, again, and again. It took me a few seconds to actually recover from that, then, when I put my two feet on that wooden floor, I felt like it was so cold, like, it has never been that cold ever.

At the very moment I actually put my feet on the floor, I heard her stop typing, suddenly standing up, and walking. But I was exhausted, I was literally drained, fed up, and just wanted to eat something, go home, and sleep, especially since I was feeling so slow this morning. Hopefully, I still had my clothes on. And, when I actually took my phone, wanting to check what was on the news today, I heard her opening the door, so I immediately turned myself. And, yeah, I saw her. Same as me, barely wakened up. Surprised, she looked at me, sat on the bed, and said:

"Oh, here you are, sleeping beauty?"

"Hey," I smiled at her.

"You were sick all night! Oh my god, I really don't understand how you managed to actually sleep like this. I came many times to check on you, check if you were still okay and alive, because..."

"Oh, was that so terrible?"

"Trust me..."

"Damn..."

To be fair, I could see on her face that she had a rough night. All the makeup she wore yesterday was gone, and... it actually displayed a more masculine look. Right now, she was just wearing a top, at the colour of the Guns'n'Roses. A black one. And given that she was wearing women underwear, I have the confirmation that she actually had surgery. But she seemed very tired, her eyes were red, and as she yawned at the very end, I mean, just before I said my "damn". She must have been transitioning for a while now. After she yawned, well, she just checked over me, and... At the same time, I saw my shoes left near the window, dropped adequately.

"Oh, before to go... I really hope that you took some other clothes..." she made the remark.

"Oh, why?"

"Well, it's kind of snowing outside! And there are no taxis available out there!"

"Oh, shit. Okay, I'll find a way, thanks!"

Holy crap, yeah, I forgot that I saw the weather forecast yesterday and they said it was supposed to snow today. Well, forecasts are forecasts, and you never expect forecasts to actually take place. When she left, I stood up. I wasn't going yet,

I was just about to unplug my phone and take it with me, but it became problematic when I put my two feet on the floor because one more time I was feeling dizzy. After I took my phone, first, I looked at the time, 10:10am. Wow, so the might must have been long, I guess. I really have no idea at what time I started to sleep. That was the lock screen, and underneath and I could actually see that, well, "4 missed calls" only. Okay, who called me? I unlocked the phone, opened the telephone app, and there, yeah, no surprises: Mum called me twice, once in half-past seven and then at eight forty. Clarisse called me five minutes after my mother's second call, and Florent ten minutes ago. If my twin called me before Florent, it means that there's a problem. And, I curiously have an idea on what the problem may be. Yeah, "what are you doing, you're not at school?". Oh, fuck off...

Immediately afterwards, after having looked at my missed calls – no voicemails by the way... surprising – I went back to the main screen, to open my GPS. To know precisely where I was. I opened the app, and I saw: I was located in some hotel close to the Champs-Elysées avenue. Fine, and I checked the metro, which seemed to be working. Ugh! It's not suspended. But I think I should better hurry up before it is stopped. Hopefully, the closest station is George V, a station on the first line, my line to go back home, so it's going to be fast. As we say, it's time to take the French leave! Yeah, because as it's snowing... okay, even if it's underground, but they should shut it soon because parts of my metro line are over the ground, especially towards where I live. Anyway, with my phone on my hand, I went towards the door, and I reached a small hallway leading to the rest of the hotel suite, which was a sort of living room, still curiously plunged into thick darkness. This corridor, rectangular-shaped, led through that living room, and on the left was the main door, after the coat rack, where my coat was hanging. My handbag as well, all them next to her jacket and her purse. Okay, so, this is here. On the right, I assume it's the bathroom or something, as, well... Yeah.

I didn't really pay attention to the living room, even though I saw that Allison was still on her computer because I could hear the constant typing on the keyboard, I just wanted to know where the bathroom was, because, well, I tried to pee. I also wanted to know where my coat was, and I found everything. I still had my phone in my hand when I entered. And I quietly closed the door, taking care not to make any noise, and I felt that the floor was literally icy. Yeah, well, if it's snowy, it's sure that the temperature dropped dramatically, I wouldn't be homeless at that hour. I will enjoy coming back home, I guess. Well, the first thing I did, because it was the toilets, even if there was a bathtub next to it, I went to seat on the bathroom, and once sat, well, I immediately felt like delighted just by the fact to let my bladder emptying itself. And, now, just like most of the time, I am peeing. I assume it's the same for the rest of the humankind now. At the same time, I checked on my phone, especially on the RATP website (the authority in charge of public transportation in Paris), to check if they scheduled closures of some lines due to the weather conditions. But it looks like there's nothing, I mean, no lines affected, except the bus, most of the buses are now no longer working. Suddenly, as I was scrolling back, I received a call. Clarisse... Oh, Clarisse... here you are, back again...

"*Hallo, sestra!*" I immediately replied after having taken the call.

"Hy honey, what's up? Oh, and mostly, where are you now?"

"I'm fine, and I am near the house. I mean, on my way back home."

"Okay. You'd better hurry up because they said they plan to close the metro after twelve."

"Okay, I was just checking. But thanks. Is Claire at school now?"

"Nope!"

"What about Kelly?"

"She's here, yes."

"Okay."

"Wanna speak to her?"

"No, darling, I don't want to have your phone dirty."

"Okay. Also, mum is not working today, because of the weather, and this morning, she was pissed because you were not at school, so she's waiting for you now..."

"Jesus fucking Christ. And there are gonna be no ways to avoid her since it's snowing out there..."

"Well, actually, yeah, there are no ways out..."

"Fine, I'll confront her... One more time..."

"Okay. Anyway, I'm coming back home now, I'll see you there, then."

"Okay darling, see you at home," I concluded before hanging up.

There is this thing I never understood, in American TV series or films (I don't know why I am suddenly thinking about that), they never say "bye" before they hang up. That's so fucking disrespectful. Anyway, yeah, there's also this, Clarisse always tells me that it's disgusting to be on the phone while peeing. Is it? Everybody does that nowadays; come on. I mean, I hope so. Anyway, regarding my mother, yeah. Well, even if I wanted to go to school, it would have been aborted, given the fact that it's snowing outside, and I really don't understand why she's so pissed. Last Tuesday, I cut school because I was sick, and she didn't say anything. Now, she wants to piss me off for some details, again. I don't really understand; on Tuesday, she was friendly with me, and suddenly, she switches.

On the other hand, I still didn't apologise from what I said last Sunday and, erm, yeah. Whenever she finds something that she can use against me, she will use it. She's so moody, I am fed up to have to deal with that.

Once I was done, so a few seconds later, I left the toilets, when I actually had an idea: there was an empty bag near the sink, next to two packages of medicine, I assume her hormonal treatment. Well, if I were her, I wouldn't leave that here, but it's up to her. This small plastic bag came from a pharmacy, and I think, well, this bag can confirm something, actually: what is that person hiding from me. I am sure she is a cop. To be honest, she was playing her game very well, and... It's hard to describe, as she looked in her twenty-five or something, but I tend to think that she is older than twenty-five. Over the sink was a small closet, and it seemed like quite full: a lot of makeup product, razors, a lot of creams, like... She certainly had more cosmetic products than I had in my own bathroom. That could be explained by the fact that she's transgender; obviously, you can easily recognise a trans woman by her overuse of makeup, thing that "classic" woman does not do (and, no, that's not a cliché). But curiously, I saw yesterday that her makeup seems to be discreet. And I saw her face this morning, she doesn't seem to have any skin problem or anything—Hum, curious.

So, I blew on that bag, making sure that it would be fully inflated, and hide it behind me. Meanwhile, I kept on hearing her, and she was still typing on her keyboard, she always seems to be working. I just didn't flush, not to make any noise, so she couldn't expect me to suddenly leave the toilets as she is so into her work. Seeing her will be quick, because she was sitting on a small desk that is along the wall of the main door, typing on her laptop. And... Yeah, I know, that's an old prank, but today it's a vital prank. Suddenly, I opened the door, making sure that I was opening when she was still typing. It went rapid: after I opened the door, I swiftly looked at her to make sure that she'd be busy as the door doesn't make that much of a noise, I took the bag, and with my two hands, made it explode very unexpectedly. It made like a kind of loud "bang" noise... But what I wanted to observe is her reaction to that prank. When she suddenly looked at me, so the direction where the bang came, she saw me, smiling. However, I noticed that after the bag exploded, with her left hand, she actually put it at the level of her pelvis, like she wanted to grab a thing that she didn't have. I was curious... It works for real, it's crazy.

"The fuck!" she started to yell, surprised after she quickly placed her hand back to her laptop.

"That was just a little prank. Good morning!" I was happy, I had results.

"Yeah, good morning!"

Well, well, yeah. That is funny. She actually relaxed, like, breathed... and, yeah. Meanwhile, deep inside, I was happy, I got my answer: she can be either a criminal, either a cop, given the fact that instinctively, under the surprise of a loud bang, her first reaction was to actually seek a weapon to defend herself that she may have with her, even if she doesn't have anything on her except her clothes. This is why I blew up that bag, to scare her. When people are scared, it reveals their true nature. That confirms why she didn't sleep with me then.

"Are you okay?" I still asked, just in case.

"Yeah, I'm fine, yeah, erm... Do you want a coffee or anything?"

"Hum, yeah, that would have been with pleasure, but, as I am kind of scared that transports would stop at some point today."

"Meh, you still have a minute, don't you? Moreover, you'd better eat something as you were sick, and you look like a zombie right now."

"By the way, what do you mean, when you say I was sick?"

"Well, I think you drank a little too much. But be not afraid, you didn't throw up, you just fell asleep when we came back here and, erm... You were mumbling some words; I just couldn't understand. And, you've been coughing all night, coughing at the point you almost chocked yourself many times."

"I mumbled some words?"

"Yeah, but it was almost inaudible. I didn't get anything of what you said!"

"Okay."

"Did it ever happen to you, like choking as you did?"

"Nope, that's a first one."

"If I were you, darling, I'd see a doctor."

So, I mumbled things. On the other hand, the next day, when you throw up, you feel weird, you feel like you threw up. And I didn't feel like I did that, so she may have told the truth. What she might be hiding is, the words I have said. Given the fact that lying is a reality for me, and also given the fact that I blacked out for a second time, I may have escaped details that she actually heard and will keep secret as things that I mumbled thus she didn't listen. Whatever happened, I will certainly never know the truth, because if I gave out sensitive things that night, well, she would never tell me, so I am not scared, she will keep it for herself.

"Okay, I'll see what I can do," I continued, thinking about the things I mumbled.

"Okay, erm... You still don't want a coffee? I mean, the metro will stop at twelve, you still have an hour."

"Okay then, but if we can make it quick?"

"No problem."

"I appreciate it, thanks."

At the same moment, when she actually stood up to go somewhere, well, I went to get my bag and my coat, so I was now ready to go. I still have my pumps in my bag, so I took them, because, yeah, it's snowing. My feet will be frozen, I should have thought about today, and... took the weather forecasts a bit more seriously. I went back to get my shoes in the bedroom to place them in my handbag. When I thought that, well, Florent is undoubtedly home. I hope not, but he is surely waiting for me at home. Well, if I get a dress... I don't know, I'll tell him something, I have no idea what. Geez, I am so done with him, it's crazy, always justifying myself on what I do, I am really done with that. Well, I can tell him that I was invited to a party yesterday, and I slept at a friend's place, and... Geez, yeah. I am done with this. I am so done with that.

At the same moment, I mean, after I placed my shoes in my handbag and closed it, at the same time, I heard the first coffee coming. Well, a Nespresso machine and the capsule breaking... I have the same at home. I just hope that this is good coffee, because, as I do not drink that much coffee, I am more into teas or hot chocolate, I have very restricted taste in coffee. I love Clooney's favourite, the one he is talking all the time on TV... And, I remember, I even asked when mum ordered the last time in our local store if even George could deliver the coffee straight. They said that it would probably be a bit more expensive and includes delivery charge. "My favourite, very nice choice", well I must admit that he knows how to choose his coffee, though. Anyway, meanwhile, I saw a mirror just next to the toilet door.

Obviously, curiosity took over, I looked at myself. Well, as I had my coat, well, I could see that my dress was somehow folded and, my hairs were messy. I still had my makeup from yesterday, it was almost intact, it didn't move that much. But, my hair, oh my god... It's been a while that I didn't comb them, I am sure that the next time I will do that, it's gonna be hilarious. Especially since I am a damn pussy and yell all the time something hurts me, or I have to untie my hairs... It's why I never tie them, because... Well. Usually, when I wash my hairs, they look like untied and perfect. I'll do it later today, maybe. But, yeah, as my makeup remained intact, it is proof that nothing actually happened. I just hope that Florent will not see me like this because this will raise questions. Maybe I will make sure that I will text him to actually know where he is whenever I am close to home. I hope that he is still at his mum's, and for once, it is okay if he remains trapped there for like a couple of days. I need to do sensitive things, and having him in my feet won't make my life easier.

I didn't want to enter into her living room, I actually wanted to remain near the entrance to leave fast. Staying there would mean that I am in a rush, but curiously, I was in that mood that, honestly, whether I find Florent or not when I come back home, I don't really care. Well, if I have to have an argument with him, then let it be. Sometimes, it's good to actually clear things, and... Ironically, to be fair, I do not feel like I am in a relationship right now. I am and always will remain a free bird. He's just my boyfriend (I mean, fiancé, but I don't know if that really counts), he's nothing else. And, well, the fact that I am pregnant now, well. Meh. Anyway, I actually leaned next to her mirror, and I could see how her living room was set up, and yeah, it was like a hotel suite. She does not live here, or unless she is wealthy, but I don't think that's the case. Or her employer pays for here, this can actually be possible. She didn't personalise anything, her living room was just soulless like she just passed and was supposed to leave soon.

There was not a lot of things in her living room, though. I don't really know where the kitchen was, indeed hidden somewhere, but there were not many things. The decoration was relatively modern, I mean, furniture in this room seemed to be quite modern, probably coming from Ikea. The small desk, stuck on the wall where the main door was, stood in the middle of this wall, just before some huge closet or wardrobe, but it was opened. Astonishingly, it's where her clothes were. It was open, so I could see everything. There was a sofa in the middle of the room, standing a bit far from the windows behind... I assume it was a balcony or something like this. But given the fact that there was absolutely no personalisation of this room, she didn't want to personalise anything, I assume that obviously, this was a cover-up, she was not living here and was here temporarily. At least to welcome us. So... I waited in there. Seeing that room confirmed what I actually thought, she was a cop. But, not like a classic cop working for like the local precinct. No, she was a particular cop. This is why Claire told me to go to her.

In addition to that, I didn't really know anything about her, that was, yeah. Because I am sure that what she said was basically more or less than a smokescreen. I think she must be around twenty-five, but I think, yeah, she must be older than this. Because to be fair, she doesn't look like her age. And, moreover, her accent doesn't lie, even if she pretends to hide it, I can still hear that she's Irish. Hum... Let's see what's next, maybe she will call me back, I don't know. Well, if she plugged my phone... I think she must have taken my number, or... She may have asked Claire and knows me well already. Anyway... I was still leaning in the entrance for maybe like a minute when she actually finished her two coffees. Suddenly, she shouted:

"Hey, Charlotte, your coffee is ready, come here!"

"Hum, thank you, but I really don't have time, do you think you may give it to me here?" He said to me, happy to serve me.

"Okay, how many sugars?"

"Two should be fine."

"Okay."

She came a few seconds later with her two coffees. She put it in mini cups, it was, well... So, I actually drank it fast, it was just an expresso, it's not something that takes time to drink. Even though it was hot. And, before sipping her coffee, she came to me and gave me an envelope:

"Here you go. This is for you, erm... Joris has had his part, already."

"Cool, but I don't want it," I didn't take it.

"Are you sure, that's, erm...?"

"Trust me!"

"Okay, then. Well, that was fun, and erm... I'll call you soon, actually."

"You'll call me soon?"

"Yeah, I may need to talk to you more, there are things that we need to discuss. Just, expect my call!"

25 *Renegade*

// *Back home, Neuilly-sur-Seine.*

// *Friday, 18th of January 2013, 11:54*

Well... You know, that's life. I have been raised and actually really trained by my parents that, basically, whatever happens in your life, just take it, and shut up. And deal with it. I must admit that given my current situation, this was quite useful now. When I was a kid, I remember, my parents wanted me to see a psychologist. To give the perfect metaphor to this, basically, I went to see them because I was peeing when I slept. After a few seances and really so much money given away, I still pee at the bed. But now, I just don't really give a crap.

When I walked down, I actually realised that the situation into which I was currently involved was, well, of course perilous, but, well, I just have to carry on and deal with it. My girlfriend is trapped in a basically human trafficking scheme, just because she met an evil human, and now, I am here to deliver here. Honestly, I was thinking about atrocious things when I left the hall of the quite luxury hotel Allison was currently living: my deepest desire was to actually, not to kill Kelly. If it were legal, oh my god, she'd better hide. What I'd love to do would be to actually kidnap her, and torture her for days, and keeping her alive with so much medicine that even dead, she would be still alive and endure the pain until the very last second and her very last breath. Using excellent tools such as... Oh, my, there are so many things. And Joris, I'd removes his own testicles with a simple pair of scissors and make them eat with the sauce of his choice. What actually killed me at that moment was, Claire was in pain for something she didn't deserve. And attacking her, it's like attacking me. I just, yeah, I can't forget the despair I could see in her eyes yesterday.

And, today, well... Well, to be honest, I think it's time: I know that mum is waiting for me, with her mood swings, and I don't think I will stay there for long. Because, as it's for school, again, and again, I really don't want to talk about it. I have things to tell to Claire, I think that is a great moment to speak with her. So, I think, well, once at home, I will pack up some stuff, and I will take the weekend at Claire's house. I want to be with her. Just like old-time, because, well, now... I need my girlfriend; I need my girlfriend back. I want to have at least a weekend with her.

And regarding Florent and everything, now that I have my exit strategy, he is part of it: I will dump him on Monday, my decision is taken. I love Claire, and I know that she loves me back, and I don't see why I shouldn't be with her. I want life to have a sense, to be meaningful. I am done with a shitty life.

It's why, when I actually left that hotel, I was absolutely overwhelmed by the situation. This was still a lot since everything started, this was a damn lot, but unfortunately, I am so trained that so much more is actually required to make me collapse. Using Claire is like psychologic torture, but I can endure suffering, I think, because I know the capacity of my mind, and I know that I am so strong. Claire isn't that tough, and she must be destroyed. It's why, when I was out, discovering Paris under the snow, on my way to the metro, I decided to call her.

"Hey, honey!" I said when she took the call.

"Hi, love," she seemed sad, like usual.

"How are you? You okay?"

"Hum, well... I'm just out of the GP, and erm... No, I'm not okay, no..."

"What's going on?"

"I just went there to talk and... Because I can't sleep, I'm tired, and... Hopefully, I am home for the weekend, he finally decided to leave me this weekend, so... Anyway, it's nothing, I am just... I'm tired, that's all."

"Hum... You think I may come by later today?"

"Hum... How? They are planning to close the metro at twelve or maybe later this afternoon?"

"Well, darling, even if I had to walk to your place, I'd do it. I need to speak to you, and it's quite important. And erm... If you want, I can even stay for the weekend?"

"Well, I'd say yes, but... I just don't see how you may come. But, well, if you want to come, yeah, sure. We could... I just need to cook something, and... Yeah, sure!"

"I don't really mind eating. I just want to be with you... Just like old times. Sharing some time with you, having fun, and watching movies in the mattress that you will put in the living room!"

"Okay then, sure. But if you can help me with the mattress, to bring it downstairs..."

"Of course, no problem."

"Okay, then. Erm... See you later then."

"See you later... I love you," and I hung up before she would have the opportunity to reply.

When I arrived at the station, I actually saw that they planned to close their stations at twelve, and then close the service step by step. I could have enough time, I think, to be back home, change myself, pack up some stuff, and leave. If anything, I'll take my shower at Claire's. I'm not gonna take a thousand things because, given the fact that it was snowing quite heavily, I don't really think we may go out for a couple of days. Which is actually even better.

But the snow... Okay, I've seen snow in Paris already, but today, it was quite unusual. When I walked, I couldn't run, because the floor was icy and I may slide and fall, so I want to avoid a journey by the hospital, but... Wow, it was actually bizarre. I don't know for how long it has been snowing, but there was maybe certainly more than ten centimetres of snow on the floors. I just had a street to cross to actually join that station, George V, and even if it were maybe something like sixty metres away, I could already see people leaving their cars to actually walk. It must have started early in the morning. Moreover, it was frigid, the air was not that cold, but what made the weather icy was the snow agglutinated on the floor. The cold was coming from down, not up.

I walked down the streets very slowly. And it's funny, it was like the apocalypse. That reminded me, well, when I was younger in Montpellier, and it snowed, and dad had to come to pick us up at school to go back home. He couldn't do otherwise but by foot and we had to make quite a long walk under the snow. And, we had to pass through a roundabout where tramways were circulating... And, I still have that picture in my mind, this tramway had all its light switched off, and cars were left in the middle of the road like there was a zombie attack or something. That actually shocked me, just seeing that blue tramway being abandoned, just like that. Okay, I was young, I was maybe seven or something, and yeah. We had to walk along the tramway tracks at some point, and we could see even more being abandoned like this. I was almost like; this was so spooky. I don't remember precisely when it was, but, yeah, just that image of cars being abandoned on the banks of the roads and those tramways being left almost in an emergency, yeah.

But apparently today, it seems to be a nationwide problem. My phone has news alerts, and it was said that Marseilles and Lyon were also paralysed, just like Paris. They said it's like, yeah, massive. No wonder buses are already closed, and they are going to shut down the metro. I was sauntering, and... Well, maybe if I leave before twelve, I may have enough time to go to Claire's. Or... Well, I'll find a way. The journey for going back home wasn't that long, certainly less than fifteen minutes. In the metro, I received a text from Florent, stating that basically, given the fact that he woke up late and as he was still at his mum's, he may stay there for the weekend, or at least until public transports services are restored. I just shrugged off, and wondered, do whatever you want, not my problem. That's what I replied. I also think it's highly likely that Clarisse would stay at her boyfriend's place, as he lives near our College and... Well, so at least mum is gonna have the house for herself all alone. I also thought that, basically, thanks to the snow, Joris would leave us alone for at least a couple of days. I hope until Sunday.

And, finally, I arrived at my station. And the floor was slippery. I really didn't have the correct shoes to walk in the snow, but, well. It was why I was cautious. I walked towards the exit, and, well, again, in here, I didn't hear any sounds, which was quite astonishing when you are living in a big city. I walked out, and a few minutes later, at least after having walked almost two hundred metres and ensuring that I didn't fall, it was quite heroic, to be fair. Oh, and, yeah, the fancy thing of this morning was basically that, as all cars were left on the side of the road... I could walk freely on the road. That was really fun. Hopefully, at home, I have boots that are better to walk on the snow. And once arrived home, I had to go to the security office before, and, finally, within the building, it was warm. Trust me, to go back there, I know I'll wear heavy clothes. And that's what I did. After I walked towards the lift, took the lift, saw my legs wet and my feet were literally frozen, I finally managed to arrive home. And once I arrived, I didn't hear any sound, too. No TVs switched on, nothing. I closed the door whilst still remaining vigilant just if she may be waiting for me somewhere, and I may be trapped, as she uses to do sometimes. I actually walked, checked the living room, nothing. At the same time, I checked the kitchen and nothing too. Oh... Is she really there? I actually walked towards my bedroom with a kind of feeling of freedom, will I escape her? I hope so. And then, I walked towards my bedroom. And then, I opened the door. And then, guess who did I saw sitting on my bed? When I opened the door, she stood up.

"Charlotte!"

"Oh, damn, you found me!" I was startled.

"Where the hell are you coming from?"

"Oh, hum... Apparently, from the monkey, if we believe Darwin and the socialists."

"Tell me the truth, for God's sake!"

"You want the truth? Okay... Hum... Kennedy has not been killed by Oswald."

Hum, yeah. Maybe taking her for an idiot wouldn't be a great strategy, especially since she seemed like really pissed. But to be fair, I didn't mind. This morning, I was feeling free for once, I was feeling light, and I was okay. Ironically, she didn't seem that much pissed because I cut school this morning. There was something else. Especially since I could clearly see her hiding something, hiding her hands in the back. At the same time, I actually looked at my bathroom door, and it was open. And the light was turned on. Hum... If she was pissed if she was... Oh, my...

Don't tell me she's been smart enough to actually find it? On the other hand, well... Oh, I see, I understand several things now. It's my mistake when I left that bathroom after having found out what it was... Holy shit, I actually fucked up. I left it near the sink, and I just didn't pay attention. That explains why Florent went to his mum's and is acting kind of weird now because he doesn't text me just like he does all the time and... the fact that she is so pissed, because, I am sure she knows my intentions. Clarisse wouldn't have betrayed me, I know that, so it leaves only one person that could have done that: Florent. And, trust me, he's gonna pay for that.

"What the hell is this?" she showed me my pregnancy test.

"This is a pregnancy test!" I actually pretended that this thing was unknown to me.

Fuck, how could I have forgotten such a thing? I mean, this is basically a gross mistake, and I couldn't imagine that it would... That she would actually find out. I mean... Yeah. Okay, so, now, how turn things at my advantage? He could have spoken to me straight, I mean... Okay, well, now, everybody knows. I can deny it's mine, but it would be gross, I mean, I am sure she found the package open down there and, she's not stupid. I can also confront her, on, how comes that she found this and no matter what it is, this is my private life thus none of her business... Damn, I need a strategy. I need one now. Or I could refocus her, on actually trying to speak of the matter but I am sure her next move would be, why did I hide it. I really hope this is not coming from Clarisse, but damn... I have been so dumb; I shouldn't have forgotten this. Why did I conceal the fact that I am pregnant!

On the other hand, I don't really understand Florent's move, the very last thing he'd say to my mum would be that he knocked me up. It doesn't really make sense in some ways. His behaviour actually incriminates him, but... If I were Florent, why would I come to mum in law and say that, well, my girlfriend is pregnant, and I feel like she's hiding something? To convince me not to abort, maybe, but this doesn't make sense, I know Florent, and he would have confronted me first. This is really weird from Florent. Anyway, let's see how things go before actually making a decision on how to counter-attack.

"I assume that this thing belongs to you!"

"It actually depends where you actually found it."

"And given the fact that I found it into your bathroom, then I assume that this is yours!"

"Hum... Yeah. I guess this is mine!" I was seeking a strategy or a way to make sure that she would attack me first. Because if I attack first, it's done for me.

"Charlotte, are you pregnant?"

"I might."

"Why are you hiding it? Florent found it, and he told me that he was actually scared to confront you. He was not so confident, because he knew that confront you on this point... So, I don't understand, Charlotte, clearly. Why didn't you speak about your pregnancy if you are pregnant?"

"Well, I just found this out a couple of days ago!" I actually moderated the situation to make sure she would attack and confirm my pregnancy whilst not admitting it. "I just wanted to keep that for me, to make sure that this would be actually none of your business. I didn't want Florent to know because that is not something that actually concerns him. And, I don't want that baby, I'm gonna abort," I actually decided to spread gasoline so she would ignite the fire.

"Oh... Did I hear that right?"

Basically, and we can't really blame her for that, mum is coming from an old Catholic family. Because she was the only daughter and has been raised with those values, homosexuality and abortions are two crazy sins in her family. A couple of days ago, she said that basically abortion is like killing a human being and should be forbidden. A man against abortion doesn't really make sense to me, but to be honest, a woman against abortion, it's just... Well, I have no example to compare to the aberration this actually is. It looks like if you say that the Earth is the centre of the Universe, it is flat and the sun turns around it. If you say that, it's going to become evident that you are a brainless worthless moron. Women against abortion, it's basically the same process to me. And even, we are in 2013, the law was adopted in France in 1975, and now... It's not even a question to me on whether I am for or against abortion.

Nevertheless, there are still people that believe abortion is a sin and... they must be respected because otherwise, you're racist or ...-phobic or something... Unfortunately, there are no words for people that hate morons. Which is my case. So, stating abortion... It was like Galileo that actually said to the inquisition that Earth spin on itself. Except that, Inquisition, I openly pee on them.

"Yes, you heard that right, I'm gonna abort. And, let me clarify this point, whether or not you're okay with that, I do not give a shit!" I actually proudly looked at her and smiled.

"You cannot do that!"

"Oh, why? God disagrees with me? Damn it, I forgot him..."

"This is Florent's baby as well, and I do think that as the father, he is perfectly entitled to have his word on it. You were two to have this baby, and Florent may certainly want to have his word on this!"

"This is Florent's baby... I'm not really sure of this..."

"I BEG YOUR PARDON?"

"I was kidding, come on... chill!" I actually laughed.

LOL.

Anyway, let's pretend that this is the truth because she thinks that guys actually care today, that's breaking news. I recall that say when I made that prank, suggesting that I was pregnant, he was panicking on the phone. He said that he wants a baby, but we are both not ready to be parents, because our couple is not stable. On the other hand, she confirmed that she knew that from Florent, and thus, it becomes clear that Florent wants certainly to use my mother to actually put pressure over me. Obviously, because he wants me to keep that baby. That's very coward from him, it's surprising. Either way, this is not going to work, I am sorry.

"He certainly doesn't have his word to say. None of us is ready to have a kid because we are not a strong couple. I don't really love him, I tried, I did my best, but I don't love him. I can't have a child with him," I actually started to defend myself, on the purpose that she may report that to him.

"This is genuinely unwholesome... This is his baby, he is also part of this, no matter what you say. Whether you loved him or not, you still have that baby now," she actually curiously remained calm and tried to explain.

"It was an accident! I just forgot to take my pill for a couple of days and, that was an accident!"

"Charlotte, for God's sake, a child cannot be an accident. It was not an accident when I was waiting for you and your sister, I was proud of it, and the situation for me by that time was even worst, we were both with your dad looking for a job, and I didn't even speak French, which made things worse for me, and we didn't have all the money you have!"

It's actually at that moment that I had an idea. The word accident inspired me, because this pregnancy is, erm... I know some other pregnancy that actually turned into an accident. My stepsister is the perfect example of it. And if I just say the word "Aurelie", which is her name, I don't think she's gonna love it. Because Aurelie basically ruined her marriage, I am sure that she considers her life worthless and if she could have been aborted when she was an embryo, that wouldn't have been a problem for her. Let's see how it goes... Oh, and Aurelie is basically our stepsister, which means she's Clarisse and my sister's, and... She lives in Pau, in the south of France with our dad and her mum. Well, at least that's what I know from several years ago since I didn't hear about dad for the last six years. Obviously, mum hates my stepsister (shocking...) and hates her father and mother. If she had a gun, for sure, I know who would be her three first targets.

"And what about Aurelie?"

"Why on Earth are you talking to me about that little cunt!"

"She must be sixteen right now, by the time, right?"

My point is, by refocusing on my stepsister is, I want to personify her. By this, it recreates the image she can have or her into her mind. Using those details, like her age, like... her name, basically, she's still terribly upset and hugely angry against all them. And this is my point, using her anger against her will definitely spark whatever argument she may have against abortion and leave me alone. In the meantime, it would make sure she would have a wrong time, which is something that I actually kind of like somehow.

"Why the fuck are you talking about that piece of trash?" she started to lose control.

"She must be happy, with her dad and mum... Certainly, she would start College, just like I did a couple of years ago. Having a boyfriend..."

"Okay, go to your point, now!" she actually now lost control, as I saw her swiftly turning red.

"I am sure you would definitely be tenfold fortunate is that piece of trash, as you said, would never have been born!" I actually felt like I gained control over the conversation.

Yeah, basically, that's the problem with Catholics... Do what I say, but don't do what I do. Same with politicians or scammers. More or less. Fucking religious... Because the point is, she does agree with me on that very point. Surely, she would have been tenfold more fortunate if my stepsister would have never existed. She may have never discovered that my father was an unfaithful waste. Yes, there are a couple of lives that are definitely worthless for a couple of people. I mean, if that kid would have never existed, that would have certainly saved her wedding. And indeed, made me a better person, even though it was already fucked up for my part. Han... I was like, now, you're screwed, you basically cannot reply by any other thing but bollocks. And, honestly, I was kind of proud of myself on that.

"That is not the same, Charlotte, come on!" she actually wanted to redirect me.

"That's exactly the same. Dad put his dick on someone else's vagina and after having leaked the magic fluid, nine months later came that magic surprised called Aurelie. I mean, come on, you already forgot how things are going?" I redirected her back from the main topic, this time a bit more harshly to actually trigger an attack coming from her.

"Shut up, Charlotte, SHUT UP! This... That... This is completely different!"

"My body, my womb, my choice. That's exactly the same because I don't want to give birth to a kid that will have both his parents fighting over his control and hearing all his life that his dad is a son of a bitch and his mother is a whore. Just like you guys did when you split up and divorced. If someday I have a kid, which is unlikely to happen, I would certainly do not make the same as you."

"You'll never forgive us, huh?"

"Why would I forgive two wankers that pretended once to be stable and split two twin sisters apart?"

"The two wankers, as you said, are your parents, first. Second, Charlotte... I know you are different; you won't be the mistakes that your parents did. I know you'll never mess up with your kids."

"I don't want to have kids, final point."

"Charlotte, you are pregnant! Come on, you must deal with that, this is part of your responsibility!"

"And I am already dealing with that, my first appointment for abortion is already booked."

No, it's not booked yet. I just have to make the call, but... I am kind of busy right now, I'll certainly do it next Monday. The thing is, I just want her to know that I am determined and given the fact that I broke all her possible arguments, she basically doesn't have anything. She's screwed because no matter what I say, I am right. But, curiously, this morning, I was feeling her like giving up, almost shrugging off to what I may say on the future. She just looked at me, but... This was a weird fight, I mean, I was already defending myself, I was already preparing how to take over the conversation, but I feel like... I don't know. She seemed despaired, like totally giving up the fight, I thought that would be tougher because mum is somewhat resistant to my manipulation, but curiously... I felt like she was, I don't know, yeah, giving up. That is actually very curious. Somehow, she sees that she cannot win and whatever happens, I will remain in control of what I want, and I won't be influenced. When, suddenly, she stood up from my bed. And, on a surer and certainly calmer tone, she restarted:

"There are no reasons that could actually change your mind anyway, huh?"

"Nope!" I remained clear.

Then, she slowly walked towards me. And it was just in space on a few microseconds, I have seen nothing coming as I was focused on looking at her straight into her eyes. When, yeah, suddenly, I felt a hard impact on my right cheek. It was so violent that it made me turn the head and slightly lose my balance, for a couple of seconds later. I actually felt like if millions of tiny wasps were stinging my cheek. This was just unexpected; I couldn't say anything. In the meantime, in my mind, I felt like, okay, she slapped me, fine, then I made her really upset. I actually touched my cheek, absorbing the slight humiliation, and thinking already about the retaliation, because there will be one. After maybe a few seconds, after she obviously slapped me and after I touched my cheek, she was somehow proud of her:

"Keep on fucking up your life, Charlotte. Someday I am sure you'll regret it!"

26 *Wake me up when you need me*

// Claire's house.

// From Friday to Sunday, 20th of January 2013.

The thing in manipulation is, whatever happens, you must never get defeated, you must always seek the perfect equation that will finally find a way to triumph yourself over the person you're manipulating. Otherwise, you are a pathetic manipulator. When you want to be a great manipulator, the proper thing is to find a solution until the very last minute. Like a pilot, you must always find a solution before to crash to save lives. Even though sometimes crash is inevitable, you must deal with a solution, and this until the very end... But usually, when you are an excellent manipulator, things actually never end. It's just maths, more or less. To compare the pilot with the manipulator, the equation is basically more or less straightforward: the crash is the end of a relationship with the person you are manipulating. Lives on board are representing your interests. And, since in both cases it's just a question of maths, if you're gonna be good or not, you must always save your own interests and cover your arse. Oh, yeah, because the first rule is, the people you are manipulating are basically, well... just tools to finally get what you want. You want to be a great manipulator, consider people like credit cards or... whatever you want from them. But do not consider the human side. Otherwise, it's gonna prevent you from sleeping at night.

Free Expensive Lies: Prologue

So, basically, my mother actually told me more than I could ever expect: Florent's betrayal, because I was at least expecting from him that he would deal with my pregnancy discreetly, now, I had the perfect argument to finally dump his arse. They thought that I was fucked, it's just that, well, basically, I am like a phoenix, I always come back from my own ashes. But, ironically, this story kind of helps me: as my relationship with my mother is breaking down, now I have the perfect argument to actually trigger a war with my mother, dumping Florent simultaneously, which will make Claire's come back ways easier. We just do what I planned yesterday evening, and then, we just go to Roissy, take the first plane, and get the fuck out of here. I will be hated, my mother will never want to talk to me again, well, that doesn't sound a big deal for me. Florent will see me like a whore... It's a shame because I wanted him as a friend, but, fine, fair enough, I'm okay with that. We cannot please everyone anyway. Anyway, I planned to leave already, but now I may have an opportunity to go with Claire, which actually sounds better than what I expected.

But now I needed to implement that. I don't know if Allison will call me back again, but at least for now I am alone, so I think that Claire is trustworthy for that kind of job. I could hear her, like, since everything started, I know that this is absolutely atrocious for her and I want to pull her out of this. But she's gonna be perfect for that job, given the fact that she's morally exhausted of what happened. She's just done with everything, and it makes her the ideal candidate for that. Even if she knows what's at stake, I think I will just not tell her the whole strategy, I will monitor her instead, push her to go to Joris, explaining part of what I want, explaining precisely that I want her to sleep with him so he can get the statutory rape charge. Still, I will not explain to her how I want her to go there, I will just let her do her stuff. Because this must not appear as like a bait, this must appear as unsuspicious. If I tell Claire what I want from her, I am sure things will appear to Joris as usual and whenever he sleeps with her... Well, we'll see at this point who's fucked the most.

Hum, yeah, I know, she's my girlfriend, and she's the one I love. Using her for one of my tricks doesn't actually make me have fun because she will have to endure everything. She will have to sleep with Joris, she will have to do lots of things, and it doesn't please me at all, I just don't want her to do that. I don't want her to do that, but this is the only way out. In the meantime, as she's not feeling good, she needs at least a weekend of confidence. She needs to understand that I am backing her, and no matter what, I will be there. This is why, after that argument, I packed my stuff, I actually changed myself to get a bit more comfortable as I will have to walk outside. I took like my everyday stuff, like my black and pink pullover, black trousers and some big boots, and over it, I took the oversized orange coat that I bought for going in the French Alps a couple of years ago. And, yeah, I left.

Hopefully, I could leave right on time, which means that I could finally catch almost the last train going southbound, and I was also lucky enough to actually get the last metro. It was practically empty, I mean, the carriage into which I sat was merely unoccupied. And when I took the metro in the line going towards her place, I decided to call her when I was actually sure to go to her home. At least for letting her know that I was on my way to her place. Because to be honest, this weekend, I want her to be okay, and to think about something else. And it was with a kind of weak voice that she actually replied:

"Yes, Cha?"

"Hey. Hum, I am sure you'd be glad to know that I could finally manage to get a metro to actually come to your place!" I was somehow amused.

"Oh, that's great, I wasn't expecting you to finally come. Well, I'm just back from shopping, I bought some stuff for lunch, and we can make a raclette together tonight. I'm not sure if mum will be there, but Either way, we can make it together, what do you think?"

Raclette is a typical French dish that we eat at a party. That's just some special melted cheese on baked potatoes, I love it. It's usually a winter dish, but it will certainly make the thing more magic since it's snowing today. I like her mum, I mean, she's a fantastic lady, and... Because she works in a hospital, I'm not really sure that she can make it through tonight. Well, if we are only together, that can be good, I think.

"I think that it's an excellent idea, honey," I confirmed.

"Did you call me 'honey', or I had a hallucination?" she was actually surprised.

"No, I said it. And erm, Claire. We need to talk," I wanted her to actually understand that something is going to happen this weekend.

"Oh, Cha, please don't say that; I really don't need a bad thing, I know what you mean when you usually say that we need to talk, I'm not in the mood," she actually defended herself.

"I know you're not in the mood. That's why we need to talk."

Free Expensive Lies: Prologue

"Please, I'm just not feeling good at all today... So, I just... Well, we can also talk here."

"Well, I prefer it to be private. And face to face."

"Okay then, erm... Well, then, I'm home, and waiting for you."

"Sure. I'll be certainly there in a minute!"

"Take your time. Anyway, see you in a bit, I love you, bye."

"I love you too, bye," and I hung up.

Because, yeah, basically I have a plan. Here, too. We cannot call this actually a plan, but, well, anyway.

It didn't take long before I arrive. I was like, yeah, last time I actually went there, it was before everything starts. I just cannot believe that we've been there, I mean, so many things happened. It's odd; when I was at school and playing sinister plans to piss off someone, Claire used to be mad at me, but, now, I am sure she will swiftly change her mind.

When I finally arrived at the Ivry Townhall station, well... The street was desert, but I could see that the snow became actually kind of heavy. I mean, there was at least more than twenty centimetres of snow on the floor. It's always fun to walk in the snow, I mean... As long as you wear good shoes, your feet get frozen even if you wear appropriate shoes. You have to walk quite slowly, make sure you do not rush, and lift your legs relatively high otherwise you're trapped and cannot move forward. I kind of like it, because it seems like the snow is making a soft floor and, whenever you walk on it, it collapses under your feet. The problem is, the road levels, and given the fact that the main road I have to cross to go to Claire is covered with potholes, I need to be extra careful upon walking. Hopefully, her house is just behind a small square in front of the station, so not much to walk. Especially since my backpack is quite heavy as I took quite a few stuff... Even if I don't think we're gonna leave her house for the weekend, as the snow seems thick and I don't think it's gonna melt during the next night or the next day. It may take a while.

And then I arrived at Claire's house. It was almost 1.30. The travel was quite long, especially since they were closing the station. I knocked at her door, and I was at the same time covering my face with the fleece hood of my coat, as the wind started to raise, which made the cold basically harsher. I didn't hear that much noise from outside, except the TV on and she was watching the news flash, just like every day when she's not at school. I heard her walking, at least standing up from her sofa and walking towards the door; she was in her living room. And, yeah, she opened. And, at the moment she opened the door, well... I saw her face. She was pale, it doesn't seem like she ate recently. She was feeling sick, except that she wasn't ill at all. She was wearing an old blue pyjama that she has for a long time, and... She seemed exhausted. Like, literally shattered, I could see her mental exhaustion through her facial expression. Well... It's why I started with humour, as my coat was orange, I impersonated Kenny McCormick and his mumblings as I covered my face after I saw her face. Almost detached and merely depressed, she barely replied:

"Oh my god, they killed Kenny..."

"You bastards!" I uncovered my face, laughing.

She actually let me enter. I closed the door behind me, and, upon entering, I was feeling like arriving on another planet. She basically drew all the curtains, she put herself in total darkness, the only thing that provided light was her TV. And, on the table, I saw something I never saw... Especially from Claire that never wanted to take this: antidepressants. But, like the strong ones. Doors were closed, the living room was slightly messy, and, yeah, a box of tissue just next to where she sat. Some used tissues...

On the other hand, when she opened, her eyes were red, like slightly red, she basically just cried. Her phone was also turned, like thrown forcefully on the floor, behind her table... And not in her hands as it used to be. I just entered, saw her going back where she was sitting, and I observed things. I dropped my bag, removed my coat and gloves, and yeah... When I entered in the living room to see all this after I observed her phone on the floor, I actually started taking the bulls by the horns:

"Oh, wow... What is it like, depression party today? You planned to open your veins in half an hour? How does this work today?" I remained detached, like pushing her to actually stop depressing.

"Oh, please!", she actually almost whispered, "Spare me your touches of sarcasm. I'm not okay today, shit happens."

"And what happened, someone broke up with you?"

"Charlotte... Sometimes I wish I'd be like you, not caring about human lives and just focusing on results and getting what you actually want!"

"Meh, it's just a question of training. But I think I know what's the problem. Just give me a minute!"

"Wait, what are you doing?" she actually turned her head to see what I wanted to do.

Yeah, because she knew just like me that she could be listened. And as she's like me and a bit paranoid especially when it comes to new technologies, as you never know whether your phone is actually listening to you instead of you listening to it, I went behind the table and grabbed her phone. I took mine out of my pocket and then went to her kitchen. Simultaneously, she actually stood up because she was intrigued: she knows that I know. So, she just wanted to see if I was doing the right thing. Remember the Faraday cage? I took both our phones and put them in the microwave. Obviously, I unplugged the microwave and closed the door, so at least, no reception and no possible incident. At the same time, she just looked at me, she was like, "you're weird", and I closed the door of her kitchen. Now, you're free to speak. Because phones can be a particular threat, and I want to kill that threat. At least, now, we can talk freely.

"Okay, so what's the problem now?" we went back into the living room.

"Why did you put my phone in the microwave?" she was feeling like a new problem was coming.

Claire is not someone who speaks, especially when there is a huge problem or something she's ashamed of. When she wants to hide something, she will hide it very well, even if you prove that she's somehow related or responsible for that problem, Claire will never talk. But since I know her for seven years, and I basically know how she works, and obviously how to get what I want from her, the position was now perfect: I went to her sofa, at the place she was sitting, and sat. At the same time, she was standing behind her other couch, and I know that this is intimidating for her: whenever we had an argument, and whenever she lost the fight, she was always standing, and I was always sat. It's like a kind of a destabilisation process to her, seeing me sitting when she is standing, basically, in her mind, we do not have the same strength. This is bad, it's somehow putting her under pressure, but I want to know the truth, I need to know the truth. So, it's the reason I continued speaking, now with a more aggressive tone, almost interrupting her, to increase the pressure over her, mostly since she is completely lost and destroyed now:

"Your phone is like my phone, right now, we both know that we are spied on by some jerk. You know that, and I also know that. Because you are not stupid, because I am not stupid, and because I know the truth and I also know that just like I am, you are also blackmailed. Someone wants you, and this is why I am here today. Yesterday, you sent me to that person, Allison or whatever her name is. This person... It means something, and I want to know why. Listen, Claire... Having sex with weirdos is not something that amazes me just like you. We both do things that we do not want to do. And if I accepted to do that, when your fucking friend named Kelly pushed me into that... It was only for you, for saving your damn arse! So now, unless you want to keep hiding shit from me, I want to know, and I want to know what THE FUCK is going on with you!"

At that same moment, she went to sit, she came just next to me. I didn't want to be aggressive with her, I didn't want to push her into that, but I need to know what she's hiding because so far, all I have are just suppositions. These are only deductions, and I want to know if my conclusions are right to start to implement the exit strategy. And... Regarding the fact that we broke up, there are quite a few things I actually want to know. Again, this is not to piss her off. This is to confirm the truth.

She came closer to me and started to cry. To reassure her, to tell her that I am by her side, I took her immediately in my arms. Maybe my monologue was said with fierce and strength, perhaps in a regular time it would be like, I don't know, but this time, it actually broke her into pieces. Seeing her crying... this is something that first makes me upset and second destroys me. For me, Claire is all that matters, she's the only human on this planet that worth it. I just can't stand seeing her crying, it's just too much, and it's something that makes me upset, it makes me feel like I want to kill whoever made her cry. I had that feeling at that moment, but I needed to remain strong and override this to stay the one in charge, whatever it costs me.

"Charlotte, I'm fucked!"

"No, you're not. I'm here, honey, okay?"

"I am so sorry, but I didn't have any other choices, it's just... They forced me, they pushed me, they manipulated me... I am so sorry, Cha..."

"It's fine, darling. I told you that even if someday you stab me, I'd forgive you," I used now a more maternal tone, so she could feel that I was here.

"I fucked up everything..."

"Shhh... Calm down, it's fine... Calm down, and talk to me."

For some moment I was feeling like, I don't know, real tears. When I saw her face when she opened the door... and to recollect the fact that she's no longer coming at school, she's crying most of the time... the "I am sorry" when she gave me the envelope that last day. Everything literally exploded under my arms. It's gonna take months before she passes through this. But I don't care, I'll be there, as always, as I've always been. I promised her that I'll always be there for her. Maybe she wept for like, yeah, ten minutes, but those were ten intense minutes. And at the end... after I passed her maybe the twentieth tissue, she actually started confessing everything:

"Cha... You remember the day we had an argument about Kelly, just... well, the night when I actually, erm... made that mistake," she restarted with her weak voice.

"Yeah?" I was listening carefully.

"It went exactly the same way as you. Kelly, I was out with her, and she pushed me to some guy we had to meet, and the guy drugged me, and... You know me, I'd never sleep with anyone, even though I was mad at you that evening, I would never do that. And, even, this morning when you were downstairs..."

"I never really understood why you broke up with me... Okay, you cheated on me, it would take time for me to go through that, but at least I tried to understand!"

"A few days later, basically, I received a call, an anonymous call. This guy, he named himself *Raising Sun*, and forced me to basically break up with you and do what he wanted me to do, otherwise, as I have been recorded that night, this would end up in social networks and dark web's porn websites. As I received the video as an attachment in my phone, I understood this was serious!"

That's what I thought. She's been forced to break up with me. I didn't actually speak, because... well, hearing the truth from her was somehow painful. And... So, they did the same to her. This is why she decided to break up with me, she's been forced. I just understood that a couple of days ago, I... well I suspected this already because it didn't make any sense, that she would break up with me albeit she cheated on me. I just let her continue.

"Then it was... I slept with those guys, I... I have been raped many times, I just... This was why I took drugs. It has just become terrible, the last few months. And, when Kelly wanted to push you..."

"Claire... Why didn't you talk about this to me earlier?" I tried to understand.

"I was scared! I was so scared! Basically, if I spoke to anyone about what I was doing... This guy was putting me under more pressure, it happened once when I spoke with Sophie, that I was scared to tell you that because you would judge me because you would... And because I knew what Kelly had in mind for you and... She wanted to trap you on your birthday, and she forced me to trap you, so we could split and..."

"Okay... Okay, I see."

So, it's why Sophie took so many precautions to actually talk to me on that birthday night. I don't know if she was aware of what was ongoing... But curiously, since this happened, she actually disappeared, I mean, I didn't see her again. But why would she... Hang on, Sophie knows when I started dating Florent. But why would she blackmail me? What's her interest? Sophie being worse than Kelly, or Sophie being a tool of Kelly? Hang on, I know Sophie for much longer than I know Kelly, and, yeah, it makes sense, because she used to be a lot with Claire after we broke up, just like Kelly, they both became close friends. But I don't get why she would be blackmailing me, I mean, I never attacked her. Well, on the other hand, Joris remains the very first suspect, but the question is, why she would disappear, I mean, the very last time I heard from her was during the nightclub's party. That is actually curious. Some things make sense, but a couple of them do not. Like the wordings, I mean, when I had my blackmailer by phone, it was not Sophie's wording, it was not even a female wording, it more seemed like a guy. I still need to confirm that.

"But hang on..." Claire actually resumed. "You said earlier that you accepted to do that... what does it mean?"

"It means that... It means what it means. The day I saw you almost under the pressure of Kelly... I know that this whore was on a bad influence on you. I could just have shrugged off and let the blackmailer do whatever he wants, and disappear, I have enough money for disappearing and pretending I am dead and... But I fought for you."

At that moment, she actually raised herself and looked at me. Her eyes were still red but at this time full of hope. Because she knows me, and she also knows that I can change my relationship quickly with people depending on the interests I have with them. And, given that she knows that I am a cold-blooded psychopath, I am sure that she didn't expect that from me because she is a sentimental person. She's hugely sensitive to affection, and given the fact that now I have the proof that she still loves me... It's why she actually looked at me for a couple of seconds, and then, said, hesitating:

"But... What about Florent?"

"Florent, erm... I'm gonna break up with him next Monday. I never loved him anyway. It's why I wanted to be here, with you, this weekend..."

"Why?"

"I, erm... Anyway, it doesn't matter."

"No, no, wait... I think I know what you mean. You are telling me that you did that for me. You actually engaged yourself in that shit because you wanted me to actually be safe and to be out of this, you want to destroy Joris and Kelly's activity..."

"I just want you to have a normal life, and turning eighteen without this..."

"No, no, no... This is rubbish!", she smiled at me. "Come on, admit it... You know you have the skills to actually destroy that. You are not someone like me that let herself wrecking by events. You are a fighter... You did it for me, huh?"

"I already said that I did it for you..."

"Oh, my..." she felt suddenly impressed.

Yeah, I am sure she suspected that, but she just wanted to hear that for me. Well, I think now she has maybe a real understanding of my situation. I just didn't mention the big issue ongoing, that I was now pregnant. I don't know if I should tell her that because she'll know too much. I'll say to her someday, but not now. At that moment, she was just like... We just looked at each other, and suddenly, I could see something I've never seen in her for a while now: she was hoping. She was happier and certainly delighted that I was fighting for her. As she said, she knows me, she has seen me manipulating people on many occasions, she knows what I am capable of. And disregard what she's done or who she has slept with, I was still here for her. Her day was certainly cloudy and full of shit, but at least, now... the sun was shining, and there was a new day, a beautiful new day ahead.

"Cha..." she started, whilst still containing her tears, but now tears of joy or solace.

"Yeah?" I was now expecting she would ask me out again.

"Hum... I, erm... I think I cannot say thank you enough, it's just... I mean, I, hum... I am just impressed, after what I did, after... you could have let me deal with my shit..."

"I promised you one day that no matter what happens, Claire, I will always fight for you. Okay, we are no longer together, but still. I don't care if it has to cost me a boyfriend or a dignity, all I want is... You, to be safe!"

"You're my hero, Cha..."

"Oh, shut up, I ain't a damn hero or anything..." I actually for once remained modest.

"I, erm... anything you want. Whatever you want, Cha, erm, just ask me!"

And now, I was like... Literally, anything?

"Anything... Like, anything I want?"

"Yes, honey, yes!" she was feeling better.

"Okay, then two things. First, why don't you ask me out again as it's been months that you're craving for it!"

"Oh, hum... Will you be my girlfriend again, Charlotte?"

"Don't call me by my full name, and yes, I want to be your girlfriend again," I smiled at her but remained detached, just to tease her.

"Hum... Okay. Anything else?"

"Yes, I'm starving. And cold!"

"I think this is something I can deal with!"

At that very moment, she hugged me, like... And cried again. Obviously, I told her to stop crying, but I was feeling her, it was now a considerable relief. Now, we were back together, just like old-time, and she knows that together, we're invincible. There is a threat, but she's not alone anymore, she's with me again, and... Okay, she cheated on me, okay, she did that, but I did the same and even worst within the last months, so whatever happens, I think the balance is now back to zero. Now, we're back together. And it's all that matters. But even if I must admit that... Oh, no, the first time, I asked her out, now she asked me out, so now, yeah, we're even. Florent is gonna enjoy the breaking news. Mum as well. But I don't care. Fuck that.

And, again, she kissed me. I forgot how beautiful it was, it was like... Every time I kiss her, it's like different, it feels like the truth, it feels like the right thing. The truth is now back, the balance of the universe has now been restored. I think this was the only magic moment, for now, a couple of months, when she kissed me, I was feeling backed, I was feeling like she was giving me the strength I needed, the fuel I ran out for a long time, this was actually a priceless moment. I just couldn't stop kissing her, I just didn't stop, the flame was burning again, warming our hearts from the avalanche that happened a couple of days ago. Now, back together, we are going to be invincible. And, back together, I know that she will have the strength to do what I want her to do, and to finally push her out of these troubles she has been into for now too long. Even if it has to pass through, well... This. But if this could make sure we would actually have our lives back and ensure we can maintain a good life later, I consent to this.

And yeah... after the hug, it was actually something else that disturbed us: my stomach. Making some weird noises, meaning that I was starving. For the rest of the day, well... The flame now burning again, we went to the kitchen... we left our phones into the microwave, and we actually cooked some lunch. Nothing specific, we just ate sandwiches, and... As we were both relatively tired, we went upstairs to grab her mattress and bring it downstairs, just like old time. But we decided to remain into the darkness, because, well, there was nothing else to do. But this afternoon, it was, yeah, like living in a dream.

I recovered actually... The pleasure of being with her. Hugs, kisses, all those moments that I so needed so far from the last months. At some point, we actually fell asleep, but we remained so close to each other. I felt like everything was more robust than before, my baby was back, and this was something tremendous. We didn't sleep that long, maybe in the middle of the afternoon for like two hours, but when we woke up, it was by the sound of the TV two hours later. And, the most significant thing, I mean, the vital thing for me, was just seeing her face in the dark, her eyes looking straight at me, and her saying only "I love you". We actually maybe recovered from all the moments lost between those last four months, lost because of Kelly and Joris. It's odd, I mean, we know each other for seven years, and, still, every time I see her, it feels like I am in love with her like in the first day, and today was a kind of a new first day. I was fine, and I needed it. At that moment, there were no problems. There was just nothing, just us. Isolated from a mad world, protecting each other, like recreating a kind of dome to actually face up the world ahead. And whatever people may say about us, whatever they may think about us, it was just her and me. And nothing else mattered. I was undoubtedly her hero as she said, and as she kept on saying, but now, we actually terribly needed each other. Because we were both down. And... She's like my diamond in the middle of the ocean, even if everything is dark, she's the only one to actually remain so bright.

Towards the end of the evening, well, I actually took a shower, and now, the mood was to relaxation. I just didn't want to talk about anything, until things are resuming. Or at least until I take my phone back. We actually played games. At least before dinner, we played Monopoly. Usually, I feel the need to cheat on Monopoly, as always when someone is playing with me, I'm consistently cheating, today I didn't care. It basically ended up over a dispute on the two most expensive street we could buy, between *Rue de la Paix* and the *Champs-Elysées*. As she purchased the Champs-Elysées... But, well, anyway. Then after we ate. The raclette that she promised. And yet again, we just lit some candles, we didn't turn on any lights, we just had a bath later, and went back to sleep downstairs after for finally finishing that quite challenging day that was this Friday.

Saturday, we actually woke up pretty late, maybe around twelve. As the curtains she has are so thick that it doesn't let through any lights, it could allow us to sleep a bit longer. And it was a bit cold today. And, it's Saturday, I mean, on regular times, we'd feel like going outside, maybe eating in some restaurants as we used to do, but now, because of the snow of yesterday, everything was still partially closed. And moreover, we didn't feel like going out, we were still feeling like staying inside. Our phones were still in the microwave, and we didn't feel the need to actually take them. However, she took her laptop, and received a message from her mother (because as she was not responding any texts, she sent her a mail instead), saying that she'd certainly be back tomorrow as it's too dangerous to actually drive. Yeah, it may form ice on the road because of the snow and then be fatal if she's problems. She replied, okay. She wanted to tell her mother that we were back together, but I told her that she shouldn't do anything for safety measures. After that, she took her antidepressants.

For the first time of the weekend, she actually went outside, I mean, in her garden. She drew the curtains, but it was freezing out there. Obviously, when we went to her terrace, I just couldn't resist. I threw her on her back a snowball. Which ultimately led to a battle of snowballs, and... Yeah, until the moment she actually grabbed me and put one big ball in my top, and I was frozen. That was fun, I mean, for four months we've been battling against each other, and now, we gained our complicity back again. It was good to have her back. For the rest of the afternoon, well... I actually took her laptop to go to the Internet, whilst she did various things, for example doing her bank stuff, and all this. After it was maybe around three, we went back together to the bathroom and had another bath. And we talked.

"What do we do after this?" she actually started, after maybe a couple of minutes, whilst everything was quiet.

"What do you mean?" I had her in my arms.

"Once we're done with everything?"

"Oh, well... Why don't we actually get the hell out of here? I mean, we take the first plane for abroad, we choose, and... We just leave?"

"Why not. I really want to go over this, I just... I just want a change!"

"Well, the departure boarding at Roissy shall tell us where we can head after. Just pick a city, and we just get the hell out!"

"And what about... the family and everything?"

"Claire. I really don't see how we may get out of this without any scandal. The truth will explode, no matter what. I have a plan, I have an exit plan, but...

Unfortunately, we must brace for a big scandal. For our reputation to actually be tarnished forever. This is why, leaving together is the best option, and restarting somewhere where nobody knows us."

"What do you mean? What's your exit plan?"

"On Thursday, after we talked when we were at Kléber, Joris expressed the desire to actually be with you, and sleep with you!"

"I know, it's been days that he's like flirting with me. That evening, he invited me to the restaurant..."

"As a matter of fact, you're still seventeen, and basically... This is statutory rape!"

"I thought about the same," she actually started to confess. "Maybe giving him what he wants and after reporting that. I was scared that he might retaliate after I do that."

"This is the only way out. We both need to talk to the police, stating that he forced us to prostitute, basically reporting him as a pimp. And as a rapist. He may retaliate, yes, but at least, you won't have to undergo... This, this constant thing! At least we'd be free and able to restart a new life."

"That will not be that easy. They broke me. I'm broken."

That is the problem today, maybe since yesterday we were feeling better, but... She's broken. She confessed to me that she had suicidal thoughts because she was feeling like raped and didn't want to talk about all the time she slept with someone. I didn't force her to tell me this, she needs to see a specialist for that. It's odd, I'm always criticising psychologists, but for once I admit that she needs what she has, her antidepressants, and she needs to talk to someone. Even, she looked at me weird, but what she went through, it's just massive, she cannot just shrug off and pretend this was nothing, otherwise someday she will wake up and having a big problem. She needs to talk about what happens, but with someone else. Because... if I hear just a second what she had... I don't think I can actually bear it without killing someone. I am not the right person with whom she should talk, and I told her anyway.

At least antidepressants help her to cope with the messy situation. It's a legal alternative to drugs, but she must have it. She told me that she wanted to poison herself a couple of days ago, and this, me coming back, is the only thing that prevents her from doing that. She even prepared her death note because she's at the end. To be honest, I believe she would have done that because she didn't talk about anything to anyone. People who really want to kill themselves are never talking, they remain silent until the very end.

"And what's your exit plan, for this?" she asked after we talked about her current psychologic state.

"Just offer Joris what he wants, and after, I will back you when we're gonna go to the police!"

"You promise me you'll be there?"

"I promise you, honey. I want you safe!"

The weather was still threatening outside. Even though there was some strong wind, the sky was still very cloudy. When we left her bathroom, maybe after a certainly two hours bath and our fingers were all palmed, we actually went back downstairs, and back in the bed. The mood was different, I mean, it was the first time she confessed about her psychological state, for the first time since we broke up. At least, because she has become paranoid, I still had something quite important: her trust. At least she still trusts me.

We went back downstairs, and, well, once we once again drew all the curtains, we went back on the mattress, and watched some movies, for thinking about something else. At the moment we actually realised that, basically, there would be nothing to eat tonight. She completely forgot yesterday when she went shopping that, well, we may eat tonight. On the other hand, we were not really hungry, and by that time it was already 6pm, so it was okay. We watched movies, we intermittently fell asleep, until we actually finally fall asleep by 10pm.

And Sunday... Well, we actually woke up at around nine. But now we were hungry. So, well... Hopefully, we had breakfast, so we had breakfast, and in the meantime, she turned on the TV. For once, whilst she was preparing the breakfast, I used her laptop, and checked the metro, it was in service again. Weather was excellent too, and I hate nice weather. Temperatures slightly increased, which made the snow melting a bit. At least, since yesterday, it melted by half. When I proposed, shall we have dinner outside today? Today, we've been in lockdown, and why not going out today, I think that would be a great idea. She said yes. So, we had breakfast, I didn't have tea today but a hot chocolate with oat milk. She made me try it once, and I kind of liked it. Hopefully, she has a coffee machine that can heat correctly that milk and I do not. It's the reason why I don't try oat milk at home.

Moreover, Claire is really fancy with all those alternative shitty kinds of milk such as coconut, almond and blah, blah, blah. Sometimes, when she has her coffee with coconut milk, the smell of that milk heated up makes me almost sick as it so smells terrible. On the other hand, I hate coconut, tastes like shit to me.

So, the metro has fully reopened, that was perfect, I was just looking for a good restaurant. Upon looking on the Internet, I actually found some restaurant on the bank of the Seine, just near the Invalides. I showed that to her, and she said, why not. As we've never been there, I was maybe like, let's give it a try. Because I was thinking about the rest of the day that I will have: having to go back home, facing up everybody, my mother, I had to think about what I will tell Florent, his betrayal over my pregnancy and... Why he didn't want to deal with me straight over this. This, again, would be a tough day. Maybe I'll stay with her until the end of the day, I don't actually know, I will see.

But obviously, I needed to call the restaurant to book a table. So, I asked Claire if she could bring me back my phone, and maybe a couple of seconds after she actually took it out of the microwave... Well, basically, my battery was deficient. I left it a minute to update the last messages and calls received as it was deprived of its network for two days. When, after quite a few minutes of seeing it vibrating (even with Claire, we were like... what the hell) I saw, "17 missed calls", "79 new messages" amongst 70 of Florent and 9 of my mother. Fine, so, they are now worried, good for them. Especially Florent, if I were him, I'd feel like... I mean, come on, seventy messages! Even Claire never sent so many messages. Well, through this, I may assume that this is the guilt that is coming out. I didn't read any of them, I actually didn't read any of the messages that I received from any of them, I just wanted to see who texted me and that was it, for the rest, I don't care. And the calls... Yeah, whatever they wanted, I also don't really care.

Curiously, Clarisse didn't call. Well, on the other hand, she's at her boyfriend's, and I feel like she has better things to do instead of pissing me off with their crap. Clarisse knows that I am fine now; otherwise, she'd have called me. Anyway, when I actually unlocked the phone and was entering that restaurant's phone number to actually dial it, I unexpectedly received a call... It was written on the phone, "Confidential". Hum... It usually says a private number, not confidential. Well, well, let's actually answer, and let's find out what it actually is.

"Hi, Charlotte," a voice (normal voice, not a distorted voice like my blackmailer) actually said.

"Hi, hum... Who is that?" I just replied, curious.

"Allison. You don't remember me?"

"Oh, sorry, Allison. What is up? How did you get my phone number by the way?" I remained detached but curious.

"More or less, and regarding your phone number, well, I have my ways. You, what's up?"

"Same old. What can I do for you, darling?"

"I need you to come tonight late at night. Like, between one and two of the morning. I need to talk to you."

"Talk to me?"

"Yes, it's, erm… I cannot tell you by phone. I need to talk to you, so come between one and two tonight, and don't ask any questions."

"Hum, sure."

"Oh, and no need to come with your skirt and heels. Just come like, natural. I just wanna talk to you, that's all, nothing more."

"Okay, then!"

"Good. Looking forward to seeing you, and I will text you the address. See you tonight. Bye."

27 *Truth*

// Room 303, George V hotel, Avenue des Champs-Elysées, Paris.

// Monday, 21st of January 2013, 01:20.

She told me to meet her late at night, in a kind of fancy hotel in the Champs-Elysées. Somehow, that confirms what I think of her; she's a cop. Then, she sent me the text. "Room 303 at George V. Come for 1 am and be discreet. Make sure nobody sees you." Hum, yeah. Fine, then I don't need a special outfit, the one for today should be fine.

There were twelve hours to go, between the moment I received the text message and the moment I had that meeting with her. When we went to the restaurant, we had quite a long chat with Claire regarding Allison and why she sent me to her. She doesn't know exactly who she is, but she knows that she's seeking information regarding our blackmailer. At least, she told me she introduced herself as someone who was seeking someone, which is why it was maybe a couple of days ago when she met her, she talked about me, because she knows that I may fight back. At least she was assuming that I would fight back and explained that having Allison help fight back with me would certainly be really helpful; at least a valuable help. I didn't share my opinion with her. I just heard and gathered all the information, but my supposition is actually correct: Allison is undercover, so she's a cop, but hides her cards very well. We also talked about implementing my strategy, and I let her know that I was to meet Allison tonight. I told her, wait. Maybe Allison has something important, she certainly has some information that I may not have and could help me actually fight back, using Claire as bait. I just told her, because I thought about that, that whenever she would receive a text from me that quotes, "fool me once, shame on you", she would respond "fool me twice, shame on me". Meaning that she would confirm that she invited Joris, so we can start the operation.

But now my exit strategy actually started to become simpler: I will use Florent and Claire against my blackmailer. Why Florent? Astonishingly simple. I now know that I cannot rely on him on keeping such an important secret. As he spoke with my mother regarding my pregnancy. Fine, I still didn't give him any update on where I was and what I am doing, despite his numerous amounts of texts left, some of them quite threatening. He is worried, this is evident. When I am back home tomorrow, he will be waiting for me. Obviously, when he wakes up, he will ask me questions on where I have been this weekend, and this is where the argument will happen: he is scared of me, and I will just scare him more. Using his fears against him. (That is sadistic, yes, but at least this is for having talked to my mother about my pregnancy). Whenever he is scared, he will act quite quickly, and if I lead the thing correctly, he should be breaking up with me. Why Florent must break up with me and not otherwise? Because I am under surveillance, my blackmailer hacked my phone. And I want to play this card at my advantage. If Florent breaks up with me, this will be more credible to him that I may be affected by him breaking up and explaining the rest of my plan that follows.

After that, the plan will be simple, but it must take place on a couple of days, no more, it must be swift. In between, tomorrow (tomorrow is Monday), Claire must call Joris, and proposing him a date. But she will ask him like, she will not explicitly ask him, I told her how to do and suggest him on a date, but this day must take place the next day, so on Tuesday evening. Why? Because something is actually scheduled on Monday evening already.

And what is scheduled on Monday evening will be this: through Monday, I will pretend to be on a bad mood because Florent will break up with me, and I will make sure to actually trigger the argument in a certain way that I am supposed to lose it. Pretending that I am overwhelmed, I am so sorry, and that I'd do anything to have him back. I will harass him all day, so I can have a discussion with him on Monday evening. I will just go to school, but openly display that there is something wrong, because I want to show Kelly that I am in a bad mood. Kelly, communicating with my blackmailer, will then report that and I will just pretend that, well, things are just out of my control and I am losing my mind. If he's bright enough and I think he is, my blackmailer will understand that he is winning the game. Obviously, I will not explain anything to anyone, even to Clarisse, because she must believe something huge has happened. Anyway, I will be kind, I know how to get Florent's attention. This Monday evening, I will invite him to get some food, and I will talk to him. And then, I will reveal the dark secret that is ongoing since the 9th of January, that I am trapped. Why I will disclose this? Remember when I told you that he couldn't keep a secret? He will talk, and this is precisely what I want him to do.

Next day, because obviously, he will be terribly upset, he will call my mother. And tell all that happened, because I will specifically suggest to him that he must not talk to anyone. Reverse psychology, I don't think he could keep this. And moreover, my mother will start wondering what's going on. So, they will talk, and the scandal will very quickly explode: my mother knowing my new activities, I will first deny, and then tell the truth, and tell that I am in danger. I will specifically talk about Claire, so both our names are in the same scandal. Why making this scandal explode? Because mum loves me and will defend me no matter what. She knows good lawyers, who will back us up. Which will, naturally, lead us to Wednesday morning, when Claire and I will go to the police for our joint statement regarding Joris and Kelly for statutory rape, blackmailing and pimping. We will have lawyers with us, and this... Oh, yeah, because of Joris and Claire... Yes, Claire would be raped on Tuesday night. If we have lawyers, witnesses, this case may likely go through. Because also... Another reason why I want this scandal to explode: my blackmailer won't have anything to keep me under pressure anymore.

Oh, I'm not proud of this. But I don't see any other plans.

This is what we decided with Claire, this is our exit strategy. And after... After, it's later. Restarting a new life. We will implement this from tomorrow morning. Obviously, tonight, there's Allison. I don't know what she wants. But, given what she tells me... No matter what, the plan will be implemented tomorrow, and there will be no changes for the strategy. We will just let things go naturally. And allowing predictable reactions from people remaining predictable. And obviously oriented.

Free Expensive Lies: Prologue

So, I went there that night. It was cold and dark, as it was the middle of the night, and I stayed at Claire's all evening. The plan was ready to be implemented, and we all knew and repeated what we all had to do. We obviously made sure that we knew and didn't have to communicate, but this time... Well, Claire had the easy job to do. I had the hardest, but it's okay for me. The priority remains the priority. But I went there, to the George V hotel, taking the bus as it was during the night, carrying my small bag where I had my stuff for the weekend. More or less I was wearing the same outfit than Friday, when I left for Claire's place, I didn't really change myself, and my last shower was, well, Saturday. When I had my bath with her. I was in a different mood now because, yes, we had to strike back even though we were together. Even if that plan is quite safe and relatively easy to implement for me, it may still fail, and if it fails, I will have to seek another solution again to actually make things right. Undergoing a scandal is not something that scares me, especially this, I am not scared of what is due to happen, I am simply frightened for her, because even if it sounds fun, it will impact her, and... I'd better be ready for her not to collapse.

The George V is a hotel in Paris, near the Champs-Elysées. That was a long journey. I mean, I had to take a bus, then a metro that I never take, then the Paris Overground (or Regional Train, whatever they call it). To make two stops and arriving where I had to go, to finally walk and coming maybe forty minutes later, where I was supposed to go. She actually gave me a meeting in a five-star hotel in Paris. And this hotel is curiously not that far away from her place, (but it is not her place...), at first I didn't really understand why she actually wanted to meet me in a neutral area, to make sure that she wouldn't be listened or anything like this. As it was late, I was tired, I mean, I wasn't really in the manipulation mood or anything, usually, when I am tired, I am more likely to be rude or mean.

And, today, I didn't come back home. I decided that it can wait until this meeting, anyway I didn't really have any reason to actually come back home. We went to that restaurant near the Invalides, it was fine, we had time to speak and elaborate our strategy further, we talked and agreed on the plan, this would be the plan. Later we came back home, and Claire wasn't feeling pretty well, she was actually sad and cried at least a good part of the afternoon. I really don't know why, but every time she cries in front of me, she feels ashamed, and I usually tell her, come on, it's okay to weep, it's not because I can't do it that it should be a sign of weakness. And, really, that's what I think, crying is somehow a way to actually express yourself when you are under pressure, not feeling good just like she was, it's nothing to be blamed for. The thing was, I knew why she was crying, and it just made me upset. But anyway, we just had dinner together, and I stayed at her place, at least until midnight, to gather my stuff in my bag and getting ready to go. Florent texted me that he was home and waiting for me, I replied that I'll come back in the night. It's just when he asked me where I was for the umpteenth time that I didn't answer. I just said, tomorrow, we need to talk. But he's intelligent, he knows what I want to talk about. And if I were him, I wouldn't sleep on my two ears at that moment. Or at least I would brace for an argument because I want him to dump me.

Anyway, I left, and basically, when I left, I was already struggling not to fall asleep, and Claire told me, see you in a couple of days and thank you for everything. I just replied that I'll see her Wednesday morning. As for now, that is the plan. I took this bus, metro, and regional train, and I arrived there. The floor was still very icy; hopefully, I was wearing hot stuff and fully covered, because even though my gloves and scarf, I was still actually pretty much cold. On the other hand, it's winter, and God knows how I love winter and hate summer. It was so cold that I was almost feeling the cold stinging on my face, it was odd. But hopefully, the walk was not that long. The Champs-Elysées avenue by night is somehow magic but actually pretty dangerous, even now, to be honest, I wasn't feeling safe. And when I think that I have to retake the bus to come back home and sleep. Anyway, at some point, I entered the hotel, and yeah. I reached a great hall, fully illuminated with this yellow incandescent light appearing as chandeliers hanging from the ceiling... And the vast hall where, in the middle of it, was the small round office, the receptionist office. I went there and asked for room 303, where Allison actually gave me a rendezvous. The third floor, lifts are on the corridor over there. Fine. But whilst speaking to him, I had an idea.

Because as I think Allison is a cop, I am sure she just wants to question me. Unlike other days, I have an optimistic hunch regarding that meeting, I don't think she's going to expect anything from me other than answers in her investigation. Especially when I had her on the phone, she precisely mentioned the word "meeting", then it means what it means. If she wants to talk to me, I will talk about the ongoing plan, and since I cannot trust my phone, I actually asked the receptionist if he could keep my phone for a couple of times. He placed it in a safe, I think, as I heard a thing under him being opened. And then, I left. Because, yeah, after all, if something happens, I still have the phone in the room, connected straight to the receptionist room. But I think a terrible event is unlikely to happen.

Free Expensive Lies: Prologue

So, yeah, I went upstairs. The third floor. Obviously, this is a five-star hotel, so the entire floor was covered with a thick carpet, a red one, absorbing all possible footsteps noise. Walls were covered with a kind of yellow wallpaper, and all the doors were closed. It was so quiet on that floor.

On the other hand, we are in an hour where I think everybody bust be sleeping. There was not that much of door, I just took on the right when I entered, as it was indicated that the room was on the right, and then, well... Basically, through that door, I actually heard some music, but some kind of relaxing music. Yeah, she was awake and also waiting for me. I just knocked; I didn't waste that much of time trying to listen through the door. I don't know if I was on time or not, but suddenly, I heard her walking, standing up from somewhere, and standing, walking towards the door. As she opened quite quickly, I assume that the door was not that big. And, when she opened the door, I discovered her under a new visage.

"Hi," I shyly started.

"Hi, Cha. Come on in!"

Ironically, I found that she was pretty sad. Her too was in a casual outfit, I mean, just a grey sweater, a pair of black pants and white sneakers. She recently straightened her hairs, I could see that, but no makeup, nothing of the sort. Basically, we are pretty much the same, maybe I am slightly taller than her, but she looks the same as me, corporally speaking. We certainly have the same weight, (as she's trans I assume her weight is something she takes extra care about) but she had shorter hairs, like, she went to a hair-dresser recently, I suppose she must be kind of feeling weird. On the other hand, she's Irish, and, well, I guess she's been here for a long time, and Ireland may miss her. She may miss her country like my mother feels sometimes, she's never happy when we have to come back to France. Same as me, everything is ways much simpler in the UK. Anyway, I assume this was her problem, for the last couple of days, maybe she's progressing in her investigation, and she misses being in Ireland.

Yeah, I usually go to the hair-dresser for the same reasons. When I am feeling down. It's pretty unusual, and the very last time I went there was maybe a while ago, but she did something to her hairs.

Anyway, I was expecting this meeting to take place elsewhere than here, I mean, I thought she'd tell me to go at her place, but yeah. No, I was now in just a simple hotel room, completely different from the previous one. Apart from the bed, the walls' primary colour was a light burgundy, a small office on the left-hand side of the bed and the wide French window on the opposite side; nothing to actually say about that room. If she wanted me to come here today, yes, there was a reason, and I am sure this was because it's far from her last place, the place she was before, certainly to remain anonymous. This also confirms that she's a cop, it does make sense to me now more. Especially since I saw that she had a kind of a black wallet on her trousers' back pocket. So, I entered, and actually saw her office first: not a lot of stuff, but still quite messy. She didn't have any laptop, just an iPad that she set like a screen, there was next to it a small box which I assume is a Bluetooth speaker, as there was some music playing, pleasant, relaxing music, by the way. On the same small desk, looking more like a small cabinet than any other thing were left several notes and papers, anyhow. And a big folder, a purple folder, which seemed to be full of documents as it was literally voluminous and certainly about to explode, on which I could read "Case 15-9786". A small drawer was underneath, it seemed closed, but not correctly, I assume she's hiding something in it. Or wants me to glance inside, but... Checking police files, in front of a cop, when you're not a cop, I really don't think this would be very wise.

The bed was neat. I mean, not completely neat, but it seemed to have been unused. She didn't sleep here. When I went towards it, it seemed perfectly neat, I don't think she has slept here, or she is going to rest here. However, I could see on the foot of the bed that someone sat here, probably for quite a few moments, as I could see the trace of someone seating. She didn't, as the chair of her small desk moved, like, it was not properly under the desk. That's why, so far from what I have seen at her place, she seems to be an organised person, she's not messy just like me, she wants everything to be functional. But she received someone else earlier that evening, and according to the footsteps that I could see on the carpet covering the floor, it was a guy. Long shoes, with footprints looking like trainers... She had some guy coming in. But I assume this would be work-related, the reason for the visit, according to the shoes. But as seen as I could see the "print" of his arse on the bed, I assume that this guy didn't leave a long time before I arrive, certainly five to ten minutes before I am here.

As I said, the room was just temporary. Two more things were almost confirming me that idea: the bedside-tables on each part of the bed, and the colossal furniture in front of the bed, leaving a relatively big gap between the mattress and this furniture, almost covering the entire wall, to access from each side of the room. First, there was strictly nothing on the bedside-tables, except the lamps, nothing more. Second, absolutely no drawers have been opened on that furniture and (there was a hole with a big flat screen in the middle of that furniture), the TV was off. Speaking of the TV, the TV remote was placed correctly on one of the bedside tables. So, I assume that she will leave that place after our meeting.

Whatever this meeting is for, I don't think this may be dangerous. I don't feel her like hostile or wanting to harm me. No, as she was somehow depressed because even if her hairs were different, they were, however, quite messy and according to her face, she was also tired, just like I was. But she kept herself awake with the small cup that I could see next to her iPad... She had coffee multiples times. Problem is, given that I could see this cup has been used and reused without being cleaned, I could see that she had more than one espresso in the same cup.

Anyway, I walked in, dropped my bag next to her bed, and sat in the middle of the bed, precisely at the same place the guy sat before I arrive. At the same time, after she closed the door, but left it unlocked, she actually came in front of me, leaning on that furniture, looked at me and said:

"How are you, you okay?"

"Yeah, hum... Tired, but yeah, I'm fine!"

"Cool..."

"And you, what's up?"

"Well... I'm doing okay, actually!"

"Great!"

Curiously, she reminded me at that very moment, Jodie Foster, in *The Silence of the Lambs*. I mean, I don't know why, but I was looking at her, and... Okay, the first time I met her, I actually didn't process this detail, but as I was normal now, not drugged, or anything, I was impressed: same hairs, same corpulence, same way to speak... Meanwhile, as she stood in front of me, I tried to look at her eyes, analyse her body language, and perform a cold reading. Obviously, this would have been easier if I weren't that tired. But the way she was standing, as she was moving around, it was not nervous from her, it was just that she was looking for a way to speak to me. Because, from her eyes, I could actually find out that... Yeah, if she tells me that she investigated me, I will indeed not be surprised because I feel like she knows who she's about to talk to. She certainly knows me a bit better, because I am sure that Claire told her a lot about me. And I could see, she was seeking her words because she really wanted to enter into direct contact with me and was aiming for a way to start talking to me. I mean being more persuasive by direct contact, so more convincing because she knows that she will not get anything if she fails to convince me. Because she wanted to reveal who she is, she tried to tell me that she was an undercover cop, but... As I said, she knows who she is talking to, and she knows that I am definitely the least of all the morons with whom she's ever been speaking to.

And I really like Jodie Foster. I wish I could speak French like her. That is really impressive, after eighteen years in France, I am still fucked by this accent. That reminds me, that's also a good question... Is it her that doubles her voice when her movies are in French, or someone else? I have seen many of her films, and honestly, I do not see any difference in her voice tone, whether in English or in French. And god knows how I hate watching American or even foreign movies in French, I am just obsessed with the movements of the actor's lips and the wordings that do not match. But, anyway, that is something completely different.

Anyway, so, to actually open the conversation as I saw she was hesitating on how she would be opening, I did something that doesn't really look like me. I broke the ice. Maybe, then, it would be easier for her to lead me to where she wants to go.

"So... Why did you want me to actually come so late? I mean, it's not that I don't like you, but I'd rather like to be sleeping in my bed right now!"

"I know, and I understand... I am really sorry about that, I mean, asking you to come late... Is the music okay for you?"

"Hum... Yeah. Yeah, of course!"

"Do you have any preferences?"

"Oh, hum... Whatever you want, as long as it's classical music because I don't want anything that may keep me awake right now. Put some Beethoven; that should be fine!"

Beethoven has a kind of complicated music that keeps you awake. Mozart, (my baby boy) would also be fine, but the problem is, it switches my mood. And Bach makes me fall asleep, just like, well, most of the composers. But I also see why she wanted to play music; because she knows that my phone is under surveillance and thus doesn't want me to be heard, she wants this conversation to remain confidential. I also thought about this detail, a couple of minutes earlier, this was why I left my phone to the receptionist downstairs. Remember? Because I am not dumb and I know that every room in a hotel has a phone linked to the receptionist desk in case something happens. But as I said, I don't think she has hostile intentions, and I could fully assess that at that very moment.

Anyway, even though she didn't want to be heard and spoke not very loudly, the music was too weak, I mean the music's volume, it probably wouldn't make any difference. As the music volume was soft and our voices would automatically be louder than the music, if I had my phone in my pocket, that would slightly disturb me from listening to the conversation. She put some piano concerto; I don't know which one because I don't know Beethoven enough to know everything unlike Mozart and went back standing in front of me. I was still sat. Playing music was actually clever because as this is a police investigation; but mostly, as she is not officially interrogating me, this is just a meeting because she seeks information, she is basically not allowed to ask me for my phone. And she knows the rules, rules are the rules, and she cannot derogate it without any good reason. And, also, she cannot do anything since I am not under arrest. So, music would be actually an excellent way to disturb the fact that I am listened to.

And this was also quite a big issue for her since she also knows that I know the rules; just like her. She knows that I know. And she also knows that as I am so unpredictable, nothing obliges me to actually give my phone as I am not under arrest. But more importantly, she won't dare to ask since she needs to gain my trust, and eavesdropping on me is definitely not the correct way to gain my confidence. Take my phone, and all that she wants to build will immediately fade away. But, again, it's up to her. Astonishingly, I was right to break the ice the first time, because now... Shyly, she actually restarted:

"Okay... So, do you know why I asked you to come right now?"

To be more efficient when you actually practised cold reading and when you know that both of you have the same weapons in your hands, you need to be really careful about what you say. Basically, now, she was about to enter into the conversation, she was like opening a door, and it was up to me whether I entered. The problem is, if I enter, it's like submitting myself entirely to her, so becoming her puppet. What I want is her to join in the room she wants to open, and me talking to her from the threshold. Keeping my distance from her. If I say no, that will basically show that I pretend that I don't know, and then I am taking her for an idiot, and she will use that against me. If I say yes, this will show that I am actually more than comfortable speaking to her and I may use that to try to reverse the conversation, but ultimately will end up with me failing. But since the conversation is like poker (what finally matters are not your cards but what you do with them), there is still another option: nuking her cover. Because she knows that I know, but she doesn't know precisely what I know. And this is actually the thing that will make the actual difference!

Then, more confident, and now a bit less tired, I confidently looked at her and then, started:

"Yeah, you asked me to come because... You're a cop, and I am having some weird activities with weird people, that apparently are illegal..."

"I'm not a..." she wanted to deny but actually couldn't because that would be too obvious otherwise and block her maybe further in the conversation. "How do you know that?"

"Oh, no... Your cover was perfect, I swear to God, that was fine, don't worry about that. It was just a deduction from me, hum... Remember last Friday when I woke up at your home? I noticed a total absence of decoration, nothing personal, it just didn't match a student personality. When I saw your makeup, the tons of products you had in your bathroom, it was just insane, it could be first because you're trans. You guys have an excessive need for being feminine. On the other hand, it indicated that you hide behind some personality quite often, as your makeup wasn't completely matching. And, when I blew up the bag I inflated, this was the thing that confirmed the rest, basically, when the bag exploded, the first thing you did with your hand was looking for your weapon. That are just deductions, nothing more... When I met you, I thought you were just someone looking for something, but when I saw your home... I deducted this."

"All right then!"

"Yeah... I like observing a lot of things, I'm surprisingly good at this."

"Yeah, I can see that. That confirms what I heard from many people around you, you're apparently a great and dangerous manipulator!" she said that whilst smiling, meaning that she didn't want to attack me on that.

"Meh, sometimes we have unhappy customers, that's business, shit happens, you know..."

"Always hiding behind some cynic humour and despise absolutely everyone around you..."

"Oh lord, you checked the review of the after-sales department!"

"Now I see who I have in front of me..."

"Meh..."

"Anyway, you were right. I am the police."

Suddenly, she took her wallet from her back pocket. And, yeah, here it was. She actually opened it, and obviously, as expected, it was not a wallet, it was her plate from the police. Yeah, what a surprise, I knew that already. But wait... The badge was grey and blue, but mostly grey, made of a metallic plate and written in letters... I could read underneath the word "*heireann*". Hum... That sounds like Ireland but written in Irish, so okay, she may be a cop, but she cannot arrest me here because Paris is not her jurisdiction. Next to the insignia, her identification card, with her picture, and I could read her name, "Heather Reed", an agent working for the Garda in Dublin, ranked as an Inspector. But something was weird because she was apparently affiliated for the Irish Police but as an agent of the Garda Foreign Crime Unit. So, her name is not Allison, it's just a cover name. Okay, I see. This is a foreign investigation, I mean, the Irish Police is investigating over my blackmailer, apparently. It must be then a more significant case than I thought. She must be here as an observer or be mandated by Interpol to help in the case, as the branch into which she is working may have some extra power than regular police. But why an Irish cop? Well, I assume Ireland is the country where this blackmailer emerged. Oh, I am sure she's gonna give me an explanation, because, well, Irish Police investigating in Paris, that sounds a bit odd. Since Paris is the jurisdiction of the French Police.

"Hum, Irish Police, weird..." I actually shyly added, after having examined her insignia.

"So, you know us..."

"But how comes the Irish police actually is in Paris to investigate on me? I mean, how comes that you guys are here? You must be supervising something I guess, that would be the only explainable reason since you do not have jurisdiction in here. I know the law."

"All right then, let me clarify this. I am working in a special branch of the Garda, created not long ago in cooperation with different polices in charge of law enforcement within the EU. I am also mandated by Interpol; this is why I am here. Ireland is in charge of a massive human-trafficking investigation. And I am in charge of that case, I am just here to supervise the French police collecting information on our behalf."

"Jesus Christ... The EU. Such a wonderful thing... I really hope someday we leave that bloody mess."

"Tell me about it. My real name is Heather Reed, and on behalf of Interpol and the Garda, I am currently investigating a massive human-trafficking network. This is monitored by someone that uses blackmail, threats to actually force generally 16 to 18 years old girls just like you to fall into prostitution."

"Oh..."

"This is basically an international case, I mean, crimes are happening a bit everywhere across the planet. They operate in small clusters, such as the one you are part of. It's something big, for instance, to give you an idea, we basically found more than five different clusters in Paris, and the biggest one was made of ten girls, in which the youngest girl was basically 14 years old."

"Holy crap…"

"Yes. Your girlfriend, or ex-girlfriend, whoever she is for you, has been trapped, through the same process. This network is basically operating this way: some random girl that makes friend with you, and then she traps you. I assume you already know that Claire Cobert has been trapped by Kelly Royer. As you have been trapped the same way, according to my information."

"Yeah…"

"So, I have a couple of question to ask you tonight. You can ask for a lawyer if you like, but… Or maybe I can conduct an official interview in our office in Lyon; but anyway, this is not to attack you or to suspect you of anything. I know from Claire that you are also a victim, and I just want to hear your part of the story. What happened to you. This is important for the investigation."

That is actually still very confusing for me, but I think I understood how this works. She may have a mandate from Interpol or must be affiliated to Interpol somehow for actually being allowed to show her police badge elsewhere than her jurisdiction. Because Interpol is not a supranational law enforcement agency. And as I saw on her card, she works for the Irish *Garda Síochána* (It's the word for *police* in Irish, and don't ask me how to pronounce it) but may have a card from Interpol at that moment because the Gardaí are investigating the case. But I mean… Ireland is investigating the case? I thought at the beginning that nothing like this would have happened on that island! She may have both cards, but as the Gardaí doesn't have jurisdiction in France, showing that she's also affiliated to Interpol would be maybe more speaking to people. Well, Either way, this thing seems to be actually messed up. Because the thing is, she speaks French, I heard her speaking in French on the morning I woke up at some point, whilst she was typing on her keyboard, I remember I heard her speaking in French. Well, anyway… Things seem to be seriously fucked up, because as she said, these clusters terms, these countries where there are victims, Ireland being in charge of the investigation, well… it doesn't seem to be actually good, and clear as well. In the beginning, I thought it would be something like, someone close to me attacking Claire and me, but no, this is big. It's bigger than I may think. This is why, okay, she is with Interpol and supervising French Police agents. So, she has questions, why blocking her investigations? She actually may be helpful in the near future. And by near future, I obviously mean, really close.

Yeah, because I thought that Claire would be raped by Joris and then we would report that the day after... what if Joris is actually caught straight on the day he commits his crime? This is why I continued; she may be accommodating.

"Okay, then. Ask me anything you want; I have nothing to hide!"

"Great. I basically checked on you, your background, your personal history, your bank accounts... and found out pretty much a lot of things. Anyway, first thing first; how long have you been in a relationship with Claire Cobert?"

"Wow. Quite a long time."

"You and she have been in a relationship, and recently broke up, you guys broke up in September last year, right?"

"That's correct."

"Why did you break up, exactly?"

"Claire actually broke up with me. She has been trapped by Kelly, as you said. Basically, she's been drugging her, and push her to sleep with someone else."

"What happened next?"

"Well, she cheated on me. The thing is, I really love that girl, and... Yeah, well, I was just unable to think about revenge. Deep down, I felt like there was something weird, I mean, Claire and I had many arguments throughout our relationship, but never, never any of us have been thinking about cheating on the other. We used to do this, like, we used to communicate a lot, we used to talk a lot whenever there was a problem, we basically never slept pissed at the other. It never happened. Well, until that night."

"How long has Kelly been in her life?"

"Well, when we started College, basically... Yeah, she never actually took an interest in Kelly at the beginning, we were still really close to each other, we weren't like the kind of people going towards the people, you know. But, yeah, I think, their friendship, if I may say so, actually started maybe in July last year. But, yeah, we know Kelly for pretty much two years now! But less than a month that she's been involved with Claire."

"Claire mentioned that you never liked Kelly for some reason. You became extremely jealous when they started being a friend. Is that true?"

"I feel people," I actually started thinking. "And yeah, I never liked Kelly because I knew something was wrong with her."

"Tell me more about this, Kelly. Claire mentioned she had a kind of important role within this cluster, like, a kind of recruiter or something."

"The night of my birthday, yeah, she... She was like monitoring the situation. Plus, I heard this weekend that she actually pushed Claire to break up with me."

"Hum. Okay. Are you blackmailed?"

Stupid question, basically. But that's the thing of a cop, asking the same questions several times but under different forms, just to check in case, you may say rubbish. Of course, she knows that, of course, she wants me to confirm, I really hope that she doesn't suspect me... Well, on the other hand, how may she imagine me? That just doesn't make any sense. I just confirmed.

"Yes."

"Is Claire blackmailed too?"

"She is, yes..."

"Basically, I have been talking with Claire about the organisation of that cluster. She told me that Kelly was more or less the recruiter, and Joris was the operation supervisor. Could you tell me more about this?"

"Basically, yes, I assume Kelly is a kind of recruiter within that because, the first time I talked to her, she proposed me a mission that I declined. I heard her saying to me that she needed girls somewhere. So... She proposed me something else, and, well, I had to accept."

"Would you say that she is the recruiter or also the supervisor?"

"I don't really know, to be honest. She may be both, given the fact that, as I told you, she spoke about that, that she needed a girl somewhere..."

"When you have to do something, to whom do you give the money?"

"To Joris. Joris is the cashier of that. We sleep with people; he gets his part of that. But Joris, well... He proposed to me to come on Thursday, at the party we met. Otherwise, he is not in charge of any missions, I mean, placing us."

"Did you meet any other girls within the cluster?"

"Nope."

"Okay. Also, Claire described her blackmailer's voice as being some regular French guy, no accent, or at least French accent, hidden behind a voice distorter. Was that the same for you?"

"Yeah, well, basically, yes. This guy seemed to be French, at least from what I heard, but as he was distorting his voice..."

"How often did he call you?"

"Only twice. First, he called me when I had this incident, like the very next day of my birthday. At first, I thought it was a prank call because someone was playing with a voice distorter wishing me a happy birthday and I got it wrong. He called me on a private number. This was weird. But he gave me some warning, like today is the first day of the rest of your life or something like that, I mean, I remember he was kind of threatening, but I didn't take it seriously. Regarding prank calls, it was not the first, and certainly not the last."

"Hum, and what about the other time?"

"The other time was basically when I received through the post a letter that contained pictures of me, obviously taken that night. There was a phone number attached to that..."

"A phone number?"

"Yes. I assume a prepaid phone number. Because when I called him, Clarisse checked at the same time the provenance of that phone number. You know, on this app, erm... *CheckMyNumber*."

"Yeah."

"And it was a prepaid phone. So, we couldn't identify it."

"Could you send me that phone number?"

"Sure, I'll forward it to you. Anyway, during that call, basically, he told me that given the pictures he had of me, he was ready to send it to all the members of my family if I didn't accept Kelly's offer that I rejected a couple of days earlier. Her offer was that basically, the next day after that incident happened and I got trapped, she proposed me money because, well, that evening, the thing I didn't know was that I acted as a, well... You got it."

"I see, yeah. Was this blackmailer basically well informed about you?"

"Pretty much, yes. Basically, I am not on social networks, Facebook, Twitter, or other shit like this. I'm not even using WhatsApp; I hate all those silly apps spying on you. So, I am not someone that exposes her privacy, and as my boyfriend, Florent, is on those social networks, I expressly asked him not to mention me on any of these networks, 'cause I don't want Zuckerberg to know anything about my life. And I am checking quite often if Florent puts any information that concerns me by far on those shit, and he doesn't."

"Okay, and what is the link between this and your blackmailer?"

"I'm coming to it. As nobody can trace me on these social networks, how comes that basically, this guy knew where precisely my grandparents lived in the UK? And how comes that he knew a day that strictly nobody knew except my boyfriend and I, the day we actually starting our relationship? This is just insane, I mean, giving me that information, it's simply crazy. This is where I took all this very seriously. There's absolutely no way he could basically know my life, know such private details of my life unless he is a relative or someone to whom I talk about this. And I am not someone that talks."

"Hum... And what did he ask you, after this?"

"He gave me a delay, something like 24 hours to accept Kelly's offer; otherwise, he'd ruin my life."

"Hum, I see. Did you guys have other contacts since even?"

"No... That was the last. It was on the 12th of January, something like that."

"Hum, that's quite recent. And did he give you a name to identify himself? Or a nickname, or something?"

"Oh, yeah. Erm... Basically, he nicknamed himself, erm... Something like, erm... *Evening Sun... Morning Sun...*"

"*Raising Sun?*"

"Yes, *Raising Sun*, that's right!"

I tested her, pretending that I didn't remember the name he gave me on the phone. And that worked, she gave me the nickname she was seeking, to actually confirm who he may be. So, she had the blackmailer name. And she had the full dimension of the problem now: some guy that basically knows everything about me, a great manipulator. She may or may not know the only problem, but whoever is my blackmailer, I never accepted to become a victim, I accepted his offer to counterattack and save my girlfriend's arse. This guy, my blackmailer, is a great manipulator, I must admit it, he is a good one. The problem is that it's a manipulator against the manipulator, and one of them is taking the other for an idiot. And the question is, I think I am right, but he also thinks he's right, this is why I am so careful. The problem with him is that he never contacts me, except these two calls, but other than that, he never calls me. This is why the threat is real, we are both playing chess, we just don't know what's the next move for each other.

Anyway, even if I kept my mind relaxed and remained cool-blooded, seeing Claire in that state, and having to do this was not something that amazed me. I still remember the very first time, and it's still pretty hard for me. I am somehow exhausted; this is why I will launch my counterattack offensive from tomorrow. Whatever happens. Whilst I saw her standing in front of me, listening carefully to what I was saying, for once I somehow felt the need to actually confess. And the problem is... If I want this to have more impact... Like, to show this is real...

"I am exhausted, Heather, I just want this to actually end!" I restarted.

"I know. And the reason why I wanted to see you tonight, it's because I think that one of you, between Claire and you, is now in serious danger."

"What do you mean, in serious danger?"

"Well... Let me show you something, actually. It's maybe better for you to understand."

She actually went to grab her iPad, which was still on the office. And I don't know what she was doing on this, but she seemed focused. What does she mean, by danger? If the threat is having us exposed on weird websites, well... But if she had pictures, it meant that the risk was elsewhere.

"This girl is named Natalie Dubois. She was, more or less your age. Last year, she disappeared one night without leaving any traces. Two months later, she was found dead in a square in central Paris."

"Oh, my..."

"After investigations, police actually found out that she was engaged in some prostitution activities, for months before her death. She has been blackmailed, and her leaked videos in porn websites on the day she was reported as missing. The blackmailer, someone using the nickname 'rising sun', does that tell you something?"

"Yes... Oh, my... Why has she been killed and disappeared?"

"Because she started to rebel against her blackmailer. Refusing to do some jobs and, here it went. She was basically eighteen. Had a boyfriend, and was, yeah, full of life. Just like your girlfriend."

The picture that she actually showed me was a body, a white girl, brown hairs, found dead on a grass. At that moment I was just like... Okay, this guy is not only a pimp, but he's also a serial killer. Well, fine, I mean, what should I say. The body had no marks of mutilation, I mean, we could still recognise her face, nothing weird like... No, she was fully dressed, I mean, entirely... she had a dress, and I didn't really pay attention to the rest of her clothing, but I noticed that there were three bullets around her heart, disposed in a kind of a triangle. It's actually weird to see pictures like this, bodies and everything, it kind of impressed me. It's erm, almost disgusting. And, I love watching crime series, but, when it comes to real crimes and real murders, I mean, okay, this is still through a screen, but... Well. I think I get her idea. She scrolled for the next image, and at the same time, continued speaking:

"Another example. This was Lauren Sutherland, from the UK. Found dead in Chelsea's home, a morning when her parents went back from a weekend abroad. I think this example may talk more to you: her father was a successful entrepreneur, her mother, a doctor, and they had pretty much a good situation. Until that day, they found her daughter dead in her living room. The same process killed because she was blackmailed and started to rebel against authority. Contrarily to Natalia, she didn't disappear. Instead, given the several marks on her body and several haematomas, she's been tortured for hours. At least this is the report given by the Metropolitan Police, given next to Scotland Yard, and then to me."

"Tortured?"

"Oh, yeah. Pretty much quite a lot of stuff, apparently, they attached her on a chair and plugged her on a battery for minutes, but it was not only that. It was horrible. Apparently, they actually tortured her because, she was like you, trying to organise a rebellion within the cluster. Oh, and she was seventeen."

"Oh, Jesus..."

Hum... Tortured. Well, I know what I may expect then, now for sure I need her protection. Because, well, if I pull on the trigger with my plan and if things go out of control, I don't really want to end up like this. Well, as this guy seems intelligent, for sure he's gonna target Claire since she cannot defend herself, he's Going to punish me by this. So far, from what I understand, this Natalie and this, erm... Whoever she is, they acted alone. With Claire, we are part of a team, so unless this guy has several hitmen under his control... Targeting two people at once may be tricky.

Moreover, my plan is designed to be quick, and mostly, he's not supposed to see it coming as it will start from something insignificant. I don't mind being attacked, I just want them to leave her alone, I still have my superpower: speaking. And this can ultimately save my arse. I was actually thinking, I may change my strategy, mostly the end, because I will need immediate protection from the police for Claire and me. I will negotiate it. Anyway, I let her just continuing:

"I also have a different one. Let me introduce you, Valentina Baumann, from Germany. She was living in Hamburg. She was gay, just like you guys, seventeen as well, single, died last September. Also blackmailed and overwhelmed by events, unlike the two other girls killed, she actually committed suicide. But when we actually found out in her death note that she mentioned this *Rising Sun* guy, well... You know, it rose our interest..."

"You're scaring me, now..."

"All this to say, Charlotte, I don't want either your name or your girlfriend's added on that death toll. I already placed your girlfriend's house under surveillance from Interpol. She's under protection, and under surveillance, this is why she's been instructed not to leave her house until we finally catch this guy. Or at least someone that will lead us to this guy."

Okay, so it's big. Well, it does and doesn't really surprise me to be fair. All those stories, Interpol... I think it's better if we get the hell out quick, this is why I carefully studied the plan, it should work. I hope its gonna work. Geez, Claire, in what kind of troubles did you put yourself? Hopefully, I'm a fighter, I'll fight back; hopefully, I'm here. Now I hear some murders stories or suicide... Well, on the other hand, it seems to be the purpose of it all. I am sure, if I didn't fight back, if I didn't engage myself in that fight, this would have been the outcome of that current situation. It's a bad thing, but it's also a good thing that this happened, even if it cost me quite a lot. But, well... I'm here for her anyway, a promise is a promise.

Anyway, I don't know why, but I was feeling like dizzy after all those revelations. People died, others killed themselves, and... Things are actually more important than I ever thought. This is why, once this is over, now I will ask for protection. Because that is sure, if we destroy a cluster, there will be retaliation, as he won't lose a battle without fighting back. So, I should cover our areas. It's why I was kind of, erm, confused now:

"What you're telling me... It's big. It's like, big. And erm..." I was seeking my words. "I really don't know what to say, I mean, I really feel like..."

"I prefer talking to you about this because, from Claire, I know that you are kind of specialised in manipulation. And, yeah, I have been investigating on you, on who you are, and several people said the same. I even talked to the Dr Marcovic, a psychiatrist that followed you when you were younger and found out you're actually a cold-blooded psychopath."

"Who do you mean, by several people?"

"Just some people. The only thing that actually came out was that you never cared about other people as long as your interests are fulfilled, and you have answers to your questions. You are a specialist in harassment, lies and ruining lives doesn't prevent you from sleeping as long as you get what you want. You only value Claire's life, because she's the only one that matters to you, somehow you love her. Yeah, I read your psychiatrists reports. Apparently, you are a dangerous person if not managed properly."

"If you are telling me that I blackmail Claire, this is rubbish!"

"No, I never said that. I know you have been targeted, and I know you are a victim of this thing, I know you are not like *Rising Sun*."

Yeah, but she says that I look like him. I mean, come on, listen to her, I know that people like me are generally evil and don't really care about anything, but come on... In this war I am like the United States during World War II, I entered into war because I have been attacked, and finally I see that I have interests to actually save, so I'm gonna win this war. Well, if I'm gonna win, I'm not sure, I confident it should work, but now I know that either I win, whether I die. So... But no matter what, I must still fight. But, dangerous, come on, I mean, yes, it's not that wrong, but I am manipulating people to save my girlfriend. I wonder if there would be a lot of manipulators doing the same as me. Okay, yeah, Claire is part of my interests, but I will save a human life! Yeah, I heard what you think, "like she cares..." well, I think it's better to laugh about this drama instead of having to cry for it. And... If I undergo torture or be killed for her, it is still a significant result, it will ultimately prove that I love her. Meh... This is why, yeah, I defended myself:

"Well, what you say is true, I don't give a shit about other people, I really don't. But Claire, she's the one I need. Claire is my drug, she's my reason to actually be alive. I need her. And whatever happens, I don't really care about my own life, if I have to live or be tortured for her, then I'd do it, as long as she is safe, that's all I want. This world is a mess, there's nothing beautiful in it. But Claire, she is the only person that makes this life liveable to me. And I want to save her life whatever the price is. I will fight for her."

"I know. I know, and she knows. And given all the information I have on you, I really want to use you to catch the son of a bitch who did that to you."

Notwithstanding, I am sure that this case goes beyond like a simple investigation for her. She must have personal interests in it, or she must have been humiliated by this guy. Besides, it's one of her major cases, I mean, according to my cold read, she has been promoted recently, and I really feel from her a personal involvement. Not only because she called that guy a son of a bitch, I feel like... Yeah, this meeting at 1 am, well, it doesn't sound like it is clear from her, she really wants his head. This is why my strategy can only go in her interest. I just continued:

"Well, that is your job. On the other hand, that is massive. That's huge, I mean, in the beginning, I thought that it was someone just targeting me, or Claire, for some reason. I just didn't think it was all across Europe."

"There have been deaths in the US too. For the moment, we have been counting more than a hundred victims. Ten were in France, and fifteen in the UK. But it may be bigger than we think, as we could identify more than fifty clusters across the world. And we don't know who's behind this, for the moment... All we know is that the murderer is someone that kills the victims with three bullets, positioned in a triangle shape, in the abdomen. Around the heart. It's the signature."

"So, it's bigger than Joris. And..."

"That is big, Charlotte. It's big. Bigger than you may imagine."

Well, I see what I am attacking. It's actually a machine. But her help will be paramount because it may change the events scheduled on Tuesday evening. If Claire gets ready, if I tell her what's gonna happen on Tuesday, she could have an additional pressure and actually mess up, because she will be impatient, and Joris will feel it. It's the reason why we should keep the surprise for everyone, even to Claire (well I have no plans to actually inform her and even, I think it's better this way). Now, I have my goal, I have something that she cannot actually refuse because it will bring her Joris and I feel like she didn't have any head of clusters yet, so if she catches Joris, he will speak, that is sure. And as he will have to defend himself on the charge of statutory rape, there's nothing he can actually do. He just can't get away. Since things will explode from a way he may not expect, well...

No, I think, we're clear to start, actually. Let's play because this is the last fight. This is why I just looked at her and then said:

"Okay. Then what can I do for you, as a cold-blooded psychopath manipulator?"

"We would like to actually catch Joris. For now, the problem is that we just have suspicions, we don't have anything that clearly connects him, and we know that if we talk to him, it will put you both in danger and ruin my cover. I just need to catch Joris, so I can put you two in a safe place."

"Hum. If I give you Joris for statutory rape, you think that should work?"

"That should be perfect. Do you have any idea on how we may catch him?"

"Yeah, hum... I just need some guarantee, before. I want to have your word that Claire and I will be safe, that you may find us a safe place where we can actually restart our lives. And I want Claire to have a psychologist, because... It may take years before she recovers from that, and I want her to actually be followed. To have someone other than me so she can talk... Because if she talks to me, Joris and Kelly will be both dead!"

"I will put you two on a safe place at the moment Joris is under arrest. Regarding Kelly, we will catch her later. And for the psychologist, there will be someone for both of you, that doesn't seem to be a problem!"

Oh, I don't need a psychologist, trust me... I'm like a phoenix, I can be reborn from my ashes. That will be a waste of time and time cannot be wasted, especially if I have to protect my girlfriend more closely because that will be sure, after that, my blackmailer will seek revenge. Now, I have her word, she will save me. So, let's talk more seriously now.

"Okay, then. So here is the plan..."

28 *Still alive?*

// Hôtel George V main hall, Avenue des Champs-Élysées, Paris.

// Monday, 21st of January 2013, 03:14.

It was that or die.

Well, now, I have something that I didn't actually include in my plan, and that will change absolutely everything: I have back up. I basically did the very last changes in my plan implementation, a few ones. Still, as I cannot communicate with Claire, it's better to keep this thing secret after having genuinely thought about it. She's already under pressure, if I add this, it will make her explode, and she will fail, so let's do the same way as I will do with Florent within a few hours now, let's, erm, yeah, let's let her heart speak.

Now, everything will actually be determined on Tuesday afternoon. I am just waiting for the code to have everything, but I already explained everything. Basically, as I cannot communicate, I agreed that she would also be listening to my phone, she implanted a kind of software that actually listens to me. It's okay if she does. She knows the drill. And whenever Claire sends me the code, she will understand that she must go at her place through various messages that I will say. And as she's already listening to Claire, the new plan is that Claire must provoke him, so she will push him to make a mistake and assault her. I told her to be as provocative as possible because it will work: Joris is a misogynistic sociopath and sees Claire as a piece of crap that as he trapped, she may not defend herself, and if he rapes her, he thinks that she will be obedient and more scared. He wants to have control with fear, but the thing he actually cannot resist is a woman's charms. Claire has this power, so I want her to use this power against him. And it's precisely when she will be assaulted that she will come in with some police agents, and they will catch him. Caught in the act. Like, fucked. Basically. And literally.

Free Expensive Lies: Prologue

A new day was there, and now, it was time to implement the plan. I have to take control of everything now, we've been talking quite a long moment about how I may implement my plan, and she made sure that I was fully aware of what I was doing. I mean, she doesn't really know me, but I must say that I have been entirely convincing. Because she needs to get Joris, and she doesn't really have any other proofs than our testimonies. Even these are not official, she doesn't really have guarantees on him, so this plan may be the only way she could actually get the head of a cluster. It's been five years the case is still on, and ever since, all the time she's been trying to catch a criminal, a head of the cluster or someone related to this, she always had this person dying or dead already. We basically have different priorities on Tuesday afternoon, she wants Joris alive, whilst I want to save my girlfriend. But she said, if she has to have Joris dead, then, well, she will try to focus on Kelly. But in any case, I had her words, and she told me that she will have a bodyguard for us and open a safe house to restart while they are at war. We just have to proceed now.

Anyway, this conversation kind of wake me up, but it was time to go home. I was now feeling less tired, and, well, planning this, talking about this... it's like, yeah, awakening. It's the first time that I actually set up such a plan, I mean, I already manipulated people, but I never set such a goal, very precisely, to be as accurate as possible. I left her room certainly an hour after I entered, still carrying my bag, and, I already thought since it was almost 3am, how will I get back home because I seldom took the night bus. I definitely need to go downstairs to pick up my phone. So, I took the lift, and, yeah, corridors were still noticeably quiet, even the light was dimmed. We were undoubtedly in the middle of the night; certainly, the night staff started their shifts or were in the middle of it. Anyway, I took the lift, and I arrived in that ground hall. I needed to take my phone back from the reception desk, so I approached. And there was a charming brown-haired lady, certainly thirty, that welcomed me.

"Hello!" I approached her.

"Hi!" she smiled at me.

"Erm... I left my phone at your office about an hour ago, there was a gentleman... Any chances you can actually give it back to me?"

"Oh, erm... Yeah. May I have your name, please?"

"Yeah, erm, Kominsky. Charlotte Kominsky."

"All right, just give me a second then..."

"No problem!"

And, yeah, I guess she went to look underneath her, again, where the safe was... I was leaning on that office at the same time, looking all that was behind. The night will be short, like, truly short. That's what I was thinking about, now. I mean, once back home, I will sleep, my alarm is already set up at 6.30am, and given the fact that it was already 3am, it then leaves me basically, erm, yeah, more or less three hours. But I don't know how long it will take for coming back home, so, maybe, I should more bet on two hours sleep. And, yeah, sleepless nights are, well, harsh, because it will ruin my day tomorrow, I will just be exhausted, and as I want to talk to Florent tomorrow, then I will have to stay awake until late, and... Huh. Yeah, that's gonna be tough. Anyway, apparently, I was not the only one to have left something at the reception, because after maybe ten seconds she was still seeking.

When, unexpectedly, at the very same time I was thinking about how short my night will be, like popping out of nowhere, I suddenly heard...

"CHARLOTTE!" I heard my mother's voice screaming.

"Oh, for the love of God..." I whispered, intensely astonished.

This was a total surprise. When I heard that, my muscles froze, receiving a kind of electrical shock throughout my body. I looked immediately in the direction where my name has been pronounced when I saw her, Mum. Swiftly dressed in her blue jeans, her black sneakers and a black top, the actual very first thing I could read on her face was colossal anxiety. Messy hairs, even her eyes, oh gosh, her eyes were concerned enough: I saw her, she was not angry, but she was worried for me. Now the very first question emerged, how comes that she found me here? I mean, nobody knows except Claire and... Obviously Allison, I mean, Heather, how comes that she could find me? This was the real surprise, I didn't really mind about the rest, how did she manage to know that I was here? Because she saw me leaving on Friday, I told her that I'd be back soon, and... Oh, my, don't tell me that she called her recent date, who's a PI... And had me followed. Well, if she did that, then... Then, it's even better, now all the conditions are reunited so she can be concerned over me and then I may let this scandal explode more quickly, they are all worried. This would explain why Florent kept on harassing me, and... Hum, okay. Apparently, I don't need to throw some fuel on the floor to burn the building down, it seems that my task may be more manageable. Anyway, I saw her approaching, and I showed a disappointed face. Immediately, she replied back:

"Yeah, you can swear, I don't even care," she was saying after having heard me whispering.

Free Expensive Lies: Prologue

"How the hell do you know that I was here now?"

"How could I know? You're kidding, right? I mean, you'd better be kidding me, right?"

"Not a second, Amelia!" I called her by her first name to actually have more impact.

"No? You called me ten times two hours ago and left me four messages to tell me that you were in danger, that I needed to come as soon as I could. And of course, when I called you back, you obviously didn't answer!"

"What?"

"Come on, Charlotte, don't be dumb. So, what the fuck are you doing there?"

How could I call her two hours ago to actually tell her that I was in danger? Well, there might be an explanation for that, as my blackmailer couldn't listen to my phone. I assume he doesn't really know who I was with (because if Heather called me with her standard phone, she sent me a message through another phone number, the message to tell me where I could meet her and when), then I assume this is a strategy for *Raising Sun* to disturb me. Because, as I managed to make sure our phones would be out of his reach, then... Oh my, he did that. The receptionist gave me my phone, and the first thing I did was check my calls and messages. I didn't call or message anyone in the last five hours. Hum, interesting, well, I believe my mother. Okay, this is surprising. After I checked my phone, and I raised my head, she just looked at me and remained interrogative:

"Could I know what you were doing here, at such an hour?"

"I... No, actually, you can't." I couldn't tell her why, otherwise the pressure may not raise, and I want to leave her under pressure.

"I am your mother, and I want to know what you were doing here at that hour!"

"That is great. Personally, I want a hot girlfriend kissing my arse and a purple aeroplane, so we are both going to keep on dreaming, all right?"

"What the hell is wrong with you, Charlotte, why are you acting so weird for the last two days? You told me on Friday that you'd be back on Saturday and still now, I find you here! Could I have an answer to my question?"

Mum, I can promise that you will know this in less than forty-eight hours. That is a promise that I can actually make, yes.

"Last time I checked, I was eighteen, right?"

"You don't like me, fine. I am totally fine with that. But Florent, it's been two days that we are worried for you, and now I received that text, I was like, something happened to her..."

"Great, you guys were worried for the last two days, and then what?" I remained indifferent.

"You really don't care, do you?"

"That you guys were worried? Well, that is the very least of my problems, yes, to be honest with you!"

"Oh yeah?"

"Yeah. Anyway, you wanna drive me home now? Fine, let's go home!"

29 *Zombies*

// My bedroom, Neuilly-sur-Seine.

// Monday, 21st of January 2013, 07:30.

Hum, I see. Well, basically, now, between my blackmailer and I, it's more or less who is taking the other for an idiot. Well, anyway, despite our small argument, she actually drove me home, which was better.

And it was seven. Like almost the entire flat, the bedroom was plunged into almost total darkness and deafening silence. Nobody was awake, and even the street sounded like quiet. Since my return late in the evening, I was struggling to sleep, I actually didn't sleep at all. When I arrived last night, after all the emotions and the plan that continued to be elaborated in total secrecy, Florent was sleeping already, and he seemed sleeping like a log. I looked at him, and, in some way, I was feeling sorrow for him, because, okay, he betrayed me on my pregnancy, but he doesn't deserve what will happen to him in the next day. The only difference is, he just doesn't know, but I do. And I just hate to think about what I am doing. But this is manipulation, and in manipulation, you need to focus on results, not on damages. And Claire, and everything, the fact that Mum found me at the George V, now, yeah. Yeah, now, the truth is getting dangerously closer to me as it has never been since the ninth of January. This is why, things must explode now, we just cannot live any longer with that. So, this was almost a sleepless night, although I was already exhausted, I just turned myself in the bed, at some point I took my headset to actually listen to some music and watch movies on YouTube, but I just couldn't sleep. I thought I could sleep, but my brain was overworking. I was not under pressure; I was just bracing myself for the controlled avalanche that will come after. This is the only way out.

I was feeling the situation as if it was a building through which we placed explosives all across. And we are about to blow it up. I cannot even postpone the thing because now, the situation is already under pressure, I mean, when he wakes up, he will ask me why, what happened, and this will lead to an argument. The bottle of water is already under massive pressure, and I just cannot add some more water, it's gonna explode. It's the explosion that I must control. The thing is, for that, how to actually start, because... As I said, this is already bad, this is already... fucked up. The problem is, I want him to break up with me, this must be the first situation, this must be the thing that is due to happen if he doesn't break up with me... Well, when I will reveal him tonight what I did, he will break up with me, that is sure, but I must ensure today that we have a serious argument, and I must beg him to actually come back. How to trigger the bomb so it can be powerful enough, but not wholly destructive? Hum...

On the other hand, I am not in the absolute best situation in my couple right now. Let's imagine that I would save my couple, what would I do now? Oh, I think I have an idea.

But my intentions were clear, and I remained very calm, nothing could change my mood. He was just next to me, sleeping deeply, wearing his black top, and, yeah, I guess he must have had a terrible weekend. He was asleep at my place and turned to the window, and I was quite reluctant to touch him. It's funny, he always uses to sleep at my place when I am not there, always seeking my smell, but things were already different when I came back late last night. Hum, maybe he must be feeling that the end is near. Sometimes, it's like death, we used to say that people feel when they are about to die, or when the end of the line is near. I remember, when I broke up with Claire, certainly days before, I felt that something was ongoing, and seeing Kelly coming closer made me actually panic. Things were not reassuring me, and, yeah, I was acting different, I didn't really care about myself anymore, I was just like, "let it be" because Claire didn't really have that much of interest with me, she found me boring. This is why it changed me, when I broke up with her, I was really pissed. When you break up after seven years of relationship, it's not the same, it's not like a typical ending. Hopefully, Florent and I have been together for less than three months, and even though he proposed me for marriage, even though I am technically his fiancée, as I still have this ring around my finger... Well. It's not like we've been together for long. And, I thought about it, things between him and I just cannot really work.

But the suspicions of my mother were now awake, because of my phone being hacked. I don't think she will ask me many questions; she already did yesterday (I mean... obviously, earlier in the day) when she drove me home. And I know my mother; whenever she will see things exploding with Florent, she will ask him what's going on, she won't ask me, because she knows that she may face a dispute otherwise. Curiously, I am not really sure about whether Clarisse is here or not. I don't really think so, since she spends a lot of time with her boyfriend, it's why I need to keep her updated over the situation. Well, I will see her at school today anyway. I also hope mum will be late tonight or see someone outside, one of her colleagues because I really need to be alone with him tonight. I cannot afford to have someone in the flat at that moment. Obviously, I will have observers through my phone because both my blackmailer and Heather will carefully listen to tonight's ongoing events. But this is different.

Anyway, Florent was still sleeping. It's been a couple of days that I didn't have any news of him, I mean, I don't really know what he is currently doing, like, for a living. He was still wearing his old dark pyjamas, completely faded, and almost destroyed, but he loves this one, he has it for a while now. It has holes practically everywhere, as it was manufactured in Bangladesh, maybe around six or seven years ago, probably by child workers. However, he still keeps it anyway, even if this thing is everything but totally ordinary. I kept on looking at him, and he was sleeping soundly, he basically did not move that much. As if no problems or worries could ever reach him, I imagine that his face's features were all relaxed, it was the calm before the storm. And I looked one more time at my phone, to check at the hour: my alarm is due to ring in less than one minute. I just breathed, I only, well... The alarm is gonna wake him up, or maybe not, I don't know if he is to actually wake up with me, but... I just breathed. But I was already feeling sad, feeling sorry, because there will be things that won't be said, and yeah.

My approach was decided. How I will approach things with him. I must be sad, and, basically, I must cope with whatever he wants. I just cannot be the one who decides today, I must leave him taking all decisions he wants because I am the one who made a mistake and I am also the one seeking to be forgiven. So, given that, whatever he wants, I have to cope with it, I have to deal with that. And, this situation already happened before, I mean, when we had an argument, and I did some bad things and on the process for things to go on, well. I offered him what he wanted, sex. But, usually, after sex, things use to go back to normal, he just forgives what I did, and we just go back as if nothing actually ever happened, but now, things are just too big. First, I am pregnant, and he's going to ask explanations about, well... This, and... Why I disappeared and didn't answer to his texts. Yeah, now, especially since I must be cautious of what I say. Well, I took my phone, waited for the alarm to actually ring, and when it rang, I immediately switched it off. I don't want him to be awakened by this, I actually want to wake him up. Well, at least it will somehow be the "goodbye"—my way to say goodbye.

There is still a detail I actually didn't think about: where will I sleep tonight? Because I do not feel like sleeping in here and being in the middle of the scandal when it will explode. Hum... I will see Claire, she told me she's due to come back to school today, so I just hope she's going to come. Maybe I should sleep at her place? That would certainly be better, because if I am trapped in here when things are just blowing up, well, that will be slightly funny. Basically, I want the thing to explode, but I don't really know how my mother will react to this. She will badly react, that is obvious, but how she will respond... Maybe if I stay here, she will forbid me to go outside, and as I specifically requested to be there when Joris are arrested, this will lead to some issues. Because tomorrow will be an important day, and Claire will need me, and I just can't leave her dealing with all that shit alone. And I need to be there, she will need me after that, because that will be undoubtedly horrible, even though... Well, I honestly don't know how Joris will defend himself after being arrested. Tomorrow is going to come with a bunch of surprises.

One minute past the moment, I was due to wake up. Basically, I know that today, I start at 10. Thus, it leaves me plenty of time to actually let that thing happen, and I was enjoying the very last moment of silence and calm, as I know that complete mayhem, or pandemonium, will break out in a very bit. It was still cold and obscure in there, although the curtains were not totally drawn, and a lot of light actually came in. The sun was rising now; indeed, the city was starting its daily Monday routine by working. And I was there. Wearing still the top I have now been wearing for the last six days, still carrying Claire's smell, and... Yeah. It was my very last moment, and suddenly, I had a kind of a strange feeling, it was odd. What if I fail? What if things do not go as they were to go? Meh, let's not think about this, let's live the moment instead because as I said, this is a kind of comes what may.

Rapidly, I turned myself back to him. As he was turning his back to me, I actually placed him flat back. But, damn, he was so heavy, and he almost fell like a sack of stone. Things may actually work, I don't know, but at the moment I turned him, I was like observing him from the side, and he was softly opening his eyes. The thing was, I didn't really want to actually leave him time to figure out what happened, I immediately put my hairs on a side they may not disturb me. I immediately give him an exceptionally soft, almost elusive kiss. Once, twice, it was somehow a way to reassure him when he was still coming back to his mind, certainly disturbing him from reality. I felt like he was always responsive, as suddenly I felt his hand touching my back, then caressing my back. It's true, things were different now, deep down I felt like this was all an illusion, I wasn't feeling anything, it was like giving a kiss to the first stranger that comes (and no, I never did that... Okay, once, it was just a bet, and it doesn't count). He was caressing my back, whilst I started leaning more and more against him because I was freezing, I was seeking heat, and, it was when I actually stopped kissing him, I took him in my arms. He used to love being wakened up this way, but today seemed different, according to his facial expression... He just started to mumble.

"Hmmm... Charlotte?" He said while he was opening his eyes.

"Shhh!" I whispered as I didn't want to let him speak.

"Hmmm, you're back?"

"Shhh, shut up and let me do what I want!"

"Yeah, but..." I basically blocked his arms so he couldn't repel me.

Good, it goes actually fine so far. The thing was to not leaving him time. I resumed kissing him, and yet again he was still very responsive and seemed to enjoy that somehow, whilst I started to move my hand very slowly towards his belly, and this very slowly. Well, if he didn't want that (that happened once), he would have pushed me already, especially since he is more robust than me. On the other hand, though, he is a guy and, we all know how they work, he cannot be insensitive to that. I just let things going naturally, everything was just fake, but it's not the first time that I have sex with him and pretends that I enjoy, I am kind of used to that. I was not really excited; I was quite okay and kept thinking that he had to react a certain way when I actually slid my other hand under his pants. He was just breathing normally, I mean, according to his breath, he seemed very confused, he seemed kind of, yeah, shared between the fact that he wanted to speak to me, but given the fact that I had my hand on the disturb button, he actually thought that we might talk later about this. I am sure, I would have tried to do the same to Claire, I would have first her hand in my face, then I would have to explain myself, and then, maybe something might be possible, depends on which I have been convincing.

Anyway, whilst my hand slowly reached the sensitive point, I actually stopped kissing him, and kept on overriding his own control: I sensually whispered to his left ear...

"I just want you now!"

"Oh, do you?" He immediately reacted.

Obviously, this was simple psychology. All information perceived by the left ear goes to the right brain hemisphere, in charge of the creativity and imaginary... Yes because his left hemisphere still hates me (the one dealing with logic and reason), I want to actually create a conflict. As a man, Florent works this way, logic and reason is paramount, so at some point, if I override this, this may leave me a couple of minutes. As he still has this kind of misogynistic side, even small, he will figure out that I tried to calm him down and then, he's gonna be more upset with me.

I actually kind of come increasingly closer to him, almost sticking my entire body against his, to show him that he had no way to run. I kept kissing him, and over and over again, taking now full control of himself as my other hand was now in a strategic place. His arousal exploded, I mean, this is a kind of fantasy for him, being wakened up with this. But he was not actually fully ready, for the moment he was just breathing, but he kind of remained under my control, just didn't want to get away, like reduced to a sort of strengthless state, he just couldn't do anything. I actually stopped kissing her, putting now my head over his torso, and continuing playing with him, I was feeling like so powerful, and nothing could reach me. I was playing this game, letting things actually explode. Let the bomb blow up. Now that he understood what I was seeking, as it was apparent, after a few second of feeling him now reduced to a total inability. With a mischievous smile although kind of perverse, I started to remove my hand from where it was, to actually pull slightly down his pants, everything obviously under the cover. I didn't want to see anything, to leave him now totally exposed, like he has no ways to hide. Now I feel like he is ready, I feel like if I stop, that would be a terrible mistake, so I just pushed his pants down, thinking, now, you can't get away.

At the moment when I actually did that; indeed, all the pressure increased radically. His breathing increased, his lungs were seeking for more air, and as he remained relatively slow in his moves, basically aroused, I knew that he was certainly starting to be ready. Now... I actually kind of stopped, I kind of removed my hand, as, well, I saw him, yeah, being hard and he was, yeah, even if this was all hidden under the bedsheets, I was just thinking about, is it right or is it wrong? And, when he noticed that I withdrew my hand, in a spare of a moment, he was just recovering his breath by basically whispering a few words:

"What? One week without sex, and you're already stopping?"

Because now, in my mind, I was thinking about this, it's been almost two weeks that we didn't have sex, or maybe more, and on the other hand, since what happened with the Russian guy, I was not feeling like doing it. So, should I proceed? If I do not, well, this will lead to a fight because he's gonna be frustrated, and if I do, this will lead to a conflict because he will figure out that this was a smokescreen. On the other hand, I know him, and I know that this will be very quick because it's been two weeks we didn't do anything. It's been two weeks that I am wandering around, and he cannot touch me, now he can... And then I will be frustrated, I will explain my frustration. Yeah, that could be an excellent way to lead to what is going to happen. Telling him that he is a joke, insulting his sexuality, for like every man, talking about how bad they are at bed, yeah, they kind of don't like it. On the other hand, nobody likes it. Meh...

"I had a cramp in my hand, hold on!" I cynically replied back, still showing as uninterested, another provocation from my part.

I must admit that, for someone that actually have quite a few things to think about, I remained quite enterprising with him, I mean, I am not usually like this. I placed my hand back where it was, and I felt like, is that what you want? And even if he was still on his way to correctly wake up, well... He was on that part already ready to attack. And, yet, touching him, well, it doesn't feel like really natural to me. But for him, whilst I was more confidently doing what he wanted me to do, I was feeling it, the pressure was raising, raising, on and on. I cannot stop anything anymore, I was like, yeah, tired, and... Well, on the other hand, given the fact that he actually started the race quite fast, well I don't really think he may remain that long. This seemed merely weird to me at that moment, I mean, every time it happens, I think about the same, this is just not rational, and this is just, well, weird. I just plunged my hand in his pants, kept on kissing him, and I was feeling like in a kind of automatic mode, like, basically like I was making dinner or playing on my iPad, it seemed to be the same, just observing a procedure and applying it. I honestly don't know if I am good at it and I don't really care. Still, the thing is, just doing this reminds the advice that Sophie used to give me at the very beginning I was with Florent. That for whatever guy, (because she says that they are all the same, and given the fact that for me, people are all the same), it's not the same perception, if you are well dressed and good looking, then you are good at bed. And, well, I wasn't dressed very well now, but yeah. Knowing that is just depressing.

While I remained in some kind of automatic mode, certainly delivering the shittiest of myself on this, I felt him. His heartbeat increased rapidly. He was breathing faster and was shivering. He remained there, just letting things going, almost motionless, well not entirely motionless, he was only obeying to that moment. Basically, he was more than ready, the thing was, I wanted the pressure to grow exponentially. I mean, this was insane, it's almost the first time that I am doing what I am currently doing, I never did that to him before, like, touching him how I did it. I wasn't experimenting anything, because these are not fancy things I love to experiment, but, well, on the other hand, I was actually really feeling him, and this thing confirmed me this morning what it confirms since I started that relationship with him: this is not what I want. But, well, at this point he was so hot, he was, well, this is what I thought, well, now, he is more than ready.

As he was already flat back, it was certainly more comfortable. I lifted up the sheets, stopped kissing him, and it was now the moment to actually realise what he dreamed for the moment I started this, the final. I basically jumped over him and put my leg on the other side to be over him, but I did it quite slowly. Yeah, I basically did that in the same state of mind that I would have if I had to clean my mess, more or less, it was a waste of time for me, but apparently not for him, but, well, now that I engaged the situation, it would be cruel to actually leave it as it is. But somehow, I felt like my hand was dirty (I mean, now, it was), but it was, well, it was like I put my hand without any gloves in a weak acid, it was itchy. But, hopefully, once I was over him, I didn't have that charge of, well, he was basically driving himself into where he was due to go, I didn't really have nothing to do on that point. Which is why, when I actually felt it, well, I just let myself down, closed my eyes and breathed a bit faster just to pretend that I am also in the game. I touched my hairs because I know that this is something he loves (Claire too... it's funny), and, well... As usual, feeling this hurts because I was not acutely ready, but, well.

After this, I was basically sat over him, and for a short time, he just stared at me, smiled, and after I reopened my eyes, I smiled back at him. I was there, now, I was ready to go. And, after this very swift moment, when I felt like it was the calm before the storm, when I was feeling him down there and almost as I never felt him before, he started to, well, do what he had to do. It was painful, but I am used to it; on the other hand, it's the first time we do it without anything, it's not like I can get pregnant a second time. He was pushing, again, and again, whilst I started to bend slowly towards him, keeping my arms straight, and I closed my eyes. At the same time, he actually put his hands on my butts, well, I think to make the cadence of the movement going as he likes. However, although he was going softly, although he remained quite gentle initially, it was still horrible, which is why I closed my eyes and very swiftly and silently moaned. Still, if he thought it was because I was okay, he was wrong. This was fucking painful. Unfortunately, maybe after a few seconds, not even a minute, I was feeling like, well, he was accelerating, because, well, even to me, I was actually feeling him like, yeah, for real, and, yeah... I raised the pressure too hard. At that moment, he grabbed me this time a bit more fiercely, a bit stronger, and was suddenly accelerating. Somehow I kept on having this flashbacks in my head, reminding me what happened barely a week ago when I was trapped with this two weirdos, that I couldn't do anything, that I couldn't go anywhere, I just had to live the moment and shut the hell up. He was accelerating, because, yeah, it's been too long that I am wandering around and cannot do anything, it's been too long that he is dreaming about that moment. And now he could have it, well...

And, well, curiously, as I predicted, after maybe less than a minute... I saw him moaning, one last time, and I felt down there that he was over. As usual, whenever it's done, I usually go towards him, I unbent my arms, and I collapse to him too, and I let him take back his breath. I was, yeah, relieved. Relieved that this was done, I mean, relieved this was done for the very last time ever since sex has been the less enjoyable part of our relationship, in my opinion. I pretended to be out of breath too, maybe to show him that somehow, I was aroused too, and I wanted to go further, and it is where I will actually trigger the conflict. Even if I just couldn't wait for it to finish because I wanted to pee badly and, also because, yeah, I was just impatient for it to be over. I mean, the thing now was to attack him, the logic following the plan, attack him on his atrocious performance. This is why, after a few seconds, when he regained back his respiration, I started to strike:

"Geez, you better be kidding me, right?"

"Oh, come on, that happens," he just didn't expect me to say such a thing, I was hearing, because it took him a couple of seconds to actually think about what he would say.

However, I remained quiet. I fell back onto where I slept, whilst removing him from me, and, well. Now, it was time to make him feel guilty. I don't know, I mean, those flashbacks, even if they were short, it actually switched my mood, I was feeling upset. At the same time, he was so hot that he was terribly sweating, he was just, yeah, the bed was wet. I left him just regaining his respiration, for maybe... well, more than the short time through which we had sex, I just placed myself under the sheets, and looked through the window, the light of the new day coming. And cars passing through the street, life just restarting... I just heard this. I wanted to pee, but it could actually wait. It actually turned me down, I was feeling weird, like depressed for some instants, I felt like, this is the end of a life that I accepted for too long to please people. We say that hunger justifies the means, well, I guess this is true now. And, after some point, once he was now calm, and he put his pants back, I just, well, again, broke the ice.

"So, what's up today?"

"I don't know..." he slowly replied, laconic, and also seeking his words

"Well, that doesn't tell me anything."

"I have been panicking all weekend, I have been seeking you all weekend, I have been calling you, texting you..."

"Well, I wasn't far away!"

"Now you just leave and, come back, do that, and pretend like nothing happened?"

"Well, from what you did this morning, yeah, basically, nothing happened!" I was laughing, to make sure he'd perceive this as an attack.

"You better be kidding me, Charlotte..."

"Should I?" I really hope this was not too obvious.

"Cha, I... we need to talk."

Well, the "we need to talk" actually marked the very end of the waking up. On the other hand, he was now fully awake, and, basically, I knew that I couldn't get away from this sentence, it was sure that he wanted to talk to me. The problem is, on what? My pregnancy, or the fact that I went missing that weekend? That's not really clear yet. Well, the thing was; hopefully, I didn't really think about what I would answer to any of these. I was thinking, maybe I should tell him the truth, that I went back at Claire's place and we spent the weekend together, obviously without saying what happened, but as he is smart enough, I am sure he would make the deduction on his own. Or erm, I actually don't know. Well, I'll do what I do the best, improvisation. But damn, why am I feeling like this poor king Priam, letting coming in his town a gigantic wooden horse?

"Okay, I understand... Tell me, what do you want to talk about," I changed my mood and stopped fooling around, placing myself now at the place I was supposed to have, the victim.

"Where have you been this entire weekend? I have been worried, to have no texts, no calls from you, nothing!"

"Oh, erm... You know, I wasn't there, well, because erm... It's complicated, let's say that I needed some air, I just took the weekend for myself" I was seeking my words.

Basically, we were both facing each other in the bed, both having an arm between our heads and the pillow, we basically had the same position. But the way he looked at me was now quite strange: sex didn't really appease him, as it was short, and as it was disappointing, and especially since I seemed weird to him, he was looking at me like, I better give the right answer because he seemed fed up. Deep down I am sure he suspects that I went back at Claire, because he's not stupid, where shall I go in this town for like two days except than Claire's place? I don't have any best friend, and he knows that I haven't been with Clarisse, so it leaves only one supposition to him. I felt like he just wanted to have my word, he just wanted me to say that I was at her place. The question is, on what purpose? Oh, I am sure that this is to piss me off. My phone was quite far away, and... Meh, I think I may tell him what would explain why he had such a horny wakeup call in his mind. He didn't reply to what I finally said, he just breathed and looked at me, puzzled. Making myself confused was actually good, this is why, after having sought my words, I quickly launched the strike:

"Okay, you want the truth, right? I was with Claire for the weekend."

"Oh yeah?" immediately, his face changed, he was now disturbed.

"Yes, but it's not what you think..." I started using reverse psychology, to make sure that yeah, it actually was what he thinks.

"Oh, fucking hell..."

"It was just, you know, to see someone else, I kind of had a hard week last week, and, she called me, and I said, why not, it was just to actually change my mind!"

"Oh, you had a tough week, huh?"

"Yes, I did!"

"Does this tough week have any relationship with the pregnancy test that I discovered in the bathroom the other day?"

Okay, I think I have it now. Oh, well, you know, on mornings, I am usually kind of slow to actually start.

"I am so sorry, I was just, I wanted to talk to you about this!" I changed my voice, feeling like weak, fading away, to give him the impression that I actually did something wrong.

"Why? Why did you hide this from me?"

"I don't know, I was just, this was just unexpected! It's just, I just don't want to have a baby, I don't want to be pregnant, and now, well... I fucked up, that's all, it's just... When Claire called me, it was just that I wanted to escape!"

"To escape... Do you mean, escape from me?"

"You just fucking betrayed me! I thought I could trust you, and when I came back home on Friday morning as I was out all night, mum talked to me about that, and I was just... How could you? You could have sent me a text or talking to me straight, no, instead, you talk to mum about this! So, yes, it was, yes, escaping from you!"

Hum, I think I shouldn't continue in that way, because I actually gave him an explanation, and if I go on this way, I will win and won't have what I want. Because, yes, this is his fault, basically, he just cannot really say anything. Well, there was still another thing, and I saw that he paid attention to this: on Thursday night, the night when he went to his mother's place, I told him that I was home. The night of the day when he actually found that pregnancy test, and I assume that mum called him on that morning, and, well, anyway. That Thursday night was the night I met Heather, aka Allison, but I told him that night that I was home and sleeping. Now, I kind of betrayed myself on purpose to say to him that I was lying. Obviously, he immediately paid attention to that:

"You lie to me. You told me last Thursday that you were at home, and now you tell me that you were out all night. Obviously, I wasn't here."

"I... No. Hold on, what are you exactly insinuating?" I started defending myself, showing a fake panic.

"It's been days that you disappear without notice, you act weird, we don't sleep together... Since your birthday night, you are acting weird. You lied to me about that party, you just spend your time lying to me. Moreover, on Thursday, when you were at school, I found some clothes that I didn't see you wearing on the dirty linen basket when I found that pregnancy test. Every time I ask you something, you just act weird. Same, where have you been on the day before your mum's event here? I still don't know, missing, and I couldn't have time to actually talk to you about this. You're acting weird, I feel like you're hiding from me now. And, your sister, everything... You just look weird those recent days. And, yes, I am starting to ask myself some questions regarding what is actually going on."

"I, erm..." I showed some confusion. I was actually bewildered; I didn't know what to respond.

"And now I learn that you were with Claire all weekend. I would learn that you were with Claire for your birthday night party that I wouldn't be surprised!"

"That is not true!"

"So where have you been on that night? Your birthday night?"

"I, erm... I was, erm... Yeah, I was with Sophie?" I babbled.

He was just looking at me now with a huge disappointment. So, well, so far, he had the truth, and he had, well, that I have funny outfits when I disappear, and I am also pregnant. Well, he is not stupid, I think somehow, he must be aware of the situation. He just wants me to confess, and I will, but this is too early. Now roles were clear: he was winning, and I was losing, just as expected. The problem is, I can still reverse the situation if I say something like an "I love you", or if I give the real truth. I may talk, it may be, well... Instead, I just wanted to feel sorry about my fate. With a low, almost inaudible voice, like I have been caught stealing, I continued:

"I just thought that you'd be happy this morning!"

"Happy of what?"

"Well... Having me back, making love, and..."

"Why, you think that may erase all the suspicions?"

"No, but..." I nervously smiled.

"Okay... FINE!" he abruptly switched.

I was still lying next to him when I suddenly felt the mattress moving, as he suddenly turned back. He wanted to get up. Immediately, okay, things were becoming much more dangerous: he was not only quitting the bed because he wanted to go to the bathroom for peeing, as he uses to do in such a situation. No, now, at least the way he actually stood up, he was upset, it became apparent.

I actually felt like the real danger was coming out, it was now the precise moment when everything was crucial. I couldn't remain like this without fighting: I started to grab his arm, in such a short time, as he was about to leave, and I wanted him to actually feel like, I want to defend myself, but I cannot tell the truth. And, immediately, at least when I took his hand, I looked at him, like, please, don't do it. I somehow started to beg him, when I saw him, it was actually dire, I was taking him for an idiot, and he was just done with that... But he didn't repeal me at least. A good sign, or a bad sign? I don't know. Anyway, so once I gripped myself to his arm, he just looked at me, and although I was still looking at him, remaining serious-minded, I started to say, staying quite imperative:

"No, stay here."

"What for? Hearing your craps over and over again? I am just done with that, you don't want to tell me what's going on, then fine!"

"But, sweetheart, what do you want me to say? I mean..." I tried the sentimental approach... I never usually call him sweetheart.

"I'm tired, I am done with your bullshit. The next thing I want to hear from your mouth is the truth."

"But how did you know?" I wanted to confuse him now, to show him that I was actually lost.

"How did I know what?"

"I mean... How do you know? Well, how do you... damn, I just can't... Why, oh yes, here I am, I have it. Why do you think that I, well... I mean... I am lying?" I was now much more confused, and he looked at me like, damn, she's weird.

"Look at you... I don't even understand what you mean."

"No! No, that's not that, I mean, yeah. I'm only tired, it happens. You see, you see my face!"

"Yeah, you are tired because of the lies you actually serve to everyone... Yes, I can see that. You lie to your mother, to your sister, and now to me... You are... And now covering everything up with sex, like I am that dumb?"

"You just said, 'you are', and you stopped. I am what?" my tone changed into something more offensive.

"You are... Well, it doesn't matter."

"It does, actually, what am I?" I started to seek problems.

"I am just tired of you!"

"Oh, you're tired of me. So, after I gave you my home after I lived with you for a couple of months, you are only tired of me?"

"And now, you are diverting this into bullshit. All the problems are coming from you, and you are putting things back to me!"

Hum... Okay, you caught me.

"No, baby, I am sorry!" I calmed my passive-aggressive mood. "But, I mean, honey... Geez, I really don't know what to tell you!"

"Oh, dear, you can actually try something straightforward, you'll love it!"

"And what is it?" I was trying to find a way out.

"The truth."

"Baby..."

"But you feel like you don't want it, fine. Fair enough. Keep on bullshitting me, yeah, that is the right thing to do..."

I must confess, even if this was controlled, seeing this is incredibly sad. Basically, it's sure that if I tell him the truth, this will hurt him. Because, yes, somehow, I can see he loves me on his way, I just realised when I was playing that game with him that this was so true, I just never really loved him. From this morning that I touched his, well, and I just felt disgusted, yeah, somehow, I must be a terrible person. I just used him, he was just an illusion, he was only here with me because I actually need to have someone with me. After all, otherwise, I cannot bear the fact of being alive. Florent was just my antidepressants, and even if I was manipulating him now, I felt like, this is just horrible from me. But things were to explode someday, because, for some reasons, it just couldn't work out. We are too different, we do not have the same opinions, do not have the same common interests, do not have anything, and just feel like I am his girlfriend to show off because I am what I am. I never felt that passion, the same passion I have with him that I used to have with Claire, these are two different things. And even though I was just pretending to fight, deep down I was feeling like, well, it's better this way. Seeing my old couple crumble before my eyes was obviously not satisfying, but it's the best way both him and I may have; we are not meant to be together.

So, what's next? Now, the actual point was, well, he was already pissed that I was lying, but I was still using feelings. I planned another way, I planned something else, but the pressure was raised, and it was undoubtedly time to actually cut down everything. Anyway, I can use this against him to blow up things, I know him, and I know what he wants foremost: the truth. And the thing is, I know how to present it. But I was now decided, I wanted to launch another attack, and this time, the very last, actually. It was time to wrap it up and to make sure things would really become critical. As he was standing up, I also stood up, and, well. I wanted to attack him at last, to show him that basically, this will end up in a stalemate that will be during the entire day, until the moment I start begging him to come back so I can tell him the truth. But for now, things must go to a stalemate. As Florent wants the truth, that is the only thing he is looking for, so I'll hold him through the day with this.

"So, okay, this is it? You just badly fucked me, because that was bad, and then, you tell this to have good reasons to throw me away?"

"Oh, come on. Please! You act like a bitch, and then, it's my fault. That is so pathetic!"

"I beg your pardon?" I reacted to his insult almost immediately.

"Oh, come on, like this upset you. Nothing can upset you; this is crap."

"You said, I act like a bitch?"

That may be true, but, this is not something to say. I mean when I hate people... I don't really remember having insulted someone. Even though sometimes some people just deserve it, especially Kelly. Second, well, given what happened this morning, I mean, we did it, and now, well, being insulted just after that. No, I mean, you may or may not manipulate people, starting insulting people is terrible, because this will automatically be returned against myself, it will show my weakness. It showed his, so, well, fine. It's not like I deserved it. But if he wants to play on that game, well, I may be better than him. Anyway, he just continued.

"You're right, just don't change anything, you're perfect the way you are, Charlotte," I was somehow feeling him giving up.

"Stop calling me by my first name. You know how I hate when you do that."

"Fine, then stop lying to me. And then we'll have a deal."

"Oh, come on, you too lied to me more than once before. And I have always forgiven. So, please."

"I never lied to you, this is rubbish, I've always been honest, and even, why would I lie to you? It just doesn't make any sense!"

"Oh, come on, everybody lies, that is a fact, a truth, and... Anyway, I am not lying to you, and if you think I am lying to you, then you know what to do!"

"Oh, yeah? Then what shall I do?"

"Do whatever you want, I don't care anymore..." I was honestly giving up, after having suggested him to finally punish me for what I did.

I was feeling kind of lost. Just, between the fact that I have been caught lying, I was just cold-headed and just applying some process. By ruining something beautiful for him deliberately only with the sole power of suggestion, I felt like a serial killer coldly executing one of his victims. I used the attachment/detachment like Claire had actually used when I was with her, and when I was with that situation, I am attached but feeling like I cannot defend myself. That is quite common for French girls, using this. But, well... Now, in the space of the last ten minutes, I think by far, we are good already. I think the stalemate was reached, we were now looking at each other, and I could see despair and hope in his eyes. He was seriously fed up with me, and wanted to strike, he just wanted to punish me. He resumed, after a moment looking at each other:

"You know what? Well, if you don't care anymore, I won't care as well. I'm leaving!"

"Honey, please..." I now kept a low voice, expressing fatigue and the fact that I didn't want to reach that point.

"I am done with you, you pathological liar!"

"Honey, come on, we can still find a solution to that, can't we?"

"We will find a solution on the moment you will stop bullshit ting me. In between, there are no solutions!"

"Honey, please!"

"Don't, Charlotte. Please don't. That's it. Call me back when you want to finally tell me the truth, I just don't want to hear anything from you anymore until you finally become honest with me, okay?"

I just remained there, standing, and watching the buildings exploding from my perspective, monitoring the situation being out of control. Honestly, well, seeing this was a kind of deliverance, as I didn't actually know how to end a relationship that does not work. He just went back, opened the wardrobe, his part of the wardrobe, and quickly took some clothes, for the day. Well, it was just bluffing, he just wants to put pressure over me, and that was all. I only remained by my side of the bed, observing the situation, and remained still, I just didn't want to say anything anymore. He is done with me, he is done, I'm also done with him. He picked up a pair of blue jeans, a white top, some black sweater, took his trainers, and, still standing and remaining motionless, I just watched him dressing up. Yeah, this is just bluff to me. So, let it be.

I didn't actually know what to do, from the very deep of me, because even if I was manipulating and I just wanted to pretend to be in love, I just looked at him with repulsion and hate. His body, I just don't like everything of him. He did talk to my mother, about this sensitive topic, it was the thing not to do. And now, well, I just didn't convince myself enough, this was fake and join my interests. I feel it, I really feel it now, I just didn't love him, and I certainly never will, I tried, the only problem is, he just doesn't have the right gender. He doesn't have the right attributes to make that I may love him, although he's good-looking. I just can't, it's just over my strength, and I tried, I really did. This is why, when I was looking at him, yeah, repulsion was the thing I felt, even though, I like him, but after what I will tell him tonight, I think that expecting a friendship is really unlikely. Florent is the kind of regular guy that, basically, well, he will judge me, I am sure of it, I already feel him judging me. That's why, I was just standing over there, still trying to focus on my task that, I have to direct him towards the door and just saying that, no, please stay, but deep down I was highly relieved. I just felt like, please, leave, please, go, and please, come back tonight but after, just don't come around anymore.

At this point, I sat back in my bed, staring at the barely drawn curtains of my window. He was done dressing, and, well, somehow, I was feeling weird, to do that, I had something, some voice in my mind that what I may do may not really be moral. I mean, I don't know, I felt like, yeah... Yeah, I was feeling remorse. Meh, once I was basically carrying my head, sat on the bed, and whilst I was hearing him doing *je-ne-sais-quoi* behind my back, I actually whispered:

"So, it has to end up this way," I continued, somehow desperate.

"It doesn't have to end up this way, it's just that as long as you will keep on acting this way and hiding stuff, yes, you will have a problem with me, yes."

"I... I am confused?"

"Oh, don't worry, today, we will do this, you and me: you will go to school, alone, and I'll do my stuff all alone. And I will come back only when you are ready to tell me the truth, and only the truth. I think we both need time to think about ourselves. To reflect on the other, how we consider our relationship. For you to think whether it's a good idea to continue to hide me your goddamn things and for me to think whether it's a good thing to remain engaged with you."

Oh man, this was actually mean, but fair enough. Well, this is how it ends, hopefully without lawyers. Anyway, he wants something that I cannot give him at the moment and, well, we are actually both at the same point. I had what I wanted, so it was okay. But, yeah, I was also feeling pissed, at that moment, but at least, now, here's the situation: as things have exploded between Florent and me, and as my phone wasn't far away, it allows Claire to get back, to get the place someone stole from her. I stood up and looked at him one more time. Ironically, yeah, this is our first big argument, but none of us yelled at the other. It was a discreet argument; I was honestly expecting it to be worst or less on control. That's fine. Actually, it's better than I could expect.

On the other hand, I wasn't feeling like yelling at him, it was a kind of a soft breakup. He doesn't deserve me yelling at him. But, yeah, when I saw him this morning, he didn't pack his stuff from the wardrobe, he just took his things on the purpose of leaving all day, well. If I were him, and I am sure somehow, he must feel like it, I'd instead get myself ready to actually brace for what I am gonna tell him

tonight because this is gonna be huge. It's gonna be crazy, and, that is sure, he will not like it. This is why he was pissed at me, he was just, yeah, an argument has exploded, this was what I wanted, more or less. Now, the balance of the universe has changed, I may proceed to the second phase of my plan. It's why, when I saw him on the threshold of my door, I was satisfied with what I had. I just very coldly replied:

"Okay, then. Okay, fair enough. Do whatever you want, it's fine..."

30 *A dark sky full of clouds...*

// Living room, at home, Neuilly-sur-Seine.

// Monday, 21ˢᵗ of January 2013, 20:11.

It may sound odd, but I felt weird, even if I remained cold-blooded and kept on thinking about the plan, but, well, I am usually someone who does not like when things change. When I broke up with Claire, I felt the same, besides sadness: as in the last months I got used that Florent was part of my life, now, it's over, and I am getting back with Claire. This ambiguous relationship is no longer existing because we are back together. And I got used to Florent, having him around, him teasing me all the time. I am not gonna miss sex, of course, but yeah, his personality, his light humour, himself, yeah, I'm gonna miss that. I have no hope of having him as a friend, especially with what I am about to tell him tonight, but, well. This is life, a cycle of births and deaths, you just have to adapt yourself in every crisis to survive. Now I have Claire back, a new ruined and destroyed version of herself. I just have to be there to mend broken pieces. I also have Florent, a star recently born but not sustainable enough to survive and slowly enter into a supernova.

And I actually started to feel that at the very moment he left this morning. Well, I thought, being in a bad mood would be more exacting than that, but Florent actually somehow ruined my day. Somehow, I had compassion for what happened, I was really feeling weird. So, when I left the room, Clarisse was actually in the kitchen, already drinking her tea and seeing that, well, more or less witnessing the situation. Florent didn't even say goodbye to anyone. Mum was curiously still sleeping, which is quite funny, she's always awakened at that hour. But, well, we drank our tea, we discussed that, and... After I dropped my cup in the sink, I went to my bathroom, to get dressed—still my usual white shirt, black waistcoat, black trousers, and pumps. I got my coat, and I took my bag and my books. And everything. And when I checked my phone, I received a text from Claire, stating... The text that I actually wanted to see. "Fool me once, shame on me" with a small heart next to it. She did her part of the job, and as things went right, she didn't add any comments. So, Joris is booked for tomorrow, everything is now fine. And, more importantly, under control. It made me smile, and I acknowledged, by replying "Fool me twice, shame on me". And I sent you another text, "I'll see you at school, honey, take care!"

As usual, I took the metro, certainly for the last days, because I am not sure it should be a good idea to keep going at school when the scandal will explode, but now I was feeling actually fine. I still showed that I remained melancholic, but I was actually okay from the very within because things were working, and now, nothing could stop us to be set free. Clarisse was still here, following me, but was not aware of any of the manipulations currently ongoing. She saw me this morning, remaining exhausted, pissed, and, still here like what happened actually affected me, but I have been talking to her. Without obviously entering in the details, I told her (because she asked me) that I have been with Claire all weekend, and, more or less I told her about our new situation, but I promised that I will explain to her what is going on within days. But, well, we cannot actually kill suspicions, and I am sure that she guessed that we were back together but pretended to remain innocent. She just said that this was sad for Florent, but he will move on. She's not stupid, I mean, she can see that I am not fulfilled and, as long as Claire is around, there will be no ways that I may restart my life without fighting for gaining her back. Which is why she ended up the conversation with her so useful defence parade, "You know what, actually, I don't really want to know. This is your business!"

But today was a cloudy morning, almost foggy, and when we arrived at school a couple of minutes later, because it was 10am, the doors were closed, and I saw Claire with a bunch of our schoolmates standing in front of the door. There was Claire... But Kelly was there as well. It was actually curious to see her today, I mean... I don't know what I did this weekend to her, but I could see she drastically changed. Today, I mean, at least when I saw her, I was, I actually couldn't contain my smile, just the fact of seeing her, being back, even if I discreetly smiled, I was feeling so happy and relieved that she was my girlfriend again. And, now we were back as girlfriends, just having her around was just bringing me some peace of mind and comfort, as, well, curiously, I kind of needed that.

Taylor Harding-Jenkins

She was stunning, as usual. I mean, if I looked at her today, I wouldn't believe a second about what is happening to her. Those provocative outfits that she used to wear to piss me off, well, it was now over, I could see her as more relaxed and certainly more confident. This morning, she was feeling actually okay—all in black. No, literally, she had a black blazer, black trousers (not a jean) and some black shoes, I mean, like sneakers. Only a white shirt, but her brown hairs untied, curiously she didn't have any makeup. She usually wears some exceptionally light and discreet makeup for coming, because she always says that she wants to look like a human being whenever she goes outside, but today, nope.

On the other hand, despite her relatively new outfit, I mean, dressed like an entrepreneur, it's quite odd, but it seems okay for me. Her hairs were quite messy, at least I could see that she didn't comb her hairs. It shows that she kind of woke up late, or stayed at bed until late, she almost prepared herself at the last minute. Also, for the first time in a while, I see her glasses, she was wearing her black glasses. She knows, I mean, I always said and even considered that glasses are the ultimate accessory that makes someone's charm, especially of a woman, she knows that it wouldn't let me indifferent to this. And it didn't. At least, today, given the fact that she had some good news, as things are going as we want them to go, she was smiling. And it was my most outstanding achievement.

But ironically, when I saw them, they were both split apart. Sophie was there, and Kelly spoke to her; both were chatting with Elise, one of our classmates. Nevertheless, it seemed like their relationship was at the threshold of a cold war. But, if they were like this, it meant something actually happened, and given the fact that how Kelly was behaving, I am sure this was related to Joris. It couldn't be related to anything else anyway. And, moreover, when I arrived, unlike before, she used to be on her phone. With Kelly around, this time, no, it was like completely different, her phone was in her pocket, she was having her arms crossed and was just looking around, like checking everybody, I felt like she was like before, something has changed. And she didn't look at Kelly a single moment, which was, well, quite impressive.

But, when I looked at her, I mean, Kelly, I felt like, yeah, a new time has come, at least a new day is dawning. She was completely different from the last time she arrived at school, which was quite surprising. Today's look was quite a surprise, just her hairs untied like before, no makeup at all, I felt like something was worrying her. Like Claire as well, her hairs were still pretty messy, she didn't comb it. It was icy today, and all I could see was a grey coat that she used to have for a while but didn't wear for a time as well, a black legging and white trainers. Her jacket, at least the hood of the coat, was basically made of fake fur. Still, as she was crossing her arms along her body, I assume that even if she was wearing warm clothes, she was still pretty cold whilst discussing with the other girl, maybe she was definitely recruiting someone. Geez, Kelly, always into something. However, her face, well, what was intriguing me was the absence of makeup, it really doesn't look like her, just like Claire, it was quite surprising. Because if Claire keeps a kind of small makeup, relatively discreet, Kelly is never afraid to actually be exuberant. Meh, anyway. Hopefully, stability will be back within a few days, and she is scheduled for disappearing from our lives.

But we agreed, we could speak to each other, but we must not show any sign of affection during this. First, avoid the casual homophobia in the air amongst the brainless student that this college contains. And second, the most important, to make sure that Kelly will not report to Joris that we are back together, so we avoid any suspicions, and then the plan still goes on. Anyway, I actually came closer to her, and when I arrived, I smiled at her. Clarisse remained next to me.

"Here you are, you're back! I haven't seen you in ages!" Clarisse notified her of her long absence, remaining enthusiast.

"Huh? Oh, hey, Clarisse!" Claire was obviously daydreaming, and, seemed to have her mind elsewhere.

"Oh, erm... What's up?" she continued.

"Hum... More or less. And you, what's up?" she was actually deep down despondent.

"I'm fine... Glad to see my ex-sister-in-law!" she kind of whispered that to her.

Suddenly, we both look at each other, surprised, both with like big eyes. Claire looked at me like, "I really hope you did not tell her!" and even me, I was like, the same. Because this is Clarisse, sometimes alluding to actually preach the false to get the truth. Simultaneously, I quickly looked at Kelly, still speaking with Sophie and another girl, but hopefully, she didn't seem to have heard what Clarisse told. Yeah, I know, sometimes she really misses great occasions to actually shut the hell up. Claire pondered what my twin said:

"Clarisse, be careful, nobody still knows here, I mean, except Kelly, but I don't really want people to know that I am lesbian if you know what I mean!"

"Of course, it does make sense. Hum... But seriously, how long are you guys continuing taking me for an idiot? You spent the weekend together, and curiously this morning, an argument explodes between Charlotte and her boyfriend... It looks like you are back!" Clarisse pursued.

On the other hand, she made sure that nobody would hear what she said, she made sure to speak really close to us. Because other than Kelly, as we are now in a sad period where homosexuals are most rejected because of these gay marriage stories; homophobia is at its paroxysm (how many times we recently heard that gays people shouldn't get married...). This is definitely not the right moment to actually come out. And regarding Clarisse, well... I know she won't say a word to anyone, but given that things are ongoing and threats are everywhere, even in our pockets, I preferred keeping a low profile because they listen to us. This is why, Claire actually restarted, but suddenly I placed my hand in her arm, to interrupt her, and I override the conversation. Also, to make sure that I would be as transparent as possible and to make sure nobody here would understand, I spoke in English:

"Clarisse, I have been to Claire's place this weekend because she was feeling bad, and as you can see, she looks quite sad."

"Sure, but... It still looks suspicious, look at her, I mean, she seems different," she also replied in English, whilst Claire was looking at us, as she doesn't understand or speak English.

"Just please don't ask any questions, okay? I was just at her place as a friend, that's all."

"As a friend, of course, and I am in line to become the next Prime Minister," she remained doubtful. "You guys just can't be friends, that's impossible!"

"You know what, think whatever you want, that's your problem," I showed my detachment to this.

"Yeah. Yeah, it must be!"

At the moment our conversation ended, someone opened the door of the college. And, as we walked in, my girlfriend asked me what she basically said, and I just replied, well, I think she must have a lack of sex or something. She laughed.

Anyway, as we entered the college to go for our two first hours of maths, it was curiously a bit hotter inside. I mean, what I kind of like with this building is, as it is an old one, stones are kind of keeping the temperature whether it is in summer or in winter, it's never too hot or too cold. Unfortunately, classrooms have been all refurbished and basically, it's not the same into these rooms. So far, winter is better, it's more liveable because summer in Paris is actually more challenging than it seems. The problem with summer is that you are always seeking coldness, which is why you do not sleep properly, spend hours under the shower to be actually hot minutes later, and... Yeah, basically, I prefer winter. Anyway, as we walked, together with Claire, my twin went to one of her friends behind, I was just daydreaming. I mean, we weren't talking with Claire, and yeah, with all the herd following us (I mean, we were among them), I kind of heard someone walking fast behind us. But. I didn't really pay attention to that person, it was just, yeah, my thoughts were more substantial than this silly details. When suddenly, I felt an arm crashing above my shoulders. It actually pulled my hairs. Then... At the moment I rose my head, I heard... her. She found us.

"Ladies, so you think you can come back here without saying hello?"

"Oh, sorry, we just didn't see you," Claire coldly retorted.

That was actually quite surprising, I mean, the tone she used to reply was quite dramatic. Yeah, their friendship was definitely a thing of the past, I mean, if there is still a friendship or if we can even call that friendship... I may actually call this partnership. Well, anyway, Kelly continued:

"What's up, girls?"

"Meh... I didn't really sleep last night, not in a good mood, to be honest!" Claire replied.

I pushed her arm out of my shoulder, I really cannot bear this cunt touching a strand of hair of mine.

"Do I look like being okay?" I showed my anger.

"You never look like being okay..." she was somehow amazed... "What's her problem, Claire?"

That literally shows the kind of person I don't like, you see that someone is not okay, and you ask someone else what's going on. On the other hand, it's not the first time that she does this, I mean, she knows that I am not likely to talk to her and thus if she wants to have her answers, she naturally seeks Claire, so knows me better. Geez... Anyway, but it was actually better, we needed to show a particular dimension of me being not okay at all, then more inclined to be submissive... No, it's okay. Claire knows what to do in that situation.

"She is just breaking up with her boyfriend, it's not a good day for her..."

"Oh, Claire, please, she doesn't need to..." I acted like she wasn't supposed to know.

"No, no... She needs to know; otherwise, she's gonna piss me off just like you until she knows. So, for both of you, now I know how to deal with you girls!"

she smiled at me, like... you know, take that in your face, with all due love and respect.

"Ha, ha, you know me now! Anyway, I am really sorry for you, Cha, erm... If anything, just let me know..."

"Yeah, of course, like you are really sorry. Anyway, I don't need your help. And I think your help would be the last thing I'd seek!"

"Meh," she remained detached.

"Yeah, anyway, could you get the hell out? You're stealing my air, and I need to breathe!" I continued my attacks.

"Your air doesn't belong to you, necessarily. Anyway, on Wednesday, I have some party, erm... Some guy needs two girls, and we actually thought about, you know, what about you two?"

"Yeah, we'll talk about it later, if you do not mind..." Claire was now embarrassed.

"Oh, sure... Yeah, of course, but you would be okay?"

"As she said," I used another tone, "we're gonna talk about this later!"

"Okay, okay, erm... no need to attack me, of course!"

An admirable attempt to embarrass us, obviously, we were in the middle of the classroom. Everybody could hear us even if others were talking with each other. It was producing quite a loud noise, but... Like she wants to reveal the truth now, I mean, she knows that it will also splash her if she reveals the truth. But, fine, I don't really care. Claire had the excellent reaction, and to be honest, trust me, I think on Wednesday, Kelly, you may have other problems than dealing with your stupid party. But... According to how she sees it, how she took with detachment my concerns and her current behaviour, it looks like she doesn't see or may expect what is actually going on. If I were her, I would be actually scared. Like, really scared. Because even though the main target remains Joris, she will be involved in that too since she organises things. Ignorance is bliss, and as I could see her, I tend to believe that it's actually a real source of happiness. Anyway, to ruin her insistence, I continued, this time, to make her go away.

"You know, it's funny, I mean... Last night, I had a dream. You were dating Ted Bundy, and at the end, some police found you with your head in a gutter and a poodle peeing on you... That seemed actually pretty realistic!"

"Really funny. Ted Bundy? Who's that guy?" she ignorantly replied.

"Oh, come on, what do you do on your Sundays? Get the fuck out of here, for Christ's sake!"

"Oh, come on..."

But, no, she remained... So, I actually started to speak about something else, deliberately ignoring her. I said to Claire:

"I'm gonna get a new phone. I'm done with mine..."

"Yeah. I think about that too, it may give like a new restart."

"But I was thinking, not buying a smartphone. You know, going back to basics, like old phones that you can fold... Those that do not have all that bunch of crappy options, and a safe phone so I cannot be spied on and going taking the metro and being safe with..."

"That's quite cheap. But, why not, sometimes, going retro is quite fancy..."

"Hum, I'm also thinking the same..." Kelly invited herself in the conversation. "But, well, I want a fancy phone like yours, but... Well, on the other hand..."

"Are you sure you can even afford it?" I coldly looked at her.

"Do I look like poor, Charlotte?"

"Poor, I don't know, I didn't really check your mind. But pathetic, definitely!" I was inspired.

"Fuck you, Cha..."

"My pleasure!"

And finally... Yeah, pathetic is not a word she likes. I like using that word, because, yes, I am sorry, Kelly is all that is pathetic to me. I mean, I just open the dictionary, I look at the "pathetic" definition, and I see her face! It's crazy. Anyway, it took us a while to arrive in the classroom, and as Clarisse was busy, we sat at the end of the classroom.

That was not that much a long morning. I mean... It could have been longer, but, well, during math course, we were just elsewhere, I mean, we didn't even listen to the teacher or anything. As we couldn't speak because of our phones, instead we wrote at the end of our notebook various stuff like where do you wanna eat for lunch, what do we do for this afternoon in case we do not come back at school, and we just pretended to follow up the course. The more I listened to the teacher, the more I was like, this is just nonsense. I mean, he was teaching us stuff that first I already knew, and second, he got so confused in his explanations that it made everything much more complicated. I think today's lesson was about prime numbers or something related to it (I guess because what he said was just jibber-jabber and I could only see that he was explaining something about 2, 3, 5, 7, 11, 13... which are prime numbers, so I assume he was talking about this), but... Meh.

Making complicated something that is relatively easy when you understand the logic. No wonder why they give the baccalaureate nowadays.

I understood the prime number a couple of years ago when I was watching that movie, Cube. A stressful film, by the way. But understanding a prime number is more or less than if you divide whatever number by two (for example, seven) and if you find a number ending by .5, you do have a prime number. It's just the term that appears as, well, hard to understand. I mean... That's how I understood them, many people may get me wrong... But this is not a good example, because if you divide two by two, you get one, and... I know there's a rule on this. The prime number, "prime" means one, so if you get one or a number in .5, it smells the prime number. But okay, there are more to do with prime numbers. It seems harsh to understand, but it's pretty easy.

However, Claire tried to catch up with the thing. The problem with her is that she is an artist. She is not a scientific even though she is relatively interested in this. She basically chooses scientific because she wanted to remain with me. Because, last year, it was the three choices, between scientific, economic, and literary, and the two others were not really tempting her. The problem is that scientific remains quite a challenging section, and it's been two years that she is not really following. It's still very hard for her, even if I helped her to understand the fabulous world of mathematics, she tried... but events that started last September in her personal life made that, well, she just dropped out. The thing is, I can afford not to care about baccalaureate because I still have a financial backup that makes that I can stay at home for the rest of my life, spend a life without working. It's, unfortunately not her case. Okay, you may say, many people were successful without the baccalaureate, or A-Level, or whatever you call it depending on whatever country. Yeah, that is true.

I believe that this is not absolutely necessary to be successful, but at least in this country, now... This is ridiculous, whenever you are a cashier in a supermarket, nowadays they ask you for a baccalaureate. You need a baccalaureate to scan articles before a laser and counting cash at the end of the day. Knowing the importance of a prime number is required to scan items and say that it will be 65.75 euros. French logic, I know, don't ask me. I assume the reason is for saying that 65.75 is not a prime number to the customer. Even though... I don't remember any cashier notifying me of this. Meh, again another reason to make sure that youth unemployment remains high, I guess, and make sure that it's always the same with chances and not any other person. That looks like the France I know.

Free Expensive Lies: Prologue

Anyway, even if we wrote in our books, drew many hearts and things like this. It was twelve at the end of the course, and none of us was actually hungry. There is still a small shop next to the college, where we used to stop. We left our phones in the locker, went there and bought just two bottles of water (a big for me and a small for her) and, then... after a short conversation...

There was this park, where we used to go, like, when we were on break, we just had to cross the Seine River, to arrive on Clichy. Basically, it's not really a park, as some railway tracks pass over it, through which some trains are passing quite often, I mean, we used to love going there. Time was scrolling, again, and again, and maybe if we were to restart courses in perhaps less than ten minutes, we were feeling like, let's go over there, we didn't actually want to go back at school. And, on the other hand, we have plenty of time. We arrived with our food, and like usual, even if it was cold, even if cars were passing around, even if trains were above our heads and even if it was probably about to rain, we both had the same feeling, we just didn't care. We went there like before and lied into the grass. Phones were still in college, we were free.

Today, having her back was... well I was supposed to be pissed and really in a bad mood, but I didn't actually feel like it. Even if Kelly was there, it looks like she found a new friend because she kept on talking to some girl from the class... Well, whatever she's into, I just don't care. I was just feeling my girlfriend, being utterly different. She wasn't like before, glued to her smartphone, talking for saying nothing, now, it was different. She was laconic, seemed happy, but maybe her depression is a good thing because she looks ways more mature. Even, more than before. Even if before, she was not the idiot she's been those last months, I was feeling her maybe much more thoughtful. And, after we lied in the grass, not even eating... That, whilst I heard the noises all around, I just asked her:

"So, what's next... What do we do after this?"

"Well, we can start by forgetting all this story!"

"Yeah, yes of course, yeah, I also thought about this, obviously... But... How do you want to forget that? I was thinking about booking a flight, going elsewhere... I mean, after the 10th of March, as you can't travel right now..."

"I can't travel? Of course, I can!"

"You're still seventeen, darling. You cannot go anywhere without mummy's consent, bear that in mind."

"Meh... Okay, so where do you want to go? I want to leave here; I want to move out of this shithole!" she insisted.

That is not really surprising, I mean... I'd be indeed the same if my girlfriend was a foreigner. Well, it's the case, actually. But, I mean, yeah, I'd be curious to explore other countries and other cultures. Although last time I went to the UK was last summer, I went there several times even though we were together. She was stranded in France because she could not join us, then she doesn't really know my other country. The only images she has of the UK is Westminster Abbey, Kate and William, the Queen, a tenner that I brought her three years ago with the Queen on it, the Union Jack, the double-deck buses and London Underground's roundel... And her English courses.

To me, the UK sounds more like Shoreditch and those many pubs where you can get fucked up for, well, quite a few quid and then, well... Our house is in Shoreditch, this is why I love this place. But she doesn't really know anything more than Paris, even in her own country she doesn't know that much as she never really left Paris, so exploring the world around her might be great therapy. And it would be entertaining and playful as well. When we were young, we imagined our adult life as living in London and travelling worldwide. We still may, I mean, it's not too late. We still have our entire life. I mean, the rest of our lives.

"I understand, with all what happened, it became just too much now!" she continued.

"Yeah. So where do you want to go?"

We had many travel ideas when we were younger. Like the Great Wall of China, the United States, travelling through the US... I have always been curious about the Mississippi. I was honestly more interested in Canada. I don't really know why, certainly the cold. Or Scotland and Iceland. Well, I travelled once to Edinburgh, but we stayed there only one day, (it seems spooky, by the way, especially during the night), but we spoke about this a lot. There is this lake I am inquisitive about, it's in Russia, the Lake Baikal, the deepest lake in the world. However, I am just not really confident next to a water body, and I am scared of depth—perhaps, a reason why I don't like Kelly.

After a slight moment of thought, she continued:

"You remember when we were younger, and we used to tell each other that once we would turn eighteen, we would take two months and explore the US. From East to West?"

"Yeah. Yeah, I remember. That was a good thing... Well, it's never too late, actually. We can still do that!"

"The problem is, we still have school, and we still have... the baccalaureate at the end of the year!"

Yeah, well, it's not like I care about the future, as I said, I have enough money so I can afford not to work for my entire life. But that is not her case; however, I am relatively confident: will all objectivity, Claire may have been my first love and, I think, with what we recently went through and even though we "broke up" and this, I really believe we are a healthy couple. We just proved it; nothing can really tear us apart. So, well... Moreover, we can pass it anytime. Maybe it's better to postpone until when we can finally bounce back from our pains. This is why I continued:

"Claire... Do you really think, after all that happened, we could still remain focus on our studies and act like nothing happened? I may get mine, but... Look at you, after this, you need holidays, you just need to disconnect yourself."

"Hum, true..."

"Second of all, now they almost give us the baccalaureate, whether you worked for it or not, so you may pass it as a free candidate. This is not something that is actually... You can still pass it later, it's not because you don't pass it today that it is fucked up. And to be honest, no-one cares about this, this is just a piece of paper that attests that you may work in France. And I remember you telling me on many occasions that you were not interested in remaining in there, as it was becoming too dangerous!"

"Yeah. Fuck it."

There was a bit of wind. And cars were passing around us, we were like in a small cocoon, nothing could actually disturb us. We were both lying in the grass, next to each other, looking at the sky and thinking. Our bags were next to us, and, well, for once, I was kind of enjoying this small moment of peace. I didn't really know what time it was, and I didn't really care about. Still, as I was watching over me, I could hear a train passing on the bridge next to us and, in the meantime, clouds, above us, made of some kind of white, almost translucent filaments were moving because of the wind in high altitudes. It was cloudy this morning, but now, the weather improved, and as clouds were in a kind of a low altitude, they seemed thin. At the same time, when I was kind of trapped within my thoughts and observing the clouds, thinking that we are all living in prison called Earth, Claire suddenly restarted.

"It's curious because... Well, I don't know that since I started that treatment, for now, a few days, I feel like everything has changed. You are back, I mean, by you I mean, we are back, I don't know. When I woke up this morning, for once I didn't even touch my phone, I just stayed at the bed, looked at my ceiling and telling myself, what the fuck is this!"

"Yeah. That happened to me, too, someday, when I was thirteen."

"Yeah, it was actually pretty mad, I just looked at my ceiling for like, I don't know how long, and... I don't know, I kind of question myself, on literally everything..."

"Everything?"

"Yeah, I mean... Not you, don't be scared, I need you, I mean, with what you're doing, I just... But it's just everything, everything for the last couple of months has been turned upside down. I just feel like I just don't care anymore."

"Yeah. I know what you talk about..."

"Yeah, I know you know, you were born this way!"

"Feeling like the world has literally no beauty, is empty and people are pathetic is just part of my daily routine, darling. As someone said, people that have been assaulted or aggressed may hate the humankind. It only takes a great mind to hate it beforehand," I acknowledged.

"Well, now I am the one I am, and I don't care. I mean, except you, I just don't feel like I need people, I don't feel like I need to be surrounded by people, I just want everybody to leave me alone. I just want you next to me, and that's it!"

Yeah, life is life, and we have to deal with it. I have some problems and some challenging issues, but I also have fantastic parents taking no responsibility for this. They just don't care, they just have their issues, and as their problems are much more crucial than mine for some reasons, I suffer in silence. Yes, I have the same treatment as Claire, the difference is that I am supposed to take it on morning and evenings, but the thing is, well, I genuinely questioned myself on that and, does that worth it? I am kind of trained for endure mental pain, this is part of my daily routine, and it has severe consequences on my life, I don't have friends, I just have Claire, and when I lost her, yeah, it was a real drama, this is why I went to Florent straight away but, that was a mistake. For both of us. Enduring pain, yes... I went to a psychologist, it didn't work. I drank, it didn't work. I took drugs, it didn't work, there is still something that pushes me down. I identified the problem, I saw it, I marked it, the problem is, it's just too much. My parents are not reliable people, Claire is but... Yes, I have depression, but the only thing I can do is live with it. Until the day it will end, and indeed, kill me. This is why I really do not wish living old. The sooner it is over, the better. And Claire already knows what I want for my funerals.

"Honey..." she continued, "how do you deal with that?"

"Oh, well... I just face up things. When things are coming, I just face them up, looking for a solution on how I could get rid of it, and that's all, brace for the next shit that will happen. Life is basically in my point of view from one shit to another. And, well... Now you understand what I feel since my parents broke up. Obviously, my parents' divorce is just a minor problem compared to yours, but it may have been a small problem, it actually opened my eyes on quite a few things..."

"Like?"

"Like, at some point I asked myself the same question, especially when you broke up with me, I woke up one day and felt like, does it worth it? They say that what doesn't kill you make you stronger, this is just pure bollocks..."

"I just feel like nothing does make sense right now. It's, I don't know... I kind of see things differently..." she was inspired.

"What do you see differently?" I was curious.

"I see that you are a manipulative bitch able to make simple plans to destroy things and people as long as it doesn't affect us and as long as it may save us... In my case, I kind of love it, this is what attracts me from you, your bad-girl side. But I know you will always protect me or try to save my arse. I really should have listened to you about Kelly, you just knew it, and I was just idiot by that time because all what you said was right!"

"Meh, it's fine, shit happens!"

"How did you know this about Kelly?"

Observing people. That's what I do the best, watching people, and then going to a conclusion. Inspired, I just replied:

"Well, one day, you will also realise that nowadays, thanks to smartphones, Facebook and all those fantastic creations we all have available, people are just all working the same way and do not change. They just cannot change, and it's not their fault, it's just because now, they don't have time to live and enjoy their lives. They are all under control. Every morning, they just go to the same coffee shop and take their same disgusting flat white served by their same antipathetic barista, in their same cup, asking for that always all the time in the very same rude way. They take their same overcrowded metro every day where they always see the same people in the carriage, entering it through the same door, seating if they can at the same place. They join their offices, being the victim of the same shitty boss that pretends he has leadership whilst he or she doesn't even know the meaning of that word. They come back home alone, and for entertaining themselves, after all, they all watch the same programs on TV, watch the same porn on the Internet. Or watch the very same memes on Facebook and quote that shit as inspirational, and then sleep in the same bed all alone, see the same people... People just don't change, but you cannot blame them, this is how it is, they are just not aware of that, they are all in denial. Even better, that is the life their teachers at school promoted because they would make money and be happy. They make money that they spend in shitty and completely useless stuff... Welcome in the 21st Century, darling. A world full of zombies under antidepressants."

"Yeah."

"Today, only a stupid Latte, a customised top and a Facebook wall is enough to build a personality. This is why everything is just fucked up! A world full of pre-designed personalities made only for you available for purchase in your local store today!"

"True..."

"It's just when you realise this that actually, maybe you have been part of this world or not, when you just realise it, you just see that this world is totally empty. So, does that worth it? I have no fucking idea, but as this is life, as this is modern life, personally, I am not really interested to know any further!"

She just didn't reply. I mean, there was nothing more to add, we all work for an ideal we would never have. This is not something that we see in movies, and we read in books, this is the world, and there's nothing we can change about it. After a moment, I just continued.

"This is why Claire. This is how it is. This is how the world is, and when you pass through such events, well... Now you just open your eyes. What you may do within days is, just define what you want, what you don't want, and more importantly, what you do not want anymore. And then, you will not be a prominent personality, it will make no difference between you and someone else, it will just set you free!"

"I don't really care of being different or not!" she continued.

"They may be convincing you as well that there are hell and paradise. Given how this life does look like, I honestly don't see the difference between this life and hell..."

"This is... This is a new life, I mean, I feel like we are starting a new chapter of this life, and... Whatever it is, it is. But how do you do when things are wrong?"

"Well, there's nothing you can actually do. Just live the moment. You will have some moments when you're gonna be fine when everything is going to seem like life is fantastic, and you're gonna have some other moments when life will push you so down that you will just think that the luckiest people on Earth are those that are six feet under. Just live things as they appear. And get ready to fight. Because you will have to fight!"

"Fight for what?"

"Fight for your rights, fight for what seems correct to you, fight for what you want to fight, for your convictions. Remember, Claire, you have a life with many people. You have no allies, and no clearly identified enemies, it makes that everybody is a potential threat."

"No allies? And you, why should I remain with you if I have no ally, Charlotte?" I somehow felt her offended by my words.

Oh, well, yeah, of course, saying such sentences, sometimes I forgot people do not have the same sense of interpretation as I do. On the other hand, of course, I am a damn ally, it's not like I didn't prove anything. Well, given my statement, it is still possible that I may believe that Claire would be my blackmailer. But, seriously, I think that would be very obvious and with a low strategy. I don't feel her as an enemy, I mean, why would she take antidepressants? But, no, I think I showed myself more than enough as a trustworthy ally, and... I think she can see that. Still, I feel that trust has been broken on both sides. Even though we trust each other, we are still very wary of each other, because, what if I get betrayed? It's the same for her, and a betrayal would definitely be the very last thing. I mean, I don't think I may survive to this. But we still trust each other, I mean... At least I trust her, For the last seven years I had with her, that seems gross that she would fuck me this way. It looks very awful. And if it is the case, it would mean that I am the biggest idiot on Earth. Unable of perspicacity and clear-sightedness. It is why I justified myself:

"Well, when I meant no allies, I meant the rest of the world, apart from your relatives and me. Of course, I will be there for you, and... With what we are currently doing, I don't think you should have a doubt about this..."

Both lying flat-back, certainly drinking the words of each other like they were a precious remedy, we just looked at each other. I just looked at her brown eyes, her face, her facial expression that seemed relaxed in that ocean of stress she was currently passing through, hidden behind the frame of her dark glasses. She was lost, I mean, I never saw her this way. I honestly don't know how to explain that feeling, now, I was feeling like, somehow, this shit made us more robust than ever. It made our couple just unbreakable now, nothing could ever happen to us anymore. The wind was making her fragile hair flying, her eyes bearing a vast, tremendous burden that seemed to fade away progressively the more I was next to her. Because passion is more vital than everything, and love was back, tenfold. I really don't know how I was appearing in front of her, but I just smiled at her, it was something that I did not actually control. And, swiftly, there was something that told me... Kiss her. This was just what we both wanted at that moment.

It's true, Claire went through a lot, and now, she is broken into thousands of pieces, and it is also true, both of us need time to actually step back and go through it. I just had, when I was kissing her, my eyes closed, that image of her face, bouncing back and forth in my mind. Well, this was the end, somehow, and maybe somehow, we needed that. Maybe we needed that huge test to actually assess our future self. Even seven years of relationship, seven years that we've been together and even, now, it's just like our couple is just invincible. Because, it's odd, but all the time I see her, even if it's been all that time that I know that girl, and I know her in her most profound intimacy, it's like I am discovering her like it was the first time, every moment is the first moment. And, I just cannot believe how she has changed. Love is forgiving, it's true, she's been doing many things, she ignored my advice on Kelly and now... I just feel like I cannot be a bitch with her, we just have too much together. Kelly just disrupted this, but, as the Natures loves when everything is in balance, she just couldn't expect that I wouldn't leave Claire without a fight. I honestly think I have been stupid, I only... Even me, I mean, that birthday night, I remember Sophie coming to me and warn me about Claire's activities, I just couldn't believe it. I knew about Kelly, but I was still like, I just couldn't think that Kelly brainwashed her at that point, to the point of depriving her of any morality. It just didn't really make any sense to me. But, well, like the US took time to actually be involved into World War II, took time to free France, well, somehow, I was feeling like Ike starting his plan to free up her dignity. That is my duty, I just cannot let her down, it's beyond being a responsibility. She was here when I was down, now it's only the time to return what she gave me.

That girl is my drug, she's just what I need to live. And, being deprived of that drug affected me, I screwed up. I really fucked up. And she did too. I always thought there was something magnetic between us. And now, I can just see it, magnetism is back, and... And after that kiss, I just looked at her, and she just said after seeing those small muscles of her face drawing a shy smile:

"It may take a while before we could resume life as it used to be before. I mean, I just feel like crying all the time, and... Don't expect anything from me, like, sex and... you know!"

"I know honey, I know. All I want from you is to get better, and I know it will take a while, but I don't care. I just want to see you smile, that's all that matters to me."

"So, we will ruin our scholarship tomorrow, we are going to take big holidays when I turn eighteen, and what's next? Cha, I really hope you're gonna take me elsewhere, I just don't want to remain in Paris!"

"No, we can move to London. But... You're gonna have to speak English!"

"Well, it's not like you cannot teach me!"

"Oh, I can... I honestly think that working, like, getting a real job, might be great therapy. Just maybe for a year or something, you should work. I'm sure you can find this in London! And regarding studies, well... Let's bounce back, and after, comes what may."

"Yeah, true. And you, what about you?"

"Oh, don't worry about me, honey. I'll survive!"

31 *Needle in a haystack*

// My home, Neuilly-sur-Seine.

// Monday, 21st of January 2013, 20:14.

Well, well, well... On those philosophic words, it was now time to make a scandal explode.

I must confess, I was in a kind of a weird mood today. Not happy, not depressed, it just that I was feeling like, I only didn't realise the situation as it was in its entirety. Claire's back, Florent's out, I was genuinely feeling overwhelmed by what was going around. I used to be kind of laconic when it happens, like, well... More thinking, focusing on my task and not doing anything else. And life... Well...

An hour before I finish school, mum texted me, she told me that I would be alone tonight, with Florent certainly, because she has to do quite a lot of things at work and, therefore, finish late. That is even better. During the afternoon, once we were back from the park with Claire, I started texting Florent, I actually texted him throughout the afternoon. And, well, many texts... Most of them I was telling him sorry, and, somehow, I promised him to tell him the truth, tell him what was going on. And without lying. I promised him to tell the truth and only the truth.

A reality that he will have trouble to accept, but when I think about this, well... On the other hand, I had to take Claire's truth, so it will be his turn to accept mine. Or not. And honestly, I hope not. At the end of our conversation, I asked him if he could come tonight at eight, so I would make dinner or something to eat and buy drinks, and tell him what is going on. And I had an idea at the same time because I was feeling like, you know, even for me, it's kind of embarrassing to actually confess my crimes, since my crimes also involve my intimacy. Well, this is a dirty job, and someone has to do it, and I prefer doing it myself rather than being served by someone else. He asked me, why not calling, and I told him, to make this certainly more dramatic and to make him understand that what I was hiding was not like I stole a bottle of water at the nearest store, I told him, I want to take you face to face. He accepted. And as he agreed, we could now proceed.

So, this is why I came back home alone. I spoke with Clarisse, asking her if I could have the flat tonight, as I have to talk with Florent, and she understood. She went to her boyfriend's place instead. The thing is, she can go anytime, she has the key to his flat. And, when I came back home, well, first, I stopped by the supermarket to get some food and drinks, and then... Well, I came back home. The flat, when I arrived, was, I don't know, silent. I came here, like, I don't know, with some strange hunch, like it was one of the last times for a while that I would go here. This silence was surprisingly meaningful, it was somehow ending some years of my life. I mean... It is true, tonight I sleep at Claire's place, and then after... We still don't know what is going to be the next step. What will be next, I actually don't really know. But, I entered that place and had this feeling, like, I lived some part of my life here, certainly the hardest so far from that moment, but now I was feeling like this place, I don't know like I do no longer belong here anymore. The silence made a kind of white noise in some farthest outpost that I was the only one to be able to hear, and, for once, it sounded scary. In any case, what will happen tonight will be the end of something, and the start of another thing, and whatever it was, is or will be, I don't feel like this will be okay. But I made a choice already, so far, I just cannot go back from what happened.

For most of the evening, I actually kind of enjoy that silence. I was making myself to it, when I came back home, I just removed my coat, put the stuff in the fridge, and then went to lie down in the sofa next to me. And, as hours passed, I kind of watched, through the enormous windows, with curtains wide open, the night falling. I actually didn't fall asleep; I just cleared my mind. Like, resetting it into a kind of warrior mode, where I manipulate people. But sadness remained, and, although the warmth of the sofa was corrupt by the deep coldness of the outside, hours were scrolling, I still kept an eye on the DVD reader that was displaying the time under the TV and, slowly, the final hour was coming closer.

And then, seven. But it was time to prepare everything, preparing the living room (I want the living room as a neutral place... Too many things occurred in my bedroom), and getting myself ready to brace for the moment. I want him to actually feel like I am doing everything, such as cleaning the place, preparing dinner and everything, to show him that I have something to blame myself, but something big. And as in our couple, I occupy the other side of the bed, so I have to be creative. At seven, I actually turned on the light, and, I was thinking, the light is too strong, why not using candles, it may be more intimate? Then, the table was quite messy, I actually put everything back where it was supposed to be, and then, okay, tablecloth. Then I looked at the coffee table, and I was thinking, we may not sit at the table, I prefer sitting on the sofa, close to him, making it more intimate, the table makes it too formal. So, I placed three candles on the big table and two on the bedside table. Candles will provide a dim light, so it will make it much more comfortable and more intimate. Now, table, everything was in the oven, I need to choose the tablecloth... Red? May be too aggressive. There was a white... White seemed too neutral. He likes the blue colour, so blue, more like navy blue, it should do it. Or wait... I also have a burgundy one... Less aggressive than red, and much more comfortable, it should suit with the light, making the table then almost black. That will do it. For the rest... Damn, such a headache. I made sure that there would be nothing annoying, such as unattended mess... But, no, nothing. The living room was already perfect. The thing was to create an atmosphere, I want him to be in the most comfortable situation to actually take advantage of me. More or less, I want him to feel that he is the winner, and he will win over me.

Whilst the food was underway, and the living room was now ready, candles were burning, and the table was set up, I took this time to actually prepare the most important part of this meeting, myself. For tonight, there must be no wrong note, as I must pretend to fight for the survival of our couple. And as since this morning I am not in the best position, tonight must be the final act. As I need to be careful on my words, I also need to be cautious on my appearance. The thing was, if I just tell the truth without any guilt, at least without displaying any remorse, he will take as "she's a whore" and that will be it. Whilst, if I confess the truth with actually creating this atmosphere, being nice to him and appearing as nice and desperate as I was in my texts, he will feel like, yes, I am still a whore, but at least he will be involved. And if he is implicated, he will feel the need to talk to mum, and this is what I precisely want. The problem was that, also, I need to cry. And that is not easy at all. I may have wept once or twice in my life, but all the time, it was on manipulative purposes.

On the other hand, I can show a stern face, like the fact that I am sad and desperate without necessarily crying. He knows that I am totally unable to weep, then if I sob, it will show that I am obviously controlling the situation. Yeah, he knows, he was even shocked when he saw me smiling because some guy was in deep troubles because of some stuff and after seeing wars on TV. So, no, I cannot cry. And, appearing as natural as possible is also challenging since it's not a secret that I am everything but a natural person. Well, I will see how he wants to go, I will let him start the conversation, and... Yeah, maybe it may appear like a typical day. Like, yeah, like if nothing happened, we can perhaps begin like this.

Yeah, I know, so many things, colours, all those details and everything... It's not the first time that I do that, but believe it or not, but colours have incredible power over the subconscious. I didn't make like proper dinner; instead, I bought something quick, and easy to eat, because he will clearly be starving, whilst I am not hungry at all. Something that we can eat while talking. This was when I went to my wardrobe, exploring. Tonight, well, as I said, I am not in the dominant position, then I must appear as pretty, but not provocative. I think a dress with my pumps should do it. No heels, because it just be too much, and I want him to remain focused on what I will tell him. I am not supposed to make him asleep to accept the truth, I want him to be shocked by the reality.

I had that red dress that I had for a while, it was actually subtle, neat, classic, and I will get my red pumps. Red, because red somehow shows guilt, as red is the colour of many things amongst which love, it will show that I take care of him one way or another. Oh, and that is the truth, somehow, I really do care about him. Red make-up... Red, I must be red tonight. And my hairs untied. Particularly important. Once I tied my hairs, I always heard that I look extremely strict, and I want to appear as someone to whom he wants to talk.

So, yeah, I went to actually take a shower, getting ready, and, yeah, bracing for that evening. When I was preparing myself, there was no music, for once I turned the light on (better for make-up, actually), it was quite surprising because I was feeling incredibly stressed. Tonight, the goal is to make sure my phone is next to me to be heard because I literally want to ruin my blackmailer's plan to put me under pressure. This is why mistaking is not an option. And the more I discovered myself a bit more under this artificial beauty that brings me make-up and the more I was thinking, does that really worth it? I mean... Tonight, he's gonna hate me forever. But I know that I am right, I am just correcting a mistake I made in my life, everybody makes a mistake, even me.

The thing was, I wanted everything to look like our first date. Recalling good remembrances, because I know him, as soon as he arrives, he will be like, the dominant male. He will want to show he's in the dominant position, that he has the control, and triggering those souvenirs to him will be like weakening him. He cannot resist those details; even I know that he just can't resist. Speaking of which, he was late. I mean, once I was all ready, I went back to the living room, and sat on my place on the sofa, and... Waited in the silence. For our date, I have put music in the background to play down the situation and make this less stressful for me, but now... I honestly felt like I needed silence, I need calm and quietness.

And, yeah, I sat. It was cold within the flat, I mean, the atmosphere here was somehow contradictory. It was cold, silent, but somehow the table, the candles and everything made it warm. Unintendedly, I made it correctly showing my current state of mind. But now it was the time, even if he was late, he still has the pass for downstairs, the key for here, I just need to get myself ready to play the comedy. Convincing myself that I am the victim, so I actually made it through. I was just visualising deep down three different situations: first, the one, my very feeling when I woke up on the 10th of January, after all that happened. Second, the moment when I was there, in that weird room in the South of Paris with the two guys. And the second, this morning. I mean, just the fact of thinking about this made me recall that I was just a damn monster, and I am going to hurt him tonight. And third, my pregnancy, when I had that test in my hand. This just sounds horrible to me. But, to make sure that I would really feel shameful, I actually focused on a specific detail on each of the scenes described before, first, the feeling of the sheets on the bed on the morning when I woke up after my hangover. Second, I was feeling a hand pulling out a strap of my dress, of my current attire, even if this hand was purely imaginary, I was still feeling the hand of that Russian guy acting with me like I was just a stupid piece of meat. And third, yeah... The pregnancy. In my mind, whilst time was scrolling, I kept on having these three different things scrolling again and again on my head that, well, at some point, it made me feel actually terrible.

And then, corrupt by the white and loud silence, at some point, maybe ten minutes later, I heard the lift being called and going down. Here it was, it was him. And now... I closed my eyes, took a deep breath, and... Yeah, now, I was into it. Somehow, I felt like it's actually odd, some part of me was really feeling guilty and bracing for living a challenging moment. It's actually a bizarre feeling. For someone that has literally no guilt and that is deep down rotten to the core.

And then, once the engineering machine of the lift suddenly stopped maybe a couple of seconds later, I actually had in some ways the confirmation that it would be him. As it stopped on our floor. Immediately, and also still very discreetly, I almost walked on tiptoes towards the door, to actually hear the footsteps. He knew that I was there. I heard him walking, then stopping at my door. In the meantime, I was crossing the living room to enter in the entrance, and suddenly, it almost surprised me, I heard him knocking at the door three times. Hum... Let's not make him wait. I unexpectedly arrived, and finally opened that heavy door.

And I found him. Unlike our first date when he came with his lovely and neat suit, today was quite different. He just had his white sweater, some blue jeans, and black sneakers. He still had his coat, a long black jacket... And I actually looked at his face now, and yeah. I cannot honestly describe which mood he was now; it was actually pretty tough to say. He didn't smile when I opened, but on the other hand, he was standing in front of the door, and even if I didn't open the door wide, he was still standing there and waited for me to allow him to pass. That is pretty odd, I mean, he is still at his place too, but now, maybe there was something different. I don't know. On the other hand, from both him and me, there is still in the air a kind of a goodbye feeling, we are both here for something that none of us wants to share or hear.

I actually hide most of myself when I opened the door, I just opened the door very shyly, hiding my body behind it, I just let my face appearing at the moment. But still, he could see my face, and that I was wearing some dress, he could see a strap of my dress. I actually smiled, quite nervously to be honest, and then... There was still no reaction from him. So, yeah, he was severely pissed. Slowly, maybe taking a kind of a friendly approach because I didn't actually know how to react, I just started to softly voice a slight...

"Hey..."

"Hey..." he remained cold and seemed pragmatic.

Free Expensive Lies: Prologue

I followed his eyes, and he could actually see behind me that lights throughout the flat were entirely turned off, it would be only us tonight. He just quickly glanced at this before watching me back. Suddenly, I opened the door a bit wider, to actually show myself to him. And yeah. My charm still operates. In some ways, I was doing that to calibrate him and assess how I could succeed: he was looking at me, quite quickly, but still trying to keep his distances, this actually meant that whatever I say, he will listen. Because he desperately wants the truth from me, but in some other ways, I saw him being relatively quick and trying to remain cold-headed. Because he knows me, he also knows that this is one of my strategies to dissimulate something. Or play down something. He looked at me, again, very swiftly, but even this swift glance, I could feel a strong desire from him. The problem with him is that, and now I can feel this and have the confirmation, he loves me for what I actually look like, not for who I am. This is actually most of the men, he is like them, he wants to see me pretty and pleasant all the time; otherwise, there are no interests. However, as soon as he looked at me back straight in the eyes as he used to try to keep control over the situation, I could really feel some exhaustion. Some, "she's pissing me off", as I was destabilising him. That was not my attention.

I actually discreetly stepped back, and, with my hand, showed him that he may enter. I pushed myself, so he could enter, and then, I closed the door. I didn't lock the door to have a way out and show him that I could trust him, but once was actually unusual, as usual, I used to smell around. Very discreetly, and there was a powerful smell of coffee around. It was actually a mix between his mother's place' smell and coffee. That is actually quite unusual, he was indeed coming back from work or at least from a trial shift in someplace where we make coffee. If he was working today and had a trial shift, it would mitigate his sentiments or feelings for me.

On the other hand, when I was texting him, he was actually relatively slow to answer initially and quite fast when I sent him the last texts, and at first, I thought that he may think about what to answer, trying to deal with me. I didn't feel that it could have been a possibility that he may have been busy at that moment, working. Especially since I called him towards mid-afternoon, I didn't do anything on the morning on purpose, so... Yeah, that would explain a lot of things.

Anyway, when I was around him, I felt him actually being observing around when I was closing the door. The problem with this door is that it is so heavy that it always takes me some moments to actually shut it properly, given the fact that I have no strength. And, well, in the meantime, I assume he was observing around and could notice that it was dark all around because at the moment I closed the door and was behind him, turning myself to him, he starkly muttered:

"So, what is it, depression party, tonight?" he attacked.

"No, it's just that I wanted to make things nice, like candles, like... You know, like our first date," I immediately calmed himself down, using a relieving voice.

"Hum..." he was disarmed.

"I mean, as far as I recall, it was like this, and maybe making this moment one more time would make it certainly different, I don't know..."

He spoke steadfastly, using quite a confident voice, deep as well, and seemed overly aggressive towards me. Perhaps, to show his dominance towards the situation and the fact that he was in a strong position, I actually used quite a slow voice, very soft, to reassure him. I spoke quite slowly, showing my worries and showing that I was frankly worried. Speaking slowly, I was also using an exceptionally high voice, not showing any foreign accent or signs that I may be tired, literally, I wanted to show myself hesitating. Using "I don't know", or their *je ne sais pas* was a deliberate attempt to show my confusion and discomfort with these ongoing events. And, speaking about our first date here, even if the atmosphere was totally different at that moment as it was more into a great dinner and then disappointing sex for me, now maybe associating some good remembrances... It was purely a suggestion, it was just evoking that moment, as he was now seeing me. He was turned towards me and saw me in that red dress, in his mind, according to the very shy and almost tough to distinguish smile that drew itself on his face, I am sure that he was now thinking about this moment. I was also dressed in red, but not in that dress and not wearing those shoes. And the flat was too dark, candles everywhere, but... Yeah, things were different. It's why, after I saw his micro-smile being drawn on his face, he actually started to say, now with less anger:

"Yeah, it's true. But you were different that evening..."

"Yeah. That was a good moment. True..." I was thoughtful. "Anyway, would you like to come with me to the living room?"

"Sure..."

Something was actually quite surprising, and to be honest, I wasn't expecting that reaction: I was literally driving him. By driving, I mean, physically, I invited him to step in the flat, now I was showing him the living room so he could come and sit, this was surprising, he knows that even here, he is and will always be home. Whatever happens, he is at home here, and I always told him so. Usually, he comes without asking for permission, he goes in the living room and sits, like... Yeah, basically, this was exactly like our first date, like when he didn't know the flat and was just waiting for my permission to go somewhere or do what he wants. He was timid on the first month when he came here, although I told him that. But as days passed, he took actually much more confidence, and now I feel like he was just a guest in his place. Like, everything was already over. I cannot clearly say whether he came here today intending to break up with me, or maybe it was not obvious, but... I can say that he must feel that things will be over soon, which may explain why he behaves like he is a guest. Anyway.

So, after I showed him how he already knew for joining the living room, surprisingly, he sat by himself at the precise place where I wanted him to sit. He was actually quite surprised to discover the atmosphere, I mean, after three months of a relationship and especially that very first date when we had sex on that very same sofa, he found a table covered with candles and food. And drinks. He sat, and, meanwhile, I turned around the table, to sit at the exact spot where I sat whilst waiting for me now five minutes ago.

So, now, here it was. Even though I didn't use any of the same elements of that very first date, what he could see in front of him was somehow a reminder to actually appease him. If I didn't create this atmosphere, he would be ways more nervous, and if I would have told the truth just like this... I really don't know how this may have ended up. Now, he was certainly more relaxed. I mean, at least less nervous than he already was, he could see that basically, I made something for him, I thought about him, I cleaned the flat for him, I prepared myself quite well for him, I wore make-up for him, anyway, I did quite a lot of stuff for him. Even if I let him start speaking when I opened the door and let him come in, now it was my turn to speak, because if I do not start, he will begin straightforward with, "so what did you want to tell me?". And, the harsh truth, yeah, why not, he's gonna find it anyway, but I prefer starting with light topics before. To appease the situation a bit more for him, not to manipulate him, but... I did it for that purpose: let's imagine you are in a car, and that car is launched at one hundred kilometres per hour against a wall, and your steering wheel is not responding. It's gonna be harsh. Now let's imagine that we put some big foam plate between your car and the wall. It's still gonna be challenging, but maybe a bit less. This is why, I was slowly adding some foam by just starting, as soon as I sat next to him, my legs folded on the sofa, my arm towards his neck and entirely turned to him, whilst he was just sat towards the TV:

"So, how was your day?" I started promptly after we sat.

"Meh... Not really fun. What about you?"

"Well, to tell the truth, it was not really fun either. I mean, school, back home... You know, the classic routine," I was already speaking with him like we already broke up.

"Yeah..."

"What did you do today?"

"Oh, well..." he promptly replied, "I went at my mother's... Saw some friends, this afternoon I had a trial shift in some coffee shop near Montmartre..."

"Oh, really?"

"Yeah... But, you know, customers are jerks, and I was not in the mood to actually cope with them... Coming straight to you, disrespectfully, asking for their shitty lattes in their reusable cups... Without even saying hello, please, how are you and goodbye. It was okay, but, you know, I was just not in the mood to actually go through it..."

"Yeah, I know. I mean, I think. Working in customer service might be tough. But you know what we say, the customer is the king..."

"Yeah, the customer is the king, my arse..."

"But I agree with you, some customers should bear in mind or maybe be reminded that some kings were beheaded a while ago for gross misconduct and abuse of power..."

"Yeah... Exactly..." he laughed.

Yeah, well, customer service, I recall when I was in high school, we had those professional integration weeks that we had to do, and I chose to do it in some clothing shops. For a full week, you will work, but you are not paid for this. It was just one week, just to give like a final report at the end once back to school about what you did that week. Well, it was actually fun, you could get discounts on clothes you buy (and by that time I didn't inherit, and I used to be broke). The only thing I used to recall today was rude customers, becoming aggressive when you do not have something available at the moment or coming to you and not even saying hello or I am sorry to disturb... Yeah. Consumerism... Hopefully, it was just a week. That enhanced experience convinced me that capitalism is not really... When you are on the other side of the till and not working in an office, people just see you as a total waste.

At least, in this tensed situation, I still made him laugh. But, anyway, as he was looking for a job, I was kind of happy. For the time he desperately seeks something, because... He doesn't want to loan from me... Well, on the other hand, given the situation, I may understand. I never had a rich boyfriend or girlfriend, for some reason I am the other side of the bed, so... I was still quite happy for him. I mean, I know he is hard worker, he will succeed, I am sure.

"Well, that's a great step for you. I am happy, and I really hope that it worked out well for you..."

"Well, I didn't take the job..."

"Oh, really, why?"

"Because... I've been thinking, to be honest, today... And there are quite a few things that... You know, since I discovered that you were apparently pregnant..."

Yeah, here we go. Now let's get this drama started, I mean... On the other hand, I may find maybe a thousand escape routes to divert this, he came here tonight for that. I also went for this, I mean, this is why we are here for tonight.

Obviously, my pregnancy is back. The first thing. Well, this is just the tip of the iceberg. Now, let's drain the water to make the ice fully discovered. With currently a lower and certainly graver voice, more seriously, my smile disappeared. It was time to tackle this.

"Oh, erm..." I showed some embarrassment.

"You're pregnant, you've been concealing that from me, and now, I don't know, I am actually kind of lost. I... I just don't know what to say or even think..."

"Honey, I..." I shyly started.

"Yes?" everything became suddenly quiet when he responded.

"I, erm... I am so sorry for having concealed that from you. I, erm... This is... Yeah, I actually failed to tell you, because... Well, there are many things, but, okay we may have a situation, okay we may have like a house, we have already whatever we want, and even better because I am kind of a lucky woman but... I am just not ready for that!"

"I understand. But why didn't you tell me this earlier, I mean..."

"Because..." I kept my confusion going on, "Because, I don't know, I, erm... When I actually found out, I just, I was terrified of your reaction, it stressed the shit out of me, and I was just... You know..."

"I know what?"

Yeah, well, the "I didn't tell you because I was not feeling ready" strangely, even to me, seemed like a kind of a flimsy excuse. It is true, I do not feel like having a baby and being a mum, he already knows that and most of all, he knows that I do not want to get pregnant. Still, going in this way, yes, some part was correct, but it is a weak truth, and since for me deceitful facts lead automatically to lies, telling him something that I could have said this morning, it just doesn't make sense. Whilst actually still keep on turning around the problem without entering it, I just continued, disheartened:

"I was stressed, that was it. I needed time to actually think about that, and you scare me with your envy to have a baby right now. I understand you are still older than me, and you do not have the same expectations than I do, but I am barely major, now, and, I just want to wait, that's all..."

"Okay, but you still could have told me, I mean, I am your boyfriend, and... As I said this morning, since your birthday party, you're just acting weird with everybody. You know, everybody starts wondering questions..."

Everybody? What do you mean, "everybody"? On the other hand, except me that acts as a solitary wolf here, I should still bear in mind that the alpha here is my mother. This is why I asked, now in a different tone:

"Everybody?"

"Yes, you know that we talk with your sister and your mum, and... We just find you are acting weird. This is why, you disappeared all the last weekend without giving any sign of life, any notice, and suddenly you reappear, like nothing happened and like you've been here, and everything is normal."

"Hum... It's true that... That may sound odd, true..."

"So, we all want to know, and especially me, as your boyfriend, as someone that proposed you also to marry me... What the fuck is going on, now?"

That's what I said, that wouldn't work for long. On the other hand, I think even without wanting, I kind of take the right approach, explaining things softly... Starting with this. But, as we say sometimes, it was time to face up the truth... And putting my hands into shit.

To be honest, okay... My plan included, I will now tell him the truth, and then he will break up with me. Yes, this was the plan, and so far, it is quite successful. The thing is, there are still some emotions. And even though I am what they call a psychopath and thus, not set up to actually experience or feel emotions, I was still feeling some stuff. I remained still quite sensitive to some feelings, and the emotion I was exposed to now was the fact that, yeah, what I am about to say is actually not that easy to say. Even to myself, admitting that I slept with strangers for money, even if it was... well, actually only once, but it was still enough, I still did it. I did prostitution and saying that, well... Whatever approach I will use to make the bomb explode, it was not that simple. The more critical now was, the phone was on the table, next to the plate, and the recorder still pointed right at me, so I was sure that whoever was blackmailing me, was now carefully listening to me. And now, I just cannot escape again, I cannot find a way to actually not telling the truth. I may be fucked, but, when I really think about that, there are other people for whom it's not in their best interest if I speak. Worse than mine.

So, now, let's start to actually end where it was meant to end, and this from the beginning. From the moment everything started, it was meant to end up this way. I mean, after all, what I went through... And now after having genuinely thought, there wouldn't have been any other ways through which I could have escaped that mess without sacrificing Florent. So, after a moment of thought, when I stopped touching my hairs nervously because I was bracing for this moment, very slowly but audibly, I started to make the bomb finally explode:

"Okay, erm... Okay, you want to know, and I cannot do anything otherwise. So, fine, let's tell you the truth..."

"I need it, Cha..." he suddenly turned himself towards me, understanding that now, I would give him what he wants to hear.

"Of course, I do understand, I totally do, I, erm... Could you make me a promise, though?"

"Sure?"

"Okay, what I have to tell you, darling, it's big. It's, erm... It's massive. And, I want your word that you will not repeat this to anyone," I made sure to say this as clearly as possible, for the phone, insisting on each word towards the end of my speech.

"Erm..." he was hesitating. "Yeah, yeah, of course!"

The exact way he answered... things that he said, the way he looked at me, I mean, his facial expressions actually confirmed at that moment to me that... Mum is monitoring him. They spoke together, that is sure, because he needs to know, of course, but she wants to know much more. The problem, she is unable to face me up, so she is using him instead. He somehow sought his words, he didn't say something like "of course, Cha" or "No, no, of course,"; instead, there were some moments of hesitation before actually saying yes. I always thought that given his behaviour, if he lives with me, he is a tool that my mother uses to spy on me and monitor me, and, what he actually said... He blinked his eyes quite rapidly suddenly, he was obviously trying to recall something that I don't know, so... he will talk, I can almost be assured of this. Mainly what I am about to tell him is much more than he may expect. But he doesn't know that yet. He will. So, after having observed this, I continued:

"Okay, then, erm... Do you recall the night of my birthday, I mean, not our night, the night when I went out?"

"Yeah, when you told me that you were with your friend Sophie? Who I am sure does not exist, by the way?"

"Oh, she's an existing person, nice, ask Clarisse, she knows her. But, well, yeah, I was with her. But I was with Claire too, and Kelly. Okay, you do not know any of them, I mean, you know Claire, but..."

"Yeah, birthday party with your ex-girlfriend... Of whom I am petrified of, and I threatened you many times that if you would see her outside of school once I would leave!"

"It started in the morning; I just took the metro when she called me. And pissed me off to actually come to a party with her. Trust me, at first, I was reluctant, truly, because within the last months' Claire has become, I don't know, a weird person. But... She insisted, repeatedly, and..."

"And you said yes..."

"I did. I know, this was really bad, I am so sorry, I mean... I shouldn't have given in, I mean, I was just fed up to have her around, and... At first, it was just supposed to be a couple of drinks at her place, and that would be all. Then, on the morning of that day, Sophie told me that she actually needed to talk to me; apparently, it was something important, and she couldn't say that much for some reasons, I was curious."

Obviously, I must start this by revealing Claire is a prostitute. This was not to make the situation a bit more dramatic, it was for my blackmailer. If he was listening... Then, starting by Claire would also justify my actions, even though it shouldn't be explained. In the meantime, okay, he was pissed that I was with my ex during my birthday night... I mean, who wouldn't... But he remained still curious. Because, yeah, if I spent the evening with my ex, yes, it's terrible, but it's not a crime. He was conscientious about what I was now saying. I literally had all his attention. I deliberately adopted a stressful and uncomfortable posture, like breathing not like usual, speaking almost confused. Slowly, I was getting to my point.

"Nice, so now I learn that you were with Claire that night..." he started, without wanting to hear my explanation.

"Honey, I am so sorry, it's just that I couldn't tell you the true reason why, I mean, you would be seriously pissed, and I just couldn't, that was all!"

"Hum... Okay, so what was this thing that this Sophie or whoever she is wanted to tell you?"

"She, erm..." I started to seek my words and pretended that I was confused and revealed something sensitive. "She basically started to mention that as Kelly was involved in some weird activities, such as prostitution, escorting, all that kind of stuff, she suspected that Claire would actually be involved too."

"Oh... So, as I know you, you wanted to know a bit more..."

"Yeah, I am curious, and curiosity killed the cat... Erm, I know... I just couldn't believe that I mean, okay, Claire changed, but at the point to become a prostitute, I mean, I just can't believe it. I couldn't believe it, I mean. So, I went to that party to actually know a bit more. Because, yeah, this triggered my curiosity and... Wait..."

But he raised an important point, actually, why didn't Sophie tell me the truth at school, why was it so important to say to me during that party, especially at Claire's place? I didn't really suspect Sophie initially because, well, to be honest, my vigilance was at its lowest point, but I should indeed have paid much more attention. Sophie never really seemed suspicious, but... Some things seem weird from her. I think I will ask her tomorrow. I actually thought about it, and... when I stopped speaking after having mentioned that important word, "prostitution", I had much more attention. This is why, when I thought about that and stopped talking, he was listening carefully:

"Wait, what?"

"Erm, nothing. Just thinking about some details..." I was thinking but took back the conversation swiftly. "Anyway, I went to that party, and at some point, I must admit that I drank a bit too much. And the Kelly I mentioned, at some point she asked us if we wanted to go out to some nightclub, and, I was just fucked up, I followed. I really wanted to go home at that point, and honestly, I should have listened to myself, but you know... I was just stupid. I was foolish!"

"A nightclub... You hate nightclubs..." he looked at me, realised that it is the truth.

"Exactly. I do hate those places, and I told you why. But as I said, I was just drunk. And I thought it would be fancy to actually try this. I just, couldn't expect that, basically... Well... Once arrived, Claire and Kelly dragged me towards some guy, some guy that I actually didn't know but they seemed to know pretty well, and, erm, at some point they went dancing, and, erm..." I remained still thoughtful, leaving him time to realise that...

"Wait, you hate nightclubs, and above all, you hate dancing. I haven't seen you dancing ever. These are things you hate; you are just insensitive to that... What the fuck have you done that night?"

Okay, now we get to the part when I tell that I was a shameful and unfaithful girlfriend. The problem is this guy obviously drugged me... Or maybe he didn't as I was actually really fucked up that night, but for sleeping with me, there must have been some assistance taken... such as drugs. But, well... Okay, how to tell you this, dear Florent? It is true, I've never been to a nightclub in my life, I hate those places, and above all, I hate dancing. I hate those places where music is being too loud, and... Yeah. Although before that I've never been in one, those were just preconceptions, but I must admit that I was pretty much right.

Well, in any case... Well, he is not stupid. As I was sat with some guy, drunk, and he knows how dangerous it can be especially since he knows how many guys are turning around me when I am dressed in the way I was when I went to that nightclub, and... It's like Claire, learning what she has become was actually a shock for me, but I suffered in silence. For him, he is everything but the kind of person that suffers in silence. And, given that he asked me that question almost straight away, like, what the fuck have you done that night, he knew that something was not actually smelling good. And... Even saying that it's my fault, even saying that I cheated on him even though I didn't want, even though it was a real mistake, it was... I would have never done that in the standard time since I am faithful in a relationship (except that night and what followed, I never cheated on anyone, that is a fact) and I cannot accept someone being unfaithful... I just wanted to avoid saying that straight. I cannot tell him that nothing happened, this is rubbish, and... And I think he wants to hear it from me, maybe. I saw him, when he said, what "the fuck" have I done that night, when he said, "the fuck", it was... it was like, really accusative. His breath rate increased, I assume the same as his heartbeat, I could see his face, body language; he was clearly getting ready to hear something that he would not like to catch. He was already defending himself towards that situation. Okay... This is why I tackled the thing with other words that meant the problem:

"I just don't know. I don't remember. I blacked out... I recall having sat with that guy, drinking again and again, and... I blacked out..." I used a low voice, full of shame.

Free Expensive Lies: Prologue

This was not pleasant at all for both of us. Revealing that you mistook, telling a concealed truth... I was precisely feeling like Claire on the morning when I went to her place and found out that she slept accidentally with someone else. He was undoubtedly feeling the same as I did, I just wanted to crucify her. I don't want to imagine how I would actually be in his mind at this very moment.

Because suddenly, I saw his lips becoming ways tenser. I also saw him blushing, his breath rate increased, and I could see him moving fast, or at least not staying in place. After what I said, he didn't really want to speak because he knows what this blackout means, especially in that exact situation. He is not stupid. After I said that I blacked out, there has been a small, but to me dramatically long silence. I was honestly really embarrassed to say this, I was really uncomfortable with this situation. I knew that it wouldn't be easy at all. He was just breathing, and I just looked at him. His eyes... He didn't look at me, he was exclusively focused on watching the switched-off TV, the TV screen, because... I saw that, already, he was feeling deep hate and repulse towards me. At the same time, I didn't really know if touching him, at least trying to take his hand, or doing something was actually an excellent idea. I was reviving something that I lived the last August, except that I was in a wrong position this time. He certainly wanted to break something... And, after a short silence that appeared to me as awfully long... He just started to say...

"Don't tell me that..."

"I am so sorry..." I started making my voice fading away.

"Holy cow... Don't tell me that..." he put his two hands covering his face.

"I am so sorry, honey, I woke up the following day, in some weird bed, some weird place, and he was there, and then... I am so sorry, honey..."

To be honest, I would have loved to be able to cry now. At least, this would have been the moment, but absolutely nothing came to my mind, nothing except some mathematic equations on how I can manipulate and how I can escape that shitty situation. I just saw his fury as the result of a thousand and a thousand chemical reactions that were ongoing within his brain, and it was... I just realised that, well. When I opened the door, the last August, when I took Claire on the fact that she was in tears, she was begging for my pity, she was imploring my forgiveness, and I was just unable to do anything, having been shocked by what I saw. It would have been a perfect tragedy, and I was catching myself playing a simple disaster. I know that I was playing the comedy because, yes, it was hard to explain, yes it was hard to tell him what happened. After all, I still keep in mind that we were starting a relationship. But the feeling of guilt and remorse were absolutely not destabilising me at all. And if I was proud of it? Absolutely not.

At that moment, slowly, I started to take his hand, because I was still living the thing, I was living the moment. I was really ashamed of what I said, and he just didn't deserve this. I was just cruel, to tell him that. Somehow, for him, well, it was like everything was put upside-down, everything was suddenly reversed, and it couldn't be changed. I actually didn't feel the need to thoroughly look at him or even analyse him any further, I could feel the fury and smell it. Yeah, now, I was in Claire's place, if he could kill me or harm me, he would do it. But he won't, he is the rare kind of guy who cannot hurt a woman, this is something... I think the only thing I have respect for him is that he is not a coward or an animal of that sort.

For once, certainly one of the first time in my life, I lowered my head, spontaneously. I know what it means, it's generally a sign of submission, lowering your head, and, even if he was heads up, he wasn't looking at me. What pissed me off at that moment was, I really want him in my life, I mean, he is a valuable friend, and I really do like him, I do appreciate him. After what has been done, it's evident that nothing is gonna be the same anymore. I mean, I really wish I have a friend like him, I really do. He remains someone trustworthy, and I also wished to have him as a close friend, someone I could have full confidence. Because I don't really have any friends or people trustworthy except Claire, and Claire, well, she's more than a friend, and... I just broke everything. Well, given who I am, I mean, I don't think I could actually have a friend someday, because people are still seeing me like a dark and dangerous person. And... And if I am not a dark and hazardous person, then I look like a brainless wannabe, and it's painful, I mean, somehow, I suffer from the image I have. Well, I do not suffer, I mean, it's much more complicated. Anyway, after a brief moment, when he finally came back from his thoughts, and I imagine what it would be because I passed through this, he certainly imagined me having sex with this person that I do not fully recall, over and over again. Whilst looking at the window and the streetlights reflecting this darkness slightly brightened by the candles inside, and whilst I was still lowering my head, next to him, almost unable to move because I was feeling weird. I was deep inside trying to gather all the data that I have so far to find a positive escape route from that situation... I suddenly heard, deeply inspired, a...

"You fucking bitch..." he launched this so harshly towards me.

"I am so sorry, honey, I am just so sorry, I just... I just fucked up, and I was unconscious of what was going on, I am... I just, I cannot really say anything..."

Yeah, I can imagine. He must be continuously imagining those guys and me again and again, and, I know, this is something crazy, feeling betrayed at that point. There is nothing worse than betrayal, and, yeah, he was living it. I cannot really say, because, this is weird, I didn't think that he'd love me actually, as I felt in his breath, in his reaction now, and, in some other things, yeah, he was feeling betrayed, and that was horrible. It meant that he loved me in some ways. He loved me in his manner. Well, this is the way the world ends. Once again, I tried to take his arm, but immediately he repelled me, this time more violently and more explicitly. He was in deep shock, I mean, I could see it, I was more or less the same when I was in his position, and, I must admit, this must have been torture for her as well. The thing is, I am less involved emotionally, so it reduces the impact this may have on me, my rational mind always takes it all, but still, for once I was feeling like a traitor, and this was not really peasant. It may not prevent me from sleeping tonight, but still, this was not funny. And the "bitch", yeah, usually I don't really care when I heard that said to me, but now... I actually cared about.

Anyway, after I tried to grab his arms, I understood that any possible friendship I may have with him, any potential future we may have together, everything was just torn apart. After he prevented me from taking his arm as a sign of "I am sorry", he immediately said:

"Don't touch me... Just, don't..."

"Please, listen to the rest of the story, because..."

"Oh, wait, because this is just the beginning?"

He just looked at me, obviously with a shocked air, and... And, come on, I already mentioned prostitution, what did you expect, seriously? I didn't even say yes, I shook my head for yes three times, and... I nervously smiled. His eyes were red, I mean, there was nothing now that may survive. He also raised his voice, a sign of deep anger, which went accordingly to the betrayal that I did, and his breath went back to fast... Yeah, this was really messed up. Meh... So, after I nodded my head, he continued.

"So, you cheated on me, you slept with some weird son of a bitch that I don't even know, and... Now you are telling me that this is not over?"

"Honey, please, listen to me..." I used a kind of desperate, deep voice without even paying attention.

"Okay, so you cheated on me, then what's next?"

Something that you're not gonna enjoy. But, well, at the point you are now, I don't think this may make a difference, honey. I continued:

"Okay, so... You remember, at some point, the next day, I received a call, and I had to leave... Basically, Claire called me. She was meeting with Kelly, and they both knew that I was fucked, they knew what I did last night, and I wanted this to remain hidden. And the guy... She gave me an envelope... There was some money inside, and..."

"Holy shit..."

"This was... This was the greatest insult that I have ever had in my life, I mean... This was..."

"Fuck..."

It's curious, at this precise moment, I was feeling like... Yeah, I recalled that moment, basically, and it triggered a kind of intense, excessively big repulsion that I may have for him, or even for guys in general. Even this morning, during sex, I was feeling at my ease, but now, yeah, I think this was confirmed. Is it trauma or something? On the other hand, I used to bury deep down in my mind unpleasant moments of my life, such as this one. I mean the experience with the two guys or my parents' divorce, it's like into a big graveyard in my mind that I leave, so it doesn't prevent me from thinking correctly. What depresses me is when I come closer to this, and I see that it's actually quite broad. This moment, I think it will be the same, it will go to the same place. That is the problem when you have an over rational mind or the advantage I don't know, having little or no space for emotions helps you go forward.

But, yeah, now, he knew the truth. I think that's all he needs, he doesn't need any further. We're done, now, I guess. I have what I want, he has what he wants, I think it's time to wrap up again. We are both satisfied, I mean, if I may say so. Now, it is time to let him be upset, be really upset, at the point that he will feel the need to take his revenge, then he's gonna speak to my mother, and... Or my mother will call him, I don't know how this is going to happen. For me, I think it's time to sleep now. I am actually quite tired, and... I think I played the comedy quite well, and my plan goes as I want. The first day went fine, now it's time to brace for the second. But, before wrapping up, I still need to justify myself, on my motives, so he understands the dramatic dimension of this.

Even though he just wants to kill me in a very nasty, dirty way, and... And, I understand him, I'd be on the other side of the sofa... I'd do the same. Hopefully, he is not aware that this is one of my fool's game, I am the only one to know the truth. And given that this was relatively smooth and seemed natural, there are no chances that someone thinks or guess that all this is just rubbish. He'd be distraught otherwise. Like, really pissed. Hopefully, no-one will ever know. Innocently, I started to give justifications, even if I were clearly aware that this wouldn't change anything to the situation.

"This is why I couldn't speak about it. I just thought at first that this would remain an isolated incident, and I was just so mad at Claire that, well, I just didn't talk with her, I just... I was just furious. And... And then I've been blackmailed."

"You've been blackmailed?"

"Yes..."

"By whom?"

"I don't know. Some bastard that basically took pictures of me cheating on you, and threatened me to basically release everything if I'd talk or not do what he wanted me to do..."

"Fuck, Charlotte, why didn't you go to the police or... Do anything?"

"Because... Because, I basically learned that Claire is basically being forced to do the same, and... Come on, like they care about some silly blackmail story, you know that in your fucking country, there is no justice for that!"

Hum... Forgive my French again. He knows that I do not like this country anyway, that's not a secret; I don't feel right here. And it's true, I mean, there are rapists still free here, there are terrorists released from prisons, people defrauding institutions even outside, everything is corrupt here, it's like a vast corruption place. There's no wonder why Joris is a cop and a pimp at the same time, in my opinion. It's funny, every time I talk about France, I always feel the same, a wave of enormous anger comes from nowhere. Anyway, is he serious, I mean, in what world does he live, given that this is a compact system, does he really think that if I start filing a lawsuit against some guy I don't even know, something magic will happen? Come on, mate, open your eyes, for fuck's sake! Or, even, suing a cop... I am an eighteen-year-old bobo girl as they say (bobo means... well, rich, and, basically, all what I am), against someone who is part of the machine? Mate... It would never happen, I have no chances to win, come on! It's better if I use my tools against them instead of using legal witchcraft, their system is rotten to the core. Anyway, after this very slight digression, because, yeah, I am also angry to have betrayed him and sometimes, when I hear silly things, it triggers some astonishing reactions... He just continued. Because, at now, I could see him, even him, he just wanted to leave. So did I.

"Okay... Just... Just answer to my questions, Cha..." he was breathless.

"Yes, sure, erm... Yes!"

"Did you sleep with people for money?"

"Yes..."

"How many?"

"I don't know, maybe, two... Three..."

To be honest, I remained as clear and concise in my answers as possible, because now, to make sure the impact of my solutions would be maximum. So, he could be really pissed and then really talk to my mother. He continued:

"Why did you lie to me?"

"I just didn't want the truth to explode... That's all!"

"Does Clarisse know about what's going on?"

This is a tricky one, because, well, if I say yes, he will take this as a double betrayal from my sister and me, and if I say no, it will come to him that I lied. And, saying yes would also have consequences to my sister, given the fact that she was aware of colossal stuff and didn't say a word about this, more or less she turned a blind eye on this. And, I am sure, as this will come to mum, she will also try to interrogate Clarisse about this, and how comes that she knew and said nothing. Well, on the other hand, the thing is, this scandal is due to explode, and since it is massive, I think everybody must have his part. Sorry, Clarisse. I am gonna ruin some friendship.

"Yes... She does..."

"Holy fuck..."

"I am so sorry..."

"Is the baby mine?"

Well, it was quite sure that this would lead to this question. I mean... Yeah, of course, given what I did, given a lot of things, given the fact that our sex life was quiet for the last two weeks, that would become obvious that he would ask that question, as my pregnancy was kind of unexpected. I still can lie, because this is basically the most tragic into all this. I can tell the truth, but the truth will not be, I mean, the thing he'd expect or would be ready to hear, or... This is why, I was just like, at this point, yeah. It's over anyway, and if he knows that the baby is his, or thinks that it might be the case, I think that would still be an excuse for any possible further harassment. I actually remained thoughtful for like a couple of seconds, in front of him, looking at him straight in the eyes, and... I dropped the bomb, the ultimate one. He suffered enough this evening; this was why it was time to end up the palliative cure.

"I am not sure..."

Free Expensive Lies: Prologue

Suddenly, he took a deep breath and also stood up from the sofa. Yeah, he was broken, I mean, I have never seen him like this. Those four words were actually enough to literally wipe out an entire relationship, because now, obviously, I am the evillest creature he has ever met, he now wants to kill me or hurt me badly, but now... Yeah, the end has arrived. It was not a pleasant moment, but deep down, I just, yeah, okay, I was heartbroken of that and not proud of it. Still, I kept on telling myself that I am not the only one on that planet, and there are also millions of other women, and I am sure he will find someone right for him, someone he deserves. I was just not the right person, and, even, when I started this relationship, some voice in my head was telling me that it was a mistake because I kind of had a hunch that it wouldn't end in a right way. Now, well, I didn't think at that moment that I would ever do that in some future, but, yes, that is the truth, and, yeah, he must cope with this. We must cope with that. It's gonna take time, but on the other hand, this is just a break-up, a break-up from a three-month relationship. He will not die from this.

Anyway, when he stood up, I felt like, whatever I say, it will not change anything, my job was done now. I did what I had to do, I just have to wait for the aftermath now, which should be coming within hours, as the bomb I dropped was massive. After thinking about it, I think it was actually a good idea to reveal the truth about my pregnancy and tell him the raw truth. We say that the truth will set you free but first will piss you off, after all, he just wanted the truth and nothing else. Sometimes, I really believe that a small lie is better than a devastating truth, this is why, unlike most people, I have a better acceptance when people are lying. As I lie. And I think that this evening was the best example to illustrate that. Now, our relationship is over, but it's what's best for both of us. I cannot be a wife, and I cannot be with him, this just doesn't match any natural laws. This is why, when he stood up, I only remained calm, still motionless, like, yeah. I would be in love, I would definitely react another way, but let's face the truth, I just don't love him, especially since I am back with Claire, my true love, and the love of my life. He, yeah, he just stood up, looked at the window, and in a kind of desperate voice, even if I didn't move because I didn't want to and also because whatever I do, it won't change shit, I just slightly uttered:

"Baby, please..."

"Shut up, just shut the fuck up... Just... Just, fuck you. Screw you. I don't want to hear from you anymore. I'll come soon to get my stuff, meanwhile, I just want you out of my life!"

"Florent!"

"Leave me alone..."

And he left. Furious. Well, I wouldn't do better, I assume. The dirty job was done, now, let's brace for the aftermath. After he left, there was this small glass of water that I poured before he comes. I don't know why, but my jaws were tights, just like I am when I am furious. Now, time to get some stuff and go to Claire's place, because I'd rather not sleep here tonight. I didn't even finish my glass, I mean, I poured the rest of the water in the plant behind the sofa, but now I was thinking, this is done, the task was successfully completed. And I really don't know why, but... Why was I feeling like this poor king Priam letting entering in his city a gigantic wooden horse?

32 *Once upon a time...*

// Still at home, on my way to Claire's house.

// Monday, 21ˢᵗ of January 2013, 22:33.

Anyway, the wind blows...

At the moment he left, I threw my water in the plant, and I stood up. My phone was still near me, and I actually took it. It was also the moment for me to get out. When I recalled that my books for school tomorrow are still in my locker there, I basically just need some clothes for tomorrow. If I am gonna be back tomorrow, I don't actually know, even tomorrow, yes, after Joris and Claire's meeting, I don't really know where we're gonna go. Also given the fact that the scandal will explode and... Maybe we should take a hotel in between. And, even, I know her mother works tomorrow as she just does night shifts at the hospital, I don't feel like Claire is gonna be willing to sleep at the place she's gonna be assaulted, or at least where this happened. I don't fucking know, and, to be honest, I prefer staying with her for a couple of days, because obviously they're gonna start to seek revenge and Claire will be the first target, or I would be, so...

On the other hand, last night, I agreed with Reed that we would have a safe place and an escort for a couple of days, just the time things calm down... The question was, should I take clothes for a couple of days or just for tonight? Because, yeah, somehow, I had a kind of a hunch, that I wouldn't be back here for actually a specific time.

Free Expensive Lies: Prologue

I went back to my bathroom, to actually remove my makeup. And still, my phone was quiet, even the flat, we could just only hear me. Nothing, except the noise from the outside. It's odd, I mean, I was already feeling weird, and somehow this evening, this meeting, this breakup... I felt like it was the end of something, something was curiously ending, and I couldn't clearly identify what. Or at least the thing that would end would actually be more significant than what I may expect. That heavy atmosphere didn't mean anything good, to be fair. Maybe I was just paranoid, but generally, it's never a good thing when I have a hunch. So, I started removing my makeup, then I went back to the bedroom to get some better clothes as I have to take the metro and I am gonna get cold, when suddenly, from the bathroom, I heard something vibrating. I started to rush towards there to actually see what it was, and when I saw it... It was my mother. Displayed on the phone was Amelia, my mother's name. I never put mum or something like this. Geez, what does she want, isn't she supposed to be at work or with some friends of her or dating some guy? I took the call.

"Hey, honey..." she started.

"Hey..." I replied... as always, analysing because I was aware that something might be ongoing.

"You okay, darling?"

"Still carrying my cross, what about you?"

"Oh... Carrying your cross? What do you mean?"

Okay, so she had a calm voice, not aggressive, even almost friendly, mostly because she called me honey when I took the call. It meant that she was in a pleasant place with an agreeable person. According to the background noise, as I heard people speaking and almost no music and no cars driving around, she was undoubtedly precisely in the terrace of a restaurant. So, she was probably either on a date, or either on a dinner with one of her friend or colleague, but given the fact that she called me honey, she seemed really appeased and the terrace of the restaurant, I'd personally rather bet she's on a date. The question, why the fuck is she calling me? Maybe the person she's currently dating went elsewhere, for instance, going to pee or something, and she's getting bored. Or... I don't know. I didn't really want to dwell on details about what carrying my cross currently meant, so I cut it short:

"Yeah, no, I am just a bit tired..."

"Oh... Well, then go to bed!"

"Yeah, I'm on my way. Anyway, why are you calling me that late?"

"Oh, well, I actually wanted to give you some great news, I mean, great news for me until you manage to ruin it... I finally met someone!"

"Oh, really? I didn't think that meeting people on dating apps could be successful, especially according to your standards. That's quite intriguing, actually..."

"Well, we didn't meet through that, and erm..."

Last time I checked (I didn't personally check but I heard feedback), dating apps were more designed to have a one-night stand than a long-term relationship, since people are there only for sex. I mean, comfortable meeting hidden behind screens, dating apps are like you go to a McDonalds, you want there just to get fast food, without really caring whether it's good or not; you just want to eat, and quick. So it means that if she was relaxed, I mean this way, especially given that (yeah, come on, I know it's my mother but still) I hardly imagine my mother sleep at the first night, she wants guarantees... She basically looks for boyfriends like she would buy a new washing machine, it must be performant and intuitive. It means that she knows that person already for a specific time and tonight is maybe their first date as a couple. It excludes the fact that she may have met him through whatever app or anything. Oh, wait... She actually told me that for... Oh, shit, sorry... I restarted by what she actually wanted to hear. Meh, why would I ruin her mood, let her actually enjoy her happiness, I am not a bitch.

"Oh, hum, my bad, erm... where are my manners? Congratulations, that's what I wanted to say. Or you wanted to hear, I don't know."

"That's fine, I am kind of used to it."

"So, who's the doomed?"

"Oh, well, he is, erm... He's basically the friend of a friend of mine, we actually met at that party, and he was the guy with whom I talked at a certain time?"

See...

Well, yeah, maybe I saw him, but that night, I actually saw more than fifty people, as we were quite a lot during that evening, so finding one person in the middle of it all was actually quite a lot. I can try to recall everything, as luckily, I have quite a good memory, the problem is, I am just too lazy for that. Certainly, someday I will meet him, and I will recall him, but for now... She certainly talked with him, but all I remember was just seven people and amongst which there was mostly his boss and new partners for work. Though... There was still a guy, who seemed slightly younger than her, I mean certainly thirty-five/thirty-seven... A pretty nice guy, I mean, he seemed nice to me. I remember having seen him avoiding Clarisse and me, so... That may be him. Well, symptoms are pretty much apparent, a guy turning a forty-years-old mother and avoiding her two eighteen-years old twin daughters is very certainly a boyfriend in coming. Anyway, I don't really mind whatsoever, she does whatever she wants, I am gonna move out soon regardless. I am not gonna be a problem for them anyway.

"Oh, that's great. So, I guess he already knows me. And I saw you speaking to quite a few different people, so except your boss and your partner in work that I already know, I, erm..."

"Yeah, he knows you. But it's fine, I invited him for dinner tomorrow, and I hope you're gonna be here. At least I asked Clarisse, and she told me she'd be here. But he may come late, something like 9pm..."

Hum, yeah, erm, it's not like I already have some stuff to do tomorrow. I mean, I know that Claire's stuff is around six, so the time I save her arse, it should be by seven or eight. Yeah, I cannot save the world and meet my future father-in-law (well, maybe not future father-in-law, for now, he is still just the random guy that have sex with my mum) at the same time, I mean, it's quite challenging, that's the problem when you are a superhero, you're always busy. Oh, well... There's also something that she still doesn't really know at the moment, is that tomorrow at around something like 9pm as she said, she might really hate me. Meh, I prefer saving the surprise, keep that for a surprise. This is why I very calmly continued:

"I might be late too... But erm... Yeah, I'll be there, yeah, definitely."

"You might be late?"

"Yeah, some business to set up, it shouldn't take long. I mean, I hope."

"What business?"

"Meh, you'll know eventually. Anyway, his name is?"

"Oh, he's Frank, erm... He's my age, pretty much. A nice guy, you're gonna love him. Oh, and you guys have some interests in common, by the way, I forgot to mention..."

"Oh, really?"

"Yeah, he's a psychologist!"

RIGHT. There are technically millions of guys in that damn country, even billions of guys on this planet, and what did she choose to date? A damn shrink. Like, seriously, you've got to be kidding me. Well, let's imagine that I come to the dinner tomorrow, it will be like, erm... Sigmund Freud versus Bernard Madoff. Oh, my God. Hopefully, some events will disrupt the usual way of things being supposed to be done so I may not have to sit on the red sofa and wait for a full analysis to finally state that I am evil and dangerous. On the other hand... Since she dates him... I am sure my case has been widely exposed already, and he knows much more than I may believe. Meh... So, I continued:

"Oh my... Are you sure you really want us to meet? I mean, for the sake of your couple!"

"Of course I want! I mean, you're my daughter and erm... Do not be afraid, he already knows you're a lunatic psychopath. I kind of told him, already. He's not scared!"

"Yeah, of course. And then he will talk to me, and we will see! Oh, that reminds me, did you also tell him that I still pee sometimes at bed?"

"He's used to it, trust me, he has seen much worse than you..."

"Hum... Nice. And I am sure you told him about most of my life, and now he dreads meeting me because he thinks I am a monster or some kind of it!"

"Ah, no... He explained to me how to deal with people like you, and that's fine, now I know!"

"Oh, neat. So now you know how to approach lesbians psychopaths, that's actually fancy. Could he teach me how to approach neurotic shrinks because I am kind of intrigued..."

"You see, you're already judging him..."

"Oh, well, tomorrow evening will be a kind of a dinner with some kind of psychoanalysis on the background for me, so... I just don't really want to be part of some experiment, or I don't know..."

"Darling, I swear to God, you won't be part of an experiment. Anyway, are you coming or not?"

"I told you that I will."

"Great. Thank you very much, darling, I appreciate it. And I really hope you guys will get along..."

"Oh, yeah, of course, I think. I mean, I hope so... Too..."

Yeah, erm... Yeah. I think it's cool to actually pretend that nothing is gonna happen, especially since... Since I didn't speak too much about my strategy for tomorrow, and, no, no, I think I am doing well at the moment. At this moment also, I was telling myself that whoever was on a date with her was taking quite a long time to pee, since I didn't hear anyone walking close to her. Maybe he was back, and... I didn't listen to it, that is also possible. Meh... Anyway, after having reassured her on whether I was still part of this family, she actually restarted with a question... something that she usually never asks:

"Anyway, I might be late tonight, erm... Do you guys have everything at home?"

That is curious. Florent still didn't call her, nothing. Meh, by tomorrow morning, he may call her. That's too big. But one thing was sure, she wasn't aware of the situation if she asked that question. The thing is, "you guys", it's sure she was talking about Florent and me. She would have spoken about Clarisse, and then she would have mentioned her name. So, she is aware that Clarisse is not home, which means she is mindful that Florent and I are settling down some business. Before anything, I just wanted to make sure that I was right.

"Oh, and by 'you guys' you mean Florent and I, right?"

"Oh... Let me guess... It didn't get along..."

Hum, her call was not that innocent, now I have the proof. She basically innocently called to actually take the temperature, see how things were going. Mostly since she guessed almost immediately at the moment when I mentioned Florent. Okay, now you know. Problem is, how does she know that? According to her wordings, the lack of sarcasm that I use to have with her when she speaks to me and obviously her deep relaxation at the moment, it just doesn't make any sense. Or she indeed called me because he texted her already informing me that we broke up and... But he didn't give any details yet. And as she's scared to talk with me because she knows that she won't have anything from me, she told him that she may call him later and... Yeah, she was just checking on me. On how I was feeling. More or less monitoring me. Interesting. This is why I wanted to destabilise her, she will never admit that she received any texts or anything... Let's see how she reacts:

"How do you know that?" I started.

"Well, erm... I heard you guys having a fight this morning, and Clarisse spoke to me this afternoon. I mean... I really hope you guys dealt with your stuff..."

"You spoke to Clarisse?"

"Yeah, we sometimes speak with each other..."

"Oh. Well, yeah, on the other hand, yeah, I learned that speaking was a specific human ability, yeah..."

"Hum... Cha..."

"Meh, do whatever you want anyway, I don't really care. And, anyway, Florent and I, it's over..."

Interesting. The fact that she quickly eluded when I asked her how she may know this, then mentioning Clarisse... That's interesting. This is why I wanted to tell her that him and I, it was over, so at least I knew that she would understand that this was the very end with no possible comeback. After that, I felt in her tone that... well she was sincere at that moment with me, she was frank, but after that, I felt something weird from her, compassion. And I hate that.

"Oh, darling, I am sorry, I am deeply sorry for you. I mean, this is really sad, and... Do you want to talk?"

"Oh well, it's fine, I don't really want to talk about. And I think you're busier into trying to get at your shrink's bed than speaking to me about my shit, so..."

"Cha, come on..."

"There are priorities in life, you know. Anyway, it's fine, I am fine... You know, nothing can reach me."

"Yeah, but still... He was your boyfriend, and..."

"It's fine. I still have your so beloved friend Claire Louise Cobert, remember?"

This is the greatest mistake of some parents. When they try hard to actually get something from their children when they want to impose outdated values... Whatever she does, she cannot fight against Claire. I have respect for her, I mean, yes, but she must accept who I am. I must confess that, yeah, I was undoubtedly weaker a couple of months ago when she found out about Claire and me that we were together and caught us kissing, I kind of came out that day. Whatever she does, whether she accepts it or not, I love that girl, and she cannot fight against our love. It is now more reliable than ever. Even if I must say that, as I mistakenly thought initially, she was somehow responsible for our first breakup, she is not strong enough to actually make us collapse. I love girls, that's not my fault, this is not some kind of disease or genetic anomaly, that's just me, and she must accept it.

Anyway, within the following hours... my girlfriend will be fully back in my life, whether she wants it or not. And maybe I did not dare to actually tell her that, perhaps I didn't dare to take actions for her, but now, I really don't care. If I have to move out or if I have to leave my home for my girlfriend, I will do it. Claire is the only human that make me bear my condition as a human being, I will not be deprived of her any longer. If she's okay with it, that's fine. If she's not, then, I am sorry. There will be no wars, there will be no fight, there will be no surrender, there will be no battles anymore. Claire will be back, and I really don't give a shit about whatever she says. Whenever I free her from Joris and all this, we are going to start our life. Surprisingly, after I said that, "her dear beloved friend Claire Louise Cobert", surprisingly...

"Hum... Well, if you feel the need to talk to her, then, fine. At least you're not alone, that's what I want to know..."

And now, I was destabilised. I mean, I really didn't know what to say. Okay, she sees a shrink, but did he brainwash her? I mean, no longer than fifteen days ago I was just mentioning that name, and she was literally boiling and exploding, and now... She's okay that I spend time with her! Okay, then what will happen tomorrow, will I learn that the moon never existed, and this is just a fake?

After a moment of silence, and I must confess... Some satisfaction from my part, I just started to say, really surprised:

"Are you serious?"

"Well, if Claire could be with you... I mean... I am really sorry, I really misjudged you, and I have been unfair, and... If you want to be with Claire, I mean, tonight, it doesn't matter to me. I just want you to be safe... We'll talk about it tomorrow if you want, that's fine for me."

"Hum... I am going to Claire's place, then. Anyway, it was good to talk to you, I really appreciate, and... Well, I won't disturb you any further..." I wanted to go.

"Oh, erm... Yeah, if you want, we'll talk tomorrow."

"Hum, yeah, sure, yeah. Anyway, have a good evening, and see you tomorrow then..."

"See you, darling, bye!"

33 *Exit means exit*

// *Claire's house, Ivry-sur-Seine.*

// *Tuesday, 22nd of January 2013, 07:10.*

"Hey, love... Come on, wake up, we're gonna be late! Oh, come on, you lazy ass..." Claire's voice started to shout at me.

"Huh?"

That was really odd... I mean, it's weird, I didn't really sleep well last night, I woke up certainly once or twice to pee... And the last dream I had was strange. And even... Whilst dreaming I saw her asking me to wake up on several occasions... hum, weird.

So, yeah, confused and, well, still sleepy, to be fair, I finally opened my eyes. Lights were turned on everywhere in the room, but astonishingly I found all the troubles to actually wake up. And, I don't know, to be honest, I was feeling weird... Like my muscles were in some kind of pain, but not in pain at the same time. The very first face that I saw when wakened up, it was Claire. Her hairs tied up, little makeup on her face... I assume that I woke up late. I was fatigued today. On the other hand, I probably slept maybe three or four hours last night, so... this may explain why. And, at the moment I opened my eyes and smiled at her, she just looked at me and started to say, with some kind of exhausted face expression:

"Finally! Geez, you're so slow this morning..."

"Meh, I didn't sleep very well last night..." I mumbled.

"Oh, did you? Well, on the other hand, you spent your night turning repeatedly, you even spoke in your sleep, and you drooled. Well, same as before... Did you do that with Florent?"

"Sometimes, when I managed to sleep, so it was not really often, and... What did I say?"

"Stuff in English that I do not understand since I don't speak English, dear!"

"Huh... Okay... What time is it? Oh, and what time do we start?"

"Well, it's basically... We still have half an hour, but the time you wake up, we have breakfast... You know!"

"Well, for breakfast, it's actually fine. Waking up... Okay, just give me a couple of minutes so I can get dressed."

"Sure, I'll be downstairs if you look for me!"

"Hum... fine!"

Hum, we are late. Okay then... On the other hand, it's not like I really care about that. Anyway, I looked at her, she was already dressed. Black blazer, blue trousers, and black boots today... Hairs tied; if they are tied, it's a sign of anxiety. Even, the way she talked to me, I mean she didn't speak to me like shit, but I could clearly feel that she was quite tensed. Well, then again, if I were her and aware of what I would be doing tonight, I may understand, I would be maybe much more anxious as well. I was nervous the first time I went to do that a couple of days ago... I am also concerned about this. But I just try not to show this. It would be me, as a girlfriend, I would tell her, don't go... But I have to. Anyway, this is breaking my heart.

Now then we were late. Hopefully yesterday I took my stuff quickly, I put everything in a bag, so I knew that I had everything ready. I promptly woke up and removed my nightdress, to get my clothes for today: my regular white shirt, black waistcoat, black trousers, and black pumps. Yeah, black for today. I had my handbag ready for school. Obviously, I didn't take my water bottle, which means that we will have to stop in some shop nearby before going... I don't really know that I felt like I was in a kind of a rush. Well, waking up and get dressed straight away, it's some kind of weird... But I don't really know why she imperatively wanted to be on time today, I mean, she's been cutting school for more than a week, and now she's, hum... Oh, yeah, anxiety.

Anyway, once dressed, it certainly took me like ten minutes to get ready, I went to pee on the bathroom next to her bedroom, and in the meantime, I checked my phone. No new calls, no messages too... Even if it was eight-thirty. That's quite surprising, actually. Usually, at that hour, mum is awake. I assume that Florent went to actually drink last night to forget our breakup, so he might be fucked up at that hour, or he probably already called mum, and... Or Clarisse, or... I mean, I would be Florent... I remember the day I broke up with Claire, and I just broke quite a lot of things over anger, and...

Well, I don't really know what happened, and I cannot actually speculate on what happened. I don't really know what I would do if I were him, but... Given the fact that he was too pissed when he left, he couldn't just have concealed this. He must have spoken to someone, and I am sure his mother, as they are so close... I am sure they talked together about that. As I said, this is just too big, which leads me to think, maybe the scandal didn't explode yet, but it will, within hours or minutes from now. Because, somehow, I feel like... If mum called me twenty minutes after Florent left yesterday, this was not innocent. I feel like she knows.

Anyway, I was done, I flushed the toilets, as usual, and after getting dressed and washing my hands, I went downstairs. Through the big window downstairs, I could actually perceive that she basically turned all the lights on even though the sun was rising. We used to go to school together last year, and never she did that. On mornings, we used to use the big dining room table, and we just turned the lights of the living room on so we could have lights on the morning, but today, all the lights were on. Everywhere she went, she used to turn on the light. It was weird, she never did that. Well, she used to be scared of dark before. When everything went back as fine in her life, when we had stable adolescence together, her traumas went away, so she felt better and was not scared anymore. Still, now she's back to depression and even has a treatment to cope with that, well this may explain the lights. Claire is scared of darkness, bugs, and depth. Which is funny, as there is the Seine river here and we walk on a bridge, she used to walk fast and never look at the river because she's scared of this. We can walk on the banks of that river, it's okay for her, but crossing a bridge, then it better be fast; otherwise, she starts panicking. It makes her cute, somehow.

Now, for instance, she was sat on the table, opposite to the big window, curtains drawn, was reading, and drinking her regular morning hot chocolate. No, wait, her cup was empty, she drank it already. She sat towards the end of the table, at least towards the wall, which used to be her regular place, where she sits all the time. There were some cookies next to her, she ate some of them and left some other, I think for me... Next to that cookie box, her medicine stuff, and her handbag, I mean schoolbag next to all this. She was wakened up for a while now. Astonishingly, she was reading. I mean, she used to read a lot, but today, wait... Oh my god... Machiavelli? The Prince? I thought she found politics boring! On the other hand, I read this book when I was eleven, and it really uplifted me. I am quite satisfied that she takes interests for book that worth it. But immediately, once I was downstairs and, on my way to sit next to her, I immediately noticed that detail:

"*The Prince* of Machiavelli... You finally decided to start reading good books?"

"Yeah... I saw you reading this a couple of years ago, and as it seemed to have been uplifting for you..."

"That changes from Harry Potter, right?"

"I love Harry Potter, come on..."

"Meh, nobody's perfect, darling..." I was sarcastic.

Harry Potter, well... Oh, no, I don't want to talk about JK Rowling, please... Please, you think this could be possible? Are there other people like me that DO NOT LIKE Harry Potter? If so, please manifest yourself.

"Do you think I may have time for a coffee?"

"Well, I think so..."

"Where's the sugar?"

"In its box, darling..." she made a kind of ironic smile at me.

"Is it? You would have told me that it was in a bottle that I wouldn't have believed you. But where is this box?"

"Haha... Like you don't remember... Still at the same place!"

"Oh. Okay, sorry..."

I know, I used to have my tea on mornings, that's just a change, but as I said earlier, I have coffee when I am exhausted, which was the case today. Especially since I know that I am likely to have a big day, where I don't really know the issue. *Vulnerant omnia, ultima necat*, as they used to say.

Free Expensive Lies: Prologue

Hopefully, Claire has the same coffee machine as mine to get quick espressos, so I made one. The golden capsule, my favourite. Also, Clooney's choice, according to the ad for that brand. At the same time, I made my coffee, Claire started to bring her cup and wash it. I gave her my cup at the same time. Well, here it was, we were now ready to go. She went to get her pill, took the box in her bag as she needs to have one for lunch and 4pm, and dinner (damn... being depressive is such a business nowadays). Surprisingly, she used to be chattier on mornings, unlike me, today she was quiet. I wouldn't imagine how it would be without her medicine, though. I really hope it's gonna be better within the next days, once we are done with everything. Okay, it will take her a lot of time to bounce back on her feet, but at least I am back in her life, and I really wish I can help her deal with all that, so we can restart a life, away from that.

I actually left my bag on the stairs, I mean, down the stairs, when I went there. My phone and everything was inside, I was ready to leave. After she washed her cup and left it on the small rack as I swigged my espresso, she washed her hands another time, and, well, it was time to go. Still, when I was trying to speak with her, she was not laconic, but her answers were concise and very quick, very swift also, and this was an indication of tremendous pressure. The thing is, if she's too much tense for her stuff tonight, Joris will feel it, and he will take advantage of this, so I need to make sure that everything is actually okay. We went to the entrance, she asked me if I could switch off the lights everywhere because... yeah, fear of darkness reasons, which I did, so at the same time, the time to reach all the switches, it was leaving her plenty of time to actually open the door, as it was starting to be sunny outside. I took my red coat. Hopefully, I had the bright idea yesterday to take a black scarf because I saw that this morning's temperatures would be really unfriendly, and the time I wore it, she was waiting for me in the front door.

When I looked at her, and... Except for her little coat, she didn't take anything cold. She had a black scarf, almost the same as mine, her small pink hat with a fluffy white pom-pom over it, and her thin black gloves, she was just looking at me and... Even if she appeared as all black as she was against the light, I kind of had some burst of love coming from deep inside. It was quickly fought back by a "would you move your arse, Cha, please?". Meh. So, I did what I was ordered to do.

At the same time, when I was stepping outside and feeling the very fresh morning air coming hurting my face and my skin, in my handbag that I was carrying, something started to ring and vibrate... My phone. Whilst Claire was closing the door, busy to find the right key in her keychain as for some reasons she was carrying several keys, I took my phone and looked on the screen who was calling: mum. Okay... She has no grounds to call me on mornings, especially since she knows that I am with Claire. It means that... She knows. Ah, when I said that the scandal would explode any minutes now... I was right. And surprisingly accurate. I took the call:

"Hey hey hey..." I started almost enjoyed.

"Where are you?" she immediately replied, cold, and this time, as unusual when we use to talk, she talked to me in French.

Hum, it was kind of obvious. Talking in French, no hello, no how are you, no what's up, yeah. She knew. My strategy on this, as I thought about it yesterday in the metro when I was on my way to Claire's, was to actually pretend that I wouldn't know what she was talking about, and let the surprise take over. Because if I show that I know, it may look like I am manipulating, and I don't want to show any of that. I just want things to happen as innocently as possible. This is why I didn't reply, I just wanted to show that I was feeling okay today, by using sarcasm. Meh, I guess this is the time to actually face up reality. Let's find out, I continued, just to see what the next step would be:

"Hello, sunshine, how are you?" I kind of very sarcastically replied in English.

"When you will see my face in a couple of minutes, you will understand that I am not good at all. And you'd better not hide wherever you might be. Where the fuck are you now?"

"At Claire's... I'll be at school in a bit. I mean, the time to take the metro, and..."

"Great. Once arrived, you'd better text me and wait in front of the station. I called the school already and told them you'd be late. We need to talk. See you later."

She hung up almost immediately before I could even say something.

Okay, so she spoke six times, and... I don't know, it was a mix of anger and shock. When I do something wrong, and she's pissed, she used to counter-attack to my sarcasm, but now, no, she remained concise and deliberately didn't want to talk to me or even ignored my sarcasm. She called my school already... And she wants to see me. Yeah, she's shocked. I mean, she would be angry, she would just piss me off by phone and shrug off later, but now, no, she wanted to see me. It was undoubtedly the shock. And immediately at the moment, my mother called me,

Claire received another call. Certainly... Yeah, within seconds after mum hung up. The difference is that her phone was in her hands and she was looking at her Facebook when her phone started to ring. It was her mother.

We actually didn't start walking, we remained in place when she called as I was curious about that call. I was expecting that the scandal would explode, yes, but only for me, not for her. It means that two things could have let her mother know about that scandal: either my mother called Claire's mother and informed her about Florent stuff last night, or whether... whether the blackmailer actually triggered the final operation and... And this would be a problem, as we want to catch Joris if it's the blackmailer that sent pictures or her Facebook was hacked... But if her Facebook profile were hacked, (I mean, Facebook would be the first target of the blackmailer, destroying someone through Facebook is ways much efficient than sending letters to members of her family... If I were the blackmailer, I would definitely use Facebook, where Claire is the most popular. She almost have the three-quarters of pupils at school as friends, she has a broad audience and a wide audience can be fancy if they see porn pictures, this can spread very quickly), she would have seen it and would have talked to me. As she didn't tell me anything, I assume there was nothing suspicious... This is weird. Anyway, in her turn, she took the call:

"Hey, mum... Hum, yeah, I am with Charlotte, what's wrong?... Hum, okay, but tell me what's going on?... Yeah, we will be at school in a few. Yeah... Okay then..."

After those words, she looked at her phone, and found out the same, her mother hung up. I know, I could hear the small "beep" at the end of the call, notifying that the person hung up. Hum... I think this would definitely be my mother. They know each other, they like each other, I mean, this until we split... Well, on the other hand, it makes sense that this would come from my mother, what she may have heard from Florent, as I mentioned Claire in this yesterday when we talked, as this came from her, it's just big, she cannot conceal it without talking to someone. We may be in danger, and I am sure this must be the reason why she spoke about that... Hum that changes now quite a lot of things.

We looked at each other, and to be fair, I wasn't expecting that this would explode this way. As we are heard through our phones, now I am sure the blackmailer knows that everybody knows, so he doesn't have anything. Which leaves two options: if I were my blackmailer because I would am aware that Joris and Claire have a date tonight, and as everybody knows now... Hum, that's interesting. Will he react? Because the business is now exposed, what the blackmailer seeks foremost is secrecy, and now, Claire becomes a threat. I would be him, then I would tell Joris not to come to this date. Unless he is very dumb... Or seeks to get rid of him... What we must do now is, first, give to our mother a bone so they can get busy with this, whilst we are waiting for Joris and his next move. We must not call him; otherwise, he's gonna get suspicious that something is ongoing. Claire must date him tonight, and I can still convince Claire to actually date him. On the other hand, he really wants that, I saw that last day at Kleber when they came together, he really wants to sleep with her. So even if the blackmailer doesn't want him or even forbids him to see that, well, I know what string to pull on to finally get what I want. But, for now, we don't have any news of him, I'll see when I have some as I will spend most of my day with Claire.

After we looked at each other, she pulled her phone back into her bag. And as we started walking, she looked at me, and very nervously said:

"Okay... Erm... do you still believe that it was a good idea?"

"Oh, well, I don't see any other escape plan anyway..." I remained confident.

"I mean... My mother never talked to me like that. She was fucking aggressive..."

"Yeah, the situation may be kind of uptight, true. But, meh, I'm not afraid, I don't care, she can do whatever she wants, I don't care, she cannot do anything against me."

"Yeah, of course, you are major, and millionaire. Just as a reminder, I am still minor and bankrupt. So, I really hope that you fully assessed your thing because I really do not want to have problems with that..."

"Darling, do you trust me?"

"I do, but this is... If she knows, I'm just dead..."

"Trust me, she won't kill you, honey! Whatever happens, you are the victim of someone, you didn't do that on purpose. Moreover, she may have seen you have a treatment, and you are in depression... I really don't think you risk something. Your mother is clever, she will understand that you've been trapped and that's all. And, Claire, from the very first moment I kissed you and the first day I told you that I love you... You are the most valuable person I have on that planet, so no matter what happens, nothing will ever happen to you, I swear to whatever you want. Whoever disgraced you will pay the price for what he did to you!"

"Oh, honey... Do you really mean this?"

Free Expensive Lies: Prologue

"I do promise you, love!"

She stopped walking and hugged me. And then... I kissed her.

I really don't know what happened in my mind at that moment, and I assume this is because I love her, or this is just my overprotective side that suddenly showed up or became stronger... Or my maternal and male side of the couple, but I don't know, I had some kind of need to show her protection. Because a sort of flashback suddenly occurred very rapidly into my mind, and... It was not really pleasant at all. I did what she's been doing on a weekly basis for the last three months only once or twice, and I kind of felt her pain. I have always been overprotective over my girlfriend, which is why I had this. It is just... Whoever did that will pay. I only can't accept this, having her like this, collapsed, crushed under the weight of her own guilt because she felt like she betrayed me, she deceived her mother... Claire doesn't deserve that. Nobody deserves that, anyway, but Claire is my girlfriend, and if I had to take a fucking bullet for her, then I would do it with no remorse.

Anyway, after this quick hug and kiss, (as we still had to remain careful... we can be paranoid, but we don't even know if we are still spied on in the street or not, anyway I didn't see any suspicious cars parked in her street), we continued walking down the street. Hopefully, the metro was not far away, and slowly the coldness was freezing my hands. On the footpath, along the road, there were those trees, all of them had no leaves because of winter, all of them fell off during the last autumn, and slowly a kind of weird blue sky, with high altitude clouds, was overlooking the French capital. And my little French girl was increasingly panicked the more we were walking. It's just today, tomorrow, I think we're gonna stay at bed until late and... I don't know what we will do. But for sure, nothing productive.

We arrived at the metro, obviously as we still were in rush hours the platform was full, and trains were departing amazingly fast. We had to remain standing up as seats were quickly taken by other passengers. And, after the train left the station, whilst we were both hanging each other to those bars, she looked at me and started to say:

"What do we do? Should I lie? As I think mum and your mum are together..."

"No, just don't lie, that is the last thing to do. Now, we finally get an advantage over the blackmailer, he doesn't have any means to pressure us! So, tell the truth, the raw truth. It's better," I replied straight in her ear, as I was still kind of scared by being heard by other passengers and my phone.

"She will be... Damn..."

"Claire, this is the only way out. So now we have to face it, so we will face it together. You prefer being with me instead of being all alone in front of your mum..."

It was pretty much a long journey for going to school from Claire's place, we had to change three times of metro before reaching our destination. The problem is, doing that early in the morning... I forgot how long it actually was to go there, why we had to wake up so early. Last time we went together to school was maybe... Yeah, something like last May or something, doing that again today was a kind of remembrances from the old time. In any case, I knew that, well, at least... we don't have to go to the school that fast. But, yeah, travelling early in the morning, with those over-crowded carriages where everybody are literally stuck together, and you cannot even move or breathe, and when you see the doors, and you will have to find a way to sneak towards there, it's just, yeah...

As I took my phone in my hand for safety reasons, I received a text during the travel. Heather. "Hey, Cha... Hope you doing okay. As today is the great day, any chances we could have lunch together with Claire and you? I offer the restaurant. We need to talk!" with a smiley face. I showed that text to Claire, and she was okay with that. I replied that it was fine, and immediately I saw Claire's face being much more anxious. I reassured her if Heather is behind her and monitors her tonight, then she is safe. She replied that safety or not, she will still have to be a bait. Even if we talked about this last weekend, even if she accepted, maybe I think she was not fully aware of what it meant, to be a bait. But as Heather added a smiley at the end of the text, it meant that she had pretty much some good news to deliver us, which is... I am rather impatient to hear that from her. I already know that she engaged herself to place us under police protection after that, but maybe she wants to tell us more about this.

And yeah, at the end of an hour and more than five minutes of the journey under Paris, we finally arrived at our destination. As we were using lifts for reaching the sea level to exit the station, I immediately sent to mum, "we're here". Immediately, maybe at the end of our travel through this lift, she replied me, "I'm parked in front of the station. Get in here as soon as you're here!". As we arrived, Claire started breathing much more at a faster rate. I must admit... I don't really know how things are going, I don't really have a plan to face up this. I have been told once that I used to be better at improvisation, so... Well, I assume we will find this out today. I was definitely stressed, but as I am the strongest in the couple now,

I must show that I am confident again. Otherwise, Claire will just explode, and this is just not the day for that.

We left the station, and, again, it was a sunny day. The sun was shining, almost no clouds in the sky except this almost imperceptive layer of pollution overlooking our polluted capital, and as we left, in the road literally facing us, mum's car. Her big black SUV (almost the same as Joris) parked in the taxi space. Her window was opened, and I could see that, yeah, both Claire's mother, Laure, and my mother, were both here. All waiting for us. And now, the moment of truth... So, we went towards the car. I could feel Claire's hand, as I took her hand, slightly giving up the pressure as the stress took over. She was discreetly shaking as well. Hopefully, tomorrow, we'll be done with that. Once Joris gets arrested... Things will go back to normal.

So, I opened the door, and let Claire coming in first. Mum's car is relatively new, she bought it two years ago, as she wanted a decent car if we would travel either across France or maybe go elsewhere. Since even we still didn't have that occasion. The car's interior is, well, yeah, obviously luxury, seats are made of beige leather. They are heated up, which is quite fancy when we wear some dress in winter, at least legs do not get cold, and on the floor, those beige carpeting covering all the passenger compartment of the car. Windows weren't tinted, and now, mum turned on the AC, so it wasn't cold in here, which was much more appreciated. Claire jumped in, sat in the opposite seat, and then, I jumped in, seating, putting my bag on my legs just like Claire did, and then closed the door. Mum started closing her window, and... Well, I guess, let's get this party started now, huh? I began by speaking English, to mum:

"Yo, what's up..."

"My hand will be up in your face in a second if you don't tell me that fucking truth...", she replied to me in English. Then spoke in French to Claire's mother next to her, "Sorry... I'll speak in French!"

Laure used to complain about this, she doesn't speak English at all. Like most French people, on the other hand, they are just too lazy to learn a foreign language. As foreigners, we know how disrespectful it can be when someone comes to you and speaks a language you cannot understand. We know that with Spanish people, for instance. But I said that to take the temperature, and, yeah, it's just bloody tense at the moment. Very tight. Anyway, I only resumed speaking...

"We're gonna be late for school, mum, you know..." I started playing the sarcasm card.

"Yeah, they've been called, don't worry about it, they already know that you will be late today!"

"Okay, what truth... What do you want to know..."

"Florent called me this morning. And... Hum... I really hope this was some kind of prank or something like that but... This is also why I called Claire's mother to inform her about what I heard from him, because... I think this is big enough. Again, I really hope this was a joke from you..."

"What the fuck did he tell you?"

"Damn, even..." she started to speak slower, "even thinking about this, it's just too much... Is it true that... You are blackmailed and forced to prostitute?"

So, yeah, I thought so, and as scheduled, it perfectly worked. Florent delivered the message, as he was supposed to, so my strategy worked pretty much okay. And there would be only two approaches she might have taken. Either anger, or whether shock, and given her wording, also given the fact that she cannot conceptualise this fact (I mean... I'd have a daughter like me, and I'd certainly understand), she spoke slower but not softer, she was indeed shocked.

And believe it or not, but I took the easy way out. The coward moves. I skipped my turn. I just didn't reply, I lowered my head instead, and carefully thinking. Because if I answer, this was what she expected, she will turn mad. She's somehow unpredictable, and, I kept in mind that she certainly had an excellent evening yesterday and a very bad wakeup. According to her hairs and the fact that she was just dressed but was wearing no makeup, I say this meant that she's been genuinely disturbed by the news. It somehow disrupted her daily routine, and this was why, whatever I answer, I kind of felt that she was resigned, she was, yeah, she didn't really know what to say or even believe. She was expecting something from me, maybe not that, but she was expecting something to happen. This is why, possibly lowering the head in the animal world is perceived as a sign of submission, I was like, take it whatever you want, I just pass my turn. I couldn't even pretend to ignore, I only... I cannot even deny it. Some seconds passed, quite a few seconds until Laure... lost her patience.

"Claire!" she actually yelled.

"Yes, mum..." Claire couldn't really hide her fear now.

"Tell me it's not true... Please, tell me that's not the truth..."

"Erm..." I restarted very slowly.

We looked at each other, and I took that way that approach I was actually thinking about, what will I say. Until that moment, Claire swiftly took my hand, and it clearly meant that she needed help. This was a dangerous move because we cannot deny it; if we do, that will raise suspicions from both of them. Ultimately, the thing we want to avoid above everything would be helping the blackmailer by fixing the situation. Even, if we tell the truth, it won't really mean anything, as the blackmailer doesn't really have many options to move out of this mess. He doesn't control anything; I am in control now.

We looked at each other, and Claire started to blush. Blushing like in containing her tears, because, although I don't really care to be judged, she actually does. Since we are both lookalikes, except that unlike me she has sensitivity, the fact we are relatively prude when talking about sexuality makes that it is entirely something we don't really like to talk about. Doing that to us appeared like removing an animal's skin from its carcass to practice taxidermy, we were simply scared to get blood or whatever viscous substances on our hands.

Anyway, whilst seeking my words and looking at each other, almost deciding through mind-speaking will confirm... She actually suddenly restarted. Because someone had to do the job.

"Erm, yes, that is the truth. We... Charlotte and I are blackmailed and forced to... Yes..." she launched the missile as you would announce the death of someone.

And now... The shock actually started. The bomb was dropped, and we watched the destruction and the clouds of dust meaning from the collapsed concrete building of the city from a plane. Suddenly, respiration stopped, or got interrupted, the concertos of "oh my god" mixed up with tears, as we both looked at them, and were literally unable to say otherwise. Emotions, it took them over, and... And the shame was taking over Claire, that started to look at the window.

What actually happened was, well, my mother put her two hands before her face, whilst Claire's mum started to cry out loud. One was directly showing her emotions, the other, yeah, was resigned. I was quite disturbed by this, to be honest, I was feeling weird towards all this. Although I understood the reason why Claire has hidden this, it remains that, for them, from their point of view, I was trying to understand, they created us, they are our mothers, they carried us, and saw us growing up, it must be a huge disappointment. Even if there was the war between my mother and me, for once I was feeling complacent towards her. Even if I don't really care about my actions, for someone that actually cares about this... I was disappointing her. Shall I say that now, we're even? Yeah, I may.

But at least they understood the most important, we weren't responsible for any of these. Florent explained correctly what I wanted him to explain, that we were blackmailed so this is why we had to do that. They understood that it was neither Claire's or my fault, and we didn't do it on purpose. We've been trapped, we didn't commit any offence. So, I don't know if this will be enough to forgive us or to at least buy our redemption... But I keep in mind that we can literally buy anything, so it's okay. Moreover, Claire and her mother are both close so, I don't really think this would break or collapse their relationship in the foreseeable future. It may be like turbulences are for a plane, but at some point, I am sure things may go back to normal, even if it might take time. She may be upset because she hides this, but she will understand that there is a reason for that, and it wasn't meant to be done on purpose. Anyway, we used to say that the truth will always explode like a bomb, now the bomb exploded, but at least we were closely monitoring the explosion, so it could be worse. One way or another, they would have found out the truth and played with someone who basically never moves (this makes him a more real threat) makes things much more dangerous.

After some seconds, I guess to accept the shock, slowly, whilst we saw that... Slowly, conversation resumed. My mother:

"How long? How long, Charlotte?" my mum asked me.

"I don't know, a couple of days, maybe..."

"And you never told me anything?"

"I was just scared, that's all," I was seeking a justification.

"Honey, how long have you been... doing this?" Laure started.

And slowly, Claire was weeping. I was still carrying her hand, and, swiftly, she wanted to take her hand, but I held that stronger. She looked at me quickly and wasn't defending herself. What I meant by this was, we're in this together, this was the exit strategy we agreed, so now, we must assume this together, we're in the same boat that we both set on fire. So, before boarding the lifeboat, we must assess the situation, how many icebergs we have to break before reaching the nearest island. But, yeah, it's easy for me, at least more manageable, that's what I meant, but, of course... when we have emotions... Whilst I looked at her red eyes, her blushed face and her tears slowly flowing along her face, she replied, all covered with shame:

"I don't know... Since I broke up with Cha... Three, four months..."

"Oh my god..." she almost yelled.

Free Expensive Lies: Prologue

But the discovery remained harsh. A couple of days for me is still fine, but when it's been three or four months that you are hiding the biggest secret of your life, that it literally destroyed you psychologically, yeah, of course, it's harder. It was also hard for me to imagine this, or to actually figure out this, even to hear this, I mean, my lover being just the puppet and the sex slave of Kelly, at this moment I literally looked at the window, because... Oh my god, if Kelly was in front of me, yeah, I think I would be charged for murder, for sure. This just doesn't mean war, now, it's a war to death if I find her... For now, Joris is my preoccupation, he is my main target. Kelly, she's up next, and I swear to God, I promise her no cops or no justice, no fucking judge, or fucking lawyers. She's just fucking dead, and she should really start considering packing her stuff and changing her name and even leaving the country, because... Making my girlfriend crying, making her disgraceful, making her shameful and destroying everything literally.

Seeing that... I mean, it makes me feel like this when Claire cries. Laure, the same, I mean, I looked at both of them, they were literally in tears. Mostly, Laure is having harsh shifts in the hospital as she works by night, she indeed finished work because she was still wearing her white blouse and pale blue trousers... as she's a nurse, and now, having to deal with that. And, Kelly, her stupid iPhone in her hand all the time, just laughing at this situation, destroying a family already devastated because she lost a father and her mum lost a husband and never really recovered from that. Even if it were several years ago... How can we do that, having literally no respect for that? What type of human being can do that? Without being a real scumbag, obviously...

Sometimes, I really lose faith in this weird humankind. I love them, I mean, Claire and Laure, they are both my second family, I really consider them both, I really love them, and, somehow, I feel responsible. For not to have been able to find this out on time and not to have struggled back, even if I really know psychology, even if I am quite skilled in people's analyse, I just missed it three or four months ago. Now, she's destroyed, she literally ruined my girlfriend before my eyes. And I missed it. I just... I just didn't see anything. This fight was manipulator versus manipulator, the thing was, I just ignored there was a fight, I have been blinded by my own anger against her, and... I really should be ashamed.

This is why fighting back is the very least I can do for her, even if we have to pass through it. We had to go through this anyway, so at least the truth is not distorted. But at least both could express their feelings, my mother. Yeah, now more than ever, she wasn't saying anything, she was just profoundly stoic, and I could really see... the ultimate disappointment was there, arrived today and knocked at her door. But my relationship with my mother is already based on conflicts, so there is undoubtedly less shock than misunderstandings. I really feel like she was expecting it, and what she expected finally happened, I screwed up really bad. She was certainly prepared for this, which is why she was not crying, she was undoubtedly questioning herself and what she may have failed with me. Well, she knows because we both have our revendications in this war, and this is why... Well... Okay, fair enough. As I said, now we're even.

"How did it happen?" Claire's mother asked her daughter.

"I don't know, mum, I just... I didn't want to, this is just Kelly, and I was mad at Cha, because of... And... She pushed me to someone, and they drugged me, took pictures of me, and threatened me..." Claire was weeping so hard... I have never seen her like this.

"Oh my God..." her mother was in tears too.

"I never wanted that, mum, I swear to God, it's just... They trapped me, and now I am just their puppet... I cannot do anything!"

"I promise you, mum, this is not my fault, I never choose this, I never..."

"What about you, Cha?" my mother asked me.

"Pretty much the same..." I coldly replied.

"Oh, sweet Jesus..."

Yeah, she was definitely resigned, I could see that it was more and more evident. But I don't know, for once I didn't want to go for a clash, as neither she wanted, I could feel anyway. But slowly we were leading to the question she wanted to ask, that may lead to a clash. She asked me how long, she asked me how it happened... Now... Innocently... Seriously, she should have been a cop.

"Okay... Why didn't you guys never talk about this?" my mother asked.

"Oh well... Several reasons, I guess. First, I just found out for Claire just after my birthday, when I have been trapped the same way, she never even talked about this..."

"Cha..." Claire's mother interrupted me.

"Yeah?"

"You were close to my daughter, I mean... You had a long relationship with her, and... You never suspected anything?"

As I said, when I saw her changing and literally provoking me daily after we broke up with her clothing and her behaviour, it may have been something that would have been meaning something. I just ignored it for the reason that I was too hurt by this relationship ending. I never understood if I should have taken this provocation as an open "fuck you" or camouflaged "SOS". Usually, no details escape me, but for once, something big ran away from me. On the other hand, I didn't live with Claire throughout this period, but Laure did, and even she didn't find anything suspicious.

In contrast to that, I saw that Claire was escaping me, becoming less and less accessible to me, we kept on calling each other every Saturdays afternoon and... I just couldn't imagine this would be that big. I didn't see anything weird, except her relationship with Kelly, but she didn't have any boyfriend or new girlfriend, she has been single through this period. I literally explained everything with the wrong explanation, I ultimately failed to give a rational explanation. This is undoubtedly given my personal and affective involvement with her. Somehow, I had suspicions, but I told the truth to Laure:

"No. I mean, no..."

"Okay, what are the other reasons, as you said, there were several reasons?" Mum continued.

"Well, I, erm... Come on, mum, let's not hide this, you are just deeply intolerant, and when you found out that we were together, you started that war. You hate Claire, you just genuinely hate her just because we are in love..."

"Cha, I, erm..."

Yeah, because if Kelly arrived in force into Claire's life, it's because by the end of January until our breakup in August of the last year, we were deeply divided. And she saw the opportunity, we were not as close as we used to be, and she saw the breach, and jumped into it. We've been divided because of our mother as... She was somehow enforcing some strict rules against us, like, she used to take my phone and block Claire's number when I didn't have my phone in my hands, or sometimes she was answering the phone and making sure that Claire wouldn't talk to me... Or, obviously, forbidding Claire to come into our home like we used to do after school. She even followed me once when I was out and on my way to Claire's to finally pick me up and bring me back home once arrived. Claire was pissed because of her intolerance and, at some point, even if we were more united at the beginning, she was tired and sick of it because I was unable to tell my mother to kiss my arse for some reasons, maybe I was kind of scared to confront her. Mum found out how to take a psychological grip over me, and she used that against Claire. It unfortunately worked. So, when Claire and I couldn't even talk without fighting, obviously Kelly jumped into that breach and take advantage of it. Is my mother responsible for this? Maybe at a lesser degree, but she has her part of the cake as well. So, perhaps the scandal may explode, maybe we were having sex for money, maybe it's painful to hear... But she cannot remain out of this without, also, giving her justifications. In my sense. This is why Laure bizarrely looked at her:

"Is that true?" Claire's mum looked at mine.

"Okay, erm..." she was looking for defending herself. "Let's say... Cha, since I divorced your dad, you declared me a holy war, and you just want to wipe me out of your life."

"Oh, and what's the point in this? Maybe Claire messed up once, she never listened to me when I told her to be careful with Kelly, and you know why? Because since we kissed in the living room and when you accidentally were here, YOU managed to do your best to ruin the only beautiful thing I had in my shitty life!"

"Cha, that's not what I wanted to..."

"Oh, no?" I started to raise my tone. "You're telling me that you didn't do that on purpose? Come on, forbidding Claire to come into our house because you just don't want to see her? Doing your best to confiscate my phone so you can manage to control all the situation, and saying that I cannot say shit because I am still minor... I mean, come on! Maybe you are not the one that blackmails us... But by far you are responsible for all this mess today, as you managed to ruin everything!"

And I wanted to avoid a clash...

She may have expected me to fuck up something in my life, or maybe someday to pick me up at a police precinct, or I don't know, but at least, she had the reasons of my fight. She may have expected that from me, she may have expected to be expected from her second daughter after Clarisse (even if I was born first), but... Now, she must understand that yes, we are even, whatever she thinks. And, to my arguments, she was just listening, that was what was the most fascinating although surprising, because, yeah, when I was talking, I felt that she somehow agreed with me. I am sure, this is why she let Florent live with me because when we actually broke up, she realised that she went too far and broke the thing that she shouldn't have ever broken. She realised this recently, but as my mother calls herself a leader, she never apologises. She won't apologise to me, or at least I do not expect anything from that, but now she's facing both Claire and her mother, and her homophobic tendencies are fully exposed, as well as her wrongdoings, what will she do? I didn't have anything more to say, I didn't have much more. I just stopped talking, I just let the thing speaking for itself, this silence was... Increasingly meaningful. What will you do now? After maybe some seconds, having inspired then expired, a couple of seconds happened, before, yeah. My arguments were on the table, as well as me. Now, just defend yourself, but be careful of your words.

"Charlotte..." she restarted. "You used to tell me that I am a shitty mum, that I am doing nothing for you, that I am more a pain in the arse than a good person... Maybe you are lucky not to feel anything when you get insulted, you just shrug off and pretend this never happened, but that's not my case. When you spend evenings in your bedroom avoiding me like I am the plague or... When you are in front of me but deliberately ignore me... This hurts me!"

"Oh, shall I cry?" I pitifully replied.

"Always hiding behind your sarcasm... You know, this morning when Florent called me, I took at least ten minutes after that call for crying. Clarisse was with me, and hopefully, Clarisse has something you do not have; which is wisdom."

"Han..." I was outraged.

"I asked, what did I do, what did I fail with you? What did I miss? Unlike her, I just forgot you are totally unable to forgive. Or even forget, you still raise old grievances... And I kept on thinking, a moment, from your birth, when I had the two of you in my arms when you were crying... I was so happy at that moment. I love you, Charlotte, more than you may ever think, and whatever I do, I will always be there for you, even... Regardless of what you did. And I thought, yes, I messed up. We messed up with your father. This was when Claire entered in your life, you had a good friend, that later became your lover, and... Yes, at that moment I understood that, yes, you didn't have a mother or a father because they were both too busy fighting against each other. And, as you said, I ruined it."

Hum... Okay. Hum, the shock must have been really harsh then. I mean... That's what I thought, she indeed realised something. At least, for once, I didn't want to interrupt, I didn't even want to be sarcastic, nothing. She needed to say this. It's the first time that she acknowledges this, that she fucked up too. Her words were actually for once more federating than anything else, so... Fine. I didn't speak, I just let her continue her speech:

"All this to say, Cha, I am sorry. I didn't understand that I was failing as a mother, that I hurt you. When I found the two of you, it was just a shock for me, it was just... First, I have never seen you with anyone, I kept on seeing Claire most of the time, it was weird for me that my daughter may have someone, may even grow up. And, I know I have no excuses for that, but... I recently understood that, even if you never came out, you are lesbian. There is nothing that may ever change you, you were born this way, which is not bad, this is not your fault, this... This is just the normal way things are supposed to be, I was simply wrong, and I made a mistake to deny it. So, Charlotte, I am sorry. I am sorry to have been a dismissive, resigning mother. I know, what I have done was too much, but I just want... I just would like things to go back as normal," she started sobbing. "I would like you to have a normal life, with the woman you love, next to you!"

Now, I am shocked. I mean... I have been hoping for those words for weeks, months, years... I didn't know whether it was real or not. Did she actually say I am sorry? Did she finally surrender or decide to give up the fight? Even, her voice fading away towards the end, her very first tears, or maybe the first ones but at least there were tears... Oh, God! I just can't believe it; this is what I have been waiting for years now! It took her years to finally say that I started to suddenly think, I should make explode more scandals more often, it's crazy! Claire looked at me, we were just genuinely disturbed. It literally calmed down my anger towards her. I felt like there had never been any wars at all. All the generals capitulated all suddenly. It was just a kind of a beautiful moment, a pure and intense moment also profoundly tormented. It was the white in the black, it was the ying into the yang, it was, yeah, crazy, my mother finally comes out as tolerant. All the divine storms were away, it was just pure, and the raw truth finally came out, it was just magic. It was undoubtedly a difficult moment...

But it's fine, mum. Shit happens, that's life. At least she could recognise it. And, for once, I felt genuine sincerity, this was just not simple defence, this was only true, this was just real. This is why... I remained... Yeah... Disturbed, in the right way. Even, it was the very first time that I wanted to actually hug my mother.

"Okay, okay, hum..." I slowly restarted, "Yeah, okay. I appreciate that..."

"I just want to stop that war, Cha. Claire, please accept my apologies as well... I just... I just messed up..."

"It's okay..." she was actually also taken by surprise.

"Okay, well, now we settled down the war... Who's the next target, Russians, or Iranians?" I switched to something else.

This is, erm, what I call the perfect Trafalgar Coup. I mean, they call it this way in French, basically when you want to fuck someone, but you're finally fucked by that person, they took lessons from us during Napoleonic Wars. I mean, yeah, this was just not expected, I was literally overcome by this, it was just damn insane. I was speechless. Obviously, I concluded by a digression because, yeah, it was becoming too serious, and... Okay, erm, I mean, apologies accepted. It may take time, though, I have to apologise for the last seven years of shit so... It may take time to actually carry on, but I heard the demand.

Anyway, erm... After this intense moment full of emotions, let's get back to business.

"Okay, erm... Girls..." Claire's mother resumed after that moment of silence, "Why didn't you guys go to the police? I mean... Or at least have spoken to us?"

"Mum..." Claire resumed, "it was tensed. And, going to the police... We kind of do that already..."

"What do you mean, you kind of do that already?"

"Mum," I talked to my mother, calling her mum straight for the first time in a while, "we cannot talk at the moment, it's just... I can promise you that... It's gonna be sorted out soon!"

"How is that going to be sorted out? You don't even know who's blackmailing you, right?"

"We kind of have suppositions, but we are not really sure!"

"Then go to the police, and report that!"

"Amelia," Claire said to my mother, "If we do that, they are gonna publish stuff about us, and... It's gonna ruin our lives for sure!"

The problem is, basically... Everything is set up in secret from now, and... I am just waiting from stuff to actually happen, or at least I am waiting for daily news as they happen. They cannot help that much, because, we have targets, I have my hitlist, and Joris is the top priority. They don't know, and we cannot really dwell on details. But since they mentioned police, hum, now I have the bone they can get. Because, basically, what I need from them is the time since both seem determined to actually act and get this Kelly or going to speak to cops. I may have this, using feelings. So, they have their bone and then would leave me alone until tomorrow morning. It leaves me plenty of time to actually finally get Joris. Using emotions... They cannot refuse anything, anyway, they are not really in that position. What we need is a deal, we will get that deal.

"You need to go to the police, girls. Maybe this guy is putting pressure over you, using those pictures... Who tells you that he does really have pictures?" Claire's mum asked.

"Okay," I started to bargain. "But please... Leave us today. We both need to think about... what we want to say, and... We at least need a day to get the shock, and... Listen, mum, whatever you want, if you want to drive us, Claire, and I to the cops tomorrow, it's fine. Just leave us one day, please..."

"Okay..." she added. "Agreed."

34 *So, what's next?*

// Clichy-la-Garenne, suburb of Paris.

// Tuesday, 22nd of January 2013, 12:20.

I didn't really know what to say, I mean, the very last thing I was expecting from my mother would be an apology, to Claire and me, and, yeah, somehow it turned me upside down. I remember someone that used to say that the worst may not always be never disappointing, and... Literally after having heard that, I was feeling almost embarrassed. My mother was back, at least trying to seek another relationship with me. I am not a mean bitch, I am okay with that, it's just that... Well, imagine someone with whom you've been at war for years that suddenly becomes your friend. That's actually weird. You need to adapt to the new situation.

Anyway, we discussed a plan, a fake one. The thing we agreed on was, leave us a day, to actually feel better, to cope with that, and tomorrow we will go to the cops. For now, I still don't know what will happen tomorrow, I yet don't even know where I will sleep tonight, I mean... Mum proposed to us for dinner tonight, Claire and I, along with her boyfriend, and we said yes. But we are not really sure to actually be there. We may sleep at home tonight, I don't know, or maybe at her place again, as, erm... I think she might be kind of disturbed after the evening she's about to live. Anyway, during the morning, Heather texted and asked me to eat with us for lunch, as she needed to speak to us. Something important, apparently.

Anyway, at some point, we got off the car because we had to go to school. Obviously, the shock remained, none of us were about to have a great day, and the first thing I said when I went out of the car was, I really can't wait to be at bed tonight. Claire couldn't do anything else but confirming. And, as we walked down the street, whilst still being disturbed by what I have seen and heard this morning, I actually... There is something she needs to know. We told last day, no more secrets, no more lies, no more deception. And I think it's essential that I tell her about this. But how to tell her that I am pregnant?

"Hum, at least... It was better than I could expect, I mean... It could have been worse!" she was speaking.

"Yeah, hum... For once, my mother has been helpful!"

"I appreciate her offer, though, I am really impatient for this dinner!"

"Yeah, hum... Yeah, yeah, that will be fun, of course..."

She somehow noticed I was feeling disturbed, or laconic, I'd rather say. As I was walking down the street with my head lowered, she noticed that I had something heavy that I needed to share. Deep inside, very deep down, I wondered, will she find this news painful, as I somehow concealed this... now, soon, we're going to be in a situation where none of us can hide anything to the other this is why I kind of wonder. Even if this is gonna lead anywhere... Meh, after all, it's not like announcing the bad news. It's not that terrible. I was simply scared of any possible questions that he may raise.

"Hum, honey, there is something you actually should know, and... erm..."

"Hum... I see you are not feeling right since something is worrying you..."

"Yeah, erm... I didn't talk about this now, to avoid any, erm... dramas or, whatever... But you must know this, at least, you are my girlfriend, you are certainly about to become my wife if that law passes, and..."

"Oh, darling... You're really considering this?"

"I mean, we've been together for seven years, so I think this is the normal way things must go, to our marriage... But this is not what I want to talk about." I was still eluding. "Listen, hum... I am pregnant..."

Yeah, I know that was not she was expecting for... On the other hand, I always considered that if someone has to propose the other for marriage, it's her job, not mine. Come on, I already offered her... Yeah, I proposed her out twice, by the way, so, no, for marriage, it's her job, and she knows. But, yeah, I must confess that I was amazed for a fraction of seconds by another expression quickly drawn on her face, certainly close to the one for the wedding, but... She stopped walking and looked at me whilst I was one metre away·from her. She was not pissed, not at all, on the other hand, it's not like we've been together for the last month, but... She was annoyed. Slightly annoyed:

"Hum... What?"

"Yeah, that's exactly what I said when I found out, but..."

"Okay, okay, hum... I assume you don't want to keep the baby, I mean, as I know you..."

"Of course not, I won't keep the baby, come on!"

"Hum... Okay... Okay, Cha, it's fine. I guess you want me to be there the day you will get rid of it?"

"Please. I'd appreciate that..."

"Anything for you, love... Anything!"

"Thank you very much..."

To be honest, if she had announced to me that she was pregnant, I wouldn't take it the right way, I don't know why. She was much more understanding than me, at least she's always been. I don't know, but already thinking about what she has done already makes me feel genuinely upset to the point to kill someone, and now... I am just trying to skip that fact, turn a blind eye on it, pretending that it only and simply never happened. Especially now, I mean, I was in the kind of mood, "don't talk to me", so... Even in the street, once we left mum's car, we usually hold our hands on the roads and... I don't know why, but I felt like I kind of needed some isolation.

Still, although we resumed walking, even though we weren't far away from the school now, certainly half-way, it was reasonably cold outside, but at least there was still a few ways to walk before reaching our destination. I guess she was shocked by my announcement of this morning. But yet there was nothing she could actually do to counter this. But still, after a few metres done in the silence, curiosity took over:

"How did this happen?"

"Hum... Don't ask... Later, maybe, but please honey, don't ask right now!"

"Hum, okay..."

I was not keen on speaking about all this at all. Tomorrow, if she wants, once I call the hospital to book an appointment to get rid of that, we will talk, as long as she wants, but now, no. Yeah, as I said, in my mind, there was so much, I mean, I was still bouncing back into analyse and reflections, my mother this morning, the fact that nothing happened yet although we've been speaking and our phones were nearby... I remained still kind of impressed that Florent's trick worked, I wasn't... I mean, I knew he was not someone fully reliable, but now... Oh, I guess my faith in humanity remains the same. All so predictable, asking them something, and they will do it, that's so funny sometimes. And scary by others.

But, deep down, what was worrying me was tonight. I kind of had a hunch that I was sending Claire straight to the Devil. I don't know, this was totally odd. I really don't know how this is gonna happen, how things are going to take place, but I don't feel it as useful. Anyway, Heather wants to see us for lunch, so I assume she has something interesting to tell us. Especially today, I mean, I had her words a couple of days ago when I explained her my plan that she would be here and assist, as she is working with a special branch of the Police, so they could catch Joris straight away. But still, in my mind there is "she still has to undergo this, there are no other choices", and, my heart says don't go, but my mind says, it's the only way out, and if we do not take our chances tonight, God knows what will be our blackmailer's next move, and... I can cope with that, even if I am drained now, but for sure, Claire just cannot. Especially since we heard that this guy was apparently murdering people... If he touches to a single strand of her hairs, I swear to God...

Anyway, after a fairly long walk, through which we almost didn't discuss, we finally reached the college, one hour late. Claire might be absent for a while now and has been gone several days upon the last couple of days, but she's never been late. It's undoubtedly the hundredth time that I am late, this is why I stopped counting. And, when I entered, also deep down I was telling myself, I really hope this is the very last day I am coming here. I don't think we will return after today anyway, as I am sure the blackmailer will launch his reprisals against us. This is why, I gave her the advice because we know the outcome when we entered school earlier, make sure you empty your locker, just leave the books that they gave us at the beginning of the year in it, but take what belongs to you... Because I don't really want to have to come back in a few days. I don't have nothing in this locker except my books, (I mean... their books, I don't know abroad but in France, it's usually schools that lend you the books you need to study on throughout the year) so it's gonna be quick. But her locker... is a museum of oddities.

Anyway, we passed the gates, and, yeah, again, I had the hunch that it was the last day. Well, on the other hand, it is. I mean, after this, it's sure... Maybe we will come tomorrow, but Claire's Facebook will be hacked as I am already convinced. We will find god knows what on it, there's nothing that can stop it, so this will spread throughout the school. As our classmates are as intelligent as a nutshell, (and also because it's also mass psychology), usually we all know that whenever someone not really intelligent spread something through a mass, then it will go on and on, until the pack is totally against you. I know that... You speak to a group like you talk to a child of five, and guess what makes laugh a child of five? Yeah, porn pictures, you get it! This is why I have to protect her against this, she doesn't need to see this. We didn't really give each other's instructions for today except, appearing natural, just like how we feel. Of course, do not show any sign of love or affection, but other than that, be honest.

But as we arrived, the central courtyard was totally empty. It is usually busy when we arrive, as all the students packed in groups are all waiting for their courses. But now, just the noise of the various classrooms, and, yeah, a big silence. We arrived, and nobody was in the reception office yet. I must confess that this silence was also somehow disturbing. So, well, we knew where we had to go, on Room 114, upstairs, so... We both did just like what we do every morning... Going to the lockers, taking our books... Oh, no, this time, emptying it.

My locker is pretty easy to recognise: although they change our lockers every year because of all the damages students are doing on these (by damages, I mean, decoration, customisation...), it's the only one with no decoration on it. Just a small sticker with the UK flag on it, but that's it. It's not all the students with lockers, I mean, there are 260 lockers available for more than 320 students here, the lockers are available upon a rent of ten euros a month. I don't really need it, I mean, it's easy when you don't want to carry all the books to your home (yeah, because if you do not bring back your books at the end of the year, they charge you almost a hundred euros and if you damage your locker, about the same price), so this is why I always leave everything here. However, I am still cautious, I still keep that key and the locker locked to avoid thefts... Last year, I remembered Kelly complaining because she couldn't bring back one book and charged her for that.

So, as we approached... Our lockers are pretty far away from each, mine is the number 14 whilst hers is the number 92, so... And, as I opened, opened my bag, and started emptying it, I heard some people walking in the background. But I didn't pay that much attention. As I said, there was not a lot of things in my stuff... Just an old empty bottle of water, I just need to throw it away, oh no there was my book of economics, my workbook... No, this is mine, I mean, I always keep my schoolbooks, I want to keep it until I grow old, to see what I achieved in my life. And erm... Yeah, nothing. Economics, it was where we were supposed to go, by the way. And at the very moment I put my hand on that book to finally find a way to take it with my frozen hands in that little stuff, I started hearing a big masculine voice, totally unknown to me, talking to Claire:

"Hello, you must be Claire Cobert?"

"I am... And you are?"

"My name is Laurent Olivier; I am your new orientation advisor!"

"Oh, nice to meet you!"

"Nice to meet you too... And I assume the young lady with you must be miss Charlotte Kominsky, of whom I heard a lot about?"

I really hate hearing my name sometimes, I mean... When people are calling me, I just don't like it. I just ignored him, because, yeah, my new orientation advisor, like I care. I mean, I really don't need an orientation advisor. But he noticed that I was not replying and deliberately ignoring him. I was just dropping my books, making a bit of cleaning in that locker as there was still some packaging that I forgot for the last two months of some pastries that I bought here because I was hungry, and... And curiously he didn't insist. I especially hate when someone calls my name when I am on a "don't talk to me" mood, it makes me kind of grumpy. Instead, he went back to Claire:

"Hum... She can speak?"

"Oh, yeah, she can definitely speak, she's just too snob to actually talk to you!" Claire replied on my behalf.

It made me smile... And she's not wrong.

I remember once, it was undoubtedly last April when we were at school, and we had a new teacher, don't remember for which discipline. Anyway, we were sat in the corridor, and as the teacher passed and said hello, she talked a bit with him, and I was in the same mood. I just looked at them both and didn't say a word. Suddenly, he looked at me, and told her "and she never says hello", to which my girlfriend replied, "Oh, this is Charlotte, you don't know her. All the pleasure is for her...". Sometimes she can be quite sarcastic.

But, anyway, I was still curious. What's the matter, I mean, the orientation adviser is undoubtedly the last thing... Oh, wait, shit, yeah, this is January, I am supposed to have chosen which University I want to go, they told us when we came back to school last day... And I didn't do anything. They have their website, "Post-Baccalaureate Admission..." Yeah, they gave me a login and a password, I just completely forgot to actually log in. Oh, this is definitely the reason why he wants to talk to me... Meh, I think I have until May or something. But their choice of University is relatively short, as universities in this country are somewhat... I mean, there are none worldwide famous, so... I mean, I typed Harvard, United States, and it said there was no opening. Come on, for me? Seriously? Or Cambridge... No, they said you have to be enrolled even before your own birth for going there and meeting princes and future prime ministers.

Moreover, those universities, I am not such a fan, as I said, I just want a bit of action for my life. Believe it or not, but a military career should be impressive, at least it sounds fun to me. It always attracted me somehow. Even though it's mostly for guys... But who cares about this, seriously?

Anyway, suddenly I kind of slammed the door, as my locker was now empty. I didn't slam the door out of anger or anything, I just wanted to surprise them, to shift the attention on me, which worked. And when both of them looked at me, and I was this time locking my locker, I actually... was being really sarcastic:

"Why do I have to be Charlotte Kominsky?" I looked at him weirdly, but with the smile.

"I heard so much about you, miss Kominsky!"

"Interesting! Then, please be kind, and don't spoil me, okay?"

"Hum... You know that your course started an hour ago?"

"I know, and I wouldn't be that late if you weren't bothering me..."

Well, we know we're late. I thought they knew. On the other hand, it's mostly the reception office that knows, they do not need to inform the entire building that we are late. I don't know whether we actually meet this guy now, I mean... Why... I feel like he was looking for me. Or maybe I'm merely paranoid, that would explain that feeling. Anyway.

Anyway, after having loaded our bags, especially Claire's, she was carrying so much stuff that we had to split between her purse and mine so it wouldn't be too heavy for her shoulder, we managed to arrive in the classroom we were due to have course. Obviously, as we were late, I was curious on whether he would deny the access to us, but he seemed too inspired into his speech about some economic shit that he didn't even notice our presence. I mean, yeah, he saw it, but it didn't interrupt him any further. We sat down, at the end of the classroom, obviously, together, took our books, and, same old, we both pretended to actually listen, whilst the reality was totally different. Claire was following, whilst I was on YouTube, with my phone in my pencil-case, hidden. I was still watching videos about this guy that travels across the planet, today he was in Dubai. With the highest tower in the world, the Burj Khalifa; he took a video from the observation deck. An impressive view, to be honest. I wish I could go to this country; too bad I am lesbian... Or a woman that would never accept wearing a scarf above my head.

I saw Claire annotating stuff on her books, drawing charts, and the same diagrams displayed on the giant board from times to times. Trying to understand and to catch up, but I remained outside. I used to keep my mind busy doing something before I know something stressful is ahead, and I guess she's taking the same strategy. It was definitely the very first time of my life that I kind of felt something that actually looked like empathy, at least it tasted like empathy. And it sounded weird, almost scary, I mean, I literally had mercy for her. I never had compassion for anyone in my life. I guess this is true love, I mean, or devotion I assume, but somehow, I was feeling like the knight deliberating her princess from a dungeon guarded by some kind of dragon.

The last hour passed, or at least even less than an hour, then we had our break, which was actually the moment where we threw away much stuff that was in our bags as we didn't have time to do that earlier, then we were ready for the last two hours of maths. Oh, no, in between, I actually bought a bottle of water and a *pain au chocolat* because I was kind of hungry (I didn't eat this morning... And it's not the quick coffee that I had that was enough to fill up my tiny stomach). And although she stayed with me, I proposed her to eat, and she told me that she had enough of her breakfast and, in any case, she was not hungry at all. As I said, I was kind of hungry, because I needed to eat something, to have something. Still, if I didn't need, well, then I wouldn't have anything, because the stress somehow tied me up and if I don't eat anything, I'm gonna go for stomach problems, so... Better to avoid being sick today.

Our mere discussions were mostly about during the break, tomorrow, what do we do, after the upcoming evening. I suggested that, well, we should stay in bed for at least a moment. Then, after, maybe going to the restaurant. The problem, her place, or mine? I mean... Since things seem to go better between my mum and my girlfriend, my home would be okay, but on the other hand, she said that she doesn't really want to give up her mother, especially in such situation. She wants to remain with her. I remember Heather having told us about protection, she said we would have a bodyguard, I really hope we will, as we will take Joris down tonight, to kick him out of the game, so we will be targeted, huge targets afterwards... Since Heather didn't speak to me about anything, I haven't seen any changes. Maybe this is why she wants to talk to us today because we will have one assigned to us and brief us about what we must do and what we mustn't do. I hope she's not gonna betray us, because... If she does, then everything will be lost. But I really don't think she will, she has as many interests as we have to take Joris down.

After sketching a draft of what would be our morning tomorrow (a mix between laziness, laziness and, erm... yeah, being idle), we jumped to the classroom 214 where, yeah, maths. The last two hours before we finally speak with Miss Reed.

Well... I sat down at my usual place, Claire didn't follow me... but for the first time today, (it's to say how wakened up I was), I noticed that Clarisse, as well as Kelly and Sophie, all three weren't there. It's not that surprising from Kelly, as she's as severe as, erm... but Sophie is quite punctual, and Clarisse... she only misses school when she's sick, and... maybe she's sick, I just don't feel like it. So, I texted her, to check on her... because, yeah, I recall mum talking about her this morning, so it means that she was sleeping home yesterday. Oh, wait, yesterday evening, I left home at around ten-thirty, so it means that... oh gosh. I really hope this is not what I think it is, this is why I am actually feeling so concerned today. So, moments after I sat down, my phone straight visible in my hands, I texted her immediately. I really hope that she didn't break up with her boyfriend, as she told me that things weren't that good recently. Still, before texting, I checked at the window... in case thunderstorms are coming or a hurricane... but nope, just a blue sky.

"Yo Clarisse, what is up? You're not at school today?" was what I texted. Sue was surprisingly long to answer. She may be either on the phone or whether sleeping. But as she replied five to seven minutes later, she wasn't sleeping, I bet she was on the phone. She replied that she was feeling tired yesterday because they had a big argument with her boyfriend. Without dwelling on the details, she's pretty much "on the process of" dumping him, unless she did the job already. So, well, I mean, that's sad, I mean, I replied that she should think about it carefully before doing that. Still, if she thinks it's the thing to do, then she must not hesitate.

On the other hand, to be really honest, I don't like her boyfriend. He looks like an arse. I mean, a hipster, (don't ask my opinion... no, no, no...) vegan moreover... she can definitely find better. And what I hate foremost with him is that basically, he is ultra-sensitive on everything, and you literally cannot joke about anything with him. But, well, anyway, I know my sister, she's gonna be sad for a couple of days, then say that she will find a girlfriend because she's done with guys, then start to bargain, going to parties, be drunk, sleep with some other random guy, then this guy will become the love of her life or the guy she needs. Until she will realise that all guys are all the same, and so on, and so on. My dear twin sister... it's when I see her love life that I'm happy to be reasonably stable with Claire.

Anyway, so Clarisse mystery, solved. Now, Sophie. I have often seen her with Kelly, and today she's absent, that doesn't mean anything good. Because, amongst the missing, they were the three only. And Sophie... she was certainly absent twice since the year started. And since Kelly has lost most of the power she has over Claire, I am sure she's looking for someone else to make sure her business continues to thrive. So, I texted her, as well, I mean, calm mood, relaxed, like "Hey Sophie, what's up? I haven't heard from you in ages!", but no replies. The thing is, if she ever replies, it will be... I mean I gotta be cautious with her wordings, her way to respond; it will surely be the best indication of her mood. Also, I need to see her. Maybe, in the next couple of days, but I need to see her. As she's been a kind of a whistle-blower to me, but there are still... I never really asked her how she actually gets the information. This actually mattered, more than I could believe when she told me I was more shocked by her accusations than where she found her sources, but... I really need to talk to her.

Anyway, Claire recorded all the names of her customers in a book. There are still about three pages of names, but she actually recorded their names, addresses, professions... And I had a look on that. She documented this as she never knows, it might be useful in the future. I asked her to give me a copy of that list, as I want to start to fight back, but I am sure Heather will request it. But what she had, well... Mostly lawyers, scientists, judges, one prosecutor, bank staff and all that... The kind of office-working people. She even had a journalist, which is funny, I mean... Journalists... No comment.

I may go through that list of names, as she knows that I want to fight back, I didn't record mine, but I pretty much know who it was, and to be honest, I wouldn't really seek troubles towards those people. But making downfall a lawyer or a prosecutor, this, actually seems really exciting. One way or another, I tend to believe that our blackmailer might be one of them, or at least the response to the mystery over that blackmailer's identity might lie in this list. Because all of them knew Joris, and, I mean, come on, a prosecutor... All-day making indictment against criminals and by night going out with a pimp... And sleeping with a minor, moreover. Well, taking down that kind of piece of shit won't prevent me from sleeping. Note for me, maybe considering purchasing a bulletproof vest... Who knows?

Anyway, well, the course, well... Same, Claire seemed focused, at least... But for this we weren't seating together, we were sat at two different tables, as she used to sit with Kelly and I used to sit with my sister, but since they were both absent... I wanted to come closer to her, but since we are not allowed because otherwise, we're chatting and disrupting the course... Instead, I remained behind. He was talking about the exponential function... Meh. Again, I was still listening but what he seemed to talk about was really confusing, I'd better check this on myself, to understand it better.

Anyway, I checked the program of maths to finally obtain the baccalaureate, and it seems fun... Geometry. I hate geometry, I prefer algebra by far. Like, long strings of number... I didn't really talk about, but this is something that I have, when I was maybe four or five, one of my favourite toys was a calculator. I really don't know why, but my dad used to have a calculator that I was stealing all the time and calculating stuff all day long. Yeah, I know, I was a weird kid. But today, after having spent weeks when my brain is still like a sponge and gets all knowledge it can have, now I am excellent in maths, I never used my calculator anymore. Ask me whatever complicated stuff, and I can calculate it very quickly. This caused problems when I was in high school, especially when they started to teach us how to calculate with round brackets... I had the result just by seeing the equation, the problem was... how to explain it. That's actually cool to have this, I mean, this is something quite useful in life (at least I can scream straight away when I am not given back my good change because I count it all the time) ... But, seriously, exponential functions... Who gives a shit?

Anyway... Two hours passed. Still no answers from Sophie, and I think this is really likely that she may answer... And my phone, ten minutes before we end up that course, rang. It was Heather, notifying me that she was waiting for us downstairs. As I was seating by the window area and as the classroom was on the second floor, giving a view on the parking, I swiftly glanced through the window, overlooking the parking... that was full already, many other parents coming to pick up their kids... Oh, and here she was. I don't know whose car was hers, but I could see her sitting on one of the stones facing the main door, she was on her phone doing stuff... At the moment the course was definitely over, and everybody was standing to join the building's exit, I quickly walked towards Claire, who was still pretty late... And told her that she was waiting for us downstairs. I helped her, but she seemed... I don't know, weird. I know what it was, she was severely stressed. But... Come on, we have to do it.

So, we walked towards the exit in our turn. Astonishingly, Claire was also in the same mood as I was, the "don't talk to me". Well, on the other hand, the clock was still turning, and she was fully aware of this... so was I. So, we walked down the stairs, however, it was kind of creative, we all avoided the rush that used to be there for the first ten minutes when they are all rushing out... And went down the stairs. As Claire is still minor, she still had to show her mum's authorisation in her book to exit the building and her ID... And then we went out. Straight to Heather. At the moment we walked together towards her, she was still on her phone... But suddenly rose her head as we stopped together in front of her:

"Hello, girls... What's up?" she surprisingly seemed enthusiast.

She seemed tensed at a glance but remained, however, very calm and excited. On the other hand, it's not like she knows that if tonight is victorious, she's gonna catch a pretty big fish. But as we saw her, she seemed confident, like, noticeably confident for tonight. It's a good sign, I mean... She's supervising all this, so I am sure she knows stuff we do not actually know. If she's smiling like she is, it means that she's pretty much sure of what she's doing. Which is... Okay, tonight is relatively safe.

Anyway, today, she was relatively discreet compared to the rest of the days. She had her long brown hairs untied, slight makeup, most of which was to hide her masculine stuff, and erm... Yeah, just like us, dressed in black. Black pull, black trousers, only white sneakers. She immediately stood up as we met her, put her phone back in her pocket, and it's at that moment that Claire, thoughtful, replied:

"Meh..." Claire started.

"It's gonna be better once we go to bed, trust me!" I actually confirmed.

"Ah, come on... Okay, you want to get in? Where do you want to go?"

"I don't really mind, I'm not really hungry anyway..." I was nonchalant.

"Same here..." Claire continued. "But there's a good restaurant really close to here, we can go by walk if you prefer. We used to go there with Cha a couple of times, and it's quite nice!"

"Oh, sure, yeah, why not!"

The weather was actually fine today, it was not too hot, and not too cold at the same time. However, there was still a bit of wind that were moving the early leaves of trees that were starting to grow again, producing a very slight noise, mixed up with the traffic outside. No clouds in the sky, or at least at very high-altitude, but just a blue sky, a blue...ish sky, because as Paris remains a very polluted city and there is still a skinny layer of fine particles air floating, the sky is never blue. Always pale blue. Sometimes I miss the south of France, at that period it may be cold, but at least they have a blue sky. The worst is to think that millions of people breathe this air, and authorities do not really seem to react.

The restaurant was literally not far away from school, we just had to cross the road before the entrance and walk maybe less than ten metres to actually join it. It's okay, it's actually a typical French restaurant, but they are mostly serving seafood. They can be busy sometimes, but we used to go there with Claire or even Clarisse when we used to have time for lunchtime, and we wanted to eat good food instead of shit. It's actually not that pricey, at least for Paris it's not that expensive, but the food is delicious. And, even, the place is quite cosy, it's not a big restaurant, there must be four or five tables inside, the surface is pretty narrow, but it's good when you want to have a conversation with someone without being seen by the rest of the people. Anyway, I really don't know what to eat there... Maybe a salad should be okay. At least if they serve salad... in February. I hope so.

Anyway, we left college, there was surprisingly a lot of people in the park. We crossed the road, the same usual traffic... And we arrived in front of this place. The waitress, a tall, blonde student (she looks like a student) and I'd rather say law student as she seemed slightly posh, was welcoming us. Heather talked to her, in French (I wonder how many languages she may speak... But I am sure she speaks more than five languages) in her weird accent:

"Good afternoon, how are you?"

"We're doing fine, what about you?"

"Yeah, not bad, thank you. Do you want to sit in, a table for three?"

"Yeah, sure, we've been recommended... Table for three, please!"

"Sure. Follow me!"

Basically, the restaurant is discreet, as I said. For entering, you need to follow a corridor at the entrance, which leads to some kind of room inside. All the walls are white, burgundy, and today was icy, all lit with old artificial lightning throughout the ceiling. Upon entering, well... Surprisingly, we were taking the last table. It was probably a busy day for them, although... It didn't seem to look hectic from the outside. Either way, if the place is busy, it means that the service should be fast. I mean, they want to free tables as fast as possible to welcome new customers.

The floor consists of pretty much four tables, all tables with four chairs. On the walls, some pictures, old-fashioned French actresses and actors (that used to play in good old movies... I mean, there used to be good French movies... before) and the light is slightly dimmed. Two tables are in the middle, a table of four and a table of six, both full, I assume the table of four was a family since there was a guy, a woman that seemed unhappy so I guess they are married and two kids, at the next table there was a mix of men and women. Still, as most of them were wearing casual clothing and none were drinking alcohol, I assume they were all colleagues from the same company and were eating here, discussing some weird stuff... There are still quite a lot of offices around here, so... That would explain why. However, there was still a majority of men. And, finally, a table for two people on the corner, not far away from our table, there was a guy with a black suit reading newspapers and drinking something, I guess some coke or something. He was undoubtedly waiting for his lunch to come. He was alone. Meh. So, we sat at the table on the left, the only free table. I sat in front of Heather and Claire on her left. The waitress had the menu in her hands, and as I sat, I put my bag on the chair next to me, and Claire gave me hers... And as we sat...

"So, how do you feel? Don't tell me you guys had your very first fight since you're back together?"

"Oh, no... Not yet, that shouldn't be long," Claire remained laconic.

"No, we... We kind of had a tough morning, and erm... I don't know, I want to get rid of this mess, I want to end up that fight..."

"Hum, sure... I understand. Well, you're nearly done. I am coming with some rather good news, actually!"

At the very same time when Heather started to show her enthusiasm, Claire's phone (she took it out of her bag, and it was next to her) began to ring. I immediately looked at her face, as the phone was too far away from my sight and I couldn't read what was on it... But I saw her quite annoyed by what she was reading. I could see through her eyes; she didn't receive a text that arranged her. Something... It could be Joris... But given how she reacted, with her sudden frown, yeah, I think that must be Joris. He may be changing the conditions for tonight, but as she's not over-reacting, he is not cancelling. What she read was just putting her a bit under pressure. After maybe ten or twenty seconds, after Heather noticed that she was pissed by something too, Claire started, with, yeah, the confused voice:

"Oh, hum... Heather, there's actually some update for tonight, erm... It's not cancelled, it's just that Joris wants to meet at his place. I don't really know where it is. At first, we were supposed to do it at mine, but..."

"Oh, that's interesting, actually, erm..." she replied.

"Show me your text?" I asked my girlfriend, curious.

She immediately gave me her phone without responding. And I saw the message... Among a lot of texts. Basically, the very last he sent was "Hey darling, I thought about it for tonight, you wanna come at my place instead? It's gonna be fun, I'm gonna have a lot of funny stuff!". I quickly read some other messages... No, they look like this one. There was still a multitude of emojis everywhere... At the end of this one, the emoji with the thinking face (Curious... Joris can think, that is really interesting), there was at least five of them. From what I read in previous messages, yeah. I can see Joris as really enterprising with her throughout their conversation, I mean, he was frequently making sexual allusions. Not very direct, but indirect, and she saw that. If that guy were a colleague, I'd say he'd be sexually harassing me. But Claire played the game, it was apparent, I mean, her texts meant, catch me if you can. She was not sincere, that was flagrant, but since he doesn't know her as I know her, for him at least, it seemed real.

But in his last text, there was surprisingly no comma, no sign of punctuation, everything was written in lines, different lines, and reasonably straight. Most of his messages are using punctuation, not this one. But as he still displayed some emoji, it didn't mean that he was aware of anything, he just wants to change the rules, because he is more than impatient for tonight. He will finally sleep with my girlfriend; his dreams will become true. Or at least, that's what he thinks. No, in his text, the feeling that I had first was, he was impatient, he wants to take control, it's obvious, he wants to take control over her, make her puppet more or less. And saying no wouldn't be a great idea because he could be willing to cancel. Unless...

But to be fair, I think it would be great if things occur at his home and not Claire's house. Because, we still don't know the outcome, what he will do to her and if things are happening under her roof, she will be traumatised, and it will take her months before she accepts to come back. Maybe, making this in a neutral place for her could be more playable than anything else, at least to avoid traumatism. She is already fed up, let's not make it worse. After... I don't really know where he lives, and (maybe Claire knows) ... But if he proposes his place, it's certainly more convenient for him, for perhaps both of them. Whilst I was reading the phone, I handed back the phone to my girlfriend and looked at her, and said:

"Hum, yeah, hum, go for it!" I analysed.

"Honey, erm, I am not feeling like..."

"Yes, I know how you feel, darling," I interrupted her explaining my analysis. "The thing is, he seems much more excited to actually meet you and wants to remain the master of that meeting. If you meet at your place, he may feel that this is a trap because he may know your place, but he won't really feel at ease there. If you meet at his place, he knows his place, so it's gonna be even better to control him. Trust me... And then we can catch her much more easily as he may think that he is out of reach."

"She's right," Heather replied, "I know where he lives. He lives in a studio flat in the North-East of Paris, near Stalingrad metro station..."

"Oh, Stalingrad..." Claire was suddenly disturbed by what she heard.

Okay, I didn't think about this. Damn, as a cop, I think he was paid much better and would live in a much better place. Stalingrad, for most of Parisians, is a close synonym to the shithole. In the 19th Arrondissement of Paris, (north-east of Paris) it's basically the place where crackheads, homeless people, drug dealers and prostitutes are part of the decoration by night. The kind of spot you certainly do not want to roam by night, I mean... not alone. It's why, well, I am not really sure Heather knows Paris well, but we do, and hearing that word literally froze us. It's bloody dangerous. A bit like Soho in London... But you still prefer Soho. Oh, and the 19th, I think it's the most homophobic place in Paris. Well, on the other hand, it's not really surprising, compared to the number of waste living in a square-metre there... And by garbage, I am referring to the category I mentioned above. I am not referring to local residents, honest citizens.

Yeah well, I can totally understand why she doesn't want to go there alone. So, I really hope Heather has a solution because even I... I really don't feel her like going alone there by night. Yeah, I know, we cannot afford to postpone it. But at least I understand his strategy: I am sure he knows that she doesn't know where he lives. He may certainly give the address late, but he thinks it may be a trap: as she will go in Stalingrad, and as he believes he may have power over her, they are both aware that this is a wild place, then she has no escape for tonight and thus can do whatever he wants with her. That's pretty clever, actually. And a good strategy. This is why, let's put him straight into his own smokescreen, let's make him confident. He is clearly thinking with his genitals right now... So, let's convince him that he's right. Let's convince him that he has the power. As one of my favourite politicians of all times said, "The best way to overthrow a regime (power) is to actually be part of it". Have power, Joris, have fun with this.

"Yeah, I know, that could be a better place..." Heather resumed. "But this is where I am leading to that news. That good news. I have quite a lot of things to tell you. First, Claire, reply that it's okay. And let him send you the address."

"You better cover my arse tonight because I ain't going to Stalingrad in heels and skirts, trust me! Nobody goes there like this; it's just fucking dangerous!" she imposed her conditions.

"I'll be there, honey. I'll be following you anyway!" I reassured her.

"Yes, but... You must stay away from me because if he sees you being with me, that will sound suspicious!"

"Yes, I know, I know what I have to do... But be not afraid..."

"Claire, from this afternoon... Look at that guy over there, with a suit... Say, hello!" Heather pointed some guy in a table nearby, that looked at us.

Hum... Well, I am not really surprised. I said the guy who was reading his newspaper, waiting for his lunch; I saw that he was looking at us quite discreetly from times to times. Well, he is our bodyguard... So, Heather thought about everything. We are covered. Surprisingly, it's the first time of the day I see him, which means, he is here for now not that long. That will affect us, that's sure. I mean... Our daily life. Especially since I don't know how long we will be under police protection... Unless he is a private security guard, so he is more discreet, I don't know. But at least she kept her promise, she would provide us with security as we do not realise how dangerous our blackmailer is, especially if he intends to harm us. I think he will, but...

"Who is he?" I turned myself to Heather.

"He is gonna be part of your safety for the next months, girls..."

"A bodyguard?"

"Pretty much, yeah. I could finally have my contacts at the Police here, and they granted full protection for both of you. From now on until... Some point, they will be following you, when you are out. So, trust me, Claire, you can walk anywhere you like, you're all covered for tonight and maybe for the coming months. They will not be there when you are at school this afternoon, but they will be watching over you as soon as you are out."

Still, having a bodyguard, that's quite fancy, I mean, I feel like I am someone important. You almost feel untouchable, or something like this.

"Neat!" I started to show some joy.

"Yeah, it's true. It's not like everybody who has the chance to be on the potential list of a serial killer, true..."

Yeah, of course, I didn't see it that way, yeah. Yeah, it's true, I kind of forgot the picture she showed me on her iPad when I was at her hotel room last night, I mean... But is he alone or are they more? Because... Oh, well, at least that would be an excellent opportunity to actually live together for the next months, as we never did that. How is it gonna be, living with her? I guess that having a bodyguard will severely restrict a lot of things that we could do freely before, and now... I don't really know; she will undoubtedly brief us. After having lived with a guy for a month, now Claire is gonna "assume that position", I am simply scared this would lead to more fights or... As we both like having our intimacy sometimes. I don't really know how this is going to look like. But at least if I am with her, then I guess that it's gonna be more comfortable for her, she's gonna be less scared. On the other hand, after those eight years together, or seven, I think, if we weren't meant to live together, things would have already been exploding. I don't know.

"Yeah, erm, of course, I mean..." I calmed my enthusiasm...

"Anyway, "Heather went back to more serious business. "So, text him back, and tell him that you're okay. But set the meeting at seven tonight. If it's too early for him..."

"Yeah, I know how to convince him... He's not that hard to convince! And we were already supposed to meet at seven anyway," Claire was feeling relieved now.

She immediately replied. But, yeah, now I could see some relief in her eyes, she was feeling more confident. The fact that we are under police protection from now on, the fact that she knows that Heather will be there, at least, we have guarantees now, even though Heather didn't really reveal her plan for tonight... At least we are not only together and plunging into dark waters. We are backed. This wasn't bullshit. On the other hand, I really feel that Heather is trustworthy.

Anyway, she showed us her answer. "No problem, I'll be there, just text me your address please" with a smiley that blinks. Good, at least it shows that she remains totally innocent, especially since she asked for his address, which confirms that she is not doing anything suspicious and remains innocent. I think, it was also in this state of mind that Joris texted her, I'd be a cop, and I'd set my conditions, I'd be surprised that she would say yes and not asking for my address, as she isn't supposed to know it. But, no, she thought about that detail, which is good. The blinking smiley is also a right choice, it means, yeah, I'll be there, I trust you, we will have a good evening, it shows some confidence and some readiness to actually follow him and being willing to be his stuff tonight. Overall, that's good, I mean... That's pretty clever. Now, he has all the cards in hands, he has everything in his hands. It's his turn to deal with the power he now has. Let's see how he intends to do it now.

"Okay, girls, so I have a couple of announcements for you. Some good news overall!" Heather continued after having read Claire's response.

"Oh, great... Tell me!" I was excited.

"So, we've been working yesterday all night with the Police crew in charge here of the investigation of *Raising Sun*, your blackmailer, to finally establish a plan on how we will catch Joris. First of all, they have an IT genius within that crew that basically found the recorder on your phone and destroyed it. Which means, you are no longer listened by your blackmailer and thus, can speak freely!"

"Oh, great!" Claire started.

"Then how did you manage to break this and make sure that we didn't have problems? Because the logic would be that, as I am being listened, being no longer listened would have had consequences on us, I mean..." I was curious.

"Oh, yeah. It's quite technical, he switched your recorder by, basically, from yesterday midnight. We recorded another day that we are passing, like music, he just listens your day of yesterday right now. So nothing has changed, and nothing looks suspicious. Nothing really changes for him. He just thinks you are doing something else..."

"Oh... Okay. That's quite smart."

"Don't ask me for details, I don't really know how she did that, you know, computing and I..."

"Yeah, I know, same as well..."

So that would explain why he didn't backfire after the scandal exploded. Maybe he will realise later that he's been hijacked and... And yesterday will look like today, it may create confusion. He is still not aware that things are out of his reach. I mean, that is just speculations... But at least that would explain why I found my phone pretty slow this morning and, in the metro, Claire complained about some bugs that occurred. We don't have the same phone, but still... So, great, now we can speak freely. But what about tonight?

"So, what's the plan for tonight?" Claire was impatient to know.

"So, tonight, you guys are finishing school at 5, right?"

"Normally, yes..." I confirmed.

"So, I'm gonna catch you once you're out and we're gonna go to your house. You're gonna get ready for tonight, and I'm gonna wiretap you. So, at least I can listen closely to what will happen during that meeting."

"Okay, hum... Fine, yeah. What if he finds out that I am wiretapped? Because, as a matter of fact, he is a cop, so knows the stuff..."

"Then... This is why I'm not done, let me finish my stuff, and then you can ask as many questions as you want. We're gonna wiretap you, and then you will go. I know that his building has two entrances, the main entrance and the second is the rubbish entrance. You will pass by the main entrance, and I will pass by the rubbish entrance, with three of my colleagues. I will be listening to you at the same time, so I know when to catch him, and whilst you will be doing your stuff with him, we will get ready to actually catch him, we will be behind his door and waiting quietly."

Okay, that's her plan. That sounds good, I mean, I couldn't find any other methods... Especially since he proposed to change the rules, then I assume she carefully studied her place as well as Claire's house, just in case. But that still doesn't answer the fundamental question: Claire wiretapped, okay, but Joris is a cop. And, wiretapping someone, I am sure he will find out that she is wiretapped and if he finds this out, things are going to be really tough to manage. So, this is why, I let her finishing, as she wanted to expose her plan, and then I asked, concerned:

"But Claire rose an important point, and I think she was right on that, that sounds easy, but he is a cop, and he will feel the trap."

"Yes, and I know this. This is why I was coming to that point. When you arrive, Claire, you must make sure of two things. First, the door must remain open; open, not locked, and second, erm... well... This is the part you will not like..."

"I get it," she seemed resigned. "I must let him attack me, so you can catch him for statutory rape. I understand..."

"We identified him as a potential pimp, the only problem is that we just have clues and suppositions, we do not have charges. And if we catch him red-handed, then we will have immediate charges, and he won't be able to deny it. And regarding the tap, the device is fairly small, it will be hidden in your bra, and... that is not something... Well, if he finds out... Just, don't push him to answer specific questions tonight, even better, just don't ask any questions. Let him do what he wants you to do. We won't catch him on his confessions, we just want to catch him assaulting you. For his confession, it's the next part, but... Don't worry about that. The most important is, it must be quick. Anyway, for your attitude, the attitude you must adopt towards him, I'll brief you tonight, okay?"

"That's fine. If you need that, then..."

Surprisingly, she seemed complacent. I mean, we are still speaking about, well... assaulting, in the meaning of sexual assault, but... Weirdly, it didn't seem to bother her. On the other hand, she had some excellent training in the last two months, so... But still. She seemed relieved because we knew the plan, we knew that she's gonna be there, we knew that she's gonna be under close surveillance, and it's when he starts with her that they will catch him. She's gonna explain to her what to do tonight, so she's closely monitored. But what actually bothered me was, it will be another event that will make her memory rotten repeatedly. It will prevent her from sleeping again, and... Well... this is the plan, and we must go to the end now. This is the final line.

"Also, I may need a statement from you both. For what happened, and everything."

"Do you need that on the very same evening, I mean, tonight?" I asked.

"Oh, no... That can wait. You girls will be quite tired, I think, for the next couple of days, so... But at least within a week, if possible..."

"Yeah, of course, I mean, if we can help you..." Claire confirmed. "Just leave us at least tomorrow, because... We will have a tough evening, again, and I'd appreciate to, erm, you know, relax..."

"Of course, that's no problem. Just text me when you feel ready, and I will come to you. But, no, of course, tomorrow, just, erm... Relax, take some time for you, go for shopping, or, you know... Take some time off."

"Yeah. Yeah, we will. Definitely... We just need a break from all this."

"And you deserved it..."

Okay, fine. There is just one last problem: I just cannot stay home tonight and wait until this is over. I designed most of the plan, even if she helped, and... I know that this will be a police investigation and I should stay away from this, I won't be required, but I need to be there. I need to be the first to take her in my arms tonight when she will cry. I just... If I am away from that, it will drive me nuts, not knowing what's going on, and if something is due to happen to her... Then I want to be there.

"Heather, erm... I know you cannot really grant me that favour, but... I would appreciate something," I restarted, exhausted.

"Yes?"

"I know, this is basically a police intervention, and this is something that is, erm... None of my business, but I would appreciate that... Because I cannot remain out of this, I mean, I've been helping out a lot, and I want to be there tonight. My girlfriend is used as a bait, and I cannot just stay away from this. I cannot stay out, she's gonna need me, and... I want to be here!"

The thing... And I am sure she thought about it, it's just arresting Joris. There shouldn't be any bullets fired tonight, there shouldn't be anything... So, she thought. I think I had some excellent and pertinent arguments. This is why, after having considered, she slowly replied:

"Okay. Okay, I understand. Then I'll catch you both, but make sure that no-one recognises you..."

"Yeah, of course..."

"Well, then... We're all set for tonight! I wanted to thank you, both, because if we catch him tonight, he will be the first pimp of that organisation we will actually catch, and this will be a great achievement, so we can pursue this investigation further. It will be a huge step forward."

35 *Finish the fight*

// Towards Stalingrad, Paris.

// Tuesday, 22nd of January 2013, 18:50.

It was such a long wait, and it was cold in Heather's car. I assume her air con was broken... Which is surprising for a rental car. And... We saw Claire, arriving downstairs, slowly. The deep night has already fallen over Paris, and the rain just stopped, making streets wet, roads all covered with tiny kind of swimming pools formed on the numerous pothole that the road was containing. As soon as another car was passing through, it made this kind of weird, crystal-like noise of water flowing. I don't understand how the weather managed to change so quickly. With all this humidity floating in the air, Claire arrived. She was stressed but was hiding it. And, to look like her, I was feeling she looked like twenty-five or something. I could only admire the courage she had to do the dirty job. She slowly arrived like a businesswoman, tall, wearing her black coat and her heeled shoes that made the noise that we could hear her from the street, walking on a newly renovated footpath. All around, Haussmann-like buildings, with all lights lit on, and... A silent street, quite remoted in a busy city centre, with just the noise of the metro passing nearby on a bridge. I was just following her with my eyes, slowly walking towards the threshold of a regular building, a building that looked like its neighbour building, a two or three-floor building... Going to hell. And me, waiting for the rescue mission from hell in that cold car.

After that quick lunch, and mostly after all that news that was overall great, well, it was time to get back... And get ready for tonight.

The weather didn't change that much, it was still a sunny day, and the wind started to be slightly more aggressive. After lunch, she left us, we've been followed by our bodyguard to school, and after he left us. The afternoon started, we had literature first, and we finished with mathematics, again, just like every Tuesday. Everything has been split by a twenty-minute break in between. If we were okay? Well, we could see the hour was turning, and anxiety was rising. I mean, we never did something like that, and now, the bodyguard, it was quite impressive. Hopefully, so far, the plan works, we still had some modifications, but everything went according to the plan we enforced in secrecy. At least, I think we did it quite well.

Taylor Harding-Jenkins

When we went back to school, at least when we walked towards school, Claire submitted me an idea for tomorrow. Why not sleeping at her place, so the next day, depending on the hour we will even wake up, why not going for a walk in Versailles, in the Palace's garden. She told me that it has been a while and she wanted to be back in communion with Nature. I must say that those gardens are fantastic, I mean, I went there several times (and it's so big that I even got lost once), and I said, why not? We just have a train to get in there... And it's true, having a small break from Paris (even if we remain in the suburb) could be right. She said we could get some food there, some drinks as well, and we could go for a walk. And, walking into those gardens, that could be good for the mood. I said, yes, why not. I miss going there sometimes. And as I know that tomorrow will be a tough day, perhaps less challenging than today, but still I am sure that tonight's extreme events will remain in her mind and... And, yeah, escaping Paris would be great. And, regarding the future, well...

So, we went for two hours of literature. It was annoying, but still, I listened for once. I mean, I heard... Pretty much, because whatever it was, I couldn't get away from those thoughts: I am dreading tonight, even if now I know that it's relatively safe, sending her there is still for me throwing her to the lions. Hopefully, I could be there, so I will be here when we take her back when we deliver, and so she will be safe. But still, I kept looking at her from times to times and, I don't understand, I was trying to seek, what did we do to deserve that? I mean, what did she do? I may understand, I am not someone nice, but she is, I mean, I have always seen her as a very human person and kind, I mean, she's all the kindness of the world, and now she's destroyed. It's when I see that I lose all my faith in humanity. The human race is the evillest of Nature's creation, and will always remain, and... And I don't know what's worst, thinking that we've been part of a cluster (as Heather calls it), or remaining that there are other girls, aged the same as her or even younger, that have been trapped, tried to escape, and failed? This is why tonight's operation is essential, as Heather reminded us: if we succeed, she will capture the first head of a cluster amongst more than a hundred groups identified across Europe. If we fail... Well, the blackmailer will take his revenge, or... Joris might harm Claire or even kill her, and... I prefer not to think about this. As I said, he just touches one strand of her hairs, and I swear to God, even he won't be able to deliver his harshest judgement to him. I promise him a slow but unbearable death. Because torturing people... Well, I can have a lot of ideas and show myself as highly creative. And capture him won't be a problem for me.

Free Expensive Lies: Prologue

During the break, we sought isolation. We used to have our corner, I mean, our place, under the stairs leading to the offices above the college. As we used to go there before, we went there again today, and... And we lied down on the floor, as usual, and I took her in my arms and cuddled her hairs. I sometimes believe that I am the leader in our relationship, as I am always cuddling her... That was maybe why I felt so uncomfortable with Florent, I mean, he was taking me in my arms, I was still... I didn't like it.

The conversation, what about May? Her birthday is on the 5th of May, and she still doesn't know what to do for her eighteen birthdays. The day she turns eighteen. And I suggested that we travel abroad, she asked me for London since she knows that I go there quite often and I have never been with her, I said, why not. She still doesn't know what she wants to do as a job, and... I told her that I am not even sure about working, though I am scared of being idle somehow. I told her that I am considering a military career, even if I don't know. I want to do some sports, like fight sports... That would fit me well. I fought several times, and I kind of enjoyed it.

And after having drawn the future world slowly, even if plans might change and we still don't know if tomorrow will someday look like yesterday, we went back to maths, for the last two hours. Today, we had a test, so... After this morning, the teacher said it was related to something we did before. I like this teacher, for this reason, we may study something, and the test would fall on a day we don't know... It somehow forces us to keep on working. I don't know if I did it well or not, but... I just did it. I felt like, yeah, when you feel like you have nothing to lose, that was impressive, it made me so free... But, once the test is done, the bell rang. Time to go, it was now five. And... We looked at each other with my girlfriend and, we could just simply say to each other, "well, time to go...".

Heather was waiting for us downstairs. The meeting was set for seven, which meant we had two hours to get ready. She was waiting for us downstairs, and we jumped in her car.

Her car was rented, I mean, she rented it I guess for her time in Paris. It was a relatively small car, I mean, it was a hatchback car, a Ford car, with four seats. Her car was black, with tinted windows. I have never seen her vehicle yet, but it looked like a very ordinary car to be fair. Nothing surprising. However, I must say that the seats were kind of comfortable... surprising, for a cheap car.

We jumped in, Claire moved in front whilst I moved back, and we left College. The next stop is Claire's house. She chose her itinerary carefully, avoiding the massive *Boulevard Périphérique* circling Paris because we all know that it's massively congested at that hour, and we cannot afford to be late tonight. Instead, she took several roads, passing through Paris, avoiding big arteries of the capital to avoid congestions. She had her GPS, so she was following a precise itinerary. I was even impressed, for someone who doesn't really know Paris, to avoid congestion at that hour... It's like she's been living here for years. On the other hand, she's a particular cop, so... she certainly has some special abilities. During the journey, though, the weather changed. Although we had a sunny day today, the weather looked more threatening now. Also, during the time we travelled through Paris, another car, the same as ours, was following us. I assume it's her bodyguard. Whilst it took us merely forty minutes to finally reach our destination, towards the end, as the car was kind of silent, nobody was talking, Heather finally opened the conversation:

"Okay... So, you okay, Claire?"

"Well, I can't wait for this to end, to be fair..."

"I understand... So, this is how you must behave tonight. You must go there and appear as tired. He will force you to... well, you know, but you must decline. Make sure that he proposes several times, and you decline several times as well, so at least we can record and have the proof that you've been forced."

"Well, I am already in that kind of mood anyway."

"Yeah, well, I can imagine. So, as soon as he catches you if at any moment you want us to intervene, just make sure you say 'leave me' three times. Say it fast and clearly, so we are just behind the door, and we can come and catch him quickly, okay?"

"Leave me, leave me, leave me... Okay..."

"Remember, do never ask him any questions regarding what you may do, regarding the past... We will have his confession later. The big priority is..."

"Yes, I know, he must assault me."

"Unfortunately. Just do it as normal. Like a normal day... Like a normal date, just as you behave when you are with him, don't change anything."

"Okay..."

"Anyway, just leave on time... And don't forget, make sure the door remains open..."

"Yeah, I will. Thank you..."

And suddenly, her phone started to ring. And we heard it out loud, she still has her ringtone, some almost scary sci-fi ringtone. It surprised all of us, as we were approaching Ivry, her town. She grabbed her phone, and I could see the name displayed on the screen... Kelly. That's interesting, what does she want? Suddenly, as she also saw Kelly's name and made a disappointing face, she thought out loud:

"Oh, shit, Kelly is calling..."

"Put her on speaker!" I told.

"Yeah..."

And then she took the call. Obviously, she put her on speaker.

"Heya!" she replied.

"Hey, darling, what's up, you okay?"

"Yeah, I'm all good, what about you?"

"Not too bad... Not too bad... I just wanted to call you to take some news... It's been a while that I haven't seen you!"

Hum... The last time we saw her was yesterday, and I remember that as I kind of clashed with her, calling her pathetic. I wanted to slap her, but... No, it was not the moment. So, it's been a while, I am sure she was using that to somehow say that she misses Claire and... Yeah, trying to create a new relationship, whilst I remember that yesterday she spent her time ignoring her. She wanted to take some news... Yeah, I must admit, she's a good con artist (this is what makes her so dangerous), I mean, calling for some news, she doesn't care about her, and yesterday it seemed apparent. This was to create confidence, Kelly never calls for just taking some news, she always calls for something. I am sure her request will show up at some point. Claire immediately replied, obviously seeming detached from her, like she was upset that she ignored her yesterday. However, Claire's response remained relatively savvy:

"Yeah, I didn't see you today at school, I was wondering what happened to you..."

Clever, because she didn't fall into her trap, by saying "oh yeah I missed you", just saying that would give Kelly some power over her. As she acknowledged that she missed her, so she couldn't say no to anything, it's a kind of a psychologic trap, the purpose is "say it, you belong to me". Geez... My Claire is becoming good, she impresses me on how she manages to deal with all that shit. Now, things are into some kind of *status quo,* and nobody wins. And she doesn't take over, she has clear psychological limits now. This is why she replied:

"Oh, well, I've been quite busy. A friend of mine invited me out of Paris, we went to the Riviera on his yacht and I'm going to stay a couple of days there. You know... I'm just relaxing. We flew towards the south of France yesterday, I'm gonna stay a couple of days there!"

"Oh, sweet..."

"I was wondering, I'll be back on Saturday in Paris, and maybe we should do something together, with him. I spoke to him about you, and he is interested in meeting you!"

"Is he?" she remained without enthusiasm but was trying to hide it.

"Yeah. We could have a party together, what do you think?"

She suddenly stopped speaking and looked at me. I immediately said yes, without speaking, just by moving my head. Yes, because if she says no, it will be perceived as a kind of rebellion to Kelly. If she says that she'd think about it, it would be perceived as a postponement of decision, which would ultimately raise suspicions, and as she said yes, it means that she's still on the move with her. That's quite surprising, I mean... It was fast for her to go there. Well, on the other hand... But this is surprising that she called from a yacht in the Riviera... I am sure this is only on purpose to show off. She wants to tell her, "you see what I can do and what you can't do!", it's pure provocation. Kelly's problem is that she loves so much money that ultimately, she thinks that everybody loves money as she does, but this is not Claire's case. She's been trained a bit more... I mean, I'd take another approach at her place.

Well, on the other hand, I mean, taking this approach is not that wrong either. For the last four months, Claire changed and was slowly becoming Kelly's copy, from the outside. Always showing off as well, provoking me... So... I'm just re-educating her, to become whomever she was before. Anyway, Claire turned back and replied, this time more thoughtful:

"Oh, yeah, sure, why not. That could be fun..."

"Hey, darling, what's up? You look weird today?"

"Oh, no, I had an argument with Charlotte, but don't worry, you know that bitch. Yes, Saturday, where is it gonna be?" she refocused her.

"Yeah, she's a bitch. Hum, where is it gonna be, erm... I think he has a flat near the Champs-Elysées, I don't know the precise address, but as soon as I have it, I'll let you know."

"Great. Do you mind if I call you later, as I am kind of busy right now!"

"Oh, yeah, of course. I'll call you tomorrow anyway!"

"Sure. Have a lovely evening, darling!" Claire took her high-pitched voice to show her hypocrisy.

Free Expensive Lies: Prologue

"Have a lovely evening darling, I love you!"

Hum, she cut short that call. And, in the end, I could see on her face the signs of enormous regret. I don't know if it is regrets about this or me, but there was something. She seemed sad, was certainly containing her tears and did it pretty well. But at least I know: Kelly is due to come back to Paris on Saturday, fine. I'll be waiting for her. The thing is, there might be some change in between, I hope she manages to stay alive in between. Or she manages to find a way not to get arrested. Because whatever will happen, the next threat will be coming from me.

Anyway, as I saw her feeling weird, I started to joke:

"So, I am a bitch..."

"Cha, it was for... I just needed an excuse..."

"Yeah, yeah..." I suddenly took her in my arms. "Don't worry... I still love you, anyway. I just didn't know we had a fight!"

"No, me neither!" she smiled at me.

"So, Kelly is out of Paris... Interesting. Does Joris knows about this?" Heather asked.

"No idea..." Claire replied. "I don't even know anything about their business..."

"She's selling her arse to some rich fat cat..." I added.

"Whatever she does, it's not my problem..."

"Yeah..." Heather concluded, thoughtful. "Anyway, here we are."

And slowly, we managed to arrive in her street. Usually, there used to be her mother's car, a red coupé car that used to be parked in front of her house. But as the car wasn't there, then I assume that she was at work. On the other hand, she told me that exceptionally today, she has an early evening shift as she needs to cover one of her colleagues that caught the flu. So, she's due to come back home at around midnight. Fine.

Heather parked her car precisely at that place, and we got off the car. When I stepped outside, we heard some thunder banging in the sky, as it was becoming this time threatening. Claire stepped out as well, and immediately didn't run but walked fast to her door. The wind was loud, making the high trees next to her door and the leaves on it moving that it was still making this noise almost impersonating the rain. It was kind of nice to hear. And it was suddenly cold. A hard day finishing, the sun was gone, and the day would last certainly for a couple of minutes again, but no more, now we are entering in the most challenging part of the days, as days are becoming now slightly longer. As the sky was darkening more and more, it was time to get ready. Especially since we didn't have more than thirty minutes to get ready.

The plan for tonight is, once Claire is ready, she is due to leave her house at the same time as us. Our bodyguard will follow her, but from far, except in the metro. Meanwhile, Heather and I will take the same vehicle and go towards Stalingrad, and we will park in front of Joris's building. I mean, not in front, but in the street. I am still curious about the team, but she told me that they were already on their way. They are in a kind of white delivery van for enterprises, as a cover. And, as soon as we are here, we will start there. We are due to leave the house no later than 7.15 pm, so it leaves Claire plenty of time to catch the metro and go towards Stalingrad, and it will also leave us plenty of time to park there and wait for her to arrive. And right now, it is 6.45, so we have half an hour to finally get ready.

From the information we have and especially according to the text that Claire received from him after she asked for his address, Joris lives at the 5, *Rue du Département*, flat 4, which is right behind the station, she just have to exit the station, walk through the very small *Rue de Tanger* that is perpendicular to the station, turn and she would be here. It's a regular street, I mean, not a big artery, staying there would remain discreet. This street is, well... There are some new modern buildings mixed up with old-fashioned architecture building, and... I don't know Stalingrad; I mean I passed there a few times but... Well. For reaching there, she has to take her line, then has a few stops to actually take the fifth line and then she has a couple of stops. And plenty of time to stress a bit more and more.

Anyway, she opened the door, and we both entered. The house seemed cold; I mean... She doesn't have a big house, but still, when all the lights are turned off and everything is switched off, and especially since the sky is now dark grey and the rain is about to fall, it makes her place less hospitable than it already is. After she switched on the light, we noticed that there was a note on the table with thirty euros, I mean... One twenty and a tenner. We both came closer to check that note, and it was from her mum. "Hey darling, do you mind going to get some food so I can come home and eat something quick? I left you some cash so you can get whatever you want for yourself. I'll see you tomorrow, love you! – Mum." That was nice. Well... Well, then, after that we will have to get something... Unless we order a pizza. Well...

She took the money, and then went upstairs. As I left my bag yesterday downstairs when I came, I didn't need to follow her. And at the moment that I went to grab my bag, Heather arrived, I mean, she entered, carrying a big quite heavy black suitcase. I guess... The recorder stuff that she intends to install on Claire. I immediately grabbed the grey hoodie that I had in my bag, my pair of sneakers, and a pair of socks. When at the moment she dropped her case on the table, my phone, which was in my pocket, started to vibrate. Incoming call. I checked who it might be, and... then I saw... Mum. Damn, I forgot to tell her that I wasn't coming back home tonight. I took the call:

"Hey, darling..."

"Hey... hum, what's up?" I was quite embarrassed that she called.

"Well, I'm okay, waiting for my boy... erm... Are you coming home tonight?"

"Hum, to be honest, I don't think so. I mean, Claire is not feeling well, and I'd rather stay with her tonight. She needs me. I'll be home tomorrow."

"Oh... Okay. It's a shame, I wanted you to meet Frank... Especially since your sister is not here as she had to do some stuff with her friend or one of her friend, she told me a name but I don't recall... She told me she would come back home tomorrow."

"I know, I am sorry. I promised you I'd be there, and... And she's not good, she's been crying, and... I need to stay."

"I understand. Okay... Well, if you want, you guys can come for lunch tomorrow, or for dinner... Up to you, I mean, I took my day off tomorrow as we're going to the cops..."

"Certainly, yeah. I'll ask her, and, yeah, why not!"

"Sure. I can't wait for that. Say hi to Claire, and erm... Take care of her!"

"I will. Thank you, mum, for calling, and... I'll see you tomorrow then!"

"See you tomorrow!"

Whilst I was talking to my mum, I was hearing some noise upstairs. She was dressing up. Our call didn't last that long, and... Well, I don't know. She seemed quite excited to introduce me to her new boyfriend, but as she said that Clarisse is not gonna be there... That's surprising, I mean, earlier today, this morning, she told me that she was breaking up with her boyfriend and now she's not home... What's wrong with her today? That's surprising, I mean, I thought she was impatient to meet mum's boyfriend, and... I mean this is important, and since she's much more involved in this family than I am, well, that's surprising. Well, anyway, I wish she finds someone, or she is not alone with a bottle of beer or something. She seemed pretty pissed this morning when I had her on the phone, though. This is when I thought, things are definitely out of my reach tonight.

Anyway, I wore my hoodie above my clothes, removed my pumps and started to wear my socks and my sneakers. I pulled the phone back in my pocket when I heard Claire going to her bathroom, certainly to wear makeup. At the same time, I saw Heather, with her case open, testing her equipment. She handed me the microphone and asked me to speak into it, saying "test" several times so she could calibrate it with the headset that she had already attached to her left ear. It seems like some Bluetooth stuff, I mean... Except that, I don't know how it works, but... Well, this is IT stuff. Nothing that I may understand. Then I gave it back to her as it was calibrated and could hear properly. It took about a minute.

And then, I sat down on one of the table's chair, overlooking the stairs. She was still upstairs, but I guess, she was about to be ready. Heather remained stood up, still doing something on the micro, I didn't pay attention to what. Meanwhile, night fell. The streetlights started to be turned on, providing a yellowish light through the drawn curtains, and, although the house's lights were on as well, the harsh silence was somehow announcing a tough evening upcoming. It was now seven, she's been preparing herself, for now, fifteen minutes, there were fifteen minutes left before we take off. I was cold, I mean, as radiators were off and given the fact that her living room and her dining room is a wide open space, so it becomes cold quite quickly, it doesn't keep any heat, I put my hands in my pockets as I started to freeze. Until... Seven zero five. The bathroom door from upstairs was being opened, and swiftly... She came downstairs. And I saw her now.

Slowly, she went downstairs. I was really surprised. To be honest, she was stunning, she was really beautiful. And, well, I couldn't take my eyes off of her. I thought she would be much more provocative, but no. And, obviously, under different circumstances, she would show up like this in front of me, it would be tough for me to resist. The thing with her is, she's already beautiful, I mean according to my standards she's fantastic, and she has a powerful charm. Now, she was wearing a black skirt, tightened up by a shiny and thick belt. Above that, a white shirt with small black dots over it. She combed her hairs, having them very straight and long, she didn't tie it, and, well, her makeup was showing her excessively more beautiful. She was wearing dark tights, and now, on her left hand she was carrying her black high heels and on her other arm was carrying her black dark trench. And hum... I don't know, I mean... Her red, glossy lips, her foundation all over her face and her black eyes, I mean, yeah, as I said, under different circumstances... She didn't look like what she certainly thought she would be, but she looks different. I mean, even the other day, when we were at Kleber, when things changed between us, at that moment she was stunning. Oh, Joris will love it. Unfortunately, that outfit will be associated with a tough moment for her, certainly for a long time. I think her next appointment with her psychologist is scheduled in two or three days, but... Still.

At the moment she arrived finally downstairs, she dropped everything on the floor and went towards Heather. I just couldn't conceal my feelings:

"Wow, you are stunning..." I remarked.

"Of course, I am..." Claire smiled at me, but this was ironic. "I look like a whore!"

"Oh, don't say that..." Heather was close and had the device in her hand. "I have seen worse. Anyway, take a seat, and open your shirt!"

"Yeah..."

Hopefully, she's going to be escorted tonight, because, going to Stalingrad with that outfit, and God only knows what would happen to her. But deep down I was feeling jealous. I mean, I am not jealous, but... I am not a jealous person at all, I don't care, I don't care at all, I mean... A bit, but not. Anyway, she came to sit next to me when I could smell her perfume. Hum, she perfumed herself. Well, on the other hand, everything must look normal for tonight, he thinks it's just a date, and, whenever he will see her, I am sure he won't resist. It will drive him mad. I mean, it would drive me mad. She sat down, opened her shirt when Heather started to install the wiretap in her bra. And, I saw, it's true that the device is tiny, I mean, when I was testing it, it was so small that I almost dropped it on the floor. But when she told me the price of the thing (okay... I mean, I can buy a thousand of this, but we don't have time for that tonight) that I was really careful. And when she was doing this, she continued to brief her... again, to ensure that things are perfect for tonight:

"So, remember... What I told you, no questions, just... Let him drive you. And make sure the door remains open, as we will enter anytime..."

"I just want this to be over. And, yeah, don't worry, I will distract him enough."

"Oh, well... This is gonna be quick, trust me. From now on, you just have to take the metro, going to him, don't forget to say the four 'leave me', and... That's it. Then, we catch him, and you girls can go home, get some food, relax, sleep..."

"If you want, we'll stop by a pizzeria," I suggested. "So, we can eat quickly..."

"I don't feel like I'm gonna be hungry after that, but... Yeah, if you want... I just want to be home fast after that. Oh, yeah, we will have to stop by there, as mum wants to eat something."

"Oh, I can drop you home if you want. I mean, it's gonna be quick for me!"

"That would be lovely. Drop us here..." Claire asked.

"Sure... Here you are, you're all set!"

"Yikes!" she showed some hidden enthusiasm that was probably fake.

"So, let's catch a pimp!" I showed the same excitement.

Since it was raining outside, we decided to drop her at the metro station, to avoid her ruining her makeup. She still had an umbrella, but, well... Heather started eavesdropping by switching on her headset so she could listen to her, and now... Claire went to get her coat, her shoes, and we were ready to go. She still took her umbrella, and then we went outside. Heather unlocked her car with her key, and we rushed towards her car. I put my hood on, and for this time I jumped in front, and her at my place in the back. As we jumped in the car, we both wondered where was the bodyguard, but as soon as Heather finally locked the door of her house (as she gave her the key, she had to gather all her stuff in the case but it didn't take long), she came in the car after and told us after we asked that he was already waiting for her at the station. He will escort her.

She put her stuff in the backseat, and we started to drive. First stop, the metro station. As it's five minutes' walk from here, it wasn't long. In between, I noticed that she started to breathe harder, as the hour was coming close and the stress was now harder than ever because, from now on, she's all alone, we are just in the back, but she's not supposed to see us until we finally catch him. That's a kind of weird adventure ahead, but that's still an adventure. In the end, we can still be proud of what we've done. She ignited the engine, and we started to go.

The problem with Heather is that I don't know where she learned how to drive, but she was a fast driver. I mean, we were almost clung to our seats, especially now. Well, on the other hand, she's used to driving fast when she had to pursue someone. The thing is, Stalingrad is quite far away from here, and we are supposed to arrive before Claire, as we cannot be late. If she arrives before us, we are fucked, I mean, not totally, but we need to supervise her arrival. And as she was taking public transports and we were by car; we should be arriving before her. Especially now, we are freshly out of the congestion hour, so I hope this is not going to be that hard. Even if... Well, seven, it's still quite congested. But, well, anyway, as she surprised me on finding hidden streets of Paris at rush hours, I am sure she will find a way to sneak to Stalingrad.

Anyway, after maybe less than five minutes, we arrived in front of the metro station. It was fairly busy, I mean, more people going out than coming in, so... I don't think the metro might be congested. Either way, she received the instruction to inform her in real-time on where she was. She gave me a map of the metro so I could follow her, but she has a precise itinerary to follow. We arrived, and before she leaves, Heather finally... informed her that...

"Okay, Claire, here is your destination... And the guy with the suit, this is your bodyguard, he will remain close to you until Stalingrad. Please travel not too far away from him."

"Okay... Thank you for the ride."

"No problem. Now, good luck, and we will see you soon, okay?"

"Thank you very much. See you soon then!" she said as she left the car.

Because we are still scared of her betraying us at the last minutes. But I don't think so. On the other hand, right now, Heather was wearing at her chest her card of Police consultant. Claire got off the car, went to her bodyguard, and as I couldn't hear where she was as I didn't have the headset, we restarted, this time, to the meeting point with her colleagues.

I don't know who she hired as a bodyguard, but I was surprised. It was exactly in Men in Black, I think she hired a private security company, because... Or maybe they are cops, but special forces. As bodyguards provided by the police are just wearing casual clothing, no, this guy had a kind of special suit, I am sure made bespoke. At a glance, I mean, if I wouldn't know that he was a bodyguard, I would guess that he was someone important or something like that. A tall, white guy, no beard, hairs cut short, with sunglasses (although it was the night and raining...), with an imposing build, I mean, I wouldn't honestly piss off that guy.

After we left and were now driving northbound, the rain started to decrease, which was good. It was still very cold, and now the darkness was taking over the streets. She managed to avoid any traffic lights, although she couldn't avoid them all. And she was speeding up. I was wondering, as French roads are stuffed with automatic radars, what will happen if she gets caught? Because I was checking the speedometer from times to times, and as the legal speed limit within the town is no more than fifty kilometres per hours, she was ways above that. She must have discounts over fines, I guess, as a cop consultant... I mean, I think. I hope for her. Otherwise, I'm curious about the price of our journey. But this was something I didn't want to ask. I mean, don't bother with that. Anyway, I think this car must have been lent by the police or something, so I guess that before sending the fine through the post... They may be thinking about this. If it's the case.

But right now, my thoughts were elsewhere. As we took another way to avoid the Seine banks and thus to avoid the traffic, we passed underneath the *Boulevard Périphérique* to finally reach Paris. There was astonishingly a lot of people in the streets. And, well, at the same moment, she told me that Claire's metro barely left the station, we were far too much in advance. But it's ways better. And after she informed me about this, I suddenly asked:

"So, where are your friends, the other cops you promised us?"

"I told you they're already there. Just waiting for us..."

"Oh... You guys are well organised..."

"Of course. Listen, this is the operation of my career, I mean, I play a lot on this. And for once, it seems that we are leading the situation, so, yes, I am quite excited, and I made sure that we would catch him!"

"You never caught anybody in this investigation?"

"No, never. This is why catching him, it's like the biggest achievement... It's just incredibly important. If we do not have him tonight, then... But I feel like we will have him. Claire is perfect, and you guys played an elaborate plan, nobody has suspected anything so far."

"Yeah. We will see if it pays tonight..."

"I hope it will... I truly hope!"

"So do I."

We entered Paris through the 13th Arrondissement. From now, as the streets were dark, I was more feeling like, everybody was just going home. At that moment, as we managed to avoid big arteries of the capital for the reason of congestion and also to avoid a maximum of traffic lights, but even, many flats were now lit, and, yeah, slowly, Paris was dining and going to bed, bracing for the following day. We passed near the Austerlitz train station. It wouldn't be that long before we arrive, we just have to follow Paris's canal and we will reach our destination. But the thing is, in between, Claire was slowly reaching the Station *Place d'Italie*, where she was supposed to change for the fifth line. But she definitely wouldn't be in advance.

Whilst we crossed Austerlitz Bridge to reach the opposite bank of the Seine River, I asked... I don't know why, but I was curious:

"What's that car by the way?"

"Oh, this? This is just an unmarked car that the police lent me. I mean, as you know I am collaborating, and... That reminds me, open the glove compartment..."

"Why, what?"

"There is your badge, we made you a consultant tonight, so you can be here for the arrest of Joris. Just, wear it."

"Oh, okay."

It was 7.45 when, after having crossed the Seine river and followed Paris's St-Martin Canal, we finally reached our destination. At the moment we arrived, Claire was still in the metro but was not long before coming, she just had three stations before arriving.

The thing was, ironically, as Joris's building was maybe five metres away from where we were parked, we could see Joris's flat and window from where we were. And, at the moment, his window was open, but he was inside his flat, and all the lights were on in his flat. We couldn't see what was from the inside, but one thing was sure: his flat didn't have any balcony. Heather confirmed to me that he was renting a small studio flat, and he had just a living room, a bathroom and a bedroom, nothing more. His place was really small. I asked her, how does she know that, and she told me that she went there a month ago to place a wiretap on his place. He still didn't discover any of them. But she couldn't disclose where she placed them, but from at least a month, they are on his case, they identified him, certainly thanks to Claire's work... Or someone else. But now, from what I was seeing, it was just a simple flat, no music, only normal light... Well. I guess I'll find this out soon.

Curiously, in the street, there was some music, I mean, the street was not that silent. However the street remained quite gloomy, I mean, nobody was walking down there, there was just a series of flats where the lights were turned on, cars parks on the banks of each footpath, and overall a big silence, I mean, except this music. It was some disco music being played, no idea which tune it was, but it was the only loud noise that was currently there. However, the street seemed long, although it was crossed by several other streets, at the moment there was strictly no traffic, no pedestrians, nothing. Just us, waiting for Claire. Astonishingly, no drug dealers, homeless, or weirdos of that kind. For now, Claire was relatively safe. We were parked just in front of a big white van, and Heather took out a walkie-talkie from somewhere. She turned it on, and said something in French, mentioning that we were there, but using some specific code. Why? We still don't know who's listening, and Joris might be listening. The order was, as soon as Claire enters the building, we get off our cars, obviously, we must keep under surveillance his window in case he sees us, passes through the small rubbish room that was in front of us, open, we enter the building through this way, and make our way to his flat. As he is living on the second floor, of the three floors that compose this small building, reaching there would be fast. Claire is supposed to take the lift, and we are supposed to take the stairs. In this order, we wait in front of his door, until Claire triggers the signal, we come in, we catch him, and we get out of there. Meanwhile, whilst we enter, Claire's bodyguard is charged with spying on him through his window, making sure nothing would happen. And making sure that, yeah... Claire doesn't leave his flat through that precise window.

Ironically, he was living near Saint-Louis Hospital. Claire's mum works there, at the A&E department, in the admission bureau. The problem is; if something happens to her, and if we have to call emergencies, Claire would be transferred here, and... Her mum is gonna have suspicions about what we've been doing this evening. Well, in case she wants explanations, we will tell her that we've been with the police so there is no need to talk to the cops tomorrow. I mean... I prefer not to think about it. He'd better not touch her, because, although we're aware that she's running a high risk, and potentially a life-threatening risk... But if she's too traumatised, or I don't know in which state she will end up that mission, but... I hope that a journey through the hospital would be evitable tonight. And, even if I am really scared, I am happy to be here... Because waiting at home for the result, it would make me explode.

It was now 7.50, and Claire just arrived at Stalingrad metro station, *Boulevard de la Villette*, just behind the street. She's due to arrive in a minute. And now, Heather slightly opened her window. There was still nobody in the street, it made it certainly spookier than ever. Astonishingly, when we passed minutes earlier, I found the neighbourhood relatively quiet, I mean, except on that Boulevard, it was busy as usual, with much homeless sleeping in their sort of blue body-bags-in-become on their cardboards. Here we were, the decisive moment. And, surprisingly, as we were parked in front of the rubbish area, it was bloody smelly. I mean, it stinks. And as the humidity was floating in the air, like droplets above boiling water, it made the temperature certainly colder than ever. At this moment, I started to wear my hood, and I was observing the street. Claire is due to arrive in front of us, this is the shortest way from the station from here, so we will see her arrive... I mean, above all the cars and everything.

Free Expensive Lies: Prologue

At the same time, Joris finally showed up at his big window. He has a French window, a big one, the thing is there is a guardrail in front, protecting him from falling. At that moment, I was feeling like, hopefully, our windows were tinted so he couldn't see us. From here he seemed relaxed, he was wearing a blue top with some inscription it, from here I couldn't see what was written, and a kind of black shiny short, I mean, shiny... Not really, but, at least, yeah. He had a beer in his hand, a can of beer, which tells a lot about his style, he was seeking beer some kind of self-confidence, and a can of beer means that he wants to drink fast, and not getting drunk but being at least tipsy enough to piss off my girlfriend. The way his jaws were, slightly tights, clearly meant that he had the intention to annoy her, pissing her off. But, as he showed up at his window, with his beer in his hand, and given the fact that he was dressed this way, it means that he was certainly suspicious of nothing. He seemed relaxed, but somehow angry, at least... The problem is, he thought that he was the dominant person. That was obvious, I could see that from here, the way he was holding himself at the guardrail, leading with his arms, observing the street like he was the lord of the street, yeah, there was some self-satisfaction. Moreover, he knows that having sex with Claire, certainly the most beautiful of the three of us (Kelly, her, and I) was extremely rewarding, and... I am sure of this; he intends to rape her. That's what his dominant posture was telling me.

And then, my girlfriend finally arrived. He saw her and suddenly disappeared from his watchtower. Claire was walking, not with confidence at all, but she was focused on what will happen. Surprisingly, for the very first time, I saw her lowering her head whilst walking down. Submission? I don't think so, I think that she was so focused that she was repeating in her mind the role she would play in a couple of minutes today. She was walking normally, quite slowly, actually, and when Claire walks slowly, it means that she doesn't want to go where she's heading. Well, like everybody, same for me, (everybody can make this analysis), but it was mostly showing intense stress. And, given what I have seen from Joris, and what I see from her, I don't think this will last exceedingly long before we catch him. I couldn't see his bodyguard... Which was a good thing. I guess. But he may be violent, I mean, towards her, he will be... Hopefully, we are here.

Her coat was closed, and, slowly, she was reaching the entrance of his building. An entrance that looked like most Haussmann buildings in Paris, with a dark green high and heavy door. She opened her coat and checked on her pockets. All I could hear was the noise of her shoes and her keys that she was shaking in her pockets. And then, she arrived at the threshold step of his building's door. Here it was, now, she was knocking on Satan's door. I mean, knocking... She pushed on some button of the digital code next to the door. There was the noise of an incoming call... And when he answered:

"Hey darling, it's Claire!"

"Hey, love. Just push the door, I'm on the second floor, left door!"

"Okay!"

Then, we heard a "dzzz", indicating that the door was unlocked.

Surprisingly, she overcame the stress quite easily. On the other hand, when she was younger, when she was a teen, her mother pushed her to go to follow some theatre courses, where she played numerous characters. She did that for a couple of years, so, even if she's not a hypocrite person or she's not like me a pathological liar, she does have a clear ability for lies, and she is so good at it that when she lies, you can only believe it. This is why, she was the same when she used to go to those courses, lowering her head and thinking for long moments, she was now playing a character, it was obvious. Claire is good at playing comedy, she could be an excellent actress. The only problem is, when things escalate, she doesn't know how to cope with stress. This is why using "hey darling" with a joyful and playful tone was a clever tactic. This is why she's the best for that role. Even better than me.

Anyway, she entered. I immediately unfastened my belt, just like Heather, who took her walkie-talkie, and immediately started to say:

"Okay, guys, the falcon flew over the nest!"

"Copy that, time to protect the eggs!" a male voice answered.

I looked one last time at Joris's watchtower, and although windows were still open, he was not there anymore. I guess, he was waiting for her now. We immediately jumped out of the car, and swiftly, we headed towards the rubbish area. We rushed, but Heather and the guys in the van behind made sure to close the door silently. So did we, and as I was stepping out of the car from the side of the road, I made sure to crouch like them for passing behind the vehicle. Either way, we were so ready that in certainly less than five to ten seconds, we were all behind the rubbish area, so an area where Joris couldn't see us anymore. I just followed the move.

We are not supposed to see him, I mean, in case of an unfortunate meeting, their order is to arrest him straight away, because as Heather said, our testimonies are enough to send him to prison for a while. But meeting him now, especially since he's waiting for my girlfriend in his place, it's very unlikely. Once we were in the rubbish area, well, the smell was what became the most disturbing. I mean, I don't know when they came to collect the rubbish for the very last time, but it was appalling. The thing is, this rubbish area was quite wide, the entrance was just two shallow walls and the entire area was a kind of perpendicular compound leading to a door. But there was a lot of stacked rubbish bags, and even the floor was sticky, I have no idea of what could have leaked on it, and to be fair, I don't want to know. Moreover, as there was strictly no roof over the rubbish area (it was outdoors... The neighbourhood must love it I guess) and as we were on our way to enter the building and some of them were stacked underneath the windows, and also as it rained an hour ago... And I understood why all those windows above us were all closed. I was smelling a cocktail of putrefying rubbish, pee on the floor and certainly dead rats, I was wondering if some homeless people would sleep here as it's relatively easy to access here.

So, we were five. Three cops in uniform (I assume they were constable or something, they had their guns in their hands as they were instructed that Joris might be armed and dangerous so may need to hit back in the sad event of an attack, Heather that was carrying no weapons and me closing the procession. The three cops were leading us for safety issues, but they were still monitored by Heather, who was the head of the operation. She said we may enter the building. Curiously, I noticed that the cops didn't have their normal big rangers, instead, they had some other shoes that made that as they were walking, they made no noise or were less audible, it turned them into ghosts. Heather had the same black shoes, whilst I was really careful not to make any noise, even if mine weren't that noisy. After having found a way to sneak between those rubbishes, like slaloming, making sure that we would make the less noise as possible because we also wanted to avoid the neighbours that I think were all back from work now, the leading cop finally opened the door that led to the inside of the building. One by one, we entered. I was the last. They actually picked the lock of the door as it was closed, and as the lock was some big old-fashioned stuff easy to pick, so I guess it wasn't that bad for them, but still doing that took a couple of seconds. At the moment we entered, Claire finally managed to be in the lift and was now on her way to Joris's flat.

Anyway, as we entered, we find ourselves in a kind of narrow dark entrance. Facing us, the main door, overlooked by a kind of small semicircle-shaped window that let the night and the streetlights gloomily coming lightening the entrance. Yet again, this place seemed deserted, I mean, I am not even sure the big bulb of light upon us was even working, especially given the fact that I could find cobwebs all around it, showing themselves in the reflection of the gloomy moonlight coming from out there. The place was certainly three metres large upon seven or eight long, and on our left, we found in this order the stairs, a hole in the wall leading straight to the other floors, the lift a bit far away from everything, (an old lift, I mean... It didn't seem recent at least, surprisingly it was working), and on the right, certainly in the middle of the wall, a door leading I think to some flat. I think because there was on the top of the door a small metallic plaque indicating "1". Next to it, there was a bike, that also seemed used, it was chained to the radiator just behind it. But curiously, there was strictly no noise around, I was almost feeling like in a capsule, I mean, other than the noise of the street ahead, and of us breathing, we didn't hear anything. I remember, when I was outside, there was some light coming out of the window that was next to the door. But this place seems to be well soundproofed. This is something that we could use to our advantage.

But when I mean derelict, maybe it is a bit strong. But this is not recent, that's sure: although walls were painted in white, at certain places the paint was crumbling. So, something is sure, this building belongs to an independent landlord and everybody living here is renting the place. Or, if we have any landlord here, I guess then that those people must be fifty or above and bought the place a long ago, as... How would buy a flat here, I mean, seriously? One thing was sure, even we could smell a kind of humidity mixed up with mould perfume floating in the air here, this place needed a major refurbishment, as it was certainly on its way to becoming insalubrious. This, I mean, having seen that, it must not be something that would reassure Claire as it's the first time she's coming in there. The atmosphere here, I mean, especially since we could see that the floor was kind of sticky, or dirty, there were traces of certainly weird activities here (I mean, drug dealers or homeless sleeping here, as accessing the building was relatively easy), it must not have reassured her at all.

But we didn't have time to dwell on details, we had to reach the second floor. We took the stairs, immediately on our left. Same, again, stairs were not lit, it was total darkness, but we could still see, as Heather used her exceptionally soft light from her phone. The stairs were relatively narrow, I mean, on the other hand, that building does not seem big, and all the steps were I think made of stone or something like this. No carpets, nothing. As we were progressing one by one, leaving a gap of certainly one metre from each other, we all walked one behind the other, keeping the same order that we had from the beginning. Amongst us was reigning a deep silence, we didn't want to be heard by anyone. But still, moving through the stairs, even if we tried to remain silent, we had to go quite fast (we didn't run, we walked normally), but the friction caused by our trousers and other clothing items that we were wearing still produced a slight noise. We weren't finally that silent, but we remained discreet.

Anyway, I closed the parade. We walked through those stairs, I just followed them. At some point we turned, (the stairs were disposed of in a small spiral), and we reached the first floor, still the same. Pretty much the same style as downstairs, the only two different things were that instead of the main door there was a big window, with a small guardrail and a small planter hung on the tiny balcony, (which contained only faded flowers... I wonder who is in charge of taking care of it), but yet everything was still in the same style of this. This time, next to the lift, there was another door, leading to a flat, as it was written on it "two". The door in the facing wall was number three, and nothing was attached to the radiator, unlike the first stairs. No bike. Curiously, unlike downstairs, on the threshold of the two flats here were two different doormats, I cannot tell precisely which colour was which as we were still in the darkness and they both appeared as light and dark, however, I'd say that the flat number three had the most recent, so I assume a family must be living here. But still, same, on that floor, no noise from the inside of the building, although I know that everybody was there. I mean, I was feeling, as we could see a ray of light from each door frame.

Anyway, this was not our floor. Once arrived, we took on our right to access the second floor, where Claire was there. At the precise moment we arrived on the first floor and started turning to access the second floor, we heard Joris's door closing. At that moment we stopped for a second, as... A door being opened is a danger. And, yes, she closed the door and probably recalled that she had to make sure that it was left open. I mean, we heard the door closing, but not being locked. On the other hand, I was furtively thinking, Joris must have been severely disturbed by seeing her outfit, and given what I've been saying when I was still into the car down there, I am sure his impatience and his envy must have been taking over. But the door was closed, and in whispering, Heather started, in French, "it's all clear, we can proceed!". Now, here we were. She's in there. And, immediately, once we all reached the floor, we took on the right, to finally access the third floor.

And... The time was right ahead. My heart was beating faster and harder in my chest, anxiety was strong for my girlfriend, and tension was at its peak. We were now closer than ever to catch Joris and bring to our cluster an end. One thing was odd, here, though. And I think we may be too early, but throughout all the building, we could smell a cocktail of mould, humidity, pee, and God knows what. Exactly like in a regular metro station here in this area. And, although the smell in the rubbish area was more pronounced, here things were different. But still disgusting. If only I knew, I should have taken a face-covering mask. But this time, more slowly, we all walked through the stairs, to reach the second floor. But, regarding the smell, however, it was telling a lot about him: I don't know how much he makes monthly in terms of pay, but, living within Paris, I assume that rent here must be quite cheap. Because so far from what I have seen from him is mostly, he has a nice car, yes, he certainly paid it well or maybe borrowed to have it, but I think he's mostly the kind of person that borrows money. I assume, also, that the incomes he generates from his pimping activities must be paid in cash to avoid taxes (and mostly to avoid justifications to the tax office, because I assume that they must be asking how he managed to get that money), he must have hidden money somewhere. Because, okay, he's just like drug dealers, they may have nice cars but are living in slums... I don't know where he must be hiding his money, but... To be honest, I would be here and having incomes from my job, plus having incomes from this kind of activities, well, I honestly wouldn't live here. Which leads me to this: if he's hiding all this money (because he makes a lot of money, maybe he didn't make that much with me but given that Claire, at some point, was almost sleeping with some guy every night...), he must have refunded previous debts or stuff like this. Anyway, as someone used to say, follow the money and you will reach the source of all lies.

Anyway, as we jumped upstairs, this time much more quietly, we finally discovered where he lives. After having walked through these narrow stairs, exactly the replica from the one in the basement, pretty much, with the same crumbling paint and the smell of decay everywhere, we finally reached his floor. His floor was pretty much the same configuration as the first floor: at the place of the window, another window, with the same planter and the same wilted flowers, the same doors at the same spaces, but those named differently. The one next to the lift was number 4, and the other number 5. Finally, he lived in number four. I thought that he lived in number five... Meh, anyway.

At the moment we arrived, the three armed cops started to surround his door: the first facing his door, the second stuck himself along the wall of the window, and the third on the opposite side, in front of the lift's command, next to the doors. Heather and I, just behind, waiting now, as the moment of truth was starting. From there, curiously, we were hearing some loud electronic music, all the kind of music that Claire and I hate. But as it was fairly loud, and as we didn't hear it downstairs, we started to hear it when we were passing through the second stairs, so I assume that inside must be a damn nightclub. But the music had two purposes, either putting himself in some vibes, or the second, covering his possible crimes. Heather and I remained in front of the stairs, and the two cops had their guns in their hand, ready to intervene. Unfortunately, I was unable to hear what was happening inside, so I had no clues of what was happening, nevertheless, I was still relieved that... Claire is next door, and we are here for her.

As we waited for her signal, I took the time to observe around me: this time, there was only a doormat in front of his door, not the neighbours. And as I saw no lights under the door and strictly no doormat, and even no personal belongings anywhere, (I was not feeling as well any vibes or some possible people living here), I assume that the flat next to his must be vacant. Especially since the number five was written by hand and I could with difficulty distinguish that the small plaque similar to those on every door has been recently unscrewed. So, yes, it means something, someone left here recently. That's good, at least we won't be bothered by them. Now the danger could come only from upstairs, as there was still a floor above us. At the place whereon the basement was the door for the rubbish, there was nothing, but cobwebs on the ceiling. Regarding the stairs, surprisingly, this one was much more in a derelict state than the two others, but astonishingly it was smelling less funny. I quickly looked at his doormat, and... I only saw a dark, with literally nothing on it, nothing written like the two on the floor underneath. Most flats within buildings have a doormat in front of their doors, at least in France, and usually, doormats are a glance of the personality of the person (a very quick). And, here, nothing, I guess just a beige doormat, with nothing on it. I wouldn't be surprised if I find out that there are no pictures on the walls of his flat or anything. This guy has an obvious lack of personality, but this can be caused by a lot of things.

There were also no obvious signs of anything on him here. Except for this doormat that mentioned that someone was living here, nothing. I don't know if he receives people at his place, as, well, his doormat was basically old, the carpet pile of this stuff were all flat and thus it may indicate that it could be fairly old, but on the other hand, I could see the label stitched to it... And letters seemed well-printed, at least one could read perfectly that he recently bought it in an Ikea. So, he bought it recently. Discreetly, I came closer to it, and, well, what I could mostly see that the footsteps seemed to be most of the time the same, trainers shoes... Except that I could see heeled shoes, but it could be Claire... But this was interesting. Most of the marks left on this mat were coming from the same shoes, so it indicates that he doesn't have a visit to his flat quite often. Second, I checked the frame of the door, very quickly, and I could see something interesting: above the handle to open it, certainly at human height, maybe a bit below, there was some... hole. It was tiny, I mean... If you don't pay attention to it, you won't see it, but there was a tiny hole. This tiny hole was however not connected to the inside, so it wasn't a kind of peephole. Cops can do that, but I assume that he is inserting something barely visible, except to him into this hole once he leaves and locks the door, like a broken toothpick or something, and whenever he leaves and comes back, he checks if it is still here, to check on whether his flat has been visited when he was away. So... This must be showing some form of paranoia, but this paranoia must be explained by several things, I think the biggest must be, he knows for whom he is working. Probably he doesn't know his identity, but he knows his reputation, and he knows that this guy can kill people... And to kill him. To be honest... I am not even sure now that he knows who the blackmailer is.

I lowered my head again, and, from the inside of the door, I could hear them walking. I wonder what they could be doing. Heather started leaning against the wall, lowered her head, and was careful, at least, I saw her, she was paying attention to what was happening. No smile, no expression, she was poker-face at that precise moment. Also, I checked the frame of the door one more time, and I could see it, although walls seem to be thick, doors are relatively in a poor state and very thin and even if it was locked I am sure they could break it down by simply kicking at it. Usually, at every door floor, I could see two interruptions of the indoors lights that were passing through the frame, but now, only one. She made it successfully, she left the door open. Thus, passing would be easy. I stepped down for a few seconds because I was feeling like the intervention would be imminent. Despite the loud music, I was hearing them speaking through everything, however, I couldn't distinguish what they were saying, it was only seeming like the "hummmm, hummmm", nothing more. But I guess this was the reason why he also put the music that loud, he knows that it would make it more difficult for Heather to listen. If Claire was or would be sent for eavesdropping. So, this explains why Heather was so focused, she wasn't hearing that properly.

Then, suddenly, two things happened. Suddenly, I started hearing Claire moaning from inside of the door, speaking quite loudly, like she was complaining of something. And also, suddenly, I started hearing them both stops walking. So, he was probably assaulting her. And, at the very same time, Heather, with her hand, started to tell me to step behind her, as the intervention was imminent. I immediately stepped back her, as I don't want to prevent them to do their job, and when I jumped behind, I started to see the three cops, suddenly, becoming tenser. We were hearing what was happening, and I was hearing Claire almost shouting, or at least yelling of pain. Now was the moment, they want to catch him doing something bad... They will. Oh my god, everything worked out well. I heard Claire, I don't know, I don't know what he was doing to her, but hearing this voice was a huge pain for me, it was like I was being injured the harsh way. And, suddenly, certainly one second, two seconds, three seconds later, I heard her shouting very loud, "LEAVE ME!".

"Guys, it's green light" Heather started to say quite loud, "LET'S GO!"

Then everything went suddenly extremely fast: The cop in front of the door exploded the door with his foot, and the two on the side made their ways. He suddenly entered, and Heather and I came closer to the door. My heart was beating very loud like I was terrified, I literally couldn't move, as when the guy broke down the door, it made the noise of a very loud bang. And, from the inside, we started to hear them shouting, several times:

"POLICE! FREEZE!"

"DROP YOUR WEAPON!"

Wait, what? Weapon?

"Fuck you!"

"POLICE, DROP YOUR WEAPON, NOW!"

36 Until death do us part

// Joris's flat, near Stalingrad, Paris, 19th Arrondissement.

// Tuesday, 22nd of January 2013, 19:10

At the very moment they broke Joris's door, things dramatically changed.

I mean, I was still outside, with Heather, but their mission was clear, the capture of Joris. The only problem is, I mean, from what I heard, things didn't go as they were supposed to go, as I heard sentences such as "drop your weapon", so... It didn't reassure me. The problem was, I couldn't come inside, I was just not allowed to, and the thing was also that, I didn't know what kind of weapon he had if it was his firearm that he has from work, or if it's another kind of weapons like a knife or something. And from outside... I was exploding.

They were battling with him, for now, a minute. They were still pointing their weapon, and no bullet has been fired yet. The thing is, they can't fire any bullet. Something was curious, though, I could hear in his voice some panic. He was more panicked and was surprised by this, as it came out at the very wrong moment: as he was panicked, and as the threatening voice of the cops was ordering him to drop his weapon and he didn't, well... He's a cop, he's trained to resist to that pressure I guess, or he trained himself on his own already, but as I didn't hear any of them moving, I guess he must have been taking my girlfriend as a human shield and then... Is facing them. The problem was, cops used the word weapon and didn't use any other, so it doesn't mean anything, as I said, a weapon means a lot of tools. They would have been more accurate if they would have mentioned a pistol or a knife. They didn't. So it wasn't that helpful. Until that very moment, after an umpteenth threat from one of the three bulldogs he had in front of him, I heard that very precise threat, coming out from Joris. It changed everything:

"Leave her alone!" a cop said.

"YOU CAN KISS MY ARSE!" he replied in shouting.

"Leave her alone, I said! Drop your fucking weapon!"

"If you come closer, I swear to god that I will slit her throat straight away!" he replied this time with his panicked voice.

So, by a deduction, I guess that if he mentioned that he is about to "slit her throat", then his weapon is a dagger or a knife. The last time I checked, we can't slit any throat with a firearm, unless you're particularly good... or unbelievably bad. So, he has a knife, it's safe then. I mean, a knife against three small guns, well. To be honest I would have thought about the same, that he would have a knife, because, given his accurate sense of paranoia, he must be someone that hides his firearm in a very specific place, by the fear that someone might use it against him. A dagger or a knife is a more accessible option for him. Especially since he's been caught by surprise, he must have been taking the very first thing he had close to his hand, I mean, that would make sense.

Either way, even if he was panicked and caught by surprise, he was ready to fight or retaliate, and especially given that he was using Claire as a human shield, (I mean, that's what I think... That's what I would do if I were him), he was fucked, literally. The surprise was good, as he couldn't defend himself, and, if he attacks Claire, he will get caught. They will try to strike him, and they will be faster than him. Moreover, as I saw, police officers were wearing a bulletproof vest which means, I am sure as well, is strong enough against knives, if he tries to attack one of them, he will be caught by another, and... Whatever the scenario that will happen within minutes, he will get caught. The thing is, this stalemate can stay for hours, and we forgot to take someone especially important in that kind of hostage situation: a negotiator.

And, the problem is, none of the cops can negotiate at the moment. And even within the close future, as they are all three carrying stronger weapons than his and threatening him... Obviously, they want him to surrender, he needs to have someone that talks to him with care, attention, listening to him... Using psychology, overall. They are here to arrest him; they are not him to negotiate anything with him. They are just the handcuff part of the job, that's all. And Heather, I mean, I saw her, and she was reluctant to enter, or at least was waiting for the moment, she didn't want to enter into this right now.

And to be honest, I was almost really upset. I saw her, leaning on the wall, doing nothing, whilst the cops were there. I mean, I was not upset with her, I was just upset that for the last minute, maybe two minutes elapsed from the moment that they broke his door and from now, and I saw her, thinking, assessing the situation. The problem is that she couldn't intervene, as she was a cop, maybe, but she had no jurisdiction. The law was limiting her from intervening. Whilst me... Nothing prevents me from coming. She's my girlfriend, and I don't give a fuck about the law. Anyway, this guy will not do anything unless someone comes and talks to him, so... I think I proved that I am skilled enough to negotiate with him. Even if I may be the wrong person, and if he sees me, he will immediately think that this is a plot (which is, yeah, a plot...) but I am sure I can obtain something from him. He wants attention, I will give him all the attention he wants. This is why, once the situation calmed down for a second, out there, I immediately whispered to Heather:

"Heather, let me go..." I showed my impatience.

"No, Charlotte, I can't, they are gonna catch him..." she remained prudent.

"Let me go!"

"No!"

After all, Claire is my girlfriend. As I said many times to her, if I had to die for her, I don't care, as long as she's safe. And maybe the law prevents me, or their security bollocks prevents me from doing anything, but my girlfriend is hostage from this insane coward. Her life is being threatened, and I cannot stay here and waiting for her to get injured or, even worst, killed. And if I stay here, and something happens... She will never forgive me. And I won't forgive myself as well. So, fuck the law, I don't care. If I have to die for her, then I will. This is my duty, this is my moral responsibility, this is my commitment, she's in danger and I swore to protect her from any danger that may happen. So, fuck it, I'm going. This is why, now, with a different tone, determined, I immediately started to run around her, and said:

"You know what? Piss off, this is my girlfriend that is inside!"

"Charlotte, no!"

Whilst I ran, she wanted to catch me, but I've been faster, she couldn't. Now... I'm coming, honey. I'm coming to save you. It was just too late. And if I don't do that, this may take ages before reaching an outcome. As I don't see people carrying a gun having a deep sense of human psychology. Well, I do not have it either, but at least I am good at convincing people to do what I want them to do, so let's see if I can help here.

First of all, upon entering his flat, there was a kind of small corridor, certainly here for the purpose that stairs were just next wall, it wasn't long, certainly a few metres, three metres maximum, and yeah, that was going along the stairs. By accident I touched the wall as I had a swift loss of balance after rushing towards there, and, yeah, the walls were thick, I mean, it felt like it was made of heavy concrete or even stone. But I'd bet for concrete, as it was still smooth. Surprisingly, Heather remained on the threshold of the door, she didn't dare following me inside. Hum... Was she doing that on purpose? We just looked at each other, one last time before I reach the end of that corridor, and... We certainly said to each other, although it was by the transmission of thoughts, "Be not afraid, I can do it". On the other hand, I did it, I created that plan, so it's time now to put the cherry over the very top of the cake.

And then, I reached his studio flat. An exceedingly small room, I mean, it was ridiculously small. But how comes such a small place can welcome such an unbelievable mess? Let's start with the beginning. Along the other wall of the corridor, which was a simple partition made of plasterboard, there was a slightly big space, which was his bed. No bedside tables, just the bed. Even, the bed was not... I mean, no frame over it, over where he put his head, nothing. The bed was fitting the entire space available between that partition and another wall on the other side.

Surprisingly, the sheets were messy, the bed wasn't neat at all, and the colour... I mean, navy blue, for the cover sheet, and black for the pillowcase and the sheets... Well, no drawings, nothing that may suggest any sort of personality. Nothing. In my opinion, that navy blue would be an indication of personality, black was just a colour that he chose because he had no other options, but the navy blue was interesting. To me, it would be some colour that reassures him, so that would lead me back to his childhood. Lack of childhood? Lack of trust? That would explain his slight paranoia, and the hole in the door frame, he didn't have any childhood, so he lacks confidence. And overthrowing him would then be pretty easy.

In front of his bed, there was a big space, I'd call it his small living room. Let's assume that he uses his bed as a sofa as well, there was curiously on his very rectangular and made of steel table (although the plate of the table was made of glass... I mean, I guess) an unbelievable mess. Between letters that weren't open, other open letters, and it was invoices or unpaid bills that were claimed but nothing that was related to his job, there was a lot of papers on this table. The thing is this table isn't particularly big. I could also find the controller of his console, the TV remote, and many of the small containers of premade dishes that you buy in supermarkets when you're too lazy to cook. Given the fact that there was three of them and also given the fact that in the two other the sauces of the food seem dried, then I guess that he never cooks. Although, I took a quick look at his kitchen that was right behind me, right behind the guys so on the left-hand side when you enter his flat, and it was really dirty. Dishes weren't clean and were all stacked in the sink, the oven seemed to be dirty and the gas stove as well. There was even still a pan on it. Surprisingly, a clean pan. Anyway, messy table, apparently unpaid invoices, bank statements that didn't seem to show up a lot of money in his account, he is financially struggling, which is curious. I mean, for a pimp...

But struggling financially says a lot: cops are usually the kind of people that are overall organised in their lives, I mean, I remember, my dad used to have a friend that was a cop in the south of France, and from times to times we used to go to eat at his place and, yeah, I recall, his place was organised. And, even, cops are like the military (as a personality type), hierarchy is something particularly important, orders as well, so they are usually the type of person that is not messy at all because they don't want to mess up at work. Being a cop is something that changes and greatly affects your life, given the fact that you are responsible for the security of others, you are somehow representative of the law to a lesser degree than a lawyer or a judge or an attorney, so this is why I do not understand his messy place. People with responsibility aren't that messy, usually. But for him... Although he must be something like thirty years old, if he is messy at this age, it means that this is something that comes from his childhood. A lack of trust and a lack of confidence, a lack of organisation... I mean, when I see this place, this is what I feel. However, I noted something particularly important, his name, his full name was Joris Olivier. No middle name, nothing of the sort. Usually, you have your full name appearing on bank statements, as banks are particularly focused on your identity whenever you open an account, for fiscal purposes, and especially in France. That says a lot, the fact that his family name is a first name, the fact that he has no middle names and the fact that this place is messy, everything is connected. Everything has a link since we are in the heart of what his personality is: his living place, it's even more relevant.

Facing the bed and his dining-coffee-messy-office table, whatever he calls it, there was a big gap, at least two people could pass at a time, and there was his TV, put on a small kind of seat, looking like a chair, with underneath his console and some video games boxes. It wasn't a surprise, all the video games he has been violent. At the moment, his TV was on, the console was on as well, but he was using some kind of streaming services to get music, and it was loud. This leads me to think, whenever he is off or at home, he must be spending a considerable amount of time playing video games, maybe as an anger-frustrated way to express himself, it helps him to calm down. The thing I learned from Claire is that he works for the 19th arrondissement precinct, and this arrondissement has the reputation for being a violent one because mostly of immigration issues. So, he must be having frequently bad days at work, this is certainly why he is a pimp. And given the fact that he has no confidence to face them up... Oh, yeah, being a pimp gives him all the power he wants over us. He releases his frustration over us, this would explain why he was so mad at me when we were in the toilets at Kleber and he drugged me. Now I can frame him a bit more: he is frustrated because he cannot tell his superiors to fuck themselves, so he takes his revenge over us, and especially over Claire. But why Claire? Oh, I am sure this is related to his childhood, I have a theory, but I am not sure it is right... yet. This would also explain why he spends much time on videogames. I mean, this is a supposition. But... Well, given the fact that the controller is on his table as well as the remote, so that says a lot about the time he might be spending on it.

On the right-hand side of all that, after the table, the bed, and the TV, exactly facing the small kitchen, there was his big window. His French window.

Slightly open, and it was in a pretty deep recess, deep enough to leave a big gap also. And now, this is exactly where he was standing. As I said, with my girlfriend as a human shield. The three cops, as well as me, were on the recess of the kitchen and the bathroom, as there was a small door next to the small kitchen. Pretty much, the table was separating us. A kind of a border, that nobody should cross at the moment. If someone crosses it... There will be consequences.

Claire had the knife under her throat and was terrified. Her face was red, and she was containing her tears. Deep down, she was praying that nothing would happen to her. She has not been injured, that's the most important, however, her skirt was slightly lifted, so I assume this is proof that he attempted to rape her. We now have what we want. I took a quick look at his knife, and it was a basic kitchen knife. As he points this towards her throat, I then guess that his first intention isn't to stab her but to slit her throat. Which would take time, as this knife wasn't sharp enough. But this depends on the strength he applied, of course. But he won't do that, I mean, using Claire as a human shield is mostly because he sees that cops facing him are carrying pistols and in case someone starts to fire, then Claire would be the first attacked. He is just using her as a mean to put pressure on us. He won't attack or injure her. Otherwise, he would have done that already. I mean, if I follow my theory, that makes more sense that he would harm her sexually rather than physically. Because Claire reminds him of someone. Raping her would give him satisfaction, killing her would give him frustration. He knows that. This is why even pushed to the extremes, he will not harm her. Never.

My plan is quite simple: to convince him, as he is a coward, I must confront him first. The plan is, first, assessing the situation for him, see how things are going for him, evaluate how stressed he is, and given the results of this, we will go to the second phase. But more importantly, I must not show that I am concerned about Claire, everything must be about him. Because if I show that I am worried, he will use it against me, and I have no way to escape. I must leave him a clear space, where we both can talk. Speaking calmly, listening carefully... That's what now things are all about. So, after having observed and made slightly in my mind my deductions and my theories, and as he saw me and was surprised to see me (I mean, he wasn't expecting that), I immediately took over:

"You wanted to assault her alone? Then you'd better have chosen another night!"

"What the fuck are you doing here, you stupid slut! How comes did you manage to be there? You're a cop as well?"

Well, that is not surprising, his answer. As I said, lack of confidence (showed here by insults, he treated me of slut so I assume this must be to comfort himself), and the surprise, seeing me here, at that moment, everything is upside down in his mind, he's been caught stealing and has the childish reaction. I mean, a childish reaction would be to say that it wasn't him, but it's also to be surprised by the presence of cops and guests. And as he's paranoid, then, he thinks I am a cop. He was really surprised because now, he is betrayed by his colleagues, it's his colleagues that are pointing him with a gun, so the betrayal is complete. And me, above all, here, the person that he thought he took over because I am the tool that he has to express his frustration...

However, the fact that he insulted me also shows something: he said the word slut, which directly refers to my sexuality. If he would have used another slur, such as bitch or whore, then he would have referred to me as a whole. And the slut was said to me as a primary insult, which means, he may use another funny word after, this one will remain: he just insults my sexuality and not my personality, which means, he never took over of me. He never could find the way to have power over me and thus, as a consequence of that, he fears me. Great, so now we are two minds speaking equally to each other, he never took control of me. And he is fully aware that now, he isn't in a position where he can unless he is extremely talented. The only difference between him and me is that... Well, I fully trust myself. Instead, I decided to leave him the benefice of the doubt, to confuse him more and more:

"Could be. You never know who you meet, Joris, keep that in mind!"

"You fucking whore. I was sure that she trapped me when she recommended you!"

"Who recommended me?"

"Her!"

Oh, nice try. But I know everything already.

He was now using Claire, that was a clever move. He wanted to use her as the fact that she may have betrayed me, and she may have pushed me into this. She may have helped for that, but she did that for her purpose because she'd know that I'd have the guts to save her. The problem is, now I see, he wants to try to manipulate me. Or at least using manipulation, as a desperate move, he wanted to show me that Claire may have betrayed me and that I shouldn't trust her. Well done... But nope, it won't work. But as I said, this move was a desperate move, it means that he doesn't have anything, he already wants to attack but doesn't have anything. That's even better, that helps me. This is why, I coldly replied, with a sly smile:

"Yeah, that was a clever move. Now, leave her alone!" I ordered him.

"Oh, yeah? Why? Why should I leave her alone?"

"Well, bro, it's really up to you. I mean, you just have a knife and use my girlfriend as a human shield, facing you, you have three cops that will pull the trigger if you do anything, so it's really up to you!" I took a cynical approach.

"They do anything, and I slay your girlfriend straight away!"

"I don't think so. Let's face the truth, your knife isn't sharp enough, and a bullet will take less than a micro-second to finally reach your head and shoot you down. So, let's do the maths... And, yeah, pretty much, yeah, you're screwed. You're shattered, Joris, so you'd better give up!"

Claire started to breathe more and more, as panic was taking over and was not controllable. She'd better see a psychologist right away, because she may develop PTSD after that, which will be... Well, as she's taken as a hostage, I mean, any normal person would be like this. But fear was terrible, and now she was crying but remained silent. As threats over her life were sent by Joris and I was explaining the script the possible outcome if one of Joris or the cops starts to attack, she was certainly visualising this in her mind and was terrified. Honestly, I was terrified too, but I have to keep a cold mind if I want to get anything from him. But, as she was breathing harder, more and more, was crying but in silent... I was just... I was just feeling weird, and uncomfortable to draw the scenario of the outcome, in case she's not released. I don't know what was in her mind right now... But whatever it is...

Behind her, Joris was also thoughtful for a second, but not for the same reasons: he was also picturing the thing and was forced to admit that I was right. The thing is, I somehow uncleared his intentions, I didn't do it entirely, but he knew that I was right: it will be faster to shoot him than for him to harm her. Moreover, he was thinking about the whole situation, and I saw that as well, now he felt that Claire was literally at her breaking point, I bet he wants to use that to make me fold. That was working in silent, but I will not give in. He remained thoughtful for a second, but I didn't convince him enough. After Claire started to slightly moan because he was hurting her as he was pushing her very tight against him, I started to use this time a very calm tone. And I spoke another time, taking the risk:

"Anyway, leave her alone. You don't even want to harm her!"

"What do you know about that?" he was trying to waste time.

"I just know that that's it. This... This is just pure comedy. Tonight, you've been caught and will be charged for statutory rape. They already know that you force her to sleep on command for you. You don't want to kill her... It's not in your interest!"

"I'm fucked anyway!"

Interestingly, he was starting to collapse. His defences were now really low, as we passed through the second phase of the negotiations. He tried to bargain with me, tried to manipulate me, tried to insult me and make sure that I would get offended and even tried to scare me, but he saw that I remained unbreakable and that whatever he says, or tries to do, he will fail. Now he sees that I am determined and even if he has my girlfriend, it won't disturb me until he releases her or kills her. So, for him, we were in a stalemate. For me, things were slightly different: as he was now admitting that the situation may have an outcome that may not please him, and he was acknowledging that he was trapped, it was time to calm down the situation. I don't want him to regain confidence, though, as he was trying to open this. The purpose of his "I'm fucked" is, okay, you won. He was trying to seek mercy. The thing is, if I give him what he wants, he will regain confidence and then will use it against me. So, this is why, now I have the power, the thing is... Let's all calm down. Let's relax, let's make sure that he will make him let his guard down. So, therefore, he will be all listening to what I say and then will accept whatever I ask unflinchingly. Now, I don't want to blame him, but refocusing him on what he is currently doing and explaining what the consequences are going to be.

This is why I must use a more maternal tone, without seeking my words at any time now. I replied after leaving a moment:

"Okay, listen. You are tensed, we are all tensed tonight. Let's calm all down, okay?"

"Oh, why? WHY? You guys TRAPPED ME!"

"No, we didn't trap you. Listen, Joris, this situation, all this... It's all fucked up, right?"

"Of course, it is! It fucking is, and this, BECAUSE OF YOU, BECAUSE OF THE BOTH OF YOU!"

"It's not, and you know that..." I swiftly raised my voice before coming back to normal. "Come on, man, have you seen in what kind of activities you're into? Man, pimping, now statutory rape, child abuse... Are you aware that Claire is not even eighteen?"

"I am..."

"Imagine what it will be for her, to pass through that moment. What you're making her living, what you made her live already... It's gonna take years before she goes through that!"

"I know!"

"It was already hard for her to accept to be part of this. She's scared of you, she's not sleeping... Look at her, she's a zombie now, she's completely devastated, and you are making things worse! You don't want to do that!"

"No..."

Putting him with his mistakes and his faults, reminding him that every single minute that passes now he is more and more destroying my girlfriend... What was interesting was the fact that he stopped his insults, he used small sentences instead, with a much lower voice. He was understanding and accepting. At the moment I raised my voice, he started bending. I mean, in the conversation, I took him over. This is why, now, I resumed... because somehow, he needs to be atoned:

"Listen to me, Joris... No-one is blaming you now. We are not here to trap you; we are not here as a result of whatever plot you may imagine..."

"Oh yeah?" he interrupted me. "Then how comes that I just want to have some fun with your girlfriend, as you say, and then suddenly you guys show up to arrest me? How do you call it?"

He may not realise that what he is doing is bad. Maybe he has a different sense of reality, maybe he is greatly confused. Either way, if I want to convince him, now, I need to strike. I must stop bullshitting him, or trying to temper him because this is not gonna work. But for him, now, this is becoming obvious, and I guess, this is why he responded with short sentences because he does not realise that he is taking someone as a hostage, he must think he's in a video game. But he still thinks this was a plot, yes, it was, but... I need to shift his attention into the big mess he is currently into:

"A police investigation. You should know what it is, right? Come on, Joris... Do you realise what's going on? I mean... You attempted to rape a seventeen-years-old girl; do you know how this is called?"

"She was okay with that!"

"Was she? And even if she would have been okay with that... Are you aware that you are forcing her to prostitute on your behalf?"

"This is rubbish..."

"That's not. You forced me to do the same. Maybe not you, but your disciple Kelly did. You guys are pimps, this is what you are!"

"Oh, fuck off!"

"Oh, and, in case you may have forgotten, here, you are not into one of your numerous video games. If one of the three cops start shooting, you won't respawn in another place with the same money you have! If they shoot, life is over, for you!"

"Oh, because you think I'm not aware of this! What are you taking me for, an idiot or what?"

"Just, keep that in mind. You may not care about living your life, but Claire does, and she has nothing to do with that!"

"If they shoot, Claire and I will fall together. And you won't be able to do anything, you're not God!"

"I may not be God... But shooting down Claire won't do anything. You will just be charged with murder, and that's it. Spending your life in prison, being raped by other prisoners, or becoming their sex toy just like you did to my girlfriend... Life will be fun for you, you will regret it! It's true, cops in prison... Yeah, they have a funny life, especially since they know who you are because you placed a lot of those thugs there..."

For a second, he looked at me straight in the eyes, and I saw that at the same time, he was slightly releasing Claire, at least left her more space to breathe, he wasn't holding her tight anymore. But in his eyes, I saw a deep fury, I mean, if I were in front of him, he would certainly start assaulting me. It didn't make sense. I could certainly explain that with the frustration, first because he was not sexually fulfilled tonight, second because I was facing up to him and he just didn't like that, and third, because he saw me as a potential person that may fold before him and this wasn't happening... I feel like we are reaching a point now. An interesting point. He was breathing faster, which meant, I must let him speak, I must let him express himself. And, after some seconds, as he was now just the shadow of himself, I just let him start to let his anger being expressed. Because I knew exactly where he wanted to go. And it was exactly where I was waiting for him:

"Whatever you're accusing me of, I have no regrets..."

"Don't you?"

"Nope. I just... I just fucking hate you. Whatever you've been doing..."

I stopped there because what he said after "whatever you've been doing..." was hard to hear. In very vulgar terms, he added after that, I mean, that women were pretty much all the same and I deserved what I did because I was a horrible person and Claire deserved that too because she was meant to do that.

Free Expensive Lies: Prologue

This guy is a misogynistic bastard that wishes all women strong pain and humiliation. For five minutes he blasted me, Claire, and by extension all women with all funny words that I do not want to report. Because this was offending. Well, fine, fair enough, so that confirms what I think, it's all about his childhood.

Something surprisingly came out when he started to explain the headlines of his anti-women manifesto, though: I could see tears coming out very discreetly out of his eyes, and the fact that his jaws were very tights and he was speaking with an indescribable passion about all the pain he wishes to do to some random person, it was confirming what I was thinking about him. You may have guessed my theory, which is that he has been abandoned when he was a baby and spent most of his childhood and teenage in host families that were tough with him. And he takes his mother responsible for all his pain because she failed to take care of him and hates her. And why he does not want to attack Claire, it's because he saw his mother. And Claire's face reminds him of his mother, this is why he wanted to assault her. Everything explains my theory, the fact that he is messy, his navy blue sheets reminding childhood because navy blue reminds the dawn before the night and thus helps him to sleep without making nightmares, the mess as he hasn't been taught to be organised, the unpaid bills because he hasn't been taught how to have responsibilities, the war games because he pushed himself in a self-created broken personality, the mess in the kitchen, the fact that although he is living in a messy place he has a nice car to try to show his self-built wobbly personality and above all, the fact that his family name is the first name, as he is the result of an anonymous birth. And, above all, the fact that he hates his mother, then sees all women as responsible for his problems.

This is why I reached that point. Hopefully, for him, I can understand things without being offended. This was exactly where I wanted him to go, reveal his face under the mask. So, now, I see you! Immediately, in the great calm, I started to reply, this time pushing him into where he finally wanted to be:

"That's offending. But, fine, if you feel like it. You may hate women, as you say, you may want them to suffer... Sure. Many men are like this, now, and apparently, it comes from the fact that they hate their mother. And you see in a woman the reflection of your mother; this is why you see us as threats."

"Fuck you, Charlotte. Fuck you, with your fucking girlfriend, with your... Just fuck all of you!"

"Yeah, I could do that. Or I could also try to understand what you exactly told me. At the moment you started to insult women you started also to release

Claire. So, it means that deep down, there is a wave of genuine anger that is slowly, daily, consuming you. Am I right?" I started to extrapolate by something wrong.

"Oh yeah?"

"When I first met you in that nightclub, you seemed to me like a hunter, like someone that didn't want to be disturbed. You weren't like a womaniser, but you were here as a shark. That is the thing that surprised me. Now, I see your flat, with no pictures of any family. I saw your door, with the hole for the toothpick, all I can see is paranoia. And immediately, when I started to talk about your mother, I felt like... I reached a point."

"Come on... Go on..."

I don't remember when the law has been voted, I think that it was one of the Vichy regime law that was put into the new laws after the regime collapsed as a result of Germany losing World War II, but I know that in France, before abortion was legalised in the 70', you could have the possibility to give birth anonymously, to prevent illegal abortions carried out, or even killing of babies. So, it could give the mother free care in a hospital, and then the baby would be given to social services. But as there is a legal deadline for aborting in France of twelve weeks, it may happen that the mother does not find out she's pregnant after twelve weeks for the reason that the baby is considered as being alive by law.

And thus... I guess Joris's mother was in that case. As Joris is now thirty, or around thirty, so he was born in the '80s, so... Anyway, the fact that he is acting like this with Claire, although he knows that she's been sleeping with several people and doesn't care about this, I am sure there must be a prostitution story involving his mother and this is why he is now in charge of a cluster in this organisation. I mean... I think I am sure. He wouldn't be reacting that way otherwise.

"You wanted so hard to have sex with Claire for the sole reason that she reminds you of your mother. And you want to punish her. Because your mother was also a prostitute that abandoned you when you were a kid... This is why you do not intend to kill her, instead, you just want to humiliate her, that's all!"

"The fuck... Come on, how do you know this?"

"Come on, the night in Kleber when you wanted to talk to me about having Claire for you, and you told me that you were kidding, but deep down there was a strong desire, the fact that there are no pictures in your flat of any family or relatives means a tough childhood, and finally... The fact that you have a first name as your family name, Olivier... As I can see in your unopened letters. You have the same depression as may have a child that may be seeking his parents. And you recently found out who your mother was... And the offence was just too big!"

"Shut up!"

"And now you think that all women are all the same because your mother abandoned you so this is why, at maybe thirty, or certainly approaching your thirties, you do not have any stable relationship with anyone, you are living in a shithole in the middle of nowhere. I mean, Paris, but this place looks like you're not even in France. And you fell in love with Claire, or, maybe, something pushed you to fall in love with her, you certainly have mercy for her... I don't know. The problem is that Claire is not your girl. You must give up that idea!"

Somehow, what he finally wanted to express for years, but was maybe too ashamed for this, came out tonight. So now we know him, a desperate man seeking his mother, and destroyed because he certainly knows her identity, but for some reasons is unable to speak to her. This is why he is destroyed; he is crushed by the fact that the pain is too hard for him and cannot cope with that anymore. He is genuinely fed up. This is why, after I delivered my analysis, he started to sob a bit harder. I won the battle. I won, because now his problems are exposed, the fury that was gnawing him for years, certainly decades, were exposed, and the pain was too harsh to be coped with.

What this guy need is a good psychiatrist. Because some problems are driving him mad daily, and he needs urgent help. And the thing is, now the wound is wide open and bleeding as shit, he is too focused on stopping the bleed than to remain focus on the situation, so now I have a big opening to finally free Claire. I literally nuked him, so he doesn't have that much of opportunities: he knows that whatever it is, he cannot resist. I won every single battle on every single front. He failed everywhere, and his tears were proving it. We have him now. But maybe his wound was open and was painful, he still had her. So, this is why, I was still giving him a very last reminder, still very calmly:

"Listen, Joris. I am probably the very last person you may want to listen to today, but I can still give you some advice. Take it as you wish, but... You have two options now: surrender or die. The problem is, their order is to catch you alive, so even if you attempt something on Claire, and you may attempt to kill her, they will try to catch you. You're gonna send her to hospital, and in between, they will catch you and you will rot in jail, and then in prison, especially given the fact that it will be soon proven that you are a pimp, you're gonna stay in prison for the rest of your life. And... Trust me, especially given your situation, given the fact that you're a cop... Prison is the very last place you want to end up!"

"I don't want to harm her. I just want to negotiate..."

"Sure, you can. The problem is, you've been caught for statutory rape. Unless you can negotiate to be a snitch for the cops or something like this... Well. I'd be you, and I'd surrender. There's nothing you can do anyway! They won't let you get away tonight and pretend that nothing happened, once you release or attack Claire, you'll be in the hands of the police... And then, even worst, the justice. They came to arrest you, Joris, they didn't come to pick up Claire and turn a blind eye on what happened tonight!"

"How... Charlotte... Do you know that my arrest will lead to reprisals? If you arrest me tonight... There will be retaliation, he will retaliate!"

"Who?"

"The guy that took the pictures and recorded both of you? You don't know him... But he knows you. He knows where to find you. And he precisely knows where to attack you!"

"Oh, because you think that we didn't protect ourselves already! Of course, I know that he will attempt something on me or us, but... What shall he do?"

At that moment, once again, he was thoughtful. Tears on his face weren't dried yet that some ray of new hope was already showing up. It's the very first time that he evokes the blackmailer, and thus, this becomes interesting: what's at stake on this? I know he will strike back; this is why Claire said that she will quit Facebook tomorrow because we know that those pictures will leak. The thing is, we are already under police protection, and... what can he do? Attacking my relatives? According to Heather, this is very unlikely to happen. He's gonna be too exposed if he does that, and moreover... He can't attack mum or Clarisse at the moment: both of them aren't alone and won't be alone for the rest of the night. I don't think he might do that because, to be honest, I'd be him... I don't think he's a coward. I mean... No, I don't think it's likely to happen. He will certainly try to target us, but no...

And suddenly, yeah, as I mentioned... A ray of hope appeared out of nowhere, and more confident, showing a different personality, he started to say:

"You know what? You're right. Yeah, you're right. You won the game. That's what you wanted? When Kelly told me that it was a bad idea to recruit you, that you are a huge threat and that you will destroy us... I should have listened to her. I thought I'd be better than you, and... I just didn't see that coming!"

Free Expensive Lies: Prologue

"Yeah, they say that all the time, I know. This is flattering, though…"

"Anyway, you may have destroyed me, you may have pushed me under the bus… There are stronger people than you. And, in this stuff, in this business… I know they will come and help me at some point. But you… You're fucked. Do you want Claire? Fine, I surrender. But now, get ready. I am not threatening you, but fighting back, rebelling against what he planned for you… You may have won a battle; you just didn't win the war!"

All of a sudden, still with the knife in his hand, he immediately threw it against the bed, and everything went very quick. He immediately pushed Claire towards me. The problem was, as she still had her heels, she almost fell, but I could catch her on time before that happens. And suddenly… The pressure fell. I was relieved. Now, the mission was successful. We did it, we destroyed the cluster, Claire is alive, we are now free! And, more importantly, I saved my girlfriend, which was… Well, I don't know whether it was heroic or not, but… At least she was there.

Immediately, as I was now holding her and she immediately, with the remaining strength she had and her all wet face due to the tears she had in the last minutes, Joris suddenly kneeled and put his hands up. One of them put his gun back into his case, and went to him, handcuffing him.

But as it happened, I didn't follow. Claire was in tears in my arms and was holding me strong, I mean, I never had her holding me so hard in my arms. And, I don't know, we did it, now she was safe, now we won the war, I saved her arse and we did it, no more pressure, no more fears, we are just together now. She started weeping hard and loud, as I heard at the same time the noise of the handcuffs being put against him and the two cops speaking words that I didn't pay attention to. She was holding me, and whilst one of my arms was carrying her, the other was cuddling her hands, and I kept on saying, "it's okay, it's gonna be fine, darling, it's all right", even if I knew that nothing could relieve her at that moment. But she needs to cry, she needs that, she must cry, at least she's evacuating all the pressure she had today. I'm simply scared that she might be sick in the next couple of days as it usually happens when she's being stressed out for a long time. But now, it's fine, the job is done, we can now go home, get a pizza, have a shower, watch a Disney or something, and sleep. Even if I am not sure she might be able to sleep. It's fine, now, it's all right, we're back home. We can sleep now.

The thing was, she was shaking. I mean, her arms were slightly shaking, indicating a massive dose of fear that she overcame. Hopefully, she goes to her psychologist soon, and… I think, even tomorrow, we will go to the GP so she can get something stronger or having her prescription reviewed, because of what happened today. But the most important was... And as I told her whilst cops were now raising Joris as for some reason they put him on his belly:

"We won, baby, we did it!"

"Yeah, we did it. I love you, Cha, I love you!" she shyly whispered.

"I love you too, honey! Anyway, let's go home now!"

Now, we were done with them, it's gonna take time but we can finally go back to our normal lives. There will be consequences, yeah, but I don't care. The most important for me is, she's alive, safe, and now no longer undergoing their stupid pression. We finally managed to dismantle that thing, although I thought that it would be harder, we played very well. She did an outstanding job, I mean, I was really happy to have her as a partner in crime, and, thanks to Heather, this would have never happened. We did it, we finally brought down a prostitution cluster and, in my opinion, this is something we can be proud of. The only thing is, the return to normal life will be hard, especially for her, as she has now to cope with what happened tonight, and the last two months. I think, yeah... When this started, I was just, really sceptical, and now, I mean, I saw that... I couldn't believe that I'd do that someday.

As we were waiting for Joris to go down first, as he was supposed to go straight to the nearest precinct, we wanted to avoid him. Now, Heather is supposed to bring us back home, and... At the same moment, in the street, we heard some sirens, but ambulances sirens. There were also some police sirens... And at the moment he came closer to me, Joris immediately looked at me, stopped, Claire stepped back, and he said to me, with a kind of weird, apocalyptic voice... Like a villain looking for repentance:

"You're doomed, Charlotte. You just don't know that yet!"

"Yeah, we'll see. We'll see in a couple of days who between you and me is the more doomed... I'm not scared, to be honest."

"There is no need for that. You won't have time for being scared!"

"I won the battle anyway!"

"Yeah. You just have to win the war now!"

37 *Checkmate*

// Rue du Département, Stalingrad area, Paris.

Free Expensive Lies: Prologue

It was hard to imagine, or even to conceptualise, but, yeah, mission accomplished. Maybe it's gonna take me time to figure it out.

Anyway. We're done now, and, as they brought him downstairs where a van was waiting for him to drive him straight to custody, another van was here for Claire, as they were scared for injuries. Hopefully, she was not, I mean, she was still in a state of deep shock, but she was physically fine, and now, was even more impatient to go to bed. So do I, on the other hand. So, we went downstairs, took the stairs, and Heather with their staff was busy blocking the street downstairs. They caught him, and we waited a moment before going downstairs, seeing, or even following Joris was just too much. We preferred waiting upstairs until we heard the massive door of the van being closed and the sirens being on and hearing that car.

It's funny, I was feeling like at the end of a Die Hard movie, I mean... all the pressure accumulated today, everything was just going away, we were feeling much lighter now. And to be honest, I was starving now. I was so hungry that... oh my god! On the other hand, I didn't eat that much today. But as they were all leaving upstairs, and some other officers were waiting for us to finish our hug to go downstairs so they can start searching the place for proofs of our accusations, matching proofs I mean, once we heard the sirens, I looked at her and said, it's time to leave this place now. And she agreed.

But the exhaustion, now... somehow, yeah, it was quite an emotional moment. When we broke up four months ago, I just couldn't imagine that this moment... I mean, I would save her, and restore a normal balance in her life, I mean, yeah, I was proud. But since this mess started, I just couldn't believe we could get away, as several days ago things were so different in my life, now, yes, I was feeling like the ultimate balance of the universe has finally been restored. We went down the stairs together, in silence, hands in hands, like we were going down the main alley of a church after getting married. But, in a way, I was feeling like, maybe she's in a deep shock, but never, never, she hugged me this way. I was feeling a strong and so deep aura of love coming out of her heart, it was like the comfort of a soldier having left his country for battling abroad. We carried out that war together, and now, we can rest, this is over, we can be back to a normal life.

So, yeah. Slowly, hands in hands, we took the lift to the first floor, where the main door was wide open, and through the corridors, the yellow and blue lights of the sirens still on were dancing. We reached outside, putting the first foot into liberty, for putting the other, and finding out everybody working, rushing a bit everywhere, I think to try to contain the traffic on each side, or... I don't know why everybody was rushing to be fair. Investigators arrived, officers with different outfits... and, yeah. In the middle of this, the ambulance, with a dark blue stretcher. Although my girlfriend was walking normally, she still had to be examined, as this is the procedure, and secretly I was just hoping that it wouldn't take ages, as I was also impatient to go back home, but I guess we'll find out soon. Oh, and her escorting bodyguard was back.

Something remained however curious: although terror overcame her and even though we passed this, for now, a couple of minutes, she was still shaking but remained cold-blooded, she cried, yes, but stopped crying. There was something, like a kind of mechanism in her mind that made that, no, now, in a way or another, she was stronger. No tears of emotions, I think the fact that she shakes must be a sign that the pressure of the day, accumulated until then, I was really surprised that she didn't cry or anything. On the other hand, she underwent two months of daily sexual abuse so I guess this must be a sign that she doesn't cope with events as she used to do before. Yeah, things have changed now, my baby has become a tough grown-up, and I guess I just have to deal with that now.

At the moment we walked outside, we went to the stretcher, and two first-aiders immediately took care of her. And, for a moment, yeah, I had a moment of absence. It's weird to describe, somehow, I did not realise that now this was over and for good. Seeing this firework of sirens making what would have been a peaceful night become like a battlefield, was impressive. Deep down, the movie of all that story, starting from my birthday night with Claire being so different and lying to me, acting in such a weird personality entirely made and designed bespoke by Kelly, and now, the order is re-established. I quickly saw Claire being taken by doctors and them speaking to her, after being given this golden blanket into which she entirely wrapped herself into, started auscultating her, and... Meanwhile, I saw Heather going back far away from me, going to some other van where a cop was showing her something on a laptop, and... Claire was relieved, Heather was excited, tonight was a good evening, in terms of results. We did our job successfully, and I was feeling somehow that we've been part of something big.

Something was nevertheless odd also tonight. This is not me regretting what I did, but, discovering Joris tonight, and uncovering his full personality by entering into his place... I mean, breaking into his place and finally discovering where he lived and especially how he lived, it somehow triggered some sort of sympathy to me. I mean, sympathy, it's not, it's just that I was feeling like having been pushed a child to the balcony, and now he's dead. Seeing him living his simple life because this guy was lost, I mean, what he did to Claire was obviously unforgivable and I cannot just pass or even close my eyes on this, but I was somehow feeling regretful for him. It was like shouting in the ambulance, pretty much. But on the other hand, this was the only way out, I mean, he played the game very well, it's like Claire, I didn't see. Especially since I haven't seen that much Joris or Kelly, as they didn't play well with me. I must admit, yes, I have been psychologically disturbed when I was with the Russian guys, and then at the end of the day discovering that I am pregnant, and... Yeah, it has been tough weeks. But, yeah, I must say that when I finally saw him, found out where he lived, yeah, I had some sort of empathy. Especially seeing that his studio was mostly organised as a bedroom and his sofa was also his bed, and... This guy must have been having a shitty life. Well, he's a pimp, and he must be arrested, on the other hand. Whatever happened tonight, I didn't kill anyone, and I did the right stuff, I did what was morally right. And I do not have to regret a thing, my girlfriend is safe, that's all that matters. But it's still very surprising that I kind of develop sympathy for Joris, especially now. Meh, that's just a detail anyway.

It was a cold night, and a big visible moon, waxing gibbous as they say, it was almost fully discovered. That's the only thing we could see from far away, as we couldn't see any stars. And, still into that absence, hearing some big and confused noise, I was watching the sky, in the middle of a rush, not far away from my girlfriend. When suddenly, after a certain moment that I couldn't estimate given the fact that my mind was really confused, I felt like two hands grabbing my shoulders: Heather. I lowered my head, coming back to my earthly-attached mind and looked at her... and her big smile. And also, her big excitement that she couldn't hide tonight:

"Hum... Wow, I can just say, wow. Congratulations Charlotte!" she was somehow seeking her words.

"Meh, it's fine. She was just there, I mean, I did what I thought was right, glad I could have helped!"

Well, her achievement was becoming true. I mean, I recall, from times to times I saw her on the phone as I assume, she was speaking to her boss, and all the time I saw her smiling. She was visibly happy tonight. On the other hand, she told me that it's been years that she's on this investigation and tonight it's the very first time that they catch the head of a cluster, so... Yeah.

On the other hand, yeah, when I drew that plan, I didn't think that there would be so much at stake, especially since Heather came out as a cop. At first, she was supposed to come back, but after second genuine thought, I am sure that if we wouldn't have had cops help, something would have happened to her. As, still, there were knives ready, I didn't see where he put his gun, but I assume that it was near, something would have happened to her. Maybe he wouldn't have killed her, but he would have made her disappear, that's sure. I think this was part of the plan. Because, yeah, Claire was certainly his most attractive product, but the problem, and I think this would have been their strategy, not making me work that much to save me for later, so they can use and destroy Claire psychologically and then make sure that she would accept anything without complaining, and thus abduct her and God knows what after. Then they could focus on me and after, I don't know what. I am sure we intervened at a critical moment, and I guess, whoever between Claire or Kelly made me join that network, yeah, it was for a purpose.

I feel that tonight, we avoided a disaster. I am sure we will find this out within the next days. Anyway, after I modestly replied, as I was kind of disturbed as well, she looked at me, whilst thoughtful, and said:

"Yeah, hum, helped... Anyway, I called my boss, and your trial shift has been successful!" she was glad to announce.

"Heather, I think I already told you that I was never sleeping on a first date?"

"Cha, come on... what I mean by this is, if you need any recommendation for working with us, or if you want to consider joining us, I mean, I'll back you up! You could be an amazing consultant in this investigation. Plus, you could travel anywhere! For free!"

"Yeah, hum... If you do not mind, giving me a couple of days... I still need to mend a couple of things in my life before accepting."

"Of course, Cha, I understand. Take your time, I mean... I still need to see you for your statement anyway!"

"Yeah, of course..."

We looked at Claire, together, after that. And, she was still sat on the stretch, also looking at me, and moving her legs. Her arms crossed, all wrapped in her blanket... Astonishingly, yeah, there was no expression on her face. I mean, I couldn't read anything. This is certainly because of the shock, it paused everything in her mind. But now, yeah, she was fine. Nobody was around her, except our bodyguard that remained a couple of metres away. Then suddenly, with my hand, I said "hi", and she smiled, but it was, yeah, a serious smile. I mean, the smile that she uses to make when she loves me, the kind of smile that smells love and genuine attraction. I am fully aware that we're not going to have sex for a while, but, well... And she stopped shaking. But, well, at least the smile was back, maybe the shock was slowly being taken over in her mind, but it was still here, but at least she was feeling better. That's what I saw. This is why she needs me, I need to go. But before...

"Anyway, I think your lady is waiting for you, and I'm just waiting for the doctor to tell me she's okay, and let me know whenever you want me to drive you home okay?" she has been called by someone.

"Yeah, sure! Heather, erm... Thank you for everything, again. I mean... We're safe thanks to you, and... This means a lot for us," I told her as she was leaving.

"Oh, don't thank me. You did the biggest part of the job! Anyway, catch you later, Cha!"

"Sure!"

Slowly, we looked at each other, like we were discovering each other for the very first time. A kind of feeling of the need for protection came out and was now stronger than ever. Just like the very first day of our relationship, our very first kiss. The very first time we saw each other, and I found her pretty and amazing. Everything kind of came and bounced back in my head, our first kiss, our first hug, our first moment together, all our evenings when we used to bring her mattress downstairs and we used to watch movies on her TV in the living room, the first times when we made love, all the times I had her close to me and on those cold winter nights I used to stick myself to her to enjoy her warmth, and... And now, I delivered her from the hands of an idiot. I saved her life, and I don't know what more. All this, I could just read this in her smile. That kind of test, all those moments in life, made our couple gradually stronger, the events of today made it certainly now unbreakable. There was a kind of thread between us, now, even if people were passing in between, even if things were in the middle, there was still this thread that was connecting us, and nobody, and nothing, could be able to break it. We did it together, and... I don't know what to say.

When I arrived, I immediately took her in my arms, and we kissed. I don't know, every time that we kiss, it's magic, but this time, it was like, yeah, the very first time of a new era. I was just rediscovering her. Now our couple is like a phoenix, able to arise from its ashes, for a new life. She certainly learned the lesson, I think.

We both learned a lesson. The lesson was for her not to trust weird people, and for me, the lesson was that no matter what I must save her and never get away. Well, on the other hand, now she experienced that, I don't think that she's gonna start again, I mean... No, now, I don't know, we will wait until the next couple of days, and... We will see what happen. After I kissed her, I asked her if she could leave me some space so I could sit, and she moved. I sat next to her... And, whilst still looking at each other, still mesmerised by her charm and by her breathtaking beauty, I just could speak slowly:

"Hello, my baby," I used a soft voice.

"Hello, my love!"

"Feeling better now?"

"Well, this was, erm... it's the first time in my life I'm taken as a hostage, but, yeah, hopefully, it's over! That's an experience, I guess..."

"Yeah, that must have been badass..." I thought about it before actually correcting myself, "Challenging, I mean, challenging, yeah, that must have been tough, yeah."

"Badass, yeah... What I recall and will always recall from tonight is that you did it. You saved me, you promised me the day that we started our relationship that whatever happens, you will always save me. Whatever happens, you'd save me, you said it multiples times, and you did it!"

"Oh, well, it's okay, it was just convincing that prick, that's all... Pretty much!"

"Convincing maybe, but the result is, you promised me that you would be here, and I see that you held your promise, he was about to kill me, and, you held your promise, you did it, you came in here, defending me, and saving me, honey..."

"Darling, please, stop, I'm gonna blush..." I remained insensitive.

Still wrapped in her blanket, and I think because she was cold (well, even me, even if I had that sweater, I was starting to be freezing, and I had my hands in my pockets), she put her head on my shoulder. And, well, yeah, I did it, but... Why was I feeling invincible all of a sudden, or like a superhero popping out of nowhere? Wait... This is weird, also... Am I being modest? Me, modest? Oh gosh, what happened tonight must have been serious, then...

"You're my hero tonight, and... I love you, more than ever!"

"I love you too, honey!"

I placed my left arm around her, so I could have her closer to me. And, yeah, our two hearts were beating as one, it didn't happen for a while. And, for some instant, we were just together. No words, just the silence. Either way, she was waiting for the green light of her doctor, but it should be coming any minutes now.

But still, I had my phone in my other hand, in the pocket. And, suddenly, after maybe a couple of seconds... it started ringing. And surprise... I took it out, unknown caller. Han, now I see what it may be, my blackmailer. Now we caught Joris, now we dismantled his cluster... Well, does he know already? I immediately took the call, Claire being still in my arms. Let's see what he wants.

"Hey, hey, hey!" I was amused.

"Hey, Charlotte. How are you doing tonight?" my blackmailer, with his disguised voice, started to say.

"Hum, actually, pretty well. Like someone savouring her victory over some arsehole that pissed off my girlfriend for months..."

"Yeah, you did it very well..."

"Yeah, I must say, yeah, that was very clever. I did it very well, I played very well. Now you are very fucked!"

"Oh, to be honest, I wouldn't be so sure about that."

"Have it your way, darling. The fact is, now I saved my girlfriend's arse, that's all that matters to me, I don't care about what you will do next."

"Oh, I wouldn't be so sure. First of all, I mean, please accept my apologies..."

"Your apologies... What do you mean by apologies?"

"Oh, well, I underestimated you and I thought you would be like your girlfriend and just shut up and obey."

"Oh, that's fine. You know, shit happens..."

"I mean, I heard you were a potential threat, I just didn't expect that you would actually be so dangerous and, ultimately, blow up one of my clusters in Paris. I must say, congratulations, I have in front of me a great manipulator, very skilled."

"Meh... Apologies denied, but fair enough."

"Now, I can see your true face. And I will focus more on you, young enemy!"

For a second, whilst still hearing him talking shit, I was like, seriously, what does this guy want from us? I mean... Some people in life comes, you just don't want them, but you're just trapped with them. I never wanted him, just like Claire, we were living a quiet life, together, then they showed up, Kelly and that monster. I was also wondering, what does he want now, and especially, how comes that he has been so fast to get that information about Joris being arrested. There must have been a snitch about the operation, but whoever it is, now... Joris's fate is up to his lawyers and the law, and the judge to whom he will have to deal with. Now, he was calling me for what, I defeated him, what's the matter now? For once, now I don't care anymore. I just attacked him:

"You can suck my toe, you lame piece of work. I mean, seriously, kiss my arse. What do you want from us? You ruined my girlfriend, I mean... What sack of shit can force a seventeen-years-old girl sleeping with some random guys and blackmailing her? You're a waste of humanity, mate. You're... Rot in hell, you fucking jackass!"

"There are things that could be beyond your control, my love..."

"As I said, suck my toe. I wish I'd know you, so I could kick your arse!"

"I can promise you that, we will meet soon. That's my promise!"

"You're an inspiration for birth control, mate!"

"Oh, don't be rude, remember that I still have compromising pictures of you and your friend, and your parents can still receive it!"

"Oh, dear, because you think we didn't take any precautions? Do you think I am stupid enough to keep on concealing what I have done? Everybody knows that you forced us to be a prostitute, everybody knows! You're just deeply screwed now, Joris has been captured, they will come back to you now!"

"Oh, I am not scared. You may have money, the thing is, I have money and power! And unlike you, I am an influent person. I am a big profile; I am what you prick call a fat cat. I just give calls, and I make you committing suicide, that's it, you and your girlfriend, I have the power to wipe you out!"

"Oh, sounds exciting. When I give calls, the only thing I could get is a pizza..."

"Yeah, I heard about that. As I said, I am the power."

"Yeah, Jesus said the same. Ultimately, it led him on his cross. But fine, fair enough. Now that I fucked you, I order you to leave us alone."

At that moment, I heard him... I don't know, being mean and insulting him, it was almost a pleasure for me. Making him speak. It's not the first time that he mentions that he is someone important, and I tend to believe that he may be right. I mean, to do what he was doing, he needs to be a ghost, and thus needs money to do what he wants to do. But this guy is an amazing narcissistic, I could feel it, he may have been defeated by me tonight, he is not just pissed, he's destabilised, he didn't expect from any of us that one of the girls he has on his command would rebel against him. I was the problem in the matrix for him, and...

And the problem with this guy is, as he remained silent for most of the stuff, as we were both just workers on this mess, I do not know what he intends to do. As he used those pictures as a mean to keep us under pressure... There was still this big question, okay, we may have received it at home, but there is still the question of whether this was just bluff or not. As Heather said, this guy or maybe one of his lieutenants has killed many girls. So... I don't know what I was targeting.

"Anyway, focusing on me, there is no need for that... I don't wanna kick your ass!" I warned him.

"No, no, please. That's for me. I want to test you, to try you. I want you to show me how skilled you are in this! Oh, and... Having you kicking my arse may turn me on, so just be careful with that, darling!"

"Well, have fun touching your small spaghetti as long as you want, darling, that's fine for me. And, for testing me, as you want, what if I don't want to?"

"Well, that will be very regrettable. For example, now, your twin sister is precisely located with her boyfriend at *25, Rue Jean Jaures* in Montreuil, she is with her boyfriend, I mean her new boyfriend, since she has a new one, and is having amazing sex for at least the last half hour. Your mother is at your place, *12, Rue des Peupliers*, in Neuilly. She is waiting for her boyfriend as well, which is late because of delays on the first line."

And now... I think he showed his cards.

So... okay, first of all, at that moment, I mean I paid attention to that already, but I was not finding this relevant at first, now I do. Unlike the very first time, I could hear that he was speaking quite low (when I mean low, I mean, normally, but low as in "I don't wanna be disturbed") so it means that he was out of his place. Second of all, he didn't seem to be in a big place, given the fact that his voice was resonating as if he was in a closed and narrow space, like in a car for instance, but a car stopped and parked as there was no engine noise around. There was still a detail regarding his location that would be relevant: the street around. I heard a car passing from afar, so he is calling me from a parking lot, close to a street that is not busy.

Now... he is talking about my sister and my mother. My sister is according to him having recreational sex, so she is with someone. My mother is waiting for someone... okay, but given the time, I don't think her boyfriend is far away. As they were to meet at this time. When he stated the two addresses, I was feeling like... a danger would pop out of nowhere.

"Okay, and?"

"In the next five minutes, I will kill one of them. One of them will die. Will you be skilled enough to find out whom?"

38 *End of the line*

// On my way to my home, Neuilly-sur-Seine.

// Tuesday, 22nd of January 2013, 20:29.

In my mind, things were almost crystal clear: a clear space and the fact that he was in a car... He was in a parking lot and the quiet street near him indicated that he was waiting for me at home. He will target my mother; this was just imminent. It makes much more sense to target my mother, my sister is not so valuable to him. At least, this is the place I am expected to be within the next hours. He certainly gathered the remaining information, yesterday, when I told my mother that I'd be coming for dinner to meet her boyfriend.

To be honest, I was not expecting his next move to be that fast, I was expecting the consequences to be for tomorrow or later, another day. Because we kept this under a huge secret, Heather ensured me that this would be under control, and here we are now. I am not blaming her, don't get me wrong, what I mean is, how comes that he is moving so fast? Of course, I didn't rule out that he would target my family or Claire's, this is why we have had a bodyguard, and Heather fully assessed the situation as being dangerous and also, the plan includes that my mother and the rest of my family, as well as Claire's, would also be under close protection. But damn, how comes that he has known Joris's arrestation that fast? There must have been a snitch, I mean, I don't see anything otherwise. There is a snitch here, there has been one tonight, and... Someone spoke. Or at least someone already knew and... Everybody is a potential target now. And a potential threat. I don't understand but on the other hand... Something must be going on, and I think this is internal to the police. Anyway, out of rush, right after he mentioned that he was to attack one of them, I immediately hung up the phone and yelled very loud:

"Heather!"

"Hey, Cha, I'm here, don't scream like this, what's up?"

"Fuck, hum... That son of a bitch... He just called me. Hum... We need to go to my home; I am sure he's gonna target my mum..."

"You told me she was not alone tonight?"

"No, she isn't, but... We just need to go... How comes he knew what was going on, you ensured me that I was no longer being listened to, Claire as well."

"Fuck, I knew I couldn't trust them... Okay, jump in the car!"

Her car was still parked out of the place there. Still at the same place. Unfortunately, as they closed the street at the moment to finally let investigators make their stuff, I think it's gonna pretty hectic to get out of this mess.

As I was still standing near Claire, and as she heard the conversation at the very same time, at the moment I moved she suddenly grabbed my arm, and I looked at her. Her eyes... There was a mix of worries, concerns and huge fear, all into this. Maybe This guy was just bluffing and making a false alert, this is a scenario I was thinking just at that moment. Making me go out of here, with Heather driving me home, whilst Claire stays here, even though we have a bodyguard... That would be the perfect spot to make a perfect crime. If it's bluff... As there is a snitch here, what may guarantee me that there is not a copycat of that arsehole here, that would attack my girlfriend whilst I am away? I do not feel that Heather is the snitch... Because when I announced to her that he was targeting my mother, the very first reaction I saw from her was an immediate surprise, and nothing else. I think we came out with the same reasoning: someone here is a bitch. So, I don't care whether Claire has to undergo some medical shit or whatever: now, since the target is everywhere, I want to keep her with me at all times. In that case, in the likely event of an attack, we are still together, and... I must keep her secure.

At the moment she grabbed my arm, the tension of fear was reaching its paroxysm. Safety first, and she immediately, with an extremely low voice, terrified, and fully aware that something was going on, she said, fearing this time for her life:

"Honey, please, just take me with you. I, erm... I don't want to... Please..."

I won't let you down, honey. I won't. I immediately responded:

"Yeah, okay, come..."

"Are you sure it's gonna be okay, Claire?" Heather asked.

"Yes, I need to be there!"

"Okay then..."

"She must come with us, God knows what may happen to her next, Heather!" I immediately stressed her.

"Yeah, you're right. Come with us, and let's not waste time!"

Well, what was scheduled at first to be a quiet evening... Well, quiet, I mean, not with all that faff, suddenly became something with a lot of pressure. There was not a second to lose: we immediately rushed to her car, a couple of metres away. Claire jumped back on the back seats, I went on the front and Heather drove. She ignited the engine, and we were now ready to go.

As she turned and was manoeuvring to find a way to get the hell out of this quiet street suddenly becoming busy, I was fastening my seatbelt and was thinking, making the movie of the call again and again in my mind, trying to catch up details that I may have forgotten. Through the call, I found out that he was remaining calm, like... I don't know, so he may call me from a third location, and he has two of his henchmen doing the dirty job. Or maybe three, one of them was with us tonight. Or just two, maybe he does not intend to attack my sister, I don't know what could be on his mind. Or, maybe he was about to do the dirty job himself, which makes him a fucking sociopath. Or, yeah, maybe he is misleading me, thinking that I may analyse the environment, he mentioned that he knew me, that he underestimated me, and he wants to play with me. The thing I understood, or at least what I think I understood is, now he knows what I am capable of and he knows that I am a genuine threat to his business and... But "I wanna play with you", what do you mean, exactly?

The problem is, and I think that's what it is, there has been a snitch investigating with Heather, and she didn't identify him. Now the problem is, he is making me move, what's the next thing? There are several possibilities to that: either it was the first one with me away so he can focus on Claire as he wants to, but this is now ruled out because Claire is with us and he has no means to attack us, either... either yeah, he's gonna target my mother or my sister but I think he's gonna target my mother as... as, well, we were supposed to meet up at nine tonight and... yeah, his boyfriend is certainly there or on his way, Clarisse is with someone (I don't know who...), but I think it's unlikely that he attacks Clarisse. For several reasons, attacking my mother would be a much interesting symbol and... Oh, gosh, I am so lost, now. I really cannot assess what could be the most interesting possibility for him to attack me as there are a million. What I am sure of is, the possibility that he is bluffing is likely. The possibility that he attacks one of them is also likely. The thing is, he clearly stated that he is going to attack one of them, so it wouldn't make sense that he would attack both of them. From what I heard from him, he seems to be a loyal and genuine, man of his word, piece of crap. It wouldn't make any sense to say, I will attack someone whilst he would attack two people. Unless this is a genuine smokescreen and, in that case, he is about to win the surprise battle.

Free Expensive Lies: Prologue

We weren't escorted, and I am sure that the fact we left very suddenly surprised a lot of people there. Heather was driving extremely fast, I mean, within maybe less than a minute, we were already far away from Stalingrad, heading towards Paris Centre so we could join Neuilly quickly, I was almost clinging myself although my seatbelt was fastened. I was feeling kind of nauseous, and as the stress became suddenly unbearable within a very few minutes, and from what I saw, in the mirror, Claire wasn't also that comfortable. The thing is, I must act now: should I call my mother and tell her to run away? Let's think: she has two possible escape routes out of my building, which is the main door and the garage, the thing is, both of them are close to each other, and ultimately leads to the same way out. And calling her to tell her what is going on, she will be first, (I mean, I'd be the same), thinking that I am doing a prank call and won't take it seriously. If I insist, she will feel in danger and if she's alone, she will automatically find a way to escape, that would be the normal reaction anyone would do. You flee when you are in danger. Second, calling her to announce a danger, no, she will mess up and it will make things worse. Even if I tell her to lock herself, she will do what she finally wants and will expose herself to the danger, which I must avoid. The other thing is if I call her and let her know there's a danger and no-one shows up... Well, it's better to be afraid of nothing than having to deal with a perilous situation. No, I think I should not call her, because I must avoid her panicking. That's the best thing I can do. And if something happens... Well, then it happens.

But I need Clarisse. She must be aware of the situation, that something is ongoing, and I must tell her what's happening. The thing is, as I still don't know whether he's gonna attack... No, I am sure he wants to have me, I am the final target, as I am the one that destroyed his cluster tonight, so I am sure he finally waits for me. I think he wants to target my mother to finally target me. As Heather told me, whoever tried to rebel against him ended up either dead, whether missing, and he wants me. That's obvious. This is why, at some point, whilst we were passing in front of the Gare du Nord, still at that fast speed, I gave my phone to Claire.

"Claire, call Clarisse, please, now..."

"Hum... What's your code?"

"00428. Call Clarisse, and tell her that whatever she is doing now, she must join me at home, this is an emergency."

"Okay..."

"Cha, could you pass me the beacon... Should be underneath you, in the glove compartment..."

Yeah, because, well, driving that fast, I could see, people weren't willing to let us pass. She was honking most of the time, I mean, I am sure they thought we were some troublemakers. She had to stop at a traffic light, and I took advantage of that moment, whilst the car wasn't moving, to quickly bend myself under my seat, and... I was seeking for a second... Here it is, I finally took the blue beacon. It was unplugged, I mean, there was a wire... I gave it to her, and she asked me to open my window, so I could put it over the roof. At the same time, at the very moment, she plugged the beacon, the siren started, and... Well. That was impressive.

Well, I mean, under that pressure and in all this mess there is still something interesting: we are discovering that universe. I mean... It's not on your daily basis that you do that, it's still a good experience... somehow.

Once I placed the beacon on the roof, although we were trapped in red light and there were two cars before us, one next to us and two behind, all of them suddenly started moving to let us pass. Unfortunately, we couldn't, we had to wait for the traffic light management to turn green and leave us an opportunity to leave. And once I placed the beacon on the roof, I closed my window because it was still very cold out there, and she gave me her GPS.

"Could you do me a favour, and type your address over here, please?"

"Hum, 12, Rue des Peupliers. Come on, I thought you knew that..."

"Yeah, hum, I've never been to your place, honey..."

"True..."

Hum, on the other hand, she seemed spontaneous, and, no, she doesn't know where I live. Oh my... I just can't stop analyse, it's crazy. My brain is overheating right now, I think, that I am becoming paranoid. No, Heather is the good cop, I know that.

I started turning on the GPS, and the very first thing it asked me was the geographic position... In latitudes, everything. I know my address, not my geographic coordinates. I mean, okay, I know a lot of things, but... I need to learn that, then, now, in case something happens. So, I checked, and... Fucking hell, cops' stuff, it's like the military. I was checking, especially since I am not particularly good with informatics and that kind of stuff... I mean I could be better. But, yeah, at some point, I found it. It took me a couple of minutes. Meanwhile, we've been extremely fast, I mean, we were now at the very end of the Rue La Fayette, in a bit, we will reach the Opera Garnier and the Madeleine Neighbour. I think I have an idea where she wants to go, she wants to reach the Church of the Madeleine, for going down towards Rue Royale, and then she can reach the Champs-Elysées by the Place de la

Concorde, and then she will head straight to Neuilly. Hopefully, now we are at the right hour, and traffic is fine, if what I think is right, we should be home I think in maybe less than twenty minutes. Given the fact that the beacon is loud, we are moving amazingly fast and... People are moving their asses. Which is good.

At this moment, she started to call for help. She had a kind of... I don't know, microphone, walkie-talkie or something, connected to the Centrale, and she said, out loud, "Alpha Tango Bravo 1-4-3, request help on 12, Rue des Peupliers, Neuilly. Possible casualties on site, request help ASAP". At the moment she transmitted her message, certainly a few seconds after, whilst we were turning quite harshly from the Rue La Fayette, to finally reach the Rue Halevy (oh, and Rue is the French word for "street"...) and we were still clinging on board, hoping somehow that the car wouldn't bounce on the other side (hopefully she was an amazing driver), she finally received the response, "copy, Alpha Tango Bravo 1-4-3. Sending unit at your requested position now".

Every second passing, where we were racing through the street and the time, at that moment, I saw this majestic building that is the Opera. I have some souvenirs up there. I brought in here both Claire and Florent at some point. As I said, if they want me as a girlfriend, then they will have to bear two hours of opera. It's like a pre-requirement, and Claire enjoyed it. We went to see Don Giovanni of Mozart and with Florent a recent representation of the Magic Flute. He didn't like it... That should have told me something. The lights were illuminating the corners were windows were underneath, and... It was certainly a short moment of silence in this messy situation, a moment of remembrance, of good souvenirs of an old past. And, yeah, and...

And suddenly, Claire started getting frustrated:

"Ah, fuck... She's not answering..."

"Just keep on calling, harass her. If you call her several times, then she'll understand it's important. I just hope she didn't leave her phone in her bag..." I was thinking.

"I called her three times already..."

"Try again. Again, and again, until she answers..."

"Geez... Okay..."

The problem was, for being heard from each other, we needed to speak very out loud. The beacon was noisy, and I wasn't used to that noise. As we left the opera, I heard Clarisse making another attempt... And then getting frustrated again and make another attempt one more time. And, suddenly, at the moment she was about to hang up, as we were now heading down towards the Boulevard de la Madeleine, reaching the church on our way to the Champs-Elysées, I heard her... somehow regaining hope:

"Hey, Clarisse... Hey, it's Claire. Yeah, I'm okay, erm... Yeah, no, Charlotte is busy right now, and... She just told me to tell you that you need to come back home immediately. As there is, erm..."

"Put her on speaker..." I ordered my girlfriend.

"Okay..."

For a second the beacon stopped, but it was to restart within ten seconds. I took the advantage of that moment to speak to her. Claire put my phone on speaker, raised the sound until the maximum point, and, well, he was not lying. In the background, furtively, I heard some music, some kind of suggestive music, slow and sensual tones, so, yes, she was having fun at that moment, I can see that her break-up therapy is doing pretty well. I didn't hear that much noise, and as the music wasn't that loud then I assume that she's indoors. I have no idea with whom she can be, however, she told me about some guy she met recently, and... she told me that he was not his kind, a black guy, a bit like a thug, and she said she didn't like him. I've never met him, she said she got her phone number through Facebook but as she said that he seemed to be quite annoying whilst openly flirting with her and since it was making her then-boyfriend jealous... Well, I assume that she gave in. Meh, good for her, I mean, I don't care. But as the sound seemed to be not that much reasoning, I assume she was in a small place. Poorly soundproofed. The only problem with my twin sister is that whenever she has sex, she's fucking loud, and... I just hope she's not gonna wake up the neighbourhood. It's kind of embarrassing.

For some reasons, I started the conversation, in English. So at least, with whomever she could be, it may be tough to understand...

"What's up, Clarisse?" we spoke in English.

"Yeah, you, what's up?" she seemed exhausted.

"You need to come home as fast as you can. I strongly think that something happened to mum, and I need your help. This is not to ruin your evening, it's just... The blackmailer called me and threatened to attack mum... I have reasons to believe that this is serious."

"WHAT?"

"Yes... I know, this is fucked up. Anyway, I need you, erm... If you can come ASAP, that would be helpful!"

"Okay, give me at least half an hour... The time to take the metro."

"Sure. See you then!"

"I'll be right there!"

When I said that I was feeling like King Priam with his gigantic wooden horse... Well. It was odd, to see how things went astonishingly silent in the car, I mean, except the noise of the engine, the beacon and, yeah, I guess the street, things went silent until we arrived. We passed through the Rue Royale, before finally reaching the quite imposing Place de la Concorde, and we had to head straight now to Neuilly. It was almost a straight line now. The famous Obelisk, now standing the place where Louis XVI's head fell off, was illuminated with some kind of old yellow light, making it look older than it already was. Seeing all the hieroglyph, all these messages that have been carved into the stone hundreds of years ago, and we were just now passing in the middle of it all. And then, we turned, passing as fast as we could, slaloming between cars and green lights, and it's funny to see how people are acting weird when they hear a police beacon. Especially since in France, Police and Emergency cars do not have the same beacon, I mean they are both making a different noise, people can make the difference when Police is passing or emergency services. And it's also curious to see how drivers are more careful observing the traffic laws... Funny. It nevertheless remains that I still saw at least five drivers having their phone in their hands whilst driving, which is still unacceptable, but... After the same people will complain because roads accidents are blooming. Or because they are involved in a car accident and have to pay a bit more insurance monthly. Meh...

We rode up the Champs-Elysées avenue, to reach the massive Place de l'Etoile, passing in front of Napoleon's Arc de Triomphe, also plunged into that night without a star, but illuminated with similar yellow light, and we headed up straight to the Avenue de la Grande Armée, for maybe less than a minute later, doing the very same slalom we did between cars since we turned up that beacon, reaching the Porte Maillot and finally leaving Paris. And my anxiety raised. I just kept on thinking, what will I find once back home? Multiple scenarios are now on the table, and... And it's incredible, I mean, I was not prepared for this. But time is not for lamenting myself, time is again for acting. It was the very first time that I had an unbelievably bad hunch, although I still did not rule out the possibility that this was just pure bluff or a bait or... possibly real, at the moment we crossed the Porte Maillot to finally reach the Avenue Charles de Gaulle, and having a certain way before reaching the next roundabout for then turning left on the Avenue de Madrid, and reaching my place, I was feeling weird. The problem was, in my mind if this is bait, then he is very clever. If he is targeting my mum, then he's a coward... but a clever coward. Or if it's bluff, then he is... He cannot be bluffing, if this is bluff, then it means that I should be incredibly careful on the following days because he's gonna attack somewhere. But if this is bluff, the alert is now raised, and he knows that I may expect him somewhere.

Anyway, the road was short, until we finally reach the metro station that, once in my former lifetime I use to take on a morning basis to go somewhere in Paris until we passed in the avenue that I hated taking, and until we ultimately turn right two streets later to reach mine, Rue des Peupliers... The trip from Stalingrad has never been so fast.

And surprisingly, at the moment we arrived, a car left the parking. A car that I have never seen. Curiously, it didn't seem to leave in a rush... Could it be him, possible, especially since this car was black, a kind of luxury car, and had tinted windows. Odd, yes. It seemed to leave towards the other way, and, since the Rue des Peupliers is a private street, well... You cannot access this street unless you are granted access. I think, if he attacked my place, he couldn't have entered with a car, as he has to pass two different gates to finally enter the parking of my building. I still looked at the license plate... It can still be useful. Surprisingly, as well, the car was heading in the opposite direction than us. It was heading southbound. Meh, I got the numbers... we never know.

But we didn't enter, we just dropped the car before the first gate, and we used the small door next to them. We kind of left in a rush the car, as she didn't park, she just left her car next to the entrance, and, yeah, as we arrived, we all just got off. If he attacked my mum, there was not a second to lose.

The problem in our residence is, when you have a car, it's hard to come in. If you do not and are a pedestrian, you can enter just as you like, you do not need any pass or anything. I mean, except entering within the building. Two years ago, many landlords living in this street signed a petition to the City Hall requesting total private access to the street, complaining about the many burglaries that happened. There has been a wave of robberies in our street, but the City Hall rejected it, even if most of the residents here are, well, yeah, extremely rich. We even have the CEO of a big company living here. We didn't take part in it, since we pay for the services of the private security provided by the company that manages the street. But... Yeah. Our street is safe, and this to say that... Well, if you're clever you can still avoid the security. But since I don't know this guy and I don't know if he has a brain or not, then... I can expect everything.

Free Expensive Lies: Prologue

However, as we walked, the cold temperature was refreshing us, and the calm of the street was somehow relieving. It seemed like a normal day, at least a normal evening, at first there was nothing suspicious. Lights in my building were turned on for some flats, the security post was normal, the guy was sat down and was reading something, yes, at a glance, there was nothing that looked unusual. If there was something weird, I mean, doors would have been forced, or someone would be under alert, but now, no. Briefly, in my mind, I saw us walking and arriving in front of the door, facing a closed door and me rushing to come inside to find mum looking at me and telling, "what's wrong with you?". Which was, to be fair, the scenario that I was expecting. Heather was walking behind me, Claire next to me, slowly, after having entered through the street and having passed the big gates leading to our parking, where... Where I didn't find anything suspicious, we slowly were reaching the main door. And, suddenly, I told myself, if there was something weird going on, that's logic, at least something unusual would have happened in the parking, such as a car leaving that wasn't registered to anyone... I would have been alerted. I quickly checked my phone, as Claire gave it back to me, and since she called my sister, no new notifications or missed calls appeared on my screen. So, everything was so far perfectly normal.

After having walked down the parking, we finally reached the security office. The thing was, as Claire didn't change her shoes and we could still hear her, and since we know this guy for a while and he knows both of us, I approached the office, Heather still following me, when I checked my pocket. I don't have my badge.

"Hey mate, what's up?" I said when I showed up at the office when the guy finally took his magazine back to the desk.

"Hey boss, you okay tonight?"

"Yeah, pretty much, yeah. Hum, quick question, have you seen anything unusual recently? Like a weird car parking here, or... Someone receiving guests, some problems that would have occurred in a flat...?"

"Hum, you mean today?"

"Hum, yeah, today, or in the last half hour..."

"Well, today was a quiet day. And, in the last half hour... No, nothing. I mean I haven't been reported anything weird if that's what you mean..."

"That's what I mean. Have you seen my mother coming back?"

"Yeah, I saw her. She's there, yes."

"Do you mind ringing my flat? I forgot something upstairs and I am lazy to come up!" I didn't want to dwell on details.

He rang. Just before me. The thing is, I wanted to do that for two reasons: if she's answering, then it means two things: first, he may have distracted me to ultimately target my twin sister and in that case, I am fucked because I don't know where she is, or second... Second, that could be what I thought at first, a false bait to push me to go home so he can target Claire that would have remained alone at Stalingrad. If it's the first, I am fucked. If it's the second... Well, he fucked up very badly, but I don't think the second option to be the most likely. And I prefer staying downstairs, because if she answers the phone... Then we need to jump immediately back in the car and save my sister's arse. Or, if she doesn't answer, it means, something wrong happened. Because she strictly has no reasons not to answer the phone. Especially since she's waiting for someone. At that hour, her new boyfriend is supposed to be here for the last fifteen minutes and I know her boyfriends, they better not be late and it's very unlikely that she may be having a shower in the event of him possibly being late, especially now, they must be either chatting, either eating. She's always responding. But hold on a second, he said there was nothing suspicious? If this guy, my mother's boyfriend, that never came to my home alone or at least I am not aware of that, actually showed up tonight... he would have told me, right? That would have been something unusual, no?

And guess what happened... He tried twice.

"Well, boss, I am sorry, there might be a problem..."

I was suddenly alarmed. Because I was thinking about this, and, yes, he should have told me that he would be here. Immediately, Heather took control of the situation. She showed her Police insignia, and said in an ordering tone:

"Okay, police, open this door!"

"All right then," our guard just replied.

He opened up. The two big heavy electronically-controlled doors finally opened themselves when we entered, all of us, in that total darkness that didn't seem to be the announcement of a good thing. She was there, but not responding... I know his shift, this guy is here since 4 pm and finishes in an hour, so it means that he has seen my mother coming in and if he didn't see her going out... It means that she's still here. I mean, come on, she didn't vanish this way. Especially mum.

Anyway, we entered that vast entrance where letterboxes are, for finally reaching the small corridor and heading towards the lift. I didn't run, I mean, we didn't run, but we walked fast, whilst, in between, I was observing everything. Nothing seemed unusual, everything seemed normal. Our letterbox was closed and fine, and, even, there was no weird noise or anything weird within the building, we heard our neighbour doing their stuff in their flats. At a glance, it seemed to be a normal evening. I arrived in front of the lift, and I pressed the button to call it, Surprisingly, it was already on the first floor and waiting, so we jumped in.

Yet again, nothing unusual. I mean, it was clean... There was, yeah, a kind of detail: the floor was quite sticky. I mean, we could hear it when walking on it, it was making, yeah, that sticky noise. The moment I walked in, and I found this, I was feeling suddenly scared. But I have been taught not to be afraid, never. To never be scared. And always find the solution no matter what, that's what my grandmother used to teach me, always seek for a solution, even when you are in trouble, you can always fight back all the time. You just need to see where the problem is and then find the solution. But the moment I entered, Claire was standing in front of me, Heather next to her, and I looked at my girlfriend straight in the eyes at the moment the door closed. It was a very weird evening, I was feeling like, I don't know, something massive was ongoing, and I was just still looking for what was going on. For some reasons she had a kind of a grave and serious air, she was looking at me right in my eyes, but, yeah, I could feel that. There was a big interrogation, a big fear, it was her sweet face with the hidden message stating "protect me", she was feeling as well that something weird and not normal at all was going on. I looked at Heather as well, the saviour that fifteen days before again I still ignored the existence, and... For some reasons she was also scared, but she had her cop reaction, perhaps similar to mine. She was ready to brace for what was going to happen because two lives are at stake, mine, and Claire's. As I said, they can capture me, they can attack me, torture me, do whatever they want with me, I don't care. But Claire, they cannot touch her. Strictly forbidden. But to summarise, I was extrapolating, Claire was scared, and Heather was ready. Problem is, what's gonna happen once the doors will open again at the end of our small and short assumption.

Astonishingly, through our small journey in the lift, the tension ratcheted up very suddenly. I mean, well, this kind of situation when... you know you're about to find out something you're not gonna like, you have weird hunches, and people are looking at you like, they know, or they brace with you for the problem, well it was exactly this. I think we had enough for today, it was a tough day, but it seems that we are having some extra, it's like he wants to finally destroy us. The kind of extra nobody wants. I looked at her eyes, with her makeup destroyed because of the tears of fear she had certainly less than a second ago and her mascara that leaked on her cheeks that made noticeably black trail, and I told her, we're over soon.

But... That was what I just hoped. The very last thing I saw at that moment was her eyes full of fear and worries, before the lift stops, and the doors opened. Everything went suddenly in some kind of terribly slow motion. No, we won't be over soon. It was just the beginning, and the moment I stepped out of the lift cabin, the world stopped turning. Nothing had any meaning anymore. Everything suddenly becomes confused, like a gigantic and deafening shock of sound that paralyses you for a couple of seconds. Suddenly the asteroid hit the Earth, and nothing could escape the huge tsunamis and shock waves that were about to destroy the entire civilisation: at the moment doors opened, I saw a kind of dimmed light... not the regular light from that corridor, but the light coming from somewhere, from the left-hand side of the corridor, a light similar to the white colour of the big bulb on the entrance of my flat. The light was coming out of my flat. And there...

There Claire and Heather gave me a way to step outside of the cabin, where, I turned my head and saw my door: completely broken, barely hanging on the hinges that maintained it, but however it was still covering the entrance, it was like the door was barely open. How comes that someone broke a heavy, massive, armoured door, without making any noise? I stepped forward, and found out that a note, a big A4 paper, printed on the typical Times New Roman characters, was leaving a message:

"Young enemy, my congratulations! This is your ultimate reward for your extremely hard work. It must have been tough for you, and it's why, I am human like you, and I always give rewards when I see potential. Anyway, don't thank me... You did most of the job! I may have another surprise for you, but it's coming very soon! Okay, at first, you might find this quite distressing, you may be a bit upset against me, but someday you will understand. But it's okay, you'll be over it soon, don't worry, I am not scared for you, honey! – A long-lasting acquaintance."

I, yeah, read the note, when suddenly, a feeling of big freeze invaded me. Suddenly, I felt my heart beating extremely fast, and massive vertigo, like I was suddenly walking over a thread above a massive and deep void. He did it, he attacked it, and I felt like, although I defended myself, he was one step ahead. Warm Mediterranean weather suddenly becoming like I was naked in the middle of

Free Expensive Lies: Prologue

Siberia on a tough night of January, the shock was immediate. There were suddenly no questions coming to my mind, no analyses, my brain remained suddenly like frozen in times because I knew that something was ongoing. Behind me was still Heather and Claire, and, oh my, what happened was odd. My arms were suddenly shaking, I felt like a disarticulated puppet; no strength would come because I knew that at the moment, I would push the door, something terrible will happen.

I looked at Heather one last time before opening, and I saw her at that moment taking her gun in her hands, certainly as a precaution, as she lowered it since I was in front. And then, the moment. With the tip of my fingers of my two hands, I slowly pushed that broken door that was this time lighter than ever.

And at the moment I pushed the door, all my senses were on the alert. I just heard first the calm of that flat, like nobody was in there, There was the smell of something that was cooked recently, she cooked some beef meat, one of her recipes, it was a kind of a mix between this smell that seemed so light, and the persistent smell of cinnamon that we smell most of the time we come here. I was feeling exactly like I would come home like one of my regular days at school. I couldn't hear any music, but the smell of the meat cooking or cooked already was quite appealing, but this time my stomach was tied up. And, at the end of pushing the door, although the flat was astonishingly plunged into certain obscurity, the only light that was coming out was the one from the bulb of the living room that she switch on for being more intimate, the corridor heading towards our bedroom was dark, the kitchen diodes were on but didn't provide like a massive light... I could find on the floor right in front of me, at the moment I opened the door quite slowly, right behind some debris of wood and glass that I think came out of the broken door, maybe at a metre away from me, a massive puddle of blood. Of dark blood.

A couple of things happened at that moment, but I was now certainly blind and severely disturbed. I just heard Claire silently yelling, "oh God!" behind me as she was aware that something was not right, whilst in my mind, I was actually in an exploration mood. He assaulted my mother, but will I find her dead? Claire was submerged by the emotion, and I think it was extraordinarily strong since the very last time we saw mum alive and healthy was not longer than this morning. But, like most of the time, I must remain cold-blooded. So, this finally answered my question, was he bluffing? Apparently not. He assaulted my mother. Question is, how comes that he entered the building, broke my door as he did, and left the building, without alerting anybody? Unless he is a ghost, I don't see any other explanations.

I was disturbed, I mean, finding this was like, yeah, being on board of the Titanic at the moment she is about to be consumed by the ocean and it's already broken in two and you have thus the confirmation that it won't go any further anymore. I was suddenly cold and strengthless, and my heart beating, this made me feel almost like I could feel the blood flowing in my veins. In my mind was just passing as a band the expression "holy shit", but I was kind of reminded to remain focused. Okay... So, the blood puddle was massive, which indicates that the assault happened there, so she's been surprised by someone breaking the door. But I saw a big trail of blood, much fresh, going to the living room. Heather came closer to me as I started to walk into the entrance, avoiding putting my feet on the blood, but I kept on watching where this trail would lead me, and I think not too far away. She must be somewhere close to me.

So, I stepped inside, and as the living room is almost straight on your left when you enter, I turned my head, and suddenly discovered where she was. And how she was. She managed to crawl from the entrance to the living room. And she was lying on the floor, on her back, after maybe having crawled two or three metres. And, at the moment I saw her, as the two other girls were right behind me at the moment of my discovery, I immediately triggered the alert:

"What the fuck... Heather, call 17, and Claire, give me the towels on the table, HURRY UP!"

"Okay..." Heather replied.

"Yes..." Claire whispered, with her disturbed tone.

And, at that very same moment, I immediately rushed towards my mother. Overwhelmed by the situation, because from all that happened, because of the possible outcome of this, I kept in mind that I needed to stay focus: the priority is to determine whether she's still alive, responsive or something. Claire followed me and went to the table. Because, yeah, although I didn't pay attention, I quickly saw this detail: when I entered, I could see that she dressed the table, and has made everything ready for the dinner of tonight. There were three plates on the table, meaning that she was expecting me, and Clarisse wasn't supposed to come. Surprising, since I told her that I wouldn't come tonight and requested to postpone it. Well, anyway.

Anyway, even herself, I mean, so far, I have seen that she was wearing a dark dress, normal, she was wearing black pumps, and had her necklace like she has all the time, it hasn't been stolen. She loves that necklace and given the fact that she wears it all the time but it's not always visible, she says for safety issues as pickpockets love stealing jewellery in the metro.

As I could follow the blood on the floor, she has lost a lot. Even her skin was really white and extremely pale at that moment. As the blood seemed fresh, at least had a dark red colour, I think that the assault didn't happen more than ten minutes ago, that son of a bitch was waiting for me, I guess. And as she crawled on the floor, she first crawled face down, and has lost a lot of blood, and then turned herself in a very last effort. Right now, she seemed unresponsive, had her eyes closed, and as I approached her and placed myself on all four over her, I could hear that she was barely breathing. This was the good news, at least she is still alive.

Okay... I know what to do in that kind of situation. It is just that I must not be overwhelmed. So, let's focus. According to her dress, which was all wet because covered with blood, she's been stabbed. I mean, there aren't any signs of gun bullets in her body, and I saw that her dress was torn at five different places, all of them in her lower abdomen. It was still severely bleeding, but... I don't know if that's better or not, I ain't no doctor, but at least she hasn't been stabbed in the back or any vital organ has been touched such as her heart or anything, her chest seemed still normal, or at least there didn't seem to have any sign of assault. I was touching her belly, to check... she's been stabbed five times. So, I guess this is the reason why she hasn't been heard, and nobody heard anything here, stabbing someone is much quieter than shooting him down. The thing was, I actually started hearing her nose or mouth, and she was still breathing, but at an incredibly slow rate. Hopefully, unlike my sister that didn't want to, along with Claire a couple of years ago we both did the first aid training. The problem was, Claire was right behind me, standing with her two hands in front of her mouth just like as in a shock position, I quickly told her that since my priority is to stop the haemorrhage, I need those napkins as soon as possible.

So, she was stabbed, and it seemed to be quite deep. Surprisingly, two wounds above her navel seemed to be bleeding the most, so I put my hands over it. The thing is, I need to clean it to avoid any infections. But, I have nothing but the sleeve of my clothes. In the back, as I was now on all four above my mother, and Claire was collecting the napkins that mum placed on the plates just like she does all the time for dinner, I heard Heather speaking, calling for an emergency. The priority now is, I must wake her up. She's unresponsive, but as she still breathes, she can be wakened up, I just need to be fast. For that, two options: the common one, yelling at her ears, so she can hear me and then wake up, or the second, hurt her, place maybe my fingers in one wound so it can create a pain that may wake her up, or tore her nipples, or... many things... But that can be a bad idea and I prefer the first one, as mum reacts quite harshly to the pain.

So, still above her, my two hands trying to carry myself on the massive puddle of blood that was next to her and all around her (my hands and arms were already all covered of blood, so I don't care...), I immediately bent myself towards her left ear, and took a big breath, and started screaming:

"WAKE UP, MUM, FOR FUCK'S SAKE! WAKE UP!"

But there didn't seem to have any response. However, I could notice, as I managed to keep my face close to hers so I could hear her better, that she suddenly started breathing a bit faster, so she heard me and there was a reaction. As she wasn't not breathing at all, there was still some hope, so I must not help her in any kind, I must let her breathe on her own, otherwise, it will create more damage than any other thing. That was good, that was particularly good, an exceptionally good thing, I mean, tonight, mum is not going to die, there's no way I'm gonna lose any of my parents now. She pissed me off, but I still need her, that's the problem. So, relieved to have observed that reaction, I started to get a more angry and fierce way to have to wake her up. I bent towards her second ear, and now, I started to scream certainly as I never did before:

"COME ON, GET UP, WAKE UP, FOR FUCK SAKE! I AM NOT GONNA LOSE MY MOTHER TONIGHT!"

Two things: as it's very unusual that I scream, I screamed so loud that it was making me feel dizzy and I felt that it was weird in my throat. Like, when I force my voice. Well, if that's the price to pay for actually waking my mother up, then, it's fine for me. But the second thing, the most important was, now she was up. So, she was breathing much faster, I assume because of the tremendous pain she must be experiencing. But her two blue eyes opened again, in her white face. That was good, at least if she can be up when I try to stop her from bleeding, that's a good thing.

Claire was next to me when it happened and gave me all three towels. Now, I think, the best is, whilst I cover her wounds and try my best to keep her safe, she can help me to keep her awake. At the same time, I heard Heather, who remained at the entrance, still waiting on the phone to get an emergency. But having her opening her eyes again seemed to me like a victory, at least we are all fighting together, and I certainly avoided the worst: the death of my mother. I don't know how things are going to go, but hopefully, I have her back now, and that's the most important, as she is now responsive. Now, the next priority, trying to clean the wounds, even if I have nothing for that but... At least, I'll find a way, and covering all this. Whenever the ambulance is gonna take her in charge, then I guess they will go any further.

But the thing is, as I was still all above her, and I could see that some of my hairs took some of her blood, I must make sure that she's responding and she's not delirious or something like that. Immediately, for a second, as I saw her eyes opening again and her lips moving, certainly softly but still moving, it was time to make sure she wasn't confused, as the shock must have been terrible.

"Are you okay, mum?" I said as I was starting to first aid.

"Hey honey..." she barely voiced, visibly genuinely exhausted.

"It's okay, you're gonna be okay, mum... Don't move, okay? It's really important."

"Okay..."

With the towels in my hands, I immediately checked the wounds as Claire understood that keeping her awake would help me to get time to close her wounds, or at least to try to block the blood to keep on flowing. I have no idea how much blood she has lost, but I know that the body must lose between thirty to forty per cent of blood before any reaction. As she passed out, and also given the amount of liquid spread on the floor, along with the two puddles, I think... Yeah, she's lost a lot, which doesn't give me that much time to react. Because the more I think, and the more she will lose, and if she reaches the twenty per cent, that won't be good at all.

The thing was, she exercised when she fell, which make her lose much more blood. And I guess the reason why she exercised was the fact that our home phone is dropped next to a small cabinet next to where she fell, so I guess she tried to catch that to call an emergency. But she failed as the phone wasn't in her hand, this is why, hopefully, we arrived on time. Maybe we arrived fifteen minutes later, and she'd be dead. I checked the wound, amongst which the bloodiest, and all of them weren't that deep, I don't think he used a big knife, he may have used a dagger or maybe a small kitchen knife, but from what I could see, okay, there was five of them, all spread out like three in the front and one on each side, whoever has done that did it quickly, as he was disturbed by something. Or someone. And as she wears a dress, I cannot remove it, so I unfolded all the towels and immediately, I put them all covering the wounds.

Taylor Harding-Jenkins

As Claire was speaking to her and made her think, I quickly saw that her breathing became much more rapid and shallow. The problem was, just like all the time when you are rescuing someone, this person speaks her mother tongue in priority when she's confused. And Claire was speaking to her in French and mum was replying in English. The problem is, although Claire understands some stuff, she's not good at all in English and thus it's much harder for her to reply. One was asking stuff and the other replied something completely different, especially since Claire kept on asking her random questions and mum was complaining that she was feeling weird and was cold. And she was anxious as well, but it's good: mum and Claire didn't understand each other, which was making her slightly angry, and anger will keep her alive.

At the same time, at the very moment, I started stopping the bleeding, maybe fifteen seconds later, the towels became red. It was terrible. Even me, I was all red everywhere now, on my hairs, my arms, my hands obviously, and the harder I was holding it, I was holding them, I was thinking, deep inside, what the fuck, today. Surprisingly, I managed to stabilise her for a moment. Her heart was beating fast... But the problem was, how to keep this on a soft surface that is her belly without hurting her. My mother is the same as we are with my twin, we are all very slim, certainly caused by the fact that we don't eat that much, but... The problem is, she's been exhausted recently with me acting weird, with problems at work as she's been under pressure because she had to present her new collection and she used to tell me that she was fed up with what she was doing and complained about her colleagues because they are just simple incompetent and idiots, it broke her down. She may have met a new boyfriend, the problem is, he is not here tonight, nobody has seen him apparently, and... I don't think dating someone has counterbalanced properly the fact that she's exhausted and drained. And the recent discovery of me doing those weird stuff may have made things worse. This is why she has collapsed, I guess... And now this aggression. It's too much now. I mean, I think for her, it's just too much.

But their conversation didn't last exceedingly long as it was just leading to a quid pro quo. But very suddenly, and very swiftly, popping out of nowhere, we heard a massive, big glass exploding. And as it was loud, it may have come from someplace within the flat. I couldn't leave where I was, but we were all surprised.

"What the hell is that?" Heather was suddenly surprised.

"It seems to come from my bedroom. First door on your left!"

"Yes, let me check!"

Free Expensive Lies: Prologue

It was quite loud, and, yeah, after having reviewed it, I think it came from my bedroom. But it didn't seem like someone breaking my window, it sounded more like something falling. Not something that hit my window. That was weird, I mean... Was someone there? I don't think so, otherwise, he would have stabbed mum to death. I mean, that's what he did, but he would have made sure that she would be dead. As I said, yes, five successive stabs mean that whoever targeted my mum was seeking revenge, but as it was only five it means that he planned much better but got frustrated and disturbed by something, hence he ran away. But that noise was still curious. Anyway... I am sure that within days, I will have enough time along with guilt to analyse and decrypt what happened... Unless my flat is a crime scene. Because now... that's what it is, a crime scene.

Anyway, as I heard this noise and raised my head, at that very moment, mum tried to do the same. She was shaking very slightly, as I guess she was really cold due to the big loss. On the other hand, it was pretty cold here. But suddenly, she looked at me with some kind of... I don't know, last and final hope. It was quite tough for me to hear that:

"Cha... I love you, darling..."

"It's okay, I don't blame you, mum. Moreover, you're not gonna die, it's fine. You've been stabbed, shit happens. You're too young for that, I've been checking..."

"I am feeling weird..."

"Yes, that's a side effect of being stabbed, it's normal that you may feel weird..."

And after some moment, she kind of brutally let her head falling, on the pillow of hairs that she made for herself. She was collapsing. And the fact that she closed her eyes made me panic very quickly. So, immediately, I very violently pressed on one of her wounds, and she immediately reacted:

"Ah, come on!"

"Yeah, wakey, wakey, it's not a time for sleep yet... "

"Why do you have to be so rude to me?"

"Oh please, one day, you'll thank me... Just don't move, and erm... Claire, could you pass me a pillow, so I can lift her?" an idea came to my mind.

"Yeah, erm..."

"On the sofa, just take all of them..."

"Okay..."

Claire immediately executed. My idea was that since I don't know how long it's gonna take for Heather to finally get an emergency unless she could speak to someone, the idea was to lift her bottom, so blood can stagnate through the upper part of her body and her legs, and not going away. So maybe it can help reduce her heartbeats, as her heart was beating fast. The problem is to carry her, I may need her help, I mean, Claire's help: because she can be slim, she's just goddamn too heavy for me. And, also, I need to be careful, as I do not want the wounds to break and becoming worse... Damn, why does everything need to be hardcore tonight, for God's sake? Geez... why me? God is mad at me tonight, or how does it work?

Besides being heavily flabbergasted tonight, because of all that I found, because the battle was harder than I thought and he didn't leave me time to face this up, I just need to remain strong all the time, he is challenging me. I mean, my blackmailer... He wants to challenge me. I mean, I quickly thought at the note still pinned to my door, what does it mean, who's that acquaintance he was talking about? No, seriously, he wants to play with my nerves, tonight, as he is frustrated to be unable to finally reach me, so he seeks revenge on someone else. I don't know whom I am fighting against, but this guy became all of a sudden, a much more serious threat. This, I mean... First, I did my best to save Claire that served as a human shield, after this fucker started assaulting her, now I am saving my mother... what's next? When will all this stop? Because now, I may have good training over psychological pressure, it may be hard to put me down, but seeing all this mess, yes, now, it was annoying, it was upsetting, and it was flabbergasting.

It didn't take that long before Claire bring me back those three white pillows that were on the sofa. At the same time, quickly, she removed her shoes, as they were not the best for the occasion. And, also, at the same time, now all my arms were mostly covered with blood. I very slightly withdrew myself to remove my sweater, so I could give it to mum, I mean, at least use it as a temporary extra layer to make her feel more comfortable. But the thing was hard, I mean, my hands were all covered with blood, and I just can't wash those clothes anymore, I'll have to throw everything away. Hopefully, mum doesn't have any weird disease, so it's okay. Relatively safe. But as I removed everything, and I had my dark waistcoat and a white shirt underneath, well, it was from some parts red. I'll have a shower tonight, I guess. Even on my chest, I mean... But it's fine, I have plenty of these anyway. I don't care, it's just clothing stuff. What I care about is not burying my mother within days.

Free Expensive Lies: Prologue

So, she came back, and I had placed my sweater above her. Together, whilst I remained incredibly careful on moving so I wouldn't end up on her or make her bounce, we carried her up and placed the pillows on her bottom. Ultimately, it was done, I just came back one last time above her, and pressed the towels against her so I could maintain the pressure. After we did that operation, I could see Heather finally coming back, this time she had her phone in her hand, apparently off, and her gun in the other. She was kind of concerned at the moment she came back.

"Okay... There was nothing. I mean... Your window was wide open, but I didn't find anything... He probably entered through your window."

Hum, that could be possible. I mean, we live on the first floor and the fact that I have a balcony... And it's quite fine, I mean, if you are good at escalating stuff, then it's quite easy to access my flat through my window. And as I have those big French windows that are mostly made of glass, you can break it and then it's easy. That would explain a lot of things, though, why he entered like a ghost, why nobody has seen him, and that noise. And as my mother was somewhere close from here, he could have stabbed him. The only thing that I do not explain in this is, why is the door broken? Because, I am sorry, but breaking that heavy door without making any noise... That's weird. That's especially weird since the flat in front of us is rented by a couple of retired seventy-years old that were teachers before, and they are here most of the time. They only leave once in the morning for doing their regular shopping and that's all. Other than that, right now, they are home. And as we entered, I mean, when I left the lift, I heard as background noise their TV (always loud... One of them is almost deaf) being on, so it means that they were here when it happened. Well, the fact that they are deaf would be an explanation to why they didn't hear shit, but the problem is, a door being broken is still a weird noise. And the building is poorly soundproofed. That's an absolute mystery.

"He may have entered through my room, I mean if you heard something being broken..." I suggested.

"He did... He came out of your room..." mum said.

"Ambulance is on the way, also, I could speak to one of them, they said less than a minute... They will transfer her to Beaujon Hospital." Heather confirmed.

"Great, it's not far away from here..." I was relieved.

"Now... What was the guy looking like?" Heather asked mum.

"I don't know... He was... all black. I couldn't... I couldn't see his face... was masked..." Mum was confused and trying to speak.

"How tall was he?"

"As tall as Cha…"

"You said he was a guy…"

"Yeah… But I'm not sure."

"Slim? Fat?"

"No, no, very slim…"

"Has he been speaking? Did you hear him?"

"No… He just… I don't remember…"

So, we have a slim guy, as tall as me, that showed up masked, wearing black stuff. And she said it was a guy. That did not speak.

The thing is, I don't think this is the right moment to carry out any investigation, since she's in shock, and she's a casualty now. My mission is now to try to collect a maximum of stuff and keep it in my mind so I can work later on it. The problem is, as far as I know, as this guy signed his letter with the word acquaintance, it suggests that I know him. The thing is, guys that are as tall as me, wearing dark stuff, and slim, it's like half the guys in the city of Paris, so it doesn't help that much, and now, she won't give a precise description of the guy since pain is taking over, and unlike me, she cannot have the capacity of remaining focused for a long period and clear her mind to target what she needs to get. When she got stabbed, I am sure she didn't think about who it was, she got focused on the pain she experienced and the surprise she may have had to meet him. Because one thing is sure, I think that it happened pretty much this way: she said that the guy came out of my bedroom, so it means that she was certainly in the kitchen when everything started, and she went towards the entrance to check in my room. And it's where she came face to face with the blackmailer, who stabbed him. But as he got disturbed, it's possible that whilst she was crawling to the entrance, something disturbed him and he tried to leave and then left through my room. Or at least it must be something like that.

And, I think I may have an explanation for the letter, as mum always keeps the door closed and as he was in a rush, he wanted to leave that note on that door, so he broke it to open it. Because, when I recollect the image that I got from the door at the moment I saw it, totally broken, it seemed that it was broken from the inside, so it may be the explanation. As he managed to do this on time, then I think that, yeah, he left that note and ran away. But the problem is, what disturbed him?

I stopped Heather at that moment… I think we can proceed with this later.

"Heather, we will conduct the investigation maybe later, no? Let her recover first..."

"Yes, Cha... Yes."

Because, when I looked at Heather, I haven't seen that at the same time, she was collapsing. Her head was backward, her eyes were closed, and she was maybe about to have a seizure. And... she started breathing faster and faster. She was heading to a shock.

"Damn, she's collapsing... how long until we get someone?" Claire started to raise the alert.

"They said they're on the way..." Heather panicked.

"Holy crap... mum! Mum!" I ended up screaming again.

39 *What the day owes to the night*

// Waiting for Clarisse, still at home, Neuilly-sur-Seine.

// Tuesday, 22nd of January 2013, 21:04.

Hopefully, she didn't have seizures. She collapsed, yes, but I managed to do the right thing, and maybe a minute after she collapsed, first aiders, as well as the police, arrived here. I think, so far, I can say that, yeah, if tonight was a battle and I was in charge of leading the allied troops, I think I fought pretty well. By far, I saved my girlfriend from being abducted or god knows what, and I saved my mother's life. I mean, I saved... I did fight for her, first aiders said that she has still lost a lot of blood, but... I think she's likely to survive. From now, my blackmailer's been defeated. And the victory is still mine.

So, yeah, after she collapsed, police and first aiders were downstairs but were already instructed to come with a stretcher, as it would be just impossible to get out of the building for my mother without a stretcher. They immediately come, started to take care of my mother, whilst I went away, I just remained in the main entrance, and looked at what was going on. Police were there, and Heather instructed them regarding what happened, and, yeah, after this, I leaned against the wall, next to the big puddle of blood in the entrance and sat down. Claire went to my bedroom to get me some clean clothes for tonight and get my nightshirts, whilst, powerless, flabbergasted, disenchanted, and God knows what other feeling I experienced at that moment from the last three hours, I sat on the floor, my hands all covered of blood raising my hairs and watching the first aiders putting plasters where my mother has been stabbed after they cut her dress. They were already fighting harder for her life, and in the middle of it all, I was just like, this was surrealistic, I mean, in my mind, I was feeling guilty, because this happened because of me, and, yeah, I'm fucked now. Will she ever forgive me? I have no idea. I don't know what's the best now, I have no idea... But all I saw was that whoever this guy is, he played very well. The world was exploding before my eyes, and I was just feeling like, there's nothing I can do about this. I was honestly far, extremely far, from imagining that this would have such consequences. As he said, I guess I played.

They carried her up on the stretch, took her pulse, and started doing their medical stuff. Heather remained close to me, as the police arrived a bit later, for starting to seal my apartment because I am sure investigations are due to start. I must call Clarisse, and, well, I guess we will all sleep at Claire's tonight. Looking at that stretch was somehow a vision of horror to me: they banded all her wounds, I think they will be stitching all this once she arrives at the hospital, and in between, they attached sensors to her chest, I guess to check her heartbeat, and placed a respirator over her mouth... It was just horrible, I mean, seeing this, seeing her leaving like this, we may have arguments in the past, but right now I was feeling deeply sorry and appalling. The thing was, what will I explain to Clarisse? She knew I played a dangerous game, and she's gonna kill me, or... I don't know. Even on the phone, she seemed pissed, and now... The thing is, I tried to save her, and maybe this will help me to regain her trust, or I don't know. Honestly, I don't know, for now, yeah, we were in the middle of the North Atlantic Ocean, the water was -2.2 around, the iceberg was in front of us or nearby, and the Titanic has just hit, and I didn't have any time to reach a lifeboat. So, yeah, now, I guess the only thing I have to do is, well... Just hold the handrail and let me fall when the boat is high enough so it can kill myself before reaching the sea.

They carried my mother away, took her through the lift, as it is wide enough to carry a stretch, and I guess they are going downstairs. The fact is, they covered her with a blanket, but as it's freezing down there, it's nearly 8 degree Celsius out there, and, well I think it may help for the wound to freeze. I was considering going to the hospital, but Heather advised me to go back home with Claire, she called an escort so we will be back home by car, and she told me that she would join Clarisse at the hospital. As, now, we saw that he targeted my mother, the danger is everywhere, he can also try to target Clarisse as well, so she needs to be under police protection too. For now, she said that it was better if Clarisse was to remain with her for the night, and she said that tomorrow, we must stay at Claire's home all three of us. Hum... drama days are ahead... Anyway.

Heather remained quite a long time moving back and forth. She went to the kitchen from times to times, as she was speaking with some investigators, I guess her unit, to investigate what happened, and maybe also briefing them, and, yeah, she went in the front to check how my mother is going. Well, for now, it's just an assault investigation, depending on what happens with my mother, if they manage to do their job, it's just an assault, otherwise, it's a murder, and... Things won't be the same in the balance. She was carrying her phone in her hand, and yeah, left the kitchen and followed my mother's stretch to the lift, but she remained on her floor. I saw her discussing with the guys, and... I didn't pay attention to what she said, and... then she came back. Whilst I was still seating on the floor, thinking, or trying to clear my mind, and while Claire was still getting some clothes for me, Heather came to me, sitting down next to me:

"Hey honey... You did a good job, tonight," I looked at her and she smiled at me.

"I know, it's the second time you tell me that..."

"No, I mean, I am impressed. To be honest, I wouldn't be able to do the least of what you did tonight, and... You did it, remained cold-blooded and you just did it. That's impressive!"

"I did what I had to do, that's pretty much it!"

"Okay... I have some good news, regarding your mother, they said it's not that bad, she's lost a lot of blood but it's not that terrible. She's gonna be better soon, she just needs some sleep."

"Yeah, we'll see that in a couple of days I guess?"

"Yeah, I think so."

"Anyway, darling, you should take some clothes, and just go downstairs, my agents will escort you home, and just sleep... I'll come back to you with your sister tomorrow, as promised! Also, before you go, do you mind giving me your twin's phone number?"

"Hum, yeah, hum... Yeah, give me one second!"

At the moment I heard a parade of people coming to my apartment and the doors of the lift suddenly closing, I took my phone out of my pocket after having dried up my hand against my pants. And... Surprisingly, no calls. I wonder where Clarisse might be right now since I alerted her maybe twenty minutes ago. My last call was twenty-five minutes ago, so I guess she must be half-way now or perhaps really close from here. At the moment I opened the Contacts app and typed her name, Claire arrived right in front of me with a white bag, a white shopping bag, and some stuff inside. I don't know what she took, but, yeah, at the moment she saw me, and I was about to give Clarisse's number to Heather, she looked at me and, said like she saw a ghost:

"You have blood on your face..." Claire noticed.

"No way, Claire... No way..." I was appalled.

"Hum, Charlotte," Heather interrupted. "The phone number?"

"Yeah, here it is. I need to call her, by the way?" I pressed her contact page, so the phone number was fully displayed.

"Yeah... Sure!" Heather replied.

And, surprisingly, at the very same moment, I showed the number to Heather and she wrote it down, Claire's phone started to ring in her coat's pocket. She dropped the bag next to me and took her phone. And surprise...

"What the hell..." Claire seemed surprised.

"Maybe she was trying to call me, which is weird, I didn't get any calls..." I found out that Clarisse was contacting Claire. "Meh, take her call, maybe she wants to contact me."

"Yeah... Hey Clarisse?"

Somehow Claire seemed relieved, I don't know for what reason. Like always, whenever she gets a call that she likes, she always smiles, always remains positive to whomever she is talking to. I mean, all the time I spoke with her (except days after we broke up) she always remained positive and was always fine when on the phone. This girl is fantastic, I mean, even in depression, she always finds a way to smile. But, yeah, she said, "Hey, Clarisse", didn't ask questions such as how are you, but suddenly, her smile disappeared. Like my sister was taking over and was pissing her off or annoying her and she couldn't talk or... But her smile disappeared. The problem was, I couldn't hear, as everybody was quite noisy here, and there were certainly twenty people in my flat right now, taking pictures and walking around doing stuff, it was like I was in the middle of a busy street. And... Certainly after fifteen seconds of her remaining silent, and, I don't know becoming severely disturbed, she handed me the phone and said, with a trembling voice:

"Hum... it's for you, honey..."

I immediately started to ask myself many questions: who did that? Because, I mean, yes, Clarisse was upset, but she understood there was an emergency and wouldn't piss her off right now, I mean, there are much more different priorities at the moment, and... Unless... Oh, my, unless...

"Yo, what's up Clarisse?"

"Charlotte..." she was speaking in a low voice and was crying. "They caught me..."

Unless... Unless I was wrong from the beginning, and he let me focus on Claire to target both my sister and my mother, because, oh, fuck... there is a snitch. So this is why there was a surprise waiting for me, the surprise was not my mother, as I swiftly thought, the surprise was not another attack on Claire or trying to attack me, no, holy crap, all of it was just a smokescreen. Whilst I was busy saving Claire's arse, he was busy attacking my mother. And then, whilst I was busy saving my mother, he was busy... holy shit. And I don't even know where she is.

"Hey, honey, where are you?"

"He... he told me to tell you goodbye... I love you, Cha..." she was weeping again and again.

"Clarisse, calm down... who told you to tell me that?"

"He said, you did it well, but will you be able to find me on time... he also said that you have forty-eight hours... I'm scared!"

"Clarisse, where are you, what happened?"

I immediately stood up. That... Geez, everything was ready from the beginning, and I couldn't do anything to help that. If she cries if she's like this... It means that they have her. And I'm fucked. Again, he is one step forward.

"Clarisse? CLARISSE?"

And then... after I heard the phone moving, and Clarisse still crying, I just heard some icy laugh. Someone laughing, some guy laughing. A laugh, a long one, that left me speechless. As she's my twin, I immediately felt some kind of fear, and then, nothing. The guy hung up the phone.

We were all there, Claire, Heather, and I looked at each other one last time, and we all heard that laugh. A huge questioning was now there. Everything was a smokescreen, everything was designed like this, and whatever has happened tonight, we cannot do anything anymore, we were supposed to lose. I thought victory was mine, but I just didn't expect that to finally happen. As he said in his call, he was about to attack someone or someone else. But I shouldn't have trusted that at the moment he gave me all the full addresses of where both my mother and Clarisse where, I should have suspected something weird was going on, I should have been wary. Now, Clarisse is in danger, and... I thought it was an end, he played very well and won the battle. I thought, tonight, we could finally get rid of everything, all the problems would be gone this time forever, and we could go forward together, hands in hands, walking forward together and restart a new life with my girlfriend, after all this, just like we planned before. I thought the final chapter was written and I was done with him, but no, he may have won a battle, he didn't win the war. But no. My only tremendous mistake tonight, I guess, is to have ignored the possibility that this would just be a beginning.

Prologue **9**

Part 1 **19**

1 Forward 23

2 Another day 47

3 Oh, I am fine, you? 57

4 Speaking of which... 70

5 A normal day in a normal life 84

6 Obviously... 94

7 An amazing mess 102

8 Where are you? 114

9 Et lux in tenebris lucet... 139

10 Crimes and punishments 152

11 This means war 173

12 It's a match 189

13 Deal or no deal? 204

14 You're probably wondering... 215

15 This is gonna hurt 228

16 Listen, darling... 238

17 And God created lesbians 241

18 Self-sufficiency and sustainability 261

19 Game over 279

20 To whom it may concern 294

21 For the blue of your eyes 302

22 On the brink of collapse 320

23 Drifting universes 344

24 Gosh, it stinks! 380

25 Renegade 391

26 Wake me up when you need me 401

27 Truth 417

28 Still alive? 439

29 Zombies 443

30 A dark full of clouds... 461

31 Needle in a haystack 478

32 Once upon a time... 501

33 Exit means exit 508

34 So, what's next?   529

35 Finish the fight   550

36 Until death do us part   574

37 Checkmate   591

38 End of the line   601

39 What the day owes to the night   624

Acknowledgements   **633**

Still there? Man, I couldn't think you'd do that. I thought at first that you would have dropped the book already because you found this boring. But, okay, thanks, then, I guess.

So, first, I'd like to thank my wife and my grandmother. And my mother-in-law, (surprising, eh?) because unlike the rest of my family, they've been there until the end of this adventure. The only three people to have helped me when I was down.

Second, I'd like to thank Prime Minister Boris Johnson. Yeah, I know, but, hey, without him, without lockdown, none of this would have been possible. I mean, me working again on that book, countless agents telling me that I was "not right for their list", my depression to explode ... But thank you, Boris, at least, I could have time to improve and complete my manuscript. So, thanks.

Third, erm... Well, actually, I want to thank my depression and my gender dysphoria, to actually help me see things in another way, and it has been really helpful to write this book. I'm not gonna extend on gender dysphoria because some people may not like it.

Fourth, okay... I guess they deserve it. I'd like to thank Amazon, for finally allow me, I mean, give me a chance to finally see this book real. Thanks, guys. Even if I have no hope to sell even a single copy.

A special thank you to Andrea, for this amazing cover. Follow her on Instagram at @andreagilart

And, finally, thank you. Unlike many people who didn't have time to read this until the end, you read pretty much 290,000 words and you survived. That's an achievement! I am writing a second opus, I really hope you'd be there for the release day... unless... yeah, just check Amazon, or subscribe for alerts, I don't know how this works. And, thanks to your purchase, you could allow a near-poor trans girl to finally get some money to buy new pants at Primark, so thanks. Be proud, you've been part of something very important in the life of someone!

Great, now I have no idea when I'll publish the second part, but it should be coming anytime soon, so please stay tuned! Now, close this book, leave a review (would be helpful if you want to share), and have a good day.

Printed in Great Britain
by Amazon